PRAISE FOR CATHERINE COULTER'S
FBI THRILLER SERIES

"Fast-paced."

"This terrific thriller will drag you into its chilling web of terror and not let go until the last paragraph . . . A ripping good read."
—*The San Francisco Examiner*

"A good storyteller . . . Coulter always keeps the pace brisk."
—*Fort Worth Star-Telegram*

"With possible blackmail, intra-judiciary rivalries, and personal peccadilloes, there's more than enough intrigue—and suspects—for full-court standing in this snappy page-turner . . . A zesty read."   —*BookPage*

"Twisted villains . . . intriguing escapism . . . The latest in the series featuring likable . . . FBI agents Lacey Sherlock and Dillon Savich."
—*Lansing (MI) State Journal*

"Coulter takes readers on a chilling and suspenseful ride . . . taut, fast-paced, hard to put down."   —*Cedar Rapids Gazette*

"A fast-paced plot with numerous twists and turns . . . Only Catherine Coulter can spin such a web and tie up the loose ends in an incredibly believable manner."   —*Fresh Fiction*

"The perfect suspense thriller, loaded with plenty of action."
—*The Best Reviews*

"The newest installment in Coulter's FBI series delivers . . . a fast-moving investigation, a mind-bending mystery . . . The mystery at the heart . . . is intriguing and the pacing is brisk."   —*Publishers Weekly*

"This fast-paced thriller, featuring the author's trademark wit in counterpoint to intense action, is an excellent addition to Coulter's popular FBI series."   —*Booklist*

"An exciting, suspense-laden whodunit . . . Fans will enjoy this twisting . . . fast-paced thriller."   —*Midwest Book Review*

SECOND SHOT

CATHERINE COULTER

BERKLEY BOOKS, NEW YORK

THE BERKLEY PUBLISHING GROUP
Published by the Penguin Group
Penguin Group (USA) LLC
375 Hudson Street, New York, New York 10014

USA • Canada • UK • Ireland • Australia • New Zealand • India • South Africa • China

penguin.com

A Penguin Random House Company

Library of Congress Cataloging-in-Publication Data

Coulter, Catherine.
[Novels. Selections]
Second shot / Catherine Coulter.—Berkley trade paperback edition.
pages cm.
ISBN 978-0-425-27134-6 (pbk.)
1. United States. Federal Bureau of Investigation—Fiction.   2. Government investigators—Fiction.
3. Sherlock, Lacey (Fictitious character)—Fiction.   4. Savich, Dillon (Fictitious character)—Fiction.
I. Coulter, Catherine. Eleventh hour.   II. Coulter, Catherine. Blindside.   III. Title.
IV. Title: Eleventh hour.   V. Title: Blindside.
PS3553.O843S37 2014
813'.54—dc23
2013034262

PUBLISHING HISTORY
Berkley trade paperback edition / January 2014

PRINTED IN THE UNITED STATES OF AMERICA

10 9 8 7 6 5 4 3 2

Cover photograph by Jake Rajs / Getty Images.

CONTENTS

ELEVENTH HOUR

To Phyllis Gran. You are a tremendous publishing talent. Thank you for twelve incredible years.

—Catherine Coulter

ACKNOWLEDGMENTS

I would like to thank producer and assistant director John Isabeau for his relentless pursuit on my behalf to see my FBI books made into films. When everything finally comes together, it will be because of his efforts.

Thank you, John, you're the best.

I would like to thank Inspector Sherman Ackerson and Spokesman Dewayne Tully for showing me around the main cop shop on Bryant Street (the San Francisco Hall of Justice), and answering every question.

I would like to thank Dr. Boyd Stephens, San Francisco medical examiner, who graciously showed me his facilities and answered all of my questions, even the gruesome ones.

ONE

San Francisco

Nick sat quietly in the midnight gloom of the nave, hunched forward, her head in her arms resting on the pew in front of her. She was here because Father Michael Joseph had begged her to come, had begged her to let him help her. The least she could do was talk to him, couldn't she? She'd wanted to come late, when everyone else was already home asleep, when the streets were empty, and he'd agreed, even smiled at her. He was a fine man, kind and loving toward his fellow man and toward God.

Would she wait? She sighed at the thought. She'd given her word, he'd *made* her give her word, known somehow that it would keep her here. She watched him walk over to the confessional, watched with surprise as his step suddenly lagged, and he paused a moment, his hand reaching for the small handle on the confessional door. He didn't want to open that door, she thought, staring at him. He didn't want to go in. Then, at last, he seemed to straighten, opened the door and stepped inside.

Again, there was utter silence in the big church. The air itself seemed to settle after Father Michael Joseph stepped into that small confined space. The deep black shadows weren't content to fill the corners of the church, they even crept down the center aisle, and soon she was swallowed up in them. There was a patch of moonlight coming through the tall stained-glass windows.

It should have been peaceful, but it didn't feel that way. There was something else in the church, something that wasn't restful, that wasn't remotely spiritual. She fidgeted in the silence.

She heard one of the outer church doors open. She turned to see the man who was going to make his midnight confession walk briskly into the church. He looked quite ordinary, slender, with a long Burberry raincoat and thick dark hair. She watched him pause, look right and left, but he didn't see her, she was in the shadows. She watched him walk to the confessional where Father Michael Joseph waited, watched him open the confessional door and slip inside.

Again, silence and shadows hovered around her. She was part of the shadows now, looking out toward the confessional from the dim, vague light. She heard nothing.

How long did a confession take? Being a Protestant, she had no idea. There must be, she thought, some correlation between the number and severity of the sins and the length of the confession. She started to smile at that, but it quickly fell away.

She felt a rush of cold air over her, covering her for a long moment before it moved on. How very odd, she thought, and pulled her sweater tighter around her.

She looked again at the altar, perhaps seeking inspiration, some sort of sign, and felt ridiculous.

After Father Michael Joseph had finished, what was she supposed to do? Let him take her hand in his big warm ones, and tell him everything? Sure, like she'd ever let that happen. She continued to look up at the altar, its flowing shape blurred in the dim light, the shadows creeping about its edges, soft and otherworldly.

Maybe Father Michael Joseph wanted her to sit here quietly with nothing and no one around her. She thought in that moment that even though he wanted her to talk to him, he wanted her to speak to God more. But there were no prayers inside her. Perhaps there were, deep in her heart, but she really didn't want to look there.

So much had happened, and yet so little. Women she didn't know were dead. She wasn't. At least not yet. He had so many resources, so many eyes and ears, but for now she was safe. She realized sitting there in the quiet church that she was no longer simply terrified as she'd been two and a half weeks before. Instead she'd become watchful. She was always studying the faces that passed her on the street. Some made her draw back, others just flowed over her, making no impact at all, just as she made no impact on them.

She waited. She looked up at the crucified Christ, felt a strange mingling of pain and hope fill her, and waited. The air seemed to shift, to flatten, but the silence remained absolute, without even a whisper coming from the confessional.

Inside the confessional, Father Michael Joseph drew a slow, deep breath to steady himself. He didn't want to see this man again, not ever again, for as long as he lived. When the man had called Father Binney and told him he could only come this late—he was terribly sorry, but it wasn't safe for him, and he had to confess, he just had to—of course Father Binney had said yes. The man told Father Binney he had to see Father Michael Joseph, no one else, and of course Father Binney had again said yes.

Father Michael Joseph was very afraid he knew why the man had come again. He'd confessed before, acted contrite—a man in pain, a man trying to stop killing, a man seeking spiritual help. The second time he'd come, he'd confessed yet again to another murder, gone through the ritual as if he'd rehearsed it, saying all the right words, but Father Michael Joseph knew he wasn't contrite, that—that what? That for some reason Father Michael Joseph couldn't fathom, the man wanted to gloat, because the man believed there was nothing the priest could do to stop him. Of course Father Michael Joseph couldn't tell Father Binney why he didn't want to see this evil man. He'd never really believed in human evil, not until the unimagined horror of September 11th, and now, when this man had come to him for the first time a week and a half ago, then last Thursday, and now again tonight, at nearly midnight. Father Michael Joseph knew in his soul that the man was evil, without remorse, with no ability to feel his own, or another's, humanity. He wondered if the man had ever felt truly sorry. He doubted it. Father Michael Joseph heard the man breathing in the confessional across from him, and then the man spoke, his voice a soft, low monotone, "Forgive me, Father, for I have sinned."

He'd recognize that voice anywhere, had heard it in his dreams. He didn't know if he could bear it. He said finally, his voice thin as the thread hanging off his shirt cuff, "What have you done?" He prayed to God that he wouldn't hear words that meant another human being was dead.

The man actually laughed, and Father Michael Joseph heard madness in that laugh. "Hello to you, too, Father. Yes, I know what you're thinking. You're right, I killed the pathetic little prick; this time I used a garrote. Do you know what a garrote is, Father?"

"Yes, I know."

"He tried to get his hands beneath it, you know, to try to loosen it, to relieve the pressure, but it was nice strong wire. You can't do anything against wire. But I eased up just a bit, to give him some hope."

"I hear no contrition in your voice, no remorse, only satisfaction that you committed this evil. You have done this because it pleased you to do it—"

The man said in a rich, deep, sober voice, "But you haven't heard the rest of my tale, Father."

"I don't want to hear anything more out of your mouth."

The man laughed, a deep, belly-rolling laugh. Father Michael Joseph didn't say a word. It was cold and stuffy in the confessional, hard to breathe, but his frock stuck to his skin. He smelled himself in that sweat, smelled his dread, his fear, his distaste for this monster. *Dear Lord, let this foul creature leave now, leave and never come back.*

"Just when he thought he had pulled it loose enough so he could breathe, I jerked it tight, really fast, you know, and it sliced right through his fingers all the way to the bone. He died with his damned fingers against his own neck. Grant me absolution, Father. Did you read the papers, Father? Do you know the man's name?"

Father Michael Joseph knew, of course he knew. He'd watched the coverage on television, read it in the *Chronicle*. "You murdered Thomas Gavin, an AIDS activist who's done nothing but good in this city."

"Did you ever sleep with him, Father?"

He wasn't shocked, hadn't been shocked by anything for the past twelve years, but he was surprised. The man had never taken this tack before. He said nothing, just waited.

"No denial? Stay silent, if you wish. I know you didn't sleep with him. You're not gay. But the fact is, he had to die. It was his time."

"There is no absolution for you, not without true repentance."

"Why am I not surprised you feel that way? Thomas Gavin was just another pathetic man who needed to leave this world. Do you want to know something, Father? He wasn't really real."

"What do you mean he wasn't really real?"

"Just what I said. He didn't really ever exist, you know? He wasn't ever really here—he just existed in his own little world. I helped him out of his lousy world. Do you know he contracted AIDS just last year? He just found out about it. He was going nuts. But I saved him, I helped him out of everything, that's all. It was a rather noble thing for me to do. It was sort of an assisted suicide."

"It was vicious, cold-blooded murder. It was real, and now a man of flesh and blood is dead. Because of you. Don't try to excuse what you did."

"Ah, but I was giving you a metaphor, Father, not an excuse. Your tone is harsh. Aren't you going to give me my penance? Maybe have me say a million Hail Marys? Perhaps have me score my own back with a whip? Don't you want me to plead with you to intercede with God on my behalf, beg for my forgiveness?"

"A million Hail Marys wouldn't get you anywhere." Father Michael leaned closer, nearly touched that evil, smelled the hot breath of that man. "Listen to me now. This is not a sacramental confession. You believe that I am bound by silence, that anything anyone tells me can go no further than the confessional. That is not true. You have not made a sacramental confession; you are not contrite, you seek no spiritual absolution, and I am not bound to silence. I will discuss this with my bishop. However, even if he disagrees with me, I am prepared to leave the priesthood if I have to. Then I will tell the world what you have done. I won't allow this to continue."

"You would really turn me over to the cops? That is very impassioned of you, Father. I see that you are seriously pissed. I didn't know there was a loophole in your vow of silence. I had wanted you to be forced to beg and plead and threaten, but realize you're helpless and let it eat you alive. But how can anyone predict someone's behavior, after all?"

"They'll throw you in an institution for the rest of your miserable life."

The man smothered a laugh, managed a credible sigh, and said, laughing, "You mean to imply that I'm insane, Father?"

"No, not just insane. I think you're a psychopath—ah, I believe the politically correct word is sociopath, isn't it? Doesn't make it sound so evil, so without conscience. It doesn't matter, whatever you are, it's worse than anything doctors could put a tag to. You don't give a damn about anybody. You need help, although I doubt anyone could help the sickness in you. Will you stop this insanity?"

"Would you like to shoot me, Father?"

"I am not like you. But I will see that you are stopped. There will be an end to this."

"I fear I can't let you go to the cops, Father. I'm trying not to be angry with you for not behaving as you should. All right. Now I'm just mildly upset that you aren't behaving as you're supposed to."

"What are you talking about—I'm not acting like I'm supposed to?"

"It's not important, at least it isn't for you. Do you know you've given me something I've never had before in my life?"

"What?"

"Fun, Father. I've never had so much fun in my life. Except, maybe, for this."

He waited until Father Michael Joseph looked toward him through the wire mesh. He fired point-blank, right through the priest's forehead. There was a loud popping sound, nothing more because he'd screwed on a silencer. He lowered the gun, thoughtful now because Father Michael Joseph had slumped back against the wooden confessional wall, his head up, and he could see his face clearly. There was not even a look of surprise on the priest's face, just a flash of something he couldn't really understand. Was it compassion? No, certainly not that. The priest despised him, but now he was shackled for all eternity, without a chance for him to go to the police, no opportunity for him even to take the drastic step of leaving the priesthood. He was silent forever. No loophole now.

Now Father Michael Joseph didn't have to worry about a thing. His tender conscience couldn't bother him. Was there a Heaven? If so, maybe Father Michael Joseph was looking down on him, knowing there was still nothing he could do. Or maybe the priest was hovering just overhead, over his own body, watching, wondering.

"Good-bye, Father, wherever you are," he said, and rose.

He realized, as he eased out of the confessional and carefully closed the narrow wooden door, that the look on the Father's face—he'd looked like he'd won. But that made no sense. Won what? The good Father had just bought the big one. He hadn't won a damned thing.

There was no one in the church, not that he expected there to be. It was dead silent. He would have liked it if there had been a Gregorian chant playing softly. But no, there was nothing, just the echo of his own footsteps on the cold stones.

What did that damned priest have to look happy about? He was dead, for God's sake.

He walked quickly out of St. Bartholomew's Church, paused a

moment to breathe in the clean midnight air, and craned his neck to look up at the brilliant star-studded sky. A very nice night, just like it was supposed to be. Not much of a moon, but that was all right. He would sleep very well tonight. He saw a drunk leaning against a skinny oak tree set in a small dirt plot in the middle of the sidewalk, just across the street, his chin resting on his chest—not the way it was supposed to be, but who cared? The guy hadn't heard a thing.

There would be nothing but questions with no answers for now, since the cops wouldn't have a clue. The priest had made him do things differently, and that was too bad. But it was all close enough.

But the look on the priest's face, he didn't like to think about that, at least not now.

He whistled as he walked beneath the streetlight on Fillmore, then another block to where he'd parked his car, squeezed it between two small spaces, really. This was a residential area and there was little parking space. But that, too, was just the way it was supposed to be. It was San Francisco, after all.

One more stop to make. He hoped she'd be home, and not working.

TWO

Special Agent Dane Carver said to his unit chief, Dillon Savich, "I've got a problem, Savich. I've got to go home. My brother died last night."

It was early, only seven-thirty on a very cold Monday morning, two weeks into the new year. Savich rose slowly from his chair, his eyes on Dane's face. Dane looked bad—pale as a sheet, his eyes shadowed so deeply he looked like he'd been on the losing end of a fight. There was pain radiating from his eyes, and shock. "What happened, Dane?"

"My brother—" For a moment Dane couldn't speak, and just stood in the open doorway. He felt in his gut that if he actually said the word aloud, it would make it real and true and so unbearable he'd just fold up and die. He swallowed, wishing it were last night again, before four o'clock in the morning, before he'd gotten the call from Inspector Vincent Delion of the SFPD.

"It's all right," Savich said, walking to him, gently taking his arm. "Come in, Dane. That's right. Let's close the door."

Dane shoved the door shut with his foot, turned back to Savich, and said, his voice steady and remote, "He was murdered. My brother was murdered."

Savich was shaken. Losing a brother to a natural death was bad enough, but this? Savich said, "I'm very sorry about this. I know you and your brother were close. I want you to sit down, Dane."

Dane shook his head, but Savich just led him to the chair, pushed it back, and gently shoved him down. He held himself as rigid as the chair back, looking straight ahead, out the window that looked out at the Justice Building.

Savich said, "Your brother was a priest?"

"Yes, he is—was. You know, I've got to go see to things, Savich."

Dillon Savich, chief of the Criminal Apprehension Unit at FBI headquarters, was sitting on the edge of his desk, close to Dane. He leaned forward, squeezed Dane's shoulder, and said, "Yes, I know. This is a terrible thing, Dane. Of course you have to go take care of it. You'll have paid leave, no problem. He was your twin, wasn't he?"

"Yes, an identical twin. He was my mirror image. But inside, as different as we were from each other, we were still so much alike."

Savich couldn't imagine the pain he must be feeling, losing a brother, a twin. Dane had been in the unit for five months now, transferred in from the Seattle field office, by his request, and strongly recommended by Jimmy Maitland, Savich's boss, who told Savich that he'd had his eye on Dane Carver for a while. A good man, he'd said, very smart, hardnosed, tough, sometimes a hot dog, which wasn't good, but reliable as they come. If Dane Carver gave his word on something, you could consider it done.

His birthday, Savich knew, was December 26, two hours after midnight. He'd gotten lots of silly Christmas/birthday presents at the office party on the twenty-third. He'd just turned thirty-three.

Savich said, "Do the local cops know what went down? No, back up a moment, I don't even know where your brother lived."

"In San Francisco. I got two calls, the first just before four a.m. last night, from an Inspector Vincent Delion of the SFPD, then ten minutes later, a call from my sister, Eloise, who lives down in San Jose. Delion said he was killed in the confessional, really late, nearly midnight. Can you believe that, Savich?" Dane finally looked at him straight on, and in that instant there was such rage in Dane's eyes that it blurred into madness. He slammed his fist on the chair arm. "Can you actually believe that some asshole killed him in the confessional? At midnight? What was he doing hearing a confession at midnight?"

Savich thought Dane would break then. His breath was sharp and too fast, his eyes dilated, his hands fisted hard and tight. But he didn't. His breathing hitched, suspended for a moment, and then he made himself breathe deeply, and held himself together. Savich said, "No, it doesn't make sense to us, just to the person who killed him, and we'll find out who and we'll find out why. No, stay seated for a minute, Dane, and we'll make some plans. Your brother's name was Michael, wasn't it?"

"Yes, he was Father Michael Joseph Carver. I need to go to San Francisco. I know the reputation of the department out there. They're good, but they didn't know my brother. Not even my sister really knew him. Only I really knew him. Oh God, I thought I'd never say this, but it's probably better that my mom died last year. She'd wanted Michael to become a priest, prayed for it all her life, at least that's what she always said. This would have destroyed her soul, you know?"

"Yes, I know, Dane. When did you last speak to him?"

"Two nights ago. He—he was really pleased because he'd managed to catch a teenager who'd been spraying graffiti on the church walls. He told me he was going to make the boy a Catholic. Once he was a Catholic, he'd never do that again because he wouldn't be able to bear the guilt." Dane smiled, just for an instant, then fell silent.

"So you didn't sense anything wrong?"

Dane shook his head, then frowned. "I would have said no, that my brother was always upbeat, even when a local journalist tried to come on to him."

"Good grief, what was her name?"

"Oh no, it wasn't a woman. It was a man."

Savich just smiled.

"It happened quite a bit, but you're right, usually it was women. Michael was always kind, it didn't matter if it was a man or a woman doing the coming on." Dane frowned, fell silent again.

"Now that you think back, there is something, isn't there?"

"Well, I'm just not sure. He said something recently about feeling helpless, and he hated that. Said he was going to do something about it."

"Do you have any idea what he meant by that?"

"No, he wouldn't say any more. Maybe a confession that curled his toes, maybe a parishioner he couldn't help. But there was nothing at all that unusual about that. Michael dealt with lots of problems, lots of nutcases over the years." Dane curled his fist over the chair arm. "Maybe there was something there, something that frightened him, I don't know. I could have called him back and talked to him some more about it, pushed him when he clammed up. Why the hell didn't I?"

"Shut up, Dane. You're a cop. Don't freeze your brain up with guilt."

"It's hard not to. I'm Catholic."

A meager bit of humor, but a start. Savich said, "None of this was your fault. You need to find out who killed him, that animal is the only one to blame here, *the only one*. Now, I'll have Millie make the reservations for you. Tell me again, who's the lead inspector on this?"

"Vincent Delion. Like I said, he called me right before Eloise did last night, said he knew I was FBI, knew I'd want to hear everything they had. It isn't much as of yet. He died instantly, a shot through the forehead, clean in the front, you know, it looked like an innocent *tilak*, the red spot Hindus wear on their foreheads?"

"I know."

"But it wasn't just a red dot on the back of his head. Jesus, not on the back." His eyes went blank.

Savich knew he couldn't let Dane get sucked down into the reality of it, couldn't let him dwell on the hideous mess a bullet made of the head at the exit wound. It would just bury him in pain. He said very precisely, using his hands while he spoke to force eye contact, "I don't suppose the killer left the gun there?"

Dane shook his head. "No. The autopsy's today."

Savich said, "I know Chief Kreider. He was back here last year to appear in front of Congress on commonsense approaches to avoid racial profiling in the Bay Area. I met him down at Quantico on the rifle range. The man's a good distance shooter. And my father-in-law's a Federal judge out in San Francisco. He knows lots of people. What do you want me to do?"

Dane didn't say anything. Savich thought he was too numb with shock and grief to process what he'd said, but that would change. The good thing was that along with the rage and the pain he would have to deal with moment to moment, he would have his instincts and training kicking in. He said, "Never mind. Tell you what, head on out to San Francisco and talk to Delion, find out what they're doing. See if our office out there can help. Do you know Bert Cartwright, the SAC in San Francisco?"

"Yeah," Dane said, his voice flat as a creek-bed stone. "Yeah, I know him." There was sudden animosity on his face. At least it masked the pain for a moment.

"Yes, all right," Savich said slowly. "You two don't get along."

"No, we don't. I don't want to deal with him."

"Why? What happened between the two of you?"

Dane just shook his head. "It's not important."

"All right, you get yourself home and packed. Like I said, I'll have Millie take care of everything for you. Do you want to stay in the city or go to your sister's?"

"I'll stay in the city. Not at the rectory, either, not there."

"Okay, a hotel downtown, then. It'll be FBI approved, so you can count on it to be basic. You'll call if there's anything I can do."

"Yes, thank you, Savich. About my cases—"

"I'll see that they're covered. Go."

The two men shook hands. Savich watched Dane make his way through the large room with workstations for nine special agents, only six of them occupied at the moment. His wife, Special Agent Lacey Sherlock Savich, was in a meeting with Jerry Hollister in the third-floor DNA analysis unit, comparing a DNA sample taken from a Boston rape-and-murder victim with a DNA sample from the major suspect. If they got a match, the guy was toast.

Ollie Hamish, his second in command, was in Wisconsin consulting with the Madison police on a particularly vicious series of murders, all connected to a local radio station that played golden oldies. Go figure, Ollie had said, and started humming "Maxwell's Silver Hammer."

Savich hated crazies. He hated unsolved craziness even more. It amazed and terrified him what the human mind could conjure up. And now Dane's brother, a priest.

He dialed Millie's extension, told her to make arrangements. Then he walked over and flipped on his electric kettle to make a cup of strong Earl Grey tea. He poured his tea into an oversized FBI mug and went back to MAX, his laptop, and booted up.

He started with an e-mail to Chief Dexter Kreider.

San Francisco

At three-thirty on Monday afternoon, San Francisco time, after a five-hour-and-ten-minute flight from Dulles, Dane Carver threaded his way through the large open room toward Inspector Delion's overloaded desk. He paused a moment, studying him. The older man, with his bald, shiny head and thick handlebar mustache, was hunched over a computer keyboard, typing furiously. Dane sat down in the chair beside his desk and said nothing, just looked at the man at his work. It was like every other large cop shop he'd ever been in. Cops with their suit jackets hung over the backs of their chairs, their ties loosened, sleeves rolled up, a young Hispanic guy in handcuffs lounging in the side chairs, trying on sneers, a couple of lawyers in three-piece suits doing their best to intimidate— nothing at all unusual for a Monday afternoon. A decimated box of jelly donuts lay on a battered table in the small kitchen, a coffee machine that looked to be from the last century beside it, along with stacks of paper cups, packets of sugar, and a carton of milk Dane wouldn't touch in a million years.

"Who're you?"

Dane came to his feet and extended his hand. "I'm Dane Carver. You called me last night about my brother."

"Oh yeah, right." He rose, shook Dane's hand. "I'm Vincent Delion." He sat again, waved Dane to do the same. "Hey, I'm real sorry about your brother. I called you because I knew you'd want to hear what was going on."

The brothers had been close, Delion knew from Carver's sister, Eloise DeMarks. And Delion wasn't blind. The man was hurting, bad. He was also a Fed. All the Feds Delion had ever met hadn't seemed to feel much of anything. They all just wanted to press their wing tips down hard on his neck. Of course, he'd never seen a Fed in this situation before. Murder of a family member—something very personal, something over which he had no control at all. It couldn't get tougher than this.

Dane said, his voice effortlessly calm and compelling—it was a very good interview voice, Delion thought—"Yes, I appreciate that. Tell me what you have."

"I'm really sorry about this, but the first thing we need to do is go over to the morgue and you need to identify the body, not that there's any doubt, just procedure, you know the drill. Or maybe you don't. You ever been a local cop?"

Dane shook his head. "I always wanted to be an FBI agent. But yes, I know the drill."

"Yeah, I hear that's usually the way the thing works. Me, I always wanted to be local. Okay, Dr. Boyd did the autopsy this morning, and yeah, I was there. Your brother died instantly, like I told you last night. Boyd also says that was the case, if it's any comfort. I've spoken to your sister. She wanted to come up today, but I told her you would be here to handle things, that you'd fill her in. I'll need to speak to her, but in a day or two. I figured you'd rather take care of things."

"Yes. I've spoken to Eloise. I'll speak with her tonight. Now, about the gun—"

"No gun found at the murder site or anywhere in the church or within a two-block radius of Saint Bartholomew's, but the coroner extracted a twenty-two-caliber bullet from the concrete wall behind the confessional. So the bullet passed through your brother, out the confessional, and another six feet to the wall, not very deep, just about an eighth of an inch into the wall, and it was in pretty good shape. Our ballistics guy, Zopp—yeah, that's really his name, Edward Zopp—was on it right away. The thing is, you know, your brother was a priest, a very active, well-liked priest, and that's got priority over about everything else going on. The bullet was intact enough to weigh and measure, and Zopp was very happy about that. Usually it's not the case. Zopp said he counted the grooves and the land, and determined, of all things, that the gun is probably a JC Higgins model eighty or a Hi Standard model one-oh-one—both of those weapons are really close."

"Yeah, and they're also pretty esoteric. Neither of them is made anymore, but they're not hard to find, and they're not valuable. They're cheap, in fact."

"Yeah, that's it. Also Zopp told us it was weird because it's like the same gun the Zodiac killer used back in the late sixties and early seventies. Ain't that something? You remember, the guy was never caught."

"You're thinking there could be some sort of connection?"

Delion shook his head. "Nope. We're wondering if maybe our perp is an admirer of the Zodiac killer. Hey, it's a real long shot, but we'll see. Since we got the bullet, when we find the gun, we'll be able to match it for the DA."

Dane sat back in his chair and looked down at his wing tips. He hated this, hated it to his soul, but he had to ask. "Angle of entry?"

THREE

"The killer was sitting right opposite your brother. They were looking at each other. The killer raised the gun and fired through the screen."

Jesus, Dane thought, seeing Michael, his head cocked just slightly to one side, listening so carefully to the penitent, trying to feel what the person confessing was feeling, trying to understand, wanting to forgive. But not with this guy, Dane was sure of that. His brother had been worried about this guy. The guy just raised the damned gun and shot him right through his forehead? For a moment, Dane couldn't even think, the horror of what had happened to Michael deadening his brain. He wished it would deaden the rest of him, but of course it didn't. He felt hollow with pain.

Delion gave Dane Carver some time to get himself together, then said, "We've already started checking local gun shops to see if they still carry either of these models or have carried them in the past, and if so, who's bought one in the last few years. Our local gun shop folk keep very thorough records."

Dane couldn't imagine using such a gun to murder someone, particularly if he'd bought the gun here in San Francisco. He'd get caught in no time at all if he bought it here, but it was an obvious place to begin.

"How was he discovered?"

"An anonymous call to nine-one-one, made only minutes after the murder."

"A witness," Dane said. "There's a witness."

"Very possibly. It was a woman. She claims she saw the man who shot your brother come out of the confessional, the proverbial smoking gun still in his hand. She says he didn't see her. She started crying—and then she hung up. Nine-one-one calls are taped, so if you'd like to listen to the call, we can do that. We haven't got a clue who the woman is."

"The woman hasn't called again?"

Delion shook his head.

"She didn't say whether or not she could recognize him?"

"Said she couldn't, said she'd call if she thought of anything helpful."

Great, okay, Dane thought. At least there was someone. Maybe she would call back. He said, "Have you spoken yet to the other priests at the rectory?"

For the first time Vincent Delion smiled beneath his thick mustache, the ends actually waxed, Dane realized when he saw him smile. "Guess what? I figured you'd be ready to climb up my ass if I didn't let you in on that. So, Special Agent Carver, are you ready to move out?"

Dane nodded. "Thank you. I really appreciate this. I'm officially on leave from the FBI, so I've got time. Father Binney's got to be first. When we exchanged e-mails last week, Michael mentioned Father Binney."

"Oh? In what way? Something pertinent to this?"

"I'm not sure," Dane said, shrugged. "He just wrote of problems with Father Binney. There's something else," Dane added, raising his head, looking straight at Delion's mustache. "My brother said something to me on the phone the other night—something about how he felt helpless and he hated that. I'm hoping that Father Binney will have some ideas."

They passed the small kitchen area with microwave, coffeepot, and three different bowls of peanuts.

"Hey, you hungry? Want some peanuts, a cup of coffee?"

"Peanuts, not donuts?"

"Cops living on donuts, all sporting a big gut—that's a myth, that's just television," Delion said. "We're not big on donuts here, all of us are into fitness. We like peanuts in the shell from Virginia. Sometimes even the spicy ones."

"What's that then?"

"Well, that's just one jelly donut, probably the cleaning guy brought it in."

It was hanging off a paper plate, ready to make its final leap to the floor. Dane thought it more likely that the cleaning guy wouldn't touch it. He smiled, shook his head. "I ate on the plane. Thank you, Inspector."

* * *

THE god-awful reality of it hit Dane when he saw his brother through the glass window in the very small viewing room at the morgue. Dr. Boyd, a tall, white-haired, commanding man, with a voice to make a sinner confess, had taken them through the security door, down the short hall into the room, and drew back the curtains. There was Michael, a sheet pulled up to his neck, only his head visible. Dane felt a lurch of pain so deep he almost gasped. He felt Delion's hand on his shoulder. Then he saw the red dot on Michael's forehead; it looked so fantastical, like it had just been painted on, nothing more, just a dab of makeup, some sort of fashion statement or affectation. He wanted to ask Dr. Boyd why they hadn't cleaned it off, but he didn't.

Dr. Boyd said very gently, "He died instantly, Agent Carver. There was just the slap of the bullet, then he was gone. No pain. I'm very sure of that."

Dane nodded.

"You know that we've done the autopsy, taken fingerprints and DNA samples."

"Yes, I know."

Delion stepped back, his arms folded across his chest, and watched Special Agent Dane Carver. He knew what shock was, what anguish was, and he saw both in this man. When Dane finally nodded and stepped back, Delion said, "Chief Kreider wants to see us now."

CHIEF Dexter Kreider's secretary walked them into the chief's office. The room wasn't all that big, but the view was spectacular. The entire side wall was windows, looking out toward the Bay Bridge, a huge Yahoo! sign and a neon-lit diet Coke sign the other landmarks in view. There was a large desk, and two large cabinets filled with kitsch, something that made Dane smile, for a moment. Just about every higher-up's office he'd been into had had at least one display case. And here, there was also a touch of whimsy—in a corner stood a colorful wooden carousel horse. Utilitarian and whimsical, a nice combination.

Dane knew that Chief Kreider could never sit on that carousel horse. He was a huge man, at least six-foot-four-inches, a good two hundred sixty pounds, not much of it excess, even around his belly. He had military-short hair, steel gray, and lots of it, wore aviator glasses, and looked to be in his mid-fifties.

He wasn't smiling. "Carver? Dane Carver? Special Agent?"

Dane nodded, shook the chief's hand.

"It's good to meet you. Come, sit down. Tina, bring us some coffee."

Delion and Dane sat at the small circular table in the center of the room. The chief still didn't sit, he stood towering over them, his arms crossed over his chest. Then he began to pace until Tina, an older woman, with the same military precision as the chief, poured coffee, nodded to the chief, and marched out. Finally he said, "I got an e-mail from Dillon Savich, your boss back at Disneyland East."

"That's a good one," Delion said.

Kreider said, "Yeah, fitting. Savich writes that you're smarter than you've a right to be and you've got great gut instincts. He asks that we keep you in the loop. Delion, what do you think? You want to cooperate with the Feds?"

"No," Delion said. "This is my case. But I'll accept Carver in on the case with me, as long as I'm the boss and what I say goes."

"I don't want to take over the case," Dane said, "not at all. I just want to help find my brother's murderer."

Kreider said, "All right then. Delion's partner, Marty Loomis, is out with shingles, of all things, laid up for another couple of weeks. Inspector Marino has been in on this since Sunday night with Delion. I've given this some thought." He paused a moment, smiled. "I knew Dillon Savich's father, Buck Savich. He was a wild man, smart enough to scare a crook off to Latvia. I hear his son isn't wild—not like his father was—but he's got his father's brains, lots of imagination, and is a professional to his toenails. I respected the father and I respect the son. You, Carver, I don't know a bloody thing about you, but for the moment I'll take Savich's word that you're pretty good."

"Like I said," Delion said, "I don't mind him tagging along, sir. Hey, maybe he'll even say something bright now and again."

"That's what I was thinking," Kreider said. He paced a couple more times, then pulled up right in front of Dane. "Or would you rather go off on your own?"

Dane looked over at Delion. The man wasn't giving anything away at all. He just stared back. Dane wasn't a fool. He slowly shook his head. "No, I'd like to work with Delion."

"Good." Chief Kreider raised his coffee cup, took one sip, and set it down. "I'll have the lieutenant reassign Marino. Delion, I expect twice-daily updates."

After they were dismissed, Delion said as they walked to the garage, "Lots of the guys wonder how Kreider makes love since the guy is always pacing, back and forth, never stopping. Tough to get much done when you can't hold still."

"Didn't you see that old movie with Jack Nicholson—*Five Easy Pieces*?"

Delion rolled his eyes and laughed as he pulled the 1998 Ford Crown Victoria, white with dark blue interior, out into traffic on Bryant Street. Delion headed north, crossed Market Street, and weaved his way in and out of traffic to Nob Hill. They found a parking slot on Clay.

Delion said, "Dispatch sent a field patrol officer from the Tenth District. He notified Operations, and they called me and the paramedics. Here, our paramedics are the ones who notify the medical examiner. Because it's very high profile, Dr. Boyd himself came to the church. I don't know how well you know San Francisco, but we're near one of the gay districts. Polk Street is known for lots of action. It's just a couple of streets over."

"Yes, I know," Dane said. "Just in case you're wondering, my brother wasn't gay."

"That's what your sister told me," Delion said. He paused a moment, looking up at the church. "Saint Bartholomew's was built in 1910, just four years after the earthquake. The other church burned down. They made this one of redbrick and concrete. See that bell tower—one of the big civic leaders at the time, Mortimer Grist, paid for it. It's a good thirty feet above the roof."

"Everything seems well tended."

"Let's go inside the church first," Delion said. "You need to see where everything is."

He needed to see where his brother's life was ended. Dane nodded, but as he walked down the wide central aisle, closer and closer to where Michael had been shot, in the third confessional, Delion had told him, the one that stood nearest to the far wall, each step felt like a major hurdle. His breathing was hard and fast. As difficult as it had been to see his brother lying dead on that gurney, this was harder. He suddenly felt a vivid splash of color hit his face and stopped. He looked up at a brilliant stained-glass window that spewed a spray of intense colors right where Dane was standing. He didn't move, he just stood, looking up and then beyond the colors, to the scene of Mary and Joseph in the stable, the baby Jesus in the manger in front of them. And angels, so many of them, all singing. He could practically hear the full, brilliant chorus of voices. He drew in a deep breath. The air began to feel warmer, and the crushing pain eased just a bit. He couldn't see the confessional. Rather than a yellow crime-scene strip, they'd rigged up a tall black curtain that cut off the confessional from prying eyes and curious hands. Delion moved the black curtain aside to reveal the confessional—all old, dark wood, tall and narrow, a bit battered, with two narrow doors, the first for the penitent and the far door for the priest. The dazzling colors from the windows were shining down on it now, making it look incandescent.

Slowly, he opened the door and sat down on the hard bench. He looked through the torn mesh netting. His brother had been just there, speaking, listening intently. He doubted the man had used the kneeler, not with the angle of the bullet. Did Michael know the man would kill him?

Dane rose and walked to the other side. He opened the door and eased down on the cushioned seat where his brother had sat. He didn't know what he expected to feel sitting there where his brother had died, but the fact was, he didn't feel any fear, nothing cold or black, just a sort of peace that he let flow deeply into him. He drew a deep breath and bowed his head. "Michael," he said.

Delion stood back, watching Special Agent Dane Carver walk out of the confessional. He saw the sheen of tears in his eyes, said nothing.

"Let's go talk to the rectory people," Dane said, and Delion just nodded.

They walked around to the back of the church to the rectory, which was set off by eucalyptus trees, a high fence, and more well-tended grounds. It was quieter than Dane thought it would be, the sounds of traffic distant. The rectory was a charming two-story building, with ivy trailing over the red brick walls, the tinkling of a small fountain in the background. Everything smelled fresh.

Michael was dead and everything smelled fresh.

FOUR

Father Binney immediately rose to greet them from behind a small reception desk. He was very short, and on top of his neck sat the head of a leprechaun. Dane had never before seen hair that red, without a single strand of white. Not even Sherlock could match this. Father Binney was also nearly sixty years old. Amazing.

He stuck out his hand when he saw Delion, but in the next instant he looked like he was going to faint. He grabbed the edge of a chair, staring at Dane.

"Oh, you gave me a start." He grabbed his chest. "You're Father Michael Joseph's brother, that's it. Our sweet Father in Heaven, you're so much alike, you scared me there for a moment. Ah, do come in, gentlemen, do come in. Inspector Delion, it is good to see you again. You must be exhausted."

"It was a long night," Delion said as he followed Father Binney. He said to Dane, "I visited briefly with Father Binney this morning about eight o'clock, after the forensics team finally cleared the church for use again."

And you didn't say a word about it to me, Dane thought. He would have been surprised, though, if Delion hadn't been camping on the rectory's doorstep as quickly as possible.

"He spoke to everyone," Father Binney said. "You didn't find anything in Father Michael Joseph's room, did you, Inspector Delion?"

"Nothing that one wouldn't expect."

Father Binney was shaking his head as he led them into a small parlor. It was packed with dark-grained Chinese furniture, old and scarred and graceful, sitting on an ancient Persian carpet that was so frayed in spots that Dane was afraid to walk on it. The heavy red drapes had black dragons woven into them. "Do sit down, gentlemen." He turned to Dane. "I am very sorry for your loss, Mr. Carver. Everyone is. We loved Father Michael Joseph, it's a horrible thing. Oh my, you look so much like him, it's a shock even though I've seen a picture with the two of you—peas in a pod, the same smile. Oh my, this is very difficult. As I told Inspector Delion this morning, I'm the one who's responsible. If only I hadn't agreed to let that man come to the church for confession so late."

Father Binney sank down onto an overstuffed red brocade chair, all black against all red, except for his white clerical collar. Suddenly he covered his face with his hands. There were red hairs on the backs of his hands. Finally he looked up. "Please excuse me. It's just that I have to get used to looking at you, Mr. Carver, you're just so much like Father Michael Joseph. To have him gone, just gone, it's too much. Nothing like this has ever happened here at Saint Bartholomew's, and it's my fault."

Dane said in his deep, calm voice, "It isn't your fault, Father. It isn't mine either. It's this madman who killed him—he's the only one to blame here. Now, please, Father, tell us what you know about this man."

It steadied Father Binney. Slowly, he raised his head. He shuddered one more time as he looked at Dane. Dane saw that his feet barely reached the threadbare carpet, probably a good thing, since the thing was so tatty.

"As I told Inspector Delion, the man phoned late Sunday night, around eight o'clock, I think it was. I was on the desk for that hour, which is why I took the call. He said it was urgent, said he was very ill, that if he didn't speak to Father Michael Joseph, then he might go to hell if he died. He was very fluent, very believable. You understand, we have set times for confessions, but he pleaded with me, didn't let up."

"What was the man's name, Father?" Dane said.

Father Binney said, "He said he was Charles DeBruler, promised me he'd confessed to Father Michael Joseph two previous times, that Father had really helped him. He said he trusted Father Michael Joseph."

"What did my brother say, exactly, when you told him of the call?"

Father Binney frowned, his brow pleating deeply. "He was very angry, truth be told. He said he knew this man, that he didn't want to speak to him, not ever again. I was surprised, told him that I had never known him to fail to minister to anyone who asked for help. He didn't want to, but you see, I made him feel as if he was failing in his duty if he didn't see the man. I also told him that I never knew him to turn down a person who wanted confession, no matter the time requested, no matter what he thought of the penitent. Father Michael Joseph didn't wish to discuss the man with me, but he said he would see him one more time. If he couldn't do anything to change the man, it was the last time. Then he said something about having a decision to make, a decision that could change his life forever." Father Binney fell silent.

"What do you think he meant, Father, by 'change his life'?" Dane asked.

"I don't know," said Father Binney. "I can't imagine."

Dane slowly nodded. "The man asked for my brother three times. Why? If he didn't come to repent, then why did he want to see my brother, specifically?"

"I have asked myself that over and over," said Father Binney. "Three times he saw Father Michael Joseph. Why didn't Father Michael Joseph want to see him again? Why did he talk about making a decision that night that might change his life?"

"It sounds to me like this man had no intention of repenting his sins," Delion said. "Maybe it's possible that the man came to brag to your brother, you know, maybe he wanted to brag to someone about his crimes who was helpless to do anything about it. That's why your brother was angry, Dane, why he didn't want to see this man again. He knew the man was playing games with him. What do you think? It explains why Father Michael Joseph didn't want to see him again. Hey, am I off the wall here?"

"I don't know," Dane said. "The man came three different times." He fell silent. "The third time he killed my brother."

Father Binney's eyes filled. "Ah, but why would the man taunt Father Michael Joseph? Why?" Father Binney rose, began pacing. "I'll never see Father Michael Joseph again. Everyone is immensely saddened, and yes, angry. Bishop Koshlap is distraught. Archbishop Lugano is extremely upset by all of this. I believe he met with Chief Kreider this morning."

"Yes," Delion said. "He did." He turned to Dane. "The janitor, Orin Ratcher, found Father Michael Joseph just before the police came, right?"

"Yes," Father Binney said. "Orin has trouble sleeping, keeps odd hours. He said he was mopping in the vestry, thought he heard a pop, ignored it, then finally he came in and found Father Michael Joseph in the confessional."

"He didn't see anyone?"

"No," Father Binney said. "He said there was no one, just dark silence and Father Michael Joseph, still sitting in the confessional, his head back against the wall. Just a moment later a patrol officer came, said there'd been a call about a murder. Orin showed him Father Michael Joseph's body. Orin is in very bad shape, poor man. We have him staying here for the next couple of days. We don't want him to be alone."

Delion said, "I already spoke to him, Dane. He didn't see the woman who phoned in the murder either. Nothing. Zip."

"Father Binney, do you have that list of Father Michael Joseph's friends?"

"There are so many." Father Binney sighed and reached into his pocket. "At least fifty, Inspector Delion."

Delion pocketed the list. "You never know, Father," he said.

"Father Binney, could you tell us the dates and times of the two other visits my brother had with this Mr. Charles DeBruler?"

Father Binney, pleased that he could do something, was only gone for five minutes. When he returned to the sitting room he said, "Father Michael Joseph heard confession last Tuesday night until ten p.m. and last Thursday night until nine p.m."

Dane asked to look through his brother's room even though Delion had already searched it. At the end of nearly an hour, they had found nothing to give them any sort of clue. There was a pile of Dane's e-mails to his brother, beginning from the previous January, which he'd printed and kept, just over a year's worth. That was when Michael had finally gotten himself online and went e-mail mad. "Have your guys checked out my brother's computer?"

"Yes. They haven't found anything hidden on the hard drive, if that's where you're headed. No coded files, no deleted files that look like anything."

They spoke to two other priests, to the cook, the maid, three clerical assistants. None could add anything relevant. No one had ever spoken to or seen Charles DeBruler.

"He knew his murderer," Delion said when they were back in the car. "There's no doubt about that. He knew he was a monster, but he wasn't afraid of him."

"No," Dane said, "not afraid. Michael was repulsed by him, but he wasn't afraid of him. Charles DeBruler spoke two other times to my brother, last Tuesday and last Thursday, both in the late evening." Dane took a deep breath. "For Michael to be that upset, for him to be angry about seeing this man, it's my best guess that the man must have done something horrendous around both those other times. Delion, were there any murders committed here in San Francisco on those days or perhaps a couple of days before?"

Delion hit the steering wheel with his hand and nearly struck a pedestrian who was stoned and walk-dancing across Market Street. He gave them the finger, never breaking stride.

"Yes," Delion said, turning the Ford sharply to make the guy jump out of the way. "Damn. It makes sense, doesn't it? Why the hell didn't I think of that?"

"You're exhausted, for a start."

Delion blew that off, fingered his mustache. "Okay, Dane, let me think. We've had three murders, one a couple of weeks old. We've got the guy—a husband we believe who just wanted to collect on his wife's life insurance. That was Donnie Lunerman's case. He just shook his head when he walked out of the interview with the man. It boggles the mind what some people will do for fifty thousand dollars.

"I've got it. Last Monday night—just one night before the first confession—there was an old woman, seventy-two, who lived alone in the Sunset District, on Irving and Thirty-third. She was murdered in her home. No robbery, no forced entry, no broken windows. The guy clubbed her to death in her bed and took off. Thing's a dead end so far."

"He didn't shoot her," Dane said thoughtfully, bracing one hand against the dashboard as Delion took a sharp turn into the police garage.

"No, he bludgeoned her to death. Then, last Wednesday, and this is the one that everyone is all up in arms about, a gay activist was murdered, outside a bar in the Castro. Lots of witnesses, but no one close and no one can agree on what the guy looked like. He was straight, he was gay, he was fat, thin as a rail, old, young—you get the picture. That's not my case. The chief formed a special task force, that's how high profile this guy was."

"How was he killed?"

"Garroted."

"Okay. Blunt force, strangulation, bullet. The guy is all over the board."

"If," Delion said, "if—and this is a really big if—if the guy killed both those people and taunted your brother about them, then why would he kill him?"

"I don't know," Dane said. "I'm really not sure, but I'll betcha that our profilers would have an idea about that."

"Oh man," Delion said, screeching into a parking place in the garage, "the Feds are coming to roost on my head after all."

"They're good people, Delion." Dane paused a moment, then said, "You know, I'm wondering about that woman—the one who called in my brother's murder—why she was there at midnight on Sunday?"

"Yeah, everyone was wondering about that. No way to find her. Let's hope she calls us again."

"I wonder what she really saw."

"We'll probably never know. I don't think we'll have any luck finding her."

Dane said, "Maybe she'll be on Father Binney's list."

Delion glanced over at him. "You ever find anything out that easy?"

FIVE

She stood on the bottom step of the ugly Hall of Justice building on Bryant Street.

It was a beautiful Tuesday morning, gloriously sunny, with just a nip in the air, actually a typical winter day in San Francisco, as she'd been told many times. Yes, the air was so clear and sharp you couldn't breathe in deep enough.

She'd only been here about two weeks, and there had been other days like this. But this morning, this incredibly crisp, clear morning, she felt little pleasure. She walked slowly to the top step, people streaming around her, most of them moving fast, focused on where they were going. No one paid her any attention.

She was scared, really scared. She didn't want to be there, but she didn't have a choice. She'd tried for a solid two minutes to convince herself that Father Michael Joseph's death had nothing to do with her, but of course that was not going to work.

It was time to step up.

She went through the metal detector, made her way through the crowded lobby, and took the elevator to the fourth floor.

She'd been to the police station once before, when she'd first arrived in San Francisco. She'd had a weak moment, thought she would just waltz in and tell someone what had happened, see if someone would help her. But she realized soon enough that she was dreaming. She'd snuck away. That first time she hadn't noticed the series of black-and-white photos that lined the walls, many of them taken before the earthquake. She walked through the door to Homicide, into the small reception area. There was no one behind the high counter. She paused a moment, then walked through the door. She'd seen a lot of homicide rooms on TV and this one looked much the same except it was smaller, about a dozen big, scarred light oak desks shoved together in pairs, heavy old side chairs beside each one. There was a computer on top of each desk, stacks of loose paper, folders, books, a phone, and what looked like mounds of just plain trash. What struck her was that there wasn't much noise, no cursing, no yelling, no chaos. Just the steady low hum of a dozen simultaneous conversations. On one side of the main room were two small interview rooms, with no windows, that looked like soundproofed coffins. Finally, from one of those rooms, she heard some raised voices.

There were eight or so men in suits standing or seated at their desks, speaking on phones, working on computers. She didn't see any women.

Half a dozen other people stood around the room, some of them thumbing through the ancient metal file cabinets that lined every wall, some just studying their fingernails, some looking really worried. She wondered if they were criminals or lawyers, or maybe some of each. One young guy with purple hair and pants so low she could see that his navel was an outie, sauntered out of one of the interview rooms, winked at her, and smacked his lips. He must be really desperate, she thought, ducking her head down, to come on to her.

Other than the kid with the purple hair, no one paid her a bit of attention. She wondered if anyone would be willing to take the time even to listen to her. Everyone looked harassed, too busy—

"Can I help you, miss?"

It was a uniformed patrol officer. There wasn't a smile on her face. On the other hand, she didn't look like she was ready to chew nails either.

"I need to speak to the detective who's investigating Father Michael Joseph's murder."

The woman lifted a dark brow a good inch. "They're not detectives here in San Francisco. They're inspectors."

"I didn't know that. Thank you. May I please see the inspector? Really, I'm not here to waste anyone's time."

The officer looked her over, and she knew what the officer was seeing. It wasn't good. Finally, the officer said, "All right. I see that Inspector Delion is at his desk. I'll take you to him."

There was a man seated in the chair beside Inspector Delion's desk, his back to her. The set of his shoulders, the color of his hair were somehow familiar to her. A criminal being interviewed?

The officer said, "Hey, Vince, I've got a woman here to see you about Father Michael Joseph's murder."

"Yeah?" He looked as harassed and as impatient as every other man in the room. Then he grew quiet, his dark eyes on her face. She knew what she looked like. Was he going to sneer at her? Tell her to get lost? No, he just sat there, staring at her, fingering his mustache. He didn't say anything else, just waited.

"Yes, I need to speak to you, sir."

The man seated in the side chair rose and turned to face her. She stared at him, unable to take it in. She had to be dead, there was no other conclusion. She didn't feel dead, but who knew? Here he was, looking at her, and he was dead, she had seen the bullet hole through his forehead, seen his eyes.

She squeaked, nothing more than that, and folded up on herself, fainting for the first time in her life.

Dane caught her before she cracked her head on the edge of the desk behind her. The inspector sitting there jerked back and said, "Hey!"

"I've got her, it's okay," Dane said.

"What the hell's wrong with her?" Delion shoved back his chair, splaying his hands on his desktop. "Damnation, it's only eight o'clock in the morning. Here, Dane, take her into the lieutenant's office. She and the captain are in a meeting with Chief Kreider, so it's free."

Dane hauled her up in his arms and carried her into a small glass-walled office. Like every other free space in the area, it was lined with old gray file cabinets that had seen better days a half century before. He laid her on the rattiest, ugliest old green sofa he'd ever seen. No, there was one just as ugly in the rectory at St. Bartholomew's.

"You got some water, Delion?"

"Uh? Oh yeah, just a moment."

Dane went down on his haunches next to her. He gave her a cop's once-over, quickly done, assessment made. She looked homeless—torn jeans, three different sweaters, one on top of the other, all of them on the well-worn side, not dirty, just old and tattered. She wore no makeup, not a surprise. Her hair was a dirty blond with a bit of curl, longish, tied in the back with a rubber band. Even with all the bulky layers of sweaters, it was easy to tell she was thin, pale, no more than twenty-seven, -eight, max. Not doing well in life, that was for sure. She looked like she'd been in a closet for too long without a glimpse of the sun, or tucked away in a homeless shelter. She also looked like she needed a dozen good meals. She'd been carrying a wool cap. Even unconscious, she still clutched it in her fingers.

They had a homeless woman for a witness?

Of course, that was just the outside. What a person was like on the inside was what was important, what was real. But if her outsides gave any clue at all, it was that something bad had happened to her. Drugs? An abusive husband? Alcohol?

Why did she faint? Hunger?

"Here's some water. She show any signs of life yet?"

"Soon." Dane lightly slapped her cheeks, waited, then slapped her again.

A couple of inspectors stuck their heads in. Delion waved them off. "She'll be okay, don't call the paramedics, okay?"

A woman officer said, "She looks really down on her luck. The last person she should want to see is you, Delion."

Her eyelashes fluttered. Slowly, she opened her eyes, blinked a couple of times, and focused on Dane's face above her.

"Oh no," she said, so low he could barely hear her. She tried to get away from him by pressing herself against the back of the sofa. "Oh God, am I dead?"

Dane said, "No, you're not dead. I'm not dead either. You knew my brother, didn't you? Father Michael Joseph?"

"Your brother?"

"Yes, my twin brother. We're identical twins. My name is Dane Carver."

"You're not a priest?"

"Nope," said Delion. He brought his face down close to hers, which made her shrink back even more. Delion backed off, said, "He's the other end of the scale."

"You're a criminal?"

"No, I'm not. That was just a bit of police humor. Here, drink a bit of water."

He cupped the back of her head, brought her up a bit, and put the paper cup to her mouth. She sipped at it, then said, "Thank you, no more."

Delion pulled up one of Lieutenant Purcell's chairs, straddled it, waved Dane to the only other chair in the small room. Dane pulled it up next to the sofa.

Delion said, "You here to tell us about Father Michael Joseph? You know something about his murder? You wouldn't be the woman who phoned in the murder about midnight Sunday night, would you?"

"Yes," she said, unable to look away from Father Michael Joseph's brother. She lifted her hand, touched her fingertips to his cheek, the small cleft in his chin. Dane didn't move. She dropped her hand, swallowed tears. Dane saw that her fingernails were as ragged as her sneakers, her hands chapped. "You're so like him," she said. "I only knew him for two weeks, but he was always kind to me, and I know he cared about what happened to me. He was my friend. I'm not Catholic, but it didn't matter. I was there Sunday night, in the church, when that man shot him."

Delion said, "Why the hell didn't you come forward right away? Good God, woman, it's Tuesday morning. He was murdered midnight Sunday."

"Yes, I know. I'm sorry. I had to call you from a public phone, and I finally found one that worked by a convenience store about two blocks from the church. I called nine-one-one, told the operator what I'd seen. But I couldn't stay, I just couldn't. This morning I knew I had to come and talk to you, that just maybe I could help, but I really don't think so."

"Why couldn't you stay and talk to us on Sunday night?"

"I was just too scared."

"Why?"

She didn't say a word, just shook her head.

"Okay," Delion said, backing off for the moment. "I want you to take a deep breath. Get a hold of yourself. Now then, I want you to tell us everything that happened Sunday night, and don't leave out a single detail. We need everything. Can you do that?"

She nodded, closed her eyes a moment against the fearsome pain, the terror of Father Michael Joseph's violent death.

Dane watched her twist the old red wool cap between her long fingers, thin and very white.

She stared down at that woolen cap as she said, "All right, I can do this. I was sitting in one of the front pews on the far side of the church, waiting for Father Michael Joseph to finish."

"So you came in after the man had already gone into the confession?" Delion asked.

"No, I'd been speaking to Father Michael Joseph, and he wanted me to stay, to talk to him when he'd finished hearing this one confession."

Dane said, "Was anyone else in the church?"

"No, it was empty, except for the two of us. It was very dark. Father Michael Joseph left me, walked to the confessional, and went inside."

"You saw the person come into the church?"

"Yes, I saw him. I didn't see him clearly, mind you, but I could see that he was slender, lots of black hair, and he had on a long Burberry coat, dark. I wasn't really paying all that much attention. I saw him go into the confessional."

"Could you hear either Father Michael Joseph or the other person speaking?"

"No, nothing. There was pure, deep silence, like you'd expect in a church at night. A good amount of time passed before I heard a popping sound. I knew instantly that it was a gun firing."

"How'd you know it was a gun?" Delion asked. "Most people wouldn't automatically think *gun* when they heard a popping sound."

"I went hunting a lot with my father before he died."

"Okay, what next?" Dane said.

"Just a moment later the man came out of the confessional. I think he was smiling, but I can't be sure. He was holding a big ugly gun in his hand."

SIX

She took another sip of water, trying to get herself together. She was shaking so badly she spilled some of the water on the woolen cap in her lap. She stared at it, and swallowed.

"You okay?" Father Michael Joseph's brother said.

She nodded. "Yes, I think so."

"Do you think he saw you?" Dane asked.

She shook her head. "I was in the shadows, down under the pew. No, he didn't see me."

"Okay, when you're ready, tell us the rest," Delion said.

"When I heard the gun fire, I slipped down beneath the pew. I was terrified that he'd come out, see me, and kill me. He looked around, but like I said, I'm sure he didn't see me. I watched him unscrew a silencer off the end of the gun—he did it very quickly, like he was really proficient at it—and he slipped both the silencer and the gun into his coat pocket. Then he did something strange, and it nearly scared me to death. He pulled the gun back out of his pocket. He held it pressed to his side. I think he was whistling as he walked out of the church.

"I didn't move for a real long time, just couldn't, I was just too scared that he was waiting behind the side door to see if anyone would come out, and then he'd kill me, quick and clean, just like he killed Father Michael Joseph.

"I finally went to the confessional." She swallowed, closed her eyes for a moment. "I looked at Father Michael Joseph's face. His eyes were open wide and I could see that he was gone. Oh God, he had such beautiful eyes, dark and kind, he saw so much. But his eyes were blank, vague in death, and there was a small red hole in his forehead. It looked so harmless, that little hole, but he was dead. There was something else, something in his expression. It wasn't fear or terror, you know, from knowing in that instant he was going to die; it was something else. He looked somehow pleased. How could that be possible? For God's sake, pleased about what?"

"Pleased," Delion said. "That's odd. You're sure?"

She nodded. "Or maybe like he was finally satisfied about something. I'm sorry, I'm just not sure."

"Okay, go ahead."

"Then I heard someone coming out of the vestry off to the left. I froze. God, I thought it was the murderer and he was coming back. I thought he'd see me because I wasn't hiding in the shadows anymore. He'd know that I saw him kill Father Michael Joseph, he'd believe that I could identify him, and he was coming back to kill me, too.

"I ran as fast as I could to the side door, flipped up the dead bolt, and managed to slip outside without making much noise. I waited there, it seemed like forever, but I didn't hear or see anything. Then I ran to try to find a phone."

"Where'd you go after that?" Delion asked.

"Back to the shelter on Ellis, near Webster, Christ's Shelter."

"That's a long way from Saint Bartholomew's," Delion said.

"Yes, it is. Father Michael Joseph was very involved in the shelter's activities and the people who stayed there. That's where I met him. He, ah, was very fond of history, particularly the thirteenth century. His hero was Edward the First."

"Ah, you know about that," Dane said, and felt his voice seize up. He swallowed, knowing they were looking at him. "He loved history. I never had the knack for remembering dates, but Michael could. I remember he'd talk me into a coma, going on and on about the Crusades, particularly the one with Edward."

"That's all well and good," Delion said, "but let's get back to it, all right?" He watched Dane collect himself, and lightly gripped his shoulder.

"Are you sure you didn't see more?" Delion said. "Any thing else?"

"No, I'm sorry. The man was in the confessional when he shot Father Michael Joseph. The light was real dim—you know how the light is really soft and almost black at midnight? And the shadows, they were thick, deep, all over the church."

Dane nodded.

"It was like that. I'm sorry, but I got only a vague impression of him. The Burberry, the black hair, nothing else, really."

Dane said easily, "Do me a favor. Close your eyes just a moment and picture yourself standing inside Saint Bartholomew's. Can you see that incredible stained-glass window that shows the stable scene of Christ's birth? It's just behind the confessional."

"Oh yes, I can see it. I've stared at it many times, wondering, you know, how something made of glass could make you so aware of just being."

Yes, he thought, satisfied, she knew the window well. He said, "I saw it for the first time yesterday, stared at it, felt all those colors seep into me. It made me feel close to something bigger than I am, something deep inside that I'm rarely aware of, something powerful."

"Yes. That's it exactly."

"I can imagine how, even when it's dark in the church—that midnight dark you spoke about—how that window still shines like a beacon when just a hint of light comes through it. It would make all that black, all those shadows, take on a glow, a pale sort of shine, concentrated, as if from a long way off. I can see that. Can you?"

"Yes," she said, her eyes closed. "I can."

Dane sat forward on the chair, his hands clasped between his legs, his voice lower now, smooth as honey. "You feel like you're bathed in that light and it makes you feel warm and safe. It allows you to see everything around you more clearly because of that beautiful spray of colors."

"Yes. I hadn't realized how incredible it was."

"Which hand was he holding the gun in?"

"His right hand."

"He used his left hand to unscrew the silencer?"

"Yes."

"Was he a young man?"

"No, I don't think so. He didn't move like a young man moves, like you move. He was older, but not old, close to Inspector Delion's age, but he wasn't carrying any extra weight. He was slightly built but straight as a conductor's wand. He stood very straight, military straight. He had his head cocked to the right side."

"What was he wearing?"

"A long trench coat—you know, the Burberry. It's exactly the same sort of overcoat my father used to wear."

"What color?"

"Dark, real dark, maybe black. I can't see it all that clearly."

"Was he tall?"

"Not terribly, maybe five-foot-ten. I know he was under six-foot."

"Bald?"

"No, like I said, he had dark hair, lots of it, really dark, may be black, just a bit on the long side. He wasn't wearing a hat or anything."

"Beard?"

"No beard. I remember his skin was light, lighter than anything else about him; it was like another focal point, a splash of white in all that gloom."

"You said he was smiling?"

"Yes."

"What did his teeth look like?"

"Straight, very white, at least they looked very white in all that darkness."

"When he walked away, was he limping? Did he favor one leg over the other? Did he walk lightly?"

"He was fast, his stride long. I remember that his trench coat flapped around his legs, he was walking so fast, and he was graceful, yes, I can remember how graceful he was."

"Did he ever put the gun back in his pocket?"

"No, he just kept it held down, close against his right side."

Her breathing hitched.

Dane leaned forward and patted her hand. Her skin was dry, rough. She blinked, so surprised at what she'd remembered so clearly, seen so clearly, that she just stared at Father Michael Joseph's brother.

She said, "Your name is Dane Carver?"

He nodded.

Delion waited another couple of seconds, saw that it was over, and said, "Not bad, ma'am."

"Yes, you saw quite a lot," Dane said, and now he leaned forward and lightly touched his fingers to her shoulder. It felt reassuring, calming, that touch of his, and she realized that he knew it and that's why he'd done it. Dane said, "That was really good. Inspector Delion will call up a forensic artist next. Do you think you could work with an artist?"

"Yes, certainly. I really don't think I can identify him if you ever catch him, though."

"Now back up a minute," Delion said. "Why were you in the church at midnight?"

"Father Michael Joseph told me that he had to meet this man really late for confession, but he said he wanted me to stay, he wanted to talk to me, see if maybe he could help me work things out."

"Help you with what?"

She shook her head.

"Maybe we could help you," Dane said.

She shook her head again, lips seamed together.

"You know," Delion said, "life has a funny way of changing things around. People you don't particularly trust one day, you can confide in the next."

"Look," she said, "I don't want any help. I don't want to tell you what I was going to speak to Father Michael Joseph about. I don't want you to keep asking me about it, all right?"

"But maybe we could help," Dane said.

"No. Leave it alone or I'll disappear."

Delion and Dane looked at each other. Slowly, Dane nodded. "No more questions about you and your situation."

"Okay. Good." Suddenly she started crying. Not a sound, just tears running down her face.

Delion looked like he wanted to run.

Dane grabbed a couple of Kleenex off the lieutenant's desk and handed them to her.

"Oh goodness, I'm sorry, I—"

Dane said, "It's okay. You've had a couple of tough days."

She wiped her face, her eyes. "I'm sorry," she said again, tears thick in her voice.

She clutched the Kleenex in her right fist, sat up, and swung her legs over the side of the sofa. She took a very deep breath, looked down. She paused a moment, sniffed, swallowed, then said, "This sofa is really ugly."

Dane laughed. Somewhere deep down, there was still laughter in him. "Yeah," he said, "it's butt ugly."

"Yeah, yeah," Delion said, scooting his chair forward, crowding Dane out of the way, easy since the office was very small. "We've got a lot to talk about, Ms.— Hey, we don't know your name."

She blinked at him. "My name is Jones."

"Jones," Delion repeated slowly. "What's your first name, Ms. Jones?"

"Nick."

"Nick Jones. As in Nicole?"

She nodded, but Dane thought it was a lie. What was going on here? Was she wanted by the police in some other city? Maybe she was wanted here, in San Francisco. Maybe that was why Michael had wanted to help her. Michael had always been able to sniff out folks who were in trouble, and he always wanted to help them. He gave her a long look but didn't say anything.

"Well, Ms. Jones," Delion said, "I could arrest you, send your fingerprints off, and find out what you've done."

"Yes," she said. "You could."

She was a good poker player, Dane thought.

Delion folded first. "Nah, we'll pass on that. No more questions about your background, your own situation. You got a deal. Now, tell us, Ms. Jones, did you meet other people that Father Michael Joseph knew?"

Nick nodded. "Yes, there was another woman he was trying to help. Her name is Valerie Striker. I think she's a prostitute. She was in the church when I got there. She'd just stopped by to speak to Father Michael Joseph for a moment. I remember she left maybe five minutes before that man came in."

Delion said, "Oh, shit. Whatcha bet he saw her?"

"It's possible," Dane said.

"Did you see her when you ran out of Saint Bartholomew's, Ms. Jones?"

She shook her head.

"Valerie Striker," Delion said and wrote the name down in his book. "We'll check on her. Just maybe she saw something."

"Or maybe he saw her," Nick said. "Dear God, I hope not."

SEVEN

Nick said, "I'm really sorry you lost your brother, Mr. Carver."

Dane's hands were clasped in his lap. "Thank you," he said, but didn't look up. He said after a moment, "You said that you and my brother were friends. How close were you?"

"Like I told you, we only met two weeks ago. Father Michael Joseph was visiting the shelter a couple of days after I arrived. We got to talking. We got off onto medieval history. I don't remember how it came up, to be honest. Father Michael Joseph was very kind, and very knowledgeable. We got to talking, and it turned out that he is—he was—fascinated by King Edward the First of England, particularly that last Crusade Edward led to the Holy Land that led to the Treaty of Caesarea." She shrugged, tried to look self-deprecating, but Dane wasn't fooled for a moment. Who was she?

"He took me for a cup of coffee at The Wicked Toe, a little café just off Mason. He didn't care how I looked, didn't care what anyone else would think—not, of course, that the area is any great shakes."

She looked over at Dane, stared at him, and then she started crying again.

Dane didn't say anything this time, couldn't say anything because his throat was all choked up. He wanted to cry himself, but he wouldn't let himself, not here. All he could do was wait, and listen to her sobs.

When she'd stilled, he said, "Did my brother give you anything to keep safe for him?"

"Give me something? No, he didn't. Why?"

"Too bad."

Delion came into the lieutenant's office and said, "Valerie Striker lives on Dickers Avenue. I'm outta here. You want to come, Dane?"

Nick was on her feet. "Please, please, let me come with you. I met

Valerie, she's so beautiful, and really nice. She was unhappy, didn't know what to do. There was this man who was threatening her. Please, let me come with you. Maybe if she sees me, she'll agree to talk to you."

"This is police business, ma'am. You're a civilian, for God's sake, you can't just—"

"Please," Nick said, and grabbed Delion's sleeve. "This is so important to me, please, Inspector. I won't get in the way, I won't say a thing, but—"

"I'm an outsider, too, Delion," Dane said. "Maybe she can be helpful if Ms. Striker doesn't want to talk to us." His unspoken message that Delion got real fast was that Ms. Jones might just disappear on them again.

Delion said low to Dane, "If this was FBI business, would you let her tag along with you?"

"Sure, no problem."

"Yeah, right." He said on a sigh to Nick, "All right, Ms. Jones, just this one time. Dane, she's your responsibility."

"Sure, no problem."

"Hey, wait. Before we head on over to Valerie's place, let's just wait for the forensic artist here before Ms. Jones starts to forget."

An hour later, Jenny Butler, one of two forensic artists on staff, held up her sketch for everyone to see.

"Is that him, Ms. Jones?" Delion asked.

Nick nodded slowly. "It's as close as I can get. Will it help?"

"Remains to be seen. Thank you, Jenny. How's Tommy?"

"He's just ducky, Vince. The older he gets the more of a handful he becomes." She added to Dane and Nick, "He's my husband. See you, Vince."

"Thanks. Ms. Jones, this sketch will be printed up and distributed, and there will be no mention of you."

Delion grabbed his jacket and headed out the door, Nick and Dane close on his heels.

Fifteen minutes later, he pulled the Ford next to the curb only a block from the address they wanted on Dickers Avenue.

The three of them stood a moment staring up at the old Victorian where Valerie Striker lived.

Delion looked at Ms. Jones—homeless woman, fake name—and said, "This is great, just great. I've got a Fed and a civilian with me to interview a witness. Great."

"He's all bark," Dane said.

They watched Delion stomp up the six stairs to the front door of the Victorian, which was painted four shades of green. He turned. "Hey, come on, you guys, enough chitchat. Let's see what Valerie's got to say."

"THE place looks terrific," Dane said, touching a pale lime-green gargoyle, one of three hovering over the lintel of the front door, looking down at them. "Business must be good."

"I talked to one of the inspectors in Vice; he said eight hookers live here. Everything very discreet, very respectable, doubtful even the neighbors know anything. There's a back way in, and it's all sorts of private."

Delion rang the bell to 4B. "There's four apartments on each floor."

There was no answer.

He rang again.

There was still no answer.

"It's pretty early," Dane said. "She's probably still asleep."

"Yeah, well, we're her wake-up call." Delion pressed his thumb on the bell and kept it there.

Three minutes later, he rang the bell to 4C.

"Yes? May I help you?"

"Very polite, very discreet," Delion said under his breath, then continued into the intercom, "This is Inspector Vincent Delion of the SFPD. I know I got you up, but I'm a cop and we need to talk to you. This isn't a bust, nothing like that. We're not here to cause you any trouble. We just need to talk."

A pause, then the buzzer sounded.

The entrance was old-fashioned, dripping with Victoriana, the dark red carpeting rich and deep. Everything was indeed very upscale.

Dane glanced over at Nick Jones. She looked fascinated. Must be her first time in a hooker's nest. Come to think about it, it was his first time, too. Business, he thought, stroking his hand over the beautifully carved newel post on the stairs, was good.

They walked up one flight of stairs, turned right. The lush red carpeting continued. There was wainscoting along the walls of the wide corridor, and well-executed watercolors of the Bay were hung along the walls.

A woman in a lovely black kimono stood in the open doorway to 4C. She was young, with artfully mussed long black hair tossed over one shoulder. She wore almost no makeup. Delion looked at her, appreciated her, and guessed that five hundred bucks wasn't out of the question.

"Ms. . . . ?"

"Elaine Books. What do you want? Hey, she isn't a cop, she's homeless. I know . . . Valerie told me about you, told me you sort of hid in the shadows whenever somebody came around, that you'd only talk to this priest. And you, you're no local, just look at those wing tips; they're a cut above what local guys wear. What are you, a lawyer? What's going on here?"

Delion said, "They're with me, no problem. You really think his shoes look more expensive than mine? Nah, forget it. We need to speak to Valerie Striker, your neighbor in 4B, but she's not answering her doorbell. You seen her this morning?"

"No." Ms. Books frowned, tapped her lovely French manicure against the door frame. "You know, I haven't seen Valerie in a couple of days. What's going on with her?"

Dane said very slowly, "I really don't like the sound of this, Delion."

Delion said, "Right. Ms. Books, we'd like you to come next door with us, watch us open the door, okay?"

"Oh God, you think something's happened to Valerie, don't you?"

"Hopefully not, but we'd like you to verify that we're concerned, and that's why we're going in."

Delion knocked on 4B. There was no answer. He pressed his ear to the door. "Nothing," he said.

Delion put his shoulder to the door of 4B and pushed hard. Nothing happened. "Well made, solid wood, I should have guessed," he said. Both he and Dane backed up, then slammed their shoulders into the door. It flew inward, crashing against the inside wall.

A beautiful apartment, Nick thought, looking past them, all light and airy, so many windows, sunlight flooding in.

Where was Valerie Striker?

Dane stopped suddenly. He became very still. He turned, said very low, his voice urgent, "Ms. Jones, please stay right here. Thank you, Ms. Books. We'll take it from here."

"Hey, what's that smell?" Elaine Books jerked her head back. "Oh God, oh God."

"Stay back," Delion said. He turned to Dane. "Keep them here, all right?"

But it was too late. Before Dane could force Elaine Books and Nick Jones back out of the apartment, Nick saw two white legs sticking out from behind the living room sofa, a really pretty sofa, all white with even whiter pillows strewn across it. All over that white were dark stains, as if someone had dipped a hand into a paint can and just sprinkled the paint everywhere.

"Oh no," Nick said. "It's not paint, is it?"

"No," Dane said, "it's not. Don't move from this spot, you understand me?"

Delion went behind the sofa and knelt down. When he straightened, he looked hard, sad, and angry.

"I think we've found Valerie Striker. She's been garroted. I'd say she's dead a couple of days at least." He nodded to Dane, who herded the two women back into the hallway. He heard Delion on the phone, speaking to the paramedics.

Elaine Books leaned against the corridor wall and started crying. "I'm so sorry," Nick said. "She was your friend. I'm so very sorry. I liked her. She was kind to me, despite—despite how I look." Very slowly, Nick drew the woman into her arms and let her cry on her shoulder.

Nick looked up at Dane. "He killed her. He must have seen her, worried that when she found out about Father Michael Joseph's murder, she'd remember seeing him. He either knew who she was or he found out, came here sometime during the night on Sunday and killed her. That's exactly what happened, isn't it?"

Dane nodded. "Yes, that's probably right."

Elaine Books continued to weep, softly now, her head still on Nick Jones's shoulder.

Valerie Striker was dead. Chances were that she hadn't seen a thing, but that hadn't mattered. She couldn't tell them anything now. Nick closed her eyes as she rocked Elaine Books against her and thought, I'm the one who's supposed to be dead, not her. If only she'd waited for the cops, she would have remembered to tell them about seeing Valerie Striker, and they would have come here, maybe before the killer did, and they could have saved her.

It was her fault.

EIGHT

"She can't stay in the shelter," Dane said. "Do you have a safe house where we can stash her?"

"Yeah," Delion said, "but I don't know if the lieutenant will approve it for her. There's no real threat of danger here."

"You're wrong, Delion. When our guy sees this description—and I bet he will—he'll try to find out about the person who gave it, knowing that if he's ever caught, she can identify him. She'd be a sitting duck at the shelter."

"If she would just tell us her real name and address, we could send her little ass home."

Dane looked over toward the small kitchen where Ms. Nick Jones stood waving a tea bag in a paper cup of hot water, the frayed cuffs of her thick red sweater falling over her fingers. He could still see the tear streaks on her cheeks.

"Look, Dane," Delion said, "you're a cop. You know that since she isn't a teenage runaway, it means she's running from something or someone. That, or she's a druggie—that's the most likely. You notice she's wearing all those sweaters? She's probably hiding needle tracks on her arms.

"Maybe she's wearing them to keep warm. Whatever, it's unfortunate because our Ms. Jones seems bright and speaks well. She's well educated. It was just her bad luck that she was in Saint Bartholomew's on Sunday night, that is, if you believe the story she told us about why she was actually there."

Dane didn't say anything, kept looking at Nick Jones. "She has very nice teeth," he said. "Good dental hygiene."

"Yeah, I noticed. And that means she hasn't been on the street all that long. What? A couple of weeks? Not a month, I'll bet. She doesn't smell and her clothes aren't stiff with dirt."

"No."

"All right, Dane, I'll ask the lieutenant. Now, we've got four murders, all possibly committed by the same perp. We have a pretty fair description of him. Now we need to figure out why he did this."

"Well, we think he meant to do the first three—the old woman, the gay activist, and finally, my brother. Valerie Striker was just in the wrong place at the wrong time."

"Yes, and once we have the why, we'll have him. Let's go meet with the chief, tell him about Valerie Striker. It could have been one of her johns that killed her."

"You don't believe that for a second."

"All right, I don't."

"If the ME pins her murder down to sometime Sunday night, then we know with about ninety-eight percent certainty that the same guy killed her," Dane said. "You go see the chief. I'll speak some more with Ms. Jones."

"You know, I've always wondered why folks can't come up with better aliases. Jones, for God's sake."

"Nick is her real first name though," Dane said. "But it's not short for Nicole."

"You picked up on that lie as well, huh?"

"Oh yes. I wonder what it really is."

A few minutes later, Dane strolled over to the small kitchen. The single donut was gone. Finally tossed? Or was Ms. Jones so hungry that she ate it? He hoped she hadn't. From the looks of that critter, it would have given a buffalo food poisoning.

"Would you like some peanuts? Inspector Delion tells me that's the snack of choice here."

"But I just saw one of the men snag a donut that looked like it died last week."

Good, she hadn't eaten it.

"At least the Medical Examiner is close. Peanuts?"

She shook her head and kept waving the tea bag in the water.

"It's nearly black."

"I like tea strong," she said, but pulled out the bag and tossed it in the open trash bin. "It's hard to get really strong tea unless you do it yourself."

"You know I'm Father Michael Joseph's brother, Dane Carver. There's something else, something I don't think you've caught on to yet. I'm also a special agent with the FBI."

She dropped the cup. It splattered hot tea all over her, him, and the Virginia peanuts.

"Oh no, look what I've done. Oh no." She was grabbing paper towels, wiping him down, finally on her knees, wiping up the floor. "I'm sorry."

"It's all right," he said, pulled off another paper towel and joined her. "It's all right, Nick. I'm the one who's sorry."

"Not your fault," she said, staring down at that towel wet through with tea now.

"Hey," an inspector said, coming around the corner, "who took that last donut?"

Dane laughed, just couldn't help it. She didn't.

"NO can do," Lieutenant Purcell said, standing in her doorway. "No clear and present danger to her. You know that our budget's stretched to the limit, Delion. I'm sorry, but she's on her own."

Dane wondered if it was because she was homeless, and had less worth than someone who had a job and a bit of standing in the community. He didn't say anything. He'd already known the answer would be no and he'd also known what he was going to do.

He hadn't let Nick Jones out of his sight. She looked, quite simply, like she was ready to run. After he left the lieutenant, he went back to the small kitchen. She was still wiping up tea from the counter. "Enough," he said, took her arm, and guided her over to Delion's desk. Delion was in the lieutenant's office. Dane could see him gesticulating through the glass windows. He sat her down, came down beside her on his haunches. "Okay, tell me why you freaked out when I told you I was FBI."

"It was just a surprise, that's all. Your brother is a priest. You're at the other end of the spectrum."

She'd had time to come up with an answer, not a bad one either.

"That's true. What's your real name, Nick?"

"My name is Nick Jones. Just look in the phone book, you'll see there are tons of Joneses. Lots more Joneses than Carvers, that's for sure."

"How long have you been in San Francisco?"

"Not all that long."

"Two, three weeks?"

"Something like that. Two and a half weeks."

"Where did you come from?"

She just shrugged. "Here and there. I like to travel a lot. But it's winter, so it's best to stay in cities that don't get all that cold."

"How old are you?"

"Twenty-eight."

"Where'd you go to school?"

She didn't say a thing, just looked down at her hands, chapped and dry, and her ragged fingernails. Dane sat back in the side chair, crossed his arms over his chest. Finally, she said, "We had a deal here. No questions about me. You got that, Agent Carver? No questions or I'm out of here. I figure you need me, so leave it alone. All right?"

"It's too bad you feel that way," Dane said. "I have the FBI behind me, and you knew my brother. If you're in trouble, I can help you."

Her head came up with that. She seemed stiff all over, but it was hard to tell with all those layers she was wearing. She said, "It's your choice, Agent Carver."

"All right."

"What you need to do is find this man who killed Father Michael Joseph. Is there a death penalty in California?"

"Yes."

"Good. He deserves to die. I was very fond of Father Michael Joseph, even though I only knew him for a short time. He cared about all of us, didn't matter if you were rich or poor or a basically shitty person, he still cared."

Delion came up, shaking his head at Dane. "I had to try again. No go."

Dane said, "Inspector Delion means that there isn't a safe house for you. Given that I firmly believe you need to be kept out of harm's way, I'm taking you with me, back to my hotel. You'll stay with me until we find this guy."

"You're nuts," Nick said. "I'm homeless. No hotel would even let me through the door. Look at me, for God's sake. I look like what I am. Besides, I don't want to stay at a hotel. I'm just fine where I am."

Delion said, "The FBI undoubtedly has a safe house in the area."

"Nope, I don't want to involve them in this. Trust me, Delion, you don't either."

"The camel's-nose-under-the-tent sort of thing? That's fine by me. We don't want Ms. Jones to end up like Valerie Striker. I'm heading to a meeting with the chief now. We're organizing a task force, then we'll have more than enough manpower of our own to catch this creep."

Dane waited to say anything else until Delion was out of earshot. "You're safe for the moment. But, Ms. Jones, when the guy who murdered my brother and three other people realizes his description is out there, you know as well as I do that he'll try to hunt you down. You want to be in that shelter when you hear his footsteps coming up the stairs? There isn't anyone there who could help you."

She went nearly as white as his shirt. "I'll leave San Francisco, go south."

"No, going on the run isn't the answer. If you force us to, we'll arrest you as a material witness."

But evidently Delion wasn't out of earshot. He stopped, said over his shoulder, "You've obviously got a lot of crap going on in your life, Ms. Jones. I'd go with the big Fed if I were wearing your shoes. Let him watch out for you." Delion fanned his hands. "You don't have to worry about our asking you any more questions about your past, okay?"

"No," she said. "I'm stupid for staying this long. I've told you what I know. I'm outta here." She was out of her chair and heading toward the door in a flash.

Delion made a grab for her, but missed.

Dane sighed, said over his shoulder, "She moves fast."

One of the inspectors called out, "She must have learned that in the Tenderloin."

Dane stomped after her. He saw a flash of her red sweater as she ran past the elevator toward the stairs. He caught her just before she made it to the third-floor exit.

He didn't know what he expected, but she fought him like her life depended on it. She kicked and punched and didn't make a single sound while she was trying to kill him.

Why didn't she yell at him?

He finally managed to get behind her and force her arms against her sides. He pulled her back hard against him so she couldn't move.

"Hold still, just hold still."

She was breathing hard, but still she struggled and tugged and heaved. She was strong, workout strong. He simply held on as tightly as he could. She couldn't gain enough leverage to hurt him, but she tried.

A couple of cops came out onto the third-floor landing. "Hey, what's going on here?"

"I'm Dane Carver, FBI," Dane said. "She's trying to escape. Go ask Delion up in Homicide."

"You need any help?"

"No," Dane said. "I wish you'd come about five minutes ago, though."

"Yeah, I can see how you'd have trouble with a perp who's fifty pounds lighter than you. You want us to get Delion? Tough guy, Delion. He can stop a perp, no matter how big."

"Nah. I've finally got her pinned."

She'd quieted, just a bit, but he'd no sooner got the words out of his mouth than she went wild again. She took him by surprise this time, twisting sharply inward, and his hold on her loosened just a bit. She drove her elbow into his belly and was off again, as the air whooshed out of him.

"Yeah, you've got her, all right," one of the officers said, laughing.

Dane caught her again on the second floor just before she ducked into the women's room. "Okay, enough."

He pressed his back against the wall and jerked her back against him. "Let's try this again. That was a good move, that twist. Where'd you learn that?"

She was heaving, panting. She didn't say anything, just stood there, her head down, breathing hard. She didn't say anything for a very long time, but Dane was patient; he'd learned to be. Finally, he said, "Are you afraid the media are going to catch up with you and there'll be a photo or a video?"

"Another word about me, and, believe this—I'm gone. You have no right to question me, no right at all. No more, Agent Carver. No more."

He didn't want to drop it, but he knew he had to. They needed her. Dane sighed. "There just isn't anything easy in this life, you know? Why couldn't you have sold lingerie at Macy's? Something nice and normal?"

"I was nice and normal," she said, realized she'd let something out, and seamed her lips together.

"Oh? Maybe you were in real estate? Advertising? Maybe you were married and your old man knocked you around? All right, you got it, there won't be another word out of me."

"You've got words just waiting to spill out of you. Forget it." She leaned down and bit his hand, hard.

Dane yelled, just couldn't help himself. There were a good dozen folks on them then, half of them cops. She was homeless. There was no question who the good guy was. One uniformed officer grabbed her hair and yanked her head back.

The officer said, "She didn't draw blood, but it was close. You want some help here?"

"Yeah, could I have a pair of cuffs?"

The officer handed them over without even asking for an ID and Dane knew it wasn't because they were careless. He looked like a cop. He pulled her arms behind her and cuffed her wrists. "There," he said. "Now my body parts are safe. Thank you, ah, Officer, ah, Gordon. I'll leave the cuffs with Inspector Delion, up on four."

"No problem. You gotta watch yourself with these people. You might want your hand checked out, you never know what diseases she might be carrying around."

"Yeah, thanks, I will."

He barely understood Nick say "bastard" she had her jaw locked so tight.

"I'm not a bastard. I've got a pedigree. Now, what are we going to do with you?"

"Let me leave. I'll come back, I swear it."

"Nope. Let it go, Ms. Jones. You're with me now. Think of me as your own personal bodyguard. Just let it go. Can you do that?"

As he spoke he turned her around to face him. There was a line of freckles across her nose he hadn't noticed before, quite visible since she was so pale. But what he really saw, and hated, was defeat. She looked crushed, flattened.

He clasped her upper arms and shook her slightly. "Listen to me. I won't let anyone hurt you, I promise."

"You look so much like him."

"Yes, I know, but my brother and I were very different people. Very different. Well, not in all things, but in many."

"Maybe not," she said. "Maybe not. He promised he wouldn't let anyone hurt me either." She bit her lip. "But he's dead. Please, I wasn't responsible for his death, was I?"

She stood there, her arms pulled behind her, her wrists handcuffed, tears streaking down her cheeks.

"No," Dane said. "You weren't responsible. I do know one thing for certain—Michael's murder had nothing at all to do with you. Believe it."

"Oh shit," Delion said, coming to a dead stop about three feet from them. "I don't need this."

NINE

"What size do you wear?"

"I don't want any new clothes. Listen to me, Agent Carver, I just want to stay the way I am now. I have to, don't you understand?"

"You're going to be safer if you look like a reasonably dressed woman rather than a bag lady. This is a very ordinary, inexpensive store, Inspector Bates told me. She said we could get you a couple of things here that look like what everyone else is wearing. Don't give me any more trouble, Ms. Jones. I'm so tired I could sleep leaning against that taxi sign, and I know all the way to my wing tips that I need your help. Don't think of it as a favor to the cops. Think of it as a favor to my brother, you know, the man you really liked and admired. I need you to help me catch his killer."

He knew then that, finally, he'd touched her. He'd made her feel guilty, made her feel beyond selfish if she ran away. She wanted to catch the monster who murdered his brother. Good, whatever worked. It had taken him long enough. Maybe it would help her get over the idea that she was responsible.

What made it even better was that it was only the truth. He did need her.

"All right. Let's get some inexpensive things, then."

"And then some better things."

"I thought you said you were really tired."

"I am. But I'm staying at a good hotel, the Bennington, just off Union Square. I'd like to remain low profile. Having a bag lady on my arm would make everyone think I was some sort of pervert."

"They'd think you didn't have much money, that's for sure."

Dane didn't know where it came from, but he smiled.

Thirty minutes later, they walked out of The Rag Bag, a woman's retread clothes store just off Taylor and Post, not far from the Bennington Hotel. Of course in San Francisco, nothing was very far from anything else. She was wearing a decent pair of jeans, a white blouse, and a dark blue pullover V-necked sweater. The cap was gone from her head, her hair ruthlessly brushed back and clipped at the back of her neck.

They didn't get a single look from any of the tourists or staff at the Bennington. Once they were in Dane's room on the fourth floor, he said, "You still don't look like you're quite up to snuff. But better, much better. Would you like to shower and wash your hair or have an early dinner first?"

No big surprise. She opted for dinner. When it arrived twenty minutes later, he waved her to the small circular table with its two chairs and the room-service dinner he'd ordered up for them.

She said, "I look fine, really. No one noticed me at all. I'll just wear these clothes until you can catch this guy."

"Oh? And then you're going to trot back to the shelter? Or maybe panhandle on Union Square?"

"Yes. Whatever."

"I threw away your homeless clothes."

She gave him a long, emotionless look. "I wish you hadn't done that. They were all I had."

"When this is all over, you're not going back to a homeless shelter." He took a bite of his BLT, sat back, looked at her thoughtfully, and said, "No, you weren't going to do that in any case, were you? You're planning to hotfoot it out of town once this is over, aren't you?"

She didn't raise her head, just slowly and steadily ate her way through the pile of french fries on her plate. They were well done, brown and crispy, just the way she liked them.

She said, "You're right, yes. When this is over, I'm gone. I'm thinking about the Southwest. It's really warm there during the winter months."

"At least you're telling me some of the truth now. Hey, you like french fries."

"It's been a while since I've had any. They're wonderful."

"Michael loved french fries, too, claimed they helped him concentrate better on the football field and made girls think he was wearing a really nice aftershave lotion. Who knows?"

She raised her head. "Do you mind if I use your bathroom now?"

He nodded, took another bite of his sandwich, watched her eat one more fry, sigh, and push the plate away. She looked like she wanted to cry. "They're so good, but I just don't have any more room. I didn't know Father Michael Joseph liked french fries. It never came up."

"No, it probably wouldn't have. Do you want to go back to the shelter? Do you have anything there you need?"

"No, thank you. The fact is, if someone does have anything of value, they learn to strap it to their bodies or it's gone in five minutes."

"Sort of like car parts in a bad part of town?"

He wondered what she had strapped to her middle. Papers that would tell him who she was? What or who she was running from?

He listened to the sound of the shower running. He rose and walked to the phone. He'd nearly dialed his sister's number when he slowly laid the receiver back down. No, he couldn't imagine Eloise dealing with Ms. Jones. It would be unfair to both of them. Too much grief on Eloise's part, too much fear on Ms. Jones's. Not a good mix, too much, certainly, to ask of his sister. He'd have to trust her to stay there in the hotel while he was out with Delion. He carefully wrapped her water glass in a handkerchief. There was, at the very least, a nice clear thumbprint.

When she walked out of the bathroom nearly an hour later, Dane nearly dropped his coffee cup. The bag lady was gone. She was scrubbed, her hair clean and blow-dried, and the recycled clothes looked just fine on her.

She looked like a college kid with that fresh face of hers. He hadn't realized it, but her hair was more blond than brown now that it was clean, but there were lots of different shades, and it was on the curly side. She had it clipped again at the back of her neck. Her eyes, clear and sharp with intelligence, were a mix of gray and green. She was, he saw, quite nice-looking.

"You look fine now," he said, satisfied that he sounded only mildly pleased. The last thing he needed was for her to fear that he'd jump her. "I've got to go back to Homicide. I want you to stay here, in this room. Watch TV, or, if you want, go downstairs and buy some paperbacks, whatever. Just don't leave the hotel. Okay?"

He gave her fifty bucks even though she just kept shaking her head until he stuffed it in her jeans pocket. He realized then that she hadn't answered him.

He said again, "Listen to me. Promise you won't leave the hotel."

Finally she said, "Oh, all right. I promise."

He really hoped she wasn't a liar.

He called his sister on his cell phone on his way back to Bryant Street, listened to her arrangements for their brother's funeral.

Michael was dead. They were actually talking about burying him. Dane couldn't stand it. Instead of going to the Hall of Justice, he drove back to St. Bartholomew's, at his sister's request, to see that everything was being handled. Father Binney, red-eyed, a slight tremor in his veiny white hands, had spoken to Bishop Koshlap and Archbishop Lugano. Everything had been arranged, everyone notified. Father Michael Joseph's funeral would take place at St. Bartholomew's on Friday afternoon, since there was another funeral already scheduled for the morning, and the wake Wednesday evening. "I am so sorry," he said over and over. "If only I hadn't talked him into seeing that man, that monster. I'm so very sorry."

Dane wished he could tell Father Binney again that he wasn't at fault here, that it was the monster who had murdered four people here in San Francisco, but the words just wouldn't come out of his mouth.

He drove too quickly to the Hall of Justice and was pulled over just south of Market by a motorcycle cop.

When he handed over his FBI shield, the officer just stared down at it, laughed, then said, "Hey, you on a big case?"

Dane just nodded.

"No ticket this time, Special Agent. Just watch the speed."

Dane thanked the officer and continued to speed to the Hall of Justice, despite the choking traffic.

He was shown into the task force room, which was actually the conference room next to the chief's office. Kreider's assistant, Maggie, told him the chief wanted lots of say on this one, wanted to be the first one to know if anything broke.

There were fifteen people crowded in the room. Dane stood leaning against the back wall and listened to Delion finish up.

". . . Okay, everyone knows the drill. The guy who just came in, over by the door, is Special Agent Dane Carver, FBI. His brother was Father Michael Joseph. He's not here as a Fed, just as a cop, and so he's a part of this hunt. Anybody got anything to say? No? Okay, that's it."

Dane looked up at the time line thumbtacked to the wall, at the photos of the four people murdered. Chief Kreider squeezed Dane's shoulder on his way out.

Delion said to Dane, "I'll bet our guys even have their moms working on this thing, Dane. We'll nail the guy, you'll see. Now, we're scheduled to see the medical examiner. Dr. Boyd promised he'd do Valerie Striker first thing. How's Ms. Jones?"

"She's fine. She swore to me she wouldn't leave the hotel."

An eyebrow went up. "You believed her?"

"Short of locking her up, I really didn't have a choice, but yeah, I do."

"You get her cleaned up?"

"Oh yes. She looks like a grad student."

"A grad student? You know, maybe that's a possibility. She looks brainy, speaks real well."

Dane shook his head. "She's smart, she's too scared to hide that. Graduate student? She seems a bit old for that, but who knows?"

Delion said, "I'm told by my sister—she's a professor of anthropology over at UC Davis—that there's a lot of cutthroat stuff in academia, more vicious, she says, than the business world. Of course, she doesn't really know what she's talking about but do you think our girl could be running from a badass professor?"

"Could be," Dane said, and burst out laughing, just couldn't help himself. "A killer professor. I like that, Delion. Let's stop by and see whose fingerprints are on this glass."

"Ms. Jones?"

"Yes, a beautiful clear thumb. If she won't tell us who she is, just maybe her prints are on file. You never know. And, Delion, thanks for making me laugh."

"No problemo."

Dr. Boyd met them at the morgue counter. "Valerie Striker was garrotted," he said. "Nothing more, nothing less."

Dane said, "Can you give us a time, sir?"

"It's difficult, but I'd say it was toward the middle of the night, Sunday night."

"Good enough."

Dr. Boyd said, "Same man who killed Father Michael Joseph?"

Delion nodded. "Yeah, if that's when she died, then it was probably him. She was a loose end."

"Now for my good news, gentlemen. Ms. Striker didn't go easily. She may have got some of him under her fingernails, probably skin from his neck."

"DNA," Delion said, and did a little dance.

"Get me a match and we'll fry the guy, Inspector Delion."

They watched Dr. Stephen Boyd walk away, pause to speak to one of his investigators, then continue toward his office.

"Hot damn," Delion said. "You know, no one ever even makes a joke about that man? No Sawbones, no Doctor Death, nothing like that. He's a straight arrow, smart, does what he says he'll do. When the pressure builds, the brass are really heating things up, Dr. Boyd never panics, just lowers his head and keeps marching."

"Good for him," Dane said. "On the other hand, if he did panic, the person on the slab wouldn't be able to tell anyone about it."

"True enough. Now, if that sample's got DNA in it, it's our first real break."

TEN

Chicago

Nick had never been so happy in her life. Well, maybe when she'd had her Ph.D. diploma placed reverently into her hand, but that was more a huge sense of relief than pure, unadulterated happiness. It was because of her fiancé, John Kennedy Rothman, senior senator from Illinois. "No relation," he'd told her, a lowly new volunteer in his reelection campaign three years before. That was before his wife, Cleo Rothman, disappeared, just up and ran away with one of his senior aides, Tod Gambol. Because everyone knew he loved his wife dearly, her abandoning her husband had given him an incredible sympathy vote and he'd been swept back into office by a 58/42 margin over his opponent, who'd been portrayed as too liberal for the fiscal health of both Illinois and the country, though he really hadn't been at all. Truth was, John's overpowering charm, his ability to look straight at a person and have that person believe that he would be the best at whatever he tried, was the overriding reason he was voted in.

And now she was going to marry him. It was heady. There were nearly twenty years separating them, but she didn't care. She had no parents to gainsay her decision, only two brothers, both Air Force pilots, both in Europe, both younger than she.

She knew all about campaigning now, what it would be like to live in a fishbowl. But the media really hadn't come after her yet, and she prayed they wouldn't, at least not until after they were married and she'd be able to simply step behind John as she smiled and waved.

It was a dark night, the wind whipping her hair back from her face, because it was, after all, Chicago. When you were walking the deep canyons, buildings soaring up on either side, and the wind swept off

Lake Michigan, funneling through those buildings, whipping the temperature down, it could make your teeth chatter and your bones rattle. She ducked her head and walked faster. One more block and she'd be home. Why hadn't she taken a taxi? No, ridiculous. When she got home, she'd sit in front of her small fireplace, pull over her legs the heavy red afghan that her mom had knitted eight years before, and read some essays from her senior medieval research class.

She looked both ways, didn't see a single soul, and stepped into the street. It happened so fast, she wasn't certain what had actually happened after she was safely back in her apartment. A black car, a big job, with four doors, swept up the street, lights off, and veered straight at her. She saw that it was accelerating, not slowing, not swerving out of the way. No, it was coming straight on, and it was going to hit her.

She hurled herself sideways. She hit a fire hydrant and went crashing down on her hip. She felt the hot air, smelled the sour rubber of the tires as the sedan sped by. She lay there, pain pulsing through her hip, wondering why no one was around. Not a single person was stupid enough to be out in this weather. Oh God. Would the car come back?

She got up, tried to run, but ended up hobbling back across the street. She saw a bum in the alley just next to her condo building. He'd seen everything.

"Crazy bugger," the guy said, lifted a bottle to his mouth, and drank down a good pint.

She fumbled with her building door key, finally got it to turn, and almost fell into the lobby, so afraid that she just hung there, leaning against a huge palm, breathing hard. There was a neighbor, Mrs. Kranz, standing there. The old lady, the widow of a Chicago firefighter, helped her to her condo, stuffed aspirins down her throat, and sat her down as she built up the fire in the fireplace.

"What happened, dear?"

Dear God, it was hard to speak, hard to get enough saliva in her mouth. She finally got out, "Someone—someone tried to run me down."

Mrs. Kranz patted her arm. "You're all right, aren't you?" At Nick's nod, because she really couldn't speak, Mrs. Kranz said, "A drunk, more like it. Right?"

Nick just shook her head. "I don't know. I really don't know." A drunk? She'd felt all the way to her bones that it was someone who wanted to hurt her. Maybe even kill her. Was that unlikely? Sure it was, but it didn't change how she felt. A drunk. That might be right. Damn.

She thanked Mrs. Kranz, forgot the papers she was going to grade, and went to bed. She shuddered beneath the covers, cold from the inside out.

When she finally slept, it was only to see that big dark car again, then another and another, all around her. She saw a man driving each car, and each man was wearing a ski mask pulled over his face. There was a kaleidoscope of madness in each man's eyes, but she didn't recognize any of them. There were so many, she didn't know where to look. She was spinning around, with all the cars coming toward her. She woke up screaming, breathing hard, soaked with sweat. She jerked up in bed. As she sat there in the predawn gloom, she saw those eyes again with their stark light of madness and thought they looked somehow familiar. When she was breathing more easily, she got up, went to the bathroom, leaned over the sink, and drank from the faucet. No, that didn't make any sense. There was no one who wanted to hurt her. She didn't have any enemies except for maybe one of the ancient professors at the university who didn't believe women should know anything about medieval history, much less teach it. Her hip throbbed with pain, and putting any weight at all on that leg made her groan. She took three aspirins and crawled back into bed.

She managed to sleep another hour, then awoke feeling groggy, her hip aching something fierce. She downed more aspirins, looked at herself in the bathroom mirror, and nearly scared herself to death. She looked pale, sick, like she'd been in a really bad accident. A drunk, she said to the image staring back at her. It had to be a drunk. She stripped off her pajamas, looked at the huge purple bruise covering her right hip, wished she had something stronger than aspirin, and got under the shower. Ten minutes later she felt a bit more human. It had to be a drunk, not an old relic of a professor, not a wild teenager out to scare her, no, a drunk, a simple up-front drunk.

The eyes, the madness, that was just a dream spun out of fear.

She didn't bother reporting it to the police. She had no license plate, so what could they do? She told John about it, and he held her close, stroking her hair. He repeated what Mrs. Kranz had said. "A stupid drunk, that's all. It's all right, Nicola. It's all right. You're safe now."

She didn't sleep well after that night, not until her first night wrapped in a blanket atop a very hard, narrow cot in the upstairs dorm of a homeless shelter in San Francisco.

San Francisco

Wednesday evening, after a day of endless interviews, trying to find any connection between the murdered gay activist, the murdered old woman, and his brother, with no luck at all, Dane realized he had no choice but to take Nick with him to his brother's wake. He'd had her with him most of the day, primarily because he just didn't trust her to stay put in his room at the hotel, and she'd been a silent partner, saying very little and ordering more french fries for lunch at a fast food place in Ghiradelli Square.

But before he could take her to the wake, they had to stop at Macy's in Union Square and buy her a black dress, both for the wake that night and for the funeral to be held on Friday afternoon. And black shoes. Neither of them wanted to, but it had to be done.

They didn't arrive at the kind of Irish wake filled with a sea of voices, boisterous laughter, even louder sobs, lots of hair-raising stories about the deceased, lots of food, and too much booze. This wake was attended by more men wearing black than Dane could count, all of them somber, and only two women, Ms. Jones and Eloise DeMarks, his sister, both wearing simple black dresses, both looking pale.

Father Binney greeted them in a hushed whisper, told them that both Archbishop Lugano and Bishop Koshlap were there. Dane didn't care, but Father Binney seemed to believe it was a great honor to Michael. So be it.

Eloise, tall and thin, her lipstick looking garish on her too-pale face, was dark-haired and dark-eyed just like her brothers. Grief bowed her shoulders, and she was as silent as their mother had been for those six long months before she finally left their philandering father. Dane didn't know if their father knew one of his sons was dead. They hadn't been able to reach him. Their mother had died of a ruptured appendix while traveling on safari in western Africa. Dane remembered that they hadn't heard a word from their father then.

Dane didn't want to view his brother's body again. He simply couldn't bear it. He waited at the back of the rectory chapel, his arms hanging at his sides, not moving, just wishing it was over.

His brother was dead. He'd forget for minutes at a time, but then it would smack him again—the terrible finality of it, the viciousness of it, the fact that he would never see his brother again, ever. Never get another phone call, another e-mail, another stupid joke about a priest, a rabbi, and a preacher . . .

How did people bear this pain?

Nick was standing just behind him. She picked up his hand, smoothed out the fist he'd made. Her skin was rough but warm. She said, "They're honoring Father Michael Joseph, doing the best they can, but it's so very hard, isn't it?"

He couldn't speak. He just nodded. He felt her fingers stroke his hand, gently massage his fingers, easing the muscles.

She said, "I want to see him one last time."

He didn't answer her, and didn't look at her, until she returned to stand beside him.

"He's beautiful, Dane, and he's at peace. It's just his body here, not his spirit. I firmly believe that there is a Heaven, and since Father Michael Joseph was such a fine man, he's there, probably looking down at us, so happy to see that you're here and that you're safe. And he knows how much you love him, there's no doubt at all in my mind about that. I know he must feel sorry for your pain. I'm sorry, Dane, so very sorry."

He couldn't find words. He squeezed her hand. "Just three weeks ago—Christmas was just three weeks ago, can you believe that? Michael and I went down to San Jose to be with Eloise, her husband, and our nephews. Michael gave me an autographed Jerry Rice football. It's on my fireplace mantel. Only odd thing about it was that Jerry's an Oakland Raider now. Michael thought that was a hoot. Jerry in silver and black. I never saw him after I flew out on the twenty-seventh."

"What did you give Father Michael Joseph for Christmas? I'm sorry, but I don't think I'll ever be able to call him just Michael."

Dane said, "It's all right. I gave him a Frisbee. I told him I wanted to see his robes flapping around when he ran after the thing. And I gave him a book on the Dead Sea Scrolls, a topic that always fascinated Michael." He fell silent, wondering what would happen to Michael's things. He had to remember to ask Father Binney. He wanted to look at that book that Michael had touched, read, and see his inscription to his brother in the front. He'd written something smart-ass, but he didn't remember exactly what.

Michael should have lived until he was at least eighty, maybe as an archbishop, like Lugano, that venerable old man with his mane of white hair. But he was dead because some madman had decided to kill him. For whatever reason.

Dane stood, back against the rectory wall, watching with Nick beside him, silent now, still holding his hand. It seemed that every priest in San Francisco had come, and each of them walked in his measured way over to Dane, each with something kind to say, each telling him what a shock it was to see how much he looked like Michael.

The whole time, Dane was wondering how they were going to catch the man who killed his brother and the other people. There wasn't a single good lead, truth be told, even though Chief Kreider had told the media that all avenues were being explored, and some looked very hopeful. All of that was advanced cop talk for we ain't got diddly, Delion had said under his breath.

Delion came up to him, nodded to Nick, and stood silently beside him. All three of them stood there in black, just like all the priests.

Dane said to Delion, "I've been thinking. Three murders in San Francisco—and no tie-in among the victims that anyone can find."

"True, unfortunately. But that doesn't mean there isn't a connection. We just have to find it."

Dane looked toward his brother's coffin, surrounded by branches of lit candles. "It seems like it was all well rehearsed, no mistakes, and that got me to wondering. Do you think this man has killed before?"

Delion frowned as he said, "You mean has he done this same sort of thing in another city?"

"Yes."

"He's some sort of serial killer? He comes to a city and randomly selects victims, then leaves to go someplace else?"

"No, not really that," Dane said. "He targeted my brother, no question about that, maybe even before he killed the old woman and the gay activist. Chances are they were random. What do you think, Nick?"

She blinked, and he saw her surprise that he wanted her opinion. She said, "If that's true, then Father Michael Joseph must have been the focus, don't you think? Maybe the whole point of all this was so the guy could tell Father Michael Joseph what he'd done, and dare him to say anything. Maybe it was some sort of game to him, his selection of Father Michael Joseph, at least, determined before he did these horrible things.

I don't know. This is what you were talking about earlier and I thought a lot about it. I think you're right."

Dane said, "Yes, I still feel that way. I think it was all about the priest to him. There was planning here, his selection of my brother, or maybe any priest would do and Michael was a random choice, too."

Delion said, "So the guy thinks one day, I want to murder a priest, but before I do, I'm going to kill other people and rub the priest's nose in it when I confess it to him, watch him squirm because he's bound to silence. Do you think the perp is that sick?" Dane saw that Delion had included Nick in the question. She looked intent, like she was thinking ferociously. He didn't know why, but he liked that.

Dane said, "That may be close enough."

"Jesus, Dane. Then we've got to look for any other murders involving priests."

Nick said slowly, her brow furrowed, "I just don't know. That makes it sound pretty unlikely."

None of them said anything more. Dane watched Archbishop Lugano stare down at his brother, his lips moving in a prayer. Then he crossed himself, his movements a smooth ritual, leaned down, and kissed Michael's forehead.

Dane felt tears film his eyes. He nodded to Delion and turned abruptly away, realizing that Nick was still holding his hand. "I just can't stay any longer," he said, and she understood. They made their way through the waves of black-garbed priests and walked together from the chapel.

Chicago

Nick's eyes were wide open, she knew they were, but she couldn't see anything. No, wait. She was in a room, dark, almost black. She could feel how thick the blackness was, how heavy it was settling around her, with not a shred of light coming in. She lay there, on her back, looking up at a ceiling she couldn't really see, wondering what was happening, hoping she wasn't dead.

She tasted something sour, something that made her want to gag, but she knew she shouldn't gag or she'd start to choke. At least she was alive.

There was something in her mouth, something at the back of her throat. Then she remembered.

It had been a lovely evening in December, just a few days before Christmas, not too cold, no snow for the past three days, and the winds were fairly calm. Such a splendid occasion, perfectly orchestrated, naturally so, since John's private assistant had arranged it. Albia's birthday dinner was at John's magnificent Rushton Avenue condominium penthouse, looking out on Lake Michigan. It hadn't been just the three of them, no, Elliott Benson was there, a man she didn't trust, didn't like. He was rich and charming, supposedly a friend of John's, and she'd been told they'd known each other since college, but the truth was, whenever she had to spend time with him, she always wanted to go home and take a shower. She'd wanted it just to be the three of them, no aides, no other important people to coddle who had been or would be of assistance to John's career, but Albia had wanted him there.

Albia was John's older sister, an elegant, articulate woman, rich in her own right from ownership of several successful men's boutiques. Albia had been in John's corner since their mother had died when he was only sixteen and Albia twenty-three. She was turning fifty-five, but she looked a dozen years younger. She'd married when she'd turned thirty, been widowed just a year later. Albia had always been reserved, even standoffish with all the campaign volunteers, but since John had begun dating Nick, she'd warmed up considerably. Nick felt very close to her, indeed she was becoming a confidante.

Tonight, there was so much excitement, a feast on the dining table, a gorgeous diamond bracelet, presented by John to his sister, around Albia's wrist, winking and glittering in the soft glow of the half dozen lighted candles on the table. Elliott Benson had charmed and joked and flattered Albia, presenting her with diamond earrings that easily rivaled the bracelet John had gotten her. They were in her ears, gorgeous earrings. Elliott was trying to outdo John, it was easy enough to see, at least to Nick. Why had Albia wanted him there?

Nick's gift to Albia was a silk scarf imprinted with a Picasso painting that she'd found in Barcelona. Albia, exclaiming over that lovely scarf, had said, "Oh, I remember that Mother had a scarf very similar to this one. She loved that scarf—"

And her voice had dropped like a stone off a cliff.

Nick, filled with Albia's pleasure, pleased that her scarf had reminded her of John's mother, said, "Oh, John, you've never spoken of your mother."

John shot a look at his sister. She shook her head slightly, as if in apology, and looked back down at her plate.

"That's right, John," Elliott said, "I never even met your mother. Hey, didn't she die? A long time ago?"

"That's right," John said, his voice curt. "Nicola, you knew, didn't you? It was a car accident. It's been many, many years. We don't often speak about her."

She said, "A car accident? Oh my, I hadn't realized. I'm so very sorry. It must have been such a shock to both of you."

"Not to my father," John said.

Elliott started to say something, then chewed thoughtfully on a medallion of veal and stared at one of the paintings on the dining room wall.

Albia said, "It was a bad time. Would you please pass me the green beans, Nicola?"

Elliott told stories of college days. All of them involved girls that both men had wanted. His stories were funny, utterly charming, and many times he made himself the dupe, but still, it was a very strange thing. "Then, of course," he said, "there was Melissa—no, let's not speak of her this evening. I'm sorry, John. Another toast. To Albia, the loveliest lady in Chicago." And while he drank the toast, he looked at Nick and she wanted to slap that oily look off his handsome face.

Over a dessert of crème brûlée, Nick felt a sudden cramp, then another, this one stronger, more vicious. She had to excuse herself to run to the bathroom, where she got sick, and soon felt so ill, so utterly miserable, that she just wanted to curl up and die.

The pain was ghastly, her belly twisting and knotting. She threw up until she was shaking and sweating and couldn't stand. She remembered hugging the toilet with Elliott, John, and Albia standing next to her, not knowing what to do until Albia said, "I think we should call an ambulance, John. She's really sick. Elliott, go wait downstairs for them. Go, both of you! Quickly!"

And here she was in a hospital bed and they'd pumped her stomach. She remembered now that they'd told her about that before she fell asleep again, thanks to something very nice they'd given her. At least her stomach was calm. In fact, her belly felt hollow, scooped out, shrunk down to nothing at all. It hurt, but it was a dull ache, as if she'd been hungry for too long.

She remembered now that after they'd pumped her stomach, she lay on the hospital gurney feeling like she'd been bludgeoned with several baseball bats. Just on the edge of blissful drugged sleep, she remembered all those mad eyes staring at her from behind ski masks in her dreams, breathed in the smell of the exhaust from the big dark car that had nearly flattened her into the concrete.

It was so very dark. She turned her head just a bit and saw a flashing red light. What was that?

Then she heard a movement. Someone was in the room, close to her. She nearly stopped breathing.

She whispered around that miserable tube down her throat, "Who's there?"

A man, she knew it was a man, and his breathing was close to her, too close.

"Nicola."

Thank God, it was John. Why had she thought it could be Elliott Benson? There was no reason for him to be here.

She started crying, she couldn't help it.

She felt his hand on her shoulder. "It's all right, Nicola. You'll be fine. You must stop crying."

But she couldn't.

He rang the bell. In just a moment, the door opened, flooding the hospital room with light from the hallway. Then the overhead light in the room went on.

"What's the problem, Senator?"

"She's crying and she'll choke if you don't get that tube out of her throat."

"Yes, we have an order for that, once she is awake." She was standing over Nicola now, saying, "This isn't fun, is it? Okay, this won't be pleasant, Nicola, but it's quick."

After the tube came out, her throat felt like it was burning inside.

The nurse said, "Don't be alarmed about the pain in your throat. After all that's happened, it'll be sore for a couple more days." The nurse took a Kleenex and wiped her eyes, her face. "You'll be just fine now, I promise."

She got the tears under control. She took a dozen good-sized breaths, calmed her heartbeat. "What happened?"

"Probably food poisoning," John said. "You ate something bad, but we got you to the emergency room in time."

"But what about you? Albia? Are you ill?"

"No, we're fine. So is Elliott."

"It appears," the nurse said as she took Nicola's pulse, "that only you ate whatever was bad." She eased Nicola's arm back under the covers. "The senator believes it might have been a raspberry vinaigrette. You've got to sleep now. Senator Rothman will see to everything."

And she wondered, why hadn't John or Albia or Elliott gotten ill from the food?

John kissed her forehead, not her mouth, and she didn't blame him a bit for that. She wished she could have something to get rid of the dreadful taste, but she was so tired, so empty of words and feelings, that she just closed her eyes.

She heard John say to the nurse, "I'll be back in the morning to speak with the doctor, see that she's discharged. Oh, no, I can't. I have a meeting with the mayor. I'll send one of my people to see to things."

They continued speaking, in low voices, into the hallway. The overhead light clicked off. The door closed.

She was shut into the blackness again. But she knew this time she was alone and it was warm here, nothing to disturb her except that small nagging voice in her head: food poisoning from vinaigrette dressing? What nonsense. She'd eaten so little of everything because she was excited about Albia's birthday, the gift she'd given her, and she wanted desperately for Albia to be her friend, to accept her. She wondered as she fell back into sleep if she would have died if she'd eaten more.

She'd had food poisoning before, on a hunting trip with her dad, when she'd eaten bad meat. It hadn't been like this.

The next morning, the doctors couldn't say exactly what had made her sick. They'd taken blood tests, said they would analyze what was in her stomach, and tested both the senator and his sister, but nothing was found.

Unfortunately, Mrs. Beasley, John's cook and housekeeper, had already thrown all the food away, washed all the dishes. No way to know, the doctors said. Finally they'd let her go.

She'd nearly died. For the second time in a week and a half.

San Francisco

Nick touched her fingertips to her throat, remembering how it had hurt for a good two days after she'd left the hospital in Chicago. She turned on her side, saw Dane's outline on that wretched too-short sofa not more than twelve feet from her, sighed, and finally fell asleep in her bed at the Bennington Hotel. She was afraid, afraid those mad, dark eyes would come gleaming out of the darkness at her, just over her head, hovering just out of reach. She prayed she wouldn't have any more nightmares.

Dane, sprawled on the sofa across the room, never stirred. He awoke with a start at 7 a.m. to see Nick Jones dressed in the blue jeans and white shirt he'd bought her, feet bare, pacing back and forth in front of him. He realized he'd slept hard, which was unexpected since the damned sofa was too short and hard as the floor. The TV was on, he could see the reflection of the colors in the mirror over the vanity table, but there was no sound.

"Thank God you're awake."

For as long as he could remember, when Dane woke up, he was instantly alert, and he was now. "What's the matter, Nick?"

She blew out her breath, splayed her hands in front of her. She took a step closer to him and said, "I know what's going on. I know."

ELEVEN

Dane swung his legs over the side of the sofa and stood quickly, the blankets falling to the floor at his feet. "You know what?" His sweat-pants were low on his belly, and he quickly pulled them back up. He grabbed her hands, covered them. "What, Nick? What do you know?"

"Yes, okay. Listen, you were out like a light last night. I woke up, then couldn't go back to sleep and so I watched TV, turned down really low. It's a show, Dane, a TV show on the Premier Channel, a new one, just started probably a couple of weeks ago. It came on at eleven o'clock, called *The Consultant*. It was about these murders in Chicago and how this special Federal consultant comes in and solves them. It was kind of *X-Files*-y, you know, unexplained stuff that gives you goose bumps and makes you look toward the window if it's really dark outside. I wasn't really paying too much attention until there was this creepy guy in a confessional, and I realized he was talking to a priest about what he'd done, taunting him about the people he'd killed, and then when the priest was pleading with him to stop, he laughed and shot him through the forehead. Dane, it wasn't about murders in Chicago, it was like the murders right here, in San Francisco."

Dane rubbed his forehead, dashed his fingers through his hair. He couldn't get his brain around what she'd just said. It didn't seem possible. He said finally, "You're telling me that some asshole murdered my brother because he was following the script of some idiotic TV show?"

"Yes. When the show was over, I watched all the credits and wrote down everything I could."

Dane dragged his fingers through his hair again, drew a deep breath, and said, "I'm going to order some coffee, then you're going to tell me everything, every little detail. Oh damn, let me call Delion. You're pretty sure about this?"

"I'm positive. I just couldn't believe it. I nearly woke you up, but realized that there wasn't much of anything you could do at midnight. And you were so tired."

"It's okay."

Los Angeles

After arriving at LAX on the 9 a.m. Southwest shuttle from Oakland airport, where Nick was allowed through despite having no ID after Delion filled out papers in triplicate and spoke to two supervisors, Inspector Delion, Special Agent Carver, and the woman they introduced as Ms. Nick Jones, with no designation at all, stepped into Executive Producer Frank Pauley's corner office with its big glass windows that looked across Pico toward the ocean. You couldn't see it because the smog was sitting heavy and gray over the city, but you could see the golf course.

Mr. Pauley was slightly built, tall, pleasant looking, and very pale. Surely that shouldn't be right, Nick thought. Wasn't everyone in LA supposed to be tanned from head to toe? He looked to be somewhere in his forties, and had a nice smile, albeit a nervous one when he met them. She couldn't blame him for that.

He shook hands all around, offered them coffee, and pointed them to the very long gray sofa that lined half the wall. It must have been at least eighteen feet long. There were chairs facing that sofa, all of them gray, and three coffee tables spaced out to form separate sitting groups.

Frank Pauley said, waving toward the sofa, "I just took over. I inherited this office and all the gray from the last executive producer. He said he liked a really big casting couch." He grinned at Nick, who didn't grin back, and said, "You called, Inspector Delion, because you believe that the murders in *The Consultant* that played last night are similar to murders that were committed in San Francisco over the last week and a half."

"That's right," Delion said. "But before we discuss any more of this, we'd like to see the show, compare all the points, make a final determination. Ms. Jones is the only one of us who's seen it so far."

"This is, naturally, very disturbing. Just a moment, please." Frank Pauley turned to the gray phone, punched in a couple of buttons.

Nick said, "Thank God you've only aired two of the shows."

Dane said, "We'll watch both episodes, Mr. Pauley. If we've got a match with San Francisco, we'll find out whether there have been any crimes that follow the first episode. We have no way of knowing whether the murderer would continue if you stop showing the episodes. But I presume the studio will announce that the show's been canceled?"

Frank Pauley cleared his throat. "Let me be up front here. Our lawyers have recommended that we immediately cancel the show and provide you with complete cooperation. Naturally, the studio is appalled that some maniac would do this, if, indeed, we discover that the episode does match the murders in San Francisco."

Dane said, "We appreciate it. Naturally you will have to be concerned about legal action."

"We always are," Frank Pauley said. "They're waiting for us in room fifty-one."

"Room fifty-one?" Nick said.

"A little joke, Ms. Jones, just a little film joke. It's our own private theater. We can see the first and second episodes now, if you wish."

Delion said, "Later, perhaps we can see the third episode as well."

"That's not a problem," Pauley said, waving a left hand that sported four diamond rings. Dane felt a man's instant distaste. Hey, maybe four different wives had given them to him, one never knew, here in LA.

They sat in the small darkened theater and watched the second episode of *The Consultant*. The city was Chicago, the church, St. John's, the priest, Father Paul. Dane watched Father Paul as he listened to a man telling him about the murder he'd just committed—an old woman he'd bludgeoned to death, no sport in that, was there? But hey, she was another soul lost from Father Paul's parish, wasn't she? Two nights later, a black activist was garroted in front of a club, ah, yes, yet another soul lost from Father Paul's parish, and what was the priest going to do about it? The murderer mocks the priest's beliefs, claims the Church is the perfect calling for men who can't face life, that the priest is nothing but a coward who can't even tell a soul, because he's bound by rules that really don't make a whole lot of sense, now do they?

In the fourth and final meeting, after two more murders, the priest loses it. He sobs, pleading with the murderer, raging against God for allowing this monster to exist, raging against his own deeply held beliefs, hating his own helplessness. The murderer laughs, tells him you live like a coward, you die like a coward, and shoots the priest in the forehead.

Dane leaned forward and shut off the projector. He said to Pauley, "Your writers made a mistake here. A priest is bound to silence only when it is a real confession, that is, when the penitent truly means to repent. In a case like this, where the man is mocking the sacrament itself, the priest isn't bound to silence."

Pauley stared at him. "But I thought—"

"I know," Dane said. "Everybody believes that. But the Church makes that exception. Now, if you'll excuse me, I'll be out in the hall."

The truth was, he couldn't bear the show another minute. He leaned against the wall, his eyes closed, trying to get a grip on himself. But he kept seeing the man firing that gun, shooting the priest in the forehead.

He felt her hand on his arm. They stood still, saying nothing, for a very long time. Finally, Dane drew several deep breaths and raised his head. "Thank you," he said.

She only nodded.

Delion came out of the small theater. "You didn't miss much. We have this big-shot consultant dude with some mythical agency in Washington, D.C., come riding into town—the guy's real sensitive, feels people's pain, all that crapola—he cleans the whole mess up because the local cops are stupid and don't have any extrasensory abilities, and he can 'see' things, 'intuit' things that they can't. It ended good except for five dead people."

Dane said, "He killed two more people in the show than he did in San Francisco."

"Yes. And maybe that means then that your brother didn't stick to the script and that's why the guy shot him after the two murders. Remember, your brother told Father Binney that he was going to make a decision that would change his life forever. There's only one threat your brother could have made to shut this guy down."

"Yes," Dane said. "Michael told the killer that he was going to tell the police about what this man had done."

Nick said, "And the guy had no choice but to shoot him. Father Michael Joseph wrecked the guy's script. He stopped him."

"Your brother must have told him what he was planning to do on

Sunday night and the guy had no choice but to kill him. The other two people in the show were a guy who owned a bakery and a prominent businessman. If it hadn't been for Father Michael Joseph, there might be two more dead people in San Francisco."

"The guy kept saying that this Father Paul had lost another soul from his parish," Dane said. "Do we know if the two victims in San Francisco attended Saint Bartholomew's?"

"They're not on the membership list," Delion said. "But if the guy was following the script, the chances are good that they did attend mass occasionally. That would tie it all up with a pretty bow, wouldn't it?"

"Yes," Dane said, "it would. Not that it's any help."

Delion just shook his head. "I don't believe this. A damned script. The guy's copycatting a damned TV script."

"Not copycatting," Dane said. "Don't forget, the murders took place before the show aired. Look, at least we know for sure the guy has to be here, has to be somehow involved with the show. No outsider would know the scripts that well."

SAVICH typed on MAX's screen: *Episode One of* The Consultant—*set in Boston, three murders: a secretary, a bookie, and an insurance salesman, about two to three weeks ago.* "Dane, I'll check—Hey, wait a second. Ah, Sherlock, who was reading over my shoulder, just said these murders were not in Boston, but actually happened two and a half weeks ago, in Pasadena, California."

"Bingo," Dane said. "I'll tell Delion and he can call the cops in Pasadena. Nice and close to Los Angeles."

"Dane, the guy's officially taken this show on the road. You're now formally FBI, working this case. If you want to use the San Francisco field office, call Bert Cartwright, coordinate with him. You will remain in charge of the Federal part of the investigation, all right?"

"Yes, all right, but the thing is, Savich, the killer has to be here in Los Angeles, someone working for the studio, someone working on this specific show, or with access to it."

"Yes, of course, you're right. I'll let Gil Rainy know—he's the SAC down in LA—that you'll be coordinating with him. But you'll be calling the shots. I'll make sure everyone's clear on that."

"Thanks, Savich."

There was a brief silence, then a chuckle. "And that means you've got MAX at your disposal."

There was incredulity in Dane's voice. "You mean you're going to send MAX out for me?"

"Get a grip here, Dane. Deep-six that fantasy. No, let me know what you need and I will—personally—set MAX to work."

"Oh, so I didn't catch you in a weak moment."

"Never that weak." A pause, then, "How are you holding up, Dane?"

"Michael's funeral is on Friday afternoon."

The words were spoken with finality, cold and frozen over.

Savich said, after a pause, "Just call when you need something."

"Thanks, Savich." Dane closed his cell phone and walked into the West LA Division on Butler Avenue. It was a big blocky concrete box with an in-your-eye bright orange tile entrance, evidently someone's idea of cheering up the place. Truth be told, the building was old and ugly, but humongous, nearly a full city block, with a parking lot beside it for the black-and-whites. Across the street was another lot and a maintenance station. It was in an old part of town, with lots of weeds, old houses, and little greenery anywhere.

Dane flipped open his shield for the officers standing at the front desk, got a nod from one of them, and walked to the stairs. He heard a loud mix of voices before he even saw the signs. He met Patty, a nice older lady who was a volunteer receptionist, kept chocolate chip cookies on a big plate on her desk, and tracked all the detectives. She told him they had three homicide detectives and Detective Flynn was inside with the two cops from San Francisco. Dane assumed Delion had just rolled Nick into the mix.

He walked into the large room, much bigger than the homicide room in San Francisco. All the detectives here were stationed in this room filled with gnarly workstations and funky orange lockers against the rear wall.

Patty had told him Detective Flynn's desk was down three rows. He walked past a man whose shirt was hanging out, past a woman who was shouting to another detective to *shut the fuck up,* and then there was Flynn—impossible to miss Flynn, he'd been told, and it was true. He saw Nick sitting quietly in the corner, reading a magazine. Well, no, she wasn't reading, just using it as a prop. What was she thinking?

Dane walked up to Delion and told him, "The murders from the first episode of *The Consultant*, they were in Pasadena. Two, two and a half weeks ago."

Detective Mark Flynn didn't wait for an introduction, just lifted his phone and started dialing.

Ten minutes later, he hung up. He was about fifty, black, and looked like he'd been a pro basketball player until just last week. He said, "You must be Agent Carver." The men shook hands.

Flynn said, nodding toward Nick, who'd come up to his desk when Dane arrived, "The murders in Pasadena took place before, during, and just after the first show. They sound pretty much identical to the murders on the first episode."

"That would mean, then," Delion said, "that our guy went back and forth to San Francisco, maybe he even flew back and forth a couple of times. Or drove, what with the waits at the airports. We'll have to match the exact times of the murders in both cities."

"And then we check the airlines," Flynn said. "Looks to me, boys, like we're stuck with a real ugly case. What do you say we go back to the studio and round up everyone who had anything to do with those scripts? I'll just bet the studio honchos are shitting in their pants, what with the possibility of lawsuits they'll face from the families of the victims."

"They have assured us of their complete cooperation," Delion said.

Flynn said, "Well, that's something. Hey, it's kinda neat having a Fed around. You bite?"

"Nah, never."

"That's good, because I bite back," Flynn said.

Dane said, "I'll be heading up our involvement with the local agents. Ms. Jones is a possible witness and that's why she's here with us. We want her to look at everyone who had anything to do with this show. Just maybe we'll get lucky."

"I say it's the writer," Delion said. "He dreamed it all up. Who else could it be?"

Detective Flynn just gave Delion a mournful look. "Sorry, son, but the writer—poor schmuck—yeah, he could be the one to start the ball rolling, maybe come up with the concept, a couple of show ideas, maybe even a rough draft for the first show, but is he our perp? You see, depending on the show, there can be up to a dozen writers with their fingers in the plot. Then there's all the rest of those yahoos—the director, the assistant directors, the script folk, the producers, the actors, hell, even the grip. I know all this because I live here and my kid is an actor. He's been on a few shows so far." Detective Flynn drew himself up even taller, if that was possible. "He's a comedian."

"Which shows?" Nick asked.

"He was on *Friends* and *Just Shoot Me*."

Nick nodded. "That's fantastic."

Flynn smiled down at her from his six-foot-six height and said, "I wonder how many more episodes of *The Consultant* it would have taken before someone somewhere noticed."

"Needless to say," Dane said, "they've stopped the shows."

"The studio heads might be morons," Flynn said, "but not the lawyers. I'll bet they had conniption fits, ordered the plug pulled the instant you guys called."

Nick said, "How do they select which episode is played each week? Or are they aired in a specific sequence?"

"Since this show isn't about the ongoing lives of its main characters," Flynn said, "I can't imagine that the order would be all that important. Normally, though, I understand that they're shown in the order they're filmed. We'll ask."

Delion said, "Then that means our guy knows which episode is going to play next. And that means he's here in LA for sure."

"Yeah, over at Premier Studios," Flynn said.

TWELVE

Premier Studios was on West Pico Boulevard, just perpendicular to Avenue of the Stars. Across from the studio was the Rancho Park Golf Course. Dane was surprised at the level of security. There was a kiosk at the entrance gate, armed security guards, and dogs sniffing car interiors. Past the initial kiosk, the driveway was set up with white concrete blocks forming S-curves to force cars to drive slowly.

Detective Flynn flashed his badge and told them that the Big Cheese was expecting them, at which point the woman smiled, checked her board, and said, "Have at it, Detective."

There were giant murals painted on the studio walls: Marilyn Monroe in *Seven Year Itch,* Luke fighting Darth Vader in *Star Wars,* Julie Andrews singing in *The Sound of Music,* and cartoon characters from *The Simpsons.* There was also advertising for new shows. Nick stopped a moment to stare at the building-size paintings of Marilyn Monroe and Cary Grant.

"They've been up forever," Flynn said. "Neat, isn't it?"

The head of Premier Studios, who was second only to the owner, mogul Miles Burdock, was on the fifth floor, the executive level of a modern building that didn't look at all fancy and was close to the entrance of the studio lot.

The Big Cheese's name was Linus Wolfinger and he wasn't a man, Pauley told them when he met them in his office on the fourth floor, he was a boy who was only twenty-four years old. He believed himself a genius, and the arrogant Little Shit was right.

"Does this mean you don't like him?" Delion said.

"You think it's that noticeable?"

"Nah, I'm just real sensitive to nuances," Delion said.

"The problem," Frank Pauley said, waving that hand with the four diamond rings on it, "is that the Little Shit is really good when it comes to picking story concepts, and God knows there are zillions pitched each season. He's good at picking actors, at picking the right time slots for the shows to air. Sometimes he's wrong, but not that often. It's all very depressing, particularly since he has the habit of telling everyone how great he is. Everyone hates his guts."

"Yeah," Delion said. "Even as delicate as I am, I can sure see why."

"Twenty-four? As in only two dozen years old?" Detective Flynn asked.

"Yep, a raw thing to swallow," Frank Pauley said. "On the other hand, most of the top executives in a studio are only around for the short term—maybe three, four years. You can bet their entire focus is on how much money they can pocket before they're out. This is a money business. There are simply no other considerations. You'll have an executive producer getting his paycheck, then he'll decide to direct a show and that means he gets another paycheck. It's all ego and money."

"Why are you telling us all this, Mr. Pauley?" Flynn asked.

Frank Pauley grinned, splayed his hands. "Hey, I'm cooperating. It's better if you have some clue what motivates people around here."

"You direct shows, Mr. Pauley?" Nick said.

"You bet. I sometimes also earn a paycheck for inputting on the actual writing of an episode."

"Three paychecks?" Nick asked.

"Yes, everyone does it who can. You know what's even better? For direction and writing, I get royalties or residuals. I've got no complaints."

Flynn rolled his eyes, said, "I've got to make sure my son is clear on all of this."

Delion said, "You're telling us that money, power, and ego—are the bottom line here in sin city? How shocking."

Pauley smiled. "I hesitate to say this so cynically, but I want to be totally up front with you. This is a very serious mess we've got on our hands. If it gets out, and you can bet the bank it will, I don't want to think what's going to happen. The media will be brutal. I've kept quiet about this, just as you asked. To the best of my knowledge, no one involved in *The Consultant* has left town because the cops were here this morning. Wolfinger is expecting us on the fifth floor. That's where the Little Shit's castle is. It was a regular office until Mr. Burdock hired him on. This way."

"What do you mean a 'regular' office?" Nick asked.

"You'll see."

"Tell us about Miles Burdock," Delion said.

"He likes everyone to think he's hands-on, that if he personally doesn't like a show, it's gone, but to be honest about it, it's really Linus Wolfinger who's got all the power around here. Mr. Burdock has so many irons in the fire—most of them international—and hell, you come right down to it, we're just a little iron. He really likes Linus Wolfinger, met him here at the studio, watched him over a couple of months while Linus did nearly all the planning and execution of one of our prime-time shows when both the producer and the director proved incompetent. Then he promoted him, put him in charge of the whole magilla just like that." Frank Pauley snapped his fingers. "It caused quite a furor for a while."

They went through three secretaries, all over fifty, professionals to their button-down shirts, with not a single long leg showing, and not a single long red nail.

Frank Pauley just waved at them and kept walking down the wide corridor. Flynn said, "I would have bet no self-respecting studio honcho would have secretaries like these."

"You mean like adult secretaries? Linus fired the other, much younger secretary the day he moved in. Fact is, though, everyone needs slaves who will work eighteen-hour days without much bitching. That means young, and so usually the secretaries aren't older than thirty. That's why Linus hired three secretaries. Let me tell you, the place really runs better now."

Nick said, "How long has Mr. Wolfinger been here?"

"Nearly two years in his current position, maybe six months before that. Let me tell you, it's been the longest two years in my life."

A man of about thirty-five, so beefed up he probably couldn't stand straight, put himself in their faces, barring their way. He looked like he could grind nails with his teeth. "That's Arnold Loftus, Linus's bodyguard," Pauley said under his breath. "He never says anything, and everybody is afraid of him."

"He's got lovely red hair," Nick said.

Pauley gave her an amazed look.

"You're here to see Mr. Wolfinger?" Arnold Loftus asked, his arms crossed over his huge chest.

"Yes, Arnold, we're expected," said Flynn.

Arnold Loftus waved them to a young man of not more than twenty-two who was walking toward them. No, "strutting" was a better word. He was dressed in an Armani suit, gray, beautifully cut. He stopped, and also crossed his arms over his chest. They were coming into his territory.

"Mr. Pauley," he said, nodding, then he looked at the three men and the woman tagging behind him.

"Jay, we're here to see Mr. Wolfinger. These are police and FBI. It's very important. I called you."

Jay said, "Please be seated. I'll see if Mr. Wolfinger is ready to see you."

Six minutes later, just an instant before Delion was ready to put his foot through the door, it opened and the assistant nodded to them. "Mr. Wolfinger is a very busy man, but he's available to see you now."

"You'd think he'd be a little more interested, what with the studio lawyers going nuts," Frank said. "But it's his way. He always likes to show he's above everything and everyone."

They trailed Frank Pauley into Linus Wolfinger's office.

So this was the Little Shit's castle, Dane thought, looking around. Pauley was right. This was no ordinary executive office. It didn't have a scintilla of chrome or glass or leather. It wasn't piled with scripts, with memorabilia or anything else. It wasn't anything but a really big square room with a highly polished wooden floor, bare of carpets, windows on two sides with views toward the golf course and the ocean beyond, and a huge desk in the middle. On top of the desk looked to be a fortune in computers. There was a single chair, without a back, behind the desk.

Linus Wolfinger wasn't looking at his visitors, he was looking at one of the computer screens, and humming the theme from *Gone With the Wind*.

The assistant cleared his throat, loudly.

Wolfinger looked up, took in all the folks staring at him, and smiled, sort of. He stepped around from behind the huge desk, let them assimilate the fact that he did, indeed, look more like a nerd than not, what with his short-sleeve white shirt, pens in his shirt pocket, a black dickey that covered his neck and disappeared under the shirt, and casual pants that hung off his skinny butt. He said, "I understand from all of our lawyers, Mr. Pauley, that we have a problem with *The Consultant*. Someone has been copying the murders in the first two episodes."

"Yes," Frank said. "That appears to be the case."

"Now, I suppose you're all police?"

"Yes, and FBI," Detective Flynn said, "and Ms. Nick Jones."

Wolfinger pulled a pen out of his shirt pocket and started chewing on it. He said, "Did Frank tell you that the show is now, officially, closed down?"

"Among other things," Delion said. "We wanted to ask you first if you have any idea who the real-life murderer is, since it's very likely someone closely connected to the show."

"I do have some ideas on that," Wolfinger said, and put the pen back in his pocket. He opened a desk drawer, which was really a small refrigerator, and pulled out a can of Diet Dr Pepper. He popped the lid and took a long drink.

"Why don't we go into a conference room," Dane said. "You do have one, I assume? With chairs?"

"Sure. I've got seven minutes," Wolfinger said, drank down more soda, and burped.

"With all your reputed brains," Flynn said, "we should get this resolved in five."

"I expect so," Wolfinger said, and waved them into a long, narrow, utterly plush conference room just down the hall. Manning the coffeepot and three plates piled high with goodies was the second of the three secretaries, Mrs. Grossman.

All of them accepted cups of coffee.

Once they were all seated, Linus Wolfinger leaned forward in his chair and said, "Have you seen the third episode, the one that was scheduled to air this Tuesday night?"

"Not yet," Delion said.

Linus Wolfinger said, "It's about two particularly brutal murders that take place in western New York. There's an even more *X-Files* type of situation than there was in the first two. It's got this talking head that keeps appearing just before the victims get chopped up. It's pretty creepy. DeLoach loves shit like that. He's very good at it."

Dane and Delion looked at each other. When they'd first heard the writer's name, they'd been flabbergasted. "Why would the jerk advertise like this?" Delion had wondered aloud.

Dane said, "DeLoach? The main writer's name is DeLoach?"

Wolfinger nodded. "Yes, he's smart. Ideas keep marching out of his brain like little soldiers. He really knows how to manipulate the viewer well. I'm sure, however, that all of you already knew the head writer's name."

"Could be," Delion said.

"Sounds like you like the guy," Flynn said.

Wolfinger shrugged. "What's not to like? He's creative, has a brain, and best of all, he has a modicum of a work ethic. Why are you so excited about DeLoach's name?"

Delion, seeing no reason not to, said, "DeBruler is the alias our guy used in San Francisco, at the rectory."

"That's very close," Wolfinger said, tapping his pen on the tabletop. "But you know, despite the names being close, there's no way DeLoach is your guy."

"Oh?" Flynn said, raising an eyebrow.

"The thing is that DeLoach is a weenie. I once saw him throw away an ice cream cone when a fly buzzed near it. He—well, I guess you could say that he lives in his head, he's really out of place here, in the real world. He's got a real rich fantasy life, and that's good for Premier. As I said, he's also got a work ethic, so all of it works to our advantage. But is he a man who'd commit brutal murders? No, definitely not DeLoach."

Dane said, "It's possible that DeLoach is a dangerous weenie, that this rich fantasy life of his has somehow imploded and pushed him out of his head and into the real world. Tell us more about DeLoach. Is he the one who came up with the concept for *The Consultant*?"

"Yes," Wolfinger said. "Yes, he did. His full name is Weldon De-Loach. He's been responsible for two very successful shows in the last ten years. Well respected is Weldon, even though he's pretty old now."

"Define 'pretty old,'" Flynn said.

"He's probably early thirties, maybe even older than that."

"Glory be," Delion said. "He's nearly ready for assisted living."

Wolfinger said, "Despite what I've told you, you still think he's the primary suspect?"

"It sure looks possible," Delion said. "We'll have to look at everyone. We'll need lists from Personnel of all the writers who've been involved with the show, all the technicians, everyone who's even sniffed around the sets."

Dane said, looking thoughtfully at Linus Wolfinger, "DeBruler and

DeLoach. The killer would have known his name, whoever he was. It doesn't mean much."

Delion shook his head, back and forth. "That would be just too easy. Makes the guy stupid, and Mr. Wolfinger here says he's got a brain. Ain't no road ever that straight. But we'll talk to him, the other writers as well and all those folks involved with making the show. Get us those lists, Mr. Wolfinger. I got detectives ready to go. The FBI is sending agents here to interview, do background checks, go over alibis, that sort of thing."

Linus Wolfinger nodded. He was tapping a pen on the tabletop. Dane knew it was a different one from the one he had been chewing on in his office because it didn't have teeth marks in it. "You didn't ask me who I thought was behind this."

"Well, no, we haven't," Flynn said. "And what do you know about it?"

THIRTEEN

"Hey, it all stays in this room?"

"Sure, why not?" Flynn said. "Give it your best shot, Mr. Wolfinger."

Linus Wolfinger smiled at all of them impartially, tapped his pen one more time, and said, "I think it's Jon Franken. He's the assistant director for *The Consultant*. He's too good to be true, you know? Mr. Hollywood down to his tasseled Italian loafers. He knows everyone, is just so good at A-list parties. I know there's got to be something really nasty about him. No one that good is what he seems to be, you know?"

Delion rose, the others with him. He said, "Thank you, Mr. Wolfinger. We'll really look close at Jon Franken. Me, I can't stand a guy who's too good at his job. It motivates me to nail his ass."

Flynn said, "Now, Mr. Wolfinger, do contact either me or Inspector Delion or Special Agent Carver here if you come up with something or if you find out anything that could be useful." All of them passed their cards to Wolfinger, who didn't take them, just let them pile up in front of him, close to that still-tapping pen that was driving everyone nuts.

Dane said, wishing in that moment that he could haul the little jerk up by his dickey and throw that damned pen out the window, "It would be easier if the murderer had stayed in the same city, but he didn't. At least now no more episodes will be aired."

Wolfinger said, "I've already slotted in *The Last Hurrah,* another new show about lottery-ticket winners and what becomes of them."

"Sounds innocuous enough," Flynn said.

Pauley said, "Maybe it's someone who's out to sabotage the show itself. I've been in the business a long time, made enemies. Maybe it's someone who hates me personally, wants revenge, knows that this one is my particular baby. I've got a lot on the line here."

Dane said, "You think a man would kill—what is the count now that we know of—eight people, just to get revenge on you?"

"Put that way, it doesn't sound too likely, does it," Pauley said.

"Were there problems getting the show off the ground, Mr. Pauley?" Flynn asked. "Someone specifically who put up roadblocks?"

"There are always problems," Wolfinger said, batting his hand at Pauley to keep him quiet, "but on this one there were fewer than usual. Mr. Pauley is right that he's got a lot to lose. He's married to *the consultant's* girlfriend on the show. He pushed to have her star. If the show closes down, then so does she." Wolfinger didn't sound sorry at all.

Dane glanced over at Pauley and knew he was thinking, *Little Shit.* Pauley said, "He's right—having the show shut down won't be wonderful for my home life, but Belinda will understand, she has to. But having the media go nuts over a script murderer will be a disaster for my reputation and the studio's. We won't even mention the lawsuits."

"Certainly everyone's reputation is on the line here," Flynn said.

"Unfortunately, yes," Wolfinger said. "I trust you gentlemen will try to encourage everyone interviewed to keep quiet about this?" He laughed. "Hey, it won't matter. This is far too juicy to keep quiet about. It'll be out before the day is over." Wolfinger looked down at his pen, frowned a moment, then said, "Then there's Joe Kleypas, the star. Interesting man. A bad boy, but nonetheless, an excellent actor. Maybe you want to put him up there on your suspect list."

"Why would he kill people to ape the show he's starring in?" Delion asked. "He has to know the show will be shut down."

Wolfinger shrugged. "He's a deep guy, never know what he's thinking. Maybe he's got mental problems."

Flynn said, "All right. We'll be speaking to you later, Mr. Wolfinger. Thank you for your time and your ideas."

When they left exactly seven minutes later, Nick said, "He's an interesting man. I didn't think he was a shit. Well, all that pen tapping was obnoxious."

"That's vintage Little Shit," said Pauley.

Frank Pauley stopped to frown at a framed black-and-white photo of Greta Garbo on the wall. He carefully straightened it, then nodded. "You're right. He acted like an adult. I've seen him do it before. But I've also seen him throw a soda can—full—at somebody who said something he didn't like."

Dane said, "Mr. Pauley, are they still shooting any of these episodes?"

"No. Eight shows were shot last summer and into early fall. The way it works is that if the show is picked up, that is, if the network decides to continue with more shows, they get everyone back together and shoot six to thirteen more. They usually make this decision after three, four shows. If the ratings are good, they pay for us to write more episodes. If it's a huge success, everything is given the go-ahead and things move really fast. Oh yes, I called the AD—assistant director—Jon Franken for you."

"This is the guy Wolfinger thinks is the psychopath?"

"Yeah. Wolfinger is cute. Can you believe the damned head of the studio was talking like that? Making accusations? But again, Wolfinger does just as he pleases, usually the more outrageous the better. As for Franken, the man has both feet firmly planted on the ground, knows how to squeeze money out of the sidewalk, and if something needs to happen yesterday, he's the guy you go to. He's trusted, something so unusual in LA that people come up to pinch him to see if he's real. He also works his butt off."

"Exactly what does he do on the show?" Dane asked.

"Actually, it's Franken who has to know more about the actual show than just about anyone, including the line producer. He's in charge of setting up off-studio sites, getting everyone together who's supposed to be shooting, setting up the actual shooting schedule, holding everyone's feet to the budget fire. He listens to the stars whine about the director or sob about their latest relationship gone bad, stuff like that. He's got the big eye. Oh yes, Franken's really big into anything otherworldly; he goes for that stuff. He and DeLoach are really in sync on this one."

"Did they develop the idea together?" Dane said.

"I'm not really sure about that. I do know that they've always got their heads together."

Delion said, "I hope he's older than twenty-four."

"Yes, Jon's been around for a long time. He might even be forty or so. An adult. He started out sweeping off sets when he was just a kid. He's expecting us."

THEY found Jon Franken on the sound stage for a new fall sitcom that wasn't doing well titled *The Big Enchilada*. He was talking to one of the actors, using his hands a lot, explaining something. From twelve feet away, they could see that he was buff, tanned, and dressed very Hollywood in loose linen trousers and a flowing shirt, his sockless feet in Italian loafers. He looked to be in his forties.

Pauley waved to him, and in a few minutes he joined them. He was polite, attentive, and when they asked him about the order of the episodes, an eyebrow went up. "I've been hearing some rumors, something about some murders that are similar to an episode of *The Consultant*. Is this true?"

Delion said, "Well, so much for discretion."

Jon Franken was incredulous. "You honestly believe that this could have remained a secret? This is a TV studio. There isn't a single secret anywhere within two miles of this place."

Dane said, "Yes, you have it right, and we need your help. Frank Pauley said you know everything and everyone."

Franken said, appalled, "The higher-ups must be shitting their pants. A murderer who's copying a TV show? Incredible." He shook his head. "Only in Hollywood. I'll do my best."

"Thank you," Dane said. "We understand you're close to DeLoach. How much of the actual writing was his?"

"Depended on the episode. The first two, however, were ninety percent Weldon, since it was his idea to begin with. Oh, Jesus, I can't believe that."

Nick said, "Are the episodes to be shown in a certain order?"

"Yes, that's usually the way it's done. There's not too much week-to-week carryover, so it really doesn't matter, but yes, the episodes would remain in the order they were filmed."

"Have you seen him, Mr. Franken?" Flynn asked.

"No, he isn't working right now. He called me a couple of days ago, said his brain was tired and he was taking some time off. He said not to expect him anytime soon. He's done this before, so no one gets cranked about it, but he never calls in and I don't think anyone knows where he went. Listen now, even though the first two episodes are Weldon's, that doesn't mean he would do something this heinous. It just isn't him."

Dane asked, "Is the same episode shown all over the country on the same day at approximately the same time?"

Franken said, "The first two *Consultant* episodes were shown on Tuesday night everywhere, but Wolfinger slotted them a little differently, depending on the demographics, or maybe because of it, so they'll probably okay some more scripts. Beginning with the third one, it's not that heavily Weldon's work. Do you agree, Frank?"

"You're right," Pauley said.

Delion said, "Who can tell us what Weldon's travel schedule's been the past month?"

"That would be Rocket Hanson. She makes all the arrangements for the writers, and for everybody else for that matter."

"Rocket?" Nick said. "That's a wonderful name."

"Yeah, she was trying to break into films thirty years ago, thought she needed something unusual to get her through the door. It stuck."

Flynn said, "Has Weldon DeLoach been out of town a lot very recently?"

Franken just shook his head. "I haven't been working directly with him for several months now. You'll have to speak to other folks. We e-mail a lot and speak maybe once a week if we're not working together on a show. I heard someone say he was off to see some relatives, maybe in central California, but I'm not sure about that."

Dane said, "I don't suppose the relatives are near Pasadena?"

"I haven't a clue. Listen, believe me, you're wrong about Weldon. I know it looks bad, but you're way off course here."

Dane asked, "What is Weldon writing now?"

Franken said, "He's been writing for *Boston Pops* for about four months now."

Delion looked pained.

Franken nodded, said, "Yeah, I agree with you, Inspector. It's a dim-witted show that has somehow caught on. Lots of boobs and white teeth, and one-liners that make even the cameraman wince. It's embarrassing. Weldon keeps trying to sneak in some weird stuff, like some Martians landing on the Boston mayor's lawn, just for an off-key laugh, but nobody's buying it."

Frank Pauley nodded.

They spoke to a good dozen writers. Nothing promising on any one of the group, just a bunch of really interesting men and women who didn't have a life, as far as Dane could tell. "Oh yeah, that's true," one of the female writers said, laughing. "All we do is sit here and bounce ideas off each other. Lunch is brought in. Porta Potties are brought in. Soon they'll be bringing beds in."

Dane said when they were walking down Pico back to their two cars, "It's time for a nice big meeting, mixing Feds with locals. There's lots of folks that need very close attention."

Flynn nodded, saw some kids shooting baskets, took three steps toward them before he caught himself.

FOURTEEN

St. Bartholomew's
San Francisco

Dane and Nick were seated in the second row in St. Bartholomew's, Nick staring at Father Michael Joseph's coffin, Dane staring at the wooden cross that rose high behind the nave, both waiting silently for the church to fill up and the service to begin. They'd come back from LA the previous evening for Michael's funeral.

It was an overcast early afternoon in San Francisco, not unusual for a winter day. It was cold enough for Dane to wear his long camel hair coat, belted at the waist. The heavens should be weeping, Father Binney had said, because Father Michael Joseph had been so cruelly, so madly, slain.

Dane had taken Nick to Macy's again on Union Square. In two hours flat, he'd come close to maxing out his credit card. She kept saying, "I don't need this. I don't. You're making me run up a huge debt to you. Please, Dane, let's leave. I have more than enough."

"Be quiet, you've got to have a coat. It's cold today. You can't go to the—"

He broke off, just couldn't say it, so he said finally, "You can't go to the church without a coat."

She'd picked out the most inexpensive coat she could find. Dane simply put it back and handed her another one in soft wool. Then he bought her gloves and boots. Two more pair of jeans, one pair of black slacks, two nightgowns, and underwear, the only thing he didn't help her pick out. He just stood by a mannequin that was dressed in a sinful red thong and a decorative bra, his arms crossed over his chest.

At noon, she'd finally just stopped in the middle of the cosmetics section on the main floor. Salespeople swarmed around them. A woman was closing fast on her to squirt her with perfume, when she said, "This is enough, Dane. No more. I want to go home. I want to change. I want to go to Saint Bartholomew's and say good-bye to Father Michael Joseph."

Dane, who'd never in his adult life shopped for more than eight minutes with a woman, said, "You've done well—so far. All that's left is some makeup."

"I don't need any makeup."

"You look as pale as that mannequin in lingerie, the one with the blood red lips and that red thong that nearly gave me a heart attack. At least some lipstick."

"I'll just bet you noticed how pale she was," Nick said, and turned to the Elizabeth Arden counter.

And so Dane found himself studying three different shades of lipstick before saying, "That one. Just a touch less red. That's it."

Dane finally turned in the pew to look over his shoulder. So many people, he thought. Not just priests today, like at the wake, but many parishioners and friends whose lives Michael had touched. Archbishop Lugano and Bishop Koshlap both stopped and spoke to him, each of them placing his hand on Dane's shoulder, to give comfort, Dane supposed. He was grateful for their caring, but the truth was he felt no comfort.

He watched Bishop Koshlap stand over Michael's coffin, and he knew his eyes were on Michael's face. Then he leaned down and kissed his forehead, straightened, crossed himself, and slowly walked away, head bowed.

Dane stared down at his shoes, wondering how well they had hidden the bullet hole through Michael's forehead.

Michael was gone forever, only his body lying in that casket at the front of the church. A huge sweep of white roses covered the now-closed coffin, ordered by Eloise because Michael had loved white roses. Dane hoped, prayed, that Michael knew the roses were there, that he was smiling if he could see them, that he knew how much his brother and sister, and so many people, loved him.

But Michael wasn't there and Dane didn't think he could bear it. He focused on his shoes, trying not to yell his fury, his soul-deep pain out loud.

DeBruler, DeLoach—he just couldn't get the names out of his mind, even here, at his brother's funeral mass. A sick joke? His anger shifted to the murderer who was somewhere down in LA, someone connected with that damned TV show. He turned when he heard his sister Eloise's voice behind him. He rose again, kissed and hugged her, shook her husband's hand, hugged his nephews. They sat silently in the row behind him.

Archbishop Lugano spoke, his deep voice reaching the farthest corners of the church. He spoke spiritual, moving words, words extolling Michael's life, his love of God, the meaning of his priesthood, but then there were the inevitable words of forgiveness, of God's justice, and Dane wanted to shout there would never be any forgiveness for the man who killed his brother. Suddenly, he looked down to see Nick's hand covering his, her fingers pressing down on him, smoothing out his fist, squeezing his hand. She said nothing, continued to look straight ahead. He looked quickly at her profile, saw tears rolling down her face. He drew in a deep breath and held on to her hand for dear life.

Other priests spoke, and parishioners, including a woman who told how Father Michael Joseph had saved not only her life, but her soul. Finally, Father Binney nodded to him.

He walked to the front of the church, past Michael's coffin, hearing gasps of surprise throughout the church, for he was the very image of his brother. It was difficult for people to look at him and accept that he wasn't Michael. He went up the steps to stand behind one of the pulpits. It was only then that he saw that the church was overflowing, people standing three and four deep all around the perimeter, filling the south and north transepts, even out beyond the sanctuary doors.

And Dane thought, Is the murderer out there somewhere, head bowed so people won't see him gloat? Did he come to witness what his madness had brought about and delight in it? Dane had forgotten to say anything to Nick about keeping an eye out, just in case.

Then he saw his friends, Savich and Sherlock. Dane felt immensely grateful. He nodded to them.

Dane looked down at his brother's coffin, the white roses blanketing it. He cleared his throat and fastened his gaze just over the top of Savich's head because he just couldn't bear to speak looking directly at anyone. He said, "My brother loved to play football. He was a wide receiver and he could catch any ball I could get in the air. I remember one of our last high-school games. We were behind, twenty to fourteen. There was only a little over a minute left in the game when we got the ball again.

"All the fans were on their feet and we were moving down the field, me throwing passes, Michael catching them. Finally, we were on the eighteen-yard line, with only ten seconds left to play. We had to have a touchdown.

"I threw the ball to Michael in the corner of the end zone. I don't know how he kept a foot inbounds, but he actually caught that ball just as he was tackled hard, and he held on. He won the game, but the thing was, that hit tore up his knee.

"He lay there, grinning up at me like a fool, knowing he'd probably never play another football game, and he said, 'Dane, it's okay. Sometimes the bad things don't touch you nearly as much as the good things do. We won, you can't get gooder than that.'"

Dane's voice broke. He vaguely heard scattered small laughs. He looked down again at the roses that covered Michael's coffin. Then, suddenly, he felt warmth on his face, looked up, and saw that brilliant sunlight had burst through those incredible stained-glass windows. He felt the warmth of that light all the way to his bones. He said, voice firmer now, "Michael appreciated the good in everyone, rejoiced in it; he also understood that the bad was a part of the mix, and he accepted that, too. But there was one thing he wouldn't accept, and that was evil; he knew it was here among us. He knew the stench of it, hated the immense tragedy it brought into the world. The night he was shot, he knew he was facing evil. He faced it, and the evil killed him.

"Michael and I shared many things: Two of them were Sunday football games and tenacity."

Dane paused a moment, and this time he scanned all the faces around him. He said in a low voice, filled with despair and promise, "I will find the evil that destroyed my brother. I will never give up until I do."

There was a moment of absolute silence.

The silence was broken by a soft popping sound. Even as slight a sound as it was, in the dead silence it echoed to every corner of the church. A man yelled, "This woman's hurt!"

People jerked around, trying to see what was happening.

Nick yelled, "Oh God, it's him, Dane! He tried to kill me! It's him!"

Dane saw blood streaking down her face, felt fear paralyze him for an instant. Then he raced down the steps toward Nick, as she shoved her way through bewildered knots of mourners, yelling at them, "Stop him! There, he's wearing that black coat, that black hat. *Stop him!*"

People were turning and grabbing anyone in black, but since nearly every person was wearing black, including a good three dozen priests, there was pandemonium, people shoving, people yelling, people grabbing other people. It was madness.

Dane reached Nick, looked at the blood snaking down her face, and yelled, "Dammit, Nick. Are you all right?"

"I'm okay, don't worry. Just a graze, I guess. We've got to get him. Dane, hurry, I saw him running that way."

Dane thought he saw the man then, moving fast, darting around people or pushing through them, his head down, heading to the narrow side door of the church.

Dane shoved two priests out of his way, saw the man disappear out the side door and the door swing closed again. He nearly burst with fury. The bastard had come here, to his brother's service, probably laughing behind his hand, in madness, and triumph. And he'd tried to murder Nick.

Dane made it to the door, shoved a good half dozen people out of his way, and threw it outward. He saw Savich, a blur, he was running so fast, saw him leap, left leg extended, smooth and easy, saw his foot strike the man's kidney, solid and hard. The man fell forward, flailing his arms to keep his balance. He managed to fling himself about, to face his attacker, and that was a mistake. Savich hit him three times, in the neck and head. The man gasped with pain, shock on his shadowed face, went limp and dropped. Savich went down beside him, checked his pulse and yelled, "I've got him!"

Dane couldn't believe it. Neither could Delion or Nick, who now stood over the man.

Dane said, "He's the one, Nick?"

"I think so," she said. "Can you turn him over, please?"

Savich pulled the man onto his back, got the hat off his head.

Dane said, "This is Dillon Savich, he's my boss at the FBI. Savich, this is Nick Jones, our only eyewitness."

Savich nodded. "You'd better see to that head wound she's got. This guy's down for the count. Go ahead, take care of her, Dane. Nice to meet you, Nick." Savich looked up at his wife, gave her a good-sized grin. Sherlock put her hand on his shoulder. "That was rather dashing," she said, smiling down at him. "It's lucky you guys don't have to wear high heels." She punched him in the arm, looked over at Dane. "This is the maniac who killed your brother? This is the man who just shot Nick? Oh goodness, look at your face." Sherlock pulled a handkerchief out of her jacket pocket, gave it to Dane, and watched him very gently pat Nick's forehead. "It looks like the bullet just grazed you, but scalp wounds really bleed. What do you think, Dane? I think it's okay, just looks really bad. I'm Sherlock."

Delion glanced at Nick's face, nodded, then stared again at Savich, who was still on his haunches beside the man. He shook his head back and forth. "I don't believe this, I just don't believe this." He grabbed Savich's hand, pumped it up and down. "I always thought the Feds were pantywaists. Hey, good job."

Savich checked the guy's pulse again, rose, and dusted off his suit pants. "You must be Inspector Delion. Have you called this in?"

"Yeah, it's done," Delion said.

A group of black-garbed priests were pressing in, Archbishop Lugano at their head. He said in a voice that carried nearly to California Street, "I have a cousin who's in the DEA. She's not a pantywaist either. Well done, sir, thank you."

Savich merely nodded. "Dane, get the blood out of Nick's eyes and see if she can identify this bozo."

Dane stared at the narrow furrow the bullet had made at her hairline just above her temple. It was still bleeding sluggishly. He pulled away Sherlock's handkerchief and took out his own, folded it up, and said, "Nick, press this hard against the wound. We'll get you to a doctor in a minute."

"Let me take another look at the guy, Dane." She was still breathing hard, and there was rage in her eyes as she looked down at the unconscious man who was Father Michael Joseph's murderer. She said, "I was sitting there, listening to you, and then the light came through that stained-glass window and I knew I was going to cry. I bowed my head; then in the very next instant I felt this shock of heat on my face. I looked up and saw the light from that window was shining directly down on that man. I saw him looking at me, and then I knew, just knew."

Delion was searching his pockets. "No gun. Well, it's got to be around here somewhere." He called over two uniformed officers who had just arrived and told them to start the search.

The man groaned, tried to pull himself up onto his knees. One of the officers grabbed his left arm, another grabbed his right. They cuffed him and hauled him toward a police car at the curb.

Dane said, "Look at this crowd. How are we ever going to find that gun?"

"I think perhaps I can help," Bishop Koshlap said. He flung back his head and yelled, "Everyone please listen to me. There is a gun somewhere to be found. Please help our priests form search groups. If any of you saw this man shoot this woman, please step forward."

Dane watched all those people, at least four hundred of them, grow silent and calm because the bishop himself had given them a task, a task that really mattered. He saw Archbishop Lugano speak to the priests, saw them divvy up the crowd and set to work. Dane looked down at Nick, frowned, and took back his folded handkerchief to press it himself against Nick's face. "You weren't pressing directly on the gash. You're still bleeding. But no matter, it's nearly stopped. I can see it's not bad, thank God.

"You know what, Nick? My brother would have been very pleased about this."

Savich said to Delion, "I'm not so sure there's a gun to find. If I were the shooter, I'd have another guy here so I could hand the gun off to him."

Delion knew he was right, but they had to look, just in case. "Yeah, I know." He heard sirens, and quickly went to Nick. "The paramedics are nearly here. You can bet the media will be right behind them. I want you to go with the paramedics back to Bryant Street. The last thing we need is photos of you in the *Chronicle*. We'll meet you there."

"But, Dane, I've got to go with him to the cemetery."

Dane said, "It's okay, Nick. Delion's right. If the media see you, it will be a nightmare. I'll see you back at the police station." He paused just a brief moment, lightly touched his fingertips to the wound on her forehead. "I'm sorry."

FIFTEEN

When Delion called a halt to the search, all the mourners formed a car processional that wound a mile to the west, to the Golden Gate Cemetery. The sun was shining, although the day remained cold, and there was the heavy scent of the ocean in the air. Dane looked down at the rich earth that now covered his brother's grave and said, "We just might have gotten him, Michael. I pray that you know that." He stood there a moment longer, staring down at the mound of earth that covered his brother's body. Michael was gone and he would never hear him laugh again, hear him tell about the drunk guy who tried to steal the bishop's miter and ended up hiding in a confessional.

He didn't approach his sister, couldn't look at the pain in her eyes and say something comforting. Eloise, her husband, and her kids were clutched together, and that was good.

When at last Dane turned away from his brother's grave, he saw Sherlock and Savich. He hadn't noticed that they'd flanked him, not saying anything, just there, solid and real.

Dane drove his rental car to the police station on Bryant Street, Savich and Sherlock following. Delion had wanted Savich to go downtown with them immediately, but Savich had just smiled, shaken his head. "Important things first," he'd said, nothing more, and taken his wife's hand in his and followed Dane to the cemetery.

When Dane walked into the homicide room nearly two hours later, he immediately saw Nick, seated in the chair beside Delion's desk. He said her name and she turned. "You look like a prisoner of war with that bandage on your hair."

"It's not nearly as bad as it looks. No stitches necessary. The paramedics couldn't stop talking about what had happened, and I think they lost it with the gauze."

"All right, but you just try to relax, okay?"

She nodded.

"It still shakes me to my toes that I didn't protect you better. If you hadn't bowed your head at just that moment, the bullet would have hit you square on and you'd be dead. Jesus, I'm sorry, Nick."

Nick realized this very well, in an abstract sort of way. It hadn't really sunk in yet, which was probably a blessing. When it did, she'd probably shudder and shake herself to the nearest women's room. She said, "I wish you wouldn't try to take credit for this. Just stop beating yourself up, Dane. This wasn't your fault. Do you think this means God doesn't want me to die just yet?"

"You mean that it isn't your time? Fate rules?"

"Yes, I guess so."

"I don't have a clue. I'm just really glad he didn't succeed."

"I bowed my head because I was crying and I didn't want you to see."

He gulped, but didn't say anything more.

"What you said about Father Michael Joseph, it was very moving, Dane. Did he really catch that touchdown pass? Really tore up his knee?"

He nodded, got a grip on himself. "Yes. You know, this thing about Fate or whatever—if you like, we could get drunk one night and discuss it."

It was a slight smile, he saw it. It made him feel very good.

"Yeah," she said, "I'd like that."

Lieutenant Linda Purcell came up to them, looking resigned. "We found the bullet. That's the good news. Unfortunately, it shattered against a concrete wall. No way to know if it was from the same gun that killed Father Michael Joseph. No matter. It'll all come together anyway. Delion's doing his thing. Just hang around and listen, don't interrupt. We decided to let the guy think about the wages of sin and left him downstairs in the tank for a couple of hours. We just brought him up here. We don't have any one-way mirrors here so keep back from the doorway so he doesn't focus on you."

Dane looked toward the guy who'd shot Nick. His head was down between his arms on the scarred table. He was sobbing, deep gulping sobs that sounded like he believed life as he knew it was over. And he was right, Dane thought, the bastard.

Nearly all of the inspectors hanging around in the homicide room were close enough to the interrogation room to hear. They all looked exactly the same, excited and on the edge. Dane imagined that if they were in an FBI field office, there would be no difference at all. Women agents, in particular, didn't cut any slack to a murderer who broke down in tears. That had surprised Dane when he was new in the FBI, but over the years he'd changed the opinions he supposed he'd absorbed by osmosis all through childhood and adolescence.

Delion sat across from the sobbing man, not saying a word, just watching, arms crossed over his chest, his mustache drooping a bit. Patient, like he had all the time in the world. They watched him examine a thumbnail, heard a soft whistle under his breath, watched him trace a fingertip over a deep gash in the scarred wooden table between them.

They'd taken the guy's long dark woolen coat, hat, and gloves, which left him in a gray sweatshirt and wrinkled black pants. Dane couldn't tell if he was just like the man Nick had originally described. But he saw he was slight of build, looked to be in his forties, and had a full head of dark hair—just as she'd said. And she'd recognized him from across the church.

Finally, the guy raised his head and said between gulps, "You've been holding me for a long time, haven't spoken to me, and now I'm up here in this crappy little room with cops standing outside the door watching. What do you want from me? Why did that big guy try to kill me? I'm gonna sue his ass off. His pants'll fall right off him."

Sherlock snickered.

Both Dane and Nick drew in their breaths. The guy's face was really white, like he hadn't seen the sun in far too long. Just as Nick had said.

Delion said, "We asked you before if you wanted a lawyer and you said you didn't. You want a lawyer now, Mr.—? Hey, why don't you tell us your name."

The man tilted his head back, as if he were trying to look down his nose at Delion. He sniffed, swallowed, and wiped his hand across his running nose. "You already know my name. You took my wallet hours ago and then you just left me alone to rot."

"Your name, sir?"

"My name's Milton—Milt McGuffey. I don't need no lawyer, I didn't do nuthing. I want to leave."

Delion reached over and took the guy's forearm in his hand, shook it just a little bit. "Listen to me, Mr. McGuffey, that guy who hit you is a cop. He just wanted to keep you from running away from the scene of a crime. He was being efficient, just doing what he was supposed to do, you know? Trust me on this: You really don't want to sue him or his ass. Now, why don't you tell me why you tried to kill Nick Jones at Father Michael Joseph's funeral mass."

"I didn't try to kill no Nick Jones! Is that the broad who was bleeding all over the place? Hey, I was just standing there listening and then everything went wild and I heard her yelling. I just wanted to get out of there and so I pushed open that side door and ran. Then that big guy tried to kill me."

"I see," Delion said. "So then, tell me, Milton, why you were at Father Michael Joseph's funeral. You a former priest or something?"

He wiped his nose again, rubbed his hand on his sweatshirt sleeve, and finally mumbled something under his breath.

"I didn't hear you, Milton," Delion said.

"I don't like Milton. That's what my ma called me just before she'd whack me aside the head. I said that I like funerals. So many people sitting there trying to act like they give a shit about the deceased."

Savich touched Dane's arm to keep him from going into the room. "Easy," he said in his slow, deep voice, right against Dane's ear. "Easy."

"I see," Delion said. "So you just wandered into Saint Bartholomew's like you'd walk into a movie, any movie, didn't matter what was playing?"

"That's right. Only a funeral's free. Wish there was some popcorn or something."

"So you didn't know the star of this particular show?"

Milt shook his head. His eyes were drying up fast now.

"Where do you live, Mr. McGuffey?"

"On Fell Street, right on the Panhandle."

"Real close to Haight Ashbury?"

"That's right."

"How long have you lived there, Mr. McGuffey?"

"Ten years. I'm from Saint Paul, that's where my family still is, the fools freeze every winter."

"Hey, my ex-wife is from Saint Paul," Delion said. "It's a nice place. What do you do for a living?"

Milton McGuffey looked down at his hands, mumbled something. It was getting to be a habit.

"Didn't hear you, Milt."

"I'm disabled. I can't work. I collect benefits, you know?"

"What part of you is disabled, Mr. McGuffey? I saw you run, saw you turn around, ready to fight. You were fast."

"I was scared. That guy was really big. He was trying to kill me, I had no choice. It's my heart. It's weak. Yeah, I've decided I'm going to perform a public service—I'm gonna sue that cop; he's dangerous to everybody."

"Where did you get the silencer for the gun?"

Very slight pause, then, "I didn't have no gun. I don't even know what a silencer looks like."

"We'll find that gun, Milt, don't ever doubt that. Was it the same gun and silencer you used to kill Father Michael Joseph?"

He nearly rose right out of his chair, then slowly sank down again, shook his head back and forth. "I didn't kill no priest! I'm nonviolent. All we gotta do is respect and love each other."

"Do you prefer a gun to taking a poker and striking an old woman dead?"

"Hey, man, I don't know what you're talking about. What old woman?"

"You remember that piece of doubled-over wire? Do you like that the best, Milt? Pulling that wire tighter and tighter until it's so tight it cuts right through to bone?"

"Stop it, man. I'm nonviolent, I told you. I wouldn't hurt nobody, even a parole officer. Hey, you think I shot that broad in the head? Not me, man, not me."

Delion rolled his eyes, mouthed toward the open door, *Prime asshole.*

"What were you in jail for, Milt?"

"It was just one mistake, a long time ago, a little robbery, that's it."

"There was a guy whose head you bashed in along with the robbery. Don't you remember that?"

"It was a mistake, I just lost it—you know, too much sugar in my diet that day. I served my time. I'm nonviolent now. I don't do nuthing."

"Do you watch the show *The Consultant*?"

"Never heard of it." The guy looked up then, and there was no doubt about it, he was puzzled by the question. Genuinely puzzled. He had no clue what *The Consultant* was, dammit. That, or he was an excellent actor, and unfortunately Delion didn't think that was the case. Well, shit. That was a surprise, a bad one.

Delion leaned forward, delicately smoothed his mustache with his index finger. "It's about this murderer who kills people and then taunts a priest about it, all in the confessional, so the priest can't turn him in. He kills the priest, Milt. This guy's a real bad dude."

"Never heard of it. Not a word. I don't like violent movies or TV shows."

Delion looked up at Dane, then beyond him, to Savich. Slowly, after but a moment, he nodded.

Savich walked into the small interrogation room, took a seat beside Delion, and said, "How are you feeling, Mr. McGuffey?"

The guy pressed himself against the back of his chair. "I know who you are. You're that big fella who tried to kill me."

"Nah, I wasn't trying to kill you," Savich said, a smile on his face that would terrify anyone with half a brain, still in doubt in McGuffey's case. "If I'd wanted to kill you, trust me, you'd be in the morgue, stretched out on a nice cold table, without a care in the world. What did you do with the gun?"

"I didn't have no gun."

"Actually, yes, you did and you gave it to that other guy. You know, Milt, the thing is that I saw you. I was watching the crowd, that was my assignment from the lieutenant, to watch, because just maybe the guy who killed Father Michael Joseph would be there, to get his jollies, to make him feel really proud of himself. Sure enough you came. But you weren't there just because you were proud of your work; nope, you were there to kill Nick Jones because she can identify you. You really moved fast, didn't you? It's only been a couple of days since she gave your description to the forensic artist and the drawing of you was in the newspaper. How'd you find out it was Nick Jones?"

"Look, man, I did see that drawing in the paper, that's true, but I didn't know who the guy was. Wait, you can't really think that guy was me. No way, I don't look nuthing like that dude. Mean fucker, that's what I thought when I saw his picture and read the story."

"Yeah, right, Milt," Savich said. "Whatever. Now, don't get me wrong. That was a real slick move you made—you palmed the gun, silencer still attached, and handed it off to your partner as you ran past him. He slipped it into his coat pocket. You never broke stride. It really was well rehearsed and well executed. Only thing—I was watching. You weren't lucky there."

Savich leaned forward until his nose was an inch away from McGuffey's.

He said very slowly, "I saw you do it. They're looking for him right now. I gave a really good description. They'll bring him in and he'll rain all over your picnic." Savich looked over at the door, knew that Sherlock was close.

McGuffey's eyes followed.

Sherlock stepped right up into the doorway, gave Savich a big smile, nodded in satisfaction, and stuck her thumb up.

"Ah," Savich said, "at last. Didn't take our guys too long, did it? Just over two hours. I told you I gave them a great description. Now we have him."

"I don't know what you're talking about! I didn't do nuthing, do you hear me? Nuthing! You couldn't have caught no guy because there wasn't a guy."

Savich rose suddenly. "You can go back to your cell now, Milt. You're tiresome, mouthing all that crap, crying, for God's sake. Just look at poor Inspector Delion. He's nodding off, your lies have bored him so much. You need lessons, Milt. You weren't really all that good a show."

Savich leaned over and splayed his hands on the tabletop, got right in McGuffey's face. "We're going to hold you on the attempted murder of Nick Jones. After your accomplice talks—and he'll fillet you but good, Milt, don't doubt it—the DA is going to have a solid multiple-murder case against you. He's going to enjoy parading you in front of a jury— talk about a slam dunk. He's even got a witness, you know who she is, all right—Nick Jones. You saw her standing out there, didn't you? The white bandage around her head? She sure sees you, and believe me, she knows who you are.

"Yeah, the DA's really going to be happy about this one. You know what else is great about California, Milt? California's got the death penalty. Killing a priest and an old woman, now there's just no excuse for that at all—rotten childhood, too much sugar, chemical imbalance in your brain; none of that will work. They'll drop-kick you right into San Quentin's finest facilities. You can appeal for years, but eventually you'll exhaust everything our sweet legal system has to offer you, and then you're toast."

Savich snapped his fingers in McGuffey's face. "Dead. Gone. And everybody will be real happy when you're off the face of the earth. See you at your trial, Milt. I'll be waving at you from the front row."

Savich walked out of the room, whistling.

McGuffey rose straight up and yelled, "Wait! Dammit, wait! You can't just walk off like that!"

Savich just flapped his hand toward McGuffey, not turning around. "Wait!"

SIXTEEN

Savich smiled at Dane, and very slowly turned, a dark eyebrow raised, obviously impatient.

McGuffey said, nearly falling over his own words he was talking so fast, "He's a liar, he'd roll on his own mother, I didn't do nuthing, do you hear me? You can't believe a word he says. Old Mickey's a king shit, got no sense of right or wrong, a real moral asshole."

"Mickey seems just fine to me," Sherlock said, coming to stand beside Savich, leaning against the door frame. "I spoke to him for a good ten minutes. He seemed real upright, not a lying bone in his body. I think everyone's going to believe what he has to say, Mr. McGuffey, you know? I believed him."

"No, no, you gotta listen to me. I didn't kill no priest. I didn't kill no old woman or any gay guy. It was Mickey who hired me. I didn't hire him, I didn't. I wasn't going to kill her, just make a big noise, right? I was just supposed to scare her good, make sure she was on the next flight to China. I never murdered nobody! You've got to believe me, you've got to." McGuffey was scrambling away from the chair, trying to shove the table out of the way so he could get to Savich. Delion simply clapped his big hand on McGuffey's forearm and said very quietly, "No, Milt, you just sit right back down here."

McGuffey yelled at Delion, "Mickey Stuckey's a damned liar! Don't believe him. He set the whole thing up."

Sherlock said, "Mr. Stuckey told me you hired him, just to be his palm guy, to stand there, keeping his eyes on everything and take whatever you passed to him. He claims he didn't have a clue about what you were going to do. He's really against shooting a lady."

Sherlock shut up and stepped back, no reason to lay it on too thick. The guy looked white now, not just pale, actually white.

Milt was on his feet, trying to pull away from Delion, who'd really clamped down on his forearm and wasn't about to let go. "No! Man, you gotta listen to me. I told you, Mickey's a liar."

Savich sighed deeply, crossed his arms over his chest, and said, frowning, "All right, since I'm still here, why don't you tell me your side of it. But don't lie about it being Mickey who was the shooter because I saw you pass the gun to him. What you tell me better be right on target because I'll tell you, Milt, I'm really leaning toward Stuckey's story and I haven't even heard him tell it yet."

"Okay, okay, you gotta listen, okay? I'll tell you the truth. Here it is."

"Just a moment, Milt," Delion said. "I want to tape-record this. You okay with that?"

"Sure, sure, let's get on with it."

Delion flipped the record button. He gave his name, the date, and McGuffey's name, said, "You're willing to make this confession, no one's coercing you?"

"Dammit, yes. Let's go!"

"You don't want a lawyer present?"

"No, I just want you to hear the truth!"

Delion gave him his Miranda rights, asked him if he understood, to which Milt spewed out more obscenities before he said yes, he understood his rights, to the tape recorder.

"Okay, Milt, tell me what happened."

McGuffey said, "Look, Stuckey called me a couple days ago, said this guy down in LA wanted me to scare this broad at a priest's funeral. Stuckey said he'd give me ten grand, but I had to do it in the middle of the service, for God's sake, in front of hundreds of people, which sounded real stupid to me, but he said that was the way it had to be. I didn't want to do that, but Stuckey had me by the short hairs, you know? I owe him money, some bad investment decisions, you know? So I had to take the job or he might have broken both my legs. But it was never murder, oh no.

"Stuckey had a gun for me, and a silencer, and said the shooter had to be me, it just had to. When I asked him why, he laughed and said, 'You look just right, Milt,' that's what the guy said. 'You look just right, maybe even perfect for the role.' Whatever the fuck that means."

He really did look just right, Dane thought. A good physical resemblance. Damn, nothing was ever easy.

"You really expect me to buy this?" Savich said, lounging back in the uncomfortable chair, looking bored.

Milt sat forward, clasping his hands in front of him, like he was ready to pray. "Look, Inspector, like I told you, I had to have the money. I had to pay off Stuckey or I was in really deep shit. Then there's my disability and that jerk of a landlord is nearly ready to throw me out. Hey, I was just three days away from sitting on Union Square, leaning against the Saint Francis Hotel, begging for money. I had to take the job. A man's gotta survive, you know? A man's gotta pay off his bad investment decisions."

Delion had sat back in his chair, his arms folded over his chest, a sneer on his face. "You want us to believe that this guy specifically told Stuckey it had to be you because you just looked right? You were perfect for the role?"

"I swear it. Hey, Stuckey told me the LA guy's name was DeFrosh— weird name—you'd never forget that stupid name.

"Stuckey said the guy faxed him a photo of the lady I was to give scare to, you know, shoot her just a little bit but not kill her, I wouldn't ever do that. Yeah, the guy told Stuckey that the broad was homeless, but hey, she sure didn't look homeless in the church, but what do I know? How would the guy in LA know about that? Stuckey didn't tell me nuthing else, I swear it."

Dane looked down at Nick, who was as white as the bra he'd watched her pick out in their marathon shopping spree. It was just this morning. Amazing.

Savich said, "What did you do with the photo he faxed of the lady?"

"Stuckey has it, just showed it to me, then took it right back."

"What did it look like?"

"She was coming out of this police station with that guy who's standing beside her out there, you know, that dead priest's brother. It didn't look like no police station I've ever seen in San Francisco. Yeah, Stuckey's got it. She's a looker, I wasn't about to forget her. Like I said, she sure didn't look homeless in the church so for a while there I wasn't sure it was really her."

The bastard took the photo in LA. Dane couldn't believe it.

"So you recognized the priest's brother?"

"Oh yeah, heard people talking about how he and Father Michael Joseph looked identical and it really shook some people up. Everybody was real quiet, you know? Everyone was focused on that guy and what he was saying. Lots of them were crying just listening to him. Then she had the nerve to move—no reason that I could see, she just lowered her head right when I pulled the trigger. Jesus, I could have killed her, but thank the good Lord that it went just like it was supposed to. Yeah, the bullet just grazed her."

"Tell us more about this guy from LA."

"I don't deal with people I don't know, at least usually, and neither does Mickey Stuckey. He said he knew the guy, knew he was good for the money. Hey, he gave me five thousand up front. He told me his name was DeFrosh—I already told you that. Really weird, man."

Milton McGuffey put his head down on his folded arms and began to cry again. Everyone heard him say over his sobs, "I don't want to go to jail, but now I'll have to do time just because I put a little crease in the broad's forehead." He raised his head. "I want Stuckey to go down. I never should have agreed to do it in the church."

Delion said, "You didn't realize there would be cops there?"

"Stuckey told me there'd probably be a couple there, but if I got my timing right, I'd get away, no problem. Damned bastard, that Stuckey. I really want him to go down, he set the whole thing up."

Savich said as he himself smiled down at McGuffey, "Yes, he'll go down, all right, Milt, just as soon as we catch him."

McGuffey's jaw literally dropped open. He stared at Savich for a very long time.

He said, "Shit, man."

Then he yelled at the top of his lungs, "I want a lawyer!"

DELION looked over at Savich, who was speaking to Lieutenant Purcell. They heard her say she'd already put out an APB on Mickey Stuckey, aka Bomber Turkel, the most creative of all his aliases. Delion said, "That guy is something else, Dane. He's your boss?"

"Yeah, I've been in his unit for about five months now."

"Smooth as butter," Delion said. "I was thinking about letting you have a go at Milton, but he knew you, knew you weren't a cop, so that wouldn't have worked. And there was Savich, looking ready, even smiling a little, and I knew he had something up his sleeve. He did good, didn't he?"

"Oh, yes."

"His wife, her name is really Sherlock?"

Dane nodded, smiled. "Yes, they're quite a team."

"You know," Delion said, "I've been in court with Sherlock's dad. Now there's a tough, high-powered dude. Defense lawyers hate his guts. They bitch about having the rotten luck to end up with the only law-and-order judge in San Francisco. Cops love him, needless to say."

"Yes," Dane said. "Too bad that Milton McGuffey isn't a bit more stupid. The DA'll have trouble proving attempted murder. We need Stuckey. At least Milt verified—and it's probably the only thing he said that was true—that the guy who hired him lives in LA and his name's DeFrosh. Damn, Milton isn't the killer, Delion."

"Yeah, I know, but we're getting there, Dane. I'm going to call Flynn, tell him what happened. He's gonna love it that the creep who set this all up told Milton his name was DeFrosh."

Dane said, "Maybe he thinks we're slow—DeFrosh even rhymes with DeLoach. What is he trying to prove? Is it his goal to get up close and personal with us? Or maybe he just wants us to believe that Weldon DeLoach is the killer?" Dane stopped when he saw Nick leaning against a wall, actually against a gray file cabinet since there was no wall showing. "Hey, you okay, Nick?"

She said as she lightly touched her fingertips to the bandage on her forehead, "In this case, it really does look worse than it really is. I'm okay, just resting a bit."

Delion said, "I don't know, Nick. I think you look kind of cute. In a pathetic sort of way. If you want a safe house now, I'll bet the lieutenant will spring for it."

Dane said, "No, I'm keeping her with me. Are you in, Delion? We're all going to LA tomorrow."

"I'm ahead of you, boyo," Delion said. "I already called Franken. He said there was still no sign of Weldon. He's got everybody looking for him, but he doesn't hold much hope of finding him. Since the police are looking, too, maybe someone will see him. Franken's going to meet us at the studio at ten o'clock tomorrow morning. He's got some video of Weldon DeLoach."

"We'll finally see what the man looks like," Nick said.

"Yep," Delion said. "And there's lots of stuff to go over with Flynn. He's got a small army of people working on the personnel lists, interviews, checking alibis, possible motives. We've got a lot to tell him as well."

He looked over at Savich and Sherlock and rolled his eyes. "More Feds. It always starts with a single Fed—sort of like reconnaissance—then you look up and the Feds are converging, multiplying like rabbits until soon they're everywhere and they've taken over. Hey, FBI Director Mueller will be out here before long. He comes from here, you know. Hey, you guys coming with us to LA?"

"Count us in," Sherlock said, coming to stand by Nick.

Savich said, "What's this about the gun that killed Dane's brother being like the two possible guns in the Zodiac killer case? What was that—some thirty years ago?"

"Ain't that a kick?" Delion said. "It's got our ballistics guy, Zopp, nearly drooling he's so excited, telling one blonde joke after another." At Sherlock's raised eyebrow, he grinned. "Yeah, Zopp says blonde jokes help his synapses fire. But you know, it has to be a coincidence, has to be."

"Hmmm," Sherlock said. "Yeah, it's a coincidence, but it's a strange one."

Delion said, "Hey, Sherlock, you as tough as your daddy?"

"He likes to think so," Sherlock said, and smiled real big. There were three other inspectors standing close by, grinning like loons at her.

"Local cops really like her," Savich said, and just shook his head, and Delion thought, *Boy, that guy's proud of her.*

Savich said, "So you don't mind if we tag along to LA with you, Delion?"

"More the merrier," Delion said. "Hey, Lieutenant, any word on Stuckey yet?"

"Not yet, but we'll get him." Lieutenant Linda Purcell looked around at all the assembled homicide inspectors and said, "Everyone saw how Savich worked the guy around? How he got Stuckey's name out of him?"

There were boos and hisses from the cops. A couple of inspectors threw some peanuts.

Before Dane left, Delion motioned him aside to tell him that Nick's fingerprints weren't on file.

"Hey, at least we know she's not a criminal."

"I already came to that conclusion for myself," Dane said.

SEVENTEEN

Los Angeles

Jon Franken, assistant director of *The Consultant,* said, "We couldn't find any photos, but as I told you on the phone, Inspector Delion, we did find something every bit as good." He flipped a switch on the video feed and pointed. "That's Weldon—second guy on the left, the one just standing off to the side, arms crossed over his chest, watching everyone be idiots. He watches a whole lot, just stands back in the shadows, claims it gives him ideas. Whatever, he does have brilliant ideas."

"Freeze it," Dane said and looked at Nick as the screen held the image. The fact was she already looked frozen. She had to be afraid, looking at the man who very possibly hired Milton McGuffey to murder her, the man who might have killed his brother. Dane lightly touched his fingers to her forearm. "Nick?"

"I don't know, I just don't know." She turned to look up at Dane. "Maybe the bone structure is similar." She shrugged. "It's pretty scary."

"I know. Now, Nick, I want you to forget the hair, the tan, the eyes—it could all be cosmetic alterations. Study his face, the way he moves, how he talks using his hands."

She said finally, "Maybe, I just don't know. I just can't be sure. He looks so different."

Delion said, "Milton McGuffey—would you have spotted him if he hadn't shot you?"

"You want brutal honesty here? The answer is I'm just not sure. Probably. Yes, I probably would have said something."

Flynn said, "From everything you've told me, the reason our perp selected McGuffey is because of the way he looks—that is, he looks a lot like him. Now, Mr. Franken, you still don't have a clue where Weldon DeLoach is."

Franken shook his head. "Sorry, like I already told you, he'll be here when he wants to be here. If he's in LA, he'll be coming around. Weldon is a man of very set habits."

"Mr. Franken," Nick said, "has Mr. DeLoach always looked like this? Darkly tanned, really light hair?"

"Why, yes," Franken said. "As long as I've known him. And that's about eight years now. Why do you ask?"

Dane said to Nick, "If our guy is DeLoach, then when you saw him, he was most certainly wearing a wig, contacts. As for losing the tan, I'm not sure how that would be done except with makeup."

"But why would he bother?" Nick said. "He sure didn't expect me to be sitting in the church."

"Yeah, but he would have seen a lot of people while he was in San Francisco. Maybe the disguise was for any- and everyone."

Franken said, rubbing his elegant long fingers over his chin, "I don't think Weldon DeLoach is the murderer. He—he's just not the type to kill anyone. As I told you before, it's just not in him."

Dane remembered Wolfinger had called DeLoach a weenie. "You mean you believe he's a coward?"

"No, nothing like that. It's just—no, not Weldon."

Nick said, "The killer wanted McGuffey to look like him, Dane, and that's why he hired McGuffey to kill me. So he has to be dark and really pale-skinned."

"You're probably right, Nick." Dane asked them to zoom in to get a close-up of Weldon DeLoach, which Franken did. Wolfinger had said DeLoach was around thirty. Well, he didn't look thirty. He looked forty, maybe more. He looked like he'd lived hard, that, or certainly a lot of stress. According to other writers interviewed, he wasn't a cocaine neophyte. "But those years are over," one of the lighting guys had told them. "Weldon hasn't done bad stuff in a long time. He's been really straight."

DeLoach's dark tan really stood out against his white shirt and white pants. His eyes were a pale blue. He had thinning hair—nearly white it was so blond.

Dane said, "Do you have anything with Weldon DeLoach speaking?"

"Why?" Delion said. "Nick never heard him speak."

"Maybe she'll recognize some of the moves he makes when he's animated and speaking. Besides, I want to hear his voice, too."

When Franken ran some more footage, there was Weldon DeLoach at a birthday party being held on a set, giving a toast. He had the softest voice Nick had ever heard, soft and soothing, without much expression or accent. She studied him carefully—the way his arms moved, his hands clenched and unclenched around a cup of booze he held aloft as he spoke, the way he held his head.

When it was over, she shook her head. "I'm sorry, I can't be sure. But you know, if the San Francisco police can catch Stuckey, maybe he'll identify DeLoach's voice."

"Good idea," Dane said, and jotted it down in his small notebook. "Could you give us a copy of the tape?"

Franken nodded, said, "No problem. You're really hoping that Weldon DeLoach is the madman who's copying the scripts for *The Consultant*, aren't you?"

"Fact is," Delion said, sitting forward, "when we find him, we really want to sit down with him and have a nice cozy chat. We'll see."

"It's not Weldon," Jon Franken said again.

"Now, Mr. Franken," Flynn said, "you said the first two episodes of *The Consultant* were Mr. DeLoach's scripts, almost exactly, right?" Dane noticed that Flynn's left hand always moved slightly up and down when he concentrated, as if he were dribbling a basketball.

"Yes," Franken said, "DeLoach was really excited about the series." His cell phone rang and he excused himself. When he came back, he said, "That was my assistant. She said one of Weldon's friends just told her that Weldon was going up to Bear Lake to spend time with his dad. Said he was going to take at least three weeks and he wanted to do some fishing, too. His father's in a home up there, Lakeview Home for Retired Police Officers."

Delion said, "You mean DeLoach's father is a retired cop?"

Franken said, "Yeah, I guess so. I do know his dad's been there a long time. Once Weldon told me that his father was confused most of the time."

Flynn said, "We already knew Weldon didn't ask the people here at the studio or anyone else to make him any airline reservations. If he did fly somewhere, we would have found a record, what with all the security."

"Bear Lake," Delion said thoughtfully. "That's up in the Los Padres National Forest, isn't it? In Ventura County?"

"That's right," Flynn said. "Just an hour north on I-5, over the Tejon Pass. Well, maybe more, what with our god-awful traffic."

"And that means, of course, that DeLoach could have easily driven up to San Francisco anytime he wanted. And Pasadena," Nick said.

"Yeah, that's right," Flynn said.

"Thank you, Mr. Franken," Delion said, rising. "Detective Flynn's people have interviewed all the other writers and employees of *The Consultant*. Everyone checks out, at least on the first pass, which is admittedly shallow. Oh yes, Mr. Franken, where were *you* last week?"

Jon Franken was gently swinging his foot with its Italian loafer tassel falling to one side, then to the other. He raised an eyebrow, but answered readily enough, and with good humor, "I was right here, Inspector Delion. I'm working on *Buffy the Vampire Slayer* at present. Very long days."

Delion nodded, then turned away, saying over his shoulder, "Oh yes, what's the name of Mr. Frank Pauley's wife? You know, the one who plays the girlfriend on *The Consultant*?"

"Belinda Gates."

"We'd like to speak to her. And the star of the show, Joe Kleypas."

"Of course. Watch it with him, Inspector. Joe isn't always mellow, particularly when he drinks. He's got quite a temper, actually. If you accuse him of being a murderer, his smile might just drop off his face." He looked Savich and Dane up and down, smiled to himself, and said, "Of course, it would be interesting to see what would happen if he went at it with you guys."

JON Franken took Savich and Sherlock to the commissary for lunch. "Belinda's working a soap this week," he said as he chewed slowly on a single french fry. "A guest slot. There were some problems, so I know they were shooting today. Maybe she'll be here. If she doesn't show, I'll take you to her trailer. It's pretty rare that the bigger stars come in here. They hang out in their trailers most of the time. You probably noticed trailers scattered all over the lot." He shook his head. "What a life, not much glamour sitting in a trailer."

Sherlock said, looking around the big rectangular room, "I guess I expected a big buffet, cafeteria-style. I do like all those 1930s murals on the walls."

"I like all the ape characters from the new *Planet of the Apes* you've got set around this big room," Savich said. "They're really lifelike."

"This is Hollywood," Jon said. "We never stop advertising or patting ourselves on the back. Actually, though, this commissary doesn't compare to the one over at Universal. You can catch some really big stars over there because the place is so opulent."

Belinda Gates walked in some ten minutes later. Sherlock said, "Goodness, she's got rollers in her hair, Dillon, those big heat rollers. Do you remember the last time I used them to straighten my hair? You helped me roll them in?"

He said as he wrapped a long red curl around his finger, "Let's do it again. It was fun."

Sherlock paused a moment, remembering very clearly what they'd done just after pulling the rollers out. She said to Franken, "That's really Belinda Gates? She's very beautiful."

"Yes, that's her," Franken said, and smiled as he chewed another french fry. "She is beautiful, and most important, the camera loves her face."

Both Savich and Sherlock realized in that instant that Jon Franken had slept with her.

Sherlock said, "Tell us a bit about her, Jon."

Franken ate another french fry, shrugged his elegant shoulders. "Belinda is basically a lightweight. She learns her lines, takes direction well, and has enough talent to keep the wolves at bay—of course, now that she's nailed Frank Pauley she doesn't have to worry. She works when she wants to, which probably means that her head's less screwed up than it was. The thing is, she doesn't have much fire in the belly; she just doesn't have it in her to go for the jugular. If you're looking at her as a suspect in this mess, all disguised and made up to look like a man, I'd say she wouldn't be able to make it through the first audition. Now, if you're interested in Frank Pauley as your murderer, maybe Belinda will give you something incriminating. Pauley just might have enough acid in his gut to do something like this. The thing is, I just don't know why he'd sabotage his own show."

"And you could? Make it through the first audition?" Savich said. He ate a carrot out of his huge salad.

"Oh yes, believe it. Listen, I'd still be sweeping the studio floors if I didn't have it in me to take out a few jugulars, if I didn't want to move up in this business more than I wanted to eat, which was in question in those early years." And then he smiled again, wiped his hands on a napkin. "I'll introduce you and let you at her. A few years ago, Belinda had some problems with the cops. She might not be all that easy for you."

Jon Franken rose. "Forget what I said about Pauley. Even if his worst enemy were backing this show, he still wouldn't have the guts or the imagination to try to bring it down through this convoluted, god-awful violence. Ah, Belinda is taking her lunch out. This should be a good time. She doesn't tape for another hour or so; I checked."

Sherlock and Savich met with Belinda Gates in a small green room connected to a talk show stage. She didn't look friendly. She looked suspicious, her lips tightly seamed together.

A challenge, Sherlock thought, smiling at her, remembering what Franken had said. She introduced herself and Savich, carefully showing Belinda Gates their FBI shields up close.

"You're both FBI?"

"Yes, that's right," Savich said, sitting back so he wouldn't overwhelm, so just maybe she would relax.

"Partners?"

"Sometimes," Sherlock said, sticking out her hand so Belinda Gates was forced to shake it. "Actually, we're partners all around—we're married and we're FBI agents. Isn't that a kick?"

Belinda said, looking back and forth between them, "You're really married? To each other?"

"Oh yes," Sherlock said. "We've got a little boy, Sean's his name. He's nearly a year old now. He's walking, but he can also crawl as fast as I can walk. Besides being good parents, we're good agents. We're here to catch this killer and we need your help. We assume you know all about this, Ms. Gates?"

Belinda Gates leaned toward Sherlock, less wary and suspicious now. "Oh yes. Your husband—he looks like he could star in that new series Frank just dreamed up. It's about a sports lawyer who's a real looker and a hunk, stronger than most of his athlete clients. His clients are always getting him into trouble." Belinda cleared her throat. "Listen, I'll do whatever I can to help you find this horrible person. Is your name really Sherlock?"

"Yes, it is."

"Cool."

"Thank you," Sherlock said. "We really appreciate speaking with someone who knows the ropes and all the players. I was very impressed with your role on *The Consultant*. I only saw the first two episodes, but you were really good. Your Ellie James character was believable, sympathetic, and beautiful, of course, but you can't help that." She paused a moment, and Belinda smiled.

"It's unfortunate that the show has to stop, at least until we catch the maniac who's causing all this grief. We're hoping you can give us some ideas."

EIGHTEEN

Belinda nodded, said, "I'll certainly try, but I really don't know anything. I do know that poor Frank is really upset about the show's cancellation, but what can he do? He told me that DeLoach or some other writer involved in the scripts is killing people to match the murders in the first two episodes. Frank started calling it *The Murder Show.*"

"Catchy title," Sherlock said. "Yes, that's the essence of it."

"Well, I think that actually Weldon DeLoach came up with that title, but the powers-that-be didn't like it, preferred *The Consultant.* More uptown, you know what I mean?"

"Yes," Sherlock said. "More Manhattan than Brooklyn."

"Exactly," Belinda said, smiling. "That was Frank's take on it as well. He's been in the business a long time. He was an actor back in the early eighties, never made it big, and that was okay because he realized he wanted to make shows, not star in them. He didn't ever want to do movies. He loves TV. He's at his happiest when he's the mover behind the scenes, you know, getting scripts actually made into shows, selling the networks, doing the budgets, lining up the actors and directors. Kicking butt to keep everything moving and reasonably on budget.

"The first show he produced was *The Delta Force,* back in the mideighties, ran for about four years. Maybe you've seen some reruns?"

Savich nodded. "It was a good show."

Belinda Gates seemed to light up from the inside, gave him a big smile and pulled one of the big rollers out of her hair. A long fat curl flopped out. "I'll tell him what you said. You know, Frank tells me everything so I know probably as much as he knows about this murderer."

Sherlock said, "You're smart, Ms. Gates, you're on the inside. We know that you've given this some thought. We need your help. Do you have any idea who could have orchestrated all this?"

Belinda pulled out another roller, gently ran her fingers through the big loop of hair, decided it was cool enough, and nodded to herself as she said, "If I had to guess, I'd say it was the Little Shit, you know, Linus Wolfinger. He's very smart. But it's more than that." She paused a moment, scratched her scalp, and said, "It seems like every single day he has to prove that he's the smartest guy on the planet, the biggest cheese. It doesn't matter what it is, he's got to be the best—the fastest, the smartest—and everyone has to recognize it and praise him endlessly."

Savich sat forward, clasped his hands between his knees, and said, "Other than his need for everyone to know how great he is, can you think of a reason why he'd actually follow a TV script to murder people?"

"Because it's weird, it's different, that's why. The Little Shit really likes to think up things to show his scope, all his abilities that are so much more impressive than, say, yours or mine. A murder would be a different kind of challenge for him. If he is the one killing these people, then he had to know that the police would catch on soon enough. Hey, I bet he even set it up to get the police pretty close to him, and that would put him center stage, right in the spotlight. Does that make sense?"

"Not really," Sherlock said.

Another roller came out and Belinda scratched her scalp. "Of course it doesn't, I'm just being bitchy. If I really had to vote, though, I'd pick Jon."

"Jon Franken?" Savich said, and he knew a moment of real surprise and recognized it for the mistake it was. Everyone in this bloody studio was a suspect. Still, he hadn't put Jon Franken in the mix, not really, because he was just—what? He was too together, he was focused. He was very Hollywood, yes, that was it; he was normal in that he fit just right into this specific environment. Savich just couldn't see him at ease in a murderer's world.

He said to Belinda Gates, "Why do you think it's Jon Franken?"

"Well, Jon is one of the sexiest guys who's not an actor in LA. He's slept with more women than even Frank knows about, and believe me, Frank knows just about everything. Jon's sexual prowess has helped him really plug in to everything in LA that counts. He knows everyone, knows who's on the A list at any given time for the past ten years, and that's because he's slept with them. He knows stuff he probably shouldn't know, knows all the players, intimately, most of them, including me, not that I'm a big player, mind you. Sex is powerful. Maybe sometimes even more powerful than money."

Savich thought that was probably true. The good Lord knew that if he chanced to look at Sherlock—it didn't matter where they were or what they were doing—the chances were he wanted her right at that very minute. He remembered just the week before they hadn't even made it into the house. They'd made love against the garage wall. But to have sex color every encounter, to make it the cornerstone of your success, to have sex as a major building block to help you get what you wanted and to get you *plugged in*—no, he really couldn't relate to that.

Belinda said, "I know that all makes it sound like Jon is a real Hollywood predator, and he is, but I'm using 'predator' in the good sense."

Sherlock laughed. "I've never before heard a person described as a predator in a good sense."

"As sort of the real insider," Belinda said, no offense taken. Then she frowned. "But then there's another side to Jon. He's got a mean streak, and it's really deep inside him."

Sherlock said, "Tell us about this mean streak. We haven't seen it."

"Well, when I stopped sleeping with him, I was the one to break it off—not him. Normally it's Jon who wants to move on, but the word is that he does it very smoothly, doesn't leave a woman wanting to cut his—Well, doesn't leave a woman wanting revenge. Nope, he manages to keep his women as friends.

"Don't get me wrong, he would have been the one to move on from me, too, but it just so happened that I met Frank." Belinda leaned closer. "It still scares me when I think about it. I told Jon the truth. I remember he just stood there, right in front of me, and his hands were fists at his sides. He didn't hit me. He just said in this really soft voice that I was a bitch and no woman dumped him. I think he slashed my tires, but since I didn't see him actually do it, I can't prove it. I'd call that pretty mean."

"I would, too," Sherlock said. "But that isn't the end of it, is it?"

"Right. Then there was Marla James, a young, real pretty girl who actually had some talent. I don't know what went on between them, but whatever happened, Jon saw to it that she was kicked off her show. I heard she was pregnant—by Jon? I don't know, but she left LA."

Sherlock took down all the facts Belinda knew about Marla James.

"Then there was the guy who aced Jon out of an AD spot—that's assistant director—on this new show he really wanted. That was *Tough Guy,* lasted four years. Anyway, the guy ended up with two broken legs, couldn't do the job. Jon got it. Was he responsible? You betcha, but there wasn't any proof."

Savich said, "Are you upset that *The Consultant* has been stopped?"

Belinda smiled, shrugged, pulled out another roller, and scratched her scalp. "Poor Frank, he's the one who's really upset. This was his baby. He has a lot of ego on the line here."

Sherlock said, "Can you think of anyone who would be pleased to see the show closed down?"

Belinda pulled out the final roller, dropped it, and all three of them watched it roll across the floor.

"Pleased enough to murder people according to a pre-written script? Now that's something I haven't thought about," she said, frowned at the fallen roller, then ignored it. All the rollers were arranged like little smokestacks in front of her. She ran her fingers through her hair, over and over again. Her hair, Sherlock decided, didn't need to be combed. It looked tousled and thick and utterly beautiful, more shades of blond than she could count.

"You know," Belinda said, her voice low, all confidential now, "Wolfinger's bodyguard. He's this big guy, never says a word. His name's Arnold Loftus. I think he and Wolfinger sleep together."

"You're saying that Wolfinger is gay?" Savich said.

Belinda just shrugged.

A boy with a bad complexion stuck his head in. "They need you on the set, Ms. Gates."

Belinda took one final swipe at her hair, nodded at herself in the mirror, rose, and smiled at them. "Sean's his name? I'd like to have a little boy," she said, nodded to both of them, and walked out of the green room.

Savich said, "I got turned on watching her with those rollers, Sherlock. What do you say we buy some of our own?"

"Some really big ones?"

"Oh yes," he said, "bigger than the ones we used before," and Sherlock laughed.

Chicago

"My poor darling, how are you feeling?"

Nicola looked up at John Rothman, heard three of his aides speaking in the hospital corridor because he'd left the door ajar. His face was ruddy from a stiff Chicago wind and thirty-degree weather, his blue eyes bluer than a summer sky. She thought she'd first fallen in love with his eyes, eyes that could see into people's souls, at least see deep enough that he always knew the right things to say when he was campaigning.

"I'm okay now, John, just a sore throat and my stomach feels hollowed out."

"I'm here to take you home. I was thinking, Nicola, maybe you should just move in with me now. The wedding is in February, so why not speed some things up a bit?"

She hadn't slept with him. The one night she'd decided she was ready, they were caught making out just outside one of John's favorite clubs—*The High Hat*—his tongue in her mouth, his hands on her butt, and there'd been photos in the *National Enquirer.* Very embarrassing.

He'd only given her light pecks on the cheek after that incident.

She said, "If I move in with you, people will find out. Don't forget what happened before."

He shrugged. "All right, then. Let's move up the wedding. How about the end of the month?"

She was silent.

"I want us to begin our life together, Nicola, as soon as possible. I want to make love with you."

She was still silent.

"I saw you naked, you know. You're really quite beautiful."

She smiled up at him as he took her hand, squeezed it lightly. "When did you see me naked?"

"I came over to get you, a couple of weeks ago. I rang the buzzer but you didn't answer. I had a key, and so I let myself in. I heard the shower, and I watched you step out and dry yourself. You didn't know I was there. I don't know why I'm telling you this now, except to say I'd like to see you that way again. I'd like to lick you all over, Nicola."

Maybe it was because she still felt utterly empty inside, but she didn't

say what she probably would have said with a smile two weeks before—
Licking goes both ways.

"I'm very tired, John. Really, too tired to even think straight. I want
to go home, lie in my own bed, get myself back together. Then we can
talk about it. Did the doctor say anything more to you? About the food
poisoning?"

"After speaking to each of us extensively, we figured out that only
you had the raspberry vinaigrette dressing."

"Dressing can cause food poisoning?"

John shrugged. "Would you like me to come back and take you
home?"

Before she could say anything, one of John's aides appeared in the
doorway. "Senator, excuse me, but there's a call from the mayor. He's
looking to speak to you."

"Go, John. I'll be all right."

He leaned down, kissed her cheek. "You're so pale," he said, and
lightly touched his fingertips to her cheek. "Shall I get you a bit of lip
gloss from your purse?"

She nodded.

She watched him walk to the small table on the opposite side of the
hospital room, open her purse, and pick up the lip gloss. He looked at
it, frowned. "It's really light," he said. "You need something to make
you look healthier."

"I'll put on some colorful stuff when I get home. Will I see you
later?"

"I'm sorry, but I've got a meeting with a very important lobbying
group tonight. I put off my lunch with the mayor so I could grab a little
time to come see you. Albia is coming by to take you home. I'll see you
tomorrow."

She watched him walk out, tall, slender, so very elegant. Interestingly
enough, he ranked nearly as high with male as with female voters. She
heard the buzz of voices surrounding him, disappearing finally down
the hall.

Albia arrived two hours later, sweeping into her room, two nurses
behind her, not to chastise, but to bow and scrape and give her anything
she asked for. Albia had that effect on people. She was a princess, well,
perhaps now that she was in her fifties, she was a queen. She was regal.
She was so self-confident, so self-assured, that sometimes even John

would back down in the face of a single word from his sister's mouth. She had been his hostess before he married Cleo, and then after she ran off with Tod Gambol. She was an excellent campaigner. It was rare that a reporter would ever ask her an impertinent question.

"Albia," Nicola said.

Albia Rothman leaned down, kissed Nicola's cheek. "Poor little girl," she said. "This is so awful. I'm so very sorry." She ran her finger over Nicola's cheek.

"It was hardly your fault, Albia."

"That doesn't lessen my being sorry that it happened during my birthday dinner."

"Thank you."

Albia straightened, walked to the window, and looked out toward Lake Michigan. "This is a very nice room. John didn't even have to insist. You were brought here right after they released you from the emergency room." She looked at Nicola, then away again. Albia was a very tactile person, and now she was running her hand over the drapes, less institutional than in most of the rooms that had drapes, but still.

"I've had food poisoning before, Albia. This wasn't like that other time."

A sleek eyebrow went up a good inch. "Oh? How very odd. I suppose this sort of thing can affect a person in different ways."

"I'm just having trouble understanding what I ate that could have caused it."

"I see. Do you wish to pursue it any further then?"

Nicola wanted to pursue it all the way to the moon, if necessary, but she knew when something simply wasn't possible. She shook her head.

Albia pulled a chair close to Nicola's bed and sat down. She crossed her legs, quite lovely legs, sheathed in stockings and three-inch black Chanel heels.

"John tells me that he wants to marry you as soon as possible. He reminded me about that car that almost hit you, and now this. He wants you safe and sound, and to a man—to John—that means you're in his house, in his bed, and he's looking after you. When he's there, that is."

And Nicola said, without hesitation, "I don't know, Albia. I don't think I'm ready to rush things."

"What is this? John is an excellent catch. He has more women chasing him—both here and in Washington—and he is charming to all of them, but it's you he wants. And that is a miracle, to my mind."

"A miracle? Why?"

"He loved Cleo so very much, loved her nearly to the point of obsession. When she ran away, I thought he would simply shut down he was so devastated. I was very worried about him, for months on end."

"I remember. I felt so very sorry for him, all of the staff did as well as the volunteers." Nicola remembered how stoic he appeared whenever anyone mentioned his wife's name, how stiff and remote he became.

Albia said, shaking her head, her voice incredulous, "To think that Cleo actually ran off with Tod Gambol. Sure, he was something of a hunk, a lot younger than John, but for her to want him more than John, well, it still doesn't seem possible to me."

"I wonder where they are," Nicola said. "It's been three years and still no word?"

"No, not a thing. I'll never forget how he met her. He was taking one of his very rare vacations, a long weekend really, and she was there at the hotel, some sort of manager, and there was the fire in his room and she came to apologize. And, well, they were married one week later. I was very surprised, as was the rest of the world. They kept it all very private."

"They were together for five years," Nicola said, remembering Cleo Rothman's voice, her incredible talent for organization and management. The staff had loved her.

She said, "I remember wondering why John hadn't married until he was, what? Nearly forty?"

"That's right. He and Cleo were married when he had just turned thirty-nine. Didn't he tell you? Well, he fell in love with a girl in college—this was at Columbia. Her name was Melissa and they were going to get married when they graduated. Our father was against it, of course, because John's life was planned out for him, and that included three years of law school, and a nice long wait until our father could find him the right sort of wife, you know what I mean, but John didn't care. He wanted Melissa and he wasn't going to wait."

"What happened?"

"She died in an auto accident at the end of her senior year. John was distraught, didn't recover for quite a number of years. Actually, I don't think he recovered until he met Cleo. But look, Nicola, it's only been three years, and he wants to marry you. That is a miracle. He is very much in love with you, don't you think?"

"So much tragedy," Nicola said, aware that she wanted to cry, that her throat hurt so badly she didn't think she could speak another word. She was so hungry she wanted to gnaw her own elbow. She wanted to get out of there, she wanted to go home and curl up in her own bed. And she didn't want anyone at all to come into her condo and see her naked in the bathroom.

"I'm so tired, Albia. I believe they're going to release me soon."

Albia rose. "Yes, I've taken care of it. If you'd like to dress now, I'll take you right home."

"Thank you. I would like that very much. But, Albia, I want to go to my own place. I'm just not ready to move in with John."

NINETEEN

Dane had volunteered to drive the two hours up to Bear Lake to see what they could find out about Weldon DeLoach from the staff and, they hoped, from his elderly father. "Hey, maybe," Flynn had said, "old Weldon will be hiding in one of the rest home's closets."

Dane pulled onto the freeway, then turned to Nick. "I forgot to tell you. Flynn got a search warrant and went over to Weldon's house. Unfortunately they didn't find anything to either implicate DeLoach or give a clue as to his whereabouts. And just before we left, Delion checked in with Lieutenant Purcell. They haven't caught up with Stuckey yet, so we have no gun. There wasn't anything in Milton McGuffey's apartment either that gives us a clue to the man who called Stuckey. But it's early days yet."

She nodded, stared down a moment at her clasped hands. She had a jagged fingernail and began worrying it. "I wanted to tell you that I was really sorry I couldn't be with you at the cemetery. I wanted to say good-bye to Father Michael Joseph, too, but they rushed me off so fast I didn't have a chance to speak to you about it."

"I'm sorry you couldn't come, too. At least the media didn't catch up with you. But you can bet some enterprising souls are trying their best to put this all together. Something will leak soon from the studios, if it hasn't already. Then it's going to be really rough, with you at the epicenter."

She looked, quite simply, terrified.

Dane, impatient, said, "Look, Nick, you know this is an international story. For God's sake, you're the eyewitness to my brother's murder."

"Not really. I haven't been any help at all."

"We'll see. Now, the media thing. It's going to happen. You really need to reconsider telling me what's going on with you."

"No, I don't." She still hadn't come to a decision about what to do. She knew she couldn't be a homeless person forever; it wasn't any sort of solution at all, but what she would do, she just didn't know yet. "You made a deal. Keep your questions to yourself."

He shrugged, and she knew he was irritated, probably more than irritated. He changed lanes to avoid being stuck behind an eighteen-wheeler. He looked over at her, his expression serious. "I'm sorry, but the shit will hit the fan. It's coming. Okay, no more questions, but when you're ready to tell me, just let me know."

She said nothing, just stared at the dashboard.

"I want to thank you, Nick, for the way you've stuck with me over the last days. It's—it's been difficult, and you really helped me."

She nodded. "It's hard to believe that so little time has passed. It's been very hard for you."

"Yes." He was silent, to keep control. Damnation, it was so hard. He said, "It's been difficult for you as well."

She said, surprising him, "I remember when my father died—it was in a hunting accident—some idiot took him for a deer up in northern Michigan. Death like that, so sudden, so unexpected, you just can't figure out how to deal with it."

"Yes," Dane said, eyes on the road in front of him. "I know. How old were you when your dad died?"

"Nearly twenty-two. It was really bad because my mom had died just two years before. Sure, I had lots of friends, but it's just not the same thing."

He said slowly, "I never really thought of you as a friend."

She felt a punch of hurt at his words. "I would have thought that we've been through enough to be friends, haven't we?"

"You misunderstand me," Dane said. "No, I didn't think of you as a friend precisely, I thought of you as someone who was there for me, who understood, someone important."

She was silent for a moment, but to Dane it seemed an eon had passed before she said, "Maybe I agree with you."

Dane smiled as he slowed for a car coming onto the freeway. "Hey, you got any relatives at all?"

"Yes, two younger brothers, both Air Force pilots. They're in Europe. All these questions. Are you trying to trip me up? Is this one of your famous FBI strategies to make a perp spill her guts?"

"Nah. If I wanted to interrogate you, I'd be so subtle, so consummately skilled that you wouldn't even be aware of what I was doing."

"I've also got two uncles who drill for oil in Alaska."

"I'm sorry about your folks."

"Thank you. I think they were both surprised when I ended up with a Ph.— Well, that's not important."

Yeah, right, he thought. "What do you think of Savich and Sherlock?"

"Sherlock showed me a photo of Sean. He's adorable."

"Sean is nearly a year old now, running all over the place, jabbering a language that Savich claims is an advanced code used in rocket science. I'm Uncle Dane, only it doesn't come out that way."

"They've been here less than twenty-four hours—it's like I've known them for much, much longer. Sort of like you, only not exactly."

"I know what you mean."

"How long have you been an FBI agent?"

"Six years now. I came out of law school, went to a big firm, and hated it. I knew what I wanted to do."

"A lawyer. I wouldn't have guessed."

"You mean I don't look slimy?"

"Close enough." A lawyer, that was all she needed. Both a lawyer and an FBI agent. She'd nearly spilled the beans about her Ph.D. It looked like he didn't even need to exert himself particularly to get information out of her.

Nick didn't tell him anything more about herself, eventually just looked out her window at the passing vegetation that was getting greener as they gained altitude.

They finally arrived at Bear Lake. Set amid groves of pine trees, up a beautiful long sloping lawn that stretched up about fifty yards from Bear Lake, was a lovely old two-story building of weathered wood, each room featuring glass doors and a small terrace that gave onto the lake. There were several piers that went some fifty feet out into the calm blue water, where half a dozen canoes and several powerboats were tied up. Lovely white-painted chairs and benches were scattered over the manicured lawn. But it was winter, and even though it was in the high fifties today, no one was outside to appreciate it.

They left their rented cherry-red Pontiac Grand Am in a small parking lot set amid a grouping of pine trees and walked on a flagstone path to the discreet entrance. Nick looked up at the crystal-clear sky, at the cumulus clouds that were sweeping lazily overhead. She turned a moment to look at Bear Lake glistening beneath a noonday sun, snow glinting on the peaks in the distance. There was only a light spray of snow around Bear Lake.

Nick stood still a moment, staring out toward the lake. It was as still as a postcard. She said, "I think this is a beautiful place, but somehow, I don't know why, I just don't like it."

She turned, sped up, and entered the double glass doors, which led into a large lobby. In the center was a large wooden counter with offices behind it.

Behind the counter stood a stout woman with curly black hair and a very pretty smile. The name on her tag read Velvet Weaver. With the thin black mustache over her upper lip, she didn't look much like a Velvet.

Dane introduced both himself and Nick, showed her his FBI shield.

"Oh dear, I hope there's nothing wrong."

"This is just routine, Ms. Weaver," Dane said easily. "Just a couple of questions we hope you can help us with. Could you please tell us about one of your patient's sons, a Mr. Weldon DeLoach?"

Velvet nodded. "I suppose there's nothing wrong with that. Yes, a lovely man, Mr. DeLoach, a wonderful son. You know, he's this big TV writer in Hollywood and so it's only the best for his father."

"Is Mr. Weldon DeLoach here right now? Visiting with his father?"

"Oh no, Agent Carver, Weldon hasn't been here for a week, at least not that I know of. Of course, he could have visited when I wasn't on duty. I'll ask around for you. I was wondering just the other day when he was coming to see his father again. Not that Captain DeLoach knows when his son is here, poor man. Dementia, you know, for about the last six years now. Is something wrong with Weldon?"

Dane shook his head. "Nothing at all. As I said, this is just routine, Ms. Weaver. Now, I understand that Captain DeLoach is a retired police officer?"

"Yes, he was the captain of this small-town police department in the central valley for nearly forty years."

"Do you remember the name of the town?" Dane asked.

"Dadeville. It's a good-sized town now. Not all that far from Bakersfield. Poor man, but he's eighty-seven years old and human parts break down. It's sad, but Captain DeLoach doesn't seem to be in any particular distress about it. It's usually that way. What you can't remember doesn't hurt you."

"He's that old?" Nick said.

"Yes. Weldon was his only child, born when Captain DeLoach was already well into his forties. Captain DeLoach, when he remembers, tells everyone that it was his third marriage, and his wife was much younger.

"She died, I believe, in some sort of accident when Weldon was only four years old. Captain DeLoach never remarried. He raised Weldon. And he's a very good son; he's paid for his father to be here for nearly ten years now. Never complains about any of the extras, always comes to visit."

Ms. Weaver paused, looked a bit worried. "May I ask you why you're here, Agent Carver? I know you said it was just routine, but still—would you like to speak to our manager, Mr. Latterley? He isn't here right now, but I could have him call you."

"That's not necessary, but thank you, Ms. Weaver. We'll speak to Mr. Latterley later. We're really here to see Captain DeLoach. Will that be a problem, Ms. Weaver?"

"Not at all, but let me warn you not to expect much. Captain DeLoach normally just sits about, looking out at the lake and the mountains. It's very peaceful here, very soothing for the soul. I know he enjoys watching people water-ski. Of course, now that it's winter, there's not much of that."

Nick said, "What does Weldon look like, Ms. Weaver?"

"A lovely man, is Weldon. Let's see, I suppose he'd have to be in his early forties. He's fair-skinned, light hair, although, you know, he's always really tanned, told me once that he was real proud of that tan. And he's very creative. Always has ideas for the old folks here, things to keep them involved, to keep their brains going."

"Yes, I see," Nick said, and looked over at Dane. How could Weldon

DeLoach possibly be the man she'd seen in the church? But then, why had the man used aliases that were so like Weldon's name?

Dane walked down the long, wide, very pleasant corridor. Landscapes lined both sides of the white walls. He wondered about Weldon DeLoach. How was he involved in all this? Did someone hate him so much as to implicate him so directly in the murders?

Nick said quietly so Ms. Weaver wouldn't hear, not looking at him but at the soft watercolor landscapes, "How can Weldon be the monster? Can he be that good with disguises?"

"We'll find out."

"Here's Captain DeLoach's room," Ms. Weaver said, and raised her hand to knock. They heard a groan from inside. Dane didn't hesitate, he was through the door in under a second.

TWENTY

The old man was on the floor beside his overturned wheelchair, moaning softly, a small rivulet of dried blood on his face that had dripped off his chin and onto the floor.

Dane turned to Nick, but she was already gone, probably with Velvet Weaver, to the nurses' station to get help.

"Captain DeLoach," Dane said, leaning close, "can you hear me, sir? Can you tell me what happened?"

The old man opened his eyes. He didn't look like he was in pain, just dazed.

"Can you hear me, sir? See me?"

"Yes, I can see you. Who are you?"

"I'm Special Agent Dane Carver, FBI."

Slowly, very slowly, the old man lifted his trembling, deeply veined hand, and he saluted.

Dane was charmed. He saluted him back. Then he gently wrapped his hand around the old man's and slowly lowered it. "You fell out of your chair?"

"Oh no, Special Agent," he said in a voice that sounded other worldly it was so whispery thin. "He was here again and I told him I wouldn't keep quiet anymore, and he hit me."

"Who, Captain? Who hit you?"

"My son."

"Hey! What happened here?"

A nurse fell to her knees beside Captain DeLoach, feeling his pulse, cupping her hand around his ancient face. "Captain, it's Carla. You fell out of your chair again, didn't you?"

The old man groaned.

"All right. Now, let me clean the blood off your face, see how bad it is. You've got to be more careful, you know that. If you want to run around the room, just call one of us and we'll steer you. We'll even hold races if that's what you'd like. Now, just lie still, Captain, and I'll take care of everything."

Captain DeLoach's eyes closed. Dane couldn't rouse him.

His son?

Weldon DeLoach had hit his father and knocked him out of his chair? But Velvet had said Weldon hadn't been around for a week. She also said that the old man usually didn't know his own name. Dane held the old man's hand until Carla came back into the room. An orderly, a big Filipino man, lifted him in his arms and carried him to the bed. The old man looked like a bunch of old bones barely knit together, his pale, veined flesh wrapped in a bright blue flannel shirt and baggy pants. There were thick socks on his feet, and only one bedroom slipper. The other slipper was lying near the TV. The orderly laid him on his back, very gently straightening all those old limbs.

"All right, I understand from Velvet that you're FBI agents," Nurse Carla said, not looking at either of them. "Would you mind telling me what's going on? What do you want with Captain DeLoach?"

Dane said, "We came to the door, heard moans, and I immediately opened the door and came into the room. Captain DeLoach was lying on the floor, just as you saw."

"He's always falling out of the chair, knocking it over," she said. "But this is the first time he's hurt himself. Nasty cut on his head, but it won't need stitches. I hope he doesn't have a concussion. That could really take his brain right out of commission."

Dane and Nick watched her wash out the cut, then apply an antibiotic and a bandage. Nick patted her own Band-Aid that covered the graze made by the bullet and flopped her hair back over it.

Carla said, "Captain DeLoach? Can you hear me? Open your eyes."

The old man didn't answer her, just lay there, occasionally moaning.

"He spoke to me," Dane said. "He was quite lucid. He said that someone hit him. Is it possible that that cut isn't from his fall?"

Carla snorted. "Not likely. His only visitor is his son, and Weldon was here last week. Weldon's like clockwork, never more than two weeks go by before he comes to visit." She frowned up at Dane. "You say he was lucid? How could that be? He hasn't been lucid in days now."

"He was. Excuse me a moment, I'm going to have a look around."

"Suit yourself," Carla said. She looked over at Nick. "Did you hear him speak lucidly?"

"No. When I saw him on the floor, bleeding, I came to get you."

"Well, this is all very interesting. Captain DeLoach? Come on now, open your eyes." She lightly slapped the old man's cheeks, once, twice, yet again.

He opened his eyes, blinked.

"Do you hurt?"

He moaned again, closed his eyes.

Carla sighed. "It's really hard when their minds go. Hey, what are you doing?"

Nick said, "I was just checking the chair; it's really sturdy. How does the captain manage to turn it over? It's quite heavy."

"Good question, but he's done it before. No one's seen him actually topple over, just the aftermath. Okay, I've got this wound bandaged. When the doctor comes around I'll have him look at it. Let me give the captain a sedative to help him rest."

"He looks pretty quiet to me right now," Nick said, inching a bit closer to look at the old man's pale face.

Carla said, arms crossed over her chest, eyes suspicious, "You don't know anything about it, do you, so your opinion doesn't count. Now, tell me why two Federal agents are here to see Captain DeLoach."

"Sorry," Nick said, "it's on a need-to-know basis and you're not in the loop."

Nurse Carla harrumphed and laid the palm of her hand on Captain DeLoach's forehead, nodded, pulled a small notebook out of her pocket, and scribbled something down. She didn't say anything else.

Nick wished Dane would come back. She knew he was looking to see if there was any sign of an intruder, any sign that Weldon DeLoach had been there.

TEN minutes later, they were in Mr. Latterley's office with its long glass windows looking onto Bear Lake. He'd just returned, and was still breathing hard.

"Have you seen Weldon DeLoach recently, Mr. Latterley?"

"No. I understand he visited a week or so ago, but I didn't person-ally see him. He's very dependable, as I'm sure everyone's told you. Once every couple of weeks, he's here to see his father, make sure he's got everything he needs. Sometimes Weldon comes more often."

Dane sat forward. "Have you seen anyone, any stranger, around lately? Today, to be specific?"

Mr. Latterley shook his head. "Well, I was in town for a couple of hours, so you'll have to ask the staff. But I'll tell you, Agent Carver, there's no reason for someone to come here. Oh, we get an occasional hiker in the summer or a tourist who takes a wrong turn, but today? Not that I know of."

Nick said, "The glass doors in Captain DeLoach's room weren't locked, Mr. Latterley. Someone could have simply opened them and walked in."

"Well, yes, they could, but why? You don't think that someone actually came in and struck Captain DeLoach, do you? He's a very old man, agents. Why would anyone seek to hurt him?"

"I asked him who hit him and he told me it was his son."

Mr. Latterley blinked. "You must have misunderstood him," he said. "Or the old man was just weaving in and out and that was what came out of his mouth. No, not Weldon. That's ridiculous."

He was shaking his head, an interesting head, Nick thought, staring. Shiny, bald, and pointed. She'd never seen a bald head quite so pointed before.

"No," he said again, more forcefully this time. "Impossible. You didn't see any sign of anyone, did you, Agent Carver?"

"I can't be certain. We would like to speak to all the staff who work near Captain DeLoach's room."

Dane spent the next hour doing just that. To a person, they shook their heads and looked bewildered by his questions.

Nick sat beside Captain DeLoach's bed, holding his hand, speaking quietly to him, hoping for a sensible response, but he didn't speak. She said to Dane when he came in, "He did open his eyes a couple of times, but he looked right through me, didn't respond at all. I've been speaking to him, about lots of silly things, but he hasn't answered me."

Just before they left, the doctor came out to say, "I examined Captain DeLoach's head wound. He seems to be all right. To be perfectly honest, I can't tell if it happened because he hit his head when he fell or if someone indeed struck him. But on the face of it, it seems strange to even consider that some miscreant from the outside would come into the old man's room and smack him around."

Dane said as he walked beside Nick toward their car, "Captain DeLoach said that he told his son he wouldn't keep quiet anymore and his son hit him. I wonder what he meant by that?"

"I'm beginning to think we should try the Oracle at Delphi."

He laughed. "Not a bad idea."

"I just realized, I'm really hungry. Do you think we could stop at a Mexican place on the way back to LA?"

"Sure can."

DANE walked into Nick's connecting room at the nicely updated Holiday Inn, not far from Premier Studios on Pico.

She was on the phone. She hadn't heard him, she was so intent on the call.

He stopped cold. Who was she speaking to?

"Listen," he heard her say, "I'm calling from the *Los Angeles Times*. My editor asked me to check out for sure whether he was traveling west. Does his schedule include either San Francisco or Los Angeles?"

She sensed him, there was no other word for it, and whipped around. She met his eyes, and quietly eased the phone back into the cradle.

"I can get the number from the hotel clerk, but it would be easier if you just broke down and told me what's going on."

Nick felt a corrosive fear leap to life. She wanted to cover up with a dozen blankets or run as fast as she could.

"Go away."

He sat down beside her on the queen-size bed, picked up her hands, and held them between his. She had nice hands, short nails, no rings. The skin was smooth again. Her hair was half-dry and she was wearing a bit of lip gloss. Nice mouth, too. No, he wouldn't go there. He said, looking at her straight in the face, "Listen to me, there's a lot going on here, and on top of it all, here you are scared out of your mind about—whatever. Why won't you let me help you? My brain can handle more than one thing at a time. I can multitask as well as a woman. Come on, trust me, Nick."

She suddenly looked very tired, and flattened, yes, defeated. She looked desperately alone.

Very slowly, he pulled her against him. He felt the panic rise in her, but he didn't do anything at all but hold her, give her what comfort he could. He said against her damp hair, which smelled just like his, since they both had used the hotel shampoo, which had a girlie-girl smell, floral and soft, "You've seen firsthand that there's lots of bad stuff and bad people in the world. But you know what? Some of it we can actually do something about. We're going to catch the man who killed all those people, my brother included." He stopped. If and when she was ready to tell him about herself, then she would. Maybe it was all a matter of trust. So be it. No more pushing. He said only, "I'm here for you, Nick."

"Yes, and so is the murderer, and he's already tried to have me killed. I want to leave, Dane. You don't need me anymore."

"It's too late, Nick." He raised his finger and lightly touched it to the Band-Aid that covered the bullet graze. "That's the whole point. Milton failed so the guy who hired him will try again, count on it. You need me, if for nothing else, as a bodyguard."

"Everything is rotten," she said. "All of it, just plain rotten."

"I know. But we'll take care of things. Trust me on that. Hey, rotten is my stock-in-trade. I get a paycheck because of rotten. It gives me motivation."

She fell silent. She didn't move either, just let him pull her close and hold her. She felt the core of steadiness in him, felt how solid he was, physically, and his heart, that was solid, too. She knew he was a rock, that once this man gave his word, you could bet the bank on it.

She thought of Father Michael Joseph, his face identical to Dane's, but he was dead now. She knew Dane was alone with that and she knew he was battling each hour, each day, just to get through. Here she was leaning on him, and he was comforting her. Who did he lean on?

"I'm all right," she said, slowly pulling away from him. She looked at him then and lightly laid her palm against his cheek. "You are an estimable man, Dane. I am so very sorry about your brother."

He closed down, and his face went blank, because he had to hold himself together.

"I would appreciate it," she said, standing, straightening the sweater he'd picked out for her the previous Friday, a lovely V-necked sweater, deep red, that she was wearing over a white blouse, "if you wouldn't try to find out who I was speaking to."

She saw in his eyes that he wasn't going to ask the front desk. At least he was still willing to give her some leeway. He said, "I will find out sooner or later, Nick."

"Later," she said.

He said nothing to that, just shrugged back at her. "Are you ready? We're all meeting for dinner to exchange information."

"I'm ready," she said, and picked up the wool coat he'd bought her. He'd done too much for her, far too much, and he was offering to do more. It was hard to bear. She ran her hands over the soft wool. It felt wonderful. She kept stroking it even as she said over her shoulder, "I was always scared. I'd lie in one of the small cots on the second floor of the shelter, the allotted one blanket pulled to my ears, and I'd listen to people moving about downstairs. Sometimes there'd be yelling, fighting, screaming, and always, I huddled down and was afraid because violence seemed to be part of the despair, and the two always went together. Sometimes they'd bring their fights upstairs and they'd throw stuff or hit each other until some of the shelter staff managed to get things back under control.

"There were drug users, alcoholics, people who were mentally ill, people just ground down by circumstance, all mixed together. There was so much despair, it was pervasive, but the thing was—everyone wanted to survive."

"And then there was you."

"Yes, but I suppose you could say I was one of those who'd been ground down by circumstance."

She stopped, looked down at her left hand, still stroking her wool coat. "The alcoholics and the addicts—they were self-destructive. It's not that I didn't feel sorry for them, but they were different from the other homeless people because they'd brought their misery on themselves. And they never seemed to blame themselves for what they'd become. It was the strangest thing. One of the shelter counselors said it was because if they ever had to face what they really were in the mirror, they wouldn't be able to bear it. Everyone there had so little. But they were the ones responsible for what had become of them, responsible for where they were. And because they wouldn't face the truth, there was no hope for them.

"The mentally ill people—they were the worst off. I truly can't understand how we as a society allow people who are so ill they can't even remember to take their medications or even know that they need medication, to just roam the streets. They suffer the most because they're the most helpless."

Dane said, "I remember when one of the New York mayors wanted to get the sick people off the streets and into safe houses, but the ACLU went nuts."

Nick said, "I remember. The ACLU cleaned up this poor woman, dressed her like a normal person, fed her meds so she could pass muster, and they won. Except that poor woman lost. Within days she was back on the street, off her meds, cursing and spitting at people, vulnerable and helpless. I wonder if any of the lawyers at the ACLU lost a bit of sleep over that."

"Who are you, Nick?"

She grew very still, didn't move, just stood there when he opened the door to the Grand Am. She said, "My name is Nick, short for Nicola. I don't want to tell you my real last name. All right?"

"You mean, if you tell me your real name I would have heard of it?"

"No. It means that you have a computer and access to information."

So there was something on her, something to be found, something other than just who she was. What had happened to her?

When he was seated in the driver's seat, the key in the ignition, he turned to her and said, "I want to know who you are, not just your name."

She looked straight ahead, saying nothing, until he pulled out of the Holiday Inn parking lot onto the street.

She said, "I'm a woman who could be dead before the first day of spring."

His hands tightened around the steering wheel. "Bullshit. You're just being dramatic, and you're wrong. I think by the first of spring, you'll be doing what you were doing last month. What were you doing in December, Nick?"

"I was teaching medieval history." She didn't know why she said that. Well, he already knew she had a Ph.D., this much more wouldn't tell him anything.

"Are you by any chance Dr. Nick?"

"Yes, but you already guessed that. You know that your brother loved history."

"My brother was an impressive man, he was a very good man,"

Dane said, and shut up, really fast. He could feel himself breaking apart, deep inside, where his brother's blood and Dane's own pain flowed together. He remembered Archbishop Lugano at Michael's service, his hand on Dane's shoulder, telling him to take it just one day at a time.

He concentrated on driving. He was momentarily distracted by a girl on roller skates, wearing shorts that showed half her butt cheeks, and she was waving to him, grinning and blowing him kisses over her shoulder. He waved back, grinned a bit, and said, "That's some presentation."

"Yes indeed, you're right," Nick said. "I agree, she does skate very well."

Dane jerked around, surprised. "That was funny, Nick."

She smiled. It was a small smile, but a smile nonetheless.

"Where are we going?"

"We're all meeting at The Green Apple, over on Melrose."

Nick sighed. "Doesn't sound like they'll have tacos, does it?"

"I just hope they don't serve fried green apples. I'm an American, I love fat, but you know—my belly rebels fast if I eat even two pieces of KFC. It's a bummer."

"Don't whine. It means you won't ever have to worry about your weight."

He smiled at her, then said, "I sure hope someone has found out something useful. The bottom line is that what you and I found out just leads to more questions."

As it turned out, Sherlock and Savich had struck gold.

TWENTY-ONE

Sherlock said between bites of a carrot stick, "We dug up a guy who's a real good friend of Weldon DeLoach's. His name is Kurt Grinder. He's a porn star. Yeah, yeah, I know—the name. I just couldn't help myself so I asked him. He said it was, actually, his real name. He's known Weldon for some eight years, ever since he came to LA. He said he saw Weldon DeLoach two and a half weeks ago at the Gameland Bowling Alley in North Hollywood. Said he and Weldon went bowling together every week, on Thursday night, said Weldon told him that bowling always relaxes him. He was getting worried because Weldon hadn't called him and he couldn't get an answer at Weldon's apartment."

Detective Flynn said, "I can see by that gleam in your eyes, Agent Sherlock, that there's more to it than that, and you're just leading us slowly down the garden path."

"Enjoy it," Savich said. "Let her string it out. I promise, it's worth it."

Sherlock waved her carrot stick, sat forward a bit. "Turns out that Kurt Grinder had some problem with his bowling shoes and had to stay awhile. Weldon left before he did. When Kurt came out of the bowling alley he saw this guy stop Weldon before he got to his car. They talked for a couple of minutes. Before Kurt could catch up, Weldon and this man went off together, in this man's car, not Weldon's."

Delion said, thumping his fingers on the tabletop, "All right, Sherlock, what man?"

"Kurt said he'd never seen him before, but he got a real good look at him." She dropped her voice so everyone had to lean forward to hear her. "Kurt said he looked to be in his thirties, had dark hair, lots of it. But what really stuck in his mind was that the guy's skin was as white as a whale's belly."

"And that means," Savich said, "that if Kurt is telling the truth, and as far as I could tell he had no reason to lie, that DeLoach could be connected to the killings."

"Or maybe," Dane said slowly, "someone's setting him up. Don't forget. We can't find him. And him being the killer has always been too obvious."

Savich nodded. "One of the first things we asked Mr. Grinder was had he ever seen Weldon with black hair and no tan. He laughed, said Weldon was always changing his look, that he loved disguises, but he'd never seen him go that far. Okay, Sherlock, the *pièce de résistance*."

Everyone at the table leaned forward again.

"Kurt got his license number."

"Jesus," Flynn said, "Kurt Grinder can come work for the LAPD."

Delion said, "Okay, so who owns the damned car?"

Savich said, "Belinda Gates. Frank Pauley's wife, the costar of *The Consultant*."

No one said a word for a good three seconds.

"But it was a man who met Weldon at the bowling alley," Flynn said slowly. "The car belongs to the actress?"

"Yes," Sherlock said. "Savich was thinking that just maybe we could pay a little visit to Belinda and Frank this evening."

Nick, who'd been silent, said now, "Do you think Belinda Gates disguised herself as a man?"

"Ah, Jesus," Delion said. "My brain's getting constipated. Hey, at this point I'm ready to believe in aliens landing in the Hollywood Bowl."

"The question is, where is Weldon DeLoach?" Savich said. He looked over at Nick and Dane. "Okay, let's look at this again. Dane, tell us what you make of all those events at the nursing home."

"Captain DeLoach is demented," Dane said. "No question about that. But I swear to you, when I first spoke to him, he was lucid. Do you know that when I told him I was FBI, he saluted me? Maybe he really did fall out of his chair, maybe he really did make all that up. I just don't know."

Dane turned to Nick, who was sitting with her hands in her lap, just staring down at the remains of her chicken salad, and said, "Nick? What do you think?"

Nick said, "Everyone at the nursing home believed Captain DeLoach had fallen, and no one had been around. I don't want to agree, but what else can we believe? That's a lot easier to swallow than a son trying to kill his own father."

"If," Sherlock said, raising another carrot stick, "if Weldon really did bang him on the head and toss him out of his chair, the question remains, what wasn't the old man going to keep quiet about?"

"About the fact that Weldon was murdering people according to his own scripts," Flynn said. "That's pretty obvious."

"Maybe," Sherlock said, but she was frowning. "Maybe. But you know, that's just too easy."

"He wasn't going to keep quiet any longer about what his son was doing," Dane said slowly, spacing out each word. "It sounds possible that Weldon was telling his father he was a murderer, and the old man finally freaked."

Nick said, "But the thing is, who would believe Captain DeLoach if he told everyone that his son was murdering people? His only audience is the nursing home staff, and they all think he's demented. They'd just shake their heads and say how sad it was. They'd just give him more medication. Weldon would have to know that. Why would he hurt, maybe even try to kill, his own father when there was no downside for him?"

Over coffee and tea, Flynn told them his snitches were plugged in and would send juice his way if they found out anything. As for the writers and crew on *The Consultant*, as well as two supervising producers, there was nothing on any of them to raise red flags.

"Typical stuff," Flynn said. "An arrest for prostitution, some drugs, rehab, parking and speeding tickets, a couple of spousal abuse calls, but no charges pressed, nothing to start my gut dancing."

"Yeah?" Delion said. "What? The rumba?"

"Nope," Flynn said, "straight salsa. My wife tells me she likes to see me play basketball, but she loves to see me salsa."

Nick looked at Flynn and said, "I'm pretty good myself, Detective Flynn."

Flynn's eyes gleamed. "We'll have to try it sometime."

Savich said, "Yeah, yeah, now, what about Pauley and Wolfinger?"

"Mr. Frank Pauley has been knocking around Hollywood for going on twenty-five years. He's been married four times, and the current Mrs. Pauley, Belinda Gates, according to insiders, is in for the duration. There's nothing unusual about him, nothing we can find hiding in his closet."

Sherlock said, "Surely if Belinda is involved, her husband has to at least suspect something."

"Agreed," Flynn said. "Now, Belinda Gates. She came to LA five years ago, got some minor roles, did some commercials, a couple of soft porn flicks, even did makeup for several sitcoms. Landing Pauley really made her career.

"From what we can tell, Linus Wolfinger is indeed a boy wonder. An arrogant little prick, evidently likes boys, but that's gossip, not fact. He came from nothing; an orphan in and out of foster homes. Put himself through college—UC Santa Barbara—went to work in various production jobs at Premier Studios a year after he graduated, and somehow managed to impress Burdock at the tender age of barely twenty-three, and the rest, as they say, is history. There's nothing on him, just one damned speeding ticket—and that was on the first day he was driving his new Porsche."

"What was he doing that year after he graduated?" Savich asked.

Flynn's eyes lit up. "Don't know yet. We're checking it." He pulled a small black book from his inside jacket pocket and wrote in it. "One thing's for sure, no one involved in *The Consultant* will be making a move without our being aware of it." Then he smiled at everybody. "How about some dessert?"

Flynn and Delion ordered slices of apple pie, with French vanilla ice cream. When the two servings of dessert arrived, Flynn looked around the table. "All you pantywaist Feds, you nibble around like birds. No wonder you need the locals—we provide not only the brains, but the bulk."

Sherlock, head cocked to the side, her red hair corkscrewing out, said, "You mean that's our problem? A simple lack of sugar? I never thought of it like that." She grabbed up her fork and cut a big piece of apple pie from Flynn's slice.

Nick laughed. Dane joined in. It felt good.

FRANK Pauley and Belinda Gates actually did live in a glass house, Dane thought, staring up at the monstrosity atop a cliff off Mulholland Drive. It was filled with lights, and if someone was wandering around inside naked, people five miles away could enjoy the view.

Five cops and one civilian trooped up to the gigantic double wooden doors. Flynn knocked.

A woman answered the door wearing a French maid's outfit, replete with stiletto heels and stockings with seams up the back. She had a sexy little white cap on her head. The only thing was, she had to be at least fifty and a good twenty pounds overweight, her dark hair sprinkled with gray and cut butch.

Everyone managed to keep it together, even when she asked them to follow her into the living room.

"Sir, you have visitors. I believe they're all police officers." Then she nodded, perfectly serious, to each of them in turn and glided out on those three-inch black heels.

Once the door closed behind her, Delion said to Frank Pauley, "Nice house."

"Thanks. My second wife was an architect. She designed it and it was built to her specifications. Since my third wife and Belinda both really liked it, I haven't made any changes." He cleared his throat. "The only thing is, Belinda picks the staff and doesn't like anyone to be younger than fifty, and so we have FiFi Ann, who really is a very nice person, frighteningly efficient, and something of an exhibitionist."

"FiFi Ann?" Sherlock said, an eyebrow up a good inch.

"She decided that was the name she wanted. She's a former actress. She, ah, picked out her French maid's outfit herself, said she wanted to adjust her image. Now, why are you all here at nine o'clock at night?"

"We would like to speak to Belinda," Sherlock said. "Is she here?"

"Certainly. Her partying days are over unless she's on my arm." Pauley walked to the phone, punched a couple of buttons, and called, "Cops in the living room. Come save me."

"Cute," Flynn said.

Belinda came in not five minutes later, wearing black leggings and a sweatshirt, no sneakers. Her face was shiny with sweat, her hair plastered to her head. She was wiping her face with a towel.

"Hi, Agent Sherlock, Agent Savich. Frank, you don't need help from them. They've got a little kid who's adorable. Who are these other folks?"

Introductions were made. As usual, Dane included Nick, making her seem to be just another Federal agent.

"Are you here to arrest Frank?" Belinda said.

Flynn reached for the handcuffs in his back pocket, pulled them out, and waved them toward Pauley. "You want me to take him to the floor, ma'am? We officers of the law like to be obliging."

Belinda laughed, continued to wipe sweat off herself. She suddenly pulled off her sweatshirt. Underneath it she was wearing only a little workout bra.

The men in the room nearly expired on the spot. Nick laughed. "That was very well done. I'll bet you Detective Flynn has already forgotten the handcuffs."

Belinda just smiled. "Frank, why don't you get us all a soda?"

When everyone was seated on the stark white leather chairs, love seats, and huge long sofa, facing a fireplace Nick couldn't ever imagine using in LA, Sherlock said, "Belinda, please tell us why you met Weldon DeLoach two and a half weeks ago at the Gameland Bowling Alley, why you were dressed like a man, and where you went."

Frank Pauley jumped to his feet and walked fast to a huge set of floor-to-ceiling glass windows. Actually, since the entire living room that faced out toward the ocean was glass, he had no place else to go.

Belinda drank down her soda and said after a moment, "Isn't it strange how easily you can get tripped up?"

"Yeah, but that's how we make our living," Delion said. "What were you doing meeting Weldon DeLoach? Why were you dressed like the perfect description of our murderer?"

Frank whirled around. "I knew it, I just knew it. Weldon is crazy about you, wants to make you a star and—"

Four wives, Nick thought, getting a glimmer of reality in the glass house.

Belinda smiled toward her husband, who looked ready to break into small pieces he was standing so rigid. She didn't seem at all perturbed. "Actually, sweetie, he's not. Weldon isn't my type, you are. Now, Weldon and I had arranged to meet that night, at the bowling alley, and I was to pick him up. We went to La Pomme in Westwood, sat at a booth and brainstormed story ideas. He wanted my role in *The Consultant* to be bigger." She shrugged. "Yes, I was dressed like a man. Weldon asked me to, told me what to wear, what disguise to use. Of course, now that's academic since Weldon is nowhere to be found and the show's been yanked."

Sherlock said, "Weldon wanted to change your role to a man's? This doesn't make a whole lot of sense, Belinda."

"He was thinking about another idea, a woman who was a spy and had the international community believing she was a man. He wanted to see if I was a good enough actress to fool people into believing I was a man. Nothing more than that. I think I did well. Nobody gave me a second look. Weldon laughed and laughed, he was so tickled. You know, Frank, how he acts when he's excited."

"How did you carry it off?" Sherlock said. "You're beautiful and you've got lots of hair."

"Well, you see, I used to do makeup back in the bad old days, and I'm really good at it. That disguise wasn't much of a challenge."

Nick felt her heart crash to the floor. It sounded so reasonable the way Belinda, the actress, told it, even the wretched disguise. Thing was, Nick believed her.

"She's a hell of an actress," Flynn said to the group as he walked to his car in the large circular driveway. "We can't forget that. God, she's gorgeous, isn't she?"

TWENTY-TWO

Chicago

Nicola arrived home with a bad headache after a two-hour, very contentious staff meeting at the university. At least she no longer felt like she'd been starved and kicked around. It had been three days since the food poisoning. A week since she'd begun to see everything in a different light.

She dropped her mail on the small table in her entrance hall, went to the fridge and pulled out a bottle of diet tonic water, and got three aspirins from the medicine cabinet.

When at last she sorted through her mail, she found a single letter without a return address. Her name was written in bold cursive. The handwriting looked vaguely familiar.

Nicola picked up her two-hundred-year-old Chinese dragon letter opener that John had given her for Christmas and slit the envelope open. She pulled out three sheets of closely written pages. She read:

Dear Nicola, I bet you're surprised to hear from me.

Me who? Nicola skipped to the last page of the letter and read the clean-cut, crisp signature: *Cleo Rothman.* No, it was impossible. Why would Cleo write to her after three years of silence?

There's no easy way to say this, Nicola, but since I was always very fond of you, I'll just come out with it. Don't marry John or you'll be very sorry. He isn't what he seems. You believe, like everyone else, that I skipped town with Tod Gambol, don't you? I didn't. I have no idea where Tod Gambol is, but I wouldn't be surprised if he was dead. I ran, Nicola, I ran. John was going to kill me. You want to know why? Because he believed that I was sleeping with

Elliott Benson, that longtime crony of the mayor's and friend of John's. Are they really friends? I don't know.

Actually, I've heard the rumors that you're also sleeping with Elliott. Does John know about them? I'd bet on it. Maybe you've already realized that whatever woman John has, Elliott has to take away from him. You know, I heard he's really good in bed. Are you sleeping with him, Nicola? It doesn't really matter because John undoubtedly believes you are.

You're thinking I'm nuts, but let me tell you what happened three years ago. John was in Washington and I needed something that was in his library. I saw that his safe was open. He's the only one who knows the combination. I was curious so I looked inside. I found a journal, John's journal, and I took it. I've copied a couple of pages for you so you can see what he really is, Nicola. I don't know if he killed his mother, but I do know that he killed Melissa, the girl in college that John wanted to marry until he found out she'd slept with his best friend. And guess what? His best friend was Elliott Benson. How many other women has he killed?

Here are the journal pages, Nicola. You can read for yourself, and not just take my word for it.

Have things already started happening to you?

Run, Nicola, run. John is quite insane. Stay alive.

Cleo Rothman

Slowly, Nicola picked up the final two pages in the letter. John's journal. She read.

Enough, Nicola thought when she finished reading. It was enough. She grabbed her coat and was out the door and on her way to John's condominium in three minutes flat.

She was going to get the truth, tonight.

Los Angeles

The star of *The Consultant*, Joe Kleypas, lived on Glenview Drive in a small redwood-and-glass house set on stilts in the Hollywood Hills, surrounded by dead brush, almost-dead mesquite bushes, and straggly pines. After the third knock, Kleypas came to the door wearing only pale blue draw string sweatpants that had seen better days. He'd tied them loosely, letting them hang low on his belly, showing off his famous abs, which looked like he'd polished them to a high shine. His hair stood up in spikes, and he looked close to snarling. He was also drunk. He weaved just a bit in the doorway, waved a glass at them that was half-full of either water or straight vodka. "My, my, what have we here?"

Sherlock stuck her FBI shield in his face.

He took another drink and sneered even more. "Oh yeah, you're the Keystone cops."

"That's right," Savich said. "We're the Federal Keystone cops. We want to talk to you, Mr. Kleypas."

"Federal Keystone cops. Hey, that's funny."

"It's Mr. and Ms. Federal Keystone cops to you," Dane said.

"Very funny, hot shot." Joe Kleypas had planted himself firmly in the doorway, his arms crossed over his bare chest, a well-worked-out bare chest. Nick wondered how Dane would look if he polished his abs. She wondered if you just walked into a drugstore and asked for ab polish.

Kleypas said, "I already talked to Detective Flynn. I don't want to speak to any more Keystone cops, even Federal ones. Just get the fuck out of here now, all of you. Hey, you're awful pretty, you an actress? You want, maybe we could go someplace, have a little drink. My bedroom's got a good view of the canyon, the sheets aren't too bad."

Neither Sherlock nor Nick knew which one of them had struck his fancy. Nick said, "That's nice, but not today, thank you."

Joe Kleypas shrugged and his abs rippled a bit. "Then all of you can get out. Get out of my face." He drank down the rest of his drink, hiccuped, gave a slight shudder. Not good, Sherlock thought. The man looked about ready to explode.

They'd been told he had a violent temper. A mean drunk—no worse sort of man than that, Sherlock thought, and took another couple of easy steps back in case he did something stupid, like let loose on Dane or Dillon. Sherlock said low to Nick, "Let's go sit in the car," and tugged on her arm. "We're a distraction. Let the guys handle it." They watched Savich very smoothly force Kleypas back into his house and follow him. Dane closed the door behind them.

When Dane and Savich came out some fifteen minutes later, both of them looking disgusted, Sherlock said, "Dillon, please tell me he confessed. It really would make my day."

"Yeah, he did confess," Dane said, "to about a dozen different love-guests, all in the last month, most of the ladies married. He prefers married ladies; he told us that about four times. I think he'd like the two of you to add to his list. Charming guy. Oh yeah, he was drinking straight vodka."

"Dillon, look at your knuckles," Sherlock said, and grabbed his hand. "You hurt yourself. I don't like this."

"I didn't like his mouth," Savich said, shrugging, and flexed his hands. "He came at me, and I ended up shutting it." Nick saw him rub his knuckles, a very slight smile on his face. "Nothing out of his mouth but foul language."

"Now he can repent at his leisure," Sherlock said comfortably, and patted her husband's arm. She knew Dane wouldn't tell a soul that his boss had decked a big Hollywood jerk with shiny abs. She must remember to buy some iodine; she had some Band-Aids in her purse. She always carried them for Sean. Dillon must really have been mad to hit him with his fists.

After Sherlock finished doctoring him, Savich, with a grin at his hands that now sported two Flintstones Band-Aids, pulled the Taurus out of the narrow driveway that sat atop stilts a good thirty feet from the canyon floor, and said, "Kleypas is one miserable lad, but he's more pathetic than dangerous. He's too busy drinking to be doing much of anything else."

"The word over at the studio," Dane said, "is that Kleypas is having trouble getting work because of that drinking problem. *The Consultant* was more or less his last chance. He's really bummed that it's been pulled. He'd be the last one to submarine the show."

THE following morning, Nick was blow-drying her hair—another item Dane had bought for her—half an eye on the local TV news. She dropped the hair dryer and yelled, "Oh, no!"

It bounced against the wooden dresser, then clattered to the floor.

Dane was through the door in a flash, zipping up his pants.

"What is it—" He came to a fast stop. She was standing there, clutching her middle, staring at the TV. She didn't say a word, just pointed.

There she was, in living color, walking beside him down Pico Boulevard toward their parked car. There was a close-up of her face and the newscaster said in a chirpy voice, a voice so carefree and pleased he could have been talking about how he'd gotten laid the previous night, "This is Ms. Nick Jones, the San Francisco police department's key witness in the Prime-Time Killer murders. Sources tell us that Ms. Jones was living in a homeless shelter in San Francisco and just happened to see the killer at Saint Bartholomew's Church."

"Well, damn," Dane said. "I'm not surprised that they've got something, but all this? They've got everything, including your name and a shot of you." He saw that Nick was as white as the bathroom tile.

He walked over to her and pulled her against him. "It will be all right," he said against her still-damp hair. "You've got the fastest guns in Hollywood on your side. We'll keep clear of the reporters. It'll be okay."

She laughed, a desperate laugh that felt like a punch to his gut. She raised her head to look at him and splayed her palms on his bare chest. "I've got to get out of here, Dane. There's no choice for me now."

"No. I said I'll protect you and I will. You want more Feds around? Fine, I'll speak to Savich. He'll arrange it."

"It was luck that saved me at Father Michael Joseph's funeral, not you."

"You're right about that, Nick." Dane hated to admit it. "I'll get more folks to guard you," he said again.

She just shook her head. Then, to his astonishment, she leaned her head forward and lightly bit his shoulder. Then she pulled away from him. "I hope I didn't break that very nice hair dryer you bought for me."

"You're not going to run, Nick."

She gave him a long look, then nodded as she said, "Very well," and of course he knew she was lying. She didn't do it very well.

He said nothing, just rubbed where she'd bitten him. Did it qualify as a hickey? He was smiling as he left the room to finish dressing.

Forty-five minutes later, they were in the Los Angeles field office, in the conference room with the SAC, Special Agent in Charge Gil Rainy. Sherlock said, "Sure the press found out about the murders being based on the first two episodes, but how did they find out about Nick? Not just her name, but that she was homeless."

"Maybe the murderer himself," Dane said. "He wants to flush her out, put her in the limelight."

Delion said, "Already the media idiots—oops, I'm being redundant—have labeled the murderer the Prime-Time Killer. I swear, even if it cost lives, the media would spit it all out, no hesitation at all."

Rainy said, "I bet they sat around and brainstormed to come up with the cute handle. But, bottom line, the leak isn't any big deal. The murderer already knows about her so who cares if everyone else does, too? Still, it's like the media wants to offer her up as the sacrificial goat."

Savich said, "I called Jimmy Maitland and told him what they showed, asked him to rattle some cages, find out how this happened. The thing is—where did they get the photo of Nick and Dane? To be honest, it seems to me like a plant. I think someone sent the photo in along with specifics."

"The murderer," Dane said, and looked over at Nick, who hadn't said a word. "Who else would have?"

Flynn said, "You're right. If a reporter had found them, he would have shot some video, not just taken a photo of them, so maybe Dane's right, it was the murderer."

Dane said, "Actually, that's not what's so bad about all this." He sat forward as Nick grabbed his arm.

"No, Dane, don't."

He ignored her. "Nick was in the homeless shelter in San Francisco because she's running from something or someone she hasn't told any of us about. So I think she's got two people after her, both dangerous. Being on TV was the worst thing that could have happened to her."

Sherlock said, "Okay, Nick, then it's time for you to level with us. We're the Feds. The perfect audience. Flynn and Delion are locals, but they aren't bad either, what with all the sugar they eat. We will do everything we can for you, count on it. Now talk."

Nick actually smiled. "Thank you, Sherlock, but I can't. I just can't."

Savich said, "We could lock you up, you know."

"No, you can't," Nick said. "I made a deal with Delion and Dane. Leave me alone. This is over." Then she simply pushed back her chair and walked out of the room.

"Well, hell," Dane said, and shoved back his chair to go after her.

"Not to worry," said Gil Rainy. He spoke into his cell phone. "She won't get out of the office."

Flynn said, "But we can't hold her, can we?"

"Sure," Delion said. "She's a material witness, in the flesh."

They heard some orders, a yell, and furniture crashing over. They ran out of the conference room to see four male agents holding Nick's arms and hands, trying to protect themselves. That left her the furniture to kick, which she was doing. She'd lost control. She was fighting as if her life depended on it. Dane realized he'd pushed too hard, but he hadn't felt he'd had a choice.

Delion yelled, "Don't hurt her, dammit!"

Three chairs lay on their sides, and a computer monitor was hanging off the edge of a desk. An agent grabbed it just in time.

"Give her to me," Dane said, although he knew she'd try to kill him, too. The agents gladly handed her over. This time she didn't bite him, she tried to kick him in the groin. He heard Rainy yell, "Hey, not that!" as he quickly turned to the side, just in time, and her knee struck his thigh. He pulled her back against him and closed his arms around her body, pinning her arms to her sides, her legs against his, giving her no leverage at all. But she just wouldn't stop. She heaved and jerked and didn't make a sound.

"Hey," Dane said finally, "anybody got any handcuffs?"

"Don't you dare, you jerk," Nick said.

He grabbed her shoulders and shook her. "Listen to me, Nick. You are not going to die, at least not in my lifetime. You really might try for a little trust here." He shook her again. Rainy handed him a pair of cuffs. Dane jerked her arms behind her and cuffed her.

He thought she was going to explode. She kicked and bit and twisted until Sherlock walked right up to her, got in her face, and said, "Stop it, Nick, or I'm going to belt you. The men won't because you're a woman. You're really pushing me here."

Nick believed her. She got control of herself, but it took a bit of time before the hideous panic subsided. She was white, shaking, her breath coming in gulps. "Don't hit me, Sherlock," she said, and just went limp. Sherlock held her up.

"Somebody give me the key to these ridiculous handcuffs."

One of the agents tossed Sherlock the keys. She opened them up, slipped them off, and rubbed Nick's wrists. Sherlock said, "Okay, don't you move or I'll coldcock you. Now, Nick—"

Dane said, "Her name's Nicola. At least she told me that much. And she's a Ph.D.—medieval history."

Nick lunged for him. Sherlock grabbed her and managed to hold her, as Nick yelled, "You just had to blab it, didn't you, Dane Carver? I'm going to bite you again really good, when you least expect it, damn your eyes, just like I did this morning when you were half-naked and I bit your shoulder!"

There was complete silence, at least twenty special agents frozen in place, all ears.

Sherlock blinked, eased her hold on Nick, who ran at Dane, her fists up, ready to kill him. He was fast, grabbed her, pulled her back up tightly against his chest, and held her arms against her sides. "This is familiar," he said, remembering how he'd saved himself in the police station in San Francisco by holding her immobile just this way.

She was still breathing too fast, but at last her muscles were beginning to relax. "I'm not going to let you go just yet. I really would like my body parts intact."

One of the special agents guffawed. "Hey, Agent Carver, speaking of body parts, let's see the bite on your shoulder."

"Ah," said another agent, "the perils of being an FBI agent. I think Dane should get combat pay."

Nick growled. At least her breathing was slowing down.

TWENTY-THREE

SAC Gil Rainy assigned two agents to protect Dane and Nick. Old geezers, Gil said, who needed to do something different because they'd just about burned out on bank robbers.

"Old geezers, hell," Delion said when he met Bo and Lou, neither of them over forty-five. "I'm gonna belt Rainy in the chops."

It was just after lunch, eaten at a KFC, Nick and Dane each eating only one piece of deep-fried chicken breast, when they headed back to Premier Studios to speak to Frank Pauley. The two special agents, Bo and Lou, were hanging a good ways back.

They were at the corner of Brainard and Loomis when out of nowhere a motorcycle came roaring up to the driver's side of the car. The rider was dressed in black leather, a helmet covering his head and face. He pulled a gun out of his leather jacket and began shooting. He was fast and smooth. The window exploded. Dane felt glass shower over his head and face, felt the sting of a bullet that came too close to his ear.

"Nick, get down on the floor! Now!"

She was down instantly. The bullet missed her by no more than an inch, and shattered the passenger-side window, spewing glass shards all over her.

"Jesus, keep down!"

Dane jerked the steering wheel to the left, trying to smash the Grand Am into the motorcycle. He nearly managed it, but the bike swerved hard left, then pulled back. Dane jerked out his SIG Sauer and held it in his left hand, waiting, while he tried to control the car and not kill anyone. Suddenly, the bike came back up again, the guy firing rapidly, at least six shots, emptying his clip. He stuffed it inside his black leather jacket, pulled out another, and fired again. Dane fired back, still wrestling with the car. He felt a smack of cold against his left arm, ignored it, and fired again. In the next instant, they were at a side street. Dane jerked the steering wheel sharply right. They screeched on two tires as the Grand Am barreled onto the street, barely missing three cars whose drivers were sitting on their horns and yelling curses.

Dane managed to bring the Grand Am to a stop next to a curb in front of a small 1940s bungalow. He was breathing hard, adrenaline flowing so fast his heart was nearly pumping out of his chest.

The motorcycle flew past, revving hard and loud. The guy fired two more shots, both high and wild. Then Dane just couldn't believe it—the guy turned a bit and waved to them. In the black leather gloved hand he waved, he held a gun.

Nick was stuffed on the floor, her head covered with her hands. Blood trickled over her hands from the glass shards that had struck her. He reached out his right hand and lightly touched her head. "Nick, are you okay?"

"Yes, just some glass in my hair. Oh dear, my hands are cut a bit, but nothing bad. Are you okay?"

"Sure."

"Where are Bo and Lou?"

"They're coming up behind us right now." Dane opened the door and got out. Then he looked down at his shirt. "Well, shit."

She yelled from behind him, "You're shot, dammit, Dane Carver. How could you?"

He heard her voice shaking, felt the shock building in it, and said calmly, "I'm all right. A through-and-through shot, a flesh wound, nothing broken, everything works. I've cut myself worse shaving. It's hardly worse than what Milton's bullet did to your head. Take it easy, Nick. We're okay, both of us, and that's what's important."

"The guy waved to us. Did you see that? He actually waved to us as he was holding the gun!"

"Yeah, I know. Some balls, huh? How did you see that? I told you to keep way down."

"I just looked up there at the end. The bastard." She was starting to tremble, then shudder. He took off his bloody jacket and wrapped it around her, pulled her against his side. "It's okay. Just hang on, breathe deeply. That's right, nice and deep. Bo and Lou will be here in a minute."

"I thought we were going to be bored out of our gourds," Lou said when he trotted up. "I'm sorry, guys. We were really hanging back. We won't do that again." He looked at the shattered windows, closed the driver's-side door, and waved away the six or so civilians who were closing in on them.

"Everything's okay here, folks. Just go about your business. Hey, what's all that blood? Jesus, Dane, you got hit."

Bo said, breathing hard, "The guy clipped you, Agent Carver. Okay, let's get you over to Elmwood Hospital, it's the closest good emergency room. I took Lou there just last month."

Dane said, "What was wrong with Lou?"

"I ate too much fat over a couple of days and got a gallbladder attack," Lou said. He moved Dane's hand and pressed his own palm hard over the wound. After a few minutes, he tied his handkerchief around Dane's upper arm. Dane thought about his single piece of KFC and hoped he'd never have a gallbladder attack.

"There," Lou said, "that should slow the bleeding down. Try to remember to give it back to me. My wife gave me that handkerchief for my birthday just three days ago. It's real linen and she embroidered my initials on it. If I lose it, my goose is cooked."

"It won't be lost, Lou," Dane said, "but it will be bloody."

"My wife is used to blood. That's okay."

"I'll keep an eye on it," Nick said, looking up a moment from picking glass out of Dane's hair. She said to him, "You just have a few nicks where some glass got you. Hold still. Bo, if you'll take care of our rental car, Lou can take us to that hospital, okay?"

Bo gave Dane the once-over, nodded, then saluted. "Lou, try to get him a different doctor than the one you had." He loosened the handkerchief a bit as he added, "The guy wanted to cut Lou up right there."

"Didn't happen," Lou said. "I started feeling better and got the hell out of there. Your jacket's ruined, Dane. Hey, Nick, you got yourself together?"

"I'm nearly together, thank you," she said.

Lou looked at her more closely, seemed satisfied. "All right, we're out of here. Bo has already called in. He'll secure the crime scene until someone gets here. Dane, I don't suppose you saw the shooter? Maybe a license plate?"

Dane just shook his head. "The guy wasn't in a car, he was riding a Harley. I didn't even get a good look at the gun. I was too busy trying not to get a bullet through my head. Nick, are your hands still bleeding?"

"No, hardly at all," she said. "I'm just fine. Be quiet now, and let's get you to the hospital."

She'd regained her balance, held the shock at bay. He was proud of her.

Special Agent Lou Cutter got them to Elmwood Community Hospital in under eight minutes. He used the siren and traffic disappeared in front of them. It was an experience Nick had never had. It was, she told him, very cool.

Dane was breathing lightly through his mouth, the pain sharp and hot now, and he didn't like it one bit. It was the first time he'd been shot. By a guy on a damned motorcycle. He said to Lou, "He was probably planning to come up along the passenger side and shoot Nick. We were lucky. He couldn't get up on the sidewalk next to her, too many people. He still tried it from my side."

"If he shot you," Nick said, "you would have lost control of the car and crashed. Then he could have shot me really easily. Or maybe the car crash would have killed me."

Lou said, "Thanks to you, Dane, you kept it together and pulled both of you through. Good job. Now, you do realize that this little show is way over the top. None of us expected anything like this. It's completely different from what he's done to date."

Dane sighed. "Like you said, Lou, this performance was over the top. The guy's desperate, he's losing it. Nick, I'm sorry."

"You're the one he shot."

Lou took care of all the administrative hassles with the emergency room staff, which was a relief since Nick was focused entirely on Dane.

She supposed that Dr. John Martinez thought she was Dane's wife and so didn't kick her out of the cubicle.

"Went right through your upper arm, Mr. Carver," he said after cleaning and examining the wound, poking around while Dane watched him, his mouth tightly closed. "You were very lucky. Not anywhere near any major vessels. It isn't bad at all, when you think about how bad it could have been. How did it happen? Were you cleaning your gun or something? You know that I'm going to have to tell the cops about this."

"You already have," Dane said. He pulled his FBI shield out of his inner pocket and flipped the case open.

"FBI. I've never treated an FBI agent before," Martinez said as he injected Dane's arm. "Let's just give that anesthetic five minutes to kick in. Then, just a few stitches and that'll be it, apart from a tetanus shot." It felt to Dane like ten years passed before Dr. Martinez sank his first stitch.

Dane stared straight ahead, felt the push of the needle, the pull of the thread through his flesh. He focused on the array of bandages on the shelf in the cubicle. All sizes of gauze. In and out—it seemed like a hundred times—then, thank God, Dr. Martinez was done. Dane looked down at his arm as they bandaged it, then watched a nurse clean and bandage the backs of Nick's hands.

"The stitches will resorb, but I want you to have them checked in a few days," Dr. Martinez said. "We're going to give you some antibiotics to take for a while. Any problems at all—fever, heavy pain—you get your butt either back in here or to your own doctor." He looked over at Nick. "Hey, you a special agent, too?"

"She's above just an ordinary special agent," Dane said and sucked in his breath when the nurse jabbed a needle into his right arm.

"That's your tetanus shot," Dr. Martinez said. "Now, just one more for the pain. It should keep you smiling for a good four hours. And you're going to need some pain pills, enough for three days. Don't be a macho, take them."

"He'll take them," Nick said, her bandaged hands on her hips, as if ready to belt him if he got out of line. She was still wearing his bloody jacket. She looked ridiculous.

The nurse said something and the doctor nodded. "Since you're not his wife, you need to step out, ma'am. She's got to give him a shot in the butt."

"I've seen a lot of him already," Nick said, "but not his butt."

When Dane walked out of the cubicle, his left arm well bandaged and in a dark blue sling, he was trying to get his pants fastened with just his right hand.

Nick shoved his hand out of the way. "Hold still." She zipped the pants the rest of the way up, fastened the button, then got his belt notched. "There, you'll do." She smirked, no other word for it. "Hey, did you have Dr. Martinez check the teeth marks on your shoulder?"

"He said I didn't have to worry about infection, the antibiotic should cover the teeth marks, too. If you're rabid, that could, however, be a problem."

She smiled, a small, stingy one, but still something of a smile. She straightened in front of him, studied his face for a long time. She picked out the last of the glass and stroked her fingers through his hair to neaten it. "You're pale, but not bad. Thank you for handling that so well, Dane. I owe you."

"Yeah," he said. "You do." He leaned down, kissed her, then straightened again. "Debt paid."

She laughed, looked off-kilter for a moment, which pleased him, then took off his jacket and draped it over his back. He was about to kiss her again when Lou came up. "Everything's taken care of. Everyone's excited to have a real FBI agent in here with a bullet wound. They get LAPD occasionally, but never a Fed. I think that woman over behind that desk wants to jump your bones, Dane."

"My bones wouldn't jump back," Dane said. He felt slight nausea now even though his arm throbbed only a bit. The nurse had shot him up with Demerol. Whatever it was, it was working.

"We're going back to our Holiday Inn and I'm going to watch Dane rest until tonight."

"All right," Lou said, "but you can expect everyone to come over and see for themselves what happened."

"Oh dear," Nick said. "We'll be needing another car."

"Not to worry," Lou said. "Bo is already working on it. You'll have another car there within a couple of hours, guaranteed."

"YOU could have been killed. Very easily."

"Let it go, Nick. It's my job. The arm will be fine in just a few days, according to Bo, who, according to Lou, has reason to know. How are your hands?"

She waved that away. "I don't want you to get killed."

"I won't. Drop it. Give me one of those egg rolls. Oh, dip it first. Thank you."

She watched him eat. It was dark, almost seven o'clock in the evening. They'd been alone only for the past four minutes. Savich and Sherlock were the last to leave, Sherlock saying, "Remember, we're two doors down, in twenty-three, and it's the same phone number. Enjoy the Chinese."

"You need another pain pill," Nick said when she realized he wasn't going to eat any more. She fetched him one from the bottle on the dresser.

She didn't even take the chance that he'd try to be macho, just shoved it in his mouth and handed him a glass of water.

"That should help you sleep. You need rest, not any more talk." She stood up and stretched, then began pacing the small room, to the door and back again.

"That was really much too close."

"No," Dane said, shaking his head, "that bullet old Milton fired in the church was much closer."

"How many more times can we be lucky?"

"This second time wasn't entirely luck," Dane said.

"Yeah, yeah, you're Superman."

He said, "Promise me you won't run, Nick."

"Listen, you, I want you to stop looking into my head."

"You're real easy to read, at least right now. Running won't help you. You do realize that, don't you?" His brain was stalling out, working slower, beginning to fuzz around the edges. He couldn't be certain he'd make any sense in another minute. He felt bone tired, his body and his brain closing down.

She said, "Well, I'm not a jerk, so I won't leave you while you're down. So stop trying to figure out how you can get your paws on some handcuffs."

"Thank you," he said, and closed his eyes. At least Savich had gotten him out of his clothes. He was wearing a white undershirt and sweatpants, no socks. He liked to feel the sheets against his toes. Nick pulled the single sheet to his chest, then straightened it over him.

He had nearly died because of her.

TWENTY-FOUR

Chicago

She heard him unlock the front door, walk into the large entrance hall, and pause a moment to hang up his coat. She heard him mumbling something to himself about some contributor. When he walked into the living room, where she sat in one of the sleek pale brown leather chairs, his face went still, then lit up.

"Nicola, what a wonderful surprise. I was going to call you the minute I got my coat off. You lit the fireplace, that's good. It's very cold outside."

She rose slowly, stood there, staring at him, wondering what was in his mind, what he was really thinking when he looked at her.

"What's wrong? Oh God, did something else happen to you? No one told me a thing, no one—"

"No, nothing more happened. Well, actually, I did get a letter from your ex-wife, warning me that you are trying to kill me because you believe I'm sleeping with Elliott Benson."

"From who? You got a letter from Cleo?"

"That's right. She wrote to tell me you believe I'm sleeping with Elliott Benson, that you believed she slept with him, too."

"Of course you're not sleeping with him. Good God, Nicola, you won't even sleep with me. Besides, he's old enough to be your father."

"So are you."

"Don't talk like that. I'm nowhere near that old. You know I've wanted to sleep with you, for months now, but you put me off, and now you've begun to back away from me."

"Yes, I have, but that's not what's important here, John."

"Yes, I agree. Now, what's this nonsense about a letter from Cleo?

That's impossible, you know that. She's long gone, not with Elliott Benson, for God's sake, but with Tod Gambol, that bastard I trusted for eight long years. What the hell is this about?"

"I got the letter just a little while ago. She warned me that you would try to kill me, just like you did her. She told me to run, just like she ran. I want to know what this is all about, too, John. She makes serious accusations. She wrote about your mother's supposed accidental death, and the death of your college sweetheart—both car accidents. Her name was Melissa."

His face flushed with anger, but when he spoke, his voice was calm, like a reasoned, sympathetic leader reassuring a constituent, the consummate politician. "This is nonsense. Ridiculous nonsense. I don't know who wrote you a letter accusing me of all this, but it wasn't Cleo. She's been gone for three years, not a single word from her. There's no reason she'd write to you, for God's sake. As I recall she didn't even like you. I think she was jealous of you because, truth be told, even back then I thought you were wonderful. Don't get me wrong. I loved Cleo, loved her very much, but I thought you were bright and so very eager and enthusiastic."

She wasn't about to go there. Yeah, she thought, she probably would have licked his shoes in those days, if he'd wanted her to. She said, "John, I could have dismissed this letter as a crank, but there was more."

"What the hell are you talking about?"

"She included several pages from your journal."

"My journal? Why would she do that?"

"She said she found it by accident one day in your library safe. She read it, read your confession about killing Melissa. It's right here, John, in your handwriting. How many women have you killed?"

He stood stiff as the fireplace poker, just three feet behind her, close enough to grab to protect herself if she needed to. He said slowly, his pupils dilated, "I don't know what you're talking about, Nicola. I have a journal, but writing something like that? What, as a joke? It's absurd. No, wait. Did Albia put you up to this?"

"Oh no, John, no joke. No Albia either. No, don't come any closer to me. Not even a single step. You see this?" She waved three pieces of paper at him. "This is Cleo's letter to me and two pages she copied from your journal. This is from the woman I knew when I first came to work for your reelection campaign, a woman I liked very much. When she left you, I believed, like the rest of the world, that you were devastated, but she tells me that she ran for her life. I remember how everyone felt so very sorry for you. No, stay back, John!"

He never looked away from the pages she held. She saw he wanted those pages, wanted them badly. He said, "Yes, Cleo left me, you knew that, Nicola. If you'll show me the letter, show me those ridiculous journal pages, I'll be able to prove that it's not even from Cleo. Really, that's quite impossible."

"I don't see why it's impossible. And yes, actually, it is from Cleo. I know her handwriting. God knows I read enough of her memos when I was volunteering. She wrote that you not only tried to kill her—that's the reason she ran, because of the journal—but you're trying to kill me because you believe I'm sleeping with Elliott Benson."

"Again, John, how many women have you killed?"

"For God's sake, Nicola. Somebody else wrote you that letter, some-one who copied her handwriting, someone who hates me, wants to destroy us. Someone made up those journal pages. Don't let that happen, Nicola. Let me see that letter. Give it to me."

Nicola took a step back. She was nearly against the fireplace now. She felt the heat of the flames against her back. She said, "Cleo wrote that she doesn't want me to die. She wrote that I should run, just like she did. She didn't want to die either."

"This is utterly ridiculous." He looked dazed, as if he couldn't quite grasp what she was saying, and all through it, he was staring at those pages in her hand. "Let me see that goddamned letter."

"No, you'll destroy it and the journal pages. I can't allow you to do that."

"All right, all right. Listen to me. I didn't kill anyone—not my mother, not Melissa, not anyone. That's just insane." Still he stared at those sheets of paper, his pupils sharp black points of light, his face as white as his beautifully laundered shirt. "You've got to let me see that letter. It can't be from Cleo. She loved me, she wouldn't say such things."

"She left because you wanted to kill her and because she realized you were insane with jealousy. You believed she was unfaithful to you."

"She left me to be with Tod Gambol, everyone knows that. Listen, Nicola, let's sit down and talk this over. We can start at the beginning. We can work it all out. I love you."

"I'm going to the police, John. I suppose I wanted to confront you with the letter, hear what you had to say. I really hoped that I'd believe you—"

"Dammit, then listen to me," he said, but still he was staring at that letter. "Give me a chance. I had nothing to do with my mother's death. I was sixteen years old, for God's sake. She was an alcoholic, Nicola, and the decision at the time was that she ran her car off the road because she was drunk. As for Melissa, by God I loved her, and she slept with Elliott—the bastard has always wanted what I have—but I didn't kill her. I simply broke it off with her. It was a damned accident, it had to be. The letter and the journal—it's got to be a forgery. Give me the letter, Nicola, let me examine it."

"No. I think I'll give it to the police, let them figure it out."

"It would ruin me politically, Nicola, you must know that. Do you despise me so much that you want me to have to resign from the Senate? Spend my days being hounded by the press? I didn't do anything, dammit! You can't simply read a letter, some stupid pages from a make-believe journal, from God knows whom, and decide I'm a murderer, accuse me of killing my own mother? I was only sixteen! A boy doesn't murder his own mother!"

She said very quietly, "The boy does if he's a psychopath."

"A psychopath? Good God, Nicola, this is beyond ridiculous. Listen to me. You must realize how impossible this all is. You can't go to the police." He drew himself up, becoming the patrician gentleman, tall, slender, elegant, and he was angry, his hands clenched into fists at his sides. He looked from her to the letter, the pages still clutched in her right hand. He said softly, "You're not going anywhere, you stupid little ingrate. Just look what I've done for you—Jesus, I was going to marry you, make you one of the most sought-after women in America. You're young, beautiful, intelligent, a college professor, and not left-wing, which was a big relief, let me tell you. With you at my side, with my coaching you, showing you what to do, we could have had just about everything, maybe even the White House. What is wrong with you, Nicola?"

"I don't want to die, John, I really don't. Were you driving that car, wearing that ski mask, trying to run me down?"

"The cretin who wrote you that letter, he's trying to turn you against me. Why can't you believe that? None of this is true. A drunk nearly hit you, nothing more than that."

"And the food poisoning, John? Was that all an accident, too?"

"Of course it was! Just call up the doctor and ask him again. That damned letter isn't from Cleo!"

"Why not? How can you be so sure that Cleo didn't write me? She wants to protect me, save me from you. You did want to kill her, didn't you, John? Did you really believe she was being unfaithful to you, or was that just a ruse, or some sort of sick fantasy?"

"I'm not sick, Nicola," he said, his voice shaking with rage. She was suddenly afraid, very afraid. She eased her hand into her jacket pocket, felt the grip of her pistol.

"The truth is that the bitch was sleeping with Tod Gambol, my trusted senior aide for eight fucking years! He had the gall to sleep with my wife! They would go out to motels during the day when I was in Washington, or even when I was in Chicago and in meetings. I have the motel receipts. I'm the wronged one here, not Cleo. Dammit, you knew that, everybody knew that. Don't you remember how sorry you felt for me? You cried, I remember that. As for Elliott Benson, I don't know if she slept with him, it doesn't matter. And now you believe this insanity just because someone who hates me wrote you a letter, scribbled a confession. God, Nicola, that's just stupid."

"John, I told you. Cleo wrote that she never slept around on you, that she has no idea where Tod Gambol is, but she thinks he might be dead."

He said very quietly, "Nicola, why would you believe this letter when you've known me for four years now? I've always been kind and considerate to you, to everyone around me. Have you ever seen me lose my temper? Have you ever heard anything remotely this bad about me? Anything about my ever sleeping around on Cleo?"

"Then why didn't you tell me about your mother? About your dead fiancée?"

"Why the hell would I? They were very painful times for me, and no one's business. Maybe, after we were married, I'd have told you about them. I don't know."

"It's true that I always felt safe around you because no one ever even hinted that you played around like many of the other men in Congress, hitting on young women."

He faced her, palms spread out, and his voice softened, deepened, "Please, let's sit down and discuss this like two people who are planning on spending the rest of their lives together. It's all a misunderstanding.

You've gotten ideas that simply aren't true. We'll find out who tried to hit you in that car. It will be some drunk, you'll see. As for the food poisoning, it was an accident. There's no big conspiracy here, no mystery, other than who sent you that letter."

"I realize if I take these journal pages to the police that you and all your spin doctors could just claim I was a nutcase and wasn't it so sad, and everyone would probably believe it. If only she'd sent me the original journal pages and not copies, then maybe I'd have a chance, but not with these."

She paused. He said nothing.

"But I don't want to see you again."

Without warning, he ran at her, his hands in front of him, his fingers curved. Oh God. She whipped the Smith & Wesson out of her pocket, but he was on her, grabbing for the letter. He ripped it out of her hand, leaped back, panting hard. He stared down at the pages before he shredded each one. When he was done, he bunched the paper into a ball and threw it into the flames. He said, both his face and voice triumphant, "That's what your letter deserves."

His hands were still fists, the fingers curved inward. She would have been very afraid if she hadn't had her gun. She was shaking as she said, "I'm leaving now, John. Stay away from me."

SHE came awake that night at the sound of a noise. It was more than just a condo creak, more than just the night sounds she always heard when she was lying in bed alone, with nothing to do but listen.

She thought of Cleo Rothman's letter, now destroyed, about that car with the accelerator jammed down coming straight at her, about the food poisoning that could have put her in her grave. She thought of John coming toward her, destroying that letter.

There was absolutely no doubt in her mind that he'd wanted to kill her. But there was no proof, not a single whisper of anything to show the police.

She heard it again, another sound, this one like footsteps. No, she was becoming hysterical.

She listened intently, for a long time, and it was silent now, but she was still afraid. She thought she'd rather be in the dentist's chair than lying there in the dark, listening. Her mouth was dry, and her heart was beating so loud she thought anyone could hear it, track the sound right to her.

Enough was enough. Nicola got out of bed, grabbed the poker by the small fireplace, turned on the light, and looked in every corner of her bedroom.

Nothing, no one was there.

But then she heard something again, something or someone running, fast. She ran to her living room, to the large glass doors that gave onto the balcony. The doors weren't locked, they were cracked open.

She ran to the railing and looked down at a shadow, and it was moving.

Then she smelled the smoke. She ran back into her condo and saw smoke billowing out of the kitchen. Oh God, he had set a fire. She grabbed up her phone and dialed 911. She ran into the kitchen, saw that there was no way to put out the fire. She had time only to pull on jeans, shoes, and a shirt, grab her purse and coat, and she was out of there, banging on her neighbors' doors as she ran. She knew he was waiting downstairs, probably hiding in the shadows between the buildings across the street, knowing that she'd get out alive since she'd been on the balcony looking down at him.

She stayed close to the building, huddling with the neighbors, watched the fire trucks arrive, watched the chaos, the evacuation of everyone in the building. No one died, thank God. Actually, only her condominium was destroyed, and the one next to it slightly burned and smoke-damaged.

But he hadn't cared if the whole building had burned. He just wanted to make sure she was dead. She heard a firefighter say to the chief, "The fire was set. The accelerant is in the kitchen of 7B."

She realized in that moment that Senator John Rothman had burned her condo, or had it burned, with the hope that she'd be burned with it. He wanted her dead.

Since she had nothing left, since she had only her purse, it wasn't hard to decide what to do.

She spent the night in a temporary Red Cross shelter, watching to see if John would come looking for her. She even gave them a false name. The next morning, the volunteers gave her some clothes. She had decided during the night what she was going to do. Before she left Chicago, she used her ATM card, then cut it up.

An hour later, she was headed for San Francisco.

TWENTY-FIVE

Los Angeles

Savich and Sherlock were back the next morning with coffee and bagels.

"Nonfat cream cheese," Sherlock said, pulling out a plastic knife. "Dillon refuses to allow any high cholesterol in his unit."

Savich, who'd been studying Dane's face, said, "We've decided that you two are going to stay in today. Sorry about that, Nick, but Dane will doubtless try to go find the bad guys unless someone with staunch resolve keeps him here. You willing to take on the job?"

"Yes, he will do as he's told," Nick said as she gave Dane a bagel smeared with cream cheese.

He took one bite and turned green.

"You're still nauseous?" Sherlock said. "Not to worry, it'll ease off soon."

"How do you know?" Dane asked, staring at Sherlock. "Don't tell me you've been around another gunshot wound?"

"Well, the thing is," Sherlock said, paused, looked at her husband, then quickly away. "I sort of got a knife thrown into my arm once—a very long time ago."

"Yeah, a really long time," Savich said. "All of two and a half years ago."

"Well, it was before we were married and it feels like we've been married forever." She gave her husband a fat smile and said to Dane, "True, it wasn't much fun, but I was up and working again within two, three days."

"I think she felt nauseous," Savich said, his voice emotionless as a stick, "because the doctor gave her four shots in the butt. I remember that I cherished every yell."

Sherlock cleared her throat. "That is neither here nor there, the whole thing's best forgotten."

Savich said, "Forget the four shots in your butt or the knife wound?" He was trying for a light touch, but Dane heard the fear in his voice, a fear he still hadn't gotten over. He'd felt that fear for his brother when they'd been younger, whenever Michael had put himself in harm's way, something both of them did playing football, white-water rafting, mountain climbing. They'd done so much together before and during college. Then came Michael's time in the seminary and Dane's trip to Case Western to become a lawyer, something he'd hated to his bones. At least it hadn't taken him all that long to realize he wanted to be a cop.

Sherlock said, "Okay, no more about that incident. We've got a murderer who's running scared, so scared that he tried an insane stunt yesterday. He's insane, desperate, or both. We've been trying to find out what Linus Wolfinger did during that year after he graduated and before he came to work here and met Mr. Burdock, the owner of Premier Studios."

"And not having much luck," Savich said. "MAX is pretty upset about the whole thing. He just can't seem to find anything, as of yet—no credit-card trail, no employment trail, no purchase of a vehicle."

Sherlock said, "So we've decided to ask him, straight up. What do you think, Dane?"

"Why not the direct approach?" Dane said and shrugged. "It'll give us a story to check, not that it'll matter. I'm beginning to believe that none of them is telling the truth."

"At least everyone is consistent," Savich said.

Sherlock's cell phone trilled the leading notes to the *X-Files* theme. "Hello?"

"This is Belinda Gates. We're in really deep trouble here. Maybe."

"What happened?"

"I was watching a cable station last night, nine o'clock. I saw *The Consultant*, the third episode."

"Oh no," Sherlock said, "we are in trouble."

THREE hours later, LAPD Detective Flynn, feeling harassed, said to the group of ten people crowded into Dane's Holiday Inn room, "The program director, Norman Lido, of KRAM, channel eight locally, said Frank Pauley from Premier Studios sent him the episode and gave him permission to show it, told him they'd canceled the show, but maybe KRAM would like to pick it up. He liked the episode, showed it last night. This particular cable channel reaches about eight million people here in southern California."

"Didn't the idiot know why the show had been pulled?" Dane said. "The whole world knows."

"Claims he didn't know," Flynn said, shrugged. "Of course he's lying through his teeth. Why, I ask you, would any person with any sense of ethics want to air this show?"

The answer was money, of course, but it hung in the air, unspoken. He'd probably been paid a bundle to show the episode.

Flynn said, "When I told him it was all over the news, the jerk smirks and tells me he never watches the networks, they're a bunch of has-beens. I told him that even minor stations like his had it plastered all over their local news. The jerk just stood there and pretended to be surprised. It was really close, but I didn't slug him."

"Why didn't Belinda Gates call me last night?" Sherlock said. "Right after she saw the show?"

"We'll ask her," Delion said.

"She didn't know what her husband had done?"

Delion shrugged. "Don't know yet. But Sherlock and Savich are off to see Pauley. I can't wait to hear what he has to say. Depending on what he does say, I'm ready to haul his ass off to jail or stake him out in the middle of Pico Boulevard at rush hour."

"At least there haven't been any reports yet of any murders similar to the ones committed in episode three," Flynn said.

"No news is good news, I guess," Savich said. "When we spoke to Pauley by phone, he claimed he didn't know anything about this, that he never gave a copy of any episode to anyone. We're going to go see him again, and Belinda as well. Delion thought Sherlock would do best with her. Dane, you stay in bed and try to get yourself healed. Nick, you keep out of sight; the media is going to be crawling all over the studio."

"No," Dane said. "I'm okay, really. I want to come see Pauley with you." He paused a moment, then said, "I really need to do this, Savich."

After a pause, Savich said, "All right, Dane. We'll pick you up in about fifteen minutes. But I think this is the last time you guys should be out and about here in LA. There's just too much media interest, and

I'd just as soon not take any more chances with Nick's safety. Or yours," Savich added, looking at Dane's arm.

Nick just looked at him and said, "I'll get your clothes together for you while you take a shower."

"Thank you."

"Be careful of your arm."

FRANK Pauley stood in the middle of his office, his arms at his sides, and said without preamble to the four people who'd just been ushered into his office, "It's like I told you a couple of hours ago, I did not send that damned episode over to KRAM. I don't even know the program manager over there. I've never even heard of Norman Lido. Obviously, somebody got ahold of the tape—maybe the murderer, maybe not—and sent it over in my name to confuse things, to make you think I did it. But I did not. There's a little thing called liability, you know, and the studio will get its butt sued off if there are more murders. Jesus, I wouldn't ever do that. It's madness."

Sherlock said, "Why weren't you watching TV with Belinda last night?"

"What? Oh, I was playing poker with some guys in Malibu. It's a weekly game. There were five of us. You can check it out."

Savich waved to the very long gray sofa. "Do sit down, Mr. Pauley." He motioned Sherlock, Dane, and Nick to sit down as well. "Agent Carver was shot yesterday, so he needs to take it easy. It's likely that the murderer was trying to kill Nick."

Pauley just stared at Dane, then over at Nick. He said slowly, looking utterly bewildered, "I just don't understand any of this. It doesn't make sense. All of this is just plain crazy."

"I'm starting to agree with you," Dane said. He was feeling a bit green again. His arm was throbbing, a dull bite that just wouldn't stop. He cupped his right hand under his elbow, sat back in the comfortable gray leather chair, and held himself perfectly still.

Nick's hand hovered, then lightly touched his.

"Mr. Pauley," Sherlock said, "help us get a handle on this, please. When you got home last night from your poker game, did Belinda tell you about the show?"

Pauley looked at his fingernails, then down at the tassels on his Italian loafers. "I didn't go home last night."

"Oh?" Savich said. "Just where did you go?"

"We played poker until really late and I had too much to drink. I stayed over at Jimbo's house."

Savich raised a dark eyebrow. "Jimbo?"

"That's James Elliott Croft."

"The actor?" Nick said.

"Yes. He's also a lousy poker player. I won three hundred bucks off him."

Savich said, eyebrow raised higher, "And he still let you stay?"

Pauley said, "Hey, it's a really big house. I'm a quiet drunk, never bother anyone."

Sherlock said, not breaking the rhythm that she and Savich had set up, "When you saw Belinda this morning, she told you about the show?"

Pauley shook his head. "No, she was pissed at me because I'd told her I was coming home but I didn't. She'd left for a run before I even got back from Jimbo's house."

Savich said, "So you don't know why she wouldn't have called last night, the minute she realized she was watching episode three?"

"No clue. She's at home right now. I know that Detective Flynn spoke to her. What did he tell you?"

Sherlock gave him a nice smile. "I think I'll just keep that under my hat."

"You shouldn't wear a hat, ever," Pauley said. "It wouldn't look good on you."

"Depends on the hat," Sherlock said, still with a sunny smile.

The phone rang. Pauley shot a harassed look toward his desk, listened to it ring again. "I told Heather not to disturb me so it must be really important," he said, and picked up the phone, a fake antique affair in, naturally, gray.

When he hung up, he said, "That was Jon Franken. He says that his own personal copies of the next episodes of *The Consultant* are gone."

"What do you mean, gone?"

"Agent Savich, look, the episodes we taped of *The Consultant*—they're videotapes, and all over the place. Anyone who wants a copy can get ahold of it. All the producers, the editing department, the grips, anyone on set could get copies. They're not locked away. Jon said that someone evidently took his copies." He sighed. "Everyone knows that actual murders were committed using the scripts from the episodes. Who would steal Jon's copies?"

"How many of his episodes are missing?" Sherlock said.

"He said the next three. Look, there's just no way to hide the last three episodes we shot last summer. I'm surprised that Jon even noticed." He looked like he wanted to howl. Sherlock devoutly hoped he wouldn't.

"It seems," Sherlock said, "that the videotape was delivered by Gleason Courier Service. We spoke to the man who delivered the film and the letter. He said the package was simply left in their mail delivery drop at the North Hollywood office. Here's the letter."

She stuck it out to Pauley. He took it, stared down at it.

"Please read it, Mr. Pauley," Savich said. "Dane and Nick haven't heard it."

Frank read: *"Dear Mr. Lido, I'm enclosing an episode of* The Consultant. *We've decided to cancel the series due to many factors, and someone suggested that you might find it appropriate for your audience. Give it a try, see what you think, get back to me."*

Frank looked up. "He signed my name, and my title. It isn't my handwriting though, I can prove that." He was up fast, nearly ran to his desk and pulled some papers off the top. "Here," he said, shoving the pages into Savich's hand, "this is my handwriting."

"It's very similar," Sherlock said at last. "Even the letters are slanted the same way. It's hard for me to tell."

"Not for me."

Savich rose. "All right, Mr. Pauley. We will be in touch."

Nick just happened to look over her shoulder as she left Frank Pauley's office. He was standing in the middle of the room, his arms stiff at his sides, his hands fists. Just like he had been standing when they'd come in.

They were standing at the elevator doors when Dane said, "While we're here, why don't we drop in on Linus Wolfinger?"

"That's the plan," Savich said and punched the up button.

They went through the three secretaries, all of them the same adult crew, still showing no cleavage, just elegant suits in subdued colors. The place hummed with efficiency.

Nick nodded to Arnold Loftus, Linus Wolfinger's bodyguard, who was leaning against the same wall, looking buffed, tan, and bored. Sherlock picked up a magazine from one of the end tables and handed it to him.

Arnold Loftus automatically took the magazine. "Thank you. Hey, you guys are the FBI agents, right?"

"That's right," Sherlock said. "Does the FBI interest you?"

"Oh yeah, you guys get a lot more action than I do."

Nick smiled at him. "How's tricks?"

He shrugged. "Never anything going on. Wolfinger prances around, telling everyone what to do and how to do it, and people want to stick a knife in him, but they haven't yet because they're more afraid of him than they are of their mothers, at least that's how it looks to me. I guess if somebody got pissed off enough to go after him, I'd have to save him. Hey, thanks for the magazine."

"You're welcome. Is Mr. Wolfinger here?"

"Oh yeah, you just have to get past his guard dog."

"You're not the guard dog?"

"Nah, I'm the ultimate weapon."

Savich laughed, just couldn't help himself. "What's the guard dog's name?"

"I call him Mr. Armani, but his real name is Jay Smith."

"Now we've got a Smith and a Jones," Dane said, and looked toward Nick, who ignored him.

"I don't think," Sherlock said after they'd stepped away, "that Mr. Arnold Loftus and Mr. Linus Wolfinger are lovers."

"Agreed," Nick said. "Who was it who told us about that?"

"I'll have to look it up in my notes," Sherlock said.

Jay Smith, in a beautifully tailored pale gray wool Armani suit, frowned at them. "Mr. Wolfinger is very busy. There are a number of people waiting—"

Savich simply walked by him, paused a moment, and said over his shoulder, "Do you want to tell Mr. Wolfinger that we're here to speak to him or should I just go on in?"

"Wait!"

"Oh no, this is police business. I don't ever wait." Savich winked at Sherlock, and she put her palm over her breast and mouthed, "My hero."

Savich opened the door, stepped into the huge, bare office and stopped cold.

Linus Wolfinger was lying on top of his desk, and he looked to be asleep, unconscious, or dead.

TWENTY-SIX

"Shall we try CPR?" Nick said.

"It may be too late for him," Dane said. "Hey, he doesn't look bad, if he's dead. A real pity, he was so young."

"I think he looks very peaceful," Sherlock said. "Do you think I should maybe kiss him? See if he'll come around?"

"Like the Sleeping Prince?" Nick asked.

Jay Smith was wringing his hands behind them. He whispered, "That's not funny. He's not dead and you know it. He's meditating. For God's sake, you can't interrupt his meditation. He'll fire me if I allow it. Oh God, I'm still in hock to MasterCard for this suit."

Sherlock patted his Armani arm. "Good morning, Mr. Wolfinger," she called out, then simply brushed past Jay Smith, who looked to be on the verge of tears. "I'll be fired, for sure he'll bounce me out on my ear. What will I tell my mother? She thinks I'm a real big shot."

Linus Wolfinger didn't move, just lay still, looking dead.

Sherlock walked right up to the desk, leaned down, and said not an inch from his face, "Did you send episode three over to Norman Lido at KRAM?"

Linus Wolfinger sat up very slowly, and in a single, fluid motion, graceful as a dancer. He stood and stretched. Suddenly he looked just like an awkward nerd again, all sharp bones and angles, three pens in his white shirt pocket, tattered sneakers on his feet. "No," he said, "I didn't. I actually had no idea until Frank told me a while ago. He's very upset about it since some character pretended it was from him and forged his name."

Savich said, "Mr. Wolfinger, what did you do that year after you graduated from UC Santa Barbara?"

Linus Wolfinger pulled a pen out of his shirt pocket, listed to the right, and began tapping, tapping that damned pen against the desktop. "That was such a long time ago, Agent Savich."

"Yeah, all of two and a half years ago," Savich said. "Try to reconstruct the time for us."

Linus looked over at Dane. "What happened to you?"

"A Harley."

"A Harley hit you?"

"Nah, the guy on the Harley."

Linus looked thoughtful. "I've always thought of Harleys as being cheap Porsches, but every bit as sexy. Now, listen to me. I know you're confused, that you don't know your heads from your asses, but I don't know anything either. All of this is quite a shock. I don't need to tell you that Mr. Burdock is pissed about the whole thing. The media is sniffing around big time, invading everyone's privacy, his in particular. And our lawyers are whimpering, hiding in their offices."

"Tell us what you did during that year after you graduated, Mr. Wolfinger."

Tap, tap, tap went the pen. Linus said on a shrug, "Nothing happened. I just bummed around the western states—you know, Wyoming and Nevada, places like that. I was trying to find myself."

Savich said, "What did you live on during that year?"

"Nothing much. I was by myself, didn't eat much, just drove around."

Nick said, "You said you were driving around Wyoming. My very favorite place is Bryce Canyon. Did you visit there? What did you think?"

"Gorgeous place," Linus said, nodding. "I spent a good couple of weeks there. What else can I do for you folks?"

Savich didn't have time to continue with Linus because the door burst open and Jon Franken came running in, his handsome face red.

He came to a dead stop when he saw the four people standing there, watching him. He drew up, sucked in a deep breath, and said, "What I meant to say is that I heard that those idiots over at KRAM showed episode three of *The Consultant* last night. Why did you okay such a thing?"

"Good morning, Mr. Franken."

"Oh, stuff it," Jon Franken said. "Why did you do it?"

"I didn't. Someone sent it over saying it was from Frank."

"That's bullshit," Jon said, and dashed his fingers through his beautifully styled hair. Next to Linus Wolfinger, Jon Franken looked like a model, one with style and good taste. He looked very Hollywood with his white linen slacks, dark blue shirt, and Italian loafers, no socks. He looked long and sleek and elegant. And royally pissed. He also didn't look the least bit intimidated by Linus Wolfinger, who could have him out on his ear in about two seconds.

Linus Wolfinger wouldn't stop tap, tap, tapping that damned pen.

Jon said to Savich, "I'm sorry for bursting in here like this, but I just heard. Belinda called me. What the hell happened? Please tell me there weren't any murders."

"Not yet," Sherlock said.

"Good. Maybe this was just a distraction," Jon said, and streaked his long fingers through his hair again. His hair was so well styled that it fell right back into place.

Wolfinger showed signs of life at that announcement. "Maybe Jon has a point there. Maybe this was just another planned detour for the police, to get you all panicked. What do you think?"

"I think you could be right," Savich said. "Dane, sit down before you fall down."

Dane went to one of the two very uncomfortable chairs in the huge, nearly empty office and sat down. He cupped his left arm with his right hand.

"What happened to you?" Jon asked.

Linus said, "A Harley."

"What?"

But Jon Franken didn't wait for an answer, just began pacing. "Look, this has got to come to an end. You've got to stop the maniac. Everyone is really freaked."

Savich said, "You told us, Mr. Franken, that Weldon DeLoach is around thirty years old. When you showed us that tape, we all agreed that he looked older, forty at least."

Jon shrugged. "That's what he told me. He lives hard, what can I say? This town is really tough on some people, and Weldon's one of them. You don't understand—it sounds like a joke, but it's all too true. People who work in TV die young because they work their butts off—an eighteen-hour day is common. Lots of people just sleep here on the lot, on sets, in trailers. I found one guy sacked out in Scully's bed on stage five, his foot dangling over the side of the crib at the end of the bed. About Weldon—look, I never had any reason to doubt him. Are you saying he's a lot older than he told me?"

"He's forty-one, nearly forty-two," Sherlock said. "You've known him for eight years, right?"

"Yeah, about that. I really never paid much attention. Who cares?"

"A lot of things could hinge on that," Sherlock said. "We don't know yet."

Savich turned back to Linus Wolfinger. "It's time for a geography lesson, Linus. Bryce Canyon is in Utah, not Wyoming. So, what were you doing during that year?"

Jon Franken looked at Linus. "You don't know where Bryce Canyon is? Jesus, Linus, you're supposed to know everything."

Savich wished that Jon Franken would take himself off.

Linus just smiled and continued to tap his pen. "The agent over there told me how much she loved it and that it was in Wyoming. I wasn't about to make her look like an ignoramus. It wouldn't be very polite, now would it?"

Well, shit, Dane thought. The politicians in Washington could learn spin from these characters.

DANE'S cell phone rang just as Nick was seat-belting him into the backseat of Savich's rental car, a big dark blue Ford Taurus. They were parked on the studio lot because the media couldn't get into the studio itself, thank God. He listened, didn't say a word for a good three minutes. Sherlock, Savich, and Nick were all staring at him, waiting.

"All right," Dane said. "I'll get back to you within the hour." He pressed the end button, stared at Savich, and shook his head. "That was Mr. Latterley, the manager of the Lakeview Home for Retired Police Officers—you know, the nursing home where Weldon DeLoach's father has lived for the past ten years.

"Mr. Latterley says that Weldon DeLoach called this morning. Said he wants to come see his father late this afternoon, and was that all right. He also said that when he'd called before they told him that his father fell out of his wheelchair and hurt himself."

"But no one told us that Weldon had called before," Sherlock said.

"That's right," Dane said. He sat back, leaned his head against the seat, and closed his eyes. "No one called at all to tell us. You know, of course, that I left my card with every sentient employee at the nursing home."

Savich didn't say anything else. He pulled out of the studio and onto

Pico Boulevard, crammed with traffic and blaring horns. "First things first," he said.

Because of heavy traffic, it was forty-five minutes before they exited 405 and wound up Mulholland Drive to Frank Pauley's glass house. The surrounding hills were dry, too dry.

FiFi Ann, in her French maid's outfit, the little white cap on her hair, answered the door and stared at Dane's arm in its blue sling.

"Somebody bring you down, Agent?"

"Yeah, a Harley."

"Dangerous fuckers," FiFi Ann said, leaned down, and smoothed her black-latticed pantyhose.

"We'd like to see Mrs. Pauley," Sherlock said.

"Come with me," FiFi Ann said, straightening, and turned on her stiletto heels.

Belinda was drinking a cup of coffee by the blue swimming pool, wearing a very brief bikini, pale pink.

Both men froze in place for a good six seconds, eyes fixed on her.

Sherlock went right up to her and said, "Nice-colored Band-Aids you're wearing, Belinda."

"Yes, aren't they?" Belinda set down her coffee cup and rose, stretched a bit, knowing very well the impact she was having on the men. She grinned at Sherlock. "I like pink. It does wonderful things for my skin."

"All shades of pink look great with my red hair. Aren't we lucky?"

Belinda laughed, grabbed a cover-up, and slipped it on.

"That's better," Nick said. "Now the guys can breathe and get their pulses back down below two hundred."

"Okay, Belinda," Sherlock said, pulling her chair close, "tell me why you didn't call me last night the minute you realized episode three was on?"

She didn't say anything for almost a full minute. Then she got up and walked to the edge of the kidney-shaped swimming pool and stuck her foot in the water. She turned slowly, looked at each of them in turn, and said simply, with no attempt to excuse herself, "I wanted to see what would happen."

Nick nearly fell into a wildly blooming purple bougainvillea. "You what?"

Belinda shrugged. "You see, I never really believed that the first two episodes were blueprints for those murders. I thought it was at best a stretch, that the police and FBI had just latched onto them because they were close to actual crimes that they couldn't solve. Listen, my role in this show is a good one. It's a solid stepping-stone for me. With the show canceled nobody's going to see me, which means I'm going to have trouble getting another good part. Of course, you, Sherlock, knew I lied to Detective Flynn and Inspector Delion this morning when I told them that I'd taken sleeping pills before the show started and simply fell asleep even before the show was over."

"Yeah," Sherlock said. "They were very angry at you. I think Detective Flynn came this close"—she pinched her fingers nearly together—"to arresting you for malicious mischief. So what you're saying now is that you—just like that fool Norman Lido at channel eight—wanted to see what would happen."

"I wanted people to see me, to see what a good actress I am, to realize that they want to see more of me, not that meathead Joe Kleypas, who's always rubbing his fingers over his stomach so women will notice his abs. You know, the more I think of it, the more I think it was Joe who sent episode three to channel eight. He's hungry. He knew, just like I did, that *The Consultant* is a winner. He even laid off the booze he was so hyped about the role. Then all this happened. It isn't fair."

She toed the water, shrugged, but didn't look at them. "I'm really sorry if more people die, but who knows, maybe they would anyway."

"Don't even try to excuse what you did," Sherlock said. "It was a really low thing to do." She got up from her lounge chair, walked to Belinda at the side of the pool, looked her in the eye, and said, "I am personally very disappointed in you, Belinda." Sherlock shoved her into the water, and walked to the others, not looking back.

She heard a sputtering cough behind her, then, oddly, laughter. "Good shot, Sherlock," Belinda yelled out.

Sherlock still didn't turn around to look at her. She said, "I think it's time we went to Bear Lake. Weldon told them he wouldn't be at the nursing home until late afternoon."

Dane said, "Detective Flynn's got the place covered and Gil Rainy is there with a half dozen agents. If he shows early, they'll get him."

"I still want to go," Nick said. "I want to finally see Weldon De-Loach." She turned to Savich. "He really is over forty. Isn't that interesting? Why would he lie about his age?"

"Who knows?" Savich said. "Maybe ten years ago he thought it was necessary. Hollywood is a town for young people, after all."

"Maybe," Dane said. "But he may have had another reason to lie. I really want to look him right in the face and ask him."

Sherlock looked over her shoulder one last time at Belinda Gates, treading water in the deep end of the pool, her white cover-up ballooning around her. Sherlock called out, "I was going to show you another photo of Sean at his grandmother's swimming pool. Dillon is holding him and he's in a swimsuit, too, and you just don't know who's cuter. But I'm not going to show it to you now, Belinda."

Belinda just kept treading water. She laughed again.

TWENTY-SEVEN

It was another beautiful day at Bear Lake. There was no more snow on the ground, and the air was winter-clear and smog-free. The calm water sparkled under the late afternoon sunlight. It had taken them just a little over an hour and a half to drive I-5.

"Not bad time," Dane said. "Considering."

"Considering what?" Sherlock said.

"Considering that it's LA and there are more cars per square foot here than any place in the country," Dane said. "You wouldn't believe some of the stories Michael used to tell me when he was just out of the seminary, living in a parish in East LA. I'll never forget how he'd say that—" Dane's voice fell off. His jaw tightened and he seamed his mouth together. Control, Nick thought, looking at him, keeping control was very important to him.

Savich said easily, "Gil Rainy was telling Sherlock and me that sometimes it takes him a good hour just to commute into the field office, and he only lives four miles away. Of course, Washington, D.C., ain't no picnic either, is it, Dane?"

Dane just nodded, not ready to speak yet.

"How about where you're from, Nick? Bad traffic?"

"No," Nick said. "Not bad at all."

"And you're Dr. Nick, a Ph.D. in medieval history. Do you teach college?"

Nick said, "Yes, I do."

"Ah. I thought college campuses were usually all jammed up with all sorts of gnarly traffic," Sherlock said.

"I guess it depends on the campus," Nick said, then turned to look out the window. Dane saw that her hands were stiffly clasped in her lap.

They parked in the small lot and walked to the entrance of the Lakeview Home for Retired Police Officers, founded in 1964.

They were met by Delion, Flynn, and Gil Rainy, all wearing buttoned-up sport coats but still looking a bit chilly.

Flynn said, "No sign of him. Gil's got two agents posted out of sight at the turnoff. They'll call when he shows so we can be ready."

Dane said, "Anyone speak to Captain DeLoach?"

"No," Gil said. "A heavy woman with a mustache named Velvet Weaver said that Nurse Carla told her that he wasn't with it today, he was just sitting in his chair drumming his fingers on the wheels, humming to himself."

"I'd like to see him," Dane said.

"Go," said Savich.

As Dane and Nick walked down the long corridor, they heard laughter, lots of it. The laughter was coming from old voices, and sounded wonderful. They paused at the doorway to a big recreation room where there were several televisions, a quality Brunswick pool table, card tables, and a small library section with bookshelves loaded with paperbacks.

There was a pool competition under way, and half a dozen people were seated around, taking sides, cheering or booing. Mainly they seemed to be laughing because both players—an elderly woman in a loose-fitting loud print dress, and an old codger in gray flannel slacks and a Harry Potter T-shirt, high-tops on his feet—were dead serious about the game, only they weren't very good. Dane smiled and said to Nick, "You think maybe we'll want to come here someday?"

"I don't know. I don't play pool all that well."

They walked past the rec room and down another fifteen yards to Captain DeLoach's room.

She hadn't laughed much in the past month, she thought.

The door was closed. Dane tapped lightly and called out, "Captain DeLoach?"

There was no answer from inside.

Dane called out more loudly, "Captain DeLoach? It's Agent Dane Carver here to speak to you again."

Dane opened the door, careful to keep Nick behind him, which was really stupid, she thought, what with his left arm in a sling.

The room was empty.

Dane breathed out real slow. "Right. Let's go see if he's one of the cheerleaders back in the rec room."

They found Captain DeLoach literally holding the eight ball, the old guy in the Harry Potter T-shirt trying to get it away from him.

Captain DeLoach was yelling, "Come on, Mortie, you lost to Daisy. She beat you fair and square. You can't throw the eight ball at her or I'll have to arrest you!"

"She deserves to eat it," an old woman yelled, and thumped her cane on the floor.

Dane realized then that at least a third of the old people were women. They were retired police officers? He didn't think things were so enlightened in law enforcement forty years ago.

Mortie wasn't happy, but he fell back, obviously still fuming. At that moment, Captain DeLoach tossed him the black eight ball, laughed, and said, "Make her eat it if you want to."

"Just let him try it," Daisy yelled, shaking her fist at Mortie.

"Excellent," Dane said. "Carla was wrong. Captain DeLoach isn't out to lunch. Looks like he's with us today, thank God."

In another minute, they had Captain DeLoach off to the side.

"Do you remember me, sir?"

Captain DeLoach looked Dane up and down, stared at his left arm in its blue sling, then very slowly raised his arm and saluted him.

Dane saluted back. He smiled at the old man.

"I've got a gun," Captain DeLoach said.

"Do you?"

"Yes, Special Agent, I do." His voice dropped to a whisper. "Don't want anyone to know, might scare 'em. I bribed Velvet to buy it for me. I told her no one could prove that I wasn't attacked, and as a senior law enforcement officer I should be armed. It's even registered in her name. It's a twenty-five-caliber Beretta. Eight rounds in the clip and one in the chamber. All I have to do is pull back the hammer and I can kill anyone in the blink of an eye." He pulled his hand from his pocket and in his arthritic old palm was the elegant small black automatic pistol.

"How long have you had the gun, sir?"

"Velvet got it for me yesterday. I didn't want my son coming back to try to kill me again."

"We heard that he called yesterday, said he was coming to see you in just a little while. We want to meet Weldon. Why don't you let me deal with him, Captain? I doubt you'll have to shoot him."

"Will you shoot the little cocksucker for me then?"

"Maybe," Dane said. "Just maybe I will. Why is it that he wants to kill you, sir?"

The old man just shook his head, stared down at his arthritic fingers.

"Captain DeLoach," Nick said, "how old is your son?"

Captain DeLoach looked over at the pool match, then down at his hands and said finally, looking up at Dane, "He's so young he's barely on this earth, but the thing is, Special Agent, he just won't stop trying to keep me quiet. It pisses me off, you know?"

Captain DeLoach looked toward Daisy, who was cheering because she'd just made the three ball in the corner pocket. "They've started another game. Old Mortie doesn't have a chance. Do you know that he was once a police commissioner in Stockton? Daisy was married forty years to a desk sergeant from Seattle who died the day after their anniversary, fell over with a massive heart attack. She's got spunk." He thought a moment, then said, "You know, if Daisy weren't so old, I just might be interested."

"Yeah, you're right, sir," Dane said. "I'd guess she's all of seventy-five."

"More like seventy-seven," Captain DeLoach said. He slipped the small Beretta into the pocket of his jacket. He was wearing the sports jacket over his blue pajama tops. "I'll bet she was hot when she was younger."

"Maybe so," Dane said, and thought of his own grandmother, who'd died some years before.

Suddenly, Captain DeLoach said in a soft, singsong voice, "I can feel him. He's near now. Yes, very close and coming closer. I always could tell when he was near. Isn't that interesting?"

"Your son Weldon, Captain DeLoach, when exactly was he born? What year?"

"The year of the rat, yes, that was it. I really got a good laugh out of that. A rat." The old man threw back his head and laughed out loud. The pool match stopped. Slowly, all the old folks began turning to look at Captain DeLoach laughing his head off. "Or maybe," he said finally, wheezing deep in his chest, "it was the horse, yes, that was it. The year of the horse."

Daisy called out, "Hey, tell us the joke."

Captain DeLoach's head fell forward and he gave a soft snore.

Dane started to shake the old man, then drew back his hand. "I should take that gun," he said to Nick. "I really should."

"I'll bet you that Velvet would just buy him another one."

Dane nodded. "You're right. Let's go wait with Sherlock and Savich."

An hour later there was still no sign of Weldon DeLoach. Everyone stayed at their stations until it was dark. Then Detective Flynn and Gil Rainy called everyone in.

Sherlock said, "All a hoax. A distraction, to get us all focused on Captain DeLoach and away from him."

Gil Rainy said, "You feeling okay, Dane? You look better today than you did yesterday."

Dane just nodded. "Arm feels better. All I am is depressed. Captain DeLoach seemed fine, then he was laughing so hard I thought he'd choke on his own breath, then he was just gone, asleep, making light little snores like women make."

"I don't snore," Nick said. "You've slept close enough to me to know I don't snore."

Everyone turned to stare at her.

"Bite me," Nick said to everyone in general, and stalked off to the Taurus.

THE phone rang in Dane's Holiday Inn room at ten o'clock that night.

"Yeah?"

"Dane, Savich here. Captain DeLoach—no, don't worry, he isn't dead, but he fired a gun at someone. Maybe it was Weldon, but nobody knows. When the staff got into Captain DeLoach's room, he was on the floor, unconscious, the gun beside him, and there was a big hole in the wall just behind that small sofa. The glass sliding doors weren't locked but they usually aren't, so that doesn't necessarily mean anything."

"Is Captain DeLoach going to make it?" Dane asked.

"I think so," Savich said. "I couldn't get exact information about his condition, only just what I told you. The people there are on top of it. We'll go out there tomorrow."

"What about the two cops Detective Flynn had out there covering Captain DeLoach's room?"

"They didn't see a thing. Didn't hear a thing until the shot."

Dane cursed again, real low so Savich wouldn't hear him. "He's our only lead, Savich."

"Maybe not. Now, get a good night's sleep. Sherlock says to tell you that tomorrow you'll be ready to rock and roll again."

Dane grunted into his cell phone, laid it on the bedside table, looked over at Nick, and told her what had happened.

"I've decided," Nick said slowly as she handed Dane two pills and a glass of water, "that Weldon DeLoach doesn't exist. Maybe he's just a name Hollywood made up, someone they've all created for us like some huge Hollywood production, an epic that pits reality against art, and reality loses. You know, lots of money, all big stars, lots of hoopla, a cast of thousands, murder and mayhem."

"You know," he said once he'd swallowed the pills, "that's something to think about."

"No," she said, "it isn't. I'm just talking, all blah, blah. I guess I'm just really tired, Dane."

She turned off the overhead light in his room and went through the adjoining door into her own.

TWENTY-EIGHT

Bear Lake

"The doctor told me it wasn't an accident," Mr. Latterley said, looking distressed. His bald pointed head, Nick saw, was shiny with sweat. It was obvious he'd never had to deal with anything like this before.

"Evidently Captain DeLoach was struck just above his left temple. The doctor said that the wound wasn't consistent with his simply falling out of his chair. I've reported this to our local police and they've been interviewing everyone, but so far, we have very little. Every time they try to interview Captain DeLoach, he starts cackling like he's some old crackpot, shouts that he'll win and surprise everybody, but that's it. Over and over, that's all he says. I don't think he wants to talk to them. He won't give them the time of day."

Dane said, "We'll have two round-the-clock guards on him now."

"That's good. This is all very disturbing, Agent Carver. Violence at Lakeview. Not at all good for business." He shook his head. "And your suspect is his own son. I must say, Weldon DeLoach has always appeared to be a very nice man. Every time I have spoken to him, he's been solicitous of his father, very caring, always paid any and all charges on time. I've e-mailed him and spoken to him on the phone countless times over the years."

Dane handed Mr. Latterley a photo. "Is this Weldon DeLoach?"

Mr. Latterley looked down at the grainy black-and-white photo that they'd had shot off the VCR reel. He didn't say anything for a very long time. Finally, he raised his head, and he was frowning. "That's Weldon. Bad photo, but yes, Agent Carver. You know, it's entirely possible that it wasn't Weldon who was here today. In fact, I simply can't accept that it could have been him. He takes too good care of his father to want to hurt him."

"All right. If not Weldon, have you any idea who else it could be?" Dane asked.

Mr. Latterley reluctantly shook his head. "No, no one else visits him, at least I've never seen anyone else. We do have security here, but I suppose some criminal from Captain DeLoach's past could have gotten in."

"It would have to be a criminal with a very long memory," Dane said. He rose. "I want to speak to Daisy."

They found Daisy in the rec room, this time reading a very old *Time* magazine, chortling about Monica's semen-stained blue dress and how the president was dancing around that blow. "A hoot, that's what it was," Daisy said. "He wanted history to judge him as a great president"— she laughed some more—"now he'll be known as the moron who couldn't keep his pants zipped."

Daisy was wearing a different loose housedress today, sandals, her toenails painted a bright coral that matched her lipstick.

"I'm Special Agent Dane Carver and this is Ms. Jones." Dane showed her his FBI shield.

"I remember you two. You were here yesterday. I'm Daisy Griffith," she said, and grinned up at the two of them, a full complement of white teeth in her mouth. Nick believed they were hers. "Now, you're here because of poor old Ellison. Knocked himself out again, didn't he? Never did have a good sense of balance, did Elly. Always hurling himself about in that chair of his whenever he gets excited. Of course, he's old as dirt—hmmm, maybe even older." Daisy paused a moment, tapped her fingertips on a photo of Clinton shaking his finger at the media, and said, "I heard some of the nurses talking; they claimed it wasn't an accident, that his son tried to knock him off. Is that true?"

"We don't know," Dane said. "Have you ever met Weldon DeLoach?"

"Oh yes, nice boy. Polite and attentive, not just to Elly, but to all of us." She paused a moment, sighed. "Elly talks about him a lot, says he's real talented, with lots of imagination, a good writer. He's a Hollywood type, you know."

"Yes, we know. Did Captain DeLoach ever speak to you about his son, other than what he did for a living?"

"Well, sure. Elly said he was just too old when Weldon was born, that Weldon had been a big accident. The boy had needed a younger man to raise him, and then his mother up and died on the two of them. Here he was, an older cop, and he had a little kid to raise.

"Just last week I think it was, he said his boy hadn't turned out the way he would have liked, but what could he do? He said he was tempted, particularly now, to let everyone know what the real truth was. He said it would scare the hell out of me. I asked him what he meant by that, and he just threatened to throw a billiard ball at me. Mortie thought that was real funny, the old buzzard."

The old buzzard, Mortie, was scratching his forearms incessantly. He said, yes, of course he'd spoken to Weldon over the years. "Oh sure, Elly talked about him sometimes, but I got the idea there was no love lost between the two of them. Did you know that Elly used to be a wicked pool player? Then his hands started shaking and the arthritis got him." Mortie shook his head and scratched his forearms again.

"Would you like a pool cue, sir?" Nick asked. She chalked a cue and then handed it to Mortie. Mortie grinned and walked over to the pool table. He was hitting balls at a fine clip when Dane and Nick left the rec room.

"I thought it might keep him from scratching himself for a while," Nick said. "What do we do now?"

"Onward to Nurse Carla."

They found her at the nurses' station, scanning a chart, whistling "Silent Night." "Oh, yes," she said, "all the staff know and like Weldon. He's a very good son—considerate, kind, always visits his father. To think that he'd strike his father—nope, I just can't believe that. It had to be an intruder."

"What does Weldon look like?" Dane asked.

Carla Bender thought for a moment. "He's real blond, practically white-haired, and he's pale—like he doesn't go outside enough. I joked with him about it once and he just laughed, said his skin was real sensitive and he didn't want to get skin cancer. You know, Agent Carver, anything his father needed, Weldon always okayed it without hesitation. Good son. I just won't believe that he struck his own father down."

"I don't think so either," Velvet Weaver said as she came out of a bathroom down the hall. "Weldon's really nice, soft-spoken, and I've never seen him as being remotely capable of any violence. And what could the old man possibly do to him to make him go into a rage and strike him?"

Dane showed her Weldon's photo.

"Yep, that's Weldon."

Nurse Carla agreed.

They spoke to orderlies, to two janitors, to a group of gardeners. Everyone knew Weldon DeLoach, but no one had seen him anywhere around the time his father was struck.

"I really wish that just one person had seen Weldon," Dane said as he steered Nick back to their new rental car, a Pontiac compact. "Within a mile of this place, that would be close enough." He sighed.

"If it was Weldon, he was super careful. Or he was wearing a disguise, like the one he just might have worn in San Francisco."

Dane didn't say anything, just drove toward LA, ideas flying about in his brain, none of them leading anywhere except fantasy land. He kept his eye out for Harleys.

NICK finally fell asleep a little before midnight and was promptly hurtled back to that night in Chicago when the dark sedan had tried to run her down. Her dreams skipped to the man she'd seen leaving her condominium, the man who'd set the fire. Then, suddenly, she was staring at the man on the Harley, firing nonstop at them.

Oh God, oh God. She gasped and bolted straight up in bed, panting. It all came together. She realized suddenly that all three were the same man.

All three times, the man was out to kill her, not because she was an eyewitness to Father Michael Joseph's murder, but because the man was sent from Senator Rothman, who wanted her dead. Odd how it had all come together in a nightmare, but she was completely certain of this.

She quietly got out of bed. She pulled off her nightgown. She put on her clothes, her shoes. She looked at the adjoining door, drew in a deep breath, and quietly turned the knob.

She heard Dane breathing evenly in sleep. She didn't think she breathed at all as she stole over to the bureau and took Dane's car keys out of his jacket pocket. She saw his wallet on the bureau and took a credit card. And finally, his SIG Sauer, and an extra clip. She looked back toward him. He was still sleeping.

She looked back at him one last time, then quietly closed the adjoining door again. He'd already been shot trying to protect her. She simply couldn't bear the thought of him dying—like his brother—a senseless, vicious death. She simply wouldn't put him in harm's way. She was a target and, as long as she was with him, so was he, for the simple fact that she knew to her soul that if she were threatened, he would give his life for her.

There was simply no way she could bear that. No way at all. Besides, she had a plan. If it failed, she could disappear again. She slipped out the door, quietly closing it behind her.

It was Savich, in a room three doors away, on the edge of sleep, who heard a car's engine rev not far from their rooms. He was out of bed and standing naked in the Holiday Inn doorway, watching Dane's rental car disappear out of the parking lot.

TWENTY-NINE

Sherlock sighed. "Does she have any money?"

"She can't have much," Dane said. "And that means that she'll hitchhike. Oh damn, I take that all back. Nick's not an idiot. Let me check." He ran back into his room. After a couple of seconds he called out, "Does anyone have any handcuffs?"

"Not on me," Savich said.

Dane was back in a moment, breathing hard. "When I catch up with her, I'm not going to rely on reason anymore. It's time for brute force. Remind me to get some handcuffs from Detective Flynn. Here's the deal. She didn't just steal the car keys, she also has my AmEx and my SIG Sauer." He stopped, looked momentarily baffled. "Why did she sneak out? Nothing's really changed. Why?"

Within ten minutes, Detective Flynn had an APB out on the Pontiac, driven by a young woman with shoulder-length blondish-brown hair, gray eyes, weight around one fifteen. Well, not just gray eyes, Dane thought, they were pure gray and large, with dark lashes. But she was thin, still too thin, although she looked better than she had when he'd first met her. Good God, it was just last Tuesday. And she was wearing a pair of dark brown slacks and a light brown sweater, he'd checked. Purse? Her purse was black leather, just like her short boots. Size seven and a half, yes, that was her exact shoe size. It was important to be accurate for the APB, and so he mentioned that her eyebrows were a dark brown, nicely arched. Jesus, he was losing it. She was about five-foot-eight-inches tall—well, maybe taller because she came nearly to Dane's nose. Every officer in the LA area was alerted, in great detail.

She'd taken all her clothes—all the clothes he'd bought her. He discovered very quickly that he'd never been so scared in his life. She was out there alone and she didn't have any idea how to protect herself. She had his car and she had his gun. She wasn't helpless, thank God. He was going to tie her down when he found her and not let her up unless they were handcuffed together.

His healing arm itched. When his cell phone rang ten minutes later, he nearly fell over in his haste to get it.

NICK left the Pontiac three miles from the Holiday Inn, in the middle of a long row of cars parked in front of an apartment complex. She locked it and left the keys on top of the front driver's-side tire. Obvious place, but given Dane's resources, the chances were that the police would retrieve the car before a thief decided he was hard up enough to steal it.

His SIG Sauer felt heavy in her purse. She'd checked the clip. There was a full fifteen rounds in it. Other than that, she had twelve dollars and Dane's AmEx. She didn't quite feel like Rambo, but it was close enough.

It wouldn't be dawn for several more hours. No one had followed her from the Holiday Inn. It was dark and she was armed. With each passing minute there was more distance between her and both the bad guys and the good guys.

She saw some kids in baggy pants on the corner of Pickett and Longsworth. They were probably dealing drugs. She didn't even pause, just turned quickly and walked to the east. The freeway wasn't more than a mile away and she'd flag down an eighteen-wheeler. She'd gotten to San Francisco riding high above the ground in big trucks and keeping company with at least a half dozen truck drivers. She'd even learned how to operate a CB.

If she ran into a nut this time, she had the SIG Sauer. She flagged down a really big Foster Farms truck heading up I-5. A beefy guy named Tommy stopped because, he told her, he had to make it to Bakersfield, and he'd been driving without a stop for too long and was dead on his feet. Would she mind singing and talking to him until he let her out? She didn't mind at all.

He got her as far as Ventura County. "Hey," he said, "I think we sing a pretty mean 'Impossible Dream.'"

An hour later, a smaller supply truck loaded with linens and bathroom supplies for one of the big ski lodges picked her up and began the climb to Mt. Pinos.

It was cold in the Los Padres National Forest, but down at Bear

Lake elevation there wasn't much snow on the ground, just a white veil, and the air was clear, as it had been yesterday.

The driver dropped her off in front of Snow House, a small lodge where she could wait until the stores opened. She wasn't about to take a room. She knew they'd be tracking the card, would realize soon enough where she was.

Things had to happen soon or Dane would get to her. She sucked in a nice deep breath and walked into Snow House.

Her husband was driving up from LA a bit later, she told the desk clerk, and was meeting her here. This was where they'd spent their honeymoon and they wanted to come back. She was just here first. No, she didn't want to check in just yet. She'd wait in the lobby area, near that roaring fire. They didn't seem at all suspicious.

When the stores opened, she smiled toward the clerk behind the counter and walked out. She visited a small boutique, bought a cheap parka and gloves, and went to a general store at a filling station.

An hour later, she hiked to the Lakeview Home for Retired Police Officers.

She began to wonder if her great plan was going to lead to anything. She had to try it. She believed that Captain DeLoach had more answers than he'd given to them before. Now she was alone, and she knew she could get him to talk.

At least she prayed she'd get the old man to talk.

She walked straight to Captain DeLoach's double-paned sliding doors, and tapped on the glass. No answer.

She tried the door. It was locked.

She tapped harder on the glass and jumped when she heard a querulous old voice mutter, "Who the hell wants in now? That you, Weldon? You want to finish the job on me, you little bastard?"

The curtains were jerked back and she was face-to-face with Captain DeLoach. He looked pale, sported a small white bandage around his head, but his old eyes were clear and focused.

He stared at her a moment, nodded to himself, and unlocked the doors. She watched him wheel his chair back before she opened the door and eased in. She relocked the door and drew the curtains.

She said, "I shouldn't be here, Captain DeLoach, but I think you're where all the action is, so consider me your bodyguard."

"You're a lot prettier than that idiot I kicked out of here last night.

Overweight dolt, all he wanted to do was eat Carla's doughnuts and she was getting pissed, which means that she'd carp at me. Did you see any of the cops they put around to protect me?"

"Not a soul, but I was really careful."

"Yeah, yeah, I bet they're all asleep. Hey, I recognize you. You're an FBI agent, aren't you? The gal with Agent Carver?"

"Yes, that's right, I was with Agent Carver. I'm here to protect you. You don't need those other cops. But you've got to keep my presence here quiet, okay?"

The old man ruminated on this for a good five seconds and then slowly nodded. "I haven't had a girl around me without a needle in her hand in more years than I can remember."

"Do you remember back for a lot of years?"

"Yep. Do I salute you?"

"Yes," Nick said. Slowly, the old man saluted her and she saluted him back. She said, "Tell me about some of those years you remember, Captain."

Captain DeLoach paused again, then said in a dreamy voice, more singsong than not, "You know, young lady, some of those years are so clear in my head that it's like yesterday. I can feel what I felt then, the exhilaration, the excitement. I can see their faces as they were then, hear the yells, the screams, feel them score into me, deep, taste them, you know? I can feel all the joy and triumph, the pure sweetness of winning, and I loved that, you know?"

"No, sir, I don't know what it is you're talking about."

He gave her the sweetest smile. "So many people I knew, liked, but now they're mostly dead. All except me and mine, of course. Yep, just look who's left. That's a shame, isn't it?"

"Yes, sir, it's a real shame. Why do you call Weldon a little bastard?"

"I remember it was like yesterday that he was just a little tyke, couldn't even walk yet, and he was into everything. I was alone. What did I know about how to raise a baby?"

"I imagine it was very difficult, sir. What about Weldon?"

No answer this time. His head just fell forward. He seemed to be asleep. From one moment to the next, he was simply gone, someplace in the distant past when he'd known happiness. Poor old man. She wondered how it would feel to have your own son trying to kill you.

She didn't know what Captain DeLoach had meant with all that talk about the yells and screams. It made no sense.

She straightened, looked around the large room. It was nice and warm in there. She shrugged out of her parka, walked around a bit, getting acquainted with everything. It was like a junior suite in a hotel, only it was personalized with some photos on the end table—none of Weldon, but she and Dane had already remarked on that. Maybe she'd ask Captain DeLoach if he had any pictures of his only son stashed somewhere. Beside his bed were a few more photos—of a baby, and then that baby as a toddler. Weldon? She didn't know. But wait—that couldn't be. There was a car in the background, and the car wasn't forty years old. It was around the mid-1980s. Okay, so it wasn't Weldon. Another family member had a little kid, that had to be it.

Nick turned away from the photo, realized that Nurse Carla or anyone who worked there, for God's sake, could come tromping through the door. Where could she hide?

There was a big walk-in closet six feet from the double bed. The wood doors were slatted so she could see Captain DeLoach clearly. She spread her parka on the carpeted floor and made herself comfortable.

She'd bought taco dip, a small box of Wheat Thins, and a Diet Dr Pepper—her favorites—in the small food market inside the filling station, using up four dollars and eight cents of her twelve dollars. Before she fell asleep, her stomach happy, she wondered how long it would take Dane to track her down.

AT ten o'clock in the morning, Delion, Savich, Sherlock, and Dane were seated around Detective Flynn's desk in the detectives' room on the second floor of the West Los Angeles Police Department. Linda, today's volunteer receptionist, had given them all homemade cookies when they'd come in. "I've always admired the FBI," she'd said, patting Savich's biceps. "And you're so nice, too."

Sherlock had said, "What about me, Linda?"

"I think of you as their mascot, cute as a button with that red hair flying all over the place. As for you," she said to Dane, "you look a bit on the edge. The cookie will help get things in perspective, sugar always does."

"Thank you, Linda," Dane said. "That's what we've been hearing about sugar."

The detectives' room was, as usual, a madhouse, which didn't appear to bother anyone. Savich settled down in a side chair next to Detective Flynn's desk, MAX on his lap. He looked up after ten minutes and said, "No indication that she's used the AmEx yet, either that, or folks are just too lazy to check. Since the card's in your name, Dane, and not hers, I can't imagine anyone not checking. We just wait, nothing else to do."

Sherlock said, "You know the deal you made with her not to delve into her past? Well, we've got to find her and protect her, we've got to find out who she is. The time has come. Dillon, can you have MAX find out who she is?"

"Yes," Savich said. "We know her name's Nicola, she's twenty-eight, she's got a Ph.D., and she's a college professor. This won't be anything for MAX. Everyone on board with this?"

Delion said, "Do it. Now isn't the time for irrelevant promises."

"Yeah," Dane said. "That's what I figured."

While Savich worked, Detective Flynn was sitting back in his chair, his hands laced over his belly, a basketball on the floor beside him. He said, "I just don't understand why she took off like this. She's pulling us away from the really important stuff—you know, multiple murders, silly things like that. I'd like to get in her face when we catch up with her."

Sherlock said, "Do you think she headed back up to San Francisco? To hide herself in the homeless population again?"

Dane shook his head. "No. And I don't think she's gone back home either, wherever home is."

"Then where did she go?" Flynn asked, sipped at the god-awful coffee. His phone rang. He picked it up, barked, "Yeah? Detective Flynn here."

He wrote something on a pad. When he set the receiver back into its cradle, he was grinning. "How's this for a bit of luck? Our girl hitched a ride with a trucker. He said he always listens to the police reports on his CB. Said when he heard the APB, he knew he'd given our girl a ride."

"Where?" Sherlock said.

"Up in Ventura County."

"Hot damn," Dane said. "She's gone to see Captain DeLoach."

"But why did she just run away like that?" Flynn asked.

"I'll be sure to ask her after I handcuff her," Dane said.

"I'll provide the handcuffs," Delion said.

"I'm still gonna burn her ass," Flynn said.

MAX chose that moment to beep. Savich looked down, smiled. "MAX just told me who she is."

Savich closed down MAX, rose, and stretched. "We can be at Bear Lake by midafternoon."

THIRTY

One moment there was only the sound of Captain DeLoach's soft snoring. The next there was a man's voice, speaking quietly, right there, right next to Captain DeLoach's wheelchair.

"Wake up, old man. Come on now, you can do it. It's Weldon, and I'm here to make sure that it's over, at least for you. Wake up, you old monster, wake up. I'm going to mete out the only justice you'll ever get in this world, and I want you awake for this."

Captain DeLoach jerked awake, snorted, looked up, and whispered, "Weldon, how did you get in here? There's cops out there protecting me, lots of them. And the Feds, they're everywhere looking for you. You'd better run while you've got the chance. How did you come in through the sliding doors? I always keep them locked."

"You old fool, I have a key to the sliding doors. Not a soul saw me, for sure not that one cop chatting up Velvet in the reception area. And the other one who's supposed to be protecting you—I saw him out in the parking lot smoking a cigarette. There's just the two of them, old man.

"It's finally time for you. For more than thirty years you've thumbed your nose at everybody. Now it stops. No more time for any big announcements to anyone else from you. It's simple justice, you know it."

"You think you can manage it this time when you didn't the last two times, you little wimp?"

"I was trying to scare you, not kill you, you monster. I didn't think I'd have to kill you then. Is your brain so far gone you can't remember that?

"But this time, I am going to kill you. All your threats to tell the world what you are will die with you. After that fall you took—I really hoped you'd die, but you're still tough, aren't you? Why didn't you make your big announcement?"

Captain DeLoach said, grinning widely, "Of course I'm tough, but no one could tell that by looking at you, you little pussy. I didn't say anything because I wanted to torture you more, boy. Make you wonder, worry when the blow was going to fall. Threatening your daddy, trying to scare him—nearly to death—that's not a nice thing, you know. And you left me there, lying on the floor, my head all bloody."

"Shut up. No more abuse from you, old man, no more."

"I'm still your only daddy, you puking coward. Jesus, I can't believe that you're actually part of me, although your mother was weak, always whining, just like you. And then she died, and it was just you and me, but you weren't strong, you weren't a man, you were just like her. And then you just up and left after high school, believed you'd escaped me. Well, I was sick of you, I wanted you out of there.

"But I kept tabs on you, boy. After all, you were the only one who knew. I wanted to make sure you wouldn't ever tell anyone. And now you want to kill your own daddy."

"Quiet! Just shut up, damn you. No more threats, no more lies. I'm going to send you to hell, where you belong."

Weldon paused a moment, then said, "What I really can't believe is just how long you've lasted." He reached into his pocket.

Nick said, "No, Weldon, you're not going to do anything to your father. Step away from him."

Weldon DeLoach jerked up, appalled and surprised as he looked into the muzzle of the SIG Sauer, held in the hand of that homeless woman he'd seen on TV. What the hell was she doing here? He straightened slowly, took a step back.

The old man laughed, rubbed his arthritic hands together. "She's my own personal bodyguard, Weldon. You thought there was only two cops. Not a chance. She's here, staying right in my room. What do you think about them apples? She sharp, or what? Salute her, Weldon, she's with the Federal Bureau of Investigation. She's a special agent."

Weldon kicked at his father's wheelchair, missed, and yelled, "You moron, she's not a cop. She's a homeless woman who just happened to see things that would make her a real danger to the murderer."

"What shouldn't she have seen, Weldon?"

"The murderer just after he killed the priest in San Francisco."

"Hey, does she think it's you?"

Weldon was still blond today, deeply tanned, his eyes a pale blue. Nick wasn't at all good with guessing people's age, but if she had to, she'd say he was easily in his forties. Was it makeup? Contacts? Or was this the way he really looked? Nick simply didn't know if he was the man she'd seen in the church. Maybe disguised, but she knew she'd be useless in court. She held the gun steady, knew she had to get him down to the floor, get him tied up so she could breathe again, so she could think, get help. She was scared, almost as scared as she'd been when she had faced John Rothman.

Still, she had to try. She said, "To be real accurate, Weldon, yes, I saw you." She continued, now looking back at the old man, "Sir, I saw Weldon in a church just after he'd murdered Father Michael Joseph. And he's killed other people as well. He wrote TV scripts, then copied them in real life. I'm sorry, but he is a very evil man."

Captain DeLoach said, "Hey, you really mean that? Nah, that doesn't make any sense. Weldon's a pussy. No spine in that back of his, just mush. You really a homeless woman? Fancy that. I won't have to pay you, will I? You don't expect anything because you're not an officer, right?"

"Right, this is for free," Nick said, not looking at the grinning old man, who really did sound pleased as punch.

"You said Weldon is a murderer? He's really a criminal?"

The old man laughed. "Listen to me, girl, you're all wrong about this. Weldon couldn't kill a roach if it crawled over his bare feet and started gnawing on his toe. He's a coward."

"Sir, please be quiet." She adjusted her aim with the SIG just a bit and said to Weldon, "I want you to lie on your stomach on the floor. Now." It was aimed right at his chest.

"No," he said. "I can't. I haven't killed anyone. Don't you see? It's this filthy old man who's the monster. You can't believe the havoc he's wrought. This is justice, dammit."

"What are you talking about?"

Captain DeLoach laughed. "Yeah, tell her, Weldon. Tell her why you want to murder your dear old dad."

"No, she doesn't need to know. Listen, I've got no bloody choice. Believe me, sister, this crazy old man richly deserves it."

"Why does he deserve to die?"

Captain DeLoach started laughing again, spittle pooling in the corners of his mouth, flecked with blood.

Nick said, "Come on, Weldon, what on earth are you talking about?"

In that moment, Weldon grabbed the arms of Captain DeLoach's wheelchair and shoved hard. Nick had only an instant. As the chair rammed into her, she fired. The shot went wide, shattering the TV screen. Captain DeLoach's arm flew up to gain balance, and he struck her wrist. The SIG flew out of her hand and skidded across the floor to land just beneath Captain DeLoach's bed.

Nick froze, expecting Weldon to pull out his own gun and shoot both of them. There'd already been one shot, why not more? But he didn't have much time. Nursing home staff would burst in there in just a couple of seconds. She had to protect the old man. She raced around in front of Captain DeLoach's wheelchair.

But Weldon didn't try to shove her aside, didn't draw a gun to kill her. He just ran out through the glass doors, yelling back at her, "You've made the worst mistake you'll ever make in your life!"

Seconds later, Nurse Carla, a cop behind her, burst in to see Nick Jones racing out the glass sliding doors, a gun in her hand.

Captain DeLoach was sitting in his chair. He was smiling, looked happy as a clam, singing "Eleanor Rigby."

Nick saw Weldon racing toward a small black car, Japanese, she thought, maybe a Toyota, but she couldn't be sure. Where was that cop who was supposedly out here smoking a cigarette? She didn't see anyone. She yelled, "Stop, Weldon! Or I'll shoot, I mean it!"

But he didn't. Nick raised the gun, then realized she didn't need to fire at him. She aimed at the tires of the black car just as he flung open the driver's-side door and threw himself in.

She fired, hitting both back tires just as he gunned the engine and roared out of the parking spot, rubber and smoke spewing out of the tires. Soon he'd be driving on the rims and that wouldn't last long.

Weldon was keeping his head down, afraid she'd shoot him. She saw the instant he knew she'd hit his tires. The car swerved madly to the left. As the rubber was finally stripped away, the god-awful screeching of steel against concrete filled the air.

Nick kept firing until she'd shot ten of the fifteen rounds in the SIG.

She stopped, to save the remaining bullets. She'd hit the two back tires; that had to at least slow him. She started running. She wanted more than anything to pull him out of that car.

The car swerved wildly from side to side. The tires were smoking, grinding, the steel beneath raw on the concrete, tearing it up. The stench of burning rubber filled her nostrils.

She watched him suddenly jerk the car to the right and head it directly into the pine woods that began about forty yards from the east side of the rest home. He crashed it into a pine tree. Smoke billowed up, black and thick, and then it was quiet.

She saw him dragging winter clothes out of the car and running into the woods.

"Stop!"

Nick headed after him, the SIG still in her right hand. She realized then she wasn't wearing warm clothes. She'd run out of Captain De-Loach's room with nothing but her V-necked red sweater over a white blouse, jeans, and boots.

She didn't care. She wasn't going to fail now, she couldn't. This madness had to stop and she was the only one there who could stop it. She heard him crashing through the undergrowth ahead of her. How far? Twenty feet?

She saw Father Michael Joseph's face in her mind's eye, a beautiful face, open, rich with intelligence and humor. He was laughing at something he'd just told her about King Edward. And now, because of Weldon DeLoach, no one would ever see that smile again or hear that laugh. So like Dane, and so different, but not in the ways that counted. Both put themselves on the line for others, both had a core of honor. She realized in that instant that she didn't want to let Dane out of her life, ever.

Weldon had to be just ahead, not that far. Wait, she couldn't hear him crashing through the trees anymore. Had he fallen? Was he hiding, lying in wait for her?

Before she could react, he grabbed her around the neck and hauled her back against him. His other hand was on her arm, trying to pull the SIG out of her hand. But she wasn't about to let go. She pulled and twisted, but he pulled his arm tighter. "Damn you, be quiet. Let that gun drop. Now!"

Nick yelled at the top of her lungs, jerked as hard as she could, and drove her elbow into his stomach. He yelled, his hold loosened just a bit. She jerked the SIG down and pulled the trigger. She shot him in the foot.

He screamed, released her. He was dancing in place, trying to grab his foot, his eyes wild with pain.

Sherlock, Savich, and Dane saw the dance, saw her standing there, the gun dangling in her hand, breathing hard, staring at Weldon De-Loach. Flynn and Delion came up to stand beside them.

"Jesus, woman," Dane said, reaching her first. She turned, white-faced, and he forgot every curse word he'd stored up. "Ah, dammit, Nick," he said, and pulled her against him. "Just look at you. You're freezing, you twit."

"No, I'm not," she said against his shoulder. "Be careful, Dane, you might hurt your arm."

"My arm? You're worried about my arm?" He couldn't help it, he started to laugh. He saw Flynn and Delion pull Weldon DeLoach to the ground, Flynn pulling off the guy's boot to wrap his parka sleeve around the wound.

Flynn looked up, grinned at her. "Congratulations, Dr. Campion, you brought down the perp. They don't exactly teach you that a foot wound is the way to go, but hey, I'm not about to argue with success. Okay, Weldon, shut your trap."

"You know," she said.

"Yeah," Dane said, "we know, but it's not important now."

"It hurts, dammit!"

"Yeah, I'll just bet," Flynn said, and came down on his haunches beside Weldon. He looked straight down into that face, and read him his rights.

"No, I don't need an attorney. I didn't do anything. You've got to listen to me."

Savich, who was standing over him, said in a quiet voice, "So now you didn't do anything?"

"I didn't commit those script murders! Yes, I came up with the idea for the series, but I had nothing to do with those murders. They're horrible. I don't know who's responsible. It may be someone at the studio, someone who worked on the series. But I don't know who."

Sherlock said, "I see. So it has nothing at all to do with the fact that you seem to be trying your best to murder your father?"

"No, dammit. Do you have any idea what he's done to me all my life?"

Weldon looked ill, but he held on, sucked in a deep breath.

"No, no one knows anything," Delion said. "Listen, Weldon, someone murdered four people in San Francisco. You hired that moron Milton to kill Nick at the funeral because she saw you in the church. Then there's Pasadena. It's times like this I'm really glad I live in California and we've got the death penalty. They're gonna cook you, Weldon."

The pain was glazing his eyes. He was holding his foot, crying, pleading. "No, listen to me, I wouldn't kill anybody. I'm not like that."

Savich said, "Tell us exactly why you tried to kill your father. This time in nice plain English."

Weldon's voice was soft now, so quiet it was like listening to him again on the video. He was getting himself back in control. He'd finally managed to regain some calm, control the pain in his foot. "I can't. There's too much at stake here."

"That's not a very good start, Weldon," Dane said.

Weldon lowered his head and moaned at the pain in his foot.

Delion snorted, stood, his hands on his hips. "Sherlock has called on her cell phone and rounded up a doctor for you. Let's get you back to the parking lot. Detective Flynn and I will help you."

Weldon DeLoach tried to get up on his own, but ended up moaning again, clutching his foot. Flynn and Delion got him up and half carried him back to the facility.

Dr. Randolph Winston, a geriatrician, was waiting for them at the front entrance to attend to the foot, a thick black eyebrow arched. "A woman shot him in the foot? Here, at Lakeview?" The eyebrow went even higher when Detective Flynn just shrugged.

"No elderly person I've treated has ever been shot in the foot. Let's get him to the hospital."

Dane nodded. "We'll follow. We've got lots more to talk about with Mr. DeLoach."

THIRTY-ONE

Delion and Flynn read the riot act to the two policemen assigned to keep an eye on Captain DeLoach, then rode with Weldon to the hospital. The rest of them walked back to Captain DeLoach's room.

It appeared that Captain DeLoach's brain had faded into the ether again. Or it was all an act, one at which he excelled.

He was still singing "Eleanor Rigby." Nurse Carla said, just shaking her head, "The fact that his son tried to kill him—I think it knocked him right off his mental pins again. I was with him several times during the morning and he was with it the whole time, but not now. Poor old man. How would you like to have a son who keeps trying to kill you?"

Nick moved away from Captain DeLoach and said, her voice low, "Something is very strange here. When Weldon was in the captain's room, he called his father a monster, said he had to stop him. But Captain DeLoach, he wasn't afraid at all. He taunted Weldon."

Savich walked to the old man, who was still singing softly, vacantly, in his wheelchair.

"Captain DeLoach? You've met me before. I'm Dillon Savich. I'm an FBI agent."

Slowly, the old man stopped singing "Eleanor Rigby" and raised his eyes to Savich's face. Then, slowly, he raised his hand and saluted.

Savich, without pause, saluted him back.

"I saluted that girl, too," Captain DeLoach said in a singsong voice. "I thought it was weird to have to salute a girl, but I did it. Respect for the Federal Bureau of Investigation, you know? It's a sign of the times that the Feds would allow a girl to join up. I always wanted to be an FBI agent, but I couldn't. And now it turns out she isn't a cop, just a girl who's homeless, leastwise that's what Weldon said. Hey, is that little redheaded girl a cop?"

"She certainly is, an excellent FBI agent."

The old man gave her a toothy grin and saluted her. Sherlock didn't salute him back, just gave him a little wave with her fingers. He gave a dry, cracking laugh, shook his head. "That girl over there, the homeless one, she saved me from Weldon, the little pissant. I don't think he would have killed me. You see, Weldon's a coward. I never could teach him to be a man. He's always hated blood, wouldn't ever go hunting with me. Once I tried to get him to butcher a buck, but he vomited all over his shoes and hid. He's never even used a gun as far as I know."

"How was he going to kill you, sir?" Dane said. "I believe he struck you the first time."

"Nah, that first time, I fell over all on my own. That last time he could only bring himself to shove my chair over."

The old man started laughing, more spittle spotted with blood sprayed on his chin. "What a hoot this all is, best time I've had in years. Nah, I don't think Weldon could have killed me. But I could tell he was going to try. He was going to strangle me with a string. The girl there thought he had a gun, but he didn't. He won't touch 'em. I saw the string hanging out of his pocket, you know, real stout with little knots tied along the length? Yep, just a string because there's no blood when you strangle someone. But it's still gross. Weldon just doesn't realize how gross it is to strangle someone—all the gagging, the eyes, my God, the eyes, they bulge, you know? And you can see all the terror, the fright—it all oozes out—then the final acceptance that they're going to die. It isn't a pretty sight. No, shooting's cleaner. Only thing is, though, that the eyes fade really fast with a bullet."

Nick closed her eyes, said, "I shot Weldon in the foot. You're right, it was easier."

"For a homeless girl, she knows stuff," Captain DeLoach said, and began humming "Eleanor Rigby" again.

"Are you trying to make us think you're senile, Captain DeLoach?" Sherlock said, her palm resting lightly on the old man's shoulder. She gently kneaded the flesh and bone and the flannel shirt, all that was left of him.

"Nah, I just like to sing. I was the only middle-aged guy who liked the Beatles."

Dane said, "But why did Weldon want to kill you, sir?"

The old man looked at Dane. "I think you're probably an excellent cop, young man. You're passionate, you stick tight, you don't screw around, all are important to be successful in any job."

Dane said again, "Why does your son want you dead?"

"The little pussy thinks he's safe if I'm dead. And he would be." The old man, now as sharp as any of them, stared at Dane, his faded eyes bright with intelligence. He said, his voice so proud, "Weldon's got to know that I'll talk now, and why not? I was the sheriff, and look at what I did, no one ever had a clue. Of course, like the saying goes, a dog never shits in his own backyard." He laughed, a wheezing, scaly sound that made Sherlock's skin crawl.

"Captain DeLoach," she said, "do you pretend to be senile? Is it all just an elaborate charade?"

The old man said, "Me, senile? Hey, I haven't seen you before, have I? Aren't you the cutest little thing. My wife had the look of you. All sprite and fire and that lovely hair, so red, like blood, one could say."

"Yes," Sherlock said slowly, "I suppose you could say that, but I doubt many people would. Now, Captain, you just made a little joke, didn't you? You know exactly who I am. You were just pretending, just continuing with your charade."

He said nothing.

Sherlock said, "What was your wife's name, sir?"

"Marie. Her name was Marie, French for God's mother's name, something that always made me smile, particularly when I'd come home and my hands would still have seams of blood in the cracks. Yep, my palms would look like road maps."

"I know you were a sheriff," Dane said, "but did you have blood on your hands that often?"

"No, not just *on* my hands, Agent. There was usually so much blood it would work its way into the lines and hunker down and live there. No matter how hard I scrubbed, I couldn't get it all out. Then I really looked at my hands one day and knew I liked it. It was always a reminder to me of how much fun I had."

Nick stepped up to the wheelchair, leaned down, and clasped her hands on the wheels, got to within an inch of his face. "You killed people, didn't you, sir?"

"Well, of course, young lady. I was the sheriff."

"No, not as a sheriff. You killed people. You liked it. You liked seeing the remnants of their blood in your hands. You got away with it. And that's what Weldon doesn't want you to tell the world, isn't it?"

"Ain't you a cracker. Of course I got away with it. I might be old now but I'm still not stupid. It was easy. Once they even got a picture of me, but it didn't lead them even close to me. I was that good." He raised his hand and snapped two of his bony fingers together. "I'm eighty-seven years old. You think I care now if everyone knows? Hell, I deserve the attention, the recognition of what I did. What will they do? Put me on trial? Sentence me to the death penalty? Judging by the way I'm feeling these days, the blood I keep spitting up, I'm ready for the needle already. Not that they'd ever get the chance, a man of my age with cancer. Hey, you think I'm senile. Listen to this." And the old man started humming "Eleanor Rigby" again, saw the shock on their faces, and laughed.

Nick said, "And Weldon didn't want you to tell anyone, did he?"

"No, he claimed it'd ruin everything. He didn't want it known that his pop was a serial killer. Weldon was always afraid of me, terrified of me when he discovered what I was doing, but he kept quiet, particularly after I told him I'd nail him upside down to a tree and skin him alive if he ever told anyone. He didn't."

It was Dane who said slowly, "I remember when I first went to San Francisco Homicide after my brother's murder. Inspector Delion said they'd found out from the bullet that the gun that killed my brother was like the gun the Zodiac killer used."

Captain DeLoach laughed again, whistled something no one knew through his teeth. "I'm impressed, Agent. I read about it at the time and it kind of got me started, you know? I wanted to be better than him. The least I could do was use the same kind of weapon he used. A fine gun—my JC Higgins model eighty."

Captain DeLoach sighed, rubbed his old hands together. "Nope, I wasn't the Zodiac killer. I was really a bit more basic than the Zodiac killer was. But I liked his style. Isn't that a kick? What a handle. Trust the media to always come up with a good sound bite. If only I'd been open about what I did, maybe I would have gotten a handle, too."

The old man frowned, looked off into nothing at all, said, "Hey, do you think he's still around? Maybe he's in a nursing home, just like I am. Maybe he's here, you think?"

No one said anything, just waited.

Captain DeLoach continued singing, then he said, his voice sharp, "Your guy didn't use my gun. Nope, mine's hidden, and I'll be glad to tell you where." He gave them a big smile.

Dane said, "Weldon knows. He has to."

Savich said, for the third time, "Tell us why your son wanted to kill you, sir."

The old man laughed, smacked his lips together, and started singing again.

Nick moved close and said right in his face, "I saved your life, sir. I figure you owe me. Tell us the truth."

Captain DeLoach gave her a big smile, raised his veiny old hand, lightly touched his fingertips to her cheek. "So soft," he said. "You want to know, do you, little girl? Yeah, I guess I do owe you. Weldon wanted to protect his boy."

"His boy?" Dane said. "Weldon has a son?"

"Sure. Didn't let me near him when he was young, but then he came here to meet me. I took care of him really good, now didn't I? I got him all juiced up and now, here he is, following in his granddaddy's footsteps. Weldon wanted to protect his boy, didn't want to see him ruined, hounded by the media."

"Who is his boy, sir?" Savich said.

"You're FBI, son, it's your job to find out. I don't want to make things that easy for you." He coughed, and a trickle of blood snaked out of his mouth.

Sherlock said, "I don't want to salute you, sir."

Captain DeLoach said, head cocked to the side, "Well, after all, you're just a girl, when it all boils down to what's important."

"And I'd say that you're an evil old man."

"Oh yeah," he said. "Oh yeah, I really am. And I'm eighty-seven years old and sitting real pretty. Ain't life a kick?"

WHEN they reached the Ventura County Community Hospital, they saw Weldon, who didn't look too good. He was pale, still in pain, and he knew the dam had burst. Everything he'd been struggling with was over now, and he knew it. Dane lightly laid his palm on Weldon's shoulder. "I'm very sorry, Weldon. We're all very sorry."

"You know," Weldon said, his voice dead. "That wretched old man told you all of it?"

Savich said, "Yes, your father finally got around to telling us in simple English, once I asked him to do it, with no crazy allusions or cover-ups. He's really quite mad. I don't think he's senile, not for a moment, but he's fooled everyone else. He's a fine actor."

"He's been mad all my life. So he's finally done it. I didn't know whether or not he really meant it."

"How old were you when you discovered what he was?" Sherlock asked.

"I was ten years old. I couldn't sleep one night, and he'd left early in the evening, supposedly on a call. I waited for him. I saw him drive into the garage. I heard the kitchen door open. I started to go to him, but something stopped me, something that had scared me about him for a good long time. I stayed hidden behind some of my mother's favorite curtains in the living room.

"I heard him come in and he was whistling. I crawled to the kitchen. I saw his clothes, saw his hands—he had blood all over him. So much red, and even as I watched, it was turning darker and darker, almost black. His shirt was stiff with blood. At first I was terrified that it was his, but not for long.

"I watched him scrub his hands in the kitchen sink, watched him strip to his underwear, wrap up his bloody clothes, and tie them up in a neat bundle. It was practiced, everything he did, like he'd done it many times before. He never stopped whistling. I watched him take that bundle of bloody clothes out in the backyard. He paced off six steps from a big old elm tree. He dug down and dumped the bundle in. I saw that there were maybe half a dozen bundles down there. Then he shoveled dirt over all of it. He never stopped whistling.

"When I was twelve, I wondered if he was the one they called the Zodiac killer. I saw all about the murders on TV, but they weren't on the same days he was gone. And that insane whistling—it was always the same, always 'Eleanor Rigby.' He still hums or whistles that damned song now, only he uses it to fool people, to make them think he's senile."

"What did you do?" Dane asked.

"Oh man, I was never more scared in my life. I didn't know what to do. I was just a kid. He was my father."

Nick said, "You confronted him, didn't you? You just couldn't stand it anymore and you confronted him."

"Yes, and do you know what he did? He just stood there, looking down at me, and began to laugh. He laughed until there was spittle on his mouth. Then he just stopped and went cold. Like, with no warning, his body went perfectly still and his eyes were dead. There was no one behind those eyes and I knew it. I was twelve years old and I knew it." Weldon paused, took a shuddering breath. There wasn't a sound in that small room. "He told me in this cold, dead voice exactly what he would do to me if I said anything to anyone."

"You were brave to confront him," Nick said. "Very brave."

"Turns out I was a coward, turns out when I was old enough to kill the old monster, I didn't. I just wanted to scare him to keep him quiet. But I knew he wouldn't. This time I was going to strangle him. Would I have gone all the way until I knew that his heart was no longer beating?" Weldon shook his head, looked down at his bandaged foot, winced. He said finally, "What are you going to do?"

He looked at each of them in turn. From Inspector Delion to Detective Flynn, to the FBI agents, in a circle around him. The pain meds had finally kicked in completely and there was only a dull throb in his foot. He looked at Nick. "I don't blame you for trying to protect an old man. You didn't know."

"I wish I had shot him instead," Nick said. "But if I had, we wouldn't have learned the truth."

Weldon was shaking his head, back and forth, his eyes on each of their faces in turn. "I left home on the day I turned eighteen. I came to LA because I was a good writer and I wanted to write TV and movie scripts. I met a girl, Georgia, and we fell in love. I got her pregnant. We got married. A drunk driver killed her when our son was only three years old."

"You raised your son alone just like your father did you?"

"Of course, but I wasn't like my father, I really loved my boy. I would have done anything for him. It wasn't long before I got work writing for a TV sitcom and started making enough money so I didn't have to worry about it all the time." He paused a moment. "I kept up with the old man. Do you know that long after he was in his sixties, the people still wanted him to stay on as sheriff?"

"Why?" Dane asked.

"The old man was so mean he could face down drunk bikers. Once, I heard he'd pistol-whipped a man for hassling a woman, all the while yelling at him, 'No one fucks with my town!' That's what he always loved to say, and then he'd spit out a wad of tobacco.

"I'll bet you're all wondering why I've kept him in such a nice place for the last ten years."

No one had actually really thought about it yet, but Nick knew they would have, sooner or later.

She said, "Why did you?"

Weldon said simply, "He told me if I didn't keep him sitting real pretty until he kicked off, he'd contact the press and tell them where bodies were buried that no one even knew about, tell them where his gun was hidden, tell them all about the bundles he'd buried beneath that elm tree. There'd be so much proof, they'd have to believe him.

"I agreed. What else could I do? There was my own growing career to think about, but most important, there was my boy, my own innocent boy."

Nick said slowly, "I guess I can understand that, but was he still killing people? Didn't you realize you had to do something once you were an adult and out from under his thumb?"

Weldon said, "I tried never to think about it. He's right. I was a coward, and he knew I wouldn't say anything once I had my boy. He was still the sheriff thirteen years ago when something went wrong with an arrest, and a car ran over him, smashing his legs. He's been confined to a wheelchair ever since. So I knew the world was safe from him."

Savich started to say something, but Nick shook her head, said, "He started his threats recently, didn't he? He knew he was getting close to the end and he wanted recognition for what he'd done. He wanted the world to know just what had walked among them for years and years."

Weldon nodded, his hands clasped, so pale, so deadened, that it broke her heart. "Yes. After he told me what he was planning to do—you know, make his announcement to the press, tell everyone everything—I didn't know what to do. I reminded him that he'd sworn to keep quiet for as long as I kept him in that home. He just laughed, said he was going to croak pretty soon so it didn't matter. I knew his madness was beyond control then."

Weldon stopped cold. Then he seemed to look deeply inside himself, drew a deep breath, and said, "That's when he told me he'd had a nice little visit with his grandson. And that's when I hit him and knocked his chair over. I should have killed him then but I just couldn't do it. I threatened him, hoped to scare him into silence like I already told you, but I knew that wouldn't work. After I left, I thought about it and knew I had to kill him, there was just no other way. I failed."

Dane said very gently, "Weldon, your father visited with your boy and confessed what he was to him?"

"Yes."

"Weldon, who is your son?"

Weldon shook his head. "Listen, Agent Savich, my son isn't a murderer, he isn't."

"But you believe he is," Sherlock said, "and it's eating you alive. You think your son killed the people in San Francisco and in Pasadena, copying the scripts you wrote."

Finally, Weldon DeLoach said, "I just couldn't make myself accept that he was like his grandfather, that his head wasn't right, that something was missing in him."

Dane said, "We've got to bring him in, Weldon, you must know that. You can't let him continue doing what your own father did for so many years."

Weldon was shaking his head. "Don't get me wrong. I didn't figure it out until just a couple of days ago. And even then I didn't figure it out for myself. The old man actually bragged about how he'd finally gotten a real man in the family, how he didn't have much to teach his grandson, because—like his granddaddy—he was born knowing what to do and how to do it. He told me that his grandson came to see him, brought a Christmas present, a nice tie with red dots on it. And how perfect that was, and so he told the boy he was going to die soon and he wanted to tell him all about himself. And he laughed and laughed at how stupid everyone was, the cops especially."

Weldon fell silent, looked at them again. He said at last, "I haven't known what to do. I just knew I had to kill that obscene old man, get him buried, and gone."

Sherlock said very gently, "But what were you going to do about your son?"

"Get him help. Stop him from doing any more harm. Turn him over to the police if I had to."

Sherlock said, "We're the cops. What's his name, Weldon?"

But Weldon just shook his head. "I couldn't let him continue, not like my father had done. He was a good boy, really. I know something must have happened to make him snap, to turn him into a monster like his grandfather. I don't know what it was, but there just had to have been something. He was doing so well. He's very smart, you know, extraordinarily talented. But then there were some signs—he struggled when he was in high school, didn't like his teachers, couldn't make friends—it was enough to make me pay attention. He was violent once, when he accidentally killed a girl in college, but it could have happened to any guy, you know? Things just got out of hand. It was involuntary manslaughter. I got him help. They made him well. My son promised me he was just fine, and I wanted desperately to believe him.

"Something happened. The old man did this to him, somehow."

He looked up at each of them in turn. "Do you know I still don't know how many people that old monster killed? There were people he killed that were never found by anyone. Oh Jesus."

He put his head in his hands and sobbed very quietly.

THIRTY-TWO

"Wait! You can't go in there!"

As she pushed past him, Sherlock said, "Jay, it's time for you to go away now. It's time to take your custom suits from Armani, get another job, and pay off your credit cards."

"But he's meditating! He specifically told me he didn't want to be bothered. And I love Armani. When I wear Armani everyone knows it's Armani."

Suddenly Arnold Loftus came roaring forward. He didn't try to bar their way, he rounded on Jay Smith. "Shut up, Jay. They're here for a reason. Don't try to stop them."

"You're the damned bodyguard. Don't let them go in there, you moron, you've—"

Arnold very gently picked up Jay Smith beneath his armpits and simply walked away with him. He said over his shoulder, "The Little Shit fired me. Whatever it is, go for it."

Dane gently turned the handle. The door was locked. He turned to Jay, still held up by his armpits, and held out his hand. "Key," was all he said.

Arnold let Jay down, watched him like a hawk as he went to his desk, got down on his knees, and untaped a key beneath the center drawer. He handed it to Dane.

"Thank you," Dane said.

Dane quietly unlocked the door, slowly pushed it open. The huge office was dark, like a movie theater, and indeed, there was a movie showing, on the far white wall. Linus Wolfinger was seated in the chair behind his desk, his chin propped up in his hands, watching.

It was an episode of *The Consultant*, one they hadn't seen. He didn't look away from the screen even after all six of the people who'd come into his office were standing around his desk.

He said in a calm, conversational voice, "My dear old dad blew the whistle, I take it?"

"No," Delion said. "Your dad told us about how he'd found out that his son was a murderer, but no, he didn't tell us your name."

"That crazy old pile of bones told you then."

Savich said, "Actually, we managed to figure it out. MAX, my computer, verified for us that you were born Robert Allen DeLoach, and you attended Garrett High School here in LA. Here's a photo of you."

Savich laid the photo faceup on Wolfinger's desk. Linus didn't bother to look at it.

Sherlock said, "We also found the real Michael Linus Wolfinger. Here's his photo. He isn't you."

Linus waved a hand. "The guy died in a skiing accident, nothing more. He was an orphan. Taking his identity wasn't a problem. I wanted to work in the studio. With the year in that institution, I knew no one would hire me." Linus shrugged. "Who the hell cares?"

"Tell us about the girl in college," Dane said.

Linus shrugged again, his fingers were tapping on the desktop. He couldn't seem to keep himself still. "Silly little twit, told me she wouldn't go out with a nerd. I twisted her neck until it broke. Unfortunately my father came in before I could get rid of her body. But he helped me, told me that I wasn't like my grandfather, that he was going to get me help. I argued with him but he told me I had no choice. For my own good, he was putting me in an institution. If I didn't agree, he'd turn me over to the police."

Linus looked at them again, shrugged. "I am very smart, you know. In fact, I'm more than smart. I'm a genius. That year in the Mountain Peak Institution, in the butt-end of nowhere—well, I used that year to plan out what I wanted to do with my life. It was right after that that Wolfinger died and I took on his name and his past. Dear old dad got me a job here at the studio. Then I met Miles Burdock and impressed the hell out of him, which was tough, but I told you, I'm a genius. I've proved it. I've made lots and lots of money for the studio. That's why all the old duffers around here call me Little Shit. They're all jealous. Hey, I'm the crown prince, the best fucking thing that's ever happened to this place."

He paused a moment, looked at Savich. "I don't suppose my daddy knocked off my grandfather?"

"No," Dane said, "but he really wanted to. He still does. How did you find out about your grandfather? How did you even know where he is?"

Linus laughed. "I was at my dad's house last month and came across a paid invoice to the old folks' home. I had never met my grandfather, but I did know that my dad hated him. He told me several times that he'd never put that old man in my life, never. I suppose my dad told you that?"

Dane nodded.

"I wanted to meet him, maybe find out why my dad hated him so much. I even took him a Christmas present. Do you know what I found out from that pathetic old man?"

No one said anything, just waited.

"He told me about what he'd done. At first I just didn't believe him, it was too fantastic. But he told me stuff that sounded too real to be made up. He called my dad a coward and a wuss. Then he asked me if I was really of his blood, if I'd ever killed anyone. I told him I had. I thought the old man would crawl out of his wheelchair and dance he was so pleased.

"He cackled, blood and spittle hanging off his chin. He wagged his finger at me, told me it was in my blood, told me I had the look of him when he was young, and the good Lord knew it was so deep in his blood that now it was coming out of him. He coughed again and more blood came out of his mouth.

"I realized then that I was just like him. I told him that I'd gotten bored, and then my dad had come up with this terrific idea for a series. As I listened to him, everything came together in my mind. I knew exactly what I was going to do. I added my own ideas to the first two or three scripts, and my dad was really pleased that I was so interested and that my ideas worked so well.

"When I told my grandfather what I was going to do, he wanted all the details. He even helped me refine some of my plans. When I left, he laughed and wished me luck, said he wanted to hear how things actually went down because, he said, things never go exactly as planned, and that just makes it all the more fun. I told him he could read all about it in the newspaper." Linus shook his head, tapped his fingers some more on the desktop.

"Jesus, it was fun, particularly that priest in San Francisco, your twin brother, Agent Carver. He surprised the hell out of me. It gave me quite a start when you first came in here."

Dane wanted to kill the little bastard. He felt Savich's hand on his arm, squeezing very lightly. He fought for control, managed to keep it. He said, "It's over now, Linus, all over. You're dead meat."

Linus said, "You do know I'm the one who sent that picture of you and Miss Nick to the media. All I had to do was make a couple of calls to the SFPD to find out who she was. And now she was here, sniffing around, looking at everyone, but I knew she wouldn't recognize me."

Dane said, "But you hired Milton to kill her. You were afraid that she might recognize you eventually."

Linus shrugged yet again, his fingertips tapping a mad tattoo. "Why take a chance? Too bad Milton was such a lousy shot." He looked at Nick. "Pity he missed you. Just a graze. Bummer. But I would have gotten you, Miss Nick, oh yes, I would have killed you dead." He gave a short laugh, then turned back to the show. He pressed a button, lowering the volume even more. He said, never looking away from the episode playing on the wall, "Father Michael Joseph was my first big challenge. He told me he was going to blow the whistle on me, leave the priesthood if he had to. I was going to kill him anyway, but I had to speed things up." He looked at Dane and smiled. "It was a beautiful shot. But you know what? The damned priest looked happy, like maybe he realized that he'd saved some lives with his sacrifice. Who can say?"

Dane was breathing hard now, struggling to keep his hands at his sides, to keep himself from wrapping his hands around Linus Wolfinger's neck and choking the life out of him. He was a monster, maybe even more of a monster than his grandfather, but that would really be saying something.

"What did you do with the gun?" Sherlock asked.

He grinned at her. "Who knows?"

Dane smiled at him. "You're going to pay now, Linus. You're going into a cage and you're never going to come out except when they walk you down to the execution room to send you to hell."

"I don't think so," Linus said, lifted his hand, and in it was a gun, a derringer, small and deadly. He aimed it at each of them in turn.

"Don't even think about it, Linus," Savich said. "It's too late. We don't want to have to kill you. Don't make us."

Linus Wolfinger laughed. "Do you know running this studio isn't even much fun anymore? Nothing's much fun anymore." He said, in a very good imitation of Arnold Schwarzenegger, "*Hasta la vista*, baby." He stuck the derringer in his mouth and pulled the trigger.

THIRTY-THREE

They'd just returned to the Holiday Inn. Linus Wolfinger had been dead for only an hour. It seemed much longer.

Nick stood in front of the TV and watched John Rothman, senior senator from Illinois, face a slew of cameras and a multitude of shouting reporters.

". . . We're told it's your wife, Senator, the one everybody believed ran away with one of your aides three years ago. They found her body, but where's your aide?"

". . . Sir, how did you feel when they told you they'd found your wife's body?"

". . . She's dead, Senator, not off living with another man. Do you think your aide killed your wife, sir?"

". . . How do you think this will affect your political career, Senator?"

Nick simply stared at the TV screen, hardly believing what she saw. She felt a deep pain, and rising rage. John Rothman had finally tracked Cleo down, and killed her. To shut her up. And to get revenge for the letter she'd written to Nick?

She looked at that face she'd believed she loved, that mobile face that could show such joy, could laugh and joke with the greatest charm, a face that could hide hideous secrets. She watched him perform, no other word for it. He was a natural politician, an actor of tremendous talent. To all the questions, Senator John Rothman said not a word. He stood quietly, like a biblical martyr as stones were hurled at him. He looked both stoic and incredibly weary, and older than he had just a month before. She couldn't see any fear leaching out of him; all she saw was pain, immense pain. Even she, who knew what this man was, who knew what he'd done, what he was capable of, even she could feel it radiating from him. If she had been asked at that very instant if he'd killed Cleo, if he'd ever killed anyone or tried to kill anyone, she would have said unequivocally no. He was the most believable human being she'd ever seen in her life.

He continued to say nothing, didn't change his expression at any of the questions, whether they were insulting or not. All the questions seemed to just float past him. Finally, and only when he was ready, Senator Rothman took a single step forward. He merely nodded to the shouting reporters, the people holding the scores of cameras, made brief eye contact with many of them as he gave a small wave of his hand. Immediately everyone was quiet. It was an incredible power he had, one she'd always admired. Even before she'd met him she'd wondered how he did it.

Senator Rothman said very quietly, making everyone strain forward, shushing their colleagues so they could hear him, "The police notified me just last night that they'd found my former wife's body, that it looked like she'd been dead for some time. They don't know yet how long, but they will do the appropriate testing to find out. Then, we hope they'll be able to ascertain what happened to her. As you know, I haven't seen her in more than three years. I would like to ask for your understanding for the grieving family and friends."

He took a step back, raised his head, and nodded to the reporters.

"Your wife's name was Cleo, right, Senator?"

"That's right."

"You were married how long, sir?"

"We were married for five years. I loved her very much. When she left, I was devastated."

"How did she die, Senator?"

"I don't know."

"Did she tell you she was leaving you, Senator?"

"No."

"Are you glad she's dead, Senator?"

Senator John Rothman looked at the woman who'd asked him that. A very long look. The woman squirmed. He said finally, "I will not dignify that question with an answer. Anyone else?"

Another TV-news reporter yelled out, "Did you kill your wife, Senator?"

He didn't say anything for a very long time, just looked at the reporter, as if he were judging him, and the conclusion he'd reached wasn't positive. He said, his voice weary, resigned, "It's always amazed me how some of you in the media, in the middle of a crisis—large or small—are like a pack of rats."

There was silence, some shuffling of feet, some angry whispers and outraged faces.

Nick stared at the man she'd come so close to marrying. Some of the reporters who were furious at what he'd said started to yell out more questions, but stopped. Everyone was looking at him—his face was naked, open, the pain stark and there for everyone to see. She saw tears streaming down his face, saw that he tried to say something but couldn't. Or pretended to. He shook his head at the straining group, turned, and walked away, his aides surrounding him, a barrier between him and all the reporters. Tall, stiff, a man suffering. The reporters, all the camera crews watched him. And the thing was—no one yelled any more questions at him. The sound of the cameras was the only noise. She watched him walk out of the room, a man in pain, his head down, shoulders hunched forward. A tragic figure.

Nick was shaken. She'd never seen John Rothman cry. She felt a moment of doubt before she quashed it beneath the rippling fear she'd felt when she'd awakened from that dream and known, all the way to her soul, that all three attempts on her life had been made by the same man, the man John Rothman had hired to murder her.

The fact was that John Rothman had also tracked down his ex-wife and murdered her in cold blood. Or had he hired the same man to kill Cleo Rothman? The autopsy would show that she'd been dead for no longer than four weeks. That was when Cleo had written the letter that had saved her life. Only Cleo had died.

A local reporter turned and said with great understatement, "Senator John Rothman appears very saddened at the discovery of his wife's grave by a hunter's dog yesterday. Cleo Rothman's remains were identified this morning. We will keep you informed as details emerge from this grisly case."

Nick walked slowly to the TV and turned it off. She started shaking, just couldn't help it.

She looked up to see Dane watching her from across the room. He was leaning against the door, his arms crossed over his chest.

She hadn't heard him come in. And that was a surprise. She'd become very attuned to him over the past week. Only a week. It was amazing. She tried to smile, but couldn't manage it. She said finally, "Did you see it?"

"Yes."

"There's no proof, Dane. Nothing's changed. I know you must have found out that there's no missing-person's report on me because I did have the sense to write to my dean at the university about a personal emergency."

"And your point would be?"

He didn't move, just said when she held silent, his voice very low, "It's time to tell me all of it, Dr. Campion. There are no more distractions to keep us away from this. Linus is dead. Detective Flynn is with the district attorney deciding what to do about Captain DeLoach, and Weldon will survive. How is Senator John Rothman connected to you, Nick? I want all of it. Now."

"Up until three weeks ago, he was my fiancé."

"He was what? Jesus, Nick, I want to know how you could get caught up with a man old enough to be your father. I can't believe that—No, wait, I want to know, but not just yet." He crossed the space between them, jerked her against him, and kissed her.

When he let up just a bit, he was breathing hard and fast. Nick's eyes, once tear-sheened, were now vague and hot. She said into his mouth, "Oh, God. Dane, this is—" She went up on her tiptoes and grabbed him tightly to her. She was kissing him, nipping his jaw, licking his bottom lip, her hands in his hair, pulling him closer, closer still, pushing into him, wanting him. She groaned when his tongue touched hers.

"Nick, no, no, we can't—oh hell." He wrapped his arms around her hips and lifted her off the floor, carrying her to the bed. He'd never wanted a woman like he wanted her. There was so much, too much really. His brother, all the death, and now the damned senator, more confusion, more secrets. No, he couldn't do this, not the right time, not the right place. He pulled back, lightly traced his fingertip along the line of her jaw, touched her mouth. "Nick, I—" She grabbed him, pulled him flat on top of her.

"Don't stop, don't stop." She was kissing him all over his face, stroking him, reaching to touch all of him she could reach.

"Oh hell." He wanted to cry, to howl. He didn't have any condoms, nothing. He wasn't about to take the chance of getting her pregnant. Okay, okay, it didn't matter, getting himself off wasn't that important, at least not now. Nick was what was important. She'd been engaged to that damned senator? That old man who looked like an aristocrat, the bastard? Well, no matter, she wasn't going to marry him, she wasn't going to marry anyone.

He stripped her jeans down her hips, off her ankles and threw them on the floor. She was trying to bring him back to her, but he held her, looked a moment at the white panties she'd bought that were French cut, and he had those off her in a lick of time. She was beautiful, he couldn't stand it. He was breathing hard, so hard, and he was panting. "It's okay, Nick. Let me give you pleasure. Just hold still, no, don't try to strangle me. Lie back and let me enjoy you." He had her legs open, and he was between them, kissing her belly, then he gave her his mouth and within moments she screamed and went wild. God, he loved it, just loved it, and gave her all he could.

When at last she fell back, her heart pounding nearly out of her chest, breathing so hard she wondered if she would survive, he came up over her. He was harder than the floor, harder than the damned bed-springs, and he hurt. He also knew it was a good thing he had his pants on, otherwise he'd be inside her right this instant. But it just wasn't important, at least not now. He wondered if there was a drugstore nearby. Hey, a gas station, anyplace that sold condoms.

He pulled himself over her and began kissing her, slow, easy kisses, and he knew she could feel him. It took a long time before he slowly pulled away from her and sat up on the side of the bed. He looked down at her long legs, flat white belly, and slowly laid his palm flat. "You're beautiful," he said.

She gave a small moan, looked surprised, then smiled up at him. "So are you."

He grinned. It didn't hurt quite as much. He was getting himself back together. He forced himself to concentrate on pulling her panties back up, then working on her jeans. Just before he zipped up the jeans, he leaned down and kissed her belly again. Oh God, he wanted her. No, no. He spent several minutes easing her upright, straightening her clothes.

He paused for a moment, leaned forward, and cupped her face in his palms. "This is just the beginning. You're wonderful, Nick. But I can't believe you were engaged to John Rothman."

"At this moment, I can't believe I was either," she said, and kissed him.

She leaned forward, resting her face on his shoulder. He stroked her back, up and down. He shouldn't be surprised, he thought, but he was, closer to floored, actually. "John Rothman is far too old for you. Why would you ever want to marry a man who's close to the age of your father?"

His voice sounded back to normal, and so she got herself together and pulled away from him. "John Rothman is forty-seven in years, but much less in the way he looks at things, the way he feels about things. At least that's what I thought."

"If he paraded around naked in front of you, I can't imagine that you'd be licking your chops, would you?"

She was so surprised by what he said that she hiccupped. She said, smiling, "I don't know. I never saw him naked."

"That's good."

"Why would you care?"

"It's really very simple, Dr. Campion. I decided about three days ago that your next fifty years are mine. I saw that they found his wife's body?"

"That's right. Fifty years might not be enough."

"He told everyone that she ran away from him? Three years ago? We'll begin with fifty years, then renegotiate, all right?"

"Yes, he told everyone she ran away. His senior aide was gone as well, a guy named Tod Gambol, and everyone believed she ran away with him. Yes, all right, we'll start with fifty years, then go from there."

"Was Tod Gambol found with the dead wife?"

"Evidently not."

Dane said slowly, "What happened? Did you find out that she didn't leave him?"

"Oh no, Cleo left him, all right. I believed that, no doubt in my mind at all. She'd been gone three years, and he'd divorced her, although she'd never responded, couldn't be found. Of course I accepted it. I loved him. I was going to marry him."

"But she didn't leave him. He killed her."

"Nope. Fact is, she did leave him."

"How could you possibly know that?"

"I also know that she was alive up to four weeks ago."

Dane crossed his arms over his chest. "How do you know that for a fact? Did Senator Rothman assure you that she was alive and well and screwing around with his aide?"

"No. The bottom line is that Cleo Rothman wrote me a letter. She hasn't been dead for three years—just for a month, at the most, and the tests they'll run will prove it. No, John Rothman didn't kill her three years ago."

"Why did she write to you?"

"To warn me. She told me about the first girl John'd planned to marry, way back just before both of them graduated from Boston College. He killed her because Elliott Benson, a rival, had seduced her. He got away with it, she said, because he was smart, and who would ever begin to suspect a young man who was engaged to be married of suddenly killing his fiancée? The final police verdict was that it was a tragic automobile accident. She said that John cried his eyes out at her funeral, that her parents held him to comfort him."

"How could she have found out about that? Did he talk in his sleep? Don't tell me he confessed it to her?"

"No, she found a journal in the safe in his library. She wrote that one day she noticed that the safe wasn't locked. She was curious and opened it.

"So when she opened it and found the journal, she read it. He wrote all about how he'd killed a girl—Melissa Gransby was her name—how he'd planned it all very carefully and gotten away with it. A simple auto accident on I-95, near Bremerton. She must have written at least a half dozen times in that letter how smart John was, how I had to be careful because I was going to be the next woman he killed. She wrote that John had come to believe that I was sleeping with Elliott Benson, too, just like Melissa did, that I was betraying him, even before we were married."

"Who is this Elliott Benson?"

"He's a powerhouse in Chicago, a very rich and successful businessman, an investment banker with Kleiner, Smith and Benson. He and John have been rivals for years and years.

"Cleo wrote that she didn't know if he'd killed other women, but she knew he would have killed her if she hadn't left and she knew he was going to kill me and I should run as far away as I could, and quickly."

Dane, frowning, said, "Why would a man who's supposedly so smart keep a damned journal where he actually confesses to a murder? And leave that journal in a safe in his own home, for God's sake, and then, to top it all off, he leaves the safe open? That's really a long way from being smart, Nick. This whole thing's a stretch. It just doesn't feel right."

THIRTY-FOUR

Nick said, "I thought the same thing at first. But listen, Dane. I knew Cleo Rothman, I knew her handwriting. The letter was from her, I'm positive about that. She told me she had the journal, that she took it with her, to keep John at bay in case he wanted to come after her. It was her only leverage."

"Why didn't she just go to the police with the thing? It was a confession, after all."

"She wrote that John had many important, powerful friends, and that many of those powerful people owed him favors. She said she could just see him saying that as his wife—she knew his handwriting, of course—she had written it herself, that it was all an attempt on her part to ruin him. I could practically taste her fear in that letter, Dane, her sense that she was a coward, but that everything was against her, that she had no choice but to run. Do you think the cops would have believed her, launched an investigation?"

"They would have looked into it, of course, but it wouldn't have helped if they believed she was vindictive, that she wanted to ruin a good man, and there was no other proof but the journal. Anyway, John Rothman wrote that he killed this Melissa Gransby because she cheated on him with this Benson character?"

"Evidently so. John couldn't forgive her. The pages were full of rage, over-the-top, unreasoned rage, and Cleo wrote that she could see that Melissa's unfaithfulness had changed him, twisted him, made him incapable of trusting a woman.

"She wrote that it did make a bit of sense since his mother had cheated on his father, and it hurt him deeply. Evidently he told her this when they were first married."

"Did he tell you this? About his mother?"

She shook her head. "No, he's never told me anything."

"So Cleo Rothman found his journal, read his murder confession, and she just up and left him? With this aide? Jesus, Nick. Ain't a whole lot of credibility here."

"No, no, she wrote that she didn't leave with anyone. She said she didn't even know where Tod Gambol was. She was never his lover, had never been unfaithful to John. She loved John, always loved him, but she was terrified, and so she just ran. She became convinced that he was going to kill her, too, because she'd heard rumors that she was sleeping with Elliott Benson. Knowing this, knowing that he'd already killed a girl because she'd supposedly cheated on him, she knew he would believe the rumors and try to kill her just like he did Melissa.

"When she heard that I was going to marry him, then she heard the rumors that *I* was sleeping with Elliott Benson, she wrote that she didn't want to see me end up dead, like Melissa, and God knows how many other women."

"Okay, Nick, something else must have happened to make you go to San Francisco and become homeless."

"Just before I got her letter, someone tried to run me down. A man with a ski mask over his head, driving a black car. It was dark and I was walking just one block from the neighborhood store back to my building."

Dane stiffened. "What," he said, "were you doing out in the dark walking to the store? In Chicago? That's really dumb, Nick."

She poked her finger in his chest. "All right, you want to know every little thing? Okay, it was my period, if it's any of your business."

"Well, I can see that you wouldn't want to wait. But, you should have had the store deliver."

It was so funny, really so unexpected, all this outrage over something so very insignificant, that she laughed. And laughed again. Here she was telling him about one of the most frightening experiences of her life—until a week ago—and he was all upset because she'd walked to her local store, by herself, in the dark.

On the other hand, given what happened, maybe he had a point.

She cleared her throat and said, "As I was saying, I was walking back when this car came out of a side street and very nearly got me. There was no way it was someone drunk or a stupid accident. No, I knew it was on purpose. Then there was his sister Albia's birthday dinner. Supposedly it was food poisoning. It was really close. If I'd eaten more I would have died. The second I got that letter, I took off to his apartment to confront him about it."

"What happened?"

"I waved the letter in his face, asked him how many women he'd killed. He denied everything, said the letter couldn't be from Cleo, he just wouldn't believe that, demanded that I give it to him. Then he came at me and I thought he was going to strangle me. He got the letter, shredded it, and threw it into the fire, then turned on me. I pulled my gun out and told him I was leaving. That night, I woke up because I heard someone in my condo. I saw this guy from the balcony, running away, and realized that he'd set my condo on fire. I got myself out in time, but it was too close. I got away with my purse and that was it. I ended up in a shelter. Since I'd lost everything, since I didn't have a shred of proof, since I knew he'd try to kill me, just like he did Melissa, just like he'd wanted to kill Cleo, I decided being homeless wasn't such a bad thing. Talk about disappearing—and it would give me time to figure out what to do. That's how I ended up in San Francisco, how I just happened to be waiting in the church for Father Michael Joseph."

"So you went to San Francisco and just hid underground. You knew you couldn't remain hidden there, Nick. What were you going to do?"

"I hadn't yet decided. Believe me, I was in no hurry. Despite where I was, I felt safe until this happened."

"Who is Albia?"

"She's John Rothman's older sister. They're very close, always have been."

"What is she like?"

"Albia is some seven years older than John. After their mother died in an auto accident, Albia more or less became his mother. As I said, they're very close. Once I asked her about the family, and she told me about their mother, that she'd died tragically, that their father had died about five years ago of a heart attack."

"Lots of automobile accidents in this man's life."

"Tell me about it."

"So Albia didn't tell you about her mother being unfaithful to her father?"

"No, would you?"

"Maybe not."

"But there was something. At Albia's birthday dinner, before I got really sick, I gave her a scarf. She started to talk about how their mother had had a scarf like that and then she looked like she'd swallowed something bad. She shut up like a clam. They explained it to me that it was a touchy subject."

"No explanation at all."

"Not really."

"Nothing much there. Is that it?"

"No, there's more, and this is something I know. I remember John told me he was in love with Cleo within minutes of meeting her. When she left him, he was devastated, just couldn't believe it. He wondered and wondered why she hadn't spoken to him, told him what was wrong, but she'd just up and left."

"Hmmm," Dane said again.

She said, "You know, Dane, it was really hard for me to believe that John began murdering women just because his mother cheated on his father. Do you think it's remotely possible that he might have killed his own mother?"

"I think it's possible that someone did."

"But who else could it have been?"

He just shook his head. "There's lots here to process, Nick. Let's get Savich and Sherlock involved. MAX found out that you're Dr. Nicola Campion quickly enough. They're primed to help."

"I think that's a great idea."

THE four of them met in the Holiday Inn coffee shop.

Dane said, "Maybe you guys could consider stopping off in Chicago with us before going back to Washington."

"Actually," Savich said, "Sherlock was just about ready to call you, Nick, get all the details out of your mouth and not from MAX."

"It's a real mess," Nick said. She talked and talked, slowly covered again all that had happened, answered many of the same questions, though many of them had a different slant, refreshing her memory for different things. She realized she was being questioned by experts. It was quite painless, actually. Finally, both Savich and Sherlock fell silent. Savich was holding his wife's hand, stroking his thumb over her palm, slowly and gently.

Nick watched Savich sip his tea, frown. He said as he gently sloshed the tea around in the cup, "It's very flat, no taste at all."

Sherlock patted his hand. "I think we should start traveling with the tea you like."

Dane, impatient, said, "Well? What do you guys think?"

Savich smiled at Nick and said, "I want to cogitate on all of this for a while. But first, I need to make a phone call."

He pulled out his cell phone, dialed, waited. "Hello, George? It's Savich, and I need a bit of help."

"Who's George?" Nick whispered to Dane.

Sherlock said, "It's Captain George Brady, Chicago Police Department."

Savich waited, listened, then said into the cell phone, "Here's the deal, George. I need you to tell me about Cleo Rothman."

Two minutes later, Savich pressed the off button on the phone. He looked at each of them in turn, then said directly to Nick, "I'm sorry, Nick, but Cleo Rothman wasn't killed a couple of weeks ago."

Nick said, "What do you mean? I don't understand. I got the letter from her not more than a month ago."

Savich said, "Captain Brady said the medical examiner was just about ready to announce his findings. Fact is, Cleo Rothman was murdered at least three years ago."

THIRTY-FIVE

They spent the entire late afternoon and evening in meetings with Jimmy Maitland, Savich's boss and an assistant director of the FBI, Gil Rainy from the LA field office, and LAPD Chief William Morgan and his staff, including Detective Flynn. They had time for only a brief good-bye to Inspector Delion before he flew back to San Francisco late that evening.

The DA wasn't going to press charges against Weldon DeLoach, recognized that the man had lost his son and would probably be *persona non grata* in Hollywood. Besides, Weldon was going to show them where his father had buried all the discarded bloody clothes from so many years ago. That was, they decided, enough punishment for any man. As for Captain DeLoach, they'd tried to get details from him, but he'd acted utterly demented. Was it a game? No one knew. The fact was, though, he was dying. No one could see putting the old buzzard in jail, but the questions would continue to be asked. They would see if any were ever answered.

With Jimmy Maitland's blessing, the four of them flew to Chicago the following morning. They survived the usual hassles that accompanied traveling by air now that the world had changed. Their FBI shields were studied, their paperwork read three times, their fingerprints closely scrutinized until, at last, they were cleared through.

They rented two cars and suffered through the snarled traffic—which still didn't measure up to Los Angeles traffic—and it took them a good forty-five minutes to reach The Four Seasons. It was a treat, Savich told them, and one that Jimmy Maitland had approved. He'd told Savich they'd done such a good job with the script murderer that the sky was the limit, given, of course, that they realized the sky consisted of two regular rooms, which were still very nice in The Four Seasons. They managed to snag two adjoining rooms.

They ordered up room service first thing. Over club sandwiches, Savich's minus the turkey and bacon, he said, "Okay, I've given this lots of thought, talked it over with Sherlock and Dane on the airplane. Here's what we think, Nick: It's just possible that Senator John Rothman isn't the murderer here."

It was like someone punched her in the gut. She lost her breath. She gaped at the three of them, all of them nodding at her, said, "No, that's just not possible."

"Think a minute," Savich said, very gently, because he knew that her entire world was based on her belief that this one man had tried to murder her. "John Rothman is a very powerful man, true, with lots of clout, lots of friends who owe him favors, but despite that, he's got a lot on the line. Not just his political career, but his life. His life, Nick. For a man like him, with his skills, his place in the world, to really be that screwed up because his mom had an affair when he was a teenager, it just doesn't make sense, for any of us." He smiled at her. "Fact is, we're thinking that it just might be Albia Rothman."

Dane smiled, didn't say a word, just took another bite of his sandwich, which was quite good.

"Albia," Nick said, her voice blank, sandwich forgotten. "What on earth do you mean?"

"Well," Savich said, "to be honest here, it socked me in the face when you first mentioned her. That's why I said I wanted to think about it, discuss it with Sherlock and Dane. I'm not saying that we shouldn't immediately speak to John Rothman, because we have been known to be wrong before. Just maybe we'll change our minds. But I want us to give serious consideration to his sister as well."

Nick could only stare at each of them in turn. She drew a deep breath, took a bite of her sandwich, chewed, then said finally, "I'm not following you guys at all here."

Dane said, "Here's the deal: Older sister and younger brother are both hurt badly because of mother's infidelity. Older sister believes to her soul that she's her little brother's protector. Maybe she kills her mother, or maybe not, maybe her death just makes it all that much worse. She becomes her younger brother's biggest supporter, realizes she can't bear to ever let him go to another woman, and so when he meets someone in college, she kills her, making it look like an accident."

Nick was shaking her head. "But how can you possibly know if any of that is even close to the truth? It was all this Elliott Benson, this friend of John's who's always gone after the women John loved or wanted.

"Also, there's the inescapable fact that John married Cleo. They were married for five years. Why wouldn't Albia have killed her before John could marry her if she wanted to keep him to herself? To keep him safe from other women?"

Sherlock said, "It's likely that Albia simply didn't have enough opportunity before they married. We'll see about that. I'll bet you the last quarter of my club sandwich, though, that it was probably a whirlwind romance, and Albia didn't have a chance to stop him from marrying. So Albia had to bide her time, had to go underground with her feelings. After all, she couldn't just knock off his new wife; there would be too many questions raised. And certainly the last thing she'd want is to have her brother a suspect in the death of his wife, supposed accident or not."

Dane said, "Here's the clincher. You said that Cleo was the one who told you about Elliott Benson. Well, Cleo didn't write that letter. It's got to be Albia."

Nick looked thoughtful, her eyes on the crust of her club sandwich, all that was left. She said at last, "I know Albia, or at least I thought I did. She's always been kind to me, not chummy, because she's not like that with anyone. She's very dignified, very together, restrained."

Dane said, "Would she go to the mat for her brother, do you think?"

Nick pictured Albia Rothman in her mind, slowly shook her head. "I just don't know. I remember once in a meeting, though, Albia didn't agree with a political stand John wanted to take. She laid out her reasons, but he didn't change his mind. I remember thinking that I agreed with her. I also remember the look she gave him was vicious, but she didn't argue with him anymore."

"You said that Albia was married once, for just a short time?" Savich asked.

"That's right," Nick said. "Oh, God, her husband died very suddenly, if I'm remembering right. You don't think—no, oh no." Nick dashed her fingers through her hair. "This is very difficult. I've believed it was John from the very beginning. When he came at me that last night, his fingers curved toward my neck—and I swear to you, I saw murder in his eyes—I knew he was guilty. Not a single doubt in my mind. I was terrified. The thing is—why would he come after me if it was Albia who killed the women?"

"Maybe he didn't mean to hurt you," Sherlock said. "Maybe he just wanted that letter from his ex-wife. And he wanted it very badly, enough to attack you to get it. Nick, his career is on the line here. All he cares about can come tumbling down around his ears. He had to get ahold of that letter. Now that raises a good question, doesn't it?"

"Yes, it does," Dane said. "Did he already know that Cleo was long dead?"

"No," Nick said. "He was saying that there was no way Cleo would ever hurt him like that, no way at all. Oh, I don't know. This is too much. You guys really believe then that it was Albia Rothman who tried to kill me in Los Angeles?"

"Probably," Sherlock said. "I'd for sure bet she arranged setting fire to your condo. As for the man on the Harley, maybe she hired someone she trusted, someone from Chicago."

Nick was shaking her head. "Actually, I figured it all out in a dream a couple of nights ago. The guy in the car who tried to run me down, the guy who set fire to my condo, the guy on the Harley—I realized that they were all the same man. I'm really sure of that."

Dane said, "That makes sense. Maybe a lover, someone she felt she could really trust."

"Maybe," Savich said. "And once Linus sent your photo to the media, and she saw you on TV, recognized you, she knew just where you were. It wouldn't be hard to locate where you were staying, and to have you followed. And when the Harley attempt failed, she just didn't have time to execute another plan."

Nick leaned over and took a bite out of Dane's sandwich.

Savich said, grinning as he sat forward, "That's interesting behavior, Nick. First you bite Dane's shoulder and now his sandwich. This appears to me to be serious aggression. Can you handle this, Dane?"

"I'll manage," Dane said, and smiled at Nick even as he touched his fingers to his shoulder. "She's too skinny. Let her bite anything she wants."

"Hmmm," said Sherlock, and gave her husband a look that nearly had him shaking. It was the same look she'd given him the night before, just before she kissed every inch of him and sent him to heaven.

"That's enough of that," Savich said, both to his wife and to Dane.

"Let's get back to Cleo Rothman. She's been dead three years. I'll wager that senior aide, Tod Gambol, is dead as well. Now, who else could have sent you that letter, other than Albia Rothman? Is there anyone else remotely possible that you can think of, Nick?"

Nick shook her head. "I can't think of anyone else. But listen to me, all of you. I was absolutely certain that it was Cleo's handwriting."

Sherlock shrugged. "That's no big problem. It just means that Albia had copies of Cleo's letters, memos, whatever, and copied them. It's a real pity that John Rothman destroyed the letter. We could have run tests, figured out who wrote it, once and for all. Maybe she wrote you the letter to scare you off. Maybe she didn't want to kill you, maybe she did. Maybe she'll end up telling us. But she wanted you gone, thus the letter and the story about the journal."

"You don't believe there's a journal?" Nick asked.

"Oh no," Dane said. "It never made any sense that John Rothman would leave a journal in which he confessed to a murder, in his study safe, and the damned safe is left open accidentally. Nope, Albia made up the journal to terrify you, to get you the hell out of Dodge."

Savich said, "Regardless, it wasn't Senator Rothman who wrote the letter. He'd have to be beyond nuts to do that. Albia wrote it because she wanted you to break things off with her bro. When it didn't work, she got real serious about killing you."

Sherlock said, "Well, Rothman could be nuts, but listen, Nick, if it turns out that it's his sister who's behind all this, do you still want to marry the senator?"

Nick didn't pause for a second. "I have other plans."

Dane said, "She can't marry the senator. She bit my shoulder a second time. Not to mention my sandwich. I figure that's a really big step toward commitment."

"Sounds long term to me," Savich said.

Sherlock patted Nick's arm and smiled up at her husband. "Last night I was feeling just a touch let down, what with all the excitement over. Well, not let down in certain things, just the contrary, as a matter of fact." She gave Savich another look to make him shake, then shook her head, cleared her throat. "And now we have a bit more to keep us occupied. Then it's home to Sean. We've been away from our boy too long. He's very likely got his grandmother dancing jigs for his entertainment. Okay, what do you say, guys? Let's wrap this thing up today."

"She's an adrenaline junkie," Savich said, and hugged his wife against his side, kissed her ear. "Hey, after we see Senator Rothman, how about we go work out?"

Sherlock said, "The way this works is that Dillon will work out until he's nearly dead, then he'll smile at me and have the whole thing figured out."

Dane said, "You mean it's plain old sweat that solves your cases? Not sugar?"

"No sugar. Just sweat and pain," Savich said. "Let me call Jimmy Maitland, tell him what we're up to, see if he wants to notify the police commissioner here in Chicago. Sherlock, why don't you call Senator Rothman's office, see if he's in. I'd really like to pop in on him, just like we did with Linus Wolfinger."

Nick sat back in her chair, arms crossed over her chest. She looked from one to the other and marveled. "I just don't believe you guys."

THEY all ended up going to Hoolihan's Gym on the corner of Rusk and Pine because Senator Rothman was in Washington and not due to arrive at his office until late afternoon.

At the gym, they watched Assistant FBI Director Jimmy Maitland on the big overhead TV, flanked by the local FBI field office people, local LAPD, and the press, in Los Angeles.

Savich said, "I told Mr. Maitland that we didn't want to be part of the hoopla. He's really good at handling that sort of thing."

They watched the media pushing and shoving, all of them yelling questions at once. At least six reporters wanted to know where Dane, Sherlock, and Savich were. One even asked about the homeless woman— the supposed eyewitness—who hadn't managed to identify Linus Wolfinger.

Nick booed the TV.

Jimmy Maitland said, fanning his hand, "Sorry, people, but the special agents in question are already involved in another case. As for the homeless woman, she did just fine. She put her life on the line for us. Next question."

Delion had gone back to Los Angeles for the press conference, after being the main rep for a huge media ordeal in San Francisco at City Hall. Both Delion and Flynn were there now, standing together, smiling, Flynn's hand moving up and down like he was dribbling a basketball, freely telling the main facts of the case. All questions about Captain DeLoach were referred to the DA.

A spokesperson from Premier Studios expressed owner Miles Burdock's shock, surprise, and deep regret. He informed everyone that *The Consultant* would eventually be rescheduled. No one wanted the stars to be penalized for something they'd known nothing about.

He didn't say it was just possible that everyone would want to watch the show now, that it would get its highest ratings ever. He didn't say he was planning to use the profits the show generated to help cover the host of lawsuits the studio was sure to face from their scripts being used as models for murder by their own chief executive.

Belinda Gates and Joe Kleypas stood behind the spokesperson. It was obvious they were very pleased. The spokesperson announced finally that Frank Pauley would be assuming Linus Wolfinger's position as president of Premier Studios.

The four watching at Hoolihan's Gym in Chicago high-fived one another when the press conference was over. "Belinda was the only one who ever helped us," Sherlock said, "but even she let us down."

Savich said to his wife, "That reminds me. I haven't pulled those rollers out of your hair yet," and kissed her.

"I'll buy some tomorrow," Sherlock said.

THIRTY-SIX

An hour later the four of them were at Senator Rothman's office on Briarly Avenue in downtown Chicago. Press were hovering about in herds. "I feel sorry for the poor soul who just happens to be walking near here today," Nick said, and led them to the back of the building. "It looks like the reporters haven't found out about this back entrance just yet."

Savich said, "It won't take them long. I saw security people in the lobby. At least they can keep the vultures out of the building."

The secretary, Mrs. Mazer, jumped to her feet when she saw Nick and yelled, "Oh goodness me, you're all right! Oh, Dr. Campion, the senator will be so pleased to see you. Even though he hasn't said anything, I know he's been dreadfully worried, particularly after we all saw you on television and realized you were involved in that horrible script murder case. We all thought you were visiting your family. Oh, come in, come in. Who are these folks with you?"

"It's good to see you, Mrs. Mazer. Is John free for a moment?"

"Oh, yes, certainly. He will be so pleased to see you." She paused a moment, looking at Dane, Sherlock, and Savich, a gray eyebrow arched.

"It's all right. They're with me, Mrs. Mazer."

Mrs. Mazer said nothing more, opened the senator's door, then stepped aside.

Senator John Rothman was standing in the middle of his large office when Nick walked first into the room. She stopped, said, "Thank you for seeing me, John."

He stood stiff as a lamppost. "Nicola," he said politely. "Who are these people?"

Nick introduced each of them in turn. "Did you see the press conference?"

"Oh yes, I saw it all," Senator Rothman said. "Mrs. Mazer, please close the door and see that I'm not disturbed."

When the door was quietly and firmly closed, Senator John Rothman turned to Nick. He tried to smile at her, flanked by three FBI agents.

"It's good to see you, Nicola. Like everyone else in the world, I saw your photo on television. It was a shock, as you can imagine." He paused a moment, searching her face. "There was the fire in your condo. I was frantic but I couldn't find you. You simply disappeared. I called the university. The dean told me you'd written a letter stating that you had a family emergency, but that was a lie, wasn't it?"

"Yes, it was a lie," Nick said.

"I had no idea where to find you. I didn't think it was a good idea to call the FBI and demand information about your whereabouts. And now you've come back. Why?"

"First of all, to tell you I'm sorry about Cleo."

"Yes, I am, too. The thing is, some people believe I killed her, but I didn't. I'm sure my lawyers think they've died and gone to heaven, they're going to make so much money off this mess. Listen, I didn't hurt anyone, Nicola." His eyes never left her face. "I didn't try to hurt you."

Finally, he broke the moment, turning, when Savich said, "Senator, as Nick told you, I'm Agent Savich, this is Agent Sherlock, and Agent Carver. Since Nick helped us out on the murder cases in California, we've decided to help her out with her involvement in this particular mess."

"It is a mess," said John Rothman. He ran his fingers through his beautifully styled salt-and-pepper hair.

Dane, who'd said nothing, stood quietly behind Nick, eyeing this elegant aristocrat. He wanted to kick the man's teeth down his throat.

"John," Nick said, "do you remember that night I asked you how many women you killed?"

Dead silence.

"Yes, of course I would remember when the woman I love accuses me of being a serial killer. I assume all these Federal agents are familiar with what you think of me, Nicola?"

She nodded. She realized in that moment that she was now perfectly safe. No one could hurt her again. She drew herself up even taller.

"Did you know there was an attempt on my life in Los Angeles?"

"Of course not. How could I possibly know that?" He paused a moment, then said, "Should I have my lawyer present?"

"I don't believe so," Savich said. "Why don't we all sit down and talk this over?"

The lovely pale brown brocade grouping was expensive and charming. The coffee served in the Georgian coffeepot was fresh and quite excellent. It was Nicola who served them. Dane saw that she was very comfortable in these surroundings, pouring the damned coffee from that exquisite silver coffeepot. He'd be willing to bet Paul Revere had made the thing. He didn't know if he ever wanted to see Nick in the senator's penthouse, damn that man's sincere and honest eyes.

Dane sat forward, clasping his hands between his legs. "Nick has told us that your mother died in a car accident some three months after she confessed infidelity to your father. You were sixteen at the time. Is this correct?"

Rothman said slowly, "Why are you asking about my mother? It is absolutely none of your business. It's no one's business. It has nothing to do with anything."

"Senator, we're here as friends of Nick," Sherlock said. "Of course, our superiors also know that we're here. We rather hoped we could clear everything up today, informally." She gave him her patented smile, which no human being alive could resist. He found himself smiling back at her, taking in her brilliant curly red hair. He said, "I appreciate that, Agent. But of course I haven't killed anyone. I don't know what's going on, any more than you do. Nicola, I told you that my mother was dead, that she died in a car accident. But what does that have to do with anything? Why the questions about my mother?"

"It was in Cleo's letter," Nick said. "The one you tore out of my hand and hurled into the fireplace."

Senator Rothman looked utterly bewildered.

"You do remember shredding the letter and throwing it into the fireplace, John?"

"Yes, of course. I was very upset that night. A letter from Cleo—I simply couldn't accept that. Throwing the letter into the fire, it was an impulse, and one that I now regret."

Dane hated it, but he believed Senator Rothman. He'd really hoped, in a deep, black spot in his heart, that the senator was so guilty he'd stink of it, but he didn't.

Dane said, "Senator Rothman, perhaps we can end this very simply. Could you please show us your journal?"

Senator Rothman looked blank.

"You do have a journal, don't you, sir?" Sherlock said.

"Yes, of course, but it's more like a recording of events over the years, nothing personal, if you know what I mean. Actually, I haven't written in it in a very long time."

"May we please see it, sir," Dane said.

Senator Rothman rose, walked to his exquisite bird's-eye maple desk, opened the second drawer, and pulled it out. He handed the journal-sized notebook to Dane.

Sherlock said, "You don't keep it at home in the safe in your study?"

"Oh no, I've always kept it here. I'm hardly home enough to leave it there. As I said, I haven't written in it in a very long time, since before Cleo left—no, before someone murdered Cleo." He winced.

Nick said, "Cleo wrote that you confessed to murdering Melissa."

"Murdered Melissa? That is absurd. I wish I hadn't destroyed that damned letter. Listen, Nick, whoever wrote you that letter, it wasn't Cleo."

"We know that now," Savich said. "Cleo's been dead since she supposedly left you."

No one said anything. Dane opened the journal, a rich dark brown leather with a clasp that wasn't locked. He skimmed through it.

Rothman said, "As you can see, Agent Carver, it's more a recording of events and appointments, nothing at all sinister." He paused, said, "No, Cleo didn't write you that letter, Nicola. God, she was dead, dead all along, and no one knew." He put his face in his hands, his shoulders heaving, struggling to keep control.

No one said a word until he got himself together again, drank some of his coffee. "I apologize."

He said finally, "What the hell is going on here?"

"Haven't you wondered who wrote me that letter since Cleo has been dead for three years?" Nick asked.

He splayed his hands in front of him, didn't say anything.

"You kept insisting that last night, John, that Cleo hadn't written the letter, that it was impossible. It occurred to me that you must have known she was dead, that it was impossible for her to have written to me, that it had to be someone else."

"No, I had no idea Cleo was dead. What I simply couldn't believe was that Cleo would slander me like that, that she would make up that story about a journal and what I'd written. There was no way she could have believed that I killed Melissa, would have killed *her* as well, and now even you. All because of some rumor that you were sleeping with Elliott Benson?"

"That all three of us slept with Elliott Benson, beginning with Melissa back in college."

He shook his head. "That's absurd. Elliott is a friend, not an enemy. He's a man I trust, a man I've always trusted."

Nick looked away from the man she'd planned to marry just one month before. Now he and Elliott Benson were the best of friends? She didn't know, just didn't know.

She rose and walked to the huge window that gave onto Lake Michigan. The water was whipped up by a strong wind. She could tell it was cold and blustery from there, on the twenty-second floor of the Grayson Building. She said over her shoulder, not looking back, "I never heard any rumor about me and Elliott, did you, John?"

To her surprise, he slowly nodded, saw she still wasn't looking at him, and said aloud, "Yes, I did hear some rumors. I actually spoke to Elliott about them, and he denied them, of course. I remember I was about to leave when I turned and saw that he was smirking behind his hand. Then it was gone, and I believed I must have imagined it. Elliott would never hurt me." He rubbed his knuckles then, and Savich knew that the restrained aristocratic senator had been thinking about hitting Elliott Benson. Because he believed he was the enemy? Did he believe that Nick would do such a thing?

"Why do you think he would slander Dr. Campion?" Sherlock asked. "If, of course, he actually did."

"I don't know. He's occupied a unique position in my life, sometimes a friend, sometimes an enemy. It's been that way since we were in high school. I do know he wanted to sleep with Cleo, I know that for a fact. But she didn't want him. She told me about it." He paused, looked down at his hands, at his fingers rubbing against his palms. "But of course there was Tod Gambol."

"Who still hasn't been located," Dane said.

The senator said, "Maybe Tod's the one who killed her. Or maybe it was Elliott and he's the one who started the rumor about Nicola because he wanted her to leave me. Maybe I've been wrong about him all these years. But would he go that far? Jesus, I don't know. Do you know why he would say such a thing, Nicola?"

"No, I have no idea. Did you believe him when he denied the rumor about me, John?"

"Good God, yes, naturally."

"Are you quite sure?"

"Of course." But he dropped his eyes. He said, "Those references to my journal, to what I'd supposedly written, listen to me. I didn't write any of that, so that means she lied, but now we know it wasn't Cleo who lied, it was someone else."

"Yes," Savich said. "Yes, we think that just might be the case, Senator."

Senator Rothman looked pathetically eager. "Really? And just what exactly do you think, Agent?"

"We need to speak to you and your sister, Albia Rothman, sir," Sherlock said. "Could you perhaps arrange a meeting?"

"I'm sure Albia would want very much to see you again, Nick. Why don't all of you come to dinner tonight at my home?"

"That would be fine," Nick said. "Thank you, John."

"What's this about Albia? You think she's got something to do with this? You think she wrote the letter to Nicola, made up that journal?" His face was flushed. "That's nonsense, absolute rubbish."

"What time, John?" Nick asked.

THEY were all seated at the magnificent dining room table, which was set for six. Senator Rothman sat at the head of the table and Albia at the other end.

Dane thought she was a beautiful woman, as charming as her brother, though perhaps a touch more calculated. It was obvious to him that her brother hadn't mentioned the letter or the journal to her.

Albia Rothman had cried when she first saw Nick, hugged her, told her over and over how very worried they'd been about her, that she was utterly distraught that Nick had believed such horrible things about John.

"My dear, I cannot tell you how much both John and I worried about you. We talked and talked but nothing seemed to make any sense to us. Then you were on TV with this man here—this Federal agent—and you were some sort of eyewitness in that script murder. However did all that come about? We heard that the murderer killed himself. It must have been a horrible time for you, Nicola."

"Yes, it was very bad, Albia," Nick said.

Nick's voice was soft, a slight musical lilt to it. Dane saw that she wasn't wearing anything he'd bought her. She and Sherlock had gone shopping at Saks on Michigan Avenue, and both of them looked expensive, and, to Dane's eye, utterly beautiful. Nick's black dress was short, showing off very nice long legs, but conservative, very appropriate for these surroundings. Once again, he thought she fit perfectly in this environment. He could easily picture her as a powerful senator's wife. It made him sick to his stomach. He realized, as he looked at her, that he never would have met her if Michael hadn't died.

It was over the artistically arranged Caesar salad with glazed pecans set precisely atop the lettuce, nestled in among croutons, that Nick said, "Albia, did you write the letter to me? The letter that Cleo supposedly wrote?"

Albia Rothman raised a perfectly arched brow. She looked markedly like her brother with that expression. She frowned, just a bit, hardly furrowing her brow, and shook her head. "No, I don't know anything about a letter. What letter are you speaking about?"

Nick said, "John didn't mention the letter I received from Cleo, warning me that he was trying to kill me, that he'd also tried to kill her and that was why she ran away?"

"Good God, what a novel idea. A letter from Cleo? How very preposterous. John try to kill Cleo? Kill you? That is utterly absurd. John, what is going on here?"

Senator Rothman merely shrugged, methodically picked a pecan out of his salad, never looking at them. "The FBI agents are the ones with all the answers here, not I."

"You realize, I hope," Albia said to the table at large, "how very absurd that is. John is a very kind, intelligent man, a man to admire, a man who will make this country a better place."

Dane said, "Ms. Rothman, let's get back to whether you were the one who wrote Nick the letter."

"That means you were trying to warn me, Albia," Nick said. "You were trying to help me. Or were you trying to get rid of me?"

"Do eat your salad, Nicola. I didn't come here to discuss this nonsense."

Savich said, "We need your help, Ms. Rothman."

Albia said as she carefully laid down her salad fork, "If your friends—these Federal officers—are pushing you to do this, Nicola, then I do believe that I don't even wish to stay." She rose as she spoke, said to her brother, "John, I'm leaving. I have no intention of trying to digest my dinner with these people accusing you of murdering women. If I were you, I'd call Rockland and have him come represent you. I would also consider asking them to leave. Nicola, you have really disappointed me."

And she walked out of the dining room.

John Rothman said nothing until he heard the front door close quietly in the distance. "Well, whatever it is you were trying to achieve, that was disgraceful. Good evening to all of you."

Senator John Rothman rose, tossed his napkin over his uneaten salad, and walked gracefully out of the dining room.

They all stared at one another when they heard the front door close a second time.

"Well," Dane said, "I do enjoy the unexpected. The salad is delicious."

THIRTY-SEVEN

Dane said, "Jimmy Maitland asked us to a meeting with the police commissioner and several other nervous politicians, all of it regarding the Rothman case. Nick, you're not invited to this meeting. You're going to stay with Sherlock. She's agreed that you're more important than this meeting, so just Savich and I will go. You're to go nowhere alone, you got me?"

"I got you, but it's not fair to Sherlock."

Savich said, "Think of this as a good-old-boys butt-covering meeting. The SAC of the Chicago field office will be there, maybe even the mayor. It's all under wraps, at least it will be until the six-o'clock news."

Sherlock said to Nick, "I really don't enjoy watching a group of men in a pissing contest. But, guys, if anything outrageous is said, I'm sure you'll tell me about it." She kissed her husband's ear and gave him a little wave as he and Dane walked out of The Four Seasons lobby.

"We've got better things to do, Nick," Sherlock said when they'd reached the street. "We're going to go see Senator Rothman. Oh yes, my husband knows, but he didn't want Dane to know. Dane is very protective of you, Nick. Actually I'd have to say that he's terrified that something will happen to you if he doesn't stick to you like Grandma's toffee. You could probably have six cops with you and he'd still worry himself sick. But it'll be all right. You've got me."

Nick grinned, rubbed her hands together. "I can't imagine anyone needing more protection than you."

"I sure hope you're right about that. Okay, let's go see what we can find out. I'd much rather do this than go to a meeting, anyway."

Nick watched her check her SIG Sauer, then smiled when Sherlock said, "Dillon always says that if you aren't one hundred percent sure of what's going to happen, you just get yourself prepared."

They were at Senator Rothman's office by 9:30. Mrs. Mazer raised an eyebrow when she saw the two of them.

"Where are the big boys?"

"They're out playing with other big boys," Sherlock said.

Nick smiled, shook Mrs. Mazer's hand. "It's just us this morning. I'm here to see John, Mrs. Mazer."

"He'll be back in just a bit, maybe twenty minutes or so. I'm sure he'll want to see you, Dr. Campion. I hope you managed to avoid the media."

Nick nodded. "Yes, we came in through the back delivery entrance."

"I'm surprised they haven't found it by now," said Mrs. Mazer, and Nick didn't tell her that the media already had. "Oh dear, all this grief from the media. Senator Rothman is a very fine man, and now there are all these questions about the former Mrs. Rothman."

"The fact is, Mrs. Mazer," Nick said, "I'm really not sure about much of anything. But hopefully everything will become clear soon. Do you mind if I wait in his office?"

Mrs. Mazer wondered whether Dr. Campion wanted a few minutes to search the senator's desk. Who was she to say no? She'd left Dr. Campion alone in the senator's office many times. She said after a moment, "Why not?"

"Agent Sherlock, would you like to go with Dr. Campion or would you like a magazine?"

"What I would really like is to speak to any staff who might be here."

"Did Senator Rothman okay it?"

"I'm sure it will be all right," Sherlock said.

Mrs. Mazer pressed an extension on her phone. She spoke quietly, then raised her head. "Matt Stout is the senator's senior aide. He'll be out shortly to speak to you." She nodded to Nick, pressing a buzzer just beneath her desk. "Dr. Campion, it shouldn't be long." Was there a warning in her voice? Nick didn't know. A few minutes would be enough.

She said as she opened the office door, "Thank you, Mrs. Mazer." Nick stepped into the big office, knowing exactly where she was going to start looking. Not in his desk. One day she'd seen him kneeling in front of the drink cart, seen a flash of papers disappear through a small opening in the bottom of the cart. She walked straight to it.

"Hello, Nicola. I'm very surprised to see you here. In the camp of the enemy."

Nick nearly dropped in her tracks she was so startled. She jerked about, nearly losing her balance, to see Albia Rothman standing by the huge windows, dressed in one of her power suits, a rich charcoal gray wool with a soft white silk blouse. She looked quite elegant, rich, intimidating.

"Albia! Oh my heavens, you scared me. What are you doing here?"

"I think the more significant question is what are you doing here, Nicola? I spend a great deal of time here, but you? You ran away, left John without a word, just ran. And now you're back to try to hang him. He is a good man, a man this country needs. He is a visionary, a man of ideas, and here you are, trying to ruin him. I really won't have it, Nicola. I won't."

"No one wants to hang John," Nick said, facing the woman Savich, Sherlock, and Dane believed to be a killer. She wasn't afraid simply because she wasn't alone, not really. Sherlock was outside, as were a dozen people. All she had to do was yell and people would come running. No reason to be afraid of Albia. She could take Albia, all sleek in her three-inch high heels and tight skirt. She didn't have much maneuvering room, but she was in better shape than Albia.

Most important, there was Sherlock, her biggest weapon. She said, "But it's clear to everyone that since Cleo's body was found, and she'd been struck with something on the back of the head—there are questions that have to be answered. Cleo was John's wife. All of us have to face that reality. People think John would have had to know. Some people think John may have killed Cleo, Albia."

"How did you get in here without the media attacking you?"

"I slipped in through the delivery entrance. It was real close going, but I was lucky. The media guy who was supposed to keep his eye on it was having a coffee break. I saw him go into the deli across the street. John told me about that entrance a long time ago." Actually, both she and Sherlock had come in through the delivery entrance, but Nick didn't want to tell Albia about Sherlock just yet. She wanted to make Albia feel safe, make her feel in control. Just maybe she'd say something, admit to something.

Albia said with a shrug of her elegant shoulders, "Vultures, aren't they? But why did Mrs. Mazer let you in here?"

"I told her I wanted to see John. She suggested I wait in here, that he'd be back soon. Of course, I've waited for him many times in his office. I would have thought she'd tell me that you were here, but she didn't."

"That's because," Albia said, as she took a step toward Nick, "she doesn't know I'm here."

Nick forced herself not to move an inch. "How did you get in?"

Albia smiled at her, waved a graceful hand in dismissal. "When John took the lease on this building some ten years ago, he had the architect design a private entrance that led only to this office. Most people in his position have alternate ways of leaving their offices, in circumstances just like this one. I wonder why John didn't tell you about the private entrance? I wonder—perhaps when it came right down to it, he didn't really trust you, Nicola. Perhaps he did come to believe that you really were sleeping with Elliott Benson. You know, of course, that Elliott has always wanted any woman that John has, and vice versa, I might add. It's been a competition between them since before they went to college. And they pretend to be close friends. Did you know that Elliott was in love with Melissa, the girl John was engaged to? Turns out she wanted both of them, stupid girl. She slept with both of them until she died in that car accident. It was a terrible thing for my poor brother."

"Did he know she was sleeping with Elliott?"

"I have no idea. As for Elliott, I don't know what he felt about Melissa's death. It was a very long time before John became seriously interested in another woman. But he did, finally, and he and Cleo married. It wasn't long before Elliott got to Cleo, screwed her brains out, and everyone knew—but not John, not until after she left. I suppose she was sleeping with Tod Gambol, too, since he left when she did."

"But everyone knows now that she didn't run away with anybody, Albia. Someone murdered her. And buried her, hoping her body would never be found."

"Isn't that interesting? Nicola, did you sleep with Elliott Benson?"

Nick didn't answer her immediately. She was remembering how she once wondered how John had arrived at his office without her seeing him. A hidden private exit, what a good idea. Nick said, "Sleep with Elliott Benson? That's a novel thought. Another man old enough to be my father. Oh, he's as polished as an Italian count, as sleek as both you and John, but I'll tell you the truth, Albia. Whenever I see him I am reminded of a Mafia movie character with his pomaded hair and his expensive Italian suits. Whenever he looks at me, speaks to me, I want to go take a bath."

"Cleo didn't think he was bad at all. To be honest about this, I didn't believe so either, at least not at first. Yes, he was my lover for a time as well. Too bad it wasn't because he adored me, no, he just wanted something else that belonged to John. I suppose I'm included in that group. And, fact is, he's not a very good lover. Sure, he maintains his body well, and says all the right things, but he's selfish. He's used to expensive call girls who lick the bottoms of his feet if that's what he wants. He has difficulty remembering to give as well as receive when he's with a woman he isn't paying. And like I said, the both of them still pretend to be friends. What games men play."

"Albia, do you think it makes any sense at all to sleep with another man when you're engaged to be married? Why would you even be engaged if you wanted to sleep around?"

"Any number of women do it all the time. They want the power, the money that marriage would bring them and they want the excitement a lover brings. It's not a big mystery. Don't be coy, Nicola."

Nick walked over to John's desk, sat down in his big, comfortable leather chair. It steadied her, sitting behind his impressive desk. She picked up a pen and tapped it against the beautiful maple. She remembered Linus Wolfinger doing the same thing until everyone wanted to strangle him. She tapped the pen again, then once again. She said, seeing the look of annoyance on Albia's face, "Did you spread rumors about me sleeping with Elliott Benson?"

"Of course not. It was common knowledge."

"I see. How odd that I didn't know. I do know you are the one who wrote me the letter supposedly from Cleo. It couldn't be anyone else, and you also wrote with great detail about Melissa."

Albia was framed by that beautiful window, the sun surrounding her. She looked powerful, otherworldly, her stance, the tilt of her head identical to John's.

Nick felt the sudden taste of sour bile in her mouth. It tasted like fear, fear of this woman whom everyone saw as an elegant creature they admired and respected, a woman who was powerful in her own right. They didn't see Albia Rothman as a person who could have started off her adult life murdering someone. For John, for her little brother, whom she adored.

"I didn't write you anything, Nicola."

Nick let it go for the moment. What had she expected? A confession? She said after a moment of silence, "I can't believe Cleo ever slept with Elliott Benson. Nor with Tod Gambol. She loved John."

"Oh, but Cleo was a little harlot. John wouldn't believe me until I finally showed him photos that I had a private investigator take of her and Elliott, all cozied up in his small house on Crane Island. It's all private, you know, the nearest neighbor is a good half mile away. I might add that he and John both have used that house. If they happen to have each other's woman at that house, they make sure to leave a small token, a small trace of it. Perhaps you've been there, Nicola?"

Nick shook her head. "I don't believe it. I knew her. I really liked Cleo. She loved John, I'm sure of that." She realized that only about fifteen feet separated them. She said, "Albia, it's time to admit that you wrote me the letter, that you made up that journal confession to save me, to make me leave Chicago and leave John. You did it to help me, didn't you? Please tell me. You wanted to protect me, didn't you?"

Albia shrugged. "Yes, all right, no reason to lie about it now. Yes, I wrote you the letter, for all the good it did. You're back and now you want everyone to pay. John didn't try to kill you, Nicola."

Nick's heart was thudding so loudly she believed that surely Albia would hear it, that Albia must know she was so scared she was ready to pee in her pants. The words just came out, she couldn't stop them. "If it wasn't John, then was it you, Albia?"

A perfectly arched eyebrow went up a good inch. "Me? Goodness, no."

"You hired someone to try to run me down, to burn down my condo, with me in it."

"It strikes me, though, that just maybe you were the one to set fire to your own condo."

Nick laughed, couldn't help it. "That's idiocy."

Albia shrugged. She took a step back, leaned against the window, crossed her arms over her chest. She looked mildly amused. "So it was your lover who tried to kill you. It was Elliott Benson. I called him, you know. He told me all about you, told me that poor John had picked the wrong woman yet again. And he laughed then, a very pleased laugh."

"Albia, who killed Cleo?"

"Tod Gambol. After all, he was the one to run away, wasn't he? As I said, Cleo was a slut. John has always been so innocent, so trusting, so unsuspecting. They say people always search out the same sort of person again and again, doesn't matter if that person is rotten. John's the classic example. Melissa, Cleo. Then he chose you, and just look at what you did."

"I didn't do anything, Albia. Did you have the same man come to LA to kill me while he was riding a Harley?"

"I'm really tired of all this nonsense, Nicola. All this will blow over. John didn't kill Cleo, he didn't try to kill you, and neither did I. I want you to leave now. I honestly believe you should take yourself as far away as possible. I did my best to get you away from here. You should get away again, Nicola."

"No, I'm staying this time, Albia. I want to know who's trying to kill me."

Albia examined a beautifully manicured nail a moment. "You're not very bright, given all your education. I have no idea about any of this. However, I saw last night at that ridiculous dinner you and your FBI friends set up how you and that one agent were looking at each other. You've already taken another lover. John saw it as well. He knows you're sleeping with that Federal cop. That's really sad, Nicola. You're not at all worthy of someone as fine as John Rothman."

"Probably, from your point of view, no woman is good enough for him, Albia."

"Well, that's probably true. I've taken care of him since our mother died."

"I've wondered if your mother really died accidentally?"

"What a ridiculous thing to say. You're nothing but a little bitch with a big mouth. I'm glad you'll soon be out of our lives. And you will be, one way or another." And with that, Albia walked across the room, pressed her finger against one of the wall panels, and watched it silently open. Then she was gone, just like that, gone without another word.

Nick looked at that blank wall. What was Albia going to do? Figure out how to kill her again? Obviously she couldn't do it here, not with so many people just a short distance away. She wasn't stupid. Where was the man she must have hired? Nick's heart was still pounding. She felt a headache building over her left eye. It was time to fetch Sherlock, time to see Dane, to tell him everything Albia had said, which wasn't much of anything except for all this stuff about Elliott Benson.

First, though, she wanted to see what was behind that hidden panel. She walked to the wall, found the nearly flat button, and pressed it. The panel slid silently open. There was a dim passage that ran about six feet directly away from her then turned sharply to the right. She wanted to know what that turn led to, but there was no way she was going into that passage. She and Sherlock would check it out together. She turned to press the panel button when a large hand clapped down hard over her mouth. She fought but it was no good. She had no leverage and the man was much larger than she was, and very strong. He dragged her out of the office and into the passage. Her heart nearly dropped to her stomach when she heard the panel slide shut, and there was nothing but a tomb of darkness and a man dragging her away from safety.

The man stopped abruptly at the end of the passage and turned sharply right. Suddenly there were soft glowing lights set above an elevator door.

"She had to take a look just like you thought she would," the man said, and pushed her away to hit the wall, hard.

Albia was holding an elegant silver derringer, and it was aimed right at her chest.

"Hello, Nicola. How nice of you to open the panel."

Her throat was clogged with fear. The man—she recognized him. He was wearing the same black leather jacket. Dark opaque sunglasses hung out of the breast pocket. His hands were large, fingers blunt—strong hands. It was the same man who'd been riding the Harley in LA.

She turned and ran.

He was on her in an instant, grabbed her arms and twisted them up and back, hard, and she groaned with the pain.

He leaned down and whispered in her ear, "It's too late now, love."

"Darling, bring her here."

He dragged her back to where Albia stood, looking unruffled and elegant, still holding that derringer. "My goodness, Nicola, you are a bad girl, now aren't you? You've been trying very hard to muck things up and I really can't allow any more, now can I?"

The man eased his hold on her arms. He turned her slowly to face him. He was older, his face seamed from years in the sun. He pushed her face up, his fist beneath her chin. "You're very pretty. I always thought so, but not so smart, even with all those diplomas you have. But you know what, love? You were lucky, very lucky. I've always believed that luck ranked right up there with brains."

Nick stared up at him. "You're the man who tried to kill me."

"Well, yes, I did, and it was quite a blow when I didn't get you. Albia was very upset with me."

"Of course I was upset. You know, Nicola, you had more than your share of luck," Albia said. "Poor little Cleo, she didn't have even a lick of luck. Just as well that Dwight here sent her to her great reward. She was looking quite old there at the end. John told me that he used to love to touch her, her skin was so soft, but there, toward the end, he thought she was getting old, her skin becoming coarse."

"I thought she felt pretty nice," Dwight said.

Albia laughed. "John is very choosy. He told me he loved touching Nicola, that her skin was so very soft. He prayed that she wouldn't become coarse for a long time."

Nick jerked, felt Dwight's hand tighten around her arm. "Don't think about yelling, love, this area is soundproof, the senator's office as well. No one can hear a thing."

Nick whispered, "It was you, Albia, all along it was you."

"Yes, dear. You want to know something? You're nothing, Nicola, nothing at all. Dwight will make sure that no hunter's dog finds you. You've caused me a lot of trouble, but this will be the end of it. Yes indeed, it's so fortunate that Dwight was waiting for you to open the panel. I thought you'd come right on in, but you didn't. Still, it didn't matter. Now, that's what I call luck—for me."

Nick knew what fear tasted like, but this was more. This numbed her brain, made her shake. She didn't want to die.

There was nothing close to her, no weapon, nothing. If only she had Dane's SIG Sauer again. But Dwight was here, ready to grab her again if she even twitched.

She didn't think, she just screamed and screamed again as she shoved her fist into Dwight's belly and tried to pull free.

"That's quite enough," Albia said, and brought the butt of the derringer hard on the back of her head. Nick didn't see points of light, just instant, nauseating black. She sank to the floor.

THIRTY-EIGHT

"When did you say the senator would be back, Mrs. Mazer?"

"He should have been here by now, Agent Sherlock. I wonder if he came in through his private entrance?"

Sherlock went *en pointe*. "What private entrance?" She didn't wait for an answer. She was around Mrs. Mazer's desk in an instant, her hand on the doorknob, turning it, but nothing happened. It was locked.

"It locks automatically when it's closed from the inside," Mrs. Mazer said, rising, alarmed now. "Some years ago a reporter forced his way in, so the senator decided to make the lock automatic. What's wrong, Agent Sherlock? Oh dear, is it about Dr. Campion?"

Sherlock knocked on the door, yelling Nick's name.

"Here, Agent."

Sherlock ground the key into the lock, twisted it, and the door opened silently.

The office was empty. "Where's the private entrance? Quickly, Mrs. Mazer."

"In the back wall."

Sherlock pulled her SIG Sauer out in a flash, even as she yelled over her shoulder to Mrs. Mazer, "Call the police. Tell them your Senator Rothman has taken Dr. Campion. Hurry!"

It took Sherlock a moment to find the small button, built in nearly flat against the wall. She pressed, and the door silently eased back. She stepped into a dimly lit passage that was oak paneled, the floor carpeted with two small Turkish rugs. She paused, listening. She thought she heard something, movement, a man's breathing.

She went forward slowly in the darkness. The corridor turned once, then ended. The whole thing wasn't more than six feet long. She was facing a narrow elevator, its silver door barely visible in the dim light.

She heard the low hum of the elevator motor. He was taking Nick down. But Sherlock didn't know where the elevator let out. She punched the button again, then a third time.

And while she punched, she pulled out her cell phone, dialed Dillon's number. He answered immediately. "Hello?"

"Dillon, hurry. Rothman's building. He's got Nick. It isn't Albia. Oh God, hurry—"

The elevator door opened silently and smoothly, and she jumped inside, punched the only button. Dillon was no longer connected on the cell phone. It didn't work inside the elevator. No, it was all right, she'd said enough. Every available cop in Chicago would converge on the building within minutes.

The door opened and she stepped out slowly, fanning her SIG. She was in a dark area of the basement. There was the low hum of equipment all around her. She paused for a moment, listening. Where could he have gone? How big was this damned basement? How could he begin to hope he'd take Nick out of here without being seen? There were media nosing around.

Sherlock stood quietly for a few more seconds, but she simply couldn't hear anything except the sounds of the equipment motors all around her.

When the gun barrel slammed down, she collapsed to the floor, her SIG hitting the concrete and skidding away from her.

HER first thought, when she opened her eyes, was that she had a bitch of a headache. She felt the pain slash through her head. Not a moment later, Nick remembered—Albia had struck her with the butt of her gun. She tried to raise her hand but couldn't.

She heard the sound of an engine, loud, but that didn't make any sense. She realized she was tied to a chair, arms and ankles, really tight. The pain in her head made her nauseous, and she swallowed repeatedly until she knew she wouldn't vomit. Then she heard a moan, but it wasn't from her.

She looked up. She was in a small room, lots of wood, cramped. She looked to her left. There was Sherlock, tied to another chair, her head slumped forward.

The room lurched. Moved. She realized they were on a boat and the boat was moving fast, the engine pushing hard. She smelled the water and the diesel, heard the powerful engine, felt the boat bounce and rock as it sliced through the waves.

Boat?

"Sherlock, wake up. Sherlock? Please, come out of it. You can do it."

Silence, then, "Nick?"

"Yes, I'm all right, just a horrible headache. He got you, too. I'm so sorry."

Sherlock got herself together, closed her eyes, tried to get her brain back in gear. "Nick, I'll be okay, just give me a minute."

The boat slammed down and Nick's chair nearly toppled.

"We're in a boat, going really fast," she said.

"Yes," said Sherlock. "I can feel it. I'm very sorry I let him get me, Nick. At least I'd already called Dillon. Every cop in Chicago will be looking for us, count on it."

"We're on John's boat. I've been out on it a couple of times. It's good-sized, a sixty-three-foot Hatteras Flybridge yacht. It's really fast, Sherlock. He used to brag that it could do twenty-one knots."

"It feels like he's nearly at maximum. The man's nuts, Nick. I can't understand how a United States senator could do something like this. I can't imagine how he got both of us out of the building and here on his boat, all without being seen. He's a very well-known man."

"It isn't John, Sherlock. You guys were right, it was Albia. The guy who's driving the boat is Dwight, the man who tried to kill me three times."

Sherlock digested that. "You know something? I don't feel all that smart that we figured out Albia was behind it."

"I wonder where Dwight is taking us?"

Sherlock didn't say anything. She was afraid she knew. Dwight was going to take them to the middle of Lake Michigan, weigh them down, and toss them overboard.

It's what she would have done if she were nuts and in a hurry.

"Crane Island," Nick said suddenly. "Maybe he's taking us to Crane Island. Albia said that John owns a house there, really private."

Fat chance, Sherlock thought, unless he wanted to kill them and bury them there. She wasn't about to say that to Nick. She got her breathing and her brain together, shook her head just very slightly so she wouldn't be sick, and raised her head. "You're right, there's the boat logo over there. My cell phone, Nick, it's in my pocket. We've got to get loose and use it. Nick, how tight are your wrists tied?"

Several moments passed before Nick said, "Real tight, but my ankles aren't too bad."

"Mine are tight, too. Okay, do you think you can move yourself closer to me?"

"Yes, Sherlock."

Nick was nearly there when the boat hit a big wave and she toppled to the side. She hit her face against the thin carpet on the wood floor. She was winded, lay there a moment trying to get herself together.

"Nick, you all right?"

"Yes, but I don't know if I can still get over to you, Sherlock."

"I've been working on my ankles, they're a bit looser, maybe. Let me see if I can't get over to you."

It took time, so much precious time, but finally Sherlock was right next to Nick. "Okay, no hope for it. I'm going to have to topple myself and hope that I'm close enough to reach your wrists."

Sherlock's chair went over. She looked over her shoulder. She was too far from Nick's wrists. She wiggled, pushed, as did Nick. Finally, she could touch her hands. She was panting hard, pain shooting up her arms. "At last. Just a bit closer, Nick. Hurry. That's good."

Sherlock went to work. They were both aware of time, and too much of it was passing too fast. Dwight could stop the boat any minute, come down the wooden stairs, and shoot them. Oh God, it was all her fault. She'd been arrogant, so sure of herself—oh God, she felt low as a slug. She thought of Sean, of Dillon, and knew, knew to her soul that she simply couldn't die. She wouldn't.

She concentrated, focused. The knot was loosening, finally. "Nick, get the rope off your hands, quick. We don't have much time."

Nick pulled her hands free, got her ankles untied, then went to work on Sherlock's wrists. She was panting, but not with fear now, with hope, urging herself to move quicker, quicker.

The boat was slowing down.

"Hurry, Nick!"

Done, her wrists were free. Both of them untied Sherlock's ankles. They both pulled themselves to their feet. But they were uncoordinated, numb from being tied so long. "He took my cell phone," Sherlock said, panting. "Blast it."

The boat was coming to a stop.

Sherlock managed to get to the galley area, pulled out drawers until she found the knives. "Here, Nick," and handed her a knife. "Can you move now? Damn, I'd rather have my SIG, well, no matter, at least it's a steak knife, with a nice sharp serrated edge. The boat's stopped. We're not in the middle of the lake. We're at a pier. I was sure he'd just shoot us and throw us overboard. Do you think we're at this Crane Island?"

"Yes, we're at Crane Island," Dwight said, walking down the stairs. "Come to think of it, I wish I'd buried Cleo here. No hunters allowed, you know? Well, well, would you just look, both of you free. How very efficient of you, Agent Sherlock. Ladies, put those knives down. I want you to come up the stairs, slowly, your hands on your heads. Do it or I'll shoot you right here. Oh yes, you're going to die in a beautiful place. I'm going to bury you beneath some ancient pine trees at the back of Senator Rothman's property."

Nick dropped the steak knife. She put her face in her hands and started crying, low, ugly sobs.

Dwight laughed. He'd taken off his leather jacket. He was wearing a black T-shirt, khaki pants held up with a silver belt with a big turquoise buckle, and black boots. He laughed, watching her fall apart. "I knew once you realized that you weren't long for this earth, you'd break. I expect more from an FBI agent. I bet she won't shed a tear.

"Pull yourself together, Nicola. I'm not going to kill you right away. Think of all the trouble you've caused me and poor Albia. I've got to punish you for that. I promised Albia I would. I'm going to let the two of you wonder about the end I've got planned for you."

"What plans?" Sherlock asked.

"You'll see," he said. "I want you to go up the stairs first, Agent."

Sherlock nodded to Nick, turned, and began climbing those nine wooden steps up to the deck.

Nick just nodded, and sobbed some more. She felt his hand pushing against her back, and trailed after Sherlock. Once on deck, she kept her head down, kept the choking sobs coming from her mouth. She saw they were docked at a long stretch of wooden planking. There was a narrow strip of beach, tossed with driftwood. The land looked wild, all thick pine forests as far as she could see.

"Welcome to Crane Island. Albia assures me there won't be any interruptions. It's a perfect place, just what I needed. Come along, Nicola, don't hang back like that. Pull yourself together. I expected more from you. Even Cleo didn't carry on the way you are."

But Nick was crying harder now, completely out of control. She dropped to her knees and crawled to Dwight. She clutched at his feet, his ankles, sobbing, "Please, Dwight, let us go. I swear I'll never say a word. I'll run and never come back. Don't kill me."

"God, you're pathetic. Get up!"

But she didn't, just kept pleading, trying to grab his knees.

He leaned down to grab her and pull her upright when Nick suddenly wrapped her arms around his knees and jerked him forward. He yelled, off-balance, and tried to hit her with the gun. Sherlock, who had been waiting, straightened and turned, smoothly sending her foot hard into his left kidney. He went stiff in agony, then yelled. He turned the gun on her, but Nick was hitting his knees, trying to jerk him down again. He struck Nick's cheek with his fist, then whirled on Sherlock. He tried to back up, but her leg was up and she kicked him in the ribs. He didn't dive away, ran straight at her and managed to grab a fistful of her hair. He twisted, pulled. Sherlock yelled in pain and rage, and first slammed her fist into his gut, then her foot into his crotch. He yelled, bent over, his finger pulling the trigger of his gun. Two shots went wild. Nick threw herself at his knees, shoved him backward with all her strength. As he fell, Sherlock grabbed his wrist and twisted it hard. He dropped the gun to the deck and fell on his face. Sherlock scooped it up.

Nick dove on top of him, hitting his face, his neck, yelling, "I'm not pathetic, you murdering jerk! I wouldn't beg you for anything, you murdering son of a bitch! We got you and you're going to rot in jail for the rest of your miserable life."

Sherlock stood over them, the feeling returning to her hands and feet. "That was quite an act, Nick. Well done."

"It was, wasn't it?" Nick said, and grinned up at Sherlock.

Then, suddenly, Dwight moved, lurched up, knocking Nick backward.

Sherlock said, "Thank you, Dwight," and she kicked him in the head.

He crumbled back onto the deck.

Nick scrambled to her feet, yelling, "You bastard," and hit him in the belly, then rose and kicked him hard in the ribs.

She looked over at Sherlock, grinned until she thought her mouth would split, and dusted off her hands.

"We're good."

Sherlock hugged her close, then leaned back. "We are good, Nick. We're very good."

"No one to match us," Nick said.

"Let me get Dillon," Sherlock said and went to the boat radio. She got the Coast Guard, which was just fine.

Twenty minutes later, when the Coast Guard launch pulled up to the Crane Island dock, with both Savich and Dane ready to leap onto Rothman's boat, it was to see both Sherlock and Nick leaning over the side, waving to them.

"Why am I surprised?" Savich asked to no one in particular. "Thank God."

"I've got to start breathing again," Dane said. "Damn, I've never been so scared in my life. Just look at them, grinning from ear to ear. Is that Rothman lying facedown on the deck?"

"Oh no," Nick said. "It wasn't Senator Rothman. You guys were right all the time. It was Albia, and this is the man who tried to kill me three times."

"Four times," Sherlock said.

Dwight groaned, then slumped back on the deck.

"Hey, Dwight," Nick shouted to him. "Am I lucky, or what?"

Dwight didn't answer. With a scream of rage, he jerked upright, grabbed a knife out of his boot, and went after Nick. She froze. That knife was up, coming toward her, arching downward to her heart, and suddenly she was thrown to the deck onto her back. Dane was on him, both hands locked around his wrist, shaking, tightening.

Dwight screamed in his face, "You're the Fed cop. Hey, I nearly got you once, I'll do it again."

"Oh no," Dane said, let Dwight draw him in closer, then he drove his knee up into Dwight's groin. He screamed, fell back. Dane slammed his fist into his belly, shoved him down. He was on top of him, slamming his head on the deck. Vaguely, he heard Savich call out. He saw the blur of the knife, realized he'd let his own rage get the better of him. He rolled off Dwight, came up, and when the man came at him again, crouched over, still in bad pain, Dane kicked him in the jaw. He went down like a rock.

This time he didn't move. They all watched the knife slowly fall from his fingers.

"Good move," Savich said, and squeezed his shoulder. He watched, smiling, as Dane turned, looked at Nick, then slowly brought her against him. They didn't move for a very long time.

Sherlock said, "You know what, Dillon? I want to go buy some fat rollers this afternoon. We've put it off long enough, don't you think?"

Savich laughed.

EPILOGUE

She watched Dane place the single white lily on top of Father Michael Joseph's grave. He straightened, his head down. His lips were moving, but she couldn't hear what he was saying to his brother.

Finally, he raised his head and smiled at her. He said simply, "Michael loved Easter, and that means lilies." He paused a moment. "I will miss him until I die. But at least he's been avenged."

"It isn't enough," she said. "It just isn't enough."

"No, of course not, but it's something. Thank you for coming with me, Nicola."

"No, please, just call me Nick. I don't think I ever want to be called that other name again."

"You got it. Whatcha say we go take Inspector Delion to lunch?"

"I'd like that." She took his outstretched hand. He turned once to look back at his brother's grave. The single lily looked starkly white atop the freshly turned dirt. Then he looked back at her and smiled.

Nick said, "Inspector Delion told me about this Mexican restaurant on Lombard called La Barca. Let's go there."

He grinned down at her. "You mean all I've got to do is give this girl a taco and she's a happy camper?"

They walked in silence to the rental car. He said, "I just heard from Savich. Albia Rothman's hearing was this morning. She pleaded not guilty. And you know what? Dwight Toomer isn't rolling on her, at least not yet. We'll have to see how tough the DA is. You'll have to testify, Nick. It won't be fun."

"No, but maybe we can get justice for Cleo."

"It'll take a long time to come to court. Albia Rothman's got big-tag lawyers. They'll stall and evade and file more motions than O.J.'s lawyers. But it will happen. She will go down. It's not enough, but it's all we can do. Now, what are you planning on doing, Nick?"

"You know I resigned from the university."

"Yes, I know," he said, and waited, and thought of the huge box of condoms he had in his briefcase. He smiled even as she said, "I've been thinking I'd like to come east, maybe to Washington, D.C., see what's available for an out-of-work college professor."

He stopped, lightly touched his fingers to her cheek, smelled the fresh salty air, and said, "Yes, I think that's a fine idea. Given your record for getting into trouble, it's probably smart of you to get as close as possible to the biggest cop shop in the U.S."

"I sure hope you're wrong about that. I don't even plan on getting a parking ticket. Dane, remember you wanted the next fifty years?"

"Yes, and then we'll negotiate for more. I was thinking that someday Sean Savich will be a grown man and just maybe, if we have a girl, she and Sean could get together. What do you think?"

"Good grief. We're not even married and you've already got our daughter married! Hmmm. To Sean Savich. We'll have to speak to Savich and Sherlock about some sort of nuptial contract. What do you think?"

He laughed, took her hand, and felt a bolt of happiness fill him, deep and bright. He turned back once more to see the lily atop Michael's grave lightly waving in the salty breeze.

BLINDSIDE

To my mother, Elizabeth Coulter

ONE

It was pitch black.

There was no moon, no stars, just low-lying rain-bloated clouds, as black as the sky. Dillon Savich was sweating in his Kevlar vest even though it was fifty degrees.

He dropped to his knees, raised his hand to stop the agents behind him, and carefully slid into position so he could see into the room.

The window was dirty, the tattered draperies a vomit-brown, with only one lamp in the corner throwing off sixty watts. The rest of the living room was dark, but he could clearly see the teacher, James Marple, tied to a chair, his head dropped forward. Was he asleep or unconscious? Or dead?

Savich couldn't tell.

He didn't see Marvin Phelps, the sixty-seven-year-old man who owned this run-down little 1950s tract house on the outskirts of the tiny town of Mount Pleasant, Virginia. From what they'd found out in the hour before they'd converged on this small house, Phelps was a retired math teacher and owned the old Buick sitting in the patched drive. Savich knew from his driver's license that Phelps was tall, skinny, and had a head covered with thick white hair. And for some reason, he was killing other math teachers. Two, to date. No one knew why. There was no connection between the first two murdered teachers.

Savich wanted Phelps alive. He wanted the man to tell him why he'd caused all this misery and destroyed two families. For what? He needed to know, for the future. The behavioral science people hadn't ever suggested that the killer could possibly be a math teacher himself.

Savich saw James Marple's head jerk. At least he was alive. There was a zigzagging line of blood coming over the top of Mr. Marple's bald head from a blow Phelps must have dealt him. The blood had dried just short of his mouth.

Where was Marvin Phelps?

They were here only because one of Agent Ruth Warnecki's snitches had come through. Ruth, in the CAU—the Criminal Apprehension Unit—for only a year, had previously spent eight years with the Washington, D.C., police department. Not only had she brought her great street skills to the unit, she'd also brought her snitches. "A woman can never be too rich, too thin, or have too many snitches" was her motto.

The snitch had seen Marvin Phelps pull a gun on a guy in the parking lot of a small strip mall, pull him out of his Volvo station wagon, and shove him into an old Buick. The snitch had called Ruth as he was tailing them to this house, and told her he'd give her the whole enchilada for five hundred bucks, including the license plate number of the man taken. Savich didn't want to think about what would have happened to Mr. Marple if the snitch hadn't come through.

But Savich shook his head as he looked at the scene through the window. It didn't fit. The other two math teachers had been shot in the forehead at close range, dying instantly. There'd been no kidnapping, no overnight stays tied to a chair with a sixty-watt bulb chasing the shadows. Why change the way he did things now? Why take such a risk by bringing the victim to his own home? No, something wasn't right.

Savich suddenly saw a movement, a shadow that rippled over the far wall in the living room. He raised his hand and made a fist, signaling Dane Carver, Ruth Warnecki, and Sherlock that he wanted everyone to stay put and keep silent. They would hold the local Virginia law enforcement personnel in check, at least for a while. Everyone was in place, including five men from the Washington field office SWAT team who were ready to take this place apart if given the word. Every corner of the property was covered. The marksman, Cooper, was in his place, some twenty feet behind Savich, with a clear view into the shadowy living room.

Savich saw another ripple in the dim light. A dark figure rose up from behind a worn sofa. It was Marvin Phelps, the man whose photo he'd first seen just an hour ago. He was walking toward John Marple, no, swaggering was more like it. What was he doing behind the sofa?

When Phelps wasn't more than a foot from Marple, he said, his voice oddly deep and pleasant, "Are you awake, Jimbo? Come on, I didn't hit you that hard, you pathetic wuss."

Jimbo? Savich turned up the volume on his directional receiver.

"Do you know it will be dawn in another thirty-seven minutes? I've decided to kill you at dawn."

Mr. Marple slowly raised his head. His glasses had slipped down his nose, and with his hands tied behind him, he couldn't do anything about it. He licked at the dried blood beside his mouth.

"Yes, I'm awake. What do you want, Philly? What the hell is going on here? Why are you doing this?"

Philly? The two men knew each other well enough for nicknames.

Phelps laughed, and Savich felt his skin crawl. It was a mad old laugh, scratchy and black, not at all pleasant and deep like his voice. Phelps pulled a knife from inside his flannel shirt, a long hunting knife that gleamed even in the dull light.

Savich had expected a gun, not a knife. It wasn't supposed to go down like this. Two dead high school math teachers, and now this. Not in pattern. What was going on here?

"You ready to die, Jimbo, you little prick?"

"I'm not a prick. What the hell are you doing? Are you insane? Jesus, Philly, it's been over five years! Put down that knife!"

But Mr. Phelps tossed the knife from one hand to the other with easy movements that bespoke great familiarity.

"Why should I, Jimbo? I think I'm going to cut out your brain. I've always hated your brain, do you know that? I've always despised you for the way you wanted everyone to see how smart you were, how fast you could jigger out magic solutions, you little bastard—" He was laughing as he slowly raised the knife.

"It's not dawn yet!"

"Yeah, but I'm old, and who knows? By dawn I might drop dead of a heart attack. I really do want you dead before me, Jimbo."

Savich had already aimed his SIG Sauer, his mouth open to yell, when Jimbo screamed, kicked out wildly, and flung the chair over backward. Phelps dove forward after him, cursing, stabbing the knife through the air.

Savich fired right at the long silver blade. At nearly the same moment there was another shot—the loud, sharp sound of a rifle, fired from a distance.

The long knife exploded, shattering Phelps's hand; the next thing to go flying was Phelps's brains as his head exploded. Savich saw his bloody fingers spiraling upward, spewing blood, and shards of silver raining down, but Phelps wouldn't miss his hand or his fingers. Savich whipped around, not wanting to believe what had just happened.

The sniper, Kurt Cooper, had fired.

Savich yelled "No!" but of course it was way too late. Savich ran to the front door and slammed through, agents and local cops behind him.

James Marple was lying on his back, white-faced, whimpering. By going over backward he'd saved himself from being splattered by Mr. Phelps's brains.

Marvin Phelps's body lay on its side, his head nearly severed from his neck, sharp points of the silver knife blade embedded in his face and chest, his right wrist a bloody stump.

Savich was on his knees, untying Jimbo's ankles and arms, trying to calm him down. "You're all right, Mr. Marple. You're all right, just breathe in and out, that's good. Stay with me here, you're all right."

"Phelps, he was going to kill me, kill me—oh, God."

"Not any longer. He's dead. You're all right." Savich got him free and helped him to his feet, keeping himself between James Marple and the corpse.

Jimbo looked up, his eyes glassy, spit dribbling from his mouth. "I never liked the cops before, always thought you were a bunch of fascists, but you saved me. You actually saved my life."

"Yeah, well, we do try to do that occasionally. Now, let's just get you out of here. Here's Agent Sherlock and Agent Warnecki. They're going to take you out to the medics for a once-over. You're okay, Mr. Marple. Everything is okay."

Savich stood there a moment, listening to Sherlock talk to James Marple in that wonderful soothing voice of hers, the one she had used at Sean's first birthday party. One terrified math teacher wouldn't be a problem compared to a roomful of one-year-olds.

Agent Dane Carver helped support James Marple, until Sherlock stepped forward, and then she and Agent Warnecki escorted Marple to the waiting paramedics.

Savich turned back to the body of Marvin Phelps. Cooper had nearly blown the guy's head off. A great shot, very precise, no chance of his knifing Marple in a reactive move, no chance for him to even know what was happening before he died.

It wasn't supposed to have happened that way, but Cooper had standing orders to fire if there was imminent danger.

He saw Police Chief Halloran trotting toward him, followed by a half-dozen excited local cops, all of them hyped, all of them smiling. That would change when they saw Phelps's body.

At least they'd saved a guy's life.

But it wasn't the killer they were after, Savich was sure of that. Theirs had killed two women, both high school math teachers. And in a sense, that maniac was responsible for this mess as well. It was probably why Cooper had jumped the gun and taken Phelps out. He saw himself saving James Marple's life and taking out the math teacher killer at the same time. In all fairness, Coop was only twenty-four, loaded with testosterone, and still out to save the world. Not good enough. Savich would see to it that he had his butt drop-kicked and then sentenced to scrubbing out the SWAT team's bathroom, the cruelest penalty anyone could devise.

The media initially ignored the fact that this incident had nothing to do with the two math teacher killings. The early evening headlines read: SERIAL KILLER DEAD? And underneath, in smaller letters, because math teachers weren't very sexy: MATH TEACHERS TARGETED. The first two murders were detailed yet again. Only way down the page was it mentioned that the kidnapping and attempted murder of James Marple by Marvin Phelps of Mount Pleasant, Virginia, had nothing to do with the two other math teacher killings.

Par for the course.

TWO

Savich wasn't stupid. He knew it when he saw it, and the gorgeous woman with the long black hair pinned up with a big clip, wearing a hot-pink leotard, was coming on to him.

He didn't know her name, but he'd seen her around the gym a couple of times, both times in the last week, now that he thought about it. She was strong, supple, and fit, all qualities he admired in anyone, male or female.

He nodded to her, pressed the incline pad higher on the treadmill, and went back to reading the report Dane Carver, one of his CAU agents, had slipped under his arm as he'd walked out of the office that evening.

Bernice Ward, murdered six days before, was shot in the forehead at close range as she was walking out of the 7-Eleven on Grand Street in Oxford, Maryland, at ten o'clock at night, carrying a bag that held a half-gallon of nonfat milk and two packages of rice cakes, something Savich believed should be used for packing boxes, not eating.

There had been no witnesses, nothing captured on the 7-Eleven video camera or the United Maryland Bank ATM camera diagonally across the street. The 7-Eleven clerk heard the shot, found Mrs. Ward, and called it in. It was a .38 caliber bullet, directly between Bernice Ward's eyes. She'd been married, no children. The police were all over the husband. As yet, there was no motive in sight.

And just three days ago, the second victim, Leslie Fowler, another high school math teacher, was shot at close range coming out of the Alselm Cleaners on High Street, in Paulette, Virginia, just before closing at 9 p.m. Again, there were no witnesses, no evident motive as of yet for the husband, and the police were sucking him dry. Leslie Fowler had left no children, two dogs, and a seemingly distraught husband and family.

Savich sighed. When the story of the second shooting broke, everyone in the Washington, D.C., area was on edge, thanks to the media's coverage. Nobody wanted another serial killer in the area, but this second murder didn't look good.

Dane Carver had found no evidence that either woman had known the other. No tie at all between the two had yet been found. Both head shots, close range, with the same gun, a .38.

And as of today, the FBI was involved, the Criminal Apprehension Unit specifically, because there was a chance that a serial killer was on the loose, and the Oxford P.D. and the Paulette P.D. had failed to turn up anything that would bring the killers close to home. Bottom line, they knew they needed help and that meant they were ready to have the Feds in their faces rather than let more killings rebound on them.

One murder in Maryland, one murder in Virginia.

Would the next one be in D.C.?

If the shootings were random, Dane wrote, finding high school math teachers was easy for the killer—just a quick visit to a local library and a look through the high school yearbooks.

Savich stretched a moment, and upped his speed. He ran hard for ten minutes, then cooled down again. He'd already read everything in the report about the two women, but he read it all again. There was no evidence of much value yet, something the media didn't know about, thank God. The department had started by setting up a hot line just this morning, and calls were flooding in. Many of them, naturally, had to be checked out, but so far there was nothing helpful. He kept reading. Both women were in their thirties, both married for over ten years to the same spouses, and both were childless—something a little odd and he made a mental note of that—did the killer not want to leave any motherless children? Both husbands had been closely scrutinized and appeared, so far, to be in the clear. Troy Ward, the first victim's husband, was the announcer for the Baltimore Ravens, a placid overweight man who wore thick glasses and began sobbing the moment anyone said his dead wife's name. He wasn't dealing well with his loss.

Gifford Fowler was the owner of a successful Chevrolet car dealership in Paulette, right on Main Street. He was something of a womanizer,

but he had no record of violence. He was tall, as gaunt as Troy Ward
was heavy, beetle-browed, with a voice so low it was mesmerizing. Savich
wondered how many Chevy pickups that deep voice had sold. Everything
known about both husbands was carefully detailed, all the way down
to where they had their dry cleaning done and what brand of toothpaste
they used.

The two men didn't know each other, and neither had ever met the
other. They apparently had no friends in common.

In short, it appeared that a serial killer was at work and he had no
particular math teacher in mind to target. Any math teacher would do.

As for the women, both appeared to be genuinely nice people, their
friends devastated by their murders. Both were responsible adults, one
active in her local church, the other in local politics and charities. They'd
never met each other, as far as anyone knew. They were nearly perfect
citizens.

What was wrong with this picture?

Was there anything he wasn't seeing? Was this really a serial killer?
Savich paused a moment in his reading.

Was it just some mutt who hated math teachers? Savich knew that
the killer was a man, just knew it in his gut. But why math teachers?
What could the motive possibly be? Rage over failing grades? Beatings
or abuse by a math teacher? Or, maybe, a parent, friend, or lover he
hated who was a math teacher? Or maybe it was a motive that no sane
person could even comprehend. Well, Steve's group over in behavioral
sciences at Quantico would come up with every possible motive in the
universe of twisted minds.

Two dead so far and Steve said he'd bet his breakfast Cheerios there'd
be more. Not good.

He wanted to meet the two widowers.

Savich remembered what his friend Miles Kettering had said about
the two math teacher killings just a couple of nights before, when he
and Sam had come over for barbecue. Six-year-old Sam was the image
of his father, down to the way he chewed the corn off the cob. Miles
had thought about it a moment, then said, "It seems nuts, but I'll bet
you, Savich, that the motive will turn out to be old as the hills." Savich
was thinking now that Miles could be right; he frequently had been back
when he and Savich had been agents together, until five years before.

Savich saw a flash of hot-pink leotard from the corner of his eye.

She started up on the treadmill next to his, vacated by an ATF guy who'd gotten divorced and was telling Bobby Curling, the gym manager, that he couldn't wait to get into the action again. Given how many single women there were in Washington, D.C., old muscle-bound Arnie shouldn't have any problem.

Savich finished reading Dane's report and looked out over the gym, not really seeing all the sweaty bodies, but poking around deep inside his own head. The thing about this killer was that he was in their own backyard—Virginia and Maryland. Would he look farther afield?

Savich had to keep positive. Even though it had been unrelated, they'd saved James Marple from having a knife shoved in his chest or his head. It had come out last night that Jimbo had had an affair with Marvin Phelps's wife, who'd then divorced Phelps and married Marple— five years before. But Savich knew it wasn't just the infidelity that was Phelps's motive. He'd heard it right out of Phelps's mouth—jealousy, pure and simple jealousy that had grown into rage. The last time Savich had seen James Marple, his wife, Liz, was there hovering, hugging and kissing him.

"Hello, I've seen you here before. My name's Valerie. Valerie Rapper, and no, I don't like Eminem." She smiled at him, a really lovely white-toothed smile. A long piece of black hair had come loose from the clip and was curved around her cheek.

He nodded. "My name's Savich. Dillon Savich."

"Bobby told me you were an FBI agent."

Savich wanted to get back to Dane's report. He wanted to figure out how he was going to catch this nutcase before math teachers in the area became terrified for the foreseeable future. Again, he only nodded.

"Is it true that Louie Freeh was a technophobe?"

"What?" Savich jerked around to look at her.

She just smiled, a dark eyebrow arched up.

Savich shrugged. "People will say anything about anyone."

Standard FBI spew, of course, but it was ingrained in him to turn away insults aimed at the Bureau. And, as a matter of fact, what could he say? Besides, the truth was that Director Freeh had always been fascinated with MAX, Savich's laptop.

"He was sure sexy," she said.

Savich blinked at that and said, "He has six or seven kids. Maybe more now that he has more time."

"Maybe that proves that his wife thinks he's sexy, too."

Savich just smiled and pointedly returned to Dane's report. He read: *Ruth Warnecki says she's kept three snitches happy since she left the Washington, D.C., Police Department, including bottles of bubbly at Christmas. She gave a bottle of Dom Perignon to the snitch who saved James Marple's life, only to have him give it back, saying he preferred malt liquor.*

The booze Ruth usually gave to her snitches would probably burn a hole in a normal person's stomach. They'd been very lucky this time, but what could a snitch know about some head case killing high school math teachers? They weren't talking low-life drug dealers here. On the other hand, most cases were solved by informants of one sort or another, and that was a fact.

He tried to imagine again why this person felt his mission was to commit cold-blooded murder of math teachers. Randomly shooting company CEOs—that was a maybe. Judges—sometimes. Politicians—good idea. Lawyers—hands down, a top-notch idea. But math teachers? Even the profilers were amused about how off-the-wall crazy bizarre it was, something that no one could ever remember happening before.

He was inside his brain once more when she spoke again. He nearly fell off the treadmill at her words. "Is it true that Congress, way back when, was responsible for shutting off any communication between the FBI and the CIA? And that's why no one shared any information before nine-eleven?"

"I've heard that" was all he said.

She leaned close and he smelled her perfume, mixed with a light coating of sweat. He didn't like Valerie Rapper looking at him like she wanted to pull his gym shorts off.

She asked, "How often do you work out?"

He had only seven minutes to go on the treadmill. He decided to cut it to thirty seconds. He was warmed up enough, loose, and a little winded. "I try to come three or four times a week," he said, and pressed the cool-down pad. He knew he was being a jerk. Just because he was anxious about this killer, just because a woman was interested in him, it didn't mean he should be rude.

And so he asked, "How often do you come here?"

She shrugged. "Just like you—three or four times a week."

Without thinking, he said, "It shows." Stupid thing to say, really stupid. Now she was smiling, telling him so clearly how pleased she was that he liked her body.

He was an idiot. When he got home he'd tell Sherlock how he'd managed to stick his foot all the way down his throat and kick his tonsils.

He pressed the stop pad and stepped off the treadmill. "See you," he said, and pointedly walked to the weights on the other side of the room.

He worked out hard for the next forty-five minutes, pushing himself, but aware that she was always near him, sometimes standing not two feet away, watching him while she worked her triceps with ten-pound weights.

Sherlock, much smaller, her once skinny little arms now sleek with muscle, had worked up to twelve-pound weights.

Thirty minutes later he forgot all about the math teacher killer and Valerie Rapper as he opened the front door of his house to hear his son yell "Papa! Here comes an airplane!" and got it right in the chest.

Two evenings later at the gym, while Sherlock was showering in the women's locker room after a hard workout, and Savich was stretching his tired muscles in a corner, he nearly tripped on a free weight when Valerie Rapper said, not six inches from his ear, "Hello, Dillon. I heard that you saved a math teacher from a crazy man a couple of days ago. Congratulations."

He straightened so fast he nearly hit her with his elbow. "Yeah," he said, "it happens like that sometimes."

"The media is making it sound like the FBI messed up, what with that old man getting his head blown off."

Savich shrugged, as if to say what else is new? He said again, "That happens, too."

"Maybe you'd like to have a cup of coffee after you've finished working out?"

He smiled at her and said, "No, thank you. I'm waiting for my wife. Our little boy is waiting for us at home. He's learning how to make paper airplanes."

"How delightful."

"See you."

Valerie Rapper watched him as he made his way through the crowded gym to the men's locker room. She watched him again when he came out of the locker room fifteen minutes later, showered and dressed, shrugging into his suit coat. He wished there were more men in Washington, D.C. Maybe he should introduce her to old Arnie. He found Sherlock talking to Bobby Curling. He grabbed her and hustled her out before she could say a word.

She asked as she got into the Porsche, "What was all that about?"

"I'd rather tell you when we get home."

SAVICH brushed out a thick hank of Sherlock's curly hair and carefully wrapped it around a big roller. "I'm glad you're feeling better. I'm glad you were at the gym tonight."

She watched him in the mirror, concentrating on getting her hair perfectly smooth around the roller. He was nearly done. He really liked doing this ever since they'd met an actress who'd had a particularly sexy way with hair rollers. Of course, the rollers didn't stay in her hair all that long. "Why? What happened?"

He paused a moment, smoothed down her hair on another roller, and slowly turned it. Sherlock shoved in a clip to hold it. "There's this woman. She's not taking the hint."

Sherlock leaned her head back until she was looking up at her husband's face. "You want me to go kick her butt?"

Savich didn't speak for a good thirty seconds. He was too busy untangling the final thick hank of hair for the last roller. "There, done. Now, be quiet. I just want to look at you. You can't imagine how that turns me on, Sherlock."

She now had a headful of fat rollers, perfectly placed, and she was laughing. She turned and held out her arms. "Now what, you pervert?"

He stroked his long fingers over his chin. "Hmmm, maybe I can think of something."

"What about this woman?"

"Forget her. She'll lose interest."

Sherlock did forget all about the woman during the removal of the rollers in the next hour. She fell asleep with a big roller pressed against the back of her knee.

It was just after six-thirty on Friday morning when the phone rang. Savich, Sean under one arm while Sherlock was pouring Cheerios into a bowl, picked it up. He listened. Finally, he hung up the phone.

"What's wrong?"

"That was Miles. Sam's been kidnapped."

THREE

Don't give up, don't give up. Never, never give up.

Okay, so he wouldn't give up, but it was hard. He'd cried until he was hiccupping, but that sure hadn't done him any good. He didn't want to give up. Only thing was, Sam didn't have a clue where he was and he was so scared he'd already peed in his jeans.

Be scared, it's okay, just keep trying to get away. Never give up.

Sam nodded. He heard his mama's voice every now and again, but this time it was different. She was trying to help him because he was in big trouble.

Don't give up, Sam. Look around you. You can do something.

Her voice always sounded soft and kind; she didn't sound like she was scared. Sam tried to slow his breathing down.

The men are in the other room eating. They're watching TV. You've got to move, Sam.

He'd been as quiet as he could, lying on that stinky mattress, getting colder and colder, and he listened as hard as he could, his eyes on that keyhole, wishing he was free so he could scrunch down and try to see what the men were doing. He heard the TV; it was on the Weather Channel. The weather guy said, "Violent thunderstorms are expected locally and throughout eastern Tennessee."

He heard that clearly: *eastern Tennessee.*

He was in Tennessee?

That couldn't be right. He lived in Virginia, in Colfax, with his father. Where was Tennessee?

Sam thought about his father. How much time had passed since they'd put that cloth over his face and he'd breathed in that sick sweet smell and not really waked up until just a while ago, tied to this bed in this small bedroom that looked older than anything, older even than his father's ancient Camaro? Maybe it was more than hours, maybe it was days now. He didn't know how long he'd been asleep. He kept praying that his father would find him. But there was one big problem, and he knew it even while he was praying the words—his father wasn't in Tennessee; as far as Sam could see, there was no way his father could find him.

I'm really scared, Mom.

Forget about being scared. Move, Sam, move. Get your hands free.

He knew he probably wasn't really hearing his mama's voice in his head, or maybe he really was, and he was dead, too, just like she was.

He could feel that his pants were wet. It was cold and it itched so that must mean he really wasn't dead. He was lying flat on his back, his head on a flattened smelly pillow, his hands tied in front of him. He'd pulled on the rope, but it hadn't done anything. Then he'd felt sick to his stomach. He didn't want to throw up, so he'd just laid there, breathing in and out, until finally his stomach calmed down. His mom wanted him to pull on the rope and so he began jerking and working it again. His wrists weren't tied real tight, and that was good. He hadn't talked to the two men when he woke up. He was so scared that he'd just stared up at them, hadn't said a single thing, just stared, tears swimming in his eyes, making his nose run. They'd given him some water, and he'd drunk that, but when the tall skinny guy offered him a hamburger, he knew he couldn't eat it.

Then one of the men—Fatso, that's what Sam called him in his head—tied his hands in front of him, but not too tight. Fatso looked like he felt sorry for him.

Sam raised his wrists to his mouth and started chewing.

"Damned friggin' rain!"

Sam froze. It was Fatso's voice, loud and angry. Sam was so scared he started shaking, and it wasn't just the damp chill air in this busted-down old room that caused it. He had to keep chewing, had to get his hands free. He had to keep moving and not freeze. He couldn't die, not like Mama had. His father would hate that almost as much as Sam would.

Sam chewed.

There weren't any more loud voices from the other room, but he could still hear the TV announcer, talking more about really bad weather coming, and then he heard the two men arguing about something. Was it about him?

Sam pulled his hands up, looked closely, and then began working the knotted rope, sliding his hands first this way, then that. The rope felt looser.

Oh boy, his hands did feel looser, he knew it. Sam chewed until his jaws ached. He felt a give in the rope, then more give, and then the knot just came loose. He couldn't believe it. He twisted his wrists and the rope fell off.

Unbelievable. He was free.

He sat up and rubbed his hands. They were pretty numb, and he felt pins and needles running through them, but at least they didn't hurt.

He stood up beside the mangy bed with its awful smells, wondering how long it had been since anyone had slept in that bed before him. It was then he saw a high, narrow, dirty window on the other side of the room.

He could fit through that window. He could.

How would he get up there?

If he tried to pull the bed to the window they were sure to hear him. And then they'd come in and tie him even tighter.

Or they'd kill him.

Sam knew he'd been taken right out of his own bed, right out of his own house, his father sleeping not thirty feet away. He knew, too, that anything those men had in mind to do to him wasn't any good.

The window . . . how could he get up to that window?

And then Sam saw an old, deep-drawered dresser in the corner. He pulled out the first drawer, nearly choking on fear when the drawer creaked and groaned.

He got it out. It was heavy, but he managed to pull it onto his back. He staggered over to the wall and, as quietly as he could, laid the drawer down, toeing it against the damp wall. He stacked another drawer on top of that first one, then another, carefully, one upside down on top of another.

He had to lift the sixth drawer really high to fit it on top of the others. He knew he had to do it and so he did.

Hurry, Sam, hurry.

He was hurrying. He didn't want to die even though he knew he'd probably be able to speak to his mama again all the time. No, she didn't want him to die, she didn't want him to leave his father.

When he got the last drawer balanced on the very top, he stood back, and saw that he had done a good job putting them on top of each other. Now he just had to climb up on top and reach the window.

He eyed the drawers, and shoved the third one over just a bit to create a toehold. He did the same with the fourth.

He knew if he fell it would be all over. He couldn't fall. He heard Fatso scream, "No matter what you say, we can't stay here, Beau. It's going to start raining any minute now. You saw that creek out back. A thunderstorm'll make it rise fast as bat shit in a witch's brew!"

Drown? The thunderstorms he'd heard on the Weather Channel, that must be what Fatso was yelling about. He didn't want to drown either.

Sam was finally on the top. He pulled himself upright very slowly, feeling the drawer wobbling and unable to do anything about it. He froze, his hands flat against the damp wall, then his fingers crept up and he touched the bottom of the windowsill.

Things were unsteady beneath his feet, but that was okay. It felt just like the bridge in the park when he walked across it, just like that. He could work with a swing, even a wobble, he just couldn't fall.

He pushed at the window but it didn't budge. Then he saw the latch, so covered with dirt that it was hard to make out. He grabbed it and pulled upward.

He heard Fatso yell, "Beau, listen to me, we gotta take the kid somewhere else. That rain's going to start any minute."

So that was his name, Beau. Beau said something back, but Sam couldn't make out what it was. He wasn't a screamer like Fatso.

Sam had the latch pushed up as far as it would go. Slowly, so slowly he nearly stopped breathing, he pushed at the window.

It creaked, loud.

Sam jerked around and the drawers teetered, swaying more than ever. He knew he was going to fall. The drawers were sliding apart like earth plates before an earthquake. He remembered Mrs. Mildrake crunching together real dinner plates to show the class how earthquakes happened.

He shoved on the window as hard as he could and it creaked all the way out.

The drawers shuddered and moved and Sam, almost crying he was so afraid, grabbed the windowsill. With all the strength he had, he pulled himself headfirst through that skinny window. He got stuck, wiggled free, and then fell outside.

He landed on the ground, nearly headfirst.

He lay there, breathing, wanting to move, but afraid that his head was split open and his brains might start spilling out. He lay listening to the wind pick up, whipping through the trees. There were a lot of trees around him, and the sky was almost dark. Was it nighttime?

No, it was just the storm coming closer, the thunderstorm the Weather Channel had talked about for eastern Tennessee. How could he be in Tennessee?

He had to get up. Fatso and Beau could come out at any moment. The drawers had fallen over, no doubt about that, and the loud noise would bring them into the bedroom fast. They'd see he was gone and they'd be out here with guns and poison and more rope and get him again.

Sam came up on his knees. He felt something sticky on his face and touched it. He'd cut himself with the fall. He turned to look up at the window. It was way far off the ground.

Sam managed to stand up, weaved a bit, then locked his knees. He was okay. Everything was cool. He just had to get out of there.

He started running. He heard Fatso scream the same instant a bolt of lightning struck real close and a boom of thunder rattled his brains. They knew he was gone.

Sam ran into the thick trees, all gold and red and yellow. He didn't know what kind of trees they were, but there were a lot of them and he was small and could easily weave in and out of them. If they got too close he'd climb one, he was good at that, too good, his father always said.

He heard the men yelling, not far behind him, maybe just a little off to the left. He kept running, panting now, a stitch in his side, but he just kept his legs pumping.

Lightning flashed through the trees, and the thunder was coming so close it sounded like drums playing real loud rock 'n' roll, like his father did when he thought Sam was outside playing.

Sam heard Fatso yell, and stopped, just for a second. Fatso wasn't even close. But what about Beau? Beau didn't have the belly Fatso had, so maybe he could slither through the trees really fast. He could come out from behind a tree and jump Sam, cut his throat.

Sam's heart was pounding so loud he could hear it. He crouched down behind one of the big trees, made himself as skinny as a shadow, and waited. He got his breath back, pressed his cheek to the bark, and listened. He didn't hear anything, just the thunder that kept rumbling through the sky. He rubbed his side and the stitch faded. The air felt thick, actually felt like it was raining before the first drop found its way through the thick canopy of leaves and hit him on the jaw.

They'd never see him in the rain. Fatso would probably slip on some mud and land on his fat belly. Sam smiled.

You did it, Sam, you did it.

He'd done it all right. Only thing was he didn't know where he was. Where was Tennessee?

Even with the thick tree cover, the rain came down hard. He wondered if the forest was so big he'd come out in Ohio, wherever that was.

FOUR

It was Saturday afternoon, her day off, but with the storm coming, anything could happen. Katie Benedict was driving slowly, listening to the rain slam against the roof of her Silverado. It was hard to see through the thick gray rain even with the windshield wipers working overtime. The mountains were shrouded in fog, thick, heavy, and cold. And now this storm, a vicious one, the weather people were calling it, was on the way. An interesting choice of words, but she bet it was apt. She realized now that she shouldn't have chanced taking Keely to her piano lesson given the forecast, but she had. At least it had only just started raining, and they were close to home. She just hoped there wouldn't be any accidents on the road. If there were, she'd be up to her eyebrows in work.

She hunched forward, peering through the thick sheets of rain, Keely quiet beside her. Too quiet.

"Keely, you all right?"

"I'd like to find a rainbow, Mama."

"Not for a while yet, sweetie, but you keep looking. Hey, I heard you playing your C major scale before. It sounded really good."

"I've worked hard on getting it right, Mama."

Katie grinned. "I know, but it's worth it."

Suddenly, Keely bounced up on the seat, straining against her seat belt, and began waving through the windshield. "Mama, what's that? Look, it's a little boy and he's running!"

Katie saw him. The boy was sopping wet, running out of the woods to her left, not more than fifty feet onto the road in front of her. Then she saw two men burst out of the trees. It was obvious they were after him.

Katie said, even as she reached over and quickly released Keely's seat belt, "I want you to get down and stay there. Do you understand?"

Keely knew that tone of voice, her mama's sheriff voice, and nodded, slipping down to the floor.

"Cover your head with your arms. Everything will be fine. Just don't move, okay?"

"Okay, Mama."

Katie pulled to a stop, quickly leaned over the front seat and punched in the two numbers to her lock box beneath the back bench. She pulled out her Remington rifle, loaded, ready to go. By the time she opened the door, the men weren't more than a long arm's reach from the boy. Thank God he'd seen her and was running toward her. He was yelling, but the wind and rain wiped any sound he made right out.

The big man, his beer gut pounded by the rain, had a gun. Not good. Despite his size he moved quickly. He turned toward her, away from the boy, and raised the gun.

Katie brought up her rifle, cool and fast, and fired, kicking up muddy water not a foot from the fat man's feet, splattering him to his waist. "I'm the sheriff! Stop right there! Don't move!"

The skinny man behind him yelled something. The idiot was wearing a long black leather coat that was soaked from the rain. Katie calmly raised her Remington again and fired. This time the shot dug up a huge clod of dirt, spraying the leather coat.

The man in the coat yelled something and grabbed at the fat man's shirt. The fat man jerked away, yelled something toward the boy, and fired from his hip, a lucky shot in the fog and rain that very nearly hit her.

"You idiot!" she yelled. "I'm Sheriff Benedict. Drop your weapon! Both of you, don't move a single muscle!" But the fat guy pulled the trigger again, another hip shot, this one nowhere near her. Katie didn't hesitate, she pulled the trigger and the guy flinched and grabbed his upper arm. She'd wanted to hit him high on the shoulder, wanted to bring him down, but the rain and fog were hard on her aim.

He managed to keep his gun. She had hoped he'd drop it.

She shouted, "Come forward, both of you, slowly!"

But neither of them took a single step toward her, not that she'd expected them to. Both men ran back into the thick trees. She fired after them, once, twice, then a final time. She thought she heard a yell. Good.

The little boy, panting so hard he was heaving, was on her the next instant. He grabbed her arm and shook it.

"You can't let them go, ma'am! You've gotta shoot them again, you gotta kick their butts!"

Katie laid her rifle alongside her leg, and pulled the boy against her. "I got the fat one in the arm. Maybe I got the other one, too, while they were running back into the forest. You can count on it—the fat one's hurting bad. Now, it's going to be all right. I'm Sheriff Benedict. I'll get right on my cell phone and call for some help with those guys. Come into the truck and tell me what's going on."

Sam looked up at the tall woman who could have shot Fatso right in his big gut, but had only shot him in the arm instead. "Why didn't you kill him?"

Katie smiled at the boy as she quickly herded him back to the truck. She didn't want to hang around here. No telling if those guys would pop back out of the woods. "I try not to kill every bad guy I run into," she said. "Sometimes I like to bring them in front of a judge." She squeezed him hard. "You're okay and that's all that matters. Now let's move out of here."

The narrow bench in the back could hold no more than a couple of skinny kids. What it did have was a stack of blankets, not usually for warmth, but to soften the ride.

She grabbed the blankets and lifted the boy up onto the front seat. "Keely, we're going to make room for—"

"My name's Sam."

"We're going to make room for Sam. He's cold and he's wet." She settled him between her and Keely and covered him with five blankets. "Sweetie, don't worry about your seat belt. You just press close to him to help him warm up, okay?"

"Okay, Mama." Keely pressed against his back. Her little face was white, her voice a thin thread.

"It's going to be all right, baby. I don't want you to worry. I want you to be real brave for Sam here. He needs you to watch over him now. He's been through something bad. Can you do that?"

Keely nodded, the tears that were near to brimming over nearly gone now. To Katie's surprise, she shook Sam's arm. "Hey, who were those guys? What were they doing to you?"

Sam was shuddering.

"Not now, Keely. Let's just let Sam warm up a bit before we grill him."

Sam managed to get his mouth working, but it was hard. "What's your name, ma'am?"

"I'm Sheriff Benedict and that little girl next to you is my daughter, Keely. Did those men kidnap you?"

Sam managed to nod. He wasn't going to cry. "I squeezed through a window and fell on my head. But I got away."

"My goodness, you're really brave, Sam. Now, let's get you over to Doc Flint's. Keely, you press close to Sam and try to get him warm."

"I call him Doc Flintstone," Keely said, watched her mom frown, then grab one of the towels to dry off the little boy's head.

Sam said from behind the towel, "My mama used to give me Flintstones vitamins every morning with my toast."

"I like marmalade on my toast. I don't think smashed vitamins would taste very good."

Sam thought that was funny, but he was just too cold and too scared to laugh. He burrowed under the blankets; all he wanted to do was get warm. He pressed himself as hard as he could against Sheriff Benedict's leg. He felt the little girl squeezing against his back. He wondered if he was going to die now that he'd gotten away from those men. The little girl was pressed so hard against him, he'd bet she was going to get her clothes as wet as his.

Katie slid her rifle onto the floor behind the driver's seat. She turned the heater on high. "Okay, kids, I cranked up the heat so it'll be roasting you both in a minute. I know you're wet clear through, Sam, but the blankets should help a little bit."

"I don't like marmalade," Sam said as Katie looked at him closely.

"You'll like my mom's. It's the best." Good, the boy wasn't in shock, at least not yet. Katie put the truck in gear and started up. She had to watch her speed; the heavy rain made the road a river. As they passed where the men had disappeared into the trees, she looked carefully, but saw no sign of them.

She picked her cell phone out of her breast pocket and called Wade at the station house.

"Hello, Wade, it's Katie. No, don't tell me anything about the storm just yet. This is urgent." She told him about Sam and his kidnappers, the two men who'd been chasing him, and how she'd shot the fat one in the arm. "I'm on the south end of Delaware. Sam came out of the woods in nearly a straight line from the road to Bleaker's cabin—I'll bet that's where they were holding him. They're armed, they tried to kill me. Take three deputies and get out there fast." She gave them descriptions, then said, one eye on Sam's white face, the other on the woods, "I'm taking Sam to Doc Flint's. I'm on my cell. Let me know what you find. Did you hear any names, Sam?"

"Fatso and Beau." Just saying their names made Sam so afraid he had to concentrate not to pee again in his jeans.

"The one in the black leather coat is Beau, the other one is Fatso, that's Sam's name for him. Put out an APB on them, Wade. The one with the bullet in his arm—chances are he'll need some medical attention. Maybe the other one, too. Alert all medical facilities in the area. I'll tell Doc Flint. I'll bet he'll be putting in some calls himself. I'll check in again after I make sure the boy's all right."

She looked one last time toward the woods. No sign of either man. She pressed harder on the gas. She couldn't go any faster, it was just too dangerous. "Sam, you keep bundled up. Don't worry about talking right now. Just get yourself warm, that's right. You can tell me everything in a little while. Right now, you just think about how you saved yourself. My goodness, you're a hero."

Sam nodded. It made him feel woozy. A hero? He didn't feel like much of a hero. His teeth were chattering and that made him feel like a baby. He hadn't been a baby for longer than he could remember. And there was that little girl Keely pressed against him, two fat braids the color of wheat toast hanging over her shoulders, touching his face she was so close. He closed his eyes. He wasn't about to cry in front of the little girl. He wanted his father.

It took them nearly twenty minutes to get to Doc Flint's office in the rain. Katie kept talking to both children, keeping her voice calm and low, telling Sam about how the weather was going to be really bad until some time tomorrow, telling him how Keely was five, not as old as he was, and about how Keely could play "When You Wish Upon a Star" on the piano. Keely chimed in and told Sam she'd teach him how to play it, too, and the C scale.

Sam looked bad, Katie thought, worrying now as she pulled in front of the small Victorian house that stood at the corner of Pine and Maple, two blocks off Main Street. It was tall, skinny, and painted cream with dark blue trim. Jonah Flint lived upstairs and had his examination rooms and office downstairs. She said, "Keely, I want you to stay put until I get Sam into the office. Don't move, don't even think about moving. I'll come back for you with the umbrella."

She and Sam were already soaked, steam rising off their clothes because of the hot air gushing out of the truck heater. The little boy's face was sheet-white and his dark pupils were dilated. There was blood oozing down his cheek from a cut on his head.

She eased him across the front seat, raised the umbrella, and whispered against his small ear, "Grab me around the neck, Sam, it'll make it easier." When she straightened, he wrapped his legs around her waist. "That's good, Sam. Now, it's going to be all right, I promise you. You're with me now and I'm as tough as an old boot and meaner than my father, who was meaner than anybody before he died. You know something else, Sam? Since you're a hero, I'm not the only one who's really proud of you. Your folks will be proud, too. Don't worry now, everything's going to be all right."

She kept talking, hoping she was distracting the boy as she carried him into the empty waiting room. Katie wasn't surprised there wasn't anybody there, not even Heidi Johns, Dr. Flint's receptionist and nurse. Who would want to be out in weather like this except for Monroe Cuddy, who might have shot himself in the foot again, or Marilee Baskim, who was close to having a baby?

She called out, "Jonah!"

No answer. What if he wasn't here? She didn't want to take Sam to the emergency room.

"Jonah!"

FIVE

Jonah Flint, just turned forty and very proud of his full head of blacker-than-sin hair, came running out of the back room, the stethoscope nearly falling out of the pocket of his white coat.

"Jesus, Katie, what's going on? Who's this?"

"This," Katie said, carrying Sam into the first examination room, "is Sam and he just escaped kidnappers, believe it or not. There's a cut on his head and I think he's going into shock. I was afraid you weren't here."

"I was doing some research in the back. Now, let's see what we've got here." Dr. Flint smiled at the boy even as he peeled him off Katie and removed all the blankets, taking in all the signs and talking to Sam all the while.

"How do you feel, Sam?" He sat the boy on the edge of the examining table. "Do you take any medications? No?" He began to check him over. "Does your head hurt? I know the cut does, but do you have a headache? No, okay, that's good. I'll give you something to cut the pain. You got away from kidnappers? That's something now, isn't it? Okay, Sam, let me get you out of those wet clothes. You can just call me Doc Flintstone, okay? That's right, you help me. Now, do you hurt anywhere else? No? Good. Katie, you can step out, please, just men in here. You going to call the kid's parents?"

Sam looked shell-shocked.

Katie said, "I'll call his parents in just a bit, when you're through examining him. First things first. He's the most important thing right now." She took one last long look at the little boy who'd run out of a wilderness of maples and oaks. She picked up the huge office umbrella, lots bigger than hers, and fetched Keely from the truck.

She sat Keely on a chair, handed her the huge black waiting room bear, and called Wade again. "What's the word, Wade? You see anything out there?"

"Not yet. Where are you?"

"I'm in Jonah's waiting room. He's with Sam—that's the little boy. I don't know his last name yet. Making sure he's okay is the first priority. I've got Keely with me, too. With the two kids, there was no way I could do anything but get out of there. Have you checked out the old Bleaker place yet? That's bound to be where they were keeping him. It's hidden and nobody can hear anything for all the trees."

"I think so, too. Me and Jeffrey are out here on the road, and even with the fog and the rain, we found where the guys had come out of the woods. We found several shells, probably from your rifle. You also dropped a blanket. We're fixing to go into the woods now."

Katie wanted to be the one to go to the Bleaker cabin. It was tough, but there was just no way she could leave the kids, not yet. "Listen, Wade, you and Jeffrey be really careful. Anyone else with you? Good, glad that Conrad and Danny got there. Don't forget, these guys are dangerous. If they're still at the Bleaker cabin, it could get dicey. If they're not there, I want you to secure the place. Be real careful not to destroy any possible evidence."

"You got it, Sheriff," Wade said. "Over and out."

Over and out? Katie shook her head. Wade sounded pleased as punch that he was the lead on this. She just hoped he'd be careful. She disconnected and said to Keely, "I sure hope Jeffrey wears his glasses."

Keely said, not looking up from the bear, "Jeffrey has to wear his glasses or he'd step in the toilet. Millie likes him without his glasses, but she says it's just too dangerous."

Millie was Jeffrey's girlfriend. Katie smiled and felt her tension lessen just a bit. She fully intended to keep the boy with her as long as it took to get him safe. She hardly knew anything about him. She hated to wait before talking with him, but the child needed Jonah a lot more than he needed to answer questions right now.

Sam's parents. She'd get their names and phone number as soon as Jonah said Sam was okay. She knew they had to be frantic.

Jonah came out from the examination room twenty minutes later, smiling, holding the little boy's hand. "Sam's been telling me how his mama kept talking in his head, telling him what to do, how to get himself free."

How could Sam be okay? He looked white and exhausted, a big Flintstones bandage on his head. Katie said, "You did great, Sam, you didn't give up."

"No, ma'am, I didn't." There was a flash of pride in that exhausted little voice, and that was good. Sam looked like the little boy he was, wrapped in two very big blue blankets, a pair of Jonah's black socks on his small feet. Sam looked up at Jonah. "I want to go home, Doctor."

Katie patted Keely's head, and walked swiftly to where the boy stood. She picked him up and held him close to her. "You're just fine, Sam, just fine. Now, if Jonah is through torturing you, I'm taking you home with me. You'll be safe there until I can get your folks here."

"We're in Tennessee?"

"Yes, we are. Eastern Tennessee. Jessborough is the name of the town."

"Where's Tennessee?"

"We're sandwiched among lots of states. Where do you live, Sam?"

"I'm from Colfax, Virginia."

"A nice state, Virginia," Katie said and turned to Jonah. "It's not too far away from here. He's okay?"

"Yep, he might come down with a cold from his run in the rain, but he's a strong kid. He'll be just fine. Give him a nice big glass of juice. He needs the sugar. I don't want to take any chances that he'll crash." He patted Sam's head, ran his fingers through his damp black hair. "His clothes are still wet. What do you want to do?"

"If you could wrap his clothes up in a towel, I'll wash and dry them."

Katie realized she was rocking Sam, sort of stepping from one foot to the other, swaying, just like she did with Keely. She smiled. "I'm going to squeeze him in next to Keely and take both of them home. You like hot chicken noodle soup, Sam?"

He didn't say anything, but she felt him nod. She and Jonah looked at each other. Neither of them knew what the kid had been through, at least not yet.

"You be careful, Katie, it's coming down thicker than confetti on New Year's," Jonah said. "Take good care of my patient. Keely, you keep a close eye on Sam, too, okay?"

Keely allowed Sam to sit next to her mother, his head on Katie's leg. She pressed close to his other side. "I'll keep him warm, Mama."

"Sam," Katie said, lightly touching her fingers to his pale cheek, "you're a very lucky boy."

Sam, who felt dopey and stupid, said, "That's what my mama was always telling my dad."

"I'll call your daddy right now if you'll just tell me his name and phone number."

Sam said against the wet denim on her leg, "My dad's name is Miles Kettering. He's really cool. He can fix anything. He fixes helicopters for the government."

His father was a government contractor? Could that be why he was kidnapped?

"What's your home phone number, Sam?"

He was silent, thinking, but he couldn't get it together, and she knew his brain was closing down. "It's okay. I'll call information. Colfax, Virginia, right?"

Sam managed to nod before he closed his eyes. He felt her strong leg supporting his head. She still felt wet through the blanket she'd put under his head. He felt the sway of the truck and the little girl's body pressed close against him. He was warm. He was safe. He was asleep in the next minute.

Katie pulled the blanket more closely around his shoulders, and whispered to Keely, "He'll be okay, sweetie. You just stay there, keep him really warm."

After a moment, Keely said, "I would have saved myself, too, Mama."

"I know you would have, Keely. Now, let me get information in Virginia and find Sam's daddy."

WHEN the phone rang, Miles jumped nearly three feet. He'd been telling the agents again how the government contracts worked, who his competitors were, and how much money was involved. Agent Butch Ashburn, the lead on Sam's kidnapping, nodded to the other agent, Todd Morton, who'd just swallowed a doughnut too fast and was choking.

"Showtime," Agent Ashburn said.

Savich, who'd just gotten to the Kettering house, laid his hand on his friend's arm and said, "Everything's set, Miles. Just answer the phone. Keep calm, that's more important than I can say."

Miles Kettering forced his hand to reach for the phone. He didn't want to touch it, didn't want to because he was afraid that Sam was dead. So many children were kidnapped and so few survived. He could hardly bear it.

It had been a day and a half. This was the first word. His hand shook as he lifted the phone.

"Hello? This is Miles Kettering."

"Hello, Mr. Kettering, my name is Sheriff K. C. Benedict from Washington County, Tennessee. Don't worry, I have your boy, Sam. He's just fine. He managed to escape his kidnappers. He's with me. Mr. Kettering? I promise you, he's okay."

Miles couldn't speak. His throat worked. "I don't believe you. You're the kidnapper, right? What do you want?"

Butch Ashburn and Todd Morton were standing there staring at the phone, trying to look both calm and competent. Savich took the phone from Miles's hands. "Who is this?"

Katie understood. She said again, "This is Sheriff K. C. Benedict from Washington County, Tennessee. Sam is just fine. He managed to save himself. I've got him with me. Tell his parents not to worry, he's okay."

"This is Dillon Savich with the FBI, Sheriff. Thank you very much. Give me your exact location and we'll be there as quickly as we can."

Katie gave the man directions. She'd never before met a special agent with the Federal Bureau of Investigation. She patted Sam's shoulder, whispered, "Your daddy's going to be here soon now, Sam," but Sam didn't hear her. He was asleep.

She heard Mr. Kettering say in the background, "I want to talk to Sam."

She said to Agent Savich, "Sam's asleep. Do you want me to wake him?"

Miles Kettering came on the line. "No, let him sleep. I'll see him soon. Please, Sheriff, tell him I love him. What about the people who took him? Did you get them?"

"I'm very sorry, but they escaped. But we've got a group of my deputies in the field and they'll do their best."

When Katie hung up the phone, Keely said, nearly asleep herself, "What about his mama?"

"She'll probably come, too. If I were her, I'd beat his daddy here to get him."

"Stealing Sam was a bad thing, Mama."

"You're right." And she thought, *I should have just brought the bastard down, not given him a kiss in the arm. I should have kicked his butt like Sam said.*

SIX

Katie's phone rang at a quarter of seven that evening. It was Alice Hewett from Hewett's Pharmacy, and she was out-of-breath excited.

"Oh, Katie, that man who kidnapped the little boy—I think it was him. He just left. I called the station house and Linnie told me to call you at home."

Katie's heart started to pound, deep and hard.

"Was he the fat one, Alice?"

"No, he was the other one, tall, almost sick-looking thin, but he wasn't wearing that long black leather coat Wade told everyone about, just a white shirt and jeans, and some scarred black boots. But he had a ponytail, like you said. And he was shivering, which means he left that leather coat in his car because he was afraid to be seen in it. He bought bandages and antibiotic cream and some Aleve. And when he was leaving I saw blood on the back of his sleeve."

"He was in his forties?"

"Yes, I'd say so."

"And he had a ponytail."

"Yeah, wet and stringy-looking. He didn't say anything, just brought the stuff up to me at the register, and paid cash. He had a really big roll. I saw a couple of hundreds, lots of fifties."

"Did he just leave the pharmacy?"

"Yes."

"Did you see his car?"

"Yes, Katie, the instant I saw that blood I knew. When I heard his car, I peeked out the front window. He was driving an old van, light gray I think, but it was hard to tell with all the rain."

Katie nearly held her breath. "License number?"

"I just got part of it. He screeched out of here pretty fast. It was a

Virginia plate, the first three letters were LTD—you know, like that old Ford sedan—LTD. I think the next one was a 'three' but I can't be sure."

Katie wanted to leap through the phone line and kiss Alice. "That's just great," she said. "Now, was there anything about the man that was unusual, something that would make you remember him as opposed to another man?"

Silence, then, "He was wearing a necklace, you know, a gold chain with some sort of pendant or stone hanging off the end of it. I've never seen anything like it before. Oh yes, his two front teeth overlap."

"Alice, do you want to be sheriff when my term is over?"

Alice Hewett laughed. "No, Katie, it's all yours. Just looking at that guy made my stomach cramp up. Besides, I'm too young to be sheriff, I just turned twenty last week."

Katie was pleased, as was the rest of the town, that Alice was no longer a teenager, particularly since Abe Hewett was fifty-four years old and had three grown boys all older than their stepmama. "Well done, Alice. Thank you."

"Let me know, won't you, Katie?"

"You bet."

Katie called Wade at home, got him between spoonfuls of his wife's special pork stew. "I'm really sorry about this, Wade, but—"

"I knew you'd call, Katie. I sent Conrad over to talk to Alice, see if she remembered anything else. Man, this stew is the best." A long silence, then Katie heard Wade's wife, Glenda, say something in the background.

"Tell you what," Katie said, "stay put. Just keep close to your phone. Call Jeffrey and have him update the rest of our people, including our three volunteer deputies. Keep an eye out for that van—we've got a partial plate. It's Virginia and it's LTD three something. I'm going to call the FBI, let them check it out."

"You don't want me to go out right this minute?"

"Nah, stay put. I'll call you if something comes up."

She called the Knoxville FBI field office because she knew the Johnson City field office just didn't have the staff for this sort of thing. She got Glen Hodges, the special agent in charge, pretty fast and told him what was going on. Then she dialed Agent Savich's cell phone. He picked up immediately.

"Agent Savich?"

"Yes. Is this Sheriff Benedict? Is Sam all right?"

"Yes, he is, but listen to this, please," and she told him about the kidnapper's visit to the pharmacy. "Alice thinks they're driving a light gray van, Virginia license LTD with a possible next number of three."

"Got it. I'll call Butch Ashburn, he's the agent leading the kidnapping investigation. He'll find out who the van belongs to."

"I called Agent Hodges from the Knoxville field office, told him what was going on. He's on his way here."

"Good. You have Sam with you?"

"Yes, he's still sleeping. He's just fine." It was then she heard the deep rumbling noise. "You're in an airplane?"

"Yes, it'll take us a couple of hours since we're in a Cessna. Sheriff, I don't like the fact that the kidnappers are still local. What else is happening?"

"Here's the deal, Agent Savich. I don't like the fact that those two guys are still hanging around here either. I'm hoping that Fatso—that's the name Sam gave one of the kidnappers—is hurt bad and that's why they haven't hightailed it out of here. But if he was badly hurt, then why not take him to a doctor? We have two doctors in town. Both of them call me from home every hour so I'll know they're okay."

"Well done," Savich said.

"Yeah, but you know, the truth is, I don't know what to make of it. They've got to know that everyone is looking for them. Why would they stay local?"

"You're basing this on one witness?"

"Yes. Her set of eyes is just fine."

"You shot Fatso in the arm?"

"Yes, that I'm sure of. Then I fired several more times while they were running back into the forest. Maybe I shot him again, I just didn't see, all I heard was a yelp." She drew a deep breath. "I know where they were keeping Sam. Agent Glen Hodges said he and his people will dust the place for prints when they get here."

"I'm not too happy that they're still around, but it sounds like you've got everything under control. We'll be there soon. Be careful, okay?"

Katie pressed the "off" button on her cell. Well, she was being careful. She was keeping Sam with her, the FBI was on the way, and she'd called in all her people—with the exception of Wade, who'd already worked his butt off today. Everyone was out looking for that light gray van now.

Her cell phone played the first bars of "Fly Me to the Moon" a minute later. A man's voice came on the line. "Sheriff Benedict? This is Miles Kettering. I'm with Agent Savich. I'm sorry to bother you, but I just wanted to thank you, and . . . please take care of my boy. Savich told me he was still sleeping?"

"Yes, he's out like a light. Do you want me to wake him up?"

"Oh no, it's just that I'm—" He stalled.

"I understand, Mr. Kettering. If someone had taken my child, I'd be scared out of my mind until I actually had her in my arms. You're flying the Cessna?"

"Yes. It was the best I could do on short notice, but it's a solid little plane."

"It's pretty bad weather here, as I'm sure you know. You're coming in at Ackerman's Air Field?"

"Yes, soon now."

She checked that Miles Kettering had directions from Ackerman's Air Field to her house before disconnecting.

She got a call not five minutes later from Glen Hodges, the SAC of the Knoxville Bureau field office.

"I've got three agents in the car with me. We'll be in Jessborough about two hours from now, give or take because of the weather. Is there any more you can tell me?"

"No. Everyone's out looking for the gray van, and doing general surveillance on anyone looking like either of the two men. I gave Agent Savich the partial license plate of the van. He said he was going to call Agent Butch Ashburn."

"Yeah, Savich just called me. Agent Ashburn will get the owner of that van in no time."

"Agent Savich and Mr. Kettering, the boy's father, will be here soon as well."

"Savich didn't say what he was doing involved in a kidnapping? Last I heard he was in LA playing around in one of the Hollywood studios."

"I'm sure I don't know, Agent Hodges. I just assumed he was assigned to the case with Agent Ashburn."

"Oh no, Savich is the unit chief for the Criminal Apprehension Unit at headquarters."

"What's that?"

"He works mostly with computers, setting up databases and data-mining programs to help catch criminals. The Bureau set up this unit for him and that's what he and eight or so other agents do."

"Sounds like something I'd want real simplified."

Glen Hodges laughed. "I'm with you, Sheriff. Oops, we're starting to break up. You get in these mountains, and you're down faster than you can catch a snake. You take care of the boy, ma'am. We're coming as fast as we can."

Katie slipped her cell back into her shirt pocket. She asked herself again what more she could do. She didn't come up with an answer.

At nearly ten o'clock that night the worst fall storm in twenty years—according to the weather folk—seemed to be fizzling out. There was less rain, but the howling winds were still a nice side show, keeping people hunkered down in their homes, hoping their trees wouldn't be uprooted.

She couldn't imagine being up in a small airplane in this wind. She looked out Keely's bedroom window, north, toward Ackerman's Air Field, and said a little prayer.

All in all, they'd lucked out, Katie thought as she closed the window and walked over to Keely's bed and gave her a kiss and smoothed her eyebrows. "I can tell you're awake, sweetie. You just smiled. You love the sound of the rain, don't you?"

"Oh yes, Mama, and the wind howling like banshees—that's what Grandma says. You told me you liked it, too, Mama, when you were my age."

"Yes, I remember pressing my nose against the window, wanting lightning, more lightning, and with it, the boom of thunder—the closer the better."

"Can I go press my nose—"

"No, not tonight. You're going to sleep now, Keely."

"Is Sam okay?"

"Yep, he's just fine." One more kiss and Katie sat by her daughter until her breathing evened into sleep. Then she walked to the window and pressed her nose against the glass. It wasn't the same. Her nose was cold and she wanted to sneeze. She left Keely's bedroom, knowing she'd pass the night easily, the sound of the rain a lullaby to her daughter.

WADE had had only one emergency call some twenty minutes before from Mr. Amos Halley, who'd gotten himself stuck in his garage when the electricity had gone out and the door opener wouldn't work. Even the manual override was stuck. Wade, pulled from his dinner, had nearly cried, but he'd gone over to the Halley house where Mrs. Halley stood in the entryway, arms crossed over her bosom, shaking her head, and told him, "Leave the old man in there, Wade. If you let him out, he'll just go drinking down at the tavern."

Wade had tried his best to get the garage door open, but the sucker hadn't budged. Then the electricity came back on, and he was a hero, at least to Amos, who claimed he was near to croaking of a heart attack it was so black and airless inside the garage.

As Wade downshifted his jeep, he saw Amos Halley drive off toward the east side of town—that's where the Long Shot Tavern had been hunkered down since just after World War II.

The rain had lightened up considerably, but winds still buffeted the jeep. There would probably be some flooding, but nothing they couldn't handle. All in all, it wasn't bad. He hoped one of the deputies would spot the gray van. He'd told them to call him first.

He made it home in record time and grinned at Glenda.

But something hit him about five minutes later. It was worry, real deep worry, and he didn't know what to do about it.

SEVEN

Katie checked on Sam, then sat down with a cup of coffee after putting some more logs in the fireplace. The fire made the living room warm, shadowy, and cozy. It was as if she'd commanded it to happen. Her cell rang. "Sheriff Benedict here."

"This is Agent Hodges, Sheriff. I just got a call from Agent Ashburn. The van is a gunmetal gray Dodge, full license is LTD 3109, registered to Mr. Beauregard Jones of Alexandria, Virginia. Is this one of the men?"

"Sam said his name was Beau, so bingo, Agent Hodges, it sounds like you guys nailed it. Excellent."

"Agent Ashburn said he was heading out to Alexandria himself to check it all out. He'll let us know what he finds."

"Good. How close are you to me?"

"We're only another half-hour, maybe. Unfortunately, Sheriff, we just blew a back tire a few minutes ago. It'll take us a while to get rolling again."

She shut down her cell and leaned back. Why had Fatso and Beau stayed in the area? Why would Beau go to the local pharmacy? Were they idiots?

If bandages from the first-aid section of the pharmacy would take care of Fatso, then she hadn't hurt him very badly. Or maybe it was a bad wound and they were trying anything they could get their hands on.

Where were they holed up? Not at Bleaker's cabin, the place was nailed down tight, police tape over the windows and a deputy outside. But where had they gone? Just stayed in the van? She raised her head, frowned and listened. She heard the rain, nothing but the rain, and the wind battering tree branches against the house.

She got up, checked on Sam and Keely. They were both still sound asleep. She lightly touched her palm to Sam's forehead. No fever.

She stood there, looking down at the boy, thinking there was nothing else to do until everyone arrived. Then her breath caught. She knew why the men were still in town, and it wasn't because Fatso was too badly hurt to be moved. No, they still were after Sam. Was there that much money involved?

She pulled her SIG Sauer out of its holster on the top shelf of her closet, shoved it in the back of her blue jeans, and pulled a loose sweatshirt over it. Then she checked her ankle holster, where her two-shot derringer was held tight. If anything happened, she was ready.

All right, you bastards, come to Mama.

Her heart raced. She could feel her skin, smell the oak trees as the winds whipped through them, even hear the soft crackle of a single ember in the fireplace.

She pulled out her cell to call over some deputies as she walked to the living room window, everything inside her alert and ready, and pulled back the drapes. She very nearly fell over. A man's face was staring in at her. He looked as surprised as she was, but his gloved fist slammed through the window, and in that hand was a gun, pointed right at her chest.

"Don't even think about moving, lady."

She dropped her cell phone. Could she get to her gun before he killed her? No, probably not. "You're Beauregard Jones, I take it?"

"Shit! How do you know who I am?"

"Law enforcement is pretty good nowadays, Mr. Jones. Just about everybody in Jessborough knows who you are. The FBI is already at your place in Alexandria and more agents will be here in about three minutes." She looked behind Beau. "Where's Fatso?"

"You just shut up, lady."

"I'm not a lady, I'm the sheriff. Surely you know that. How'd you find out where I lived? What's the matter? Is Fatso hurt so bad he can't help you anymore?"

"Shut your trap, no, wait, back up, just back up. Nail your ass to that spot and don't move or I'll kill you and that cute little girl won't have a mommy any longer." He kept the gun pointed at her as he broke the rest of the glass in the window. Then he stepped through.

When he stood dripping water on her grandmother's prized

Aubusson carpet, he looked her up and down, glanced over at the fire-place and said, "You've given us lots of trouble, Sheriff. And here you are, looking all tousled and frumpy like any good little housewife on a Saturday night."

She was aware of her SIG Sauer nestled against her back, the der-ringer pressed against the ankle holster. "I haven't begun to give you trouble, Mr. Jones."

He gave her a big grin, all big white crooked teeth, the two front ones overlapping, just like Alice had said. "I like a girl with a big mouth. Fatso's real name is Clancy and he doesn't like people bugging him about that gut of his. But no matter. He's waiting for us in the van. You'll meet him soon enough. Go get the boy."

Beau realized in that instant that it wasn't a good idea to let her go off by herself. She didn't look at all tough, and she looked real young, what with her hair pulled back with a tie and no makeup on her face. But she had to have something going for her, they'd elected her sheriff of this hick town, after all. He'd been watching her through the window, watching her eyes just like his daddy had taught him before he'd gotten himself blown away during a bank robbery down in Atlanta. His daddy would have called those eyes of hers hard, the kind that saw way down deep into you, and he'd never want to drink a beer with her. He hadn't realized how his daddy would have hated her eyes until he'd seen her up really close. He thought she knew things, thought things, that he couldn't.

Beau wasn't about to take any chances with her, not with those eyes. "Wait," he said, "you walk ahead of me, don't make no sudden move-ments or I'll have to put a bullet in your back. You got that?"

Katie fanned her hands and said, "I got it."

"Let's go."

"I don't understand something, Mr. Jones."

"Walk, Sheriff, stop trying to slow things down. You might be right about the FBI coming, but hey, they're clowns, everybody knows that."

"I didn't know that. Why do you think they're clowns?"

"Just shut up." He waved the gun. "Move, now."

Katie walked out of the living room into the small front hallway. She said over her shoulder, "I told you that the FBI knows who you are, and they're on their way here right this minute. You also know they're not clowns. If you don't get out of here now, you're going to be in the deepest trouble imaginable. There's really got to be a lot in it for you to make you come here for the boy. Somebody's paying you and Fatso lots of money, right?"

"Shut up, Sheriff. Keep walking, or I'll just shoot you and get him myself. Hey, I just might take the little girl, too. Bet I could get some loot for that cute little button."

"Yes, there must be big bucks in this for you and Fatso to take this kind of risk." In ten steps, she'd be at the guest room door. And Sam was inside.

Beau grunted. "Keep moving."

She had to do something, had to do it soon. It was up to her, not the FBI, not anybody else. But he was holding what looked like a 10mm Smith & Wesson pistol, a good weapon. Patience; she had to be patient. There was lots of time before he got hold of Sam.

She opened the door of the bedroom slowly.

The room was dark—and cold. It was very cold, she could feel the wind touching her cheek. The light switch flicked on behind her.

"Damn! Where are you, boy? You come out here now or I'll kill the sheriff!"

"The room's cold," Katie said, turning to face Beau, so relieved she wanted to dance. "Don't you see? Sam heard you coming and went out through the window."

"No, that's impossible. He's just a little kid—"

"Yeah, sure, and he went out the window at Bleaker's cabin, too, got away from you and Clancy. He's long gone now, Beau. Just feel how cold it is in here. You'd best get your butt out of here now before the FBI comes and hauls it off to jail."

Beau didn't know what to do. He eyed the open window, the rain whipping the light drapes into the room, the wind making him shiver. "Gonna ruin the floor, all that rain," he said. He waved the pistol at her. "Go close the window."

Katie closed the window, taking her time. She tried to look through the thick rain, but didn't see any movement, any shadow of a little boy. Where was Sam?

She turned, hoping he couldn't see the satisfaction in her eyes. Sam was out of it, at least for now. It was just between the two of them and he was rattled. Just let him get a bit closer.

Beau walked quickly to the door and motioned with the pistol for her to come to him.

"May I suggest that you slink out of here while you still can, Beau? Or better yet, why don't you drop that gun and let me take you to my nice warm facilities?"

"Shut up, you infernal woman. What we're going to do is get that cute little girl. Maybe we can negotiate a trade."

Her heart nearly stopped. "No, take me and leave the little girl alone, do you hear me, Beau? Leave her alone or I'll kill you so slow and so hard you'll scream so loud even the Devil won't want you."

But Beau just laughed, pushed her in front of him until he himself shoved open Keely's bedroom door. "Come on out, kid! I've got your mama!"

There wasn't a sound.

Beau flipped the light switch.

Both of them looked at the lump beneath the bedcovers. Katie's heart nearly dropped to her knees, but then she saw something wasn't right here. Keely had ears as sharp as a dog's. Why was she just lying there? Beau waved Katie to the far side of the room, walked to the bed, and poked the lump with the muzzle of his gun.

"Come on out, little girl. Your uncle Beau's gonna take you for a nice long ride."

EIGHT

The lump didn't move. Beau poked his gun harder.

"Not again." He jerked back the covers. There was a pillow molded in the shape of a person, a very little person, underneath the covers.

Both Sam and Keely were gone.

Katie was nearly giddy. "Looks like my kid's pretty smart, doesn't it, Beau?" Thank the good Lord for Katie's favorite climbing tree.

"I hate this job," Beau said. "All right, the little kids aren't dummies. It's you and me now, Sheriff, and we're heading outside. When we're clear of this place, I'm going to whump your ass."

"Okay," she said, so relieved she thought she'd choke on it, "since you put it so nicely."

Where was the FBI?

At that instant, Katie could swear she heard the soft purr of a car motor. She looked at Beau out of the corner of her eyes, realized he hadn't heard a thing.

The rain had picked up again and battered sideways in through the open window Beau had smashed in the living room.

Beau didn't look happy. "You're walking too slow. Move! This is your fault, you bitch! The slower you walk, the more I'm going to hurt you."

He shoved her hard, and then, because he wasn't stupid, he took a quick step back.

"Go! To the front door, now!"

You want a hostage, Beau? That's just fine with me, you bozo.

She walked swiftly to the front door, slid free the dead bolt, and opened it.

She saw a flashlight beam aiming toward her, then a hand quickly covered it. Someone was close.

She wanted to shout that Beau was right behind her with a gun at her back, but she kept her mouth shut. Anyone watching would see him soon enough.

Beau shoved the gun against her back. "Go, move! Get those arms up, clasp your hands behind your neck. Get out there!"

She put her hands behind her neck, walked through the open front door, and stopped on the front porch. The overhang didn't help much since the wind was slapping the rain sideways. Katie shouted, "You out there, Clancy?"

Not a sound, just another flicker of a flashlight whipping around, cutting through the thick rain, its vague beam a ghostly light. She thought she heard men's voices, low and whispering. Was Agent Savich here? Or had Wade gotten worried and come over? Whoever it was, she hoped they had a good view of her and Beau.

Beau shouted, "Clancy, drive the van up next to the front porch! If you FBI geeks are out there, stay back or the sheriff's dead. You got that?"

There was no answer, just the wind, rumbling through the trees at the sides of her house.

"You hear me, Clancy? We're taking her with us. Then we'll see about the boy."

A man's voice came out of the night, off to her right. "In that case, Mr. Jones, why don't you just consider us observers. Do whatever you want to do."

Beau jumped. "Yeah, you guys just stay back. I'm taking her and we're leaving."

Katie recognized Agent Savich's voice, and there was something else in his voice, something meant for her. She wished she could see his face, then she'd know what he wanted her to do.

The big van came hurtling toward the house, its tires spewing up black mud. Fatso was at the wheel, turning it hard until the front fender scraped against the steps of the front porch. She watched the big man lean across the front seat and push the door open. "Get her in here, Beau, fast!"

Savich's voice, loud and sharp, "Now, Sheriff!"

Katie threw herself off the front porch, jerking her SIG Sauer free even as she crashed against the back tire of the van.

She heard Beau yell, heard two shots. With no hesitation, Fatso gunned the van, but he didn't get far. She saw Agent Savich turn smoothly and shoot out both back tires. Fatso skidded in the mud and crashed hard into an oak tree. She could see him hit the windshield, then bounce back, his head lolling to the side. He wasn't going anywhere.

Katie swung her SIG Sauer around toward Beau just as Savich leaped onto the porch. He was so fast he was a blur, and his leg, smooth, graceful, like a dancer, kicked the gun out of Beau's hand. It went flying across the porch, landing against a rocking chair leg. Beau grunted, grabbed his hand, and turned to run.

Agent Savich just grabbed his collar, jerked him around, and sent his fist into his belly, then his jaw.

Beau cursed, and tried to fight back. Savich merely belted him again, this time in his kidney. He shoved him down onto the porch and stood over him. He wasn't even breathing hard. "Sometimes I like to fight the old-fashioned way. Now, you just stay real still, Beau, or I just might have to hurt you. You hear me?"

"I hear you, you bastard. I want my lawyer."

Katie, her SIG Sauer still in her hand, walked slowly up onto the porch. She looked down at the man who probably would have killed her, killed Sam and Keely, without a dollop of remorse. She shoved her SIG back into the waistband of her jeans, lifted her booted foot and slammed it into his ribs.

"Here's one for Sam and Keely," she said, and kicked him again.

"That's police brutality," Beau said, gasping from the pain in his ribs. "I'm gonna sue your ass off!"

"Nah, you're not," she said. "You're in the backwoods now, Beau, and do you know what that means?"

"You marry your brother."

"No, it means *you'll* marry my brother, if I want you to."

Dillon Savich was laughing as he looked at the bedraggled woman, hair hanging down, pulled free from her ponytail, her mouth pale from cold. "Sheriff Benedict, I presume?"

"Yes," she said, already looking around for Sam and Keely.

"I'm Agent Savich. A pleasure, ma'am. You like excitement, don't you?"

"What I liked best in all of this was the sound of your voice and sight of your face, Agent Savich. Those were some cool moves you made to take down old Beau."

"I tripped, dammit!"

"Yeah, right," Katie said, and looked toward the van again. Clancy was still out of it. She was on the point of going over and pulling him out when Sam shouted "Papa!"

"Mama!"

She heard a man yell "Sam!"

"Mr. Kettering?"

"Yes, that's Miles. I ordered him on pain of death and dismemberment to stay back. And here's your little girl, ma'am."

Keely was wet to the bone, her flannel pajamas plastered to her, her hair hanging in her eyes. Katie swept her up into her arms and held her so tight the little girl squeaked.

"Keely got me, Papa! Keely woke me up and opened the window in my room to fool Beau and Clancy, then we went out the window in her bedroom. We've been hiding just over there, behind that tree. I recognized Beau and knew we had to stay hidden. Did you see Uncle Dillon? He kicked the crap out of skinny old Beau!"

Uncle Dillon? Katie smiled, kissed her daughter's wet hair, and called out, "You wet as Keely, Sam?"

"I'm wetter than a frog buried under a lily pad."

She saw Sam's smile before she saw the rest of his face. He was being carried by a big man who was as wet as he was, and who was smiling even bigger than his boy. She liked the looks of him, liked the way he held his boy.

Miles carried Sam up onto the front porch. He saw Beau lying on his back, not even twitching, and he handed Sam to Savich.

He went down on his hands and knees, closed his fist around Beau's shirt collar, and jerked him up. "Hello, you miserable scum."

"Get off me, you bastard!"

"Oh, I'm lots more than a bastard. I'm your worst nightmare, Beau. I'm meaner than the man who just kicked your ass. I'm Sam's father and do you have any idea what I want to do to you?"

"Get him away from me!"

"Oh, no," Savich said, Sam now hanging about his neck, held real close. "You deserve whatever he wants to do to you. If he wants to, he can kick your tonsils out the back of your neck."

Miles Kettering pulled Beau to his feet and sent his fist into his jaw. Beau went down and stayed down.

Miles gave him one more dispassionate look, then turned to take Sam from Savich.

"You walloped him good, Papa," Sam said, and he patted his father's face, dark with five o'clock shadow. "Can I hit him, too?"

"Nah, he's had enough. You just stay real close to me until I get over being so scared."

Sam hugged his father's neck, really hard. "This is Katie, Papa. She helped me a whole lot."

Katie stuck out her hand even as she held Keely against her with her other arm. "Mr. Kettering, you've got some brave boy here."

In that instant, Katie saw black smoke billowing up around the front of the van. "Oh no—Fatso, I can't even see him through that smoke! I forgot about him! I've got to get him." She pushed Keely into Miles Kettering's arms, and took off running toward the van.

Savich, who saw flames licking up from beneath the van, yelled, "No, wait! No, Sheriff!" He leaped off the porch and ran after her. He yelled over his shoulder, "Miles, protect the kids!"

Katie was no more than twelve feet from the van when she was tackled from behind, hard, and smashed facedown into the wet ground.

In the next instant there was a loud explosion, and the van blew up in a ball of orange, parts flying everywhere. He was covering all of her, his head on top of hers, his arms covering both their heads. The heat whooshed toward them, sucking the air out of their lungs, heavy, scalding.

She heard him grunt. Oh God, something had hit him. She heard him suck in a breath, then she did the same.

Then it was over. Everything was still again, except she could hear Keely crying, "Mama, Mama."

He'd saved her life. He'd known the van was going to blow, and he'd brought her down.

Katie said, trying to turn over, "Agent Savich, are you all right?"

He grunted again, then she felt his determination as he pulled himself off her.

She was up in an instant, standing over him as he remained on his knees, head down, breathing hard.

"Your back. Oh God, your back!"

She looked up to see that Miles Kettering had both children pressed against the side of the house, protecting them, just as Agent Savich had told him to. Had he known, too, that the van was going to blow?

"I'm so sorry, I didn't know, I'm so sorry." She was on her knees beside him now. "Just hold still."

But Savich rose slowly, managed to straighten. "I saw the flames, you didn't. We survived it. I'm all right." He could feel the rain hitting his back, feel the pain building and building. He could also feel his blood flowing, and that wasn't good. He looked over at the van, engulfed in bright orange flames, black smoke sizzling into the air, rain mixing with it, making it filthy black soot.

"Yeah, sure you are, Agent Savich. You just come with me." She was leaning down to grasp him under his arm, when she heard Beau yell, "All right, you jerks, it's my turn now!"

She whirled around to see Beau leaning against the porch railing, his own gun in his hand. She should have cuffed him—even if she believed he was dead, she should have cuffed him. "You bastard, you killed Clancy! Ain't nothing left of him but vapor. But now I'm gonna take that boy."

Sam was tucked against his father's leg, Keely against him. Miles pressed the children more firmly against the side of the house, shouted over his shoulder, "Give it up, Beau, just give it up."

"Send the boy over, or I'll have to kill you, Mr. Kettering."

"Then do it," Miles said. "Neither Sam nor Keely is going anywhere."

Katie could tell that Agent Savich was going to go after Beau again. She couldn't let that happen. She watched Beau raise his gun, watched him aim that gun at Miles Kettering. She leaned down, smoothly pulled her derringer from her ankle holster, and fired.

She got him through the neck.

"Ah" was all Beau said, clutched his throat, and turned to face her, the gun swinging her way.

She fired again, this time a death shot, even for a derringer, through his chest. Beau fell off the porch, landing on his back, his eyes open to the rainy night. The orange ball of flame flickered in his open eyes.

Miles Kettering said, his arms wrapped tight around the children's heads, "Sam, I've got to see to things here. Promise me that you and Keely won't move an inch. Keep your faces against the house, that van just might blow up some more. Do you hear me? Not an inch."

Miles raced down, pulled Savich over his shoulder in a fireman's carry, and went into the house. Both children raced after him. Good, she didn't want them to see Beau.

"Put him on his belly on the sofa. I'll call nine-one-one," Katie said and quickly dialed. She got Marge, who always sounded breathless, told her to get an ambulance out here, and Wade, too, then hung up. "Not more than ten minutes. Now, let's see how bad you're hurt, Agent Savich." But first she'd have to move her daughter aside.

Savich said, "You're Keely?" One of his arms was dangling over the side of the sofa, and his feet hung off the other end.

The little girl gently smoothed her fingertips over his face. "I'm Keely and my mama will take care of you. She takes care of everybody. Do you know they pay her to do that?"

Savich didn't want to laugh, but it came out of him anyway. It died in a gasp. His back was on fire.

"I'm glad they pay her, Keely. How bad is it, Sheriff?"

It was Miles who said, "You've got a long horizontal gash, middle of your back, just above your waist, probably from a piece of flying metal. It doesn't look too deep, Savich, but it's nasty. You just hang on. Here's the sheriff."

"We need to apply some pressure, Agent Savich—"

"Just Savich. Or Dillon, that's what my wife calls me."

"Okay, Dillon, I'll be right back. I'm going to have to put some pressure on this wound and it's going to hurt, I'm sorry."

Savich closed his eyes and willed himself far away, back with Sherlock and Sean, his own little boy.

"Miles?"

"Yes, I'm right here, Savich."

"You sure Sam's okay?"

"I'm here, Uncle Dillon," Sam said, and patted Savich's shoulder. "Keely and I are both fine. Did you see the sheriff shoot Beau? *Whap!* She got him right in the neck, then shot him again when he turned that gun on Papa."

So much for protecting the children, Katie thought as she came back into the living room with a thick towel. She leaned down and pressed the towel hard against the wound.

Savich didn't know where the moan came from, didn't know he had it in him. The woman was very strong.

"Tell me what happened, Sheriff," Savich said.

Keely, her fingers still touching his cheek, said, "I heard that bad man talking to Mama in the living room, and I knew he wanted Sam."

Katie said, "And so you made a lump in your bed with a pillow, and went to wake up Sam."

The little girl nodded. She stuck her hand out to Sam, who took it. "He shoved up the window in my room and we climbed out on my oak tree." She frowned. "Sam wanted to help you but I told him that you're really tough, Mama, and that you would fix Beau's hash. Is that Beau out there?"

"That's his sorry self, yes," Katie said. "Now, Dillon, how are you doing?"

"Okay," he said, and she heard the pain in his voice.

"You don't seem to be bleeding through the pressure. The paramedics should be here any minute. You're going to be okay."

"Make sure you keep the kids with you."

"You can count on that," Miles said, and he knew that all the adults wondered what could possibly motivate those two to come after Sam again. Money, there had to be lots of money in it for them.

Katie looked from Keely to Sam. "Now we've got two heroes. Well done, kids."

They heard the sirens in the distance.

Katie lightly patted his shoulder. "Just another minute. I guess Clancy is dead. I can't get near the van, the flames are just too hot and the smoke's too thick."

"He couldn't have survived that blast," Savich said. "Don't worry about it."

She heard men's voices outside, one she recognized. "It's Wade, one of my deputies."

"Ho! What the hell happened here? You got a dead guy out here drinkin' rain."

Katie walked to the front door. "Bring everyone inside, Wade. The paramedics will be here momentarily. Agent Savich's back was cut by a piece of metal."

NINE

Mackey and Bueller helped Savich to the ambulance—it felt like a five-mile hike to Savich, who didn't think he'd ever want to walk straight again—then eased him down on his stomach onto the gurney.

"It'll be all right, Special Agent, sir," said Mackey, so impressed with having a federal officer as his patient that he nearly stuttered. "Sheriff, are you coming with us?"

"Oh, yes. Give me a minute, Mackey." She turned to Miles Kettering who was holding Keely in one arm and Sam in the other. "Could you bring the children to the hospital, Mr. Kettering? Oh goodness, they're all wet. Could you change them into dry clothes? As you can see, Sam's wearing my sweats. You'll find another pair in my bedroom, folded in the second drawer of the dresser. They're drawstring, so you can pull them tight enough for Sam. All of Keely's clothes are in her dresser."

"Don't worry, Sheriff, I'll see to both of them. Just go with Savich. And thank you."

She kissed her daughter's cheek, wishing she hadn't witnessed all the violence, and knowing she'd have to deal with it sooner rather than later. As for Sam, at least he was with his father now.

As she walked quickly back to the ambulance, Katie said to Wade, "Glen Hodges, FBI Special Agent in Charge from Knoxville, will be here very soon with a couple of agents. Just secure the scene and if any idiots chance to come out here to stop and gawk, threaten to toss them in jail. Oh yes, Wade, do give the FBI all your cooperation. It's their case since it's a kidnapping, and it happened in Virginia."

"No problem, Sheriff," Wade said, and walked over to where Beau still lay on his back, rain splashing off his face.

"He won't be causing any more trouble. As for that van, we can't get close yet, it's still burning too hot."

"The guy inside was Clancy," Katie said. "Call the fire department, have Chief Hayes come out here and clean up the mess."

Keely called out, "Mama, you take care of Uncle Dillon."

"What?"

"That's Agent Savich," Miles said.

"I will, Keely, don't worry." So many new people in her life in a very short time, and one of them hurt because of her. She jumped into the back of the ambulance, closed the doors, and settled herself in. "I'm set. Let's go, guys."

Mackey had Savich propped up on his side and Bueller had unbuttoned his shirt and scissored his undershirt open down the front so he could attach the EKG monitors. He said to Savich, "We'll let the doctor take care of getting the clothes off that wound. Just a moment more, Agent, sir, and you'll be better. It's important to keep you still now."

Savich grunted.

When they at last settled him on his stomach, Mackey slipped oxygen clips into his nostrils. "That should feel a bit better."

It did, thank the good Lord.

"Just a little nip here in the arm, Agent," Mackey said. "I'm going to start an IV."

Mackey got it on the first try, for which Savich was grateful.

"Now, Agent, sir, we're going to apply a little more pressure to the wound," Mackey said. "You just try breathing as normally as you can and hold still."

When Savich had the pain controlled, he opened his eyes to see the sheriff on her knees beside him, holding his hand, which was hanging off the side of the gurney. Katie saw his control. He was a strong man, not just physically. She said, "Thank you for saving my life, Agent Savich."

"It's Dillon. You're welcome. You didn't have to come in the ambulance. There's lots to do back at your house."

"Oh, yes I did." She smiled at him and kept stroking his hand. She said after a moment, "I should have realized that where there's smoke—"

"Gasoline was leaking out, and the heat was building up fast. I just didn't know how long it would be before it blew. A little more time would have been nice, though."

"I wonder if that could happen with my big Vortec V8 engine."

Savich couldn't help himself, he smiled through the god-awful pain.

If she'd come along to distract him she was doing a good job. "Yeah, it could even happen with that engine."

Katie said, seeing that reaction, "She's got three hundred horses at forty-four hundred rpm. Isn't that something?"

"She?"

"My truck. I know she's female. She just doesn't have a name."

"Three hundred horses, yeah, that's something, all right."

His eyes closed a moment; it was time for her to move on, time to get serious here. She said, "My mom told me once that learning lessons always hurt, only this time you took the hit for me. I owe you, Dillon. You saved my life."

"Everything's looking good, Agent, sir," Mackey said. "Your EKG's A-okay, and the bleeding's nearly stopped. I'm sorry we can't give you anything for the pain. You hanging in there?"

"I'm hanging in," Savich said. "Katie, would you please call my wife in Washington, D.C.? She's not much into truck engines, though, so you might not want to go there."

Katie pulled out her cell phone from the T-shirt pocket beneath her wet sweatshirt. "I could teach her."

He smiled. That was good.

"Okay, give me the number."

Savich closed his eyes as he gave her the phone number, to keep the moan in his throat.

"What's her name?"

"Sherlock."

Katie guessed he wasn't kidding about her name. One ring, two, then "Hello? Dillon, is that you? What's going on? Are you all right? What about Sam—"

"I'm calling for your husband, Mrs. Savich," Katie said, and automatically lowered her voice to make it soothing and calm. "I'm Sheriff K. C. Benedict calling from Jessborough, in eastern Tennessee. Your husband asked me to call you, ma'am. Let me assure you that he's all right, Mrs. Savich. He—"

"Put Dillon on, please, Sheriff."

Katie held the phone to his ear.

Savich drew a deep breath, hoping he was wiping all the damnable pain out of his voice. Sherlock could hear the smallest sound; she could even hear Sean's breathing change before he hollered. "Sherlock? It's me. No, no, I'm okay, just a little problem. Yes, we got Sam back. He's fine. So is Miles. What little problem? Well, you see this van blew up and I was a bit too close to it. I got hit in the back by some flying metal."

He closed his eyes, feeling the pain trying to draw him in. He really wanted to give in to it, but he wasn't about to scare Sherlock out of her wits.

Katie simply took the cell and said, "Mrs. Savich, he's going to be okay. We're on our way to Johnson City Medical Center. Your husband will be all right. I'm not lying to you. I will stay with him. Don't worry."

Savich managed to say "Tell her not to come here" before his brain swam away.

He heard the sheriff talking, but he didn't know if she was still speaking to Sherlock. He knew Sherlock was scared. If he'd gotten a call like this about her he would freak himself. He saw the sheriff lift her wet sweatshirt and slip the small bright blue cell phone back into the T-shirt pocket.

He couldn't seem to stop looking at that cell phone even after she'd pulled the sweatshirt back down over it. Blue, it was a bright blue, ridiculous, really, but on the other hand, she'd never lose it. Blue for cops. He liked that. He closed his eyes, wanting very much to control the blasted pain. He could picture the sharp slice in his back, not an appetizing image. He really wished Sherlock were here even though he'd asked her not to come. Of course she'd be here as soon as humanly possible.

He was vaguely aware that Katie was speaking in a slow deep voice. "—my truck also has stainless-steel exhaust manifolds."

Manifolds?

"And a high-capacity crankshaft that's internally balanced. That reduces stress on the crankshaft, don't you know. Did I tell you it was raining so hard this afternoon that I could barely see ten feet in front of me, even though I have the remarkable high-speed and twice-as-thick grade F windshield wipers on my truck?"

He wanted to laugh and she saw it.

But Savich didn't hear any more after that, just sounds that were soothing, as she was used to speaking to someone who was hurt or not quite with it. Like him.

He didn't rouse his brain until they were in the hospital emergency room and a nurse came forward and directed the four men to lift him from the gurney onto one of the narrow beds.

He heard the nurse speaking to the paramedics, heard Bueller give her a report on what had happened, heard the nurse greet the sheriff. She checked his IV and began cutting off his clothes. "Goodness, you're dirty, Agent Savich. Not to worry, we'll clean you up. You just keep holding on to his hand, Sheriff."

"It's too bad," he said. "Sherlock just got me these slacks."

"They're sexy," the nurse said, "but they've got to go, Agent Savich. Just stay still, Dr. Able will be here in a second to examine you."

He heard Katie's voice and focused on it as the nurse checked his blood pressure, took off the old EKG patches, and put on her own.

Katie said, "My truck has two cup holders in her center console, great for the kids."

"My car doesn't have even one cup holder," Savich said. He felt cold wet cloths cleaning the mud from his legs. He wasn't cold even though he was naked, and that was odd. "I'd like to have one," he said, frowning a bit.

He was almost with her again. She said, "What kind of wheels do you have?"

"A Porsche."

"I should have known, a hotshot guy like you."

He wanted to chuckle, but it was beyond him. The nurse was talking to Katie, giving her his wallet and keys, and pulling a sheet up to his waist.

"Did you see Wade, my chief deputy? I just wish he didn't want my job so badly," Katie said, and he heard the frown in her voice. "That means I can't trust him one hundred percent, and that's too bad. But I guess you have to take the good with the bad, don't you?"

"Kick Wade's butt out of Tennessee or one day you'll find yourself sabotaged but good."

"I will surely think about that, Dillon. Thank you."

"Agent Savich? I'm Dr. Able. Don't move now. I see Linda's got you all cleaned up. You've got no other wounds, just the one across your back. The EKG looks fine. You seem to be pretty stable, and that's good. Now, I'm going to give you some morphine for the pain and examine your back."

Savich looked at the dark-faced man with tobacco-stained teeth leaning over him and wondered how a doctor could begin to justify smoking to himself. He wanted to tell him smoking was nuts. He wanted to tell him that he didn't want morphine, that he didn't want to lose himself, but maybe it would be good if he checked out for a while. He felt Dr. Able fiddling with the IV line they'd started in the ambulance. Savich hoped he knew what he was doing.

"Let's wait just a moment for the morphine to kick in," Dr. Able said. "I'm going to draw some blood, see what's going on, okay? Also we need to type and cross you. I'd say that with this wound you might be a quart low."

Savich wanted to smile because that was funny, but he could only manage a nod. He just couldn't do any more than that. He felt Katie stroking the back of his hand, and he focused on that.

As Dr. Able slipped a needle into his vein to draw blood, he said, "Sheriff, I understand there've been two fatalities?"

"Yes, Clyde. And I was almost the third. The only reason Agent Savich is hurt is because he saved my life. He tackled and flattened me in the mud when the kidnappers' van exploded. I know I look bad, but it's all on the outside. Don't come near me with any of your needles, my innards are just fine."

"Thank you, Agent Savich, for saving her neck. We need Katie. Linda said you were a mess, but not any longer. Nasty weather out there."

Savich didn't answer, didn't ever want to move again. Then the morphine kicked in and it was like someone had pulled the monster's teeth out of his flesh.

"There, we've got the blood." Savich felt a pat on his arm. "Just lie still, Agent Savich. Here's a pillow against your stomach to keep you up on your side. Another couple minutes, then we'll see what we've got. Katie, how is the little boy?"

"Sam's just fine. He and my daughter are probably out in the waiting room with Sam's father, Miles Kettering. He and Agent Savich flew from Colfax, Virginia, into Ackerman's Air Field. I'll tell you, Clyde, given the winds out there, that's quite an accomplishment."

Everyone speaks so freely. Will she even tell him we flew in a Cessna?

"An accomplishment or just plain stupid. All right now, Agent Savich, let's see just how bad this is."

The pain was a low throb, nothing more, thanks to the morphine. Only thing was, his head was emptying out and he couldn't bring himself to care a great deal about anything, himself included.

He didn't realize he'd been gone until he heard Katie say, "Dr. Able doesn't think it looks too bad. It's a real clean slice but not deep, thank God."

"We're going to take you to the procedure room, Agent Savich, not the OR. It's just on the other side of the emergency room. It's nice and sterile and quiet. Katie, you can stay with him, but first you're going to have to jump in the shower. Then put on scrubs and a mask, and those cute little booties for your feet."

She patted his hand. "Don't worry, Dillon, I'll be right back."

"They'll let you in this procedure room?"

"Since you're special, they'll allow it this time. Now, I'm going to go get hosed down. Until I get back to you, I want you to think about that really neat coolant loss protection on my truck."

Ten minutes later, thoroughly scrubbed, Katie settled herself down beside Savich, and picked up his hand. It was a nice hand, strong and tanned, with short buffed nails. She remembered that Carlo's hands were like that, powerful and strong. A pity that her former husband's character hadn't matched his hands. False advertising all around. Good riddance to him.

Savich heard a mellow baritone singing "Those Were the Days," and saw Dr. Able's face leaning over him.

TEN

"Here's what we're going to do, Agent Savich," Dr. Able said, his minty breath wafting over Savich's face. "We're not going to put you under. We're going to give you what we call conscious sedation. That means Linda here will inject some morphine and Versed into your IV. It'll keep you comfortable and sleepy. I'm now going to give you some local anesthetic. All right?"

"All right," Savich said. They'd slid him from the gurney onto his stomach on a narrow bed, a sheet to his waist.

Savich didn't feel pain, just Dr. Able's fingers probing the wound. He wanted to hear more about the sheriff's truck or maybe even hear Dr. Able sing some more, but words wouldn't form in his brain, and so he just lay there, enduring. He wished he was with Sherlock, maybe playing with those fat rollers in her hair.

Dr. Able talked as he worked. "Nothing vital seems to be cut, just your skin and a bit of muscle. You're going to hurt a while, not be able to lie on your back for up to a week, but all in all, you're a very lucky man, Agent Savich. It could have been worse, much worse, and I'm sure you know that. Okay, I'm going to set the stitches in layers now—the deep ones, and then the surface stitches. This will take a few minutes."

Savich didn't feel any pain, just the dragging pull of the thread through his flesh, an obscene feeling he hated.

"You married, Agent Savich?"

Savich wasn't up to even a yes or no answer and Katie saw it. "Yes, he is, Clyde. I have a feeling his wife is going to show up here even though he told her not to come."

"Women," said Dr. Able, "if only they were more like trucks—nice and predictable; you floorboard 'em and they go, right where you tell 'em to."

"Yeah, I can see what you mean, Clyde," Katie said. "Not only that, you buy a truck, pay for it, and that's it. But with women, you gotta pay and pay—and don't forget the interest."

"Oh yeah? What about the maintenance?"

"Lots more than your truck'll ever need."

Dr. Able laughed hard and Savich was very relieved not to hear him say "Oops."

He heard their voices, but still felt no particular pain, just the slow pulling of the thread through his flesh; his mind, what was left of it, drifted back to the interviews he'd had yesterday with the husbands of the two slain high school math teachers. It was odd, but their faces blurred together, and he had trouble telling them apart. Then his own face blurred over the both of them.

Troy Ward, tears in his voice, said, "My wife has been dead for six days, Agent Savich, the police don't have a clue who did it, so how do you think I feel? I've told them everything I know, including my mother's social security number."

Savich nodded. He didn't particularly like Troy Ward, the over-weight sports announcer. "The thing is, Mr. Ward, the FBI is involved now—"

"Yeah, I've heard all about you big boobs waltzing in and taking over. And now the TV's screaming that it's a serial killer. God, we don't need another one. That last one still gives me nightmares."

"No, we don't need another one. But I really need to know . . ."

Savich's brain floated away, and when he managed to snag some of it back again, Troy Ward seemed more overweight now than he had been just an instant before. "Mr. Ward, have you spoken to Mr. Fowler?"

"The other murdered woman's husband? No, I haven't. Two grown men sitting together sobbing, it wouldn't play well in the football locker room, now, would it? Can't you just see the guys laughing their heads off? No, not much point to that."

What did football have to do with grieving? "Did you play football, Mr. Ward? Is that how you got into announcing?"

"You making a joke, Agent Savich? Let me tell you, I wasn't always this big, and I tried out, but I never got past high school ball. They were a bunch of macho assholes anyway." He jumped to his feet, his three chins wobbling, and screamed, "I wanted to get in the locker room!"

Savich said when that scream died away, "I played football."

"Well, yeah, I can tell by looking at you. I'll just bet you had girls hanging off your biceps, didn't you, you brainless jock?"

That wasn't very nice of him to say, Savich was thinking, but then Troy Ward had a microphone in front of his mouth and he was screaming, "Go, you macho jock jerks! Run!" He yelled in Savich's face, "It's a touchdown! You see that, a touchdown!"

Savich said, "You never met Mr. Gifford Fowler or Leslie Fowler, his wife?"

Now Savich wanted to lie down on this big soft sofa and just listen to the soft rain falling against the front windows of Troy Ward's very nice house in an excellent area of Oxford, Maryland. "Nope, I already told the police I'd never heard of them. I don't think my wife, Bernie, knew Leslie Fowler either, never mentioned her name or anything, not that Bernie and I ever talked about other women all that much. She wasn't worried about me playing around on her, said I was a really bad liar and she'd know." He paused, then tears oozed out of his eyes, falling into the deep creases on his double chin. "I want you to catch the maniac who killed Bernie!" Then he threw back his head and yelled to the ceiling, "I want to be a jock asshole!"

Troy Ward was suddenly standing over him, his hand extended. "Do you want a rice cake? I'm trying to lose some weight, gotta get back into shape, you know, because, who knows, the Ravens might make the playoffs and I'll be all front and center with the players. I may be doing some locker room interviews with the guys." But he wasn't holding a rice cake out to Savich, it was a huge Krispy Kreme the size of an inner-tube swing. Savich backed away from the doughnut and Troy Ward, that officious little sod of an overweight sports announcer, blurred into the tall gaunt features of Gifford Fowler, the car dealer, who was talking right in his face. "You want to buy one of my Chevys? I've been selling Chevys right here for the last twenty-two years! I'm solid, they're solid. *Like a Rock!* Hey? Just like the commercial. Whatcha think, Agent Savich?"

"Did you kill your wife, Mr. Fowler?"

"Nah, I sell cars, I don't kill wives. You divorce wives, not kill them. I divorced two before Leslie got herself whacked. Cops are stupid, but the fact is it's just not worth the risk. I just know that if I'd knocked off

Leslie they'd get me and then I'd only have eighteen good years left before they toasted me in the gas chamber. Whatcha think, Agent Savich?"

"It's a lethal injection now, Mr. Fowler. Sometimes it's even longer than eighteen years. That's only the average. Did you love your wife?"

"Nah, she wasn't a Mercedes anymore, looked more like a real old Chevy Impala. She used to be hot pink, then got too many miles and turned a dirty gray, ready for the junk pile. Glad we didn't have any kids with me and her as parents—they'd be stealing cars off my lot, the little bastards."

"Do you and Troy Ward, that famous Ravens announcer, ever bowl together?"

"Oh yeah, I heard about his bowling—always leaves splits and someone, it was his wife I hear, always had to come in and clean them up." He laughed and laughed, slapping his knees. "Boy, is he fat, or what? None of the players or any of the coaching staff like him. He's gross, you know? Not like me. Want to see my abs?"

"That's all right, Mr. Fowler, leave your shirt on, but those cuff links, now, they really don't go with that shirt."

"Old junk-heap Leslie gave them to me. I'm wearing them to honor her—one more time, I figure she was worth it. Then I'll flush 'em down. Hey, Agent Savich, you sure you don't want to test-drive a Silverado? Cops like Silverados because they got that fancy coolant loss protection. It would fit your image, all hard muscle, really hot for the girls. Hey, let me show you my hard muscles." As he unzipped his dark gray wool slacks he softly sang "When You Wish Upon a Star."

Voices, Savich heard voices, and this time they were close and he recognized them and could even make sense of them. It was Dr. Able.

"In deference to your wife, Agent Savich, I'm closing your skin real pretty so she'll think your scar's sexy."

His brain wasn't floating anymore, it was hovering, and things made sense now, more or less. He said, "Sherlock thinks everything about me is sexy," and was pleased because it was true. "Another scar'll just give her someplace new to kiss." He'd lost all sense and his tongue had lost its brakes. He heard a laugh, from Katie. Then he saw Troy Ward again, stuffing that huge doughnut into his mouth, and there was Gifford Fowler, dangling Silverado keys in front of him, winking, and then he threw the keys, and they went higher and higher and even though Savich jumped a good three feet in the air, they kept flying away.

"A woman with great taste," Katie said. She squeezed his hand. "You guys married long?"

"I don't know about long," Savich said. "I knew her before I ever saw her. She says I'm her fantasy."

"I'd sure like to be a woman's fantasy," Dr. Able said.

"She likes to scrub me down when we get home from the gym."

"There, you see, Clyde, she treats him just like a truck—keeps him nice and clean and revved up."

Dr. Able stopped stitching a moment because he was laughing. Savich was grateful he'd stopped.

"We have a little boy, Sean. She says he looks just like me, not fair since she did all the work. All I did was just have fun, and not even think about it."

Dr. Able said, "I had a little boy once. And you know what? The little bugger grew up. Can you beat that? After all I did for him, he had the nerve to grow up on me and leave. There, done, no more needles pulling through your skin."

"Sherlock got knifed once. I watched the doctor put stitches in her skinny white arm. It shouldn't have happened. I wanted to kill her for taking such a chance."

"Did she succeed?" Katie asked.

"Oh yes," Savich said. He sounded so proud and so pissed, with a layer of dopiness over it, that she had to smile.

"I doubt you'll remember any of this when you wake up tomorrow, Agent Savich," Dr. Able said. "But, can you understand me?"

Savich nodded.

"Your antibiotics are in and the wound looks fine. We're going to keep you here tonight so that the drugs wear off, and make sure there aren't any complications, not that I expect any. Your blood tests look okay. Now, I don't want you worrying about anything, just rest. Again, you were very lucky. I know this wasn't a piece of cake for you, but if that metal had sliced your back any deeper, it wouldn't have been any fun at all. Now, I'm going to make sure you get a real good night's sleep. I sure hope you like sleeping on your stomach."

Savich never opened his eyes though he heard everything. He smelled everything, too, including a hint of lemony soap. Maybe he'd said some things that he normally wouldn't have said. Who cared? Now, he thought, he could just let go.

Life was unexpected. You woke up in the morning, fed your little kid some Cheerios with a sliced banana on top, walked out into the sun, everything going along just fine, and then *whap!*—that night you're laid out in an emergency room in Tennessee.

"You got anything to say to Agent Savich, Katie?"

She lightly touched her fingertips to his cheek. "Just that I can't wait to meet Sherlock, and you need to rest," she said as she pulled off the surgical mask. Savich wanted to say something, maybe to thank the doctor, but it just seemed too hard. He sighed, and slept.

Katie asked, "How long will he be out?"

"He could wake up at any time, but I hope not until morning, not all that long a time away. You know that sleep is the best thing for whatever ails you. Like I said, this man was lucky."

"I'm grateful to you, Clyde, and to his luck," she said. "I'll be in the waiting room with Sam, his father, and Keely. Let me know when Agent Savich is settled in. I know Miles will want to see him, not to mention Sam."

"You sure you don't want me to check out Sam?"

"Nah, the kid's fine. Real proud of himself and that's good, it'll help him keep the fear at bay."

She gave him a small salute, thanked the ER personnel she'd known all her life, and went down to the women's room to wrap her wet clothes in a towel she'd pulled out of the hamper.

She went out into the deserted hospital corridor wearing green scrubs to call in to the station. Wade was still there, just as she'd known he would be. He brought her up to date, then gave her over to Special Agent Hodges.

"We saw the aftermath of all the excitement, Sheriff. I'm really sorry we missed it."

"We're sorry you missed it, too."

"Your house is a crime scene, but we didn't put tape across your front door. Wade and some deputies boarded up the window Beau broke in. My people are finished up inside, so you can go back in. As for the van, it's still smoldering and the fire chief roped it off. Is Savich all right?"

"He will be, but he won't be doing push-ups for a while. Thank God his wound wasn't deep, just really painful. He'll be in the hospital overnight, just to make sure. Give him a week or so, says the doctor, and he'll be able to sleep on his back again."

She listened to Glen Hodges sing Savich's praises, then he laughed. "We've got a three-way bet going here as to what time Sherlock will show up in the morning, if it takes her that long."

"Really," Katie said, "there's no way for her to get here that fast, even driving."

"You'll see, Sheriff. We'll come over and visit Savich tomorrow. We're doing paperwork here, and then Deputy Osborne will take us to the local B&B—what is it called? Mother's Best?"

"Mother's Very Best," Katie said. "Mrs. Beecham's grandmother named it that back in the forties. It's a nice place—on the frilly side— and the food is to die for. If you've never had grits before, you're in for a real treat."

"Excellent. Oh, Sheriff," Agent Hodges paused a moment, then said, "I'm, er, really sorry, but there's something else that you need to know, something you might not be expecting. You know I told you the truck was roped off? Well, that was after it was checked over real good. We decided not to bother you with it right away, what with your heading off to the hospital with Agent Savich, and Wade agreed with us."

Didn't need to bother me with something?

Keeping her voice mild and easy, she asked, "What didn't you think was important enough to notify me about, Agent Hodges?"

"Well, it's not exactly that it's *not* important . . . it's like this, Sheriff: There was no body inside the van."

ELEVEN

"*What?*"

"It looks like Clancy—big gut and all—got out before the van blew," Agent Hodges said. "Of course, he had lots of motivation. Wade called all the county sheriff's offices and all area police departments, and the state police. He gave them all the particulars and a description of Clancy. We figure he's got to be in bad shape, I mean, he did crash the van hard into that tree, and Wade told me you'd shot him in the arm or shoulder, so he's got to be in pretty bad shape.

"As I said, we've already got a manhunt going. Any stolen cars will be reported directly to us. We'll find Clancy.

"I'm really sorry we've got to add this to the mix, Sheriff. As for Beau, the coroner has his body. There'll be paperwork for you to do, but I guess you know that. And I'm sure you'll be getting a call first thing in the morning from the TBI."

The Tennessee Bureau of Investigation—oh yeah, she'd get lots more than a call. But that was tomorrow. At this moment, she was so mad at Agent Hodges that if she'd been within arm's reach she would have clouted him in the head, really hard. She told herself keeping calm was her forte and she used that now, her voice still smooth and mild. "Let me see if I've got this straight. *You* decided not to bother me with this small detail, Agent Hodges? It didn't occur to you that since I'm the sheriff I should be called immediately?"

"Well, ma'am, we've got a lot going on here—"

"You just made a big mistake you will not repeat, Agent Hodges. I'm the sheriff of Jessborough, I run things here, you don't, regardless of anything my deputy might have said."

"Now wait a minute, Sheriff. I'm sorry about the delay, but it is our case."

"I don't need to speak to you any longer, Agent Hodges. Put Wade back on the phone."

"Yo, Katie. Come on now, don't be pissed."

She pictured driving her truck over him, maybe letting the back tires with their cast-aluminum wheels sit on him, really settle in and get comfortable. Savich was right. She should boot his butt to the Tennessee line and hand him over to North Carolina or Virginia or Georgia—she had lots of choices. Hey, Kentucky sounded good. She said, "You should have called me immediately, Wade, not agreed with the Feds."

"Look, Katie, you were on your way to the hospital with Agent Savich. I didn't want you to have to worry about something else. Everything's being done that should be done."

"Worrying is my job, Wade. We'll talk about this tomorrow. Right now, I want you to bring our people in. Have them go home and sleep, but keep a patrol going near my house, no, that's not enough. I want a couple of deputies sitting out in front of my house. If Clancy is alive, chances are he's hiding in the forest. If he's not badly hurt, he might double back.

"Oh yeah, tell Dicker to bring his dogs over to my house first thing in the morning if Clancy hasn't been found by then. The state police can keep looking tonight, those guys don't deserve much sleep. One other thing, check in with every family within a five-mile radius of my house. Warn them. You got that?"

"I already had Mary Lynn call all the neighbors. I do know what to do, Katie."

"He'll try to steal a car if he's able to."

"Yeah, we know that."

"He's a dangerous man, Wade. Keep reminding everyone just how dangerous."

"Yes, I have, of course. Even though I'm sending out deputies to guard your house, Katie, you be careful, too. No telling what that moron will do."

"There's something else, Wade—something very important—but I think I'll let it wait until tomorrow morning when Agent Savich is back in the land of the living. You don't need to worry about it now, Wade."

"Wait! Whoa, Katie, what do—"

"Nah, you've got enough on your plate tonight, Wade, both you and

Agent Hodges." She smiled as she hung up. *That should have him thinking and cursing about me not telling him something.*

She pushed away from the wall and walked to the waiting room. Her brain was fried, or very nearly.

So Fatso had managed to get out of the van and into the forest before the sucker blew. Well, wasn't that just peachy?

Now she had to tell Miles, though she didn't want to. She had to tell him, it was his right to help protect his child.

It was time to herd her daughter and her guests home. Maybe they should just wait and go to Mother's Very Best, just to be on the safe side. No, she was losing it. A headache started to burrow in over her left eye. Home would be safe. Home sounded like heaven right now, even with a boarded up front window and a burned-out van in the front yard.

She walked into the small waiting room that prided itself on having the oldest *Time* magazines anywhere—most of them from the Watergate period in the seventies.

Keely was wearing her pajamas, a robe, and bunny slippers over nice thick socks. Sam had on a pair of Katie's gray sweats, with the legs rolled up more times than she could count, the long sleeves of her shirt pushed up as well, so thick it looked like he had tires around his arms. He had a pair of her socks on his feet. A nurse, Miles told her, had brought them each a couple of blankets and pillows.

That would be Hilda Barnes, she told him. Hilda always took special care of any visiting children.

Katie realized Miles was the only damp one in the waiting room.

Sam was on his feet the instant he saw her. "How's Uncle Dillon, Katie?"

"He's going to be just fine, Sam. He'll be staying here tonight. Dr. Able just wants to make sure everything is okay."

Miles said, "You look sharp in your scrubs, Katie." Actually, she looked rather ridiculous, her hair in a ratty wet ponytail, the scrubs hanging off her. And she looked valiant—a strange thing to think, but it was true. She leaned down to scratch her knee. If only he'd known, he would have offered to do the scratching for her.

"They wouldn't let me in with Dillon unless I got hosed down first. Here are my clothes, wrapped in this towel."

"Mama, I think you look cuter than Dr. Jonah."

"Let's just keep that between us."

"Okay. Who is this man who needs to shave?"

"You mean me, Keely?" Miles said, momentarily distracted. "You know who I am. Your mama needs some aspirin."

How did he know that?

"No," Keely said, "the man in the picture, in the magazine."

"Oh, that was President Nixon," Katie said. "I was born just before he resigned, a very long time ago. When was it?"

"In 1974," Miles said. "I was just a bit younger than Sam."

"Does your head hurt, Katie?" Sam said, and looked up at her.

"Just a little bit. Don't worry about it. Miles, I hear there's a bet on as to how fast Sherlock will get here. Savich told her not to come."

"Doesn't matter," Miles said. "When Sherlock's on a mission, if you don't help, you'd best get out of her way. Now, kids, it's after midnight, time for both of you to be in bed—again."

"I'm not tired," Keely said immediately, and yawned.

"Sure you're not," Katie said and swung her into her arms. She smiled at Miles Kettering, a man she'd not even known existed until she'd come across Sam. His clothes looked damp and itchy, the wool smelled, and his feet squished in his shoes, but no matter, he'd made the kids comfortable.

"You look dead on your feet, Miles. Maybe close to a coma, even." Actually, even with fatigue and worry for Sam etched on his face, those eyes of his were brilliant with relief and just plain happiness. She knew to her toes that he was a strong man, competent, a good man who loved his child more than anything.

Miles Kettering was so tired after two days of little sleep and endless worry that a coma didn't sound like a bad thing. "I'm good for a few more miles yet" was all he said. He rose slowly, Sam in his arms, looking like he never wanted to let him go again. And she knew exactly how he felt. He wanted Sam close, he wanted to feel Sam's heartbeat against his palm, to know that he was safe, and with him again.

"Let me take Sam to see Dillon for a moment. He's scared and I want to reassure him. Then we'll be right with you."

At that moment, a nurse came around to let them know Special Agent Savich was in his room, on the medical ward.

"That was good timing," Miles said. "Could you get some aspirin for the sheriff, nurse?"

"Oh, sure. Katie, just a minute, I'll get you some even stronger stuff."

"Not too strong," Katie called after her. "I can't be comatose just yet."

"I want to see Uncle Dillon, too," Keely said.

Katie knew no one was about to keep the kids out at this hour. Almost everybody here had known Keely from the moment she was born, five years before just two floors up. Come to think of it, everybody knew everything about everybody within a ten-mile radius of Jessborough, with updates every couple of hours or so. You'd have to be sick or dead to be out of the loop about what happened today.

The four of them stood by Agent Savich's bed, watching him sleep. Sam lightly patted his shoulder, and looked up to his father. "Uncle Dillon doesn't look so good, Papa. Why's he on his stomach?"

"You remember, he got cut on his back, that's why. He'll be just fine, don't worry, Sam."

"I think he's handsome," Keely said. "Do you think you'd like him, Mama?"

"It's too late for us, pumpkin," Katie told her daughter, "he waited as long as he could, and then he met Sherlock and she proposed to him. She was more in need than we were. What could he do?"

Miles wanted to laugh, but he was just too tired to do more than blink.

By the time Katie walked out of Dillon's hospital room, two Advil in her system, Keely's head rested on her shoulder, and she was sound asleep. Ten minutes later, Katie eased down into the front seat of Miles's rented Ford and settled Keely on her lap. Miles fastened the seat belt. Then he paused, and both of them realized they didn't want Sam to be alone in the backseat.

It would be a tight fit, but they could do it. Miles said, "Sam, do you think you can hold real still?"

"Sure, Papa," Sam said, so tired his voice slurred like a drunk's.

"Okay, I want you to sit on my lap, but since I'm driving, you can't move a whisker."

Katie had given people tickets for such stupidity, but she didn't say a word. It would work.

Once Miles had the seat belt around both of them, Sam nearly touching the steering wheel even though Miles had pushed the front seat all the way back, Katie said, "Maybe you'd best stay at Mother's Very Best tonight, Miles. The other Feds are staying there."

He was silent for a long moment as he started the car.

"It's not that I don't want you at my house. It's something else entirely."

TWELVE

She paused, saw that both children were asleep, then said, her voice low, "Something's happened, Miles."

His hands were fisted around the steering wheel. "Tell me."

"It seems that Fatso/Clancy got out of the van before it blew. They haven't found him yet. The hunt will begin in earnest early tomorrow morning, at first light. If he's still in the forest, he might be dead of his wounds or pneumonia by morning. But I don't think we'll get that lucky."

His right hand thumped the steering wheel. Sam jerked, but didn't awaken. "So there's still danger."

"Well, yes. I felt much better thinking he was dead and accounted for, given what's happened. I'm hoping that he'll run as far and as fast as he can. At least when we catch him, we'll have a chance to get out of him why he and Beau took Sam."

"That would make me feel a whole lot better. There wasn't a ransom note. Everyone was thinking a pedophile had taken him. Now? I don't have a clue." He paused, then added, "I guess you don't think he's dead."

There was such hopefulness in his voice, but she didn't lie. "No, I don't. Life is never that neat and tidy. When you mix criminals in, things really get mucked up."

"So that's why you want me to stay at this B and B in town."

"It might be for the best."

"Wouldn't we be just as safe with you and your deputies, Sheriff?"

"Two deputies will be in front of the house all night and there will be lots of people there tomorrow. Either way, you should be fine, but it's up to you, Miles."

"If you'll have us, Sam and I would like to stay with you. He knows your house, Sheriff, he's comfortable with Keely and with you. I don't want to take him to another strange place unless I'm forced to."

"No, you don't have to. But please remember, Clancy and Beau came back to my house to get Sam again. I'm not really sure Clancy is going to hightail it out of here."

"Ah, I don't think you know this, Katie, but I was in law enforcement myself until five years ago, in the FBI. Savich and I worked together, as a matter of fact, and that's how we became friends. I can handle myself and a gun, if the need arises."

She shook her head at him. "I knew there was something about you, something that made me think you'd been in the military, or something."

"Yeah, I can just imagine how bad-ass dangerous I looked holding two children in my arms."

IT took them a good twenty minutes to get there, never going faster than twenty miles an hour. The rain had slowed to a drizzle but a low-lying gray fog blanketed the ground. The air was bone-numbing cold, pregnant with more rain.

The children continued to sleep all the way back to Katie's house, a neat two-story with a wide porch built in the forties. It was just outside Jessborough proper, along a road lined with tulip poplars, set back on five acres that were mostly covered with hardwood trees—beech, red maple, white ash, sassafras.

Miles said, "Do you know, I can't see the mountains, but I know they're there, nearly in your backyard."

"Just wait until morning. Fall is the most glamorous time of the year. So many different trees, so many bright colors, each one distinctive. Come back, say, the end of March and it isn't so pretty."

Miles pulled the Ford in behind the deputies. Katie waved to them, then handed a sleeping Keely to Miles to put on his other shoulder. She watched him pause a moment and stare at the still smoldering van and the boarded-up front window. Then he took the children into the house.

Katie was pleased the car was parked right out in front, as conspicuous as could be. No way Clancy could miss them. They also had a huge thermos of black coffee on the front seat between them, enough, they assured her, to last them until doomsday, or later.

It was nearly 2 a.m. when Katie handed Miles a cup of hot chocolate and pointed to a big easy chair.

"Why don't you drink this. I find hot chocolate always slows me down even if my brain is revving. I'll bet it'll send you right off to sleep."

"Your headache under control?"

"Oh yes. But how did you know?"

He smiled at her. "I just knew."

She couldn't help herself and smiled back. "It's been an eventful day," she said and both of them sipped the hot chocolate.

She closed her eyes in bliss as it warmed her belly.

"An understatement. Both kids were boneless. I just poured them into their beds. It's always amazed me how a kid can do that."

Katie smiled. "Thank you for taking care of Keely. My sweats are warm even if they don't fit Sam very well. I haven't had time to wash his clothes. We can do that first thing in the morning. Sam's a brave kid, Miles."

"Yeah, he is. Obviously it's you who deserves thanks for saving my son's life. I owe you, Katie, I owe you forever."

"You're welcome. Remember, Sam saved himself. It was luck that I was driving really slow and Keely saw him."

Miles said, "When I put Keely to bed while you were drying my clothes, she still had that blanket Hilda gave her at the hospital. She didn't want to give it up."

"She didn't mention Oscar? That's her rabbit. They've been inseparable since she was six months old."

"She sleeps with her rabbit?"

"Oh, sure. Does Sam have a favorite animal he sleeps with?"

"Yes," Miles said. "A big stuffed frog named Ollie. It's really ratty, but Sam refuses to let it go."

"Wait just a second." Katie left the living room only to return a few seconds later, a big green frog under her arm. "Would you look at this sitting in her closet—her grandmother, my mother, gave it to her for Christmas last year. Maybe Sam would let it be a stand-in for Ollie."

He smiled, the first one Katie had seen. "You have a name for the critter?"

"Oh yeah, she's Marie."

"Sam might not want a girl."

"Trust me. Green isn't girly. And you'll make it Martin."

She watched him close his eyes again, saw the tension flooding back over him, and waited. After a minute or so, he said, "Best I can tell, Sam was taken out of his own bed close to dawn, early Friday morning. It's been like an unending nightmare." He swallowed convulsively. Katie just let him talk.

"I went to get him up for school, and he wasn't in his bed. I thought he was in the bathroom and I went yelling for him to hurry up. It took at least five minutes before I realized he was gone, that someone had taken him. My first thought was a sexual predator, and believe me, the FBI checked that out immediately. Then we all wondered if it was some sort of revenge—after all, I'd been in the FBI myself and captured some bad guys. Since I own a good-sized company, it could have been ransom. They spoke to my sister-in-law, to some of my employees, even a couple of friends. It all takes time, so they'd really just gotten started. But no matter what the agents said, no matter what they did, all I could think about was some child molester had gotten him."

His voice broke. He opened his eyes. "I wanted to hope, to believe that the FBI would get him back, but there have been so many kidnappings, and the kids either disappear forever or they're found dead. I've never been so scared in my life."

"I'll bet. I can't imagine how I'd feel if it were Keely." She shook her head. "Did Sam tell you that his mama got him moving when Beau and Clancy had him at the cabin?"

"No, he hasn't had time to tell me everything yet."

"I hope your wife is all right."

"His mother has been dead for two years now, a car accident."

"Oh, I'm so very sorry; Sam never told me."

He smiled wearily. "It's all right. He doesn't talk about it yet. His mom speaks to him every so often; funny thing is, sometimes she talks to me, too. Of course it's just in my head, when I'm stressed out or something, and I have a problem that's all muddled in my mind, but if she spoke to Sam to help him get away, good for her." He shrugged. "Maybe, somehow, he needed her to help him help himself. And so he did. Can you tell me what happened, Sheriff?"

"Sure. Let me tell you about Sam's great escape." She spoke for maybe two minutes, then realized her audience had nodded off. She leaned down and lightly shook his shoulder. He came awake instantly, a flash of fear, then relief that Sam was okay.

"It's time for bed, Miles. I don't think my sweats would work for you as well as they do for Sam. We can go shopping tomorrow for both of you. There's a bathroom right beside Sam's room. When my dad was alive he used to visit, so you'll find guy stuff in there."

"Thank you, Katie." She watched him walk from the living room. He was a big man, fit and runner-lean, dark-haired and dark-eyed, looking rather silly with a green frog tucked under his right arm. He looked like exhaustion walking. And the oddest thing was, she felt like she'd known him for a good long time, and it felt good.

After a long hot shower, Katie checked Keely's room. Her daughter was smiling in her sleep, Oscar lying tightly squeezed to her chest, one floppy ear showing above the blanket Hilda had given her.

Katie climbed into bed with one more thing to do before she let her brain go. She opened her laptop and went to the NCIC, the National Crime Information Center, the FBI's national criminal database that could be accessed by local law enforcement. The late Beauregard Jones was a career hood who hailed from Denton, Texas, a three-time loser, with warrants that could have put him in jail for the rest of his miserable life, if it weren't over already. She couldn't find anything about kidnapping or about any family in or near Tennessee.

She had no clue what Clancy's last name was or how he'd gotten connected to Beau. She called Ossining, Beau's place of residence until a couple of years ago. She left a message for the warden to call her as soon as possible. Clancy was the key, she just knew it.

She shut down her laptop, unplugged the modem, and pulled the covers to her neck.

She dreamed that Keely was calling to her, but when Katie got close to her daughter's voice, all she saw was a long line of vans. She watched, horrified, as each of them blew up, one after the other. Then she saw Clancy stuffing Keely into a van that hadn't blown up yet. She woke up, frightened and wheezing, her nightshirt sweated through.

She couldn't help herself. She checked on Keely, then on Sam and Miles. Sam was on his side, his face on his father's shoulder, his father's arm cuddling him close. Martin the frog was sprawled on top of Miles, Sam's arm around him.

She was still shaking from that wretched dream. Beau was dead. As for Clancy, she'd get him and throw his ass in jail.

THIRTEEN

The hospital was quiet at ten o'clock on Sunday morning. Katie, Miles, and the children trooped into Dillon Savich's semi-private room that had only Savich in it.

Leaning over him was a small woman in black slacks, black leather half-boots, and a black denim jacket over a red sweater. She had curly red hair that wasn't really a red red, or an auburn, just a marvelous mix, and a very nice laugh. She looked up when she heard them coming.

Her eyes lit up. "Hey, Sam, Dillon tells me you're a hero."

Sam shouted as he ran to her, "I did it, Aunt Sherlock, I climbed out that window myself, and it was so skinny that my shoulders didn't want to fit through, but I finally wiggled free and my butt fell right out. I landed on my face in the mud. That was yucky but I ran and ran and then Katie was there—and you know that she shot those bad men?"

He finally took a breath. Sherlock grabbed him up in her arms and danced around the room with him. She kissed him all over his face as she danced.

Sam asked her when she paused to take a breath, "Where's Sean?"

"He's with his grandmother. I'd bet that right now he's sitting in church."

"That could be bad," Sam said to Katie. "Sean doesn't like to sit still."

"You're right about that," Sherlock said, and kissed him one final time. "We bribe him with graham crackers."

Sam immediately turned to Savich. "You're sitting up, Uncle Dillon. Are you better?"

"I'm just fine, Sam, just a bit stiff." Savich hugged Sam against him, doing his best not to wince when the boy's hands brushed against the bandage over his back. "Sherlock's going to spring me today, she promised. Did you and your dad sleep at the sheriff's house last night?"

"Yeah, Papa slept with me. I got hot, but he didn't want to let go of me."

"I wouldn't let go of you either," Sherlock said. "Okay, what else do you have to tell me, Sam?"

"When I woke up there was this strange frog on top of Papa."

"That was Marie," Miles said to Sherlock. "A big green stuffed frog, on loan from Keely."

Sam was outraged. "He isn't a girl frog. You said his name was Martin."

Miles said, "Hey, I thought you were so macho that it wouldn't matter. Isn't that right?"

While Sam looked uncertain, Miles said, "I told Katie that you'd be here this morning, Sherlock. How'd you manage it?"

Savich said, "She called Jimmy Maitland, our boss, told him I was in bad shape in Tennessee, and he sent her over in a Black Bell jet helicopter."

"Oh wow," Sam said. "Katie, my papa makes parts for helicopters and he can fly them, too. Can we go home in a helicopter, Papa?"

"Very doubtful," Miles said, "particularly an FBI helicopter. Every taxpayer who didn't get to ride in it would be pretty upset. Isn't the Cessna any good anymore, Sam?"

While Sam was trying to explain how much cooler a helicopter was, Katie met Sherlock.

Sherlock took her hands and just held them in hers. "Thank you so very much for saving Sam."

"It was my pleasure. However, Mrs. Savich—"

"No, just call me Sherlock, everyone does."

"I'm the one responsible for your husband being hurt. If I hadn't run toward that van—"

"No, no, that's quite enough. I'll admit I was angry at first, but then Dillon told me how you saved Sam not once but twice, by shooting Beau when it was crunch time. So we can stand here and thank each other or we can get on with things."

Katie looked at each of them in turn. "There's something I've got to tell you two you may not know yet."

Every eye went to her.

"Clancy wasn't in the van. He got out before it blew. We've got a manhunt going on. If he's anywhere near here, we'll get him."

Savich said, "Do you have dogs, Sheriff?"

"Yes, Bud Dicker has four hunting dogs. They've been out since about six o'clock this morning. No word yet."

Sherlock said, frowning, "I can't imagine he'd stay in the area unless he was badly hurt. Okay, Katie, I can see you know something more. Come on, cough it up."

"It isn't all that much just yet. I know you've all probably wondered by now why Beau and Clancy brought Sam here, to Jessborough, Tennessee, and held him in Bleaker's old cabin. Was his kidnapping connected to someone local? Or was it all just happenstance, as in there was this cabin, and Clancy and Beau knew about it, and just used it?"

Savich sighed, recognizing an excellent performance when he saw it, and didn't say anything.

Katie said, "Miles, do you know anyone local? Anyone at all?"

"No, I don't. Like I told you last night, I've never been in this part of Tennessee before in my life."

"Okay, so I thought the next step was to connect up Beau and Clancy to a local. It was no big shock to find out that neither of them came from around here, and so, no convenient relatives popped up. But they were both lifelong criminals, in and out of prison, and I just knew to my bones that's the answer. Clancy or Beau met someone in prison and that someone is from around here or has friends or relatives here. I found out from NCIC that Beau was at Ossining, so I gave them a call to see if they'd ever had a Clancy in their fine facility.

"Ossining got back to me just a little while ago, and sure enough, Clancy Edens had enjoyed their hospitality until about eight months ago—conspiracy to commit kidnapping. It turns out one of the kidnappers got cold feet and ratted out his friends.

"They faxed me his photo, and he's our boy. I had copies Xeroxed and plastered all over town. Problem is, I just haven't found any connection between Clancy Edens and someone local."

Savich smiled. "You've got a good brain, Katie. No reason to wait. Sherlock, hand me MAX. Let me see what he can find out."

Once the modem was plugged in, Savich booted up MAX. While they waited, Miles told Katie about MAX, sometimes known as MAX-INE, the laptop he used to access the data-mining software he'd worked

on for years. "Bottom line is that either MAX or MAXINE could probably find out what kind of deodorant the president smears in his armpits
if it's on a database somewhere. He's even better with computers than
I am," Miles added, "and that bums me, it really does."

"Be quiet, Miles," Savich said, not looking up. "You can do everything else better. I wouldn't know a night guidance system from a bowling ball."

Sherlock said, "I remember you took Dillon down to the mat a
couple of weeks ago."

Savich looked up. "That was an accident, Sherlock. I must have been
dehydrated or something."

Katie smiled as she said, "Sam, I can see you're fretting. I don't want
you to worry about Fatso. We'll get him, no doubt in my mind. We've
got his photo nailed up everywhere and special flyers are being printed
up as I speak. But do you know what? Your uncle Dillon is going to find
out why they brought you here real soon."

"He's got a big stomach, Uncle Dillon," Sam said as he settled in on
his father's lap.

"I know, Sam," Katie said. "His belly nearly fills up the photo we've
got out there."

Miles said, "Keely, this is the only chair. You want to climb up here,
too?"

Keely didn't hesitate to climb up on his other leg. Miles said, "They're
still so excited they can't think straight or talk about anything else.
Okay, kiddos, just lean on me and listen for a while, okay?"

Sherlock said, "Sam, I meant to tell you, you look cool. I really like
those jeans and your Titans sweatshirt. I wonder what all your Redskins
friends are going to say when they see it. Are those Nikes I see on your
big feet?"

Katie said as Sam preened, "Mary Lynn Rector—believe it or not
her father's the local Presbyterian minister—brought them over about
seven o'clock this morning. She'd heard Sam didn't have anything except
my sweats, said it was Sunday and even Kmart didn't open until ten. As
for Miles, at least his clothes are clean, no new ones yet for him."

Sam said against his father's chest, "I'm cool."

Keely looked at her mother, frowned, and stuck her thumb in her
mouth, something Katie hadn't seen her do in at least six months. On
the other hand, Keely hadn't seen a van blow up or a man shot not ten

feet away from her in the last six months either. She would have to ask Dr. Sheila Raines what do to about this. Sheila, a childhood friend, was the only shrink in the area that Katie trusted. She moved to stand beside her daughter when Sherlock said, "Mr. Maitland wanted the other FBI guys to fly here with me, you know, the ones working with us, Miles, but I convinced him to let me come out right away. But I wouldn't be surprised if Butch Ashburn showed up here today. He's a bulldog, Katie."

"Is he like Glen Hodges?"

"More so," Savich said, still not looking up. "I can just hear her now, Katie, telling Maitland that she'd get things all cleaned up herself, no reason to load the helicopter down with unnecessary personnel."

At that moment, Glen Hodges and two other agents stuck their heads in the door. Two of them had huge grins on their faces, the third looked really down. "We knew you'd be here, Sherlock. Hot-diggity, I just won fifty bucks off Jessie here. The poor stiff said you wouldn't show up until two o'clock this afternoon." There was a boo and hiss from Jessie.

"Well, of course I'm here," Sherlock said to Glen Hodges. "Where else would I be?"

"Jessie here," Savich said to his wife, "just didn't realize that you were perfectly capable of moving a mountain or two to get what you wanted."

There was a bit of laughter, then Agent Hodges said, "Sheriff, Mother's Very Best is just excellent. You wouldn't believe the breakfast she gave us. You're not looking too bad, Savich. The sheriff said you'd just be sore for a week or two. I see you're working on MAX." He eyed Sam and Keely, then said, "Do you still want to belt me, Sheriff?"

"Agent Hodges," Katie said to the rest of the group, "didn't bother telling me about Clancy not being in the van, just took charge himself. The proverbial Fed with big wing tips."

Sherlock said, "Are you serious, Katie? You're telling me that Glen didn't call you immediately when they found out Clancy wasn't in that van?"

"Well, yeah, I did call her just a bit later."

"Actually, I was the one who called Wade. Nobody called me."

"Do you want me to belt him for you, Sheriff?" Sherlock was standing nearly *en pointe*.

Katie knew Sherlock was thinking Hodges was a sexist jerk, and maybe he was. In the short term, it really hadn't mattered, but she was the sheriff of Jessborough, and yeah, she was still low-level pissed at him. "I'll deal with him, Sherlock, thanks just the same."

"Ah, if neither of you is going to hit me right away, then there's some more stuff you and I need to go over, Sheriff. Then it's out again to look for Clancy. Strange how that guy could move so fast with all that weight on him."

Savich said, "Glen, call Butch Ashburn at home, fill him in if he's still there. He'll get out here right away since he was the lead on the investigation. I know he'll really want to hear from you. Actually, he's probably nearly here by now, but give it a try."

Katie said, "Okay. Dicker is out with his dogs, and we've got a good thirty others hunting him as well. I've had Wade expand the call to all law enforcement offices in a fifty-mile radius. Any reports from them will come immediately to me."

"Er, Sheriff, despite my not telling you about Clancy, despite everything, well, you know, since this is a federal crime, it is in my jurisdiction. Do you think these reports could also come to me?"

"Now he's thinking the way he should," Sherlock said. "There's still hope for you, Glen. Tell your wife to call me."

"Why?"

Sherlock gave him a fat smile. "Just girl stuff."

"You're going to tell her to torture me, aren't you, Sherlock?"

"Good guess," Savich said, and smiled at his wife.

Glen said, "Sheriff, you got Wade all in a knot last night when you said there was something else and that you wanted to talk it over with everybody this morning. I'm here. What's that about?"

Miles said, "The sheriff started wondering why Beau and Clancy came to Jessborough, which one wouldn't necessarily consider the kidnapping center of the world. Was it a coincidence or was there someone here connected either with Beau and Clancy or just maybe connected to someone in Colfax? Well, I think maybe we've got something."

"Got it!"

Katie stared at Savich. "Not even fifteen minutes and you've got something?"

Savich said, "Sometimes things just pop. Okay, Clancy Edens was in Ossining from 1998 to about eight months ago where he shared a corridor with a Luther Vincent of Kingsport, Tennessee, which is, if I'm not mistaken, only about fifty miles from here, right? To the northeast?"

"Right," Katie said and tapped her knuckles against her forearm.

"Do you know any Vincents?"

Katie frowned, tapped her foot, and finally, shook her head, sighed. "No."

Savich said easily, "No big deal. We'll just make a note of him and I'll keep checking. I should have another one of Clancy's files in a minute."

Savich looked up a few minutes later, grinning like a bandit, and said, "Guess what? Old Clancy Edens changed his name some twenty years ago. Turns out his daddy was a real loser—beat his wife, beat his two kids indiscriminately, from the looks of it. Clancy joined the army when he was eighteen, was dishonorably discharged two years later, changed his name and commenced his life of crime."

Katie said, "Come on, spill the beans. What name did he change from, Dillon?"

Savich smiled at her. "I sure hope you've heard of someone by the name of Bird."

Katie blinked, looked down at Keely's perfect small fingers, then said, "Bird. There aren't any local Birds, at least I don't think there are. But, Bird sounds familiar." Katie smacked her thigh. "Yes! I've got it! I remember now, her name was Elsbeth Bird."

"Elsbeth Bird?" Sherlock was standing on her toes, she was so excited. "Talk, Katie."

"Elsbeth Bird married Sooner McCamy back in the early nineties and moved here. So Clancy Edens is her brother?"

"He's in his forties, so I'd say yes, brother it is."

"Thank you, Dillon. Since you're already taken, maybe I can move in with MAX. Glad to meet you, Sherlock. I'm out of here."

Sherlock said, "Hey, wait a minute, Katie. You're not going to see this Elsbeth Bird who married Sooner McCamy alone, are you?"

"It's Sunday," Katie said patiently.

"What does that have to do with anything?"

"Reverend McCamy just happens to be a local preacher. He has a small congregation who worship him and God, probably in that order. The members pretty much keep to themselves around here. I've never been to one of their services. I wouldn't say they're a cult, but sometimes you wonder. The women are supposed to be subservient and if they're not subservient enough, rumor is the husbands are encouraged to discipline them. His church is called the Sinful Children of God."

"What?"

"Yep, that's what they're called. I know Reverend McCamy will be preaching all morning—and again this afternoon and evening. Just time off for lunch. The reverend has charisma from what I've heard, and can hold an audience in the palm of his hand. I haven't witnessed the charisma when I've seen him around town. He's quiet, pays his bills on time, hasn't ever caused any trouble, and is considered quite respectable.

"Reverend McCamy is very intense—you know, he looks all dark and broody, thin, tall, like he spends a lot of time on his knees conversing with God. I've never heard of him being involved with any of the women in his congregation. Besides, Elsbeth, his wife, is one of the most beautiful women around here—long blond hair, slender, soft-spoken, does whatever he asks. It's sure hard to see either of them being involved in this."

"Hmm," Glen Hodges said, and Katie waited, just waited, for him to make some sexist remark, but he didn't. Indeed, he was frowning. "Doesn't sound true to type," he said finally.

"You're right," Katie said. "He's always polite, always pleasant, but there's just something about him, something that makes you want to take a step back, if you know what I mean."

"How many people in his congregation?" Sherlock asked.

"Maybe fifty, sixty, I'm not really sure. I'm thinking I'll just swing by their house, you know, check it out a bit, see if just maybe Clancy is hanging around out there. He's her brother, after all. Where else would he hide?"

"I'm going with you, Katie," Sherlock said and slung the strap of her purse over her shoulder. "No way are you on this little sightseeing visit by yourself."

"What about me, Mom?"

"You stay here. Oh dear." She stared blankly at Miles, who was giving her a crooked smile.

"Go get 'em, tiger," Miles said. "Keely, you and me and Sam are going to stay and play gin rummy with your uncle Dillon and maybe have some lunch in the cafeteria. Whatcha think?"

"I don't know how to play gin rummy," Keely said.

"I want to go, Papa."

"Sorry, kid, not this time. They serve who also wait, or something like that. Keely, you'll learn real fast. Now, say good-bye to your mom."

"Good-bye, Mom."

"I'll see you soon, sweetie."

"Take another pain pill in exactly thirty-one minutes, okay?" Sherlock said as she kissed her husband's whiskered cheek. "And find out if it's at all possible the McCamys could be behind Sam's kidnapping."

"A preacher wanting Sam?" Miles said as he settled Sam back onto his lap. "I can't begin to imagine why."

Katie shrugged. "I'll bet Clancy has visited Elsbeth here in Jessborough, knew about Bleaker's cabin, and that's why they took Sam there. You ready, Sherlock?"

Could Elsbeth McCamy be involved in this? Katie just didn't think that could be right. Elsbeth was a wuss, a woman who worshiped her husband, and was utterly and completely dominated by him. She never even referred to him by his first name.

Glen Hodges said, "I should go with you, Sheriff. Like I said, this is a federal case and—"

Sherlock said mildly, "I'm a Fed last time I checked, Glen. You keep heading up the search. Welcome Butch Ashburn when he arrives, wing tips polished. The women are going to the preacher's house."

FOURTEEN

As Katie turned onto Boone Street, she said to Sherlock, "That's Town Hall, where Mayor Tommy hangs out. I've got about six messages on my voice mail from him already this morning. And that's the combination Police Department and Fire Station. We're coming up on Main Street, Jessborough's main drag. You're in for a treat."

Sherlock was already craning her neck to see everything. The sky had cleared after the heavy rainstorm of the night before, and the fall leaves were in full color, with spectacular reds, yellows, and golds. Beautiful old buildings lined the brick sidewalks. Sherlock saw half a dozen churches, with spires rising above the brilliant trees.

Katie said, "There's Keely's favorite stop, The Lollipop Store, and on the right is Nancy's coffee shop, called The Cranberry Thistle." There were antiques stores and galleries, a saddle shop, several gift shops, including a quilt shop that Sherlock would have liked to visit, and an enclosed marketplace. Small restaurants were dotted in among the shops, ranging from burgers and fries to Italian cuisine.

"This is lovely," Sherlock said, turning in her seat to look back down Main Street. "Does one of these churches belong to the Sinful Children of God?"

"No, that one's out on Sycamore Road, in an old church that used to be Lutheran before Reverend McCamy took it over some three or four years ago."

"I see some gift shops. You have a lot of tourists?"

"More during the summer. We're a little off the beaten track."

"And those mountains," Sherlock said, waving her hand at them. "It feels like you could reach out and touch that blue haze. They're solid and eternal, and that's comforting, I suppose."

Katie smiled. "The Appalachians change a lot with the seasons. Fall is the most beautiful time, but they're sort of like a good neighbor who stays put, you can count on them always being there under that blue haze—well, that's why we call them the Smokies. I'll tell you, it still sometimes makes my heart skip a beat when I look up and see them."

"This is a beautiful town, Katie. No exhaust fumes, no gangs of teenagers with bolts through their noses. It's so peaceful."

"You get all those things just up the highway."

"But you're tucked away all safe and sound. Until yesterday, anyway." Sherlock rolled down the truck window and breathed in the clean crisp air.

"Yes, it's always been peaceful, until now."

"I brought my big hair rollers," Sherlock said as she watched a horse-drawn carriage pull onto Main Street.

Katie, who'd been thinking the last thing she needed was this FBI character, Butch Ashburn, trying to out-wing-tip Glen Hodges with his heel on her neck, blinked, turned to look at Sherlock, and said, "What?"

"A while back Dillon and I were in Los Angeles on a case. There was this crazy guy murdering people, copying a TV show—"

"You were involved in those TV show murders?"

"Well, yes. As I was saying, Dillon and I discovered quite by accident that he really likes to roll up my hair on those big hair rollers and then have me pull them out of my hair, one by one, and sort of toss my head and string my fingers through my mane. So I brought them along with me to cheer him up. But I think it's going to have to wait a couple of days before he's up to playing again."

Katie laughed. "Hair rollers. Hmm, I never thought of that."

"I hadn't either until I met Belinda Gates," Sherlock said. "Boy, could she pull out hair rollers. It was enough to make Dillon sweat."

"She's that actress who starred in *The Consultant,* isn't she?"

"Yep, she's the one, a real piece of work. Actually, I liked her when I didn't want to punch her out. You wouldn't believe some of the people we met in Hollywood. They were so crooked you wondered how they could walk. You've got a cute kid. What is she—five?"

"Yes, she just turned five last month. She's all mine, thank God."

Sherlock wanted to know what she meant by that, but it was too pushy to ask, at least this soon. "Tell me more about Elsbeth Bird McCamy."

Katie turned her truck off Main Street onto Poplar Drive, checked the old Ford coming up on her left, and said, "The very first thing you notice about Elsbeth is how beautiful she is—she's got this fall of very light blond hair, all the way to her waist. She always wears it loose, tucked behind her ears so you can see her Jesus earrings."

"Her what?"

"I call them Jesus earrings. They're silver—Jesus on the cross—and they hang down about an inch and a half. When she moves, they move. I'll tell you, it makes me shudder. I think she's about thirty-five now, which isn't all that young, but given that Reverend McCamy is well over fifty, it's a bit on the creepy side. Like I told you, he's very intense—his eyes blaze and nearly turn black when he looks at you."

"He's scary?"

"Well, sort of, I guess. It's just that he's so much into his own particular brand of religion. As I said, Elsbeth calls him only by his last name. It's always Reverend McCamy this, Reverend McCamy that."

"I haven't run into that before. You mean like some wives did back in the nineteenth century?"

"Yes. And he calls her Elsbeth. She treats him like he has but to speak and she'll jump to obey. Whatever he wanted, I can see her jumping through hoops to get it for him. I'd say she was close to worshiping him."

Sherlock's left eyebrow climbed up. "Is that part of what he preaches? That wives should be as subservient to their husbands as she is?"

Katie shrugged. "Yes. From what I understand of the Sinful Children of God, Reverend McCamy preaches that women, in order to do penance for their huge sin of munching on the Eden apple, have got to give their all to another human being and that human being, naturally, is their husband."

"That's really convenient."

"Well, I wouldn't swear to it, but that's what I've heard anyway. People around Jessborough are tolerant of each other. None of the members of the Sinful Children of God who live locally has ever been arrested or disturbed the peace. They're good people, respectable, and tend to keep to themselves. I think most of the members come from neighboring areas. Like you said, it's pretty convenient, at least for all the men in the congregation. Maybe that's why Reverend McCamy has been so successful. He holds up his own wife as the model all the women should try to copy."

"What happens if the wife isn't interested?"

"I guess she could refuse to join, but I know he offers some kind of counseling for wayward wives."

"Just imagine," Sherlock said. "He preaches enslavement of women and it's all tax free."

"You're right. They're a church, so no taxes."

"I wonder if there's some kind of point system here," Sherlock said as she looked at a herd of cows spread over a low green hill. "You know, points for bringing the husband a beer during a football game?"

"Or points for meeting him at the front door at night with a drink?"

Sherlock laughed. "I can't believe they're that many sandwiches short of a picnic."

"I have no idea, really. I've never been to one of their services."

Sherlock shook her head, giggling. "Come on, Katie. You want me to believe a sizable group of women actually buys this stuff? You said the congregation was fifty or sixty people. That means at least twenty-five women?"

"To each his own, I guess. Like I said, people around here are tolerant of other people's beliefs, so long as they're left alone themselves."

Sherlock was silent for a moment, drumming her fingertips on the window. "They're in the middle of a service right now?"

Katie checked the purple big-faced watch that Keely had given her for Christmas. "Yeah, for another half-hour at least. Then there's a lunch break."

"Good. We've got plenty of time to see if there's any sign of Clancy hanging around their house."

Katie took a left onto Birch Avenue, then a right onto Sassafras Road. "Once off Main Street, all our streets are named after local trees. I live on Red Maple Road."

"Can spring be as gorgeous here as the fall?"

Katie smiled, shook her head. "It's pretty here in April and May, but you're lucky to be here just now. All the colorful trees with the mountains in the background . . . it makes you feel like there's something more than just life and death, something that's endless and beautiful."

"Have you lived here all your life?"

"Oh yes. My father owned the chip mill—Benedict Pulp—until he died two years ago. Now my mom runs the mill for me. We're coming up on Pine Wood Lane where the McCamys live. I'm going to ditch the truck. We'll go in by foot, okay?"

"Sure." Sherlock pulled her SIG Sauer out of her shoulder harness, checked it, and put it on her lap. "You know, Katie, we'd need a warrant to actually go inside the house."

"Yeah, I know that."

Katie pulled off Pine Wood Lane onto a dirt road, more a path really, that went into some thick woods. "This is good enough. The house is just a bit up the road."

Sherlock followed Katie as she wove her way through the pine trees, well away from the road. The air was cold but clear, except for the blue haze forming over the mountains.

They heard a small animal scurrying away from them deeper into the forest. The birds were quiet this morning, with just a few crow calls breaking the silence.

Katie said, "Sooner inherited his house and property from an aunt who passed on not long after he married Elsbeth. It's a nice place."

"Is he from around here?"

Katie shook her head, shoved a branch out of the way. "No, he moved here maybe fifteen years ago from Nashville. I really don't know his background but I'll make it a point to find out about him now, even whether he puts butter on his popcorn. He went off and married Elsbeth, brought her back here, and then the aunt died."

They walked out of the pine trees and stopped a moment. Katie pointed to a big three-story Victorian that stood in the middle of a huge lot filled with birches, oaks, and maples, some of them right up against the sides of the house. The golds, reds, and yellows of the leaves were incredible. It was an idyllic setting, and the house was a gem, the trim painted three different shades of green. There were no cars in the driveway.

"Just Sooner and Elsbeth live here. Reverend McCamy has money from his aunt, but they don't have anyone cleaning for them as far as I know. There's a gardener who comes by, Mr. Dillard, a really old fellow with no teeth in his mouth, but he's magic with flowers. The place should be empty. Let's just check it out."

Sherlock carried her SIG pressed downward, next to her leg.

Katie stopped abruptly.

"What is it?"

"I think I saw a flash of light in one of the upstairs windows."

"What kind of flash?"

"Like someone was holding a mirror and it caught the sun."

"Let's just see if our guy's here."

They made their way to the back of the house and watched for a few minutes.

Sherlock said, "Okay, Katie, if you'd stay here for a little while, I'm going around to the front now and ring the front-door bell. If Clancy is in there, all his interest will be on the front door. You can come around the side and look in, see if you spot him. If he's in there, hey, we've got hot pursuit."

"Let's do it."

Sherlock jogged back into the forest and made her way back around to the road in front of the house, her SIG safely in her belt holster again. She started whistling when she turned into the driveway of 2001 Pine Wood Lane.

Are you there, Clancy?

She walked right up to the front door and rang the bell, whistling Bobby McFerrin's song, "Don't Worry Be Happy."

There wasn't a hint of anyone coming to the front door.

She rang again.

Was that a sound coming from inside?

She called out, "Anybody home? I've got some real great deals to offer you this morning. I know it's Sunday, but do you want a chance to win a trip to Maui? Stay at the Grand Wailea?"

She rang again. She heard something, this time she was sure. She could practically see Clancy hovering near the front door, wondering what he should do.

Open the door, Clancy.

He wasn't going to open the door, or maybe he just wasn't there. Katie should be coming around the side of the house now, looking in through all the windows. *Quiet, Katie, be careful.*

Sherlock called out again, "Hey, I can hear you in there. Why don't you want to talk to me? I'm tired, you know? Could I at least have a glass of water? I've been walking a whole lot this morning."

Suddenly, the door opened.

FIFTEEN

Katie and Sherlock faced each other.

Katie whispered, "I didn't see him. But you know? The back door was open, I kid you not. Let's just take a quick look around."

"We shouldn't be in here, Katie. We're the law and we're supposed to have a warrant."

"I know, but this is personal, Sherlock. This guy threatened me and Keely. Five minutes. Then we can drive the truck up all right and proper into the driveway and wait outside for Sooner and Elsbeth to come home for lunch. This is our best chance, before he knows we're coming."

Sherlock pulled her weapon out and the two women searched the downstairs. It took much longer than five minutes because the house was so big, with old-fashioned nooks and crannies.

Katie nodded toward the stairs, wide enough for both of them to go up side by side, but they didn't. Katie motioned for Sherlock to follow her.

Katie had been in the house a couple of times, knew there were at least six rooms on the second level. They went through each of the rooms. Five were bedrooms and each was empty. There was nothing, not a sign that Clancy had been there.

The last door on the second level was the master bedroom, and it was something else. Katie and Sherlock, after checking every corner, stood in the middle of the room and stared.

"Preacher likes his comfort," Sherlock said.

"I'll say." Katie stared at the huge bed with the white fur cover, and four pure white pillows. The only other color used was black, and that was just a single leather chair and hassock.

Sherlock raised her eyebrow. "White and black—good versus evil?"

"I guess it's an endless struggle, even in the bedroom." Katie checked the closet. It was small, too small, nothing much in it. She stood in front of it, frowning. Then she saw a small, nearly hidden latch on the back wall, and pressed it down.

Another door opened and she stepped into a room that was nearly as big as her dining room. "Sherlock, come take a look."

Katie said, "This is the biggest walk-in closet I've ever seen. And look at that marble slab in the middle—what do they use that for? Look here, Sherlock, there are drawers under it, with underwear, her sweaters. And he's got his shirts piled on top."

"Oh my," Sherlock said, stepping into the room, "you're right. This green marble slab, isn't it gorgeous, looks Italian. You know, this is odd, but I'd say that marble slab looks more like an altar than some place to stack your freshly laundered shirts."

Katie walked around the large six-foot marble slab that was about three and a half feet off the white-carpeted floor. It was a lovely richly veined green, quite expensive. She saw something tucked under one corner of the marble. She easily flipped up an open stainless-steel cuff. A cuff? She found a cuff on each corner.

Katie raised an eyebrow.

Sherlock said, "I'd say they were for wrists and ankles."

"Oh my," Katie said, fingering one of the cuffs. "I'm kind of embarrassed. I was thinking Elsbeth was a regular garden-variety kind of subservient wife, but would you look at these cuffs? I can't imagine it would be very comfortable lying on that hard marble."

"No. I wonder what they do once he cuffs her down?"

Katie shuddered. "You know, maybe that's not any of our business. This is creepy. Let's check the rest of the house for Clancy, then we can come back here. Just maybe I can bust Reverend McCamy for something."

"Nah, forget it, we're actually breaking and entering here, Katie. Hang on just a second. What's this?" Sherlock pulled two tie racks aside. She found a button and pushed it. A cabinet opened up. It was deep, maybe five feet high. On the left, there was an array of whips, artistically displayed. Next came a block of wood topped with thick fur, a netful of small silver balls, nearly a dozen dildoes of different sizes, shapes, and colors.

Near the top of the cabinet was a wide shelf with at least a dozen vials neatly lined up on it. "Illegal drugs?" Katie said, reaching for one.

"If so, maybe I can figure out how to get a warrant." She read the label. "Tears."

"Tears? What could that be?" Sherlock reached out for the vial. She unfastened the round top and sniffed the liquid. "Phew!" Immediately she started to tear up. She swiped her fingers across her eyes. "It makes tears all right, Katie. Essence of onion?"

"Probably, but for what?"

"Well, maybe if she's not crying enough while she's being whipped, he gives her a whiff of this." She refastened the cap and set the vial back on the shelf. She picked up another. "Look at this one. Of all things it's called Man's Instrument. I guess that says it all."

Katie opened the lid and sniffed. "I wonder if a guy drinks it or rubs it on."

Sherlock said, "Probably drinks it. Here's one called Woman's Gift. Pills, big red pills. I wonder what they're for?"

"Maybe these pills assist the Man's Instrument?"

"Viagra?"

"Could be."

Katie said. "Well, it looks like there's more to this than I'd ever imagined. Nothing illegal, though."

"Even if we'd found a ton of cocaine, we couldn't arrest him for it. Let's go, Katie. I'd just as soon not be caught here by either the reverend or his wife."

"There's a thought that makes me shudder."

Sherlock said as she closed the cabinet doors and rearranged the tie racks, "I guess everybody has their own version of hair rollers."

They checked the third floor—former servants' quarters, what looked like an old schoolroom, and an unfinished attic, filled with enough old stuff for a garage sale, but no Clancy.

As they let themselves out the back door, Katie said, "Whatever I saw in that window, I guess it wasn't Clancy. I was just hoping for a sign of him, anything."

"I know. I wonder what you did see."

Katie shrugged. "Thanks for breaking the law with me, Sherlock."

"No problem. Let's just keep it between the two of us."

They were back in Katie's truck and in the McCamy driveway a good ten minutes before they saw Sooner and his wife drive up in their white Lincoln Town Car.

Sherlock said, "You'll note that the car's white, not black."

"These people," Katie said slowly, "aren't exactly your garden-variety preacher and spouse."

"You're right about that. Savich isn't going to believe this."

"I hope he doesn't laugh so hard he bursts his stitches. Okay, you up for a chat with Reverend McCamy and his sex slave?"

SIXTEEN

Sherlock was fully prepared to greet Rasputin. She wasn't far off, except that Rasputin had been ill-kempt with long black matted hair, and evidently didn't bathe often. Reverend Sooner McCamy was dark, those eyes of his nearly black, as a matter of fact. He was charming, if on the aloof side, and that was a surprise to Sherlock. He made eye contact, shook her hand firmly. He was courteous, offering coffee and some cheesecake his wife had made that morning, before church. But somehow he just didn't seem to be quite all there with them. He was away somewhere, in his head. And what was he thinking? He had a smooth deep voice—charismatic, that voice, it compelled you to listen. It was hypnotic, almost, and after hearing him speak for a few minutes, Sherlock understood his power over people.

This man appeared to have boiled himself down to the very essence of what a man of God should be. He frightened her for the simple reason that she could imagine some people hanging on his every word, maybe doing things they wouldn't normally do. Or maybe he gave them permission to do things they shouldn't want to do. Did disobedient wives listen to that voice and jump back on the straight and narrow?

Or was she over the top here? Sherlock didn't know. But he sure didn't seem like a man who would open any of those vials and apply the contents to either his wife or himself. He didn't look like a man who would whip his wife with one of those riding crops with their beautifully braided handles. If he was a Rasputin, if he was evil on the inside, he kept it hidden real deep. Sherlock had to remind herself that there were more layers to people than you could ever guess.

As for his looks, she could only say that if one believed in a handsome Satan, then Reverend McCamy would fit the bill. His black hair was a bit on the long side, a bit curly, and he had a heavy growth of beard, noticeable in the early afternoon.

He looked like a monk whose thoughts were so different from hers that they weren't even in the same world. He was in his fifties, but there was no white in his hair. Did he dye it? She didn't think so. He was slender, but that was all she could tell about his body. He was wearing a black suit, a very white shirt, and a black tie. He had good teeth, straight and white.

Elsbeth was very pretty, just as Katie had told her, and that hair of hers was glorious. Thick, rich natural blond, in loose waves down her back. She was wearing her Jesus earrings, as Katie called them. When she walked the crosses swung. She was tall and slender, but big-breasted. What made alarm bells go off for Sherlock was that the woman seemed to look at her husband as if he were a god. She looked like she'd jump up onto that marble slab and offer her wrists and ankles for the cuffs, and yell as loud as he wished when he applied a whip. Sherlock couldn't help wondering how she used that block of wood with one side padded with thick fur.

"I've heard that you've had some excitement, Sheriff. The little boy who was kidnapped, you rescued him?"

"Yes," Katie said as she sipped on Elsbeth's delicious coffee. "He's just fine now. How were morning services, Reverend McCamy?"

He said nothing, merely nodded, obviously pleased with how the morning services had gone. He took a cup of coffee from his wife, not looking away from Katie. Elsbeth said, barely above a whisper, "Two new parishioners found God this morning. Two."

Not by so much as a flick of his eyelids did Reverend McCamy acknowledge his wife's words. He then turned his attention to Sherlock. "I've never met an FBI agent before, Agent Sherlock. Why are you here?" He kept his eyes on Sherlock now, all his attention focused on her. When Sherlock purposefully nodded toward Elsbeth, he said, "You asked how services went this morning, Katie. I was pleased and gratified. I'd been counseling this couple for three weeks now. With encouragement and the endless love and understanding of God, they have found their way. By God's grace, they gave their souls to Him this morning."

He sipped his coffee. He looked out of place in this lovely living room with its human beings drinking coffee. Rasputin, Sherlock thought, he was a twenty-first-century Rasputin.

"Now, Agent Sherlock, Katie," Reverend McCamy said, "tell me why you're here. How may I help you?"

"Actually," Katie said, smiling toward Elsbeth, who was sitting demurely, her knees pressed together, her face utterly beautiful in the light shining in on her from the tall front windows, her Jesus earrings still and shiny, "we're here because of Elsbeth."

Elsbeth McCamy flinched, and the dreamy look fell right off her face. Just an instant, so fast Katie wasn't certain she'd even seen it. Fear. Her fingers fluttered. "Me? I don't understand, Katie. What could I possibly know that would help you? Surely, Reverend McCamy—"

Katie pulled out a fax with Clancy's photo. "Is this your brother, Elsbeth?"

Elsbeth shook her head, back and forth, sending the Jesus earrings dancing.

"Is he, Elsbeth?"

"Yes," she said, "that's Clancy. But I don't understand—"

"We've just found out this morning that one of the kidnappers is your brother, Elsbeth—Clancy Bird, now Clancy Edens. We found out he legally changed his name when he was younger. If you have any idea where he is, please tell us."

Elsbeth didn't move, didn't blink, didn't betray anything at all. She seemed to be waiting for Reverend McCamy to speak.

And he did. He took the photo from Katie and studied it. He nodded. "No one in Jessborough knows that Elsbeth is cursed with such a worthless brother," Reverend McCamy said. "Naturally she hasn't seen him in years now."

Katie said, "That's too bad. We hoped you'd heard from him. He's badly hurt. He could die if we don't find him quickly."

"My husband is right, I haven't seen my brother in a very long time, Katie. I know he turned away from God when he was young, but he was always a support to me when I was a little girl."

"He protected you from your father?"

Elsbeth only nodded, looking down at her shoes. "He was a very bad man. Clancy protected me as best as he could. It was so many years ago." She raised pale blue eyes to Sherlock's face and touched her fingertips to a Jesus earring.

Sherlock said, "When did you last see Clancy?"

"He'd just been released from one of his stays in prison, some six years ago, I think. Naturally he was back in prison for something else after that. When I heard there were two men, one of them named Clancy, I never thought it could be my brother. Are you certain he kidnapped that little boy, Katie?"

Katie nodded. "Yes. We are certain that your brother and a man named Beau Jones kidnapped Sam Kettering and brought him here. They kept him in Bleaker's cabin until the boy managed to escape."

Elsbeth's eyes dropped to her hands, now even more tightly clasped in her lap. "I heard about it, of course. Everyone in the congregation was talking about it. We stopped at the pharmacy this morning and Alice Hewett couldn't talk of anything else, particularly since she'd sold that other man some bandages."

Katie said, "He hasn't contacted either of you for help?"

"Oh no," Elsbeth said. "Why would he do that? Surely he must know that Reverend McCamy wouldn't help him. Why, he's a devout man of God. He feels deep pain at the actions of sinners."

Sherlock said, "All right, Mrs. McCamy. I can certainly understand wanting to help a brother just as I can understand a sister not wanting to help the police find him."

"Oh no! Lying is a sin. I wouldn't do that, ever. Just ask Reverend McCamy. I don't ever lie."

Reverend Sooner McCamy said, "I assure you, my wife doesn't lie. Now, Agent Sherlock, Clancy hasn't called either of us. If he's guilty of kidnapping that little boy, both Elsbeth and I hope that you catch him and send him back to prison."

Sherlock said, "If he wouldn't call you, Mrs. McCamy, then do you have any idea whom he might contact? Does he have any friends close by? Family?"

Elsbeth shook her head. "Clancy doesn't know anyone in these parts."

Except you, Sherlock thought. *Only you.*

"How do you think he knew about Bleaker's cabin?"

"I don't know, Katie."

Katie said, "Thank you for speaking with us. If Clancy does contact you, Elsbeth, if he does ask you to hide him, if he does ask you for money, I hope you will call me immediately. You heard, I know, that his partner, Beau Jones, died last night."

"We heard that you shot him, Katie," Reverend McCamy said. "You killed him."

Sherlock heard the cold disapproval in his voice, no chance of missing it. Why?

"Hurting a man, actually killing a man, it's very bad," Elsbeth said, clearly distressed.

Katie said, "There wasn't a choice, Elsbeth. He would have killed someone else if I hadn't stopped him. Now it's Clancy who's in danger. There's a huge manhunt going on right now for him, as I'm sure both of you know. I really don't see this ending well for Clancy if you don't help us find him."

Elsbeth said, her voice shaking, nearly on the verge of tears, "I'm sorry, Katie. I don't have any idea where Clancy could be. I don't understand why he would kidnap a little boy and bring him here to Jessborough."

Sherlock said, "Obviously Bleaker's cabin is a good out-of-the-way place to store a kidnap victim. But it has to be more than that. Most likely someone locally wanted Sam Kettering brought here."

Katie said, "It's all quite a mystery. There was no ransom note left, no calls made in the two days he was gone from his home in Virginia."

Sherlock said, "Do you have any idea at all why your brother would bring Sam here, Mrs. McCamy? Other than to use Bleaker's cabin?"

Elsbeth looked from Katie to Sherlock. Then she said to her husband, "Reverend McCamy, you know that I know nothing about any of this. Could you make them believe me, please?"

"Well, the thing is, Elsbeth," Katie said before the reverend could jump in, although, truth be told, he didn't look like he was even very interested. No, fact was, he looked like he wasn't really here. "You're the only one Clancy knows in the area. Someone also reported seeing a man who looked like him near your house. I think that's enough to have a judge issue a warrant to search your house, unless, of course, you give us permission to look around right now?"

Sherlock saw that Reverend McCamy was back, all of his focus, all of his brain was back in the living room, and he knew he had a problem. He stood, looking like an avenging prophet. "You may not search my house, Agent, Sheriff. Get your godless warrant, but I really doubt you'll be able to talk a judge into it." Of course, he realized that any search would turn up his party room, and the good Lord knew that would never do.

Their chances were about nil for getting a warrant and the good reverend knew it.

For just an instant, Katie was reminded of Carlo Silvestri, her ex-husband, standing there all arrogant and righteous, just like Reverend McCamy, looking at her like she wasn't worthy to polish his shoes.

"You mean," Katie said, rising as well, "that Benson Carlysle won't grant a warrant. His brother's a member of your church, isn't he?"

"Yes. He's a good man, a fair man. He and his wife are devout members. His brother won't allow you to harass my wife and me just because someone thought he saw her brother near here."

Elsbeth said, every muscle tensed, desperate to convince them, "Even if Clancy was here, hiding, naturally, he's certainly not here now, and we knew nothing about it in any case. He's got to know that I can't have anything to do with him."

"I see," Sherlock said, and rose to stand beside Katie.

Reverend McCamy said, "Good day, Agent Sherlock, Sheriff Benedict. You do not believe what I believe. You do not behave as women should behave. I would like you to leave. I don't want my wife tainted with your presence, your suspicions, your lack of grace. However, if Clancy does contact Elsbeth, rest assured that I will call you."

Katie dug a card out of her shirt pocket and gave it to Elsbeth. "Good. Understand, Elsbeth, if Clancy does call you, you might be able to save his life. If he doesn't turn himself in he probably won't survive. You don't want him dead."

Elsbeth's eyes filled with tears, beautiful sparkling tears. She began to moan and rock back and forth on her chair. "Of course I don't want him dead. It's a sin to want somebody dead. And he's my brother."

Katie fanned her hands in front of her, so impatient she snapped out, "Elsbeth, I'm not planning on gunning for Clancy at high noon, but I'll do what I have to do to bring him in. Now, thank you for the coffee. Remember, the chances of Clancy living through this decrease by the minute."

Sherlock and Katie walked themselves to the door, Elsbeth's sobs echoing behind them. Sherlock couldn't help herself. She turned a moment to see Reverend Sooner McCamy standing in the middle of the light-filled living room, a portrait in black and white, his face impassive, his dark eyes burning.

Sherlock said to Katie as she started up her truck, "He never asked who it was claiming to see Clancy near his house."

"No, he didn't, did he?"

SEVENTEEN

"He's Rasputin."

Savich had popped a pain pill ten minutes before so he was easily able to smile at his wife.

"Yes, but what did you really think?"

"He's scary."

"In what way?"

"He's not quite here. It's like he's into an inner self where there's only his God and what he owes his God and what he can do to get other people to worship his God. The thing is, I'm not sure he includes women or if it's just men's souls that interest him."

Savich said, "An otherworldly sexist. He sounds too preoccupied with himself to be a kidnapper."

"Yeah, you're right, he does. But I haven't heard much condemnation about his ideas out of you yet."

"Hmm."

"Why don't you yell and holler that it isn't fair, that you denounce it, that you spit upon such notions?"

"It's not fair," Savich said. "I can't spit because it would hurt my back. This guy sounds very strange, sweetheart."

"Yes, he is. He's very intense, as I said, like Rasputin or, more to the point, some descendant of Rasputin. Now, since Katie and I didn't have a warrant, we just sort of wandered around outside their big Victorian house, which is really quite beautiful, and would you just look at what fell out of a window."

"Fell out of a window? Yes, if I close my eyes I can see it falling right at your feet. Come on, what have you got?"

Sherlock tossed him a vial and told him about the hidden room off the small bedroom closet.

He read the label. Salvation. He blinked, unscrewed the top and sniffed the liquid, which had a faint almond scent. "Sex with a religious theme? Are you planning on drinking this, Sherlock? Have things gotten this bad?"

She laughed, hugged him very carefully, kissed his mouth. He fastened the cap back on the vial and handed it back to her. "When all this dies down, let's send it to the lab and see what's in this salvation stuff."

"Maybe we can find out if it's manufactured or if the reverend makes it himself. There were about a dozen other vials, all with charming names like this one. I know I shouldn't have taken it but I just couldn't resist." When she finished telling him about the whips and the green marble altar and the wooden block, he said as he looked down at his fingernails, "You wonder what that wooden block with the fur on top is for?"

"Well, I'm not going to chew off my fingernails if I don't find out, but yeah, I'd like to know."

"It's to pad your stomach."

"What? To pad . . . Oh goodness, I see now. You know, Dillon, big hair rollers are one thing, but being propped up on a wooden block is quite another. No, I don't think so. Has Dr. Able been around to see you? I want to get you out of here."

"Yes, he has. I'm fine, just need to sit forward for the next year or so. Stitches come out next week. You ready to break me out of this place? I was just waiting for you to get here."

Sherlock said over her shoulder as she fetched him the clothes she'd brought from home, "Yes, but we're in a bit of a pickle, aren't we? We have no idea why Sam was brought to Jessborough and we don't know yet who hired Clancy and Beau to bring him here. The investigation is just starting. Clancy's still out there and we need to help. I think, too, that Sam and Miles probably need to remain with us. It's dangerous for Sam and Miles to go back home alone, don't you think?"

"Yes, we'll stay," Savich said, and got himself dressed. "Don't worry about a few more days. Mr. Maitland called a little while ago, told me to take it easy, not to worry about the math teacher killings."

He looked big and tough, much more like himself with his leather jacket slung over his arm. Sherlock beamed him a brilliant smile. "Can I kiss you?"

"Yeah, but don't tease me, Sherlock." He carefully put his arms around her, nuzzled her neck. "You know, I just might be ready for some hair rollers tonight. I wish we had time to check out what's in that vial, just maybe it's something we can use."

AT five minutes after three o'clock that afternoon, five FBI agents, one former FBI agent, one sheriff, and two children congregated in Sheriff Benedict's living room.

If Butch Ashburn wondered why two young children were present during a meeting, he didn't say anything, just watched the little girl for a moment—the sheriff's kid—playing with a big-eared rabbit named Oscar. His own kid was now nearly twenty, but he could remember when she'd have been on the floor playing with a stuffed animal. The years just swept over you too fast, he thought, leaving you older and slower, and your little kid a grown-up.

"I'm thinking," Savich said, "that I want to go to church. Does Reverend McCamy have a service this evening, Katie?"

"Yes, he goes all day on Sunday. The church is really nice, sort of like Paul Revere's church in Boston. Sooner also does tent revivals— every June, out in Grossley's pasture, about three miles west of Jessborough."

Katie glanced over at Miles, who still looked dead on his feet. All his attention was on his boy. After she'd dropped Sherlock off at the hospital a couple of hours before, she'd taken Miles and the kids out to Kmart to buy some clothes. Miles was wearing the black jeans, boots, and plaid flannel shirt he'd bought. He looked, she realized, really good. As for Sam, he looked like a miniature copy of his father, down to the black boots.

"Papa forgot to pack clothes for us," Sam had confided to her earlier in the truck. "He didn't think about anything else, he just wanted to get to me as fast as he could."

"I wouldn't have packed anything either," Katie said, smiling at Miles. "Not with a Kmart in the neighborhood."

Of course, Keely had to have black jeans and black boots, and her mother, knowing when to throw in the towel, had given in.

Butch Ashburn said to Savich, "If you and Sherlock plan on staying in Jessborough for a while, I think Jody and I will head back to Washington. We're still running checks and interviewing all neighbors and employees, and I want to check Beau Jones's apartment myself. Also, since Miles is former FBI, we're checking particularly violent cases he was involved in. I don't buy the idea of revenge myself, but we're checking everything." He looked over at Sam, who'd just taken a big bite of fried chicken. "I'm more pleased than I can say, Miles, that you've got such a brave, smart boy."

Miles swallowed, then nodded, and said sharply, "Sam, don't wipe your greasy fingers on your new jeans. Use the napkin."

Life, Butch thought, was always unexpected and even, sometimes, like now, not bad at all. He said, "You guys work on Clancy's connection from this end and, like I said, I'll work the other end. Hopefully, we'll meet in the middle real soon."

Katie smiled at Special Agent Butch Ashburn—*no wing tips on my neck from this guy.*

Fifteen minutes after a telephone call, Katie's mother, Minna Bushnell Benedict, arrived to take charge of the children. She won Sam over with a chocolate chip cookie the size of Manhattan, and assured both Miles and Katie that she'd keep both Sam and Keely safe, with the help of the two deputies seated in their cruiser just outside the house.

"Butch, you have a safe trip back to Washington. Miles, Katie, we're off to meet the Sinful Children of God," Savich said, and took Sherlock's hand. "Maybe we can talk to some of the congregation before the service starts."

"Find Fatso," Sam called after his father as they went out the front door. "Shoot him."

THE church of the Sinful Children of God was on Sycamore Road. Katie was right, it looked like the Old North Church in Boston—a tall wooden spire, painted all white, the roof sharply raked with shingles, the windows small and traditional.

There were maybe twenty cars parked in the paved lot behind the church, which was set back from the road, at the edge of a thick stand of maple and oak trees. And Miles found himself marveling yet again at how many trees there were in this part of the country.

The church was nearly full, maybe as many as fifty, sixty people. Men were in suits, women in dresses, hats on their heads. Children sat quietly beside their parents. The four of them sat down in the back. A couple Katie didn't recognize scooted farther down the bench, not speaking to them.

Katie realized, as she looked around at all those well-dressed people, that she didn't know very many of them. She wondered from how far away they came. It took her a while to recognize Thomas Boone, the postman, because he looked different in a suit. There was Bea Hipple, an expert quilter, sitting only shoulder high to her husband, Benny, a local mechanic. For the life of her, Katie couldn't imagine Bea being all that submissive.

She knew maybe twenty-five of the adults in the congregation, no more than that. The organist finished "Amazing Grace." Throats cleared, papers rustled, and then the church fell quiet. Hearing "Amazing Grace" played in church always made Katie, hard-assed sheriff or not, get tears in her eyes.

Reverend Sooner McCamy rose from his high-backed chair to walk up the winding stairs to the pulpit that was set on a six-foot-high dais. He stood there for a few seconds, looking out. He was wearing a lovely white robe over a black suit and white shirt.

Reverend McCamy wrapped his large hands around the corners of the beautifully worked pulpit. They were strong hands, nicely formed, with short buffed nails, black hair visible on the backs even from a distance. When he spoke, his voice reached to every corner of the room, forceful and deep. Katie was aware that people were sitting at attention now, leaning forward a bit so as to not miss a word.

"I welcome all of you back again for our evening service. It has been a full, rewarding day, and a very unusual one as well. My wife and I spoke with Sheriff Benedict and an FBI agent at our home at noon. It seems that Elsbeth's brother, Clancy, is wanted for questioning in the kidnapping of the little boy who managed to escape. Yes, Clancy Edens is indeed my wife's brother. I would ask that if any of you know of this very man's whereabouts to call the sheriff. I've been told there are posters of him all over Jessborough."

He never broke eye contact with Katie while he spoke. She found herself nodding as one by one, the congregation turned to look at her.

Reverend McCamy paused a moment, looking, it seemed, at each of his congregation. He said finally, "Our spirits need constant nourishment, just as our bodies do. We recognize this need even if we don't understand how to bring deep into ourselves the nourishment our souls require. We must pray that Clancy Edens finds the nourishment tonight."

"Amen. Amen."

"We must all first realize there is a common bond among right-thinking men, men who recognize there is something more to living than being a part of the human herd, something beyond us. It is something more precious than life itself, something that can bring us all infinite understanding and peace. And these men know that this something is our beloved God, and that it is He who is our spiritual nourishment, He who brings value to our lives, He who makes us know the path we must tread. Let us pray for him tonight, brothers, pray that he seeks this path with us."

"Amen . . . amen . . . amen."

"It is we men who must lead, who must show these sinners, as we show our precious helpmates, the way to grace and salvation, ensuring God's forgiveness for their eternal sin. All of you seated before God and His messenger here this evening know that we each have a role in this life, some of leadership and some of submission. Both will free us. I exhort all of you: Seek always to understand what it is you must be and what you must do. Let nothing stop you from attaining what it is God wants you to have, what God wants of you."

Only men can understand God? Sherlock felt Dillon lightly touching his fingertips to her arm. When she turned, he was smiling. Then he winked at her.

"There are special graces that God grants a few men on this earth that allow them to be special victims of God's grace, to actually experience his own sacrifice for all of our sins."

Victims of God's grace? What did that mean? Sherlock tuned him out until some five minutes later, when Reverend McCamy said suddenly, "Now it's time for us to divide into our Sunday evening study groups. Our topic for discussion this evening will be 'Submitting to the Path of God's Grace.'"

Katie looked at Miles, her head cocked to one side. His dark eyes were glittering, narrowed on Reverend McCamy's face. His hands were fisted, one on his thigh. She smoothed his fisted hand with her own, feeling the tension slowly ease. She would ask him what he was thinking later. It had been smart of the reverend to be up front about Elsbeth McCamy's brother, very smart indeed. She wondered if the good reverend would have said a word about Sam's kidnapping if the four of them hadn't trooped into his service.

After the congregation split into groups, Sherlock made a request to join them. Reverend McCamy looked infinitely patient. "I'm sorry, Agent Sherlock, but you must be a believer and member of this church before you can attend our study groups. Why did you come?" He looked at all of them in turn, one very black eyebrow arched up, a bit of a satyr's look, if he but knew.

Katie introduced Savich and Miles Kettering.

Reverend McCamy said nothing, merely nodded at them. He gave Miles a long look, then he looked down at the ring on his third finger—an odd ring, thick, heavy-looking, silver with some sort of carving on top. The carving was deep black. Sherlock couldn't make out what it was. Surely this monstrosity couldn't be his wedding ring.

Reverend McCamy said, "Special Agent Savich. You appear to be hurt."

How had he known that? No, that was easy, Savich thought, likely everyone in town was talking about how the federal agent got his back sliced open by a flying piece of van. Savich removed his hand from the reverend's. "Just a bit."

Reverend McCamy said, "I will direct all our congregation to include you in their prayers. Sheriff, you've known some of these folk all your life. You know they'll help if they can. Now, if you'll excuse me, I must attend to my children."

Katie looked over toward Thomas Boone and remembered a scene in the post office between him and a Mr. Phelan. They'd been arguing about the church and Reverend McCamy. She wanted to speak to Mr. Phelan.

AFTER Katie dropped Savich and Sherlock off at Mother's Very Best, Savich looking like he was nearly ready to drop in his tracks, she and Miles went for a cup of coffee at the Main Street Cafe. Beverly, with her lovely, big smile, served them. Bless her heart, she didn't say a word about the kidnapping.

"It's an amazing thing," Miles said as he sipped his black coffee. "In the space of a day and a half, I went from absolute despair to euphoria to something like dread. Do you think Clancy is still here?"

Katie nodded as she stirred some cream into her coffee. "He's hiding somewhere."

"You think the reverend and his wife know where he is?"

"I wish I could say yes, but actually I haven't the slightest idea if they do. You're a former FBI agent. What do you think?"

"As I said, I've only been here for a day."

"What field office were you assigned to?"

"Actually, I stayed in Washington along with Savich after we met at the academy. I was in the Information and Evidence Management Unit."

"You dealt with forensics."

He nodded as he looked through the big front windows out onto Main Street. "My father wasn't pleased with my choice of career, but to his credit, he encouraged me endlessly. When he died, I realized that it was time to make a change. Fact is, I was getting burned out. I remember reading John Douglas's book and being struck to my gut when he wrote about his wife cutting her finger. He wrote that what he paid attention to was the way the blood splattered, not his wife's injury. It could have been me. So, when my father died, I resigned and took over my father's business. I've been doing it now for five years." He paused a moment, sipped his coffee, closed his eyes, and said, "Fact is, I like it, and I'm good at it."

"What is it?"

"We design and build parts for helicopters, like guidance systems, primarily for the army, but we've built components for all the other branches of the military as well. I'll tell you though, after some of our negotiations with the military agencies, I've thought life was easier at the Bureau."

She laughed, and realized she liked this man. It had been so very long since she'd even looked at a man and actually saw that he was male, a male to admire and make her laugh. It felt rather good, actually. Carlo had burned her to the ground, the bastard.

EIGHTEEN

The house was quiet. All was well. Katie had made coffee for the deputies, double-checked all the locks, and looked in on Keely before sinking down beneath three blankets on a bed so soft she was convinced her mother had ordered it for her from heaven. Miles was with Sam, who had on his new, spiffy red Mickey Mouse pajamas. Miles hadn't bought anything so she guessed he was sleeping in his shorts. Now, that was a strange thought. She hadn't thought about a man's shorts in a very long time. Boxers? Katie grinned and nodded. Yeah, she'd bet he wore boxers.

Miles lay on his back, feeling Sam's heartbeat against his side, and his soft hair smooth against his neck. He still wasn't over the debilitating fear he'd felt for those endless hours before Katie had called. He wondered if he'd ever be over it. They'd been lucky, so damned lucky. He pulled Sam tighter and felt him wheeze a bit in his sleep. No nightmares, so far. He'd have to keep a real close eye on that.

Miles was so tired he felt like his skin was inside out and his brain was in a fog bank. Yet he couldn't seem to shut down and sleep. So he lay there, listening to his boy breathe.

He closed his eyes and thanked Alicia yet again for encouraging Sam to get himself out of that cabin window. He'd wondered many times if she really was keeping a close eye on her son from the other side, if there was an other side, but if there wasn't, how had Sam heard her voice? Miles knew it was Sam's subconscious that had prodded him, but it was still somehow reassuring to believe, if even for a moment, that her love for her son overcame the silence and separation of death.

The air was soft, warm. He would swear he felt a brief touch of fingertips on his cheek. He smiled as he closed his eyes.

He had no idea how much time had passed. But one moment he was thinking about the problems with the new rotor blade design on the army's new Proto A587 helicopter, and the next he was alert, ready to move. He lay there, listening.

There was a scraping sound.

It stopped. Then nothing.

Surely Clancy wouldn't come back to try yet again to get Sam. There were two cops sitting just around at the front of the house.

It was probably just a branch whispering against the side of the house in the night wind.

No different sounds now, nothing at all.

Miles drew a deep breath, and settled in again. He imagined he'd be hearing things for many years to come.

"Hold yourself real still, Mr. Kettering."

Miles's heart nearly seized. His eyes flew open. He looked up into Clancy's shadowed face, and pulled Sam closer.

"Yeah, I saw you wake up. Then I decided to wait just another minute, and sure enough, you were out again."

Miles didn't want to wake Sam. He whispered to that round white face above him, "What the hell are you doing here? How did you get past the cops outside?"

Clancy grinned, and Miles saw he hadn't escaped scot free from the van. He had a split lip with some dried blood on it, his cheek was swollen and covered with three Band-Aids. There was another cut over his left eyebrow, a Band-Aid patched vertically over it. His right arm wasn't in a sling, but he was holding it stiffly against his side.

Miles felt the muzzle of the gun, sharp and cold against his neck. Clancy leaned his face real close to Miles's, and he smelled Clancy's breath—salami and beer. He said, real low, "It was easy as kicking dirt. They were nearly unconscious last time I checked. By now, they might be dead, the morons. I've worked enough on cars to know about what not to do with a car exhaust. Pretty dangerous things, if you don't know what you're doing. Yep, nothing so easy as the car exhaust. Easy as cooking a hot dog. You see, the bozos kept the car turned on because they were too wussy to take the cold. That was when I knew exactly what to do."

"You murdered two people just to get to Sam?"

"That's right, Mr. Kettering. What's your point?"

"Who's paying you to do this? Who?"

"Well now, Mr. Kettering, that just isn't any of your business, now, is it?"

"You have to know this is insane, Clancy. Half the state is looking for you. There's no way you'll get away with Sam, no way at all."

"You know, Mr. Kettering, with all your yapping, I'm wondering if I shouldn't just pop you now." The muzzle dug in. Miles didn't move, barely breathed, and he thought, *I can't die, I can't. I have to protect Sam.* He thought of Katie just down the hall, asleep. If Sam could hear his mother, then why the hell couldn't he talk to Katie? He did, and then focused himself again. He was an idiot, a desperate idiot. Sam was too close for him to try to make a move. And it appeared that Clancy had nothing at all to lose. Who was paying him so much money that he just couldn't give up? He felt the muzzle stroking his neck now.

"You don't look too good, Clancy. I'm surprised you're even walking around. I saw the van explode. It was a burning hell."

"When the sheriff fired I slammed into that tree and knocked myself silly, but just for a minute. I saw the sheriff kill Beau and got the hell out of the van. Yeah, I wanted to pop all of you, destroying the van like that."

But Clancy didn't pull the trigger. So Clancy didn't want to kill him just yet, thank God. Why not? No silencer, that was why, and this was not the time for gunfire.

Then Miles realized Clancy wanted him alive so he could carry Sam. He wanted two hostages. *Then he'll kill me once he's gotten us away from here.*

Miles didn't even blink. He tried to unfreeze his muscles and his heart after the immense jolt of fear that had shut him down for a moment.

"Wake up the boy, Mr. Kettering. I won't ask twice."

He did, lightly stroking Sam's cheek, speaking quietly to him, telling him not to be afraid, everything would be all right.

Sam's eyes opened, focused on Clancy. "You're a bad man," Sam said, that little voice strong.

"Hello there, you little brat. Too bad you're so valuable, I'd sure like to twist off your head. You got Beau killed, and I'm going to have to pay you back for that."

"Why do you want him so badly, Clancy?"

"I just might tell you someday," Clancy said. "Not that I necessarily believe it." He took a couple of steps back to stand at the end of the bed, his gun aimed directly at Sam.

"Don't even think of trying anything, Mr. Kettering, or I'll shoot the boy. Believe me on this. I ain't got nothin' to lose here. Both of you get up now. You might as well put some clothes on, Mr. Kettering, it's pretty cold out there. The kid's just fine in his pajamas." He fell silent, watching them. "Hey, I wonder if those deputies are croaked yet. Shouldn't be long if they aren't already. We just might take their car, what do you think?"

"Why would you do that? How did you get here?"

"Never you mind about that."

Miles said, "Sam, I want you to get out of bed real slow. Stand over there, okay?"

"Papa—"

"Do as I say. Everything will be all right, I promise you that."

Clancy laughed under his breath. He watched Sam slide away from his father, off the side of the bed. He stood there, in his red pajamas.

"Hey, Mickey Mouse, those are neat," Clancy said. "Now you, Mr. Kettering. I want you to be real careful. You see where I'm aiming now? Right at the kid's head. I'll kill him if you force me to."

But would he really? Miles didn't think so. Whoever had hired Clancy wanted Sam too badly, but he wasn't about to take the chance. Miles eased out of the covers and swung his legs over the side of the bed. He was wearing only his boxer shorts. The air was chilly. Slowly, he stood. Clancy threw him his jeans. He pulled them on, fastened them. He held out his hand. "My sweater's over there."

Clancy tossed it to him. When he had it pulled over his head, Clancy said, "No shoes. I don't want you trying to make a break for it. Now, put your hands behind your neck."

Miles laced his fingers behind his head.

"Okay, now, you walk out of here first, Mr. Kettering. Sam, you follow your dad. Do it, now. Keep walking. Kid, you behave yourself."

He doesn't want Sam dead, Miles kept thinking. Everything hinges on his taking Sam alive. But why? All Miles needed was an opening, a small lapse on Clancy's part, and he could take him. He held himself ready, listened to every breath Clancy drew, realized he didn't breathe easily because he was so heavy, and he was hurt. Just how badly, Miles couldn't guess. He watched Clancy's gun, watched how it remained aimed at Sam's head.

Miles walked slowly down the hall. He barely heard Sam's steps behind him because he was wearing a nice thick pair of Katie's socks. They were nearly to Katie's bedroom door.

This is easy, Clancy, so easy. You can relax a bit, can't you now? You've got us.

They reached the living room in utter silence. Moonlight showed through the front window that wasn't boarded up. Not much, but enough so no one would trip over anything.

Slowly, Clancy motioned Miles to move aside. He grabbed Sam's arm and dragged him toward the front door.

"Papa—"

"Shut up, you little varmint!"

He held Sam with one hand, realized that he couldn't turn the dead bolt with a gun in his other hand, and stood there a minute, wondering what to do.

"Come here, Mr. Kettering. I want you to open that door or I'll hurt your kid."

He pulled Sam back against his stomach.

Miles walked to the front door and unfastened the locks.

"Open it."

Miles opened the front door. The night wind rushed in, cool, sharp.

"Put your hands behind your head and walk."

Miles stopped at the edge of the wide porch that wrapped around the house, touched his bare toe against a rocking chair leg.

"Well, go on down. We'll check out those cops, see if they're dead yet. Then we'll take their car. I still can't believe that damned sheriff ruined the van."

"How did you get back here, Clancy?"

"I already told you, that ain't none of your business, buddy. Walk down those damned stairs!"

Clancy had to know that he was running out of time. Miles had to see exactly where Sam was before he moved. Clancy and Sam were just in his peripheral vision behind him, just off to the right. Clancy had his arm around Sam's neck, held him tightly against his side.

On the second step, Miles yelled, "Drop, Sam!"

Sam went limp and dropped to the ground. In the same instant Miles turned and kicked out, his foot crushing Clancy's injured arm. The gun went flying.

Clancy screamed even as he grabbed Sam by his neck and lifted him off the ground, twisting, holding him away from him. Miles kicked again, this time in the middle of his chest. Clancy dropped Sam and went flying back, grabbing his chest, unable to breathe.

At that moment, Katie came through the open doorway, barefoot, her SIG Sauer in both hands in front of her.

She yelled, as she crouched, "Hold it, Clancy!"

"I've got him," Miles said, and she saw that he was smiling of all things, an awful smile that held raw hate and triumph.

As he moved toward Clancy, he yelled, "Katie, check the deputies. There's gas in the car, hurry!"

Miles smashed his palm into Clancy's nose, and brought his knee up hard into his crotch.

Clancy screamed and went down onto his knees, holding himself. Katie literally jumped over Clancy and went flying off the porch, and Miles winced as her bare feet struck stone and gravel, but she didn't slow. She jerked open the passenger's side door and pulled the deputy out onto the ground, then ran to the driver's side, and dragged the other man out as well.

Clancy, still bent over, staggered to his feet, his eyes on Sam, who was on his hands and knees, scooting backward toward the edge of the porch.

"It's okay, Sam." Miles jumped toward him and slammed his fist into Clancy's jaw. He felt the skin on his knuckles split, but it felt good, sending this monster into oblivion with his bare fist. He watched him fall senseless, then turned to see Katie bent over one of the deputies, listening for a breath. Sam was sitting on the edge of the porch, huddled over, not saying a word.

"Mama?"

"It's okay, Keely," Miles said. "You stay in the house, okay? Your mom will get you in just a minute. Don't move, Keely. Katie, do I need to see to the other deputy?"

Before Katie answered, she saw that Clancy was down, not moving, not even moaning and was lying on his side, facing the house. She didn't have any cuffs and couldn't leave Cole here, possibly dying. It was okay, Clancy was down and out.

"Miles, you got him good. Hurry!"

Miles kicked Clancy just to make sure he was really unconscious, and pushed his gun in his pants. "Come with me, Sam. We've got to help the deputies."

Katie raised her head a moment to say, "Cole's not dead! He's breathing!" before she moved over to the other man. Miles was aware that Keely was standing over her mom, just as Sam was standing next to him. He quickly looked toward the porch. Clancy hadn't twitched. "Sam, run inside and get my cell phone and bring it to me."

When Sam handed Miles his cell, he punched 911. A short time later, they heard sirens loud in the still night.

The paramedics immediately covered the deputies' noses and mouths with oxygen masks. "It looks to me like that was close," said Mackey. He cocked a brow at Katie. "I'd call this a crime spree, Sheriff. You're really keeping us busy. You and the kids okay?"

"I think so." She pointed to Clancy. "For a fat guy, he moves as quietly as a cat burglar. I have no idea what sort of shape he's in, though. Mr. Kettering didn't pull any punches. But he's alive, and that's the important thing. Now we'll find out who hired him. We'll need you all to transport him once we've got you a police escort."

"Nuts," Mackey said. "The jerk must be just plain nuts."

Wade showed up not five minutes later, jeans pulled over his pajamas, his shirt hanging open. "Jesus, Katie, you got him! By damn, you got the bastard."

"Actually, Miles got him. He's got some good moves. Go cuff him, Wade."

Miles was elated and exhausted. He walked to the children who were both sitting on the edge of the porch, went down on his haunches and pulled them both against his chest. He kissed Sam, then Keely, again and again. "I'm so proud of you both."

"I want Mama," Keely said against Miles's armpit.

"Let her do her job, then she'll be over here. You just hold on to me, okay?

"Sam?"

Sam burrowed closer.

"Sam? You all right?"

Sam didn't say a thing. He didn't even blink when Clancy staggered to his feet, knocked Wade off the porch, jumped onto the driveway, and disappeared into the darkness.

Katie cursed a blue streak, and ran after him. Miles leaped off the porch after her. Both of them were still barefoot. Miles heard Wade cursing, couldn't make out his words.

Then dead silence.

He heard a gunshot.

Then more dead silence.

NINETEEN

Miles watched Dr. Sheila Raines from across Katie's living room speaking quietly to Sam. He wasn't moving, wasn't meeting her eyes. His small hands were restless, pulling on his jeans, scratching his elbow, punching one of the sofa cushions.

"He's hardly spoken a single word," he said to Katie, who was sitting next to him, holding Keely in her arms, the little girl was sprawled out, asleep. Miles barely got the words out. "Too much has happened to him, just too much. And we still have no idea who is after him, and why. And that's the biggest mystery: why go through all this misery to get ahold of one little boy? Twice now they've come after him after he escaped them. Twice! And tonight Clancy came after him all by himself, and he was wounded. It makes no sense at all to me.

"If his kidnapping was for money, then why was there no ransom note? They had almost two days, surely that was enough time to make their demands known to me." He paused a moment, streaking his fingers through his hair. "I was certain it was a pedophile who'd taken him, but no, that isn't the case, and I thank God for that. And I'm as certain as I can be that no one, not even the crooks I caught when I was an FBI agent, would want revenge against me this badly. And if someone did, then why not just shoot me? That would be easy enough to do. Why then, for God's sake?

"Jesus, this whole thing is over the top. And look at Sam, silent, his eyes blank like he's really not here, like he doesn't want to be here because it's too scary, and he has all this terror locked inside him."

Katie touched his shoulder. "It's a terrible thing, what he's been through," she said. "But you know, Miles, even with the short time I've known Sam, I know he's resilient. He's a very strong little boy. Be patient. Sheila is very good. Have some faith.

"Now the motive. There is one, you know that, Miles. There always is. It's just not obvious to us yet, and just maybe we wouldn't necessarily understand it, but there is a motive, obviously a very strong one to the person or persons who had Sam kidnapped, given all the lengths Clancy and Beau have gone to. We'll keep digging and we'll find it, I promise you."

It was as if he hadn't heard her. "And it's not over," he said, still looking toward his son, "not by a long shot. Clancy is dead, and with him the name of whoever is behind this. But they're still out there, I know it and you know it, Katie. And they'll try again, you know that, too. Why stop now?"

"To be honest," Katie said after a moment, "I don't think Clancy would have said a word. Didn't you tell me that you were certain he planned to kill you after he had Sam again?"

Miles nodded. He began rubbing Keely's foot in its bright pink sock, so small, just like Sam's.

"Even so he still wouldn't tell you who hired him to do this."

"No." Miles happened to look down. Katie was still barefoot, wearing only jeans and her nightshirt with *Benedict Pulp: Nonfiction* printed across the front.

He looked down at his own bare feet and saw several cuts. He hadn't even noticed until now. He'd see to them, but not yet, not just yet. Her feet were cut, too. Who cared about feet? He looked again at Sam and Dr. Raines. His boy wasn't moving. He just sat there, looking at nothing in particular, moving his hands.

Savich and Sherlock arrived ten minutes later. Both of them hugged Sam, met Dr. Sheila Raines, then left them alone again.

Sherlock said, "You guys tell Savich what happened while I take care of the bloody feet in this room. You got a first-aid kit, Katie?"

Katie looked at her, face completely blank. She repeated, "First-aid kit?"

"Yes, so I can clean up your feet. Both you and Miles."

Katie blinked, reminded of the cuts on her feet, and shook her head at herself. "Yes, in the kitchen, in the cabinet above the fridge."

A few minutes later, Sherlock looked up to see Katie walking gingerly into the kitchen.

"Where's Keely?"

"I gave her to Miles. I think it helps him to hold her. It's bad,

Sherlock, Sam isn't speaking at all. But I trust Sheila, she's got a gift, particularly with kids. She's able to clue right into what they're feeling— their fears and where they're lurking, and how to lessen them. She's really good. Plus I've known her all my life. She's loaded with common sense—" Katie's voice caught and tears filled her eyes.

Sherlock looked at her a moment, put down the first-aid kit she'd just pulled down from a top shelf, and held out her arms. "Come here, Katie."

Katie walked into her arms. It was silly, really, particularly since she was bigger than Sherlock, but it felt good to be held, to know that Sherlock understood what she was feeling, it made a difference. She whispered against Sherlock's hair, "I've killed two men—two—since last night. I've been sheriff of Jessborough for three years now and I've never shot anyone before. Our idea of local crime here is shoplifting and maybe twenty-five DUIs a year. Mainly we herd Mr. James's cows back into his pasture, pull Mr. Murray out from under the tractor that fell on him, tug Mrs. McCulver's rat terrier off the postman, and keep traffic smooth on the Fourth of July. I've never seen a murder or a kidnapping, at least not here. This is a peaceful town. Now this."

"I know," Sherlock said, stroking her hair. "I know it's been a shock, not only to you but to all of us. But you did exactly what you had to do to end it. You saved Sam, I mean you really saved him. Just think about what would have happened if you hadn't been with Sam. Do you think now that you had a choice? In either case?"

Katie shook her head against Sherlock's face.

"Good. Now, I expect Sam to always be there for you. He owes you his life. He can push your wheelchair or help you dodder around when you're old and drooly."

Katie laughed, despite herself. "The image of that," she said, straightening, "makes me want to both laugh and cry."

Sherlock cupped Katie's face between her hands. "The realization that you, no one else, just you, put an end to someone's life—you have to just look at Sam to know you did the right thing when it counted."

"Have you ever killed anyone, Sherlock?"

"No, I haven't, but I wanted to once, real bad. Someday I'll tell you about Marlin Jones. Dillon has, and he told me it dug right into his gut. There was one time he wasn't sorry at all, when he shot a real madman, Tommy Tuttle. But you see, he got over it because he realized that a law

officer has to be able, intellectually and emotionally, to get the job done."
She paused a moment, and looked disappointed. "I'm really sorry we
weren't here to help you take care of Clancy."

Katie smiled. "Yeah, I wish you'd been here, too. He managed to
break the locks on the back door, came right up the stairs and I didn't
hear him. None of us believed it could happen. Do you know that Clancy
actually got into the bedroom where Miles and Sam were sleeping? A
fat guy who's quiet as a mouse—that's scary. The deputies didn't see or
hear him either, even when he snuck up on them. He had both Miles
and Sam out of the house before I heard them." Katie wiped her hand
over her eyes, blew out a breath. "Thanks, Sherlock. I'll be okay, I
promise."

"I've known you for only a very short time, Katie, but I am very
certain of one thing: You're a good person and an excellent sheriff. Now,
it's after midnight, your feet are a mess. Come on, let me fix you up.
Dillon needs rest, but that won't happen until he's satisfied that everything's under control."

Katie, trying for a stab at humor, said, "Maybe I can be an excellent
patient, too?"

"We'll see about that," Sherlock said. She smiled up at Katie, who
was five foot nine if she was an inch, took her hand, and walked her
back to the living room.

Once she had a bowl of hot water, soap, towels, and the first-aid kit,
Sherlock was ready. She sat on her haunches in front of Katie, holding
her ankle firm. When she finished washing each foot, it was time for the
iodine. "Hold still, Katie, this is probably going to sting."

The word *sting* wasn't all that accurate, Katie thought as she swallowed two full-bodied curses, because Keely would have heard her curse,
even in her sleep.

"Sorry. No more stingy stuff, just the bandages." Sherlock put the
iodine back into the kit.

As Sherlock bandaged her feet, Katie said quietly, "I couldn't believe
how Miles kicked the bejesus out of Clancy. He knows karate well."
Katie looked over at him as she spoke. "I've never learned a martial art,
and after watching Miles, I want to."

Sherlock said, "Martial arts is grand as long as a gun's not in your
face. Miles and Dillon used to work out together a lot. Not so often
now, maybe once a month they get together. Miles has been so tied up

with his new military contract and trying to get all the bugs out of the new guidance system design for the army. He's really quite talented. Dillon said he could fly anything as long as it had one wing."

After a moment, Sherlock added, "Miles was in the FBI, you know."

"Yeah, he told me," Katie said, looking over at Miles, who'd moved to Katie's big rocking chair, as she spoke. He was holding Keely in his arms, his cheek resting against her head, slowly rocking, all his attention on his son. She supposed she was seeing him with new eyes now. There was no particular expression on his face, but she knew he was fighting his fear for his son. He was hurting, bad. He was holding her daughter carefully, but he never looked away from Sam. It was as if just looking at him, concentrating only on Sam, he could somehow help him.

Savich was sitting next to him, leaning forward because of his back, his hands between his legs, saying nothing. He was just there with him, and that was good.

Sherlock said, "After Alicia died, Miles just retreated, I guess you could say. It was tough for all his friends to see it and not be able to do anything about it. I never really knew her, but Dillon said she was bright, always upbeat, and smart as a whip." Sherlock looked over her shoulder at him, and said thoughtfully, "Dillon also told me that Alicia sometimes did things he didn't understand, things over the top, like she'd be terrified if Sam even got the mildest cold. Once she freaked out when Sam had a slight fever. She stripped him down, examined every inch of him before she wrapped him in a pile of blankets. When Miles tried to calm her down, she lost it, screamed at him to leave her alone.

"But that doesn't matter now. What's happened to Sam would lay any parent nearly flat. Miles is holding up well, but I'll tell you, Katie, I've never seen anyone so scared as when he discovered that someone took Sam."

"I can't begin to imagine that fear," Katie said. "Thank God, I've never had to face it."

"I pray that I won't have to either." Sherlock peeled the wrapper off a Band-Aid and gently wrapped it around a cut on the pad of Katie's foot. "It's got to be a parent's worst nightmare. You know something? I'm glad Clancy is out of the picture, dead or alive. Finally. I'm glad you just got it over with. Do you believe for even an instant that he would have stopped? I can see him breaking out of prison to come after Sam again, no matter what. My God, he came two times. What would make someone do that?"

Before Katie could say anything, Miles said, to no one in particular, his voice pitched low, "Clancy said he didn't necessarily believe it."

"Believe what?" Savich said.

Miles shrugged. "I asked him why he wanted Sam so badly and he said someday he just might tell me, and then he added that he 'didn't necessarily believe it.' It sounded like someone else believed something about Sam, but Clancy didn't agree with it, or wasn't sure about it. I'd swear now that he looked baffled when he said that. Like it was something unbelievable, which makes no sense at all to me. I don't know of anything weird or unusual about Sam at all."

He looked over at Sam again, who was now holding Dr. Raines's hand. She was closer to him, too, and he was leaning into her. It looked like she was getting through to him. He felt a jolt of helplessness that he couldn't be the one with Sam, that he wasn't the one Sam was leaning against, listening to.

He looked up when Sherlock came down on her knees in front of him. "No, you won't do this yourself, Miles. You've done enough. You just sit there and let me clean up your feet. Don't rock too much or you might kick me on my butt. Now, I've finished with Katie, if you want a recommendation."

Miles said, without hesitation, "Katie, are your feet better?"

"She put iodine on all the cuts and they stung for a bit, but yes, now they're better. Trust Sherlock."

Miles smiled down at her. "She's always been a rock, just like her old man. I'd trust her to make doubly sure I'm really croaked before she let anyone pull the plug."

"That really makes me feel special, Miles," Sherlock said, and patted his knee.

"Okay, that was a bit much," he said to Katie. "I'd trust her enough to play net in tennis doubles. How's that?"

"Not as dramatic," Katie said. "How good are you, Sherlock?"

"She's a killer," Savich said, and smiled at his wife.

Sherlock just grinned. "Now, hold still, Miles. Goodness, you've got big feet. What, size twelve?"

"Just about."

"Well, you've got a big body to support, so that's okay."

"What size does Savich wear?"

Sherlock patted his arch. "A twelve."

Katie stretched out her long narrow bandaged feet in front of her. "Well, I'm nearly five-ten, not all that much shorter than you guys. Maybe someday I can wear a twelve, too. Just three sizes to go."

Savich watched his wife putting Band-Aids on Miles's feet when he wasn't watching Sam and Dr. Raines. He wanted to move from the chair to that very comfortable sofa to relieve the pain in his back. He also wanted some tea. He took everyone's order and went to the kitchen. He saw Katie start to follow him and held up his hand. "Nope, you just sit there and let those size nines recover. If you abuse them, they just might never grow. I'll find everything, and I won't make a mess."

Dr. Sheila Raines, holding both of Sam's hands, said quietly against his temple, "Your papa is so scared I think he's going to start howling at the moon."

Sam gave her a long look and said, "Clancy's not going to come back anymore, is he?"

TWENTY

That stopped the show for about ten seconds. Then Sheila answered him. "No, he's not, and that's a very good thing. He was a criminal, Sam, and criminals shouldn't be allowed to terrorize us. What do you think about him and Beau being dead?"

Sam thought about it, bit his lower lip, shot a look toward his father, and said at long last, "It's just that one minute he was yelling and then . . . he was just . . . gone. There was this gunshot, and he was dead, just like my mama. I'm not glad my mama's dead."

Oh dear. At least Sam was talking, thank God. Sheila leaned her forehead against Sam's and said not an inch from his nose, "Trust me on this, Sam. Your mama's in Heaven and I'll bet she's kicking up her heels that you're okay. All the angels are cheering and I'll bet you there's even a big smile on Saint Peter's face.

"As for Beau and Clancy, they're probably so deep in Hell that the Devil doesn't even know where they are."

Sam thought about that, pulled back and smiled at her. He said, his little boy's voice sounding strong again, "Next time Mama talks to me, I'll ask her if she's heard anything about Beau and Clancy."

"That's a great idea. You can tell the sheriff what your mama says."

Miles wanted to shout when he saw that smile and heard Sam's words. He had no idea what Dr. Raines had said to get Sam speaking again, but she'd done it and he owed her forever.

He said, "Sam, would you please come over and hug me? I'm really on the shaky side. You'd better hurry before I fall over. I don't want to drop Keely. You don't want me to do that, do you?"

Slowly, Sam slid off the sofa and walked to his father. He stood there a moment, his hand on his father's knee, and he patted Sherlock's shoulder. "Hi, sweetie," Sherlock said, and kissed his cheek. "Just look at your father's poor feet. You want to put on this last Band-Aid?"

With great concentration, Sam went down on his knees beside Sherlock and smashed the Band-Aid down. At least it covered most of the cut.

Miles picked him up and settled him on his other leg. He held both children close and began rocking slowly. He whispered against Sam's ear, "You are the bravest boy I have ever known. I am so proud of you."

Sam released a long breath and settled against his father's shoulder. "Don't drop me, Papa. Don't worry about Keely, she's not as heavy as I am."

"No, she's not. But you, champ, are all muscle and bone. You just settle in, Sam, and I won't complain."

Sherlock rose and stepped back. She looked down at Keely, whose head was tucked into Miles's neck, then at Sam, whose eyes were already closed as his father rubbed his head.

Dr. Raines said after Sam had settled in for a while, "It's not over yet for him, but this is a good start." She rose. "Mr. Kettering, I would like to see Sam tomorrow morning, if that's okay. About ten o'clock?"

Miles looked over at Savich, who'd just walked into the living room, carrying a tray. He nodded. "Yes, that would be fine, Dr. Raines. We'll be there."

"Please call me Sheila."

"Thank you, Sheila. You got him to talk again. I'm very grateful."

"He's already out like a light. Good. Sleep, that's the best thing for him right now." She lowered her voice even more. "There may be nightmares, Mr. Kettering. Sam had to retreat inside himself for a while, to protect himself, you understand, to close off the horror of what happened. I coaxed him out again, made him pay attention, but the thing is, he really wanted to come back. Being with Keely will help, and with you, of course. He's a strong little boy, you're right about that." She turned to Katie, waved her hand to keep her seated. "No, don't move, Sheriff. In my medical opinion, you should stay off your size nines."

"You're a shrink, Sheila."

"Yeah, but I did think once about becoming an internist, and then I decided I'd rather sleep at night. It's been a pleasure to meet all of you. Perhaps we'll have time to speak more tomorrow. Katie, Miles, try to keep Keely with Sam, okay? My guess is that she's more important to him right now than any of us."

Sheila laid her hand on Katie's shoulder. "If you want to talk to me about things, I'm there for you, don't forget it. It's been a horrendous few days for all of you, but the bottom line is that Sam's safe. By the way, I've always loved that sleep shirt, *Pulp Nonfiction*. Your dad gave it to you, right?"

"Yes, shortly before he died. Thank you for coming and helping, Sheila. I owe you."

"Not this time you don't. Would you look at Keely. I swear she's grown and I saw her just a week ago."

Dr. Raines didn't stay for tea, saying it was well after midnight and she would be jumping off her ceiling if she got any caffeine into her at this hour.

Savich said as he set the tray down on the sofa side table, "I just spoke to Wade, Katie. He got Clancy to the medical examiner. He sounded really impressed this time with how you got Clancy. Since I didn't know any details, I couldn't tell him much about it. Would you like to tell me exactly what happened so I'll know how close I was?"

Katie looked closely at the children to make sure they were asleep before she closed her eyes a moment, and leaned her head back against the chair. "Clancy jumped off the porch, I ran after him. He didn't get far. He was wheezing when I caught up to him. I told him to freeze and, you won't believe this, he started laughing at me, said I wouldn't shoot him like I did Beau because if I did, I'd be a real sorry bitch, said I'd be taken down if I shot him, he promised me that.

"When he caught his breath, he ducked behind a maple tree. I think he knew I didn't want to shoot him, that I wanted to know who he was working for. Unfortunately, I got too close and he charged me. I heard Miles coming behind me, but I knew he wasn't in time. I tried to aim for Clancy's knee, but when he hit me, my SIG jerked up and I got him squarely in the chest. He just stood there, staring blankly at me, as if he couldn't believe that I'd actually shot him. He tried to reach out for my gun, but I took a step back and he just collapsed. He was dead, Miles checked him, too, to make sure. It was an accident, really. I'm sorry, guys, I wanted him alive."

Sherlock said, "As I said before, I for one am vastly relieved that

Clancy is dead. I don't think he would ever have stopped. Now we need to find out who's behind it."

Savich handed each of them a cup of tea. "This is excellent tea, Katie. I was prepared to make do with a tea bag."

"I've always loved Darjeeling," she said. "My mom gave me my first cup when I was about ten years old. I've never looked back. Bless my mom, she replenished my stock just last week."

Mundane things, Sherlock thought, looking from Miles to Katie, to help them put some of this fear behind them. She thought of Sean, her own beautiful little boy, and shivered. Sometimes, the littlest things, silly things really, were just what you needed to remind you that life was coming back to normal, that life was usually just fine, thank you.

Savich carefully rose and straightened his back as best he could. "Sherlock and I will be heading back to Mother's Very Best now. If you guys need anything, call us. Otherwise we'll see you here in the morning."

For the second time, Katie and Miles went to bed, Miles with Sam sprawled over his shoulder, Katie holding a sleepy Keely, who whispered, "I wanna sleep with you, Mama."

"I was just thinking the same thing, sweetie. You won't hog the bed, will you?"

Keely gave her a big grin. "I like to sleep sideways, Mama."

Katie was smiling until it hit her again. She'd shot two men in two days, shot them both dead. Odd how it all felt rather distant now. She no longer felt that debilitating shock that had slammed through her earlier. Now she felt strangely detached. Was it because she'd done something that made her not quite human? No, that was the wrong way to look at it. She set her jaw. She would face this, she would settle it in her mind, once and for all.

TWENTY-ONE

When Katie woke up early the following morning, Keely wasn't in bed with her. She jumped out of bed and came to an abrupt halt just inside the living room. There, lying on their stomachs on a blanket, were Sam and Keely, watching cartoons, the sound turned down low.

Katie looked down at her feet. For that panicked moment, she'd forgotten her sore feet. Then she thought of Miles. If he woke up he'd be wild with panic when he saw Sam was gone.

She didn't say anything, just ignored her throbbing feet, trotted to the guest bedroom, and stuck her head in. Miles was lying on his back, the covers pushed down to his waist, his chest bare. One arm was above his head, the other hand rested on his belly. His dark hair was standing on end, witness to an uneasy night, and his face was dark with stubble. He was sleeping deeply.

She looked at the alarm clock on the bedside table and saw that it was only just after six o'clock. Let him sleep.

She stood there a moment looking at Sam's father, really looking at the man she'd come to trust and admire in just two days' time, then grabbed a couple of blankets from her bedroom and went back into the living room.

An old Road Runner cartoon was playing, but the kids weren't watching it. They'd both fallen asleep. She turned off the TV.

She pushed the kids apart, marveling at how utterly boneless they were, just like cats. They didn't stir at all. She got down between them, and managed to get the three blankets over them. She put an arm around each child and drew them close. They snuggled in. She smiled as she closed her eyes, holding their small bodies close and safe.

An hour later, Miles woke up, realized that Sam wasn't there, and came running into the living room. There was the sheriff of Jessborough lying on her side, her hair out of its French braid, loose and long, draped over a sofa pillow. She was spooning Sam and Keely was spooning her, and all three of them were sound asleep.

For a very long time Miles stood in the doorway, looking at them, then looking at the sheriff holding them, and knew to his gut that everything was changing. He'd felt frozen inside since Alicia's death, but no longer. He turned and walked into the kitchen, made some coffee and pulled out his cell phone to call his sister-in-law, Ann Malcolm. He had called her Sunday morning, to reassure her that Sam was okay, but hadn't had time to tell her much. He'd trusted Butch Ashburn to keep her informed. He wasn't planning on telling her much this time either because there was no reason to upset her with it all. He didn't want to be on the phone anyway. He wanted to be lying in that living room holding Sam.

"Hey, Cracker, it's me, Miles."

She yelled into his ear: "It's seven o'clock on a bloody Monday morning! It's about time you called again, you jerk!" Miles smiled and she was off.

Miles held his cell phone a good two feet from his ear until he heard her running down. Then she started firing questions at him. He pictured her in his mind as they talked. She was wearing one of her gorgeous peignoir sets, no doubt—that's what she called them, honest to God. Whereas her sister, his wife Alicia, who had always had both feet a bit off the ground and a song always on her lips, had worn flannel pajamas. Cracker was a part-time estate lawyer, with a big mouth and a sharp brain. She loved Sam, and that was the most important thing.

"Yes," he said, breaking in at last, "everything is okay now. I'm okay. Sam is okay. There's lots to tell you, Cracker, but you're going to have to wait for the unabridged version. Hey, do you know anyone in Jessborough, Tennessee?"

"Me? I've never even heard of Jessborough, Tennessee. What's going on, Miles?"

"That's another reason I called. I thought we'd be coming right back, but not just yet. Sam's seeing a local shrink, and I think she's really good. She came over last night after there was more violence."

Cracker nearly lost it. *"Violence? What damned violence? Are you nuts, Miles? Bring him home!"*

When he could talk over her, and assure her again that they were safe, Miles said, "I'll keep you posted. Please, Cracker, don't worry. Now, I need you to work closely with the FBI—Agent Butch Ashburn was here but he wanted to get back, to get to the bottom of this."

"This sheriff . . . what's her name?"

"Katie Benedict. She's good, Cracker, really good. She's quick, has a solid center, and she's got guts. She's probably got lots more, but that's a good start. Like I told you, she saved Sam."

"Is she like the woman sheriff in Mel Gibson's movie *Signs*?"

"Well, maybe, only younger. She's really together, like that sheriff was."

"Okay, that's great, but Miles, I want you to bring Sam home. I miss him, you know?"

"I know. Sam is seeing a shrink this morning, so that's one thing keeping us here. Plus the sheriff has a little girl, Keely. She and Sam are really tight. Dr. Raines believes Keely is very important to Sam right now. I'm not about to risk Sam's progress by separating them. And the thing is, Sam's probably just as safe here as he would be back home. So, for the next couple of days, I'm keeping him here in Jessborough. Have you thought of anything that could help?"

"No, but the FBI are checking out all your employees, which takes a good long time. They've spoken to everyone—all the neighbors, all Sam's teachers, even the postman. Give Sam a big kiss for me, Miles, and tell him I miss him like mad."

"I will. Take care. I'll call if something happens. Hold down the fort. I'll call Conrad at the office, make sure everything's running smooth, so don't worry about the business."

He got Conrad's voice mail. When he slipped his cell back into his pocket, he looked up to see Katie standing in the kitchen doorway. She had socks on her feet and a loose shirt over jeans. She'd pulled her long hair back into a ponytail. She looked fresh and scrubbed. He himself wore socks to protect his Band-Aided feet, jeans from yesterday, and his shirt with two buttons buttoned. He smiled. It felt good.

"Cracker?"

"Yeah. She's my sister-in-law—Alicia's sister. She's lived with us ever since Alicia died. She's really Sam's surrogate mother."

"Where'd she get the name Cracker?"

"She nearly blew off my foot on the Fourth of July a couple of years back, got called Firecracker, and that came down to Cracker. She's a brick. I trust her even though she's a lawyer, only part-time since Alicia died. The kids still asleep?"

"Yeah. I woke up, saw that Keely wasn't with me in bed, and nearly had heart failure. I found them both in the living room sleeping. They must have been watching cartoons with almost no sound. I checked you, got some blankets, then went back to the living room. What would you like for breakfast, Miles?"

"You checked me?"

She nodded. "I knew if you woke up and Sam wasn't there, you'd be scared, but you were sleeping so deeply I decided not to wake you. Now, what about food?"

He remembered pushing the covers down, and he'd awakened with the covers down, which meant she'd probably seen him sprawled on his back, wearing only his boxer shorts. He hoped he hadn't had a hard-on. Then he found himself wondering what she'd thought. No, that was nuts.

"Food, Miles," she said.

He blinked. "You know, I haven't thought about food for what is it, three days now, ever since Sam was taken. I'm starving."

"Good, then bacon and eggs it is. Crispy and scrambled?"

TWENTY-TWO

After Sam's meeting with Dr. Raines, Miles still wasn't sure what the best place was for Sam. What made it easier was that Sam didn't want Keely out of his sight.

Miles knew that Katie was as flummoxed as he was. He couldn't move to Jessborough and he couldn't very well take Keely back with him to Colfax, Virginia.

Because Miles wasn't about to let Sam out of his sight, that meant he also kept Keely with him, and that meant she was out of kindergarten for the moment, cleared by Katie with Keely's teacher.

Needless to say, Keely was pleased about this. Miles and the kids parted company from the other adults after lunch at Molly's Diner on Main Street, after munching on the best meatloaf east of Knoxville.

It was a beautiful day, sunny and clear, with a slight fall nip in the air. He took them to the small Jessborough park, located just a block from Main Street, bordered with trees so outrageously colorful you just stood there marveling at them. In the middle was a big swing set for the kids.

Katie went to her office to brief Wade and all the deputies on the situation. She'd no sooner gotten into her office than Agent Glen Hodges appeared in the doorway. He had his arms crossed over his chest, shaking his head at her.

She sat down behind her desk. "Good morning, Agent Hodges."

He gave her a small salute. "Hi, Sheriff. You're amazing, absolutely amazing. You took out both bad guys."

"Yeah, well, I didn't really want to, and you probably know Clancy practically admitted he was working for somebody else."

"We'll find out who that somebody is," he said. "I spoke with Butch

Ashburn. He gave me a rundown. Now I'm thinking I should go interview the McCamys."

Katie smiled. "Admittedly, I'm just a backwoods sheriff, but Agent Sherlock and I have already been to see them. I'd appreciate it if you'd let us deal with the McCamys."

He wasn't happy about that, but he nodded.

"What I'd really like you to do is come along to the briefing I'm giving to my deputies."

He wasn't happy about this either, but on the other hand, Katie wasn't very happy with him. When he left for the department's conference room, Katie called Wade in.

Wade always walked like a guy on the prowl. He was two years older than Katie and he'd wanted very much to be elected sheriff, but the truth was, the powers in town owed a lot to the Benedict Pulp Mill, and so Katie was the one to get the nod. Wade had been a deputy to the old sheriff, a good old boy named Bud Owens who'd believed computers were for wussies. When he'd finally retired, he'd told everyone he wanted Wade. Unfortunately for him, Wade didn't have Katie's education, or her experience as a cop in a big city. Certainly her desire to be sheriff equaled or surpassed Wade's. Her cop experience had been in Knoxville, for two years, and that's where she'd met Carlo Silvestri, who turned her life upside down. For one year, her life had been one screaming crisis after another. Then Carlo's father had come and they'd both left Knoxville.

Katie had taken stock, realized she was a cop to her toes, and what she really wanted was to be sheriff of Jessborough. It was what she needed, too. She loved her work. It had helped her get through the worst of her father's illness, the devastating and inevitable march of Alzheimer's, which had turned him into an angry stranger before killing him.

She watched Wade, her eyes half-closed. When she'd had enough of his fidgeting around, she said, "Well, Wade, would you like to continue working with Agent Hodges for as long as he remains here?"

"Well, sure, I'd really like that, Katie."

"Thing is, I don't really trust him to tell us stuff, to give us everything we need to know. Can I trust you to keep me filled in?"

She saw it in his eyes. Wade wasn't good at deception, not like she was. She was so good that when she was in Knoxville, they wanted to put her in undercover operations. She smiled at him and waited.

He said, one eyelid twitching furiously, "Of course, Katie. After all, I work for the Jessborough Sheriff's Department."

"Well, actually, Wade, you work for me. I am the Sheriff's Department."

He flushed, blood rushing to his cheeks. He got all stiff, but he wasn't stupid, and he knew he couldn't cross her openly or she just might fire his ass.

"Yeah, I work for you."

"Okay, you're now my liaison with Agent Hodges." She sat forward, her eyes hard on him. "Listen to me now, this is important. Don't be impressed just because he tells you something. Make sure you know everything that's going on, you got that?"

After he'd assured her he understood, he sauntered out of her office, more enthusiasm in his step.

Katie followed him after a minute. Conversation stopped when she came into the small room. She walked to the head of the table and stood behind a small lectern, her hands clasped in front of her. "There are just eight of us this morning. Nate and Jamie are at home recovering." She looked around the conference at her seven deputies, all of them looking excited and important. She wished she had a basket of candy to hand out to them, they looked so much like school kids. Linnie, her dispatcher and assistant, had already handed out coffee.

She introduced them to Agent Hodges, then went through events chronologically. It took her a good fifteen minutes. "Do you have anything to add, Agent Hodges?"

He didn't, though he wanted to. The problem was that Katie had been thorough, and thankfully, Agent Hodges had the grace to say, "No, you've covered things quite nicely, Sheriff."

"Okay, now here's what we're going to do. I found out that Hester Granby is the church secretary at the Sinful Children of God. I want Wade to get the names of the members from her. He'll split them up and each of you will go interview as many church members as you can today. If you find out anything at all interesting about church operations or either of the McCamys, leave me a message on my voice mail. Don't forget now, we have to be nice. Remember that we have no evidence to connect the McCamys to the kidnapping, it's just that they're our only lead. You already know some of their people, but the majority aren't local. That should give you a head start at least."

Deputy Cole Osborne said, "Sheriff, how will we know if we find out anything significant?"

"You're smart enough. Listen carefully, anything you hear that might sound the least bit off, that's what I want to know about."

After she'd dismissed them all, and said fond good-byes to Agent Hodges, she pulled Deputy Danny Peevley aside. He was the best-liked of all her deputies, just about magic with people. His mama would say that he could get an onion to peel off its own skin. "I have someone real special I want you to speak to, Danny. His name is Homer Bean and he lives in Elizabethton. He owns the Union 76 gas station. I saw Bea Hipple yesterday at the church and she called me, gave me Homer Bean's name. She said she liked Homer, and he'd been unhappy with Reverend McCamy. That's all she knew. Mr. Bean left the church about six months ago. Find out why, Danny. Find out what he thinks of Reverend McCamy."

Once Katie's door closed, she sat down at her desk actually happy to have a chance to look at the three active cases Linnie had left for her to review. Three cases very nearly constituted a crime spree for Jessborough. One DUI—Timmy Engels was at this moment still sleeping off his drunk in the only cell that had a soft cushion. One assault case— Marvin Dickerson was in back in a cell for beating on his wife, Ellie. Katie would keep him locked up until Judge Denver saw him at an arraignment on Wednesday. And she would speak to his wife again, beg her to press charges. But she wouldn't, she never did, so the best Katie could do was keep the bastard locked up as long as she could. And one last case: shoplifting—Ben Chivers, a kid whose parents were so poor, it broke Katie's heart. And the fact that they were usually passed out at night after drinking themselves blind didn't help matters. *I made you give back that Snickers bar you stole, Ben; now what am I going to do with you?* She closed her eyes and mulled that one over.

Then it came to her and she smiled. It was worth a shot. She picked up the phone, spoke to Mrs. Cerlew, who owned Emmy's One-Stop Grocery, named after her suffragette grandmother. That was where Ben had ineptly lifted the Snickers bar. When she hung up, she grabbed her hat, and stopped by Linnie's desk. "I'm off to see Ben Chivers. I know he's in school, and I'm going to get him out of class. It'll make his reputation if the sheriff comes to see him, don't you think?"

"He'll strut," Linnie said, then shook her head. "That's a bad situation, Katie. Those folks of his, all they do is lie around drunk and bitch."

"I've got an idea," Katie said, gave Linnie a small salute, and drove her truck to the local middle school.

SAVICH looked up to see Sherlock tuck her cell phone back in her shirt pocket. They were in their bedroom at Mother's Very Best. He was still sitting forward, trying to ignore the constant throb in his back, working on MAX.

"What did the medical examiner have to say?"

"Clancy," Sherlock said as she bounced up and down on the bed a couple of times, "was stronger than a bull, ate like a pig, and had arteries clogged all the way to his ears. Katie's bullet killed him. Nothing more, nothing less." She eased off the bed, smoothed down the covers and walked to her husband. She leaned down and kissed his mouth. She felt the immediate hitch in his breath, and stood again. "About all we can do is play with my hair rollers," she said, a wealth of disappointment in her voice.

"Where are they?"

Sherlock laughed. "You've been working on MAX all afternoon. What have you got?" She affectionately patted the laptop as she spoke. At least Dillon didn't have to worry about the math teacher killer case since Jimmy Maitland had told him to chill out until he was better.

"I've been reading about Reverend Sooner McCamy. He's fifty-four years old, born near Nashville, Tennessee, went to Orrin Midvale Junior College, married and divorced once, no children. He sold cars at the Nashville Porsche dealership, and did very well financially. Then he quit and moved to his rich aunt's house here in Jessborough. He hasn't done anything since then to earn money, I guess because he didn't have to. He married Elsbeth Bird of Johnson City ten-plus years ago when she was only about twenty-four and he was forty-four. He didn't become a preacher until about six years ago."

He tapped his fingertips together, frowned down at MAX, who was humming placidly.

"He's married to Elsbeth four years before he finds his calling?"

"Apparently. But when the calling hit him, it hit him hard. Suddenly he's the founder and leader of this pretty strange-sounding church, the Sinful Children of God."

"He didn't go to a seminary?"

"Nope."

"Hmm. What did his aunt die of?"

Savich's back was throbbing like the very devil.

She hated seeing the pain in his eyes. "You're taking a pill, buddy, no arguments."

After he'd swallowed the pill, she made him sit for a few minutes until his back stopped throbbing. He said, "Let's see about that aunt. She died something like six months after Sooner married Elsbeth. They both lived with the aunt in that lovely big house that his aunt, Eleanor Marie McCamy Ward, inherited from her husband. Ah, do you have Katie's cell? Ask her."

Katie answered immediately and listened. She said, "That's an excellent question, Sherlock. I'm in the middle of a delinquent problem right now, but I'll get back to you."

When Sherlock hung up, she said, "Katie will check it out. We're having dinner tonight at Katie's mom's. You can tell each other what you know about Sooner McCamy and she can tell us all about Aunt Eleanor Marie. Do you want Agent Hodges to come?"

"Sure, the more we compare notes the better. I think Miles is still with Sam and Keely, even though Katie's mother volunteered to watch them."

"But Miles didn't want Sam out of his sight."

"You got it. I told him to come here—"

There was a knock on the door, then Sam's voice, "Uncle Dillon! Aunt Sherlock! We're here."

Savich slowly rose. He knew the pain would knock him on his butt if he moved too fast. He took a handful of Sherlock's hair, kissed her—lust, pain, frustration in that kiss. "I want to do something with those big hair rollers later."

She said against his jaw, "I've been thinking that just maybe we can figure something out that won't hurt you too much."

That perked him up.

TWENTY-THREE

They went to Katie's mom's for dinner, a large ranch-style home built in the sixties located in the middle of Jessborough on Tulip Lane. She'd lived there for twenty-nine years with her husband. Now, she lived with two canaries, three King Charles spaniels, and an aquarium, temporarily empty. She was serving a huge tuna casserola that the kids would love, Minna Benedict had assured Miles when she met him at the front door.

"Is that the same as a tuna casserole, ma'am?" Miles asked her.

"My granny called it a casserola and that's just the way it is around here. Hello, Dillon, Sherlock. And who are you, sir?"

"I'm Agent Glen Hodges, ma'am."

She shook his hand. "Welcome, all of you. Please, call me Minna. Ah, and the beyond-perfect specimens of kidness—Sam and Keely. Come on in, and let me give you each a big hug and an even bigger chocolate chip cookie, fresh out of the oven."

"What about us, Mom? Just look at Dillon here. The man's back is hurting bad. He could probably use a cookie about now."

Minna Benedict was not quite as tall and slender as her daughter, but she had thick red brown hair even more lustrous than Katie's. She said, "All right. One for each of you, and two for Dillon because of his back. Come in, come in, don't dawdle. There's enough time before dinner. Dessert is always better than dinner any day of the week, isn't it?"

After the three King Charles spaniels had finally calmed down, their silky ears stroked by every adult and child, and the canaries were quiet beneath their night sheets, everyone trooped into the small dining room. To Miles's surprise, Sam took one bite of the tuna casserola and didn't stop until he downed two helpings and three of Minna's homemade biscuits. He and Keely had their heads together throughout the meal.

"Let me tell you one good thing I did today," Katie announced to the table at large.

Sherlock waved her fork. "Out with it, Katie, we need to hear something positive."

"I had a boy steal a Snickers bar from a local grocery. His family's poorer than dirt and both parents drink. I went to the middle school, pulled twelve-year-old Ben Chivers out of class and offered him a deal. He works for Mrs. Cerlew at the grocery three hours a day after school. She pays him minimum wage for two of those hours, then he works free for the other hour. Mrs. Cerlew is all for it, too. If he does well for a month, she'll keep him on and pay him for the full three hours, three days a week."

Miles's head was cocked to the side. "That's very good, Katie. This way the kid doesn't have to go into the juvenile system."

Katie shuddered. "Something I like to avoid at all costs. He's not bad, just helpless. This will give him a sense of worth, and a bit of money. I told him to keep his new job to himself as long as he could, or his dad would hit him up to buy some cheap wine."

Minna said, "Of course old Ben would, too. Now, Katie, Mrs. Cerlew doesn't have an extra dime, so I'll just bet that you're subsidizing his wages, aren't you, dear?"

Katie gave her mother a tight-lipped frown and didn't say anything.

How, Miles wondered, could a sheriff, on a small-town sheriff's pay, afford to subsidize a kid's wages? He was chewing his tongue he wanted to ask so badly when Katie's mom said, smiling, "After the settlement, Katie saved Benedict Pulp Mill, and a lot of local folks' jobs, and every so often, she helps folk here in Jessborough, mainly the kids."

"This is my home," Katie said very quietly. "Actually, you could have pulled the mill out of trouble yourself, Mama." She added to everyone at the table, "She's an excellent manager, something Dad just wasn't. Now, that's enough." She looked down at the last bite of tuna casserola on her plate. "Keely, you want one more forkful?"

Truth be told, the very large tuna casserola and the platter of biscuits were memories in fifteen minutes.

Miles sat back and folded his hands over his stomach. "That was delicious, Minna. Thank you very much for letting us come."

"Well, I put up with you adults just so I can get my hands on Sam and Keely. Now, who's ready for coffee and apple pie?"

Savich said, "May I give you my mom's e-mail, Minna? You can give her your recipe for the casserola and she'll give you hers for Irish beef stew." He grinned at his wife. "Then Sherlock and I can bid good-bye to our waistlines."

AFTER Minna assured the adults that both kids were lying in front of the television, glued to *Wheel of Fortune*, Katie set down her cup of coffee, pulled out a file and said, "Eleanor Marie McCamy Ward was only sixty-three when she died of a fall down the front stairs. The ME's report showed that her neck was broken and that the broken bones and internal injuries were consistent with such a fall. Neither Sooner nor Elsbeth apparently were at the house at the time of the accident. He didn't preach his first sermon for five more years, then he was invited to the Assembly of God over in Martinville. Six months after that, he established the Sinful Children of God here in Jessborough. He started with only a dozen or so worshipers. There are now a good sixty in the congregation. He's what you'd call a natural."

"He was an accomplished car salesman," Savich said. "It makes sense that he'd be a natural as a preacher. Minna, do you know anything more about Reverend McCamy?"

"I remember Eleanor told me that Sooner had been an intense, quiet boy, self-sufficient, very into himself, but when he spoke, he was always so sure of himself that people believed what he said. She said he wasn't a happy man, understandable with a bad marriage and living in that big city selling those ridiculously expensive cars. She was quite religious herself. She prayed he would find what he was meant to do in life before she died."

"But she didn't live long enough to see him become an evangelist," Sherlock said.

"No, she didn't," Minna said. "Her death was a shock to all of us. She was a fine woman. But evidently Sooner did find his calling. He's very much admired and respected by his congregation. He's a big part of their lives. Whether that's healthy or not, I won't speculate."

Katie looked directly at Sherlock. "Do you think Eleanor's fall down the front stairs might not have been an accident?"

"Let me ask another question first," Sherlock said. "Was Eleanor McCamy Ward just really well off or was she rich?"

"We could check the probate records, but everyone knows she was worth quite a bit at her death, say, maybe around five million. So, yes, I'd say she was rich."

"And Sooner McCamy inherited everything?"

Katie nodded, sighed. "I wasn't living here at the time, but I remember thinking that her death was awfully convenient for Sooner. But of course, no one could prove anything. You guys met him. He certainly looks the role of the stern country preacher, doesn't he? Dark, brooding, his eyes boring right into your soul."

"You wonder how much of it is for real," Miles said, then rose and went off to check the kids. He returned in a moment.

Katie said, "I suppose Sooner could have killed his aunt."

"Yes," Savich said, nodding as he sipped Minna's delicious Darjeeling tea. "But a push down the stairs was taking a chance. It doesn't guarantee a broken neck. If Sooner did kill her, then he probably saw the opportunity and took it without thinking it through."

Katie said, "You're right. It's not at all a sure thing, she could have come out of it with a sprained ankle."

"You know," Sherlock said after her last bite of apple pie, "I think I'm in need of some more local religion. Katie, do the Sinful Children of God meet during the week?"

"Oh yes," Katie said. "But not on Tuesdays, that's their day off."

Savich said thoughtfully, "I think a better idea is for me and Sherlock to take the kids and go visit Reverend and Mrs. McCamy. You'll know I'll be looking real close to see his reaction to Sam. And I want to know if Sam's ever seen him before. Do you guys think that's a good idea?"

Minna frowned. "If Reverend McCamy is somehow involved in Sam's kidnapping, is it wise to stick Sam right under his nose?"

Sherlock thought about that for a moment, then said, "Absolutely nothing will happen to Sam with Dillon and me with him, that I can promise you, or else we wouldn't even consider taking him over there. Just seeing how Reverend McCamy reacts when confronted with Sam, well, that could give us lots of information."

Miles said, "Minna, these two are the best, don't worry. I'm not. On the other hand, I just might hide right outside the front door, a big stick in my hand."

Katie was grinning as she said, "I agree that just maybe something will pop. After all, Beau and Clancy are no longer in the picture. If the McCamys are involved, they've not had time to recruit more out-of-work criminals."

LATE Tuesday morning, Savich and Sherlock, with both Keely and Sam in hand, knocked on the McCamys' front door.

"Who lives here, Uncle Dillon?"

"Two very interesting people I think you kids might like meeting."

"I'd rather watch cartoons," Keely said and laced her fingers with Sam's.

Sherlock said, "We're going to have lunch with your mom, Keely, and your dad, Sam. So that means you need to hang out with me and Uncle Dillon for a while, okay? I doubt any cartoons will be playing in this house, so you'll have to be patient."

"She means she doesn't want us to whine," Keely told Sam, who nodded, then asked, "Where's my dad?"

"He had some calls to make, you know, Conrad Evans at the plant. He said he needed you guys out of his hair for a while."

"He always says that," Sam said, "but then he says he can't wait to see me again."

Savich smiled. "That, Sam, is what's known as a parent's curse."

Elsbeth McCamy came to the door after another minute had passed. She stared at the two agents, then she stared at the children.

"May we speak to you, Mrs. McCamy?" Sherlock said. "Forgive us for bringing the children, but we were the only two free adults."

"Yes, of course. Do come in. Reverend McCamy," she called out, "two FBI agents are here and they've brought children."

It really was very old-fashioned of her to call her husband Reverend McCamy, Savich thought. But Elsbeth McCamy didn't look the least bit old-fashioned in her tight low-slung jeans and white tube top that left three inches of bare belly showing. She was wearing a belly button ring, a delicate circle of gold. And her Jesus earrings were shining bright in the morning light pouring through the front windows.

Reverend Sooner McCamy was wearing his patented black pants, a white shirt, and a black jacket. When he came out of his study down the hall, he looked harassed. "Elsbeth, I'm ministering to Mr. and Mrs. Coombs."

"The agents would like to speak to us."

"Take them to the living room. I'll see if Mr. and Mrs. Coombs can wait for ten minutes." He raised an eyebrow as Sherlock said, "Ten minutes sounds just fine."

Elsbeth McCamy waved them into the living room. She eyed the children again. "Hello, Keely. Can you introduce me to this little boy?"

"I'm not a little boy," Sam said. "I'm six."

"I see. And what is your name?"

"Sam. I'm Sam."

Sherlock was watching her carefully when she looked at Sam. She saw nothing but an adult being polite to a child.

"No, you're not little at all. I'm Mrs. McCamy, Sam. Welcome to my home. Do you like it here in Jessborough?"

Sam gave this some thought. "Well, those two men who kidnapped me are dead. Maybe things are better now."

"Yes, I hope so."

"We're very sorry about Clancy's death, Mrs. McCamy. The medical examiner finished this morning and he wanted me to ask you if you wanted to take care of the arrangements."

"No, I don't want to. Let Tennessee do it. Clancy had been bad for a very long time." She paused a moment, and looked down at Sam. "Did you know that Clancy was my brother?"

TWENTY-FOUR

Sam stared up at her, then he shook his head. "Really?" Sam said. "Why did your brother take me?"

"I don't know, dear. We haven't been close for many years now."

"I wouldn't want to be close to Fatso either."

"I can see your point."

Reverend McCamy said from the doorway, "So you're Sam Kettering, the little boy who was kidnapped."

"I'm not little," Sam said.

"He's six," Elsbeth said.

"You look pretty little to me," the reverend said, ignoring his wife as he walked forward to stand over Sam.

"You're old," Sam said, staring up at him. "That's why you're bigger than me."

"Do you think Agent Savich is old?" Reverend McCamy asked, not smiling, his dark eyes intent on Sam's face.

"Well, sure, he's even taller than you, but he's really strong. I've seen him and my dad throw each other all over the place at the gym. They punch each other, yell insults, and groan, and then they're laughing."

"Sam's father and I work out together occasionally," Savich said to Reverend McCamy. "Sam, why don't you and Keely check out that fireplace. It looks pretty old and big to me."

Sam said, never looking away from Reverend McCamy, "Did you push your aunt down the stairs, sir?"

There was dead silence in the living room. Bad idea to bring the kids, Savich thought, but on the other hand, you never knew what could shake loose. So much for the kids watching TV in the other room. Savich watched the reverend's face. He was pale, too pale, except for the dark beard stubble, and now, perhaps, he'd paled just a bit more. He looked like an old-time zealot in all that black with those burning eyes of his. He gave Savich the creeps.

Reverend McCamy shook his head. He reached out his hand to touch Sam, then drew it back. "Why no, I didn't. Why would you think I did, Sam?"

Sam shrugged. "I don't know, sir. Some grown-ups do really bad things. Like Beau and Fatso."

"Fatso? Oh, you mean Clancy. Yes, what you said, that's true enough, and you have good reason to know that. But I'm a man of God, Sam. My mission in life is to bring others to Him, to accept how He suffered for all of us, how He atoned for our sins, even Beau's and Clancy's. And He allows some of us to experience His own sacrifice."

"I wish you'd brought Fatso and Beau to God," Sam said, "before they took me away from my dad."

"Well, who knows? Maybe they were thinking about God when they took you. We'll never know, will we? Not all men are capable of achieving anything like goodness. Are you good, Sam?"

Sam didn't say a word, just stared up at Reverend McCamy.

Keely said, "He's a boy, but I think he's a little bit good."

Reverend McCamy said, "You're the sheriff's daughter, aren't you?"

"Yes," Keely said, hugging Savich's pant leg. "You look like a man in one of my mama's old movies, you know, black and white before there were colors. I don't like black and white."

Savich smiled, just couldn't help it, but he saw that Reverend McCamy didn't appreciate the child's wit. There was no change in his expression, but Savich felt something dark and brooding coming over him, something he didn't understand. But all McCamy said was, "Elsbeth, why don't you take the children to the kitchen and give them some lemonade."

Sherlock said, "That sounds splendid. Let me help."

Elsbeth nodded and walked out of the living room, the kids behind her.

"He's scary, Aunt Sherlock," Sam said in a low voice.

"Maybe," Sherlock said. "Sam, what's wrong?"

He'd stopped and was staring at the big staircase. Keely was running ahead behind Elsbeth McCamy. Sherlock leaned down and whispered in his ear, "Sam, what's wrong?"

"I don't like this house, Aunt Sherlock. Can't you feel it?"

"Feel what, sweetie?"

Sam frowned a moment, kept staring at that staircase, then shrugged. "I don't know, but it's kinda scary. His aunt must have fallen down these stairs."

"Yes, she did."

Sam touched his fingers to the newel post, a richly carved mahogany pineapple. "Do you think Mrs. McCamy really has some lemonade, or do you think she'll just have Diet Coke?"

"We'll see, now won't we?" Sherlock said.

In the living room, Savich remained standing. It was less painful that way. Reverend McCamy wasn't a large man, but he had presence, and that made him appear bigger than he actually was. Savich remembered the bottomless well of madness in Tommy Tuttle's eyes and wondered if there was a hint of the same madness in Reverend Sooner McCamy's dark eyes as well.

"You actually discussed my aunt's death in front of children? Discussed my murdering her?"

"We thought they were watching TV," Savich said. "We should have known better. We're cops, Reverend McCamy, and we had to wonder about the excellent timing of her demise—six months after your marriage to your wife. No illness, just a sudden fall down the stairs and a broken neck."

"My aunt was a very fine woman, Agent Savich. I loved her very much. She took me in when I was blind and couldn't find my way. She listened to me, comforted me, encouraged me to follow my heart. Her death brought me great sadness. But I knew she basked in God's sacred light. She's with Him now, out of pain, for all eternity."

"Perhaps so. But you were still alive, Reverend McCamy, as was your wife. And you were also much richer. I like your house. It's a lovely property."

"Yes, that's a fact." McCamy waved Savich to a sofa. "It's interesting how the living always regard death selfishly, isn't it? A man will grieve, then almost immediately measure what he'll gain from it. Why don't you sit down."

"Perhaps that's true. I'll stay standing. My back isn't very happy at the moment."

"I've never had back problems."

"I haven't either until Saturday night. Tell me, sir, what do you think of Sam?"

His dark intense eyes rested on Savich's face a moment before he said, "Oh, I'd forgotten that you got hurt at Katie's house. The nurses at the hospital were really excited about having an FBI agent laid out there."

Savich arched an eyebrow.

Reverend McCamy shrugged. "It's a small town, and two of the nurses in the emergency room live here in Jessborough. Gossip is rife. Now, that's an odd question, Agent Savich. What do I think of Sam? Well, he appears to be precocious, a very forthright child."

"You mean just because he repeats what he heard adults say?"

"No, not just that." Reverend McCamy paused a moment, stroking his thin fingers over the wool of his black jacket. "It's that he's somehow above the normal lies and deceptions of children."

"I've heard Sam tell a few whoppers, Reverend. He's a little boy, and that's exactly what one would expect. But the fact that he saved himself, now that's very impressive. He wasn't cowed by fear—and that's amazing for a six-year-old. I suppose you heard the story of how he slithered out of a window in the old Bleaker cabin, and took off, Beau and Clancy after him."

"Yes, I've heard several versions of the tale. All of them strike to the soul." Reverend McCamy slowly shook his head, his eyes on his fingers, which were still stroking his jacket, against the nap. He said nothing more. How strange.

Savich said, "Don't you believe it's quite a coincidence that Clancy was your wife's brother and he brought Sam here?"

Reverend McCamy raised his dark eyes to rest on Savich's face. "Coincidences are random acts that are drawn together by foolish men."

"I gather you are not a foolish man?"

"I am a realistic man, Agent Savich, but yes, like most men, I am occasionally foolish. I believe that our Lord would have us study each random act as it touches us and try to determine how it will enhance our grace. You think my wife and I were involved with the boy's kidnapping, Agent Savich? Just because Clancy was her brother?"

Savich said slowly, not really wanting to look in those black eyes, eyes that somehow seemed to absorb darkness from light, "What I think, Reverend, is that your wife's brother brought Sam to Jessborough, Tennessee, for a reason. You'll have to admit that both Clancy and Beau demonstrated a great deal of motivation. They simply didn't stop trying to get him until they were dead. That, also, is very strange."

Reverend McCamy merely nodded. He raised his right hand and stroked his fingers through his black hair. His hair was thick, long enough to tie at his nape, but he let it hang loose. Stroking his hair was a long-standing habit, Savich thought.

Savich wished he had another pain pill. "Why do you suppose they did that, Reverend?"

"I really have no idea, Agent Savich."

"When Clancy was at the sheriff's house last night, he said something unusual to Mr. Kettering. He said that he didn't necessarily believe it. Believe what, Reverend McCamy?"

"I have no idea, Agent Savich."

"Clancy also admitted to Mr. Kettering that someone had hired him."

Reverend McCamy shrugged. "Then it seems that someone was paying them a great deal of money to get the child."

"That much is obvious. But the question remains: Why is Sam so important to the one who paid them? What is it about Sam that makes him so valuable, if you will? No ransom demands, no obvious revenge motive, no pedophilia that we know of, so it must be something else. Do you know what the motive could be, Reverend McCamy?"

Reverend McCamy shrugged. "As I remarked, he is a precocious child, but I can't personally imagine anyone going to all that trouble for a precocious child."

"Then it must be something more."

The reverend's dark eyes rested on Savich's face. "I have found that there is always something more, Agent Savich. It is a pity that men are given free will. There is endless abuse, don't you agree?"

"Why do you say it's a pity?"

"Free will allows men to make disastrous mistakes without end; what they should be focusing on is gaining God's grace."

Savich said, "I think the reason for many of men's endless mistakes is a direct cause of their search for God's grace. Witness the history of Ireland, England, Spain, France—men's disastrous mistakes litter the landscape, Reverend, especially in their efforts to focus God's grace on themselves, and to deny all other men's claims to the contrary."

"That is blindness, Agent Savich, and a man's blindness can lead either to his salvation or his damnation. If a man focuses on God's grace and His suffering for us, His creatures, his blindness will last but a moment of time. Ah, here is Mrs. McCamy with some refreshment for us, Agent Savich."

"And how does a man do that, Reverend McCamy?"

"He places himself in the hands of the prophets placed on this earth to guide him."

Elsbeth McCamy closed her eyes a moment at her husband's words, and slowly nodded.

Savich asked, "Are you one of these prophets, Reverend McCamy?"

He merely bowed his head and turned his attention to the tea.

The tea tasted as dark as Reverend McCamy's eyes, and it was so hot it nearly burned his mouth. Savich didn't like it. He leaned over to place his saucer carefully on an end table, and instantly regretted it. Pain sliced through his back.

"I do think it's time that you left, Agent Savich. Neither my wife nor I have anything more to say to you."

"Thank you for seeing us," Savich said, the pain nearly bowing him over. He needed a pain pill, fast. He shook Reverend McCamy's hand, feeling the firmly controlled strength of the man. He looked for a moment into those intense eyes, eyes that either saw too much or saw things that were not of this world. Savich just didn't know which. But he did know one thing.

Sherlock nodded to both of their hosts, but didn't say anything. She had each child by the hand.

When they were out the front door and it had closed behind them, Savich said, "Please tell me you have a pain med with you."

"You'll have to swallow it dry."

"No problem, trust me on that."

Once Savich had managed to swallow the pill, and they were ready to go, Keely said from the backseat, "Mrs. McCamy gave us lemonade."

"I didn't like it," Sam said. "It tasted funny."

Sherlock turned to look at him and slowly nodded. "I thought it tasted funny, too." She waited for Savich to get as comfortable as he could with the seat belt, and started the car.

"Let's go see your mama, Keely."

TWENTY-FIVE

"She's with Mr. Kettering," Linnie, Katie's primo dispatcher, told them. Savich smiled and nodded even as she gave a little finger wave to Keely and Sam.

"Tell you what, Sam," Sherlock said, leaning down to Sam's eye level, "why don't you and Keely stay out here with Linnie, just for a little while."

"That's a good idea," Linnie said behind her hand to Sherlock, rolling her eyes. "I think they've got a problem in there."

Keely, who like every kid in the world could hear everything, said to Sam, "If your papa is yelling at my mama, she just might crack him on the head. My mama is the boss here, Sam."

I would agree, Sherlock thought, and said to Keely, "Okay, here's the deal. Your parents aren't yelling, they're just having a discussion," and she hoped it was true. There was too much stress, too much frustration, on both sides.

Inside her office, Katie was saying, "Dammit, Miles, I can't very well arrest the McCamys just because Clancy was Elsbeth's brother. For heaven's sake, you were in law enforcement, you know I can't."

Miles snarled, no other way to put it. "You know they're involved in this somehow, Katie, you know it. There's simply no one else. Maybe it's just Mrs. McCamy. So bring her in and rattle her. No, better yet, I want to talk to that woman myself. I want to face her down."

"Not going to happen. Anything else?" Katie wished she'd French-braided her hair. The banana clip was listing over her left ear.

"What are Agent Hodges and his crew doing?"

"Since they left all the interviewing to us, they're following the money trail—you know, credit cards, church accounts, money transfers, stuff like that."

"Is the TBI going to do anything at all except hassle you?"

Katie said patiently, "The Tennessee Bureau of Investigation has an obligation to see that the sheriff of a town in Tennessee didn't just decide to up and murder two men. They're just doing their job. They won't be too much of a hassle."

"Yeah, right. You've already spent hours with them."

That was true enough, she thought, and she wasn't looking forward to her next meeting with them. So far, they were satisfied that the two killings were justified, but the investigation—being cops, they wanted to know every detail of what was happening. She sighed, saying nothing.

"I want just five minutes with Mrs. McCamy. She's got to be the weak link here."

Katie sighed again. "Listen to me, Miles. The fact is we don't have any evidence yet against either of the McCamys. What's even more to the point is that none of us can come up with a single reason why either Elsbeth or Reverend McCamy would be involved in Sam's kidnapping. Until we have evidence, and a glimmering of a motive, both of them have their rights."

"There's got to be a reason," Miles said, smacking his fist against his open palm. "This is driving me nuts."

Katie dashed her fingers through her hair, dislodging the rest of it from the big banana clip. With fast impatient movements, she twisted it up again and clamped down the clip. French braiding was the only way to keep her hair on her head where it belonged, but she hadn't had time this morning. One long hank of hair was left curling in front of her right ear and she shoved it back. She said, "It's driving all of us nuts, Miles. Savich and Sherlock should be here soon with the kids. Let's hope they've got something to tell us."

Miles looked at Katie straight on. "I'm going to talk to Elsbeth McCamy myself."

Katie grabbed his arm just before he could get to the door, only to have it open in their faces. Sherlock smiled at both of them, seeing all the fear and frustration. She watched as Katie gently laid her hand on Miles's forearm. "Don't ever shoot unless you're sure you've got bullets in your gun, Miles. The McCamys are suspects, sure, and we're going to try to find out everything we can about them, but until we've turned up something, they get to sit back and watch us. Them's the rules, you know that. Hi, Sherlock. You have Sam and Keely? Are they ready for lunch?"

"I hope you've got something," Miles said and stomped out of Katie's office. "Where are Sam and Keely?"

"Linnie took them to the bathroom," Sherlock said.

Katie said, "Let me go tell my deputies where I'll be." She walked off in her long, no-nonsense stride, half her hair falling down her back, the other half tightly held in the clip.

Miles quickly realized that Savich was in pain. He was standing very stiffly, like he was afraid to move at all, and his eyes were a bit unfocused. Miles said, "Sherlock, you got some more pain meds for the Iron Man here?"

Sherlock saw that Miles was right, even though the one he'd had not more than fifteen minutes ago should have kicked in. It scared her to her toes, she couldn't help it. She touched her fingers to his cheek. "We can't have this. You're white about the mouth, partner." She pulled out a pill bottle, dumped out another pill into her palm, filled a paper cup at the drinking fountain and gave it to him. "Don't even speak to me until you've got it down your gullet."

At that moment, Savich would have taken the whole bottle if she'd given it to him.

"This is a surprise," Miles said, stroking his jaw as he looked at Savich. "He didn't even try to kiss you off."

"No, he's not stupid," Sherlock said as her fingers touched his forearm, willing her fear for him to subside.

Savich liked her touching him. It felt good. And because she knew him well, because she hated his pain, she continued to stroke him.

"He needs to rest, but of course he doesn't get enough."

"Let's have lunch first," Savich said, "and yes, Miles, we've got some stuff to tell you. Don't fret, sweetheart, I'll be okay. These pills work pretty fast." He lifted her hand off his forearm, and lightly squeezed her fingers.

"Dillon, why don't you sit down over here for just a moment?"

"Let it go, Sherlock," and she did, as hard as it was. She wished at that moment that they were lying on the beach in Maui and had nothing more to do than suck mai tais through a straw.

At Maude's Burgers, everyone ordered a thick hamburger except for

Savich, who had grilled West Coast swordfish on sourdough bread, which was interesting but had never been close to San Francisco.

"He's a vegetarian," Sherlock said to Katie. "Sometimes, on special occasions like this, he has fish."

"Why is this special, Uncle Dillon?" Keely asked, chewing each long french fry down to the grease.

"It's special because both you and Sam are heroes. And because we're all here together. Sam, it doesn't look to me like you're really enjoying your hamburger."

Sam, who couldn't speak until he'd swallowed the huge bite he'd taken, gave Savich a big, ketchup-smeared smile.

Ten minutes later, when Keely and Sam were eating chocolate chip ice cream, focused on each other and the chocolate chips they were carefully picking from the cones, Savich said, his voice pitched low, "Jimmy Maitland called just a while ago. The math teacher killer hit again, and he wants us back on the investigation. They need fresh eyes and he says we're the freshest eyes he's got. He sounds more desperate than I've heard him in a long while. The media attention had died down after they'd thrashed over the second killing, but now, with the third, they'll have 'serial killer' plastered all over the TV and the newspapers."

Sherlock said, "He also wants us to come back for a press conference at headquarters tonight. We have no choice at all in this."

"There are lots of good people," Savich said, "but when you mix three different police departments and the FBI together and try to coordinate who's going to be top dog, it can get ugly real fast."

Katie said, "I heard that after the second math teacher killing, the politicians started getting into the act."

"They'll want to ban every gun in the universe, including the one the shooter's using," Sherlock told her. "I can just imagine how difficult it is for the local jurisdictions to deal with this, particularly when the politicians are competing for sound bites."

Sherlock sighed, her eyes for a moment on Savich's plate, where most of his swordfish sandwich was left untouched. "One thing is absolutely true: Everyone is scared. Everyone wants to catch this guy, and the pressure keeps growing."

"Maitland said that the principals in the high schools in the killing areas haven't put up any road blocks if the math teachers want to leave town for a while," Savich said. "It's rather like closing the barn door after the horses have run out."

"Three people dead," Sherlock said, shaking her head. "Maitland scheduled the press conference late enough so we'll have time to speak to the third victim's husband beforehand."

"So what are you going to say at this press conference?" Katie asked as she sipped her coffee.

Savich started to say he didn't have a clue, but instead he suddenly just got up from the table and went outside. They watched him talking on his cell phone.

"My husband just got a brain flash," Sherlock said, amused satisfaction in her voice. "The last time it happened, Sean was sprawled on Dillon's chest. Dillon grabbed him under one arm and took him to MAX. An hour later, the Detroit cops arrested a man who worked behind the counter at Trailways Bus in Detroit for the murder of three runaway teenagers, all of whom had left Detroit on Trailways. He'd followed all of them and killed them."

"Why, for heaven's sake?" Katie asked.

"He never really said, just cried so hard his nose was running. Even after six months of nonstop shrinks, I don't think anyone ever understood what he was all about. He's locked away now in a state mental hospital."

Savich came back into the restaurant, sat down, took a bite of his fish sandwich, and said absolutely nothing.

Miles said to Savich, "So all of a sudden, your brain just announced— *bang!*—the killer was a counter clerk at Trailways?"

Savich looked blank until Sherlock said, "I was telling them about the Detroit case, Dillon."

He nodded. "The cops had questioned all the employees at Trailways, but they didn't spot this guy as a viable suspect. Well, I'd just been giving it a lot of thought, that's all, and I took a guess. I asked them to follow this guy for three days."

"What happened?" Katie asked, spellbound.

"He picked out our undercover agent, who was really twenty-six years old but looked fifteen, as his next victim. We got him."

"Okay, Dillon, what's the brain flash this time?"

He smiled at Sherlock, then shook his head at the others. "Too soon for me to say. Now, the big question. It's Tuesday, what do you want to do, Miles?"

"I don't know yet, but I guess I need to stay here for a while longer," and he looked over at Sam and Keely.

Savich saw that he was pissed, frustrated, and nearly at the end of his tether. "Both of you," he said, "keep us informed."

Katie became suddenly aware that both Sam and Keely were all ears, down to the last licks on their cones. "Finish your ice cream, kids," she said, and wiped a bit of chocolate chip off Keely's mouth.

TWENTY-SIX

At eight o'clock that evening, at FBI Headquarters in Washington, D.C., Savich stood beside FBI Assistant Director Jimmy Maitland, waiting for the police chief of Oxford, Maryland, to turn the mike back over to them. The police chiefs from all three jurisdictions were lined up behind the podium, trying to look confident in front of all the blinding lights and the shouted questions.

Standing beside the chiefs were the three victims' husbands: Troy Ward, looking sad and puffy in a bright blue suit; Gifford Fowler, skinny as a post, standing with a big black Stetson in his hands; and Crayton Maddox, a successful attorney, looking as pale as a ghost, still in shock. He'd managed to dress himself in a Saville Row suit that had to have set him back a couple thousand dollars. Looking at the man now, Savich thought back to the meeting he and Sherlock had with him only two hours before, at his home in Lockridge, Virginia.

He and Sherlock had driven to Lockridge High School in Lockridge, Virginia, an affluent suburb favored by many upper-level government employees. The crime investigators, local and FBI, were still there, and six officers were keeping the media behind a police rope.

Police Chief Thomas Martinez met them in the principal's office and said without preamble, "The janitor spotted a small leak late Monday afternoon, in the boiler room. He repaired it, then said he couldn't sleep for worrying so he came back early this morning, before six o'clock, to see that everything was still holding." The chief stopped and grimaced. "He smelled something. It was Mrs. Maddox, one of our five math teachers. Evidently she'd stayed late to grade some test papers because she and her family were leaving for the Caribbean in the morning. Her husband said he'd talked her into leaving because of the two killings. In any case, she never made it home. Her husband called us around nine o'clock last evening, scared out of his mind. He'd called her cell, gotten no answer. We searched nonstop for her. The janitor found her. Come this way."

It was not a pretty sight. Mrs. Eleanor Maddox, not above thirty-five, two children, and a whiz at teaching geometry, had been shoved in beside the boiler. Because the weather was cool the boiler had fired up, and that was why the janitor had smelled her body. She'd been shot right between the eyes, up very close, just like the other two women.

Chief Martinez said, "The forensic team finished up about three hours ago. The ME said if he had to guess, it was a .38, just like the other two. He also said that this time, the guy had moved her here after he'd shot her."

"No witnesses?"

"Not a one, so far."

"Not even a strange car in the vicinity?"

He shook his head. "No. I have officers canvassing the entire neighborhood. No one saw a thing. Basketball practice and the student club meetings were over, so there weren't any other students or teachers around that we know of."

Sherlock said, "I guess he didn't want her found right away. What does the husband have to say, Chief?"

The husband, Crayton Maddox, was a big legal mover and shaker in Washington, his forte forging limitless access to politicians for lobbying groups willing to pay for the privilege. Exactly what that meant, Mr. Maddox didn't explain, and Savich, cynical to his toes, didn't ask. It was nearly six o'clock in the evening, but Mr. Maddox was still wearing his robe. There were coffee stains on the front of it. He was wearing socks, no shoes. He looked like he'd been awake for a week, and none of those waking hours had been pleasant.

Crayton Maddox said, "I called all her friends, all the teachers she worked with, I even called her mother, and I haven't spoken to that woman in nearly two years." He stopped a moment, tears choking him, and stared at Savich. "God, don't you see? This just isn't right; it shouldn't have happened. Ellie never hurt a soul, not even me, and I'm a lawyer. She planned on working until we left for the Caribbean, even though I tried to convince her to stay home, not take any chances. Why did he kill her? Why?"

Savich had no answer. "I know you've already spoken to Chief

Martinez, and he'll give us all the details. We're here to ask you to join us at a press conference in a couple of hours at FBI Headquarters. I know you'll want to hear about all that's being done and it would be helpful to us if you came. I think it's important that the world see victims' families, see what devastation this sort of mindless violence can cause. Mr. Ward and Mr. Fowler, the first two victims' husbands, will be there. Will you join us, Mr. Maddox?"

Crayton Maddox bent his head and, to Savich's surprise, didn't ask a single question. Then he said, "Did you know that I called Margie, my assistant? She was here before seven o'clock this morning. She knows everything, that's what I told Chief Martinez, everything about both me and my wife." He paused a moment, glanced down at his Rolex, then out the living room window. "Good God, it's dark outside." He looked up at them. "I'm usually about ready to come home from my office at six o'clock in the evening. Ellie always got home around four o'clock. She wanted to be here when the kids got home."

They heard crying from upstairs, a woman's soothing voice. The children, Sherlock thought. There'd been no children involved in the first two killings. Why had the killer changed?

"My mother-in-law," he said, glancing up at the ceiling. "Margie called her and she was here in ten minutes. I guess we'll have to start speaking again." He stood, all hunched forward, like he hadn't moved in far too long. "I'll be at your press conference, Agent."

Assistant Director Jimmy Maitland nodded to Savich, then stepped to the podium. He spoke of the cooperation among the three police departments, spoke of the activity by the FBI at the crime scenes, and repeated the hot-line number for any information on the killings. He finished his words to the roomful of reporters with "And this is Special Agent Dillon Savich, chief of the Criminal Apprehension Unit of the FBI."

Most of the reporters knew who Savich was. Jimmy Maitland barely had time to shut his mouth before several reporters yelled out together, "Agent Savich, why is he killing math teachers?"

"Since all the victims are women, do you think it's a man?"

Savich stepped up to the podium, said nothing at all until the room was quiet, which was very quickly. He knew many of them were jotting down descriptions of him and of the grieving husbands. He said, "Mr. George, you asked why is he killing math teachers, and Mr. Dobbs pointed out that all the victims have been women. Yes, we believe the killer is a man. As to why he's doing this, we have some ideas, but it's not appropriate to discuss all the possibilities with you at this stage in the investigation."

"Is the guy crazy?"

Savich stared thoughtfully at Martha Stockton of the *Washington Post*, who had the reputation of being something of a ditz, but this time she had stripped away the nonessentials really fast. "No, I don't think he's crazy in the sense that he's frothing at the mouth and out of control. He seems to have planned these killings well enough that so far there are no witnesses. Why he's doing this, we don't know yet, but I will tell you this: We will find him. We are spending hundreds of man-hours speaking to fellow teachers and former students. We are leaving nothing to chance.

"Now, I would like to introduce to you some of the family members affected by these tragic killings. These are the widowers of the murdered teachers, Mr. Ward, Mr. Fowler, and Mr. Maddox, whose wife was found just this morning. I believe Mr. Ward and Mr. Fowler wish to make a brief statement."

Mr. Eli Dobbs of CNN yelled out, "Excuse me, Mr. Maddox, but your wife was just murdered. How do you feel about standing up there with Mr. Ward and Mr. Fowler?"

That show of crassness was par for the course, Savich thought. He raised his hand. "We will take a few questions later. This is a time of grief and shock for these gentlemen. You might consider their circumstances before you ask your questions."

Troy Ward stepped forward and grabbed the edges of the podium. "I want to thank all those who have sent me cards and e-mails. The police are doing their best, I know, and I just want to thank everyone for their support and their thoughtfulness to me and my wife's family at this terrible time." With that, he stood back from the podium, his eyes on his shoes.

"You didn't call this Sunday's Ravens game, Mr. Ward," Eli Dobbs said. "What are your plans?"

Troy answered, but without the microphone in front of him, the reporters had to strain to hear him. "I'm planning to announce the game this Sunday. My wife would have wanted life to go on."

Gifford Fowler took his turn at the podium. He said simply, "My wife was the love of my life. I miss her every moment," and he also thanked the public. He didn't step back, though, and looked like he wanted questions.

"Mr. Fowler, we've been told you're going to speak at the Rotary Club this Wednesday."

Gifford Fowler said, "They said they wanted to show their support, to share their time with me for an evening. I am very grateful to them for inviting me."

Savich cut it off, stepping back to the podium. He wasn't about to have Mr. Maddox in front of this group. His loss was too new, his control too tenuous. Besides, the world had seen them up close and personal. It was enough.

"Have your computers been of any help yet, Agent Savich?"

"Is MAX going to stand up there and announce the killer?"

There was laughter.

Savich smiled. "MAX is a tremendous tool. But here's the truth: Crimes are solved by good old-fashioned police work. And that's what we're doing, as fast and as hard as we can. Thank you for coming."

When it was all over, Savich gave Sherlock a small salute, then turned to speak to the three widowers. "I thank you for coming. I think it makes a difference. Of course there'll be more questions. I will be in touch with each of you. As soon as we know something, we'll let you know."

He shook hands with all of the men, then watched them closely as they trailed out, following an agent through the rear door.

Sherlock took his hand and said in a whisper, "That was quite a performance. Do you think it was worth it?"

He turned, cupped her face in his hands, and said, "I think so. We'll see."

LATER that night, back home in Georgetown, Sean was asleep on his father's shoulder after helping his parents eat a late dinner of his father's pesto pasta. Sherlock said while she heated some hot water for tea, "Miles called. Dr. Raines is still seeing Sam. Miles thinks it's best to keep him with her for a while longer. Also, he can't imagine separating Sam and Keely just yet."

"I can't imagine it either," Savich said. "Sam is probably as safe there as at home, and Katie has a couple of deputies around him whenever she or Miles can't be with them. I'll bet he'll get Katie to take him to see the McCamys."

Sherlock nodded. "You're probably right. And right now, I can't imagine Sam being away from Keely either."

"Yeah," Savich said slowly, as he watched her pour his tea into his favorite Redskins mug, "and I was wondering how Miles would do away from the sheriff."

Sherlock shrugged. "Two very strong people slapped together in a mess like this . . ."

"Yeah, but let's keep out of it, Sherlock. Neither of us has a clue as to what will happen between them, if anything."

"The children are very important to both of them," she said. The phone rang and she turned to answer it. It was Agent Dane Carver, to catch Savich up on his case in Miami.

ON Wednesday morning Savich was so stiff and sore, he knew he had to do something. Walking on the treadmill sounded like just what he needed. He'd forgotten all about Valerie Rapper. But evidently she hadn't forgotten him. She was there at the gym, waiting for him. Did the woman have spies? Her timing was incredible.

He raised an eyebrow at her. "It's ten o'clock in the morning," he said.

"I sometimes like to work out in the mornings. I saw you on TV last night, Agent Savich," she said, looking over at him as she pressed in ten minutes on the treadmill next to him. "Those poor husbands, I guess you really wanted to remind the public how horrific all this is, and that's why you showed them off."

Savich grunted again. His back was sore, but the walking was helping to loosen it up a bit. Sherlock had bandaged him up really well, knowing he wouldn't do anything too stupid, but since she'd been muttering under her breath at the time, he wasn't sure.

"What's wrong? You're moving like you're hurt. What happened?"

There was real concern in her voice. He looked over at her and said in his mildest, most unthreatening voice, "Nothing's wrong. Just a pulled muscle."

"I thought you were moving a bit stiffly on television last night."

"I'll be fine." He looked pointedly down at the book he was reading.

"Would you go for a cup of coffee after you're finished working out? I'm buying."

He smiled. "Thank you, Ms. Rapper, but I'm married. I don't go out for coffee with other women even if they're offering to pay."

She laughed. "Sure you can. It's no big deal. I'm not going to seduce you, Agent Savich, it's only a cup of coffee, a bit of conversation."

He shook his head. "Sorry."

"Perhaps it's time for you to loosen up a bit, have a bit of fun. I know, I know, what fun can you have over coffee? It's possible, I swear."

Savich said, "You've probably seen my wife here at the gym—red curly hair, big blue eyes. She's also an FBI agent. Her name's Sherlock."

"That's ridiculous."

"What? Hair? Name? The fact that she's an agent?"

"Her name," she said, looking into the mirror behind Dillon Savich. "Her name is ridiculous."

"Rapper's pretty funny, too."

She stopped in her tracks. "Yes," she said slowly, "perhaps it is." She looked at him again, but he couldn't begin to read her expression. She punched the stop pad, stepped off the treadmill before it stopped, and walked away. She said over her shoulder, giving him a profile that she knew was superb, "You just think about having coffee with me, Agent Savich, all right?"

She was gone before he could answer.

TWENTY-SEVEN

It was a beautiful Wednesday morning. Katie looked up at the blue sky with its fat scattered white clouds, and followed them to the ever-present wall of mountains just off to the east. They were covered with maple, poplar, beech, and sugar maples in gorgeous reds and bright yellows and golds, the pines and firs holding to their green. Even the browns looked lustrous, magical, a magnificent palette of colors. There was simply no more beautiful a spot in the world than eastern Tennessee in the late fall. It was about fifty-five degrees, just enough nip in the day for her leather jacket. She breathed in the delicious smell of leaves mixed with the smoke from wood-burning fireplaces. Moments like this made Katie wish she could put off winter, with its frigid winds and snow and stripped-down trees.

She kept the engine running as she watched Miles lead Sam and Keely to Minna's front porch. He leaned down, spoke to both children, and touched each of them—Sam's arm and Keely's hair. They both hugged him, then ran to Keely's grandmother when she opened the front door. Chocolate chip cookies, Katie thought, remembering her excitement when she'd been a kid. She watched the two deputies take their positions, guarding the house with Sam and Keely in it. She made another sweep of the area. Nothing out of the ordinary.

Sam seemed just fine to Katie, thank God. This morning he groused and complained, just like Keely, when Katie had given him oatmeal and not Cheerios, an excellent sign. Miles hadn't helped when he'd looked at the oatmeal, blinked, and said he'd always thought oatmeal was good for making grout, but not eating. The kids had laughed, and Katie, just smiling, waited, until he took a big spoonful, rolled his eyes and said, "This is the best grout I've ever eaten. Here, Sam, take a bite of this." And Sam had said he loved it, and tried to roll his eyes just like his dad. There'd been laughter at the breakfast table, and that had felt very good. She'd also found herself smiling at Miles for no good reason she could think of.

Sam would see Sheila again today, in the early afternoon, but Sheila had told her and Miles that Sam talked more about Keely now and how he'd stuffed tons of leaves down her shirt. He talked more about Jessborough and Mrs. Miggs at the quilt shop who gave the children peppermints than he did about his kidnapping or about Clancy and Beau. It was a good sign, a very hopeful thing. Sheila was sure he wasn't holding back. He was a resilient little kid.

He was more than that, Katie thought, much more than that, especially to her, and that wasn't particularly wise. She got out of her truck and walked up the driveway. All was clear.

When Miles joined her, he said, "I doubt they'll even give us a thought. Your mom is the best, Katie." He paused a moment, drew in a deep breath, reached out his hand to touch a vivid gold maple leaf and said, "How much longer will it look like God's country around here?"

"Another two, three weeks, at most," she said. "Then the storms start coming. We have snow mostly in February and March. And that's beautiful, too. But right now? This is perfect."

He walked automatically to the driver's side of Katie's Silverado, then stopped, frowning.

"No, go ahead and drive." She tossed him the keys.

He saw the lock box on the floor in the back that held her rifle, the rifle she'd used to save Sam.

He said as he fastened his seat belt, "Those two deputies, they're good?"

She nodded, feeling exactly what he was feeling. "Cole and Jeffrey will really keep their eyes open. They both saw what happened at my house when Clancy and Beau went down, so they know this is way out of the ordinary. They're so wired, in fact, I told them to stick to decaf. This was the first time either of them had been involved in any real violence professionally."

"What kind of training do your deputies get?"

"They all have a ten-week training course at the law enforcement academy in Donelson, near Nashville. My people have also taken courses at the local junior college—Walters State, you know, law enforcement and judicial courses. Wade is trying to get so many courses under his belt that—well, never mind."

"Is he the one who might be trying to get your job?"

She gave him a sunny smile. "No chance of that."

Miles liked that smile of hers, and the mouth that made those smiles, and that gave him pause. He didn't have to move the seat back much at all. He looked over at her, an eyebrow arched. "What do you mean they haven't seen violence? Violence is part of their job, isn't it?"

Katie laughed. "Jessborough isn't Knoxville or Chattanooga. The toughest thing any of them has had to do here in the sheriff's department of Jessborough is round up Mr. Bailey's cows after they were spooked by a low-flying crop duster in August. This is a small town with very few bad outside influences. No hard drugs, just some pot our locals grow, and an occasional still deep in the hills, which is kind of a tradition around here. Most people consider that good clean fun." She paused a moment, looked out the window, and said, "We had nothing but peace here until this happened. I have ten deputies, all of them men. The testosterone has been flowing madly since I got Sam on Saturday."

"Linnie is some dispatcher."

"Yes, she's excellent, knows everyone's problems, knows about all their relationships, even the illicit ones. She's the backbone of the department. I would seriously consider hurting anyone who tried to take her away from me."

She directed him to the big Victorian on Pine Wood Lane. As he looked at the house, realized who lived there, he felt his insides chill.

Her hand was light on his forearm. "We will be professional about this, Miles. Do you agree?"

He nodded. "I swear I won't tie up either of them in their playroom."

"Good."

"But I was thinking I'd like to see what they've got in there."

"You into whips and handcuffs?"

"Not that I know of." He looked thoughtful, grinned at her, and said, "I promise not to drop-kick them out one of those big front windows either."

"Good," she said again. "We got some new cards to play. If we do it really carefully, something might pop."

Katie pressed the doorbell, heard a light footfall. A few moments later, Elsbeth McCamy answered. She looked just like she always looked: hot. It always amazed Katie that she was with Reverend McCamy, who was so dark and serious and intense, his entire being seemingly focused inward on the state of his soul. Every word out of his mouth was a paean to his God, and to his notions that men should be victims of His love. Victim of love—what a strange choice of words, but now it had a new meaning to her.

Katie looked at the woman standing there in tight jeans, a red spandex top, and the Jesus earrings and thought about the sex room upstairs with that padded wooden block. She wondered what his congregation thought of Elsbeth, but truth be told, she'd never heard anything that indicated anyone thought them mismatched or that a sexpot like her shouldn't be a preacher's wife. Like nearly all people in Jessborough, they never caused trouble.

Katie nodded but didn't extend her hand. "Elsbeth."

"Hello, Katie. Why are you here?" She wasn't looking at Katie, she was studying Miles Kettering, a perfect eyebrow hiked up. "You were in church on Sunday."

"Yes."

"You're the boy's father."

"Elsbeth, this is Miles Kettering, and yes, he's Sam's father. We would very much like to speak to you and Reverend McCamy."

"Reverend McCamy is ministering to two of his flock," Elsbeth said. "Mr. and Mrs. Locke. They're in his study. I don't expect him to be free for another half hour or so."

"May we speak to you until he's free?"

It was quite obvious she didn't want to let them in, but she couldn't think of a reason to keep them out. Grudgingly, Elsbeth stepped back.

"This way," she said. "I'm making some brownies for Reverend McCamy. They're his favorite. Where is your son, Mr. Kettering?"

"Sam is at the sheriff's department, supervising all the deputies."

Elsbeth laughed. "He's a cute little boy. Is Keely with him?"

"Oh yes," Katie said. "They've become inseparable." Now, why had Miles lied about Sam's whereabouts?

"It's comforting to know what we get for our tax dollars, isn't it?"

Katie said, "I'm sorry about your brother."

"Are you really?"

"Yes. I'm a sheriff, not a killer. I can't imagine Reverend McCamy liking brownies."

"Why ever not? He has quite a sweet tooth."

Katie shrugged. "Somehow I think of him as always being too above all of life's pleasures, immersed in his work—"

"His calling," Elsbeth said, frowning. "It's not his work, it's his calling. God chose him above all others to lead the common man to Him."

"Not women, too?"

"Of course," she said, her voice cutting. Then she lowered her voice as if someone were trying to overhear. "God has granted him His grace, he is God's messenger, so special that God gave him the beauty of suffering."

Miles said, "What do you mean 'suffering,' Mrs. McCamy? How can there be beauty in suffering?"

"It can be a gift to us, Mr. Kettering. Reverend McCamy likes his brownies with pecans, lots of pecans."

When Katie and Miles were settled at the kitchen table with cups of coffee in front of them, Katie said, "I heard a rumor, Elsbeth. I'd like to scotch it and so I figured the only way to know the truth is to come out and just ask."

Elsbeth turned, a can of cocoa in her hand. "What rumor?"

"That you and Reverend McCamy are thinking about leaving the area."

Elsbeth nearly dropped the can. "Goodness, where did you hear that, Katie?"

She was aware that Miles was wondering what she was up to. She just smiled, sipped her coffee, and wondered if indeed Reverend McCamy had been seen going into a real estate office in Knoxville. She said as she watched Elsbeth's hand shake as she measured a teaspoon of baking powder into the mixing bowl, "You know rumors—they're talked about everywhere but don't seem to begin anywhere."

"Well, it's wrong. Of course we're not leaving. Reverend McCamy is very happy here, despite that nasty televangelist over in Knoxville. That miserable man happened to find out that Reverend McCamy was approached by the producers on the cable station, and now he's trying to make everyone believe he's the spawn of the Devil, the bastard."

"What's this bastard's name?"

"James Russert, a real tacky individual, right up there with most of the others who bleat on TV and collect millions of dollars from gullible people."

And Reverend McCamy's congregation wasn't gullible?

Katie had seen Russert, a loud, blustering Bible-thumping TV preacher she turned off as fast as she could.

Elsbeth looked around at them, a big chocolate-covered spoon in her hand. "We've heard that you're harassing our congregation, talking to them at work, following them home. It's disgraceful, Sheriff, disgraceful."

"We're conducting an investigation, Elsbeth. Be sensible, you're up front because Clancy was your brother. Naturally you're part of the investigation."

TWENTY-EIGHT

Elsbeth waved that spoon at them, sending some of the chocolate flying. "I want you to leave us and our parishioners alone, or we will find a lawyer who will stop you. Do you understand me?"

Suddenly, she shrugged and turned back to the brownie bowl. She said over her shoulder as she measured more cocoa into a measuring cup, her voice calm again, under control, "Neither I nor Reverend Mc-Camy know anything about this. We have told you this repeatedly. Reverend McCamy loves God. More importantly, he is beloved by God and all those who bask in His grace. He doesn't speak ill of anyone."

"He doesn't speak ill of sinners?" Miles's voice was so mild he surprised himself.

"Regular sinners—our local sinners—they know they're in trouble. They know they need Reverend McCamy to help them rise above their sins."

Miles asked in that same mild voice after a moment of silence, "I understand that Reverend McCamy believes women need more assistance than men."

Elsbeth McCamy paused a moment, then in a sharp angry movement, pulled a bag of pecans out of a cabinet and dumped the whole bag into a bowl. "Well, not exactly, but we let our righteous men guide us. Reverend McCamy is very serious about every member of his flock leading the sort of life that will grant him God's grace. As for the women of his flock, we know it was Eve who tempted Adam to abandon God's commands, and so it is women who must bear her sin."

What to say to that? Katie and Miles sat in silence, watching Elsbeth mix the ingredients together. She was humming under her breath, comfortable with what she was doing.

How, Miles wondered, watching this woman mix brownies, how

could this very strange, very beautiful woman be involved in the kidnapping of his son? But Clancy was her brother. He couldn't forget that, ever. Miles said, "My son was kidnapped for a reason, Mrs. McCamy. Perhaps you could tell us what this reason is."

She nearly dropped the bowl to the clean pale cream tile floor. Katie held very still, her face not giving away that she wanted to punch Miles. Talk about rushing fences. She saw Elsbeth's face, just as Miles did, and it was as obvious to her as it was to Miles that Elsbeth McCamy knew something. It would have been obvious to the postman. Katie realized then that Miles's unexpected question had shocked her into giving at least that much away.

Elsbeth picked up a wooden spoon and began to vigorously stir the brownie batter. She was stirring so hard he could hear the pecans crunch against the sides of the bowl.

Elsbeth walked to the oven and turned it on, still saying nothing at all. She returned to the kitchen counter and continued beating the brownie batter. There was raw fury in every whip of the spoon.

Her Jesus earrings caught the sunlight from the kitchen window when she turned suddenly. "I want you both to leave. I've been polite, but this is police harassment and—"

"Elsbeth, what are you doing in here?"

She turned very slowly, picking up the bowl as she did so, and holding it in front of her, as if for protection. Now that was odd, particularly since it was Reverend McCamy's voice, her husband's.

"We have visitors who were just leaving. I'm making brownies for you."

He came into the kitchen, those dark intense eyes fastened on that brownie batter, but he said nothing to his wife. His eyes passed over Katie, stopped at Miles, and he said, "You're the boy's father, aren't you?"

"Yes, I'm Sam's father. Miles Kettering."

Reverend McCamy didn't approach him, and Miles was glad. He didn't want to shake the man's hand. He appeared to be studying Miles, and thinking hard.

"I have wondered," Miles said, "why you have named your church the Sinful Children of God?"

Reverend McCamy said, "Because of the first sin, Mr. Kettering. A sin so grave that Adam and Eve were forever cursed and forced to suffer for what she had done." He paused a moment, looked briefly at his wife, then at Katie. He stepped over to the counter and ran a finger along the edge of the brownie bowl and licked off the batter, closing his eyes a moment. Well, Katie thought, that was certainly one kind of bliss. Then his eyes snapped open and he seemed once again the prophet ready to condemn the sinners. He said, "It is written to woman in Genesis: 'Your desire shall be for your husband, and he shall rule over you.' It is a pity your husband left you, Katie. He took away the focus of your life."

"I cannot tell you how pleased I am about that," Katie said and smiled sweetly at Reverend McCamy.

Miles thought the man was mad.

"A husband is a woman's shepherd," Reverend McCamy said, his dark eyes resting hard on Katie's face. "Without his guidance, without his support and discipline, she will fall into sin and be struck down."

Katie looked this time as if she wanted to leap on Reverend McCamy, but the flash of murder in her eyes was gone in an instant. She even smiled. "I see you love brownie batter. I do, too. Could I have some, Elsbeth?"

Miles wondered just how long Reverend McCamy had been listening outside the kitchen. Had he been afraid his wife would give something away?

Miles said, "You probably heard me asking your wife why her brother kidnapped my boy."

Reverend McCamy didn't acknowledge Miles's words. He said, "Suffering draws us closer to God, even a little boy's suffering, if it is God's divine will."

Katie said, "I don't understand, Reverend McCamy. How can a little boy's suffering conform to God's divine will? That makes no sense to me. Do you mean that God wants everyone, including children, to suffer?"

He whispered, his eyes on Katie's face, "You misunderstand. I'm speaking of our conforming to the Cross of Christ. It is written: 'Whoever does not bear his own cross and come after me, cannot be my disciple.' It is man's highest gift to suffer for the love of God, to suffer so that he can come closer to a union with the Divine. Of course, only a very few of the blessed ones are granted such divine grace."

"What do you mean conforming to the cross?" Katie asked. "As in one should want to be crucified? That would please God?"

Miles could tell that Reverend McCamy wanted to lay his hands on Katie. To bless her or to punish her because he thought she was blaspheming? He couldn't tell.

Reverend McCamy said, all patience, so patronizing that Miles imagined Katie standing up and smacking him in the jaw if she weren't so focused on what she was doing, "We must embrace suffering to lead us ever closer to God, and in this suffering, there is greatness and submission. No, God does not wish us to be crucified like him. That is shallow and blind, meaning nothing. It is far more than that, far deeper, far more enveloping. Very rarely God's grace is bestowed on a living creature and is manifested in the imitation of Christ's travails on the cross."

Katie said, never looking away from Reverend McCamy's face, "You said that God doesn't want us to nail ourselves to a cross in imitation of the crucifixion. What then is this gift bestowed on so very few?"

Reverend McCamy said, "How long does it take for the brownies to bake, Elsbeth?"

"Thirty minutes," Elsbeth said. She never looked her husband in the face, nor did she look at Miles or Katie. She slipped the glass dish inside the oven, then turned to the sink to run water in the batter bowl.

Too bad, Katie had *really* wanted a taste of that batter. It was time to push again, time to maneuver him where she wanted him to go. She said, "These individuals who imitate Christ's suffering, who and what are they? How are they selected? And by whom?"

Elsbeth whispered, "Don't you understand? Reverend McCamy is one of the very few blessed by God's grace, who is blessed by God's ecstasy in suffering."

Reverend McCamy looked like he wanted to slap her, but he didn't move, just fisted his hands at his sides.

Katie said, ever so gently, her eyes as intense as Reverend McCamy's, "You're speaking of Christ's wounds appearing on a mortal's body. You're saying that Reverend McCamy is a—what are they called?"

"Stigmatist," said Reverend McCamy.

"And you're a stigmatist, aren't you, sir?"

He looked furious that she'd pushed him to this, and Miles realized in that instant that she indeed had, and she'd done it very well. For a moment Reverend McCamy didn't say anything. Katie knew he was trying to get himself under control and it was difficult for him.

Katie said, "Homer Bean, one of your former parishioners, told us that you'd told a small group of men one evening about being a victim of God's love, about being a stigmatist."

Reverend McCamy said without looking up, "Since they have told you, then I will not deny it. Once in my life I was blessed to have the suffering of ecstasy with blood flowing from my hands in imitation of the nails driven through our Lord's palms."

Katie said, "You're saying that blood flowed from your palms? That you have actually experienced this?"

"Yes, I have been blessed. God granted me this passionate and tender gift. The pain and the ecstasy—the two together provide incalculable profit to the soul. I have kept this private, all except for those few men in whom I once confided."

Katie said, "And how is it you were chosen for this, Reverend?"

"You must recognize and accept the divine presence, Katie. You must believe that it is too overwhelming for mankind to fathom, that it must be the expression of ultimate faith. Thus the godless have sought to belittle this divine ecstasy, to trivialize it, to turn it into some sort of freak show. But it isn't, for I have had my blood flow from my own palms."

Miles said, fed up with this fanatic, his strange wife, and the damned brownies in the oven, "This is all very fascinating, McCamy, but can you tell me why Clancy and Beau kidnapped my son?"

It was as if someone flipped off the light switch. Reverend McCamy's eyes became even darker, as if a black tide was roiling up through his body. He shuddered, as if bringing himself out of someplace very deep, very far away. He said, "Your son is one of God's children, Mr. Kettering. I will pray for your son, and I will ask God to intercede." With that, Reverend McCamy turned and walked out of the kitchen. After a moment, they heard him call out, "Elsbeth, bring the brownies to my study when they're done. You don't have to cool them."

She nodded, even though he was no longer there. "Yes, Reverend McCamy."

Katie said to Elsbeth, "Sam is a wonderful little boy. I will not allow him to be taken again. Do you understand me, Elsbeth?"

"Go away, Katie. Go away and take that godless man with you."

"I'm not godless, ma'am. I just don't worship quite the same God you and your husband do."

When they were driving away from that lovely house, Miles said, "That was excellent questioning. I just don't know what it got us."

"I don't either," Katie said. "But I discovered I could pry him open."

"They're in on this, Katie."

"Yes," she said. "I think so, too."

Miles slammed his fist against the steering wheel. "Why, for God's sake? Why?"

TWENTY-NINE

Sam and Keely were playing chess, loosely speaking, given that Keely had had only two lessons. Katie had a No-TV rule during the week so the house was quiet, with just a soft layer of light rock coming from the speakers, and an occasional ember popping in the fireplace. The air felt thick, heavy. Another big storm was coming.

"No, Sam," Keely said, "you can't do that. The rook has to go in straight lines, he can't go sideways."

"That's boring," said Sam, and moved his bishop instead because he liked the long diagonal. The only problem was he stopped his bishop in front of a pawn, which Keely promptly removed. Sam yelled out, then sat back, stroked his chin like his father did, and said, "I will think about this and then you'll be very sorry."

Keely crowed.

"Killers, both of them," said Miles, happy to see Sam acting like a normal kid again.

Katie and Miles were seated on opposite ends of the long sofa, doing nothing but sipping coffee and listening to the fascinating chess moves made by two children whose combined age was eleven.

Two deputies, Neil Crooke, who got no end of grief for his name, and Jamie Beezer, who did a great imitation dance of Muhammad Ali in his heyday, were outside watching the house. When Neil called to ask if he could go unlock ancient Mr. Cerlew's 1956 Buick for him since he'd locked his keys in it, Katie said go, but get back as soon as possible.

She excused herself a moment, and came back into the living room with a plate of brownies in her hands. "They're not homemade like Elsbeth's, but I'll tell you, the Harvest Moon bakery can't be beat."

Miles took a brownie, saying, "You think they're better than the ones Elsbeth McCamy made?"

"We'll never know, at least I hope we won't. Kids? Can the chess battle stop for a brownie break?"

When the plate was empty, in just under four minutes, Miles sat back and laced his fingers over his belly. He stretched out his legs, crossed them at the ankles, and leaned his head back against the sofa. He said as he closed his eyes, "It's Wednesday night. I've known you since Saturday. Isn't that amazing?"

Katie slowly nodded even though she knew he couldn't see her, and said, "We're sitting here like two folks who've been sitting here for a very long time." Except for the SIG tucked into the waistband of her jeans and the derringer strapped at her ankle.

That was sure the truth, Miles thought.

Katie stared at the glowing embers in the fireplace that periodically spewed up a mist of color. "It seems much longer," she said after a moment. "It seems natural."

He opened his eyes and turned his head to face her. "I can't stay here indefinitely, Katie, although I'm becoming fond of your microwave and your teakettle. The oatmeal was pretty good, too. But the bed is too short, and Sam snores on occasion." He stopped, and sat forward, his hands clasped between his knees, staring at the rag rug Katie's grandmother had made in the thirties. "This still isn't over, Katie. What am I to do?"

Because Katie didn't have an answer for that, she looked over to make sure the kids were occupied. They were on their stomachs, their noses almost touching the chess pieces. She said, "The meeting with the McCamys—you did good, Miles, asking Elsbeth that question pointblank. At least we know for sure now they're involved—Elsbeth's face gave it all away. She's not good at lying. She'd lose her knickers in a poker game."

Miles said quietly, "All right, they're involved. Tell me why a preacher would have Sam kidnapped."

"Okay, let's just cut to the bone. Reverend McCamy had Clancy and Beau kidnap Sam, told them to take him to Bleaker's cabin. To wait? Why? Well, I suppose, so he could make arrangements."

"For what?"

"We don't know yet, but if that's the case, there has to be a reason, one that makes a great deal of sense to the McCamys. You know, Miles, there was something else Homer Bean mentioned. He said something about Reverend McCamy wanting a successor. No, wanting a *worthy* successor."

"If that rumor about seeing Reverend McCamy in Knoxville at a real estate office is true, and he is planning to pick up stakes, then it would be logical, I suppose, that he'd want to find someone to take his place with all the sinful children. But what does that have to do with Sam? Sam's a little young to be anyone's successor. Just last month I told him for sure that he'd be my successor, but he couldn't take over until he could spell guidance system."

Katie smiled at that. Miles watched her scuff her toe against the carpet and leaned toward her as she said, "Bits and pieces, Miles, that's what we're gathering. Soon it will all come together. We're close, I can feel it. I do wish that Agent Hodges would get back to us on the McCamy personal bank transactions and the church's books."

"Since he had trouble getting a warrant, he said it wouldn't be until tomorrow."

"There's something else. It's Reverend McCamy. I've known him a long time. This is the first time I've seen him come close to losing it. He was out of control a couple of times."

"If they're behind Sam's kidnapping, they have to know that it's just a matter of time before everything collapses."

"Check!"

Sam came up on his knees, shook his fist, and shouted, "You moved the queen like a knight, Keely, and that's cheating!"

Keely punched him in the arm, told him she was tired of chess, and got her favorite board game out of the cabinet, The Game of Life. In the next moment, they were flicking the spinner and laughing, fighting over the rules, which neither of them really understood.

Miles said, "You've done an excellent job with Keely."

"And you with Sam. Can you imagine learning chess from a five-year-old who's had only two lessons?"

"I gather you play?"

"Oh yes, my father gave me my first lesson when I was about Keely's age. There are a couple of old guys who sit out in front of City Hall playing chess, probably been there since the Depression. I've never had the nerve to challenge either of them."

He laughed and said in a voice that was too good an imitation of Reverend McCamy's, "It's a pity your husband left you and you lost your focus."

She laughed, too, but it was forced since she really wanted to spit. "Can you believe he actually said that?"

"You handled him very well."

"Maybe, but Elsbeth still didn't let me taste the brownie batter."

Miles looked at her straight on. She'd French-braided her hair again, and a few tendrils had worked loose to curl around her ears. He really liked that French braid, and those tendrils. She was wearing her usual oxford shirt and jeans, and scuffed low-heeled boots. "I saw a cream-colored straw hat on the coatrack by the front door. Do you ever wear that hat?"

"Oh yes. To be honest, there's just been so much happening, that I haven't thought of it. I'm lucky to remember my coat."

"Eastern Tennessee is a very beautiful place, Katie."

She nodded. "Yes, it is. It's the mountains, really—always there right beside you, going on farther than the eye can see. Then you'll look at this incredible hazy blue glaze over the Appalachians. You know, I've always found it strange that people think we're country bumpkins, living out here. But the fact is, we aren't exiled here. We look up and see more stars than any city person can ever hope to see, and you know what? We actually sometimes feel the urge to talk to strangers. You've seen the cows, the dairy farms, the rolling farmlands. We're rich here, Miles, more than rich, we're blessed."

Miles studied her face as she spoke. "Yes, I can see that." He paused, looked toward the kids, then said, "I won't be here in the winter, Katie."

"No," she said slowly, "I don't suppose you will."

He slashed his hand through the air in frustration but he kept his voice low so the kids wouldn't hear. "Usually I ask a woman I'm interested in to go out to dinner, maybe a show in Washington. Yet here I am living in a woman's house and I've known her for what—four days?"

"I'm the sheriff, that's different."

"Is it?"

She made a restless movement with her hand, then smoothed out her fingers along her thigh. "You know what's funny? My husband never lived here."

He let her sidetrack him, it was safer. "What did you do with the jerk?"

She turned on the sofa, tucked one leg beneath the other, and leaned toward him. "The jerk's name is Carlo Silvestri, and he's the eldest son of an Italian aristocrat, and you're right, he's a jerk all the way down to his Ferragamos."

"An Italian aristocrat? You're kidding."

"Nope. His father is Il Conte Rosso, a big shot who lives near Milan, into arms manufacturing, I believe."

"How ever did you meet an Italian aristocrat?"

She gave a really big sigh. "I still feel like I should punch myself in the head for being so stupid. Carlo and two of his buddies were visiting Nashville. They wanted to see Dolly Parton's breasts, one of them told me, so they drove east. When they landed in Knoxville, one of them, a Frenchman who must have thought it was Le Mans, was speeding like a maniac on Neyland Avenue, one of Knoxville's main streets. I stopped them after a bit of a chase. The idiot had been drinking and nearly went over the guardrail into the Tennessee River."

"So you hauled his ass off to jail?"

"Yeah, I did. Carlo decided he didn't want to leave when his buddy got sprung. He said he fell in love with me when he saw me clap on the handcuffs. It was a whirlwind romance, I'll tell you that. I was twenty-four years old, he was thirty-six, and I knew he was too old for me, knew the last thing he could ever do was leave Italy for good and live in Tennessee, but none of it mattered. I stopped thinking and married him. It didn't matter that he was a spoiled egotist, too rich to have a clue about what responsibility meant. Women do that, you know. Stop thinking."

"So do men."

"For men, it's lust. For women, it's romance. You can get blindsided by both. I got pregnant right away. The problems started probably about a week later and never stopped. When Keely was about a month old, Carlo's father, Carlo Silvestri senior, Il Conte Rosso, shows up on our doorstep in Knoxville, announces that his son called him to come and save him. I really got a good laugh out of that one. I told Carlo senior that I'd removed his son's handcuffs a very long time before."

"So what happened?"

"Daddy did something that will endear him to me and this town for the rest of our collective lives."

Miles sat up. "What did he do?"

"He offered to buy me off for a million dollars if I would divorce

Carlo without fuss, change Keely's name to Benedict—my name—and never contact them again."

"You've got to be joking."

"No, I'm not. I remember I just sat there and stared at him, trying to picture all those zeroes following a one and all those commas actually written out on a check, and wondering: Will they all fit in that little space?

"He actually believed I was playing him, that I was a tough cookie, and so do you know what the dear man did? He actually upped the ante. I'll tell you though, I made sure the money was wired into my account before I agreed. Then both Silvestris were out the door within four hours."

"What was the final buyout?"

"A million and a half big ones. I used it to put my dad's company, Benedict Pulp Mill, back on its feet, which guaranteed a lot of folks around here continued employment and thereby, truth be told, got me elected sheriff of Jessborough. I'm the first woman sheriff of Jessborough or, for that matter, just about anywhere in eastern Tennessee." She frowned at her boots, then said, "I don't know if they would have elected me without the bribe."

"It was more a by-product of the bribe, wasn't it? It's not as though you're incompetent."

"You're a sweet-talking guy, Miles," she said, laughing. "I'll tell you the truth though, I was the best-trained candidate for the job."

"Wade was the one who wanted to be sheriff, wasn't he? The one you beat out for the job?"

She nodded. "Wade's a good man, but he's never worked on the streets of a good-sized city where there's actual crime."

Sam turned around and said, "Katie, since you're the sheriff, can I be your assistant?"

"You know, that might not be a bad idea. But you might end up becoming something else, like president, so you just keep playing."

Sam chewed on this a moment, then sprawled back onto his stomach, his nose nearly touching the spinner on the game board. They heard Keely say, "If I become president, I'll make you vice president."

Sam nodded. "Okay, that'd be cool."

"I can give you orders all the time and you'll have to listen to me."

Miles sat back, crossed his arms over his chest, and shook his head. "You did good, Katie—the proper use of money. Well done."

"Thank goodness I've had no complaints since I've been sheriff." She frowned. "This is farm and dairy country—lots of cows—and tobacco country, you know, and that means lots of cheap cigarettes and lots of teenagers smoking. I've cracked down on that something fierce."

"How are you doing that?"

"I know most of the teenagers. I see one with a cigarette in his mouth and I take him and his cigarettes to jail. I can't lock him up since it's not against the law, but I call his parents. You'd be surprised at what a screaming mother can do to a teenage boy, even the mothers who smoke. It warms a sheriff's heart."

He laughed at that. "If my mom had ever caught me with a cigarette, I'd have been grounded for a month. Now, as for your mom, she makes good tuna casserola, and she didn't raise a dummy."

She was pleased, and he saw it. "Thank you," she said. "Casserola— what comfort food. I guess that's why she made it for all of us Monday night."

Katie rose and stretched. He was watching her, she felt it, and quickly lowered her arms, slouched forward a bit.

"Sorry, I didn't mean to do that in front of you."

"Think nothing of it."

"I mean, I didn't mean to preen in front of you."

"Maybe that's too bad."

THIRTY

"There, that's it. You're going to be a dentist, Sam, and I'm going to be an astronaut!"

Katie came down on her haunches beside them. "Okay, career choices are set, let me tell you that it's nearly nine o'clock. Time for you guys to get to bed."

It wasn't as much of a production as either adult expected, no more than five minutes of whining. After Katie settled Keely in, Miles did the same with Sam down the hall, they traded places, without thinking much about it, and that made Katie frown down at her toes. What did Miles think about tucking her daughter in and being pulled into reading the next chapter of *Lindy Lymmes, Kindergarten Girl Detective*?

She offered to read to Sam from one of Keely's books, but that made him gag—loudly—so she gave him a big hug and kissed his ear. If she wasn't careful, she thought, she'd fall in love with this little boy.

When Miles had gone to bed, she went outside to speak to Jamie and Neil, who'd gotten Cerlew's Buick unlocked. She gave them a thermos of coffee she'd made, checked and locked all the doors and windows, and fell into bed.

The storm hit hard around two in the morning, rattling windows, slapping tree branches against the house. It was time for a shift change in deputies guarding the house. Katie checked on Keely, who was sound asleep, and went back to bed. Katie had always loved storms, and they never bothered Keely, but tonight, Katie was antsy and wide awake. She finally gave it up, went to the kitchen and put on the teakettle. She was standing in front of the sink, looking out over the thick stand of maple and poplar trees not more than ten feet from the house, leached of their beautiful colors in the heavy gray rain.

"You got two tea bags?"

She turned around at Miles's voice, well aware that she was wearing only her nightshirt and her empty ankle holster. Even her feet were bare.

Miles walked straight to her, and wrapped his arms around her, trapping her own arms to her sides. When she pushed against him, he immediately released her, but then she simply wrapped her arms around his back. She felt his smile against her cheek, felt the strength of him against her. He was wearing only a pair of jeans and a dark blue T-shirt. She said against his neck, "You feel good," and that was a lie because he felt far more than good. And he made her feel things she hadn't felt in a very long time.

"So do you," and she could hear tension in his voice, hear that he was lying, too.

He was nuzzling her neck, and said against her jaw, "I like a tall woman. We fit together perfectly." And he kissed her.

Katie hadn't kissed a man in approximately two years and three months, and that kiss had been on the wet side with a beer aftertaste. How far back did she have to go for an astounding kiss, a kiss like this one? All the way back to Carlo.

The teakettle whistled, shrill and loud, and they both jumped. He took her arms in his hands, looked at her a moment, and stepped back from her.

"Do you drink your tea straight?"

Katie nodded. She wished the teakettle hadn't been so loud. He'd given her comfort, and so much more than that, and it had felt right, just right. And she wanted more, and she didn't want a teakettle sounding off in the middle of it. Life was strange. She hadn't even known this man before last weekend.

She watched him fetch two mugs down from the cabinet, dangle two Lipton tea bags over the sides of the mugs, and pour the boiling water over them.

He said without turning, "I like the holster around your ankle. It's sexy."

She looked down, saw that her red nail polish was chipped on her big toe. She grinned at him. "You're pretty easy, Miles."

"Not I." He handed her a mug, picked his up, and clicked it against hers. "To us," he said.

What did that mean? She sipped her tea. The wind howled, and the rain pelted hard against the windows like pebbles thrown hard by angry children.

"I get to meet with the TBI again tomorrow," Katie said, and added at his frown, "The final meeting, I hope."

"Do you need any witnesses?"

She shook her head. "They spoke to Glen Hodges again by phone this afternoon, and of course to Savich and Sherlock before they left. I suppose they might want to speak with you, but no one's mentioned it yet. And I have my deputies, all eager to defend me, even Wade, if he has a clue what's good for him. The TBI investigator checking out everything calls this case a corker—his word—and he wants to hang around. I'm hoping he gets a call from his supervisor to finish things up."

Suddenly Katie heard something, no, it was more than that. She felt something dangerous and close. She ran to the living room window and looked out through the thick rain. No deputy car was out there.

She didn't hesitate. "Miles, grab Sam, quickly!"

Miles didn't ask for an explanation, didn't hesitate. He raced to the guest bedroom to see Sam sitting up in bed, half-asleep. "I heard something, Papa. Out there."

"Come with me, Sam." Miles grabbed him up, wrapped him in blankets and ran with him back to the living room. Katie was there with Keely.

"Sam was awake. He heard something. What's the matter?"

"I don't know," Katie said. "I don't know, but something's not right. Danny and Jeffrey were supposed to show up at two, but they're not there. We're getting out of here right now."

"Katie, you're not dressed."

She was losing it. Not good, but her fear was building. "Hold the kids, let me throw on some clothes. I'll bring you a shirt and your jacket. Oh damn, the kids need clothes, too. Miles, don't let either of them move. I'll get everything."

Two and a half minutes later, both adults were on their knees quickly dressing Sam and Keely.

"We're outta here," Katie said. Miles knew she was afraid and trying hard not to let that fear transmit itself to the children. He also knew she'd give her life for any of them.

Katie smashed her hat on her head, grabbed all the coats, and said, "We're outta here, now!"

Sam whispered as he clutched his father's neck, "What's the matter, Papa? What did I hear? Are those bad men after me again?"

"If they are, I'll knock their heads together, then I'll let you stomp on them, okay?"

"Okay, Papa," Sam said, less fear in his voice, thank God.

Keely twisted around in Miles's other arm to face her mother. "What's the matter, Mama?"

"Shush," Miles said. "We've all got to be very quiet, okay?" He squeezed both children close to him.

Just as Katie fumbled with the dead bolt on the front door, there was a loud explosion behind them that sent flames and heat out at them through the kitchen hall. Someone had tossed a bomb into the kitchen, where he and Katie had been drinking tea not more than five minutes before. Miles automatically turned his back to the heat to protect the children. Katie bounced back, blinked to clear the shock out of her head, and said, so mad she was stuttering, "The house, s-some idiot just b-blew up my damned house!"

There was a crackling of flames behind them.

Katie pulled the door open and ran out. "We're alive, thanks to you," Miles said as he raced out the door behind her.

"Wait!"

Her gun was out, and she was crouched down, making a sweep. She couldn't see anything through the deluge. There was nothing else she could do. She waved them forward. Miles, huddled over the kids, raced after her.

The rain pelted them, soaking them to the skin within seconds, and there were gusts of wind that forced them to bow forward and brace themselves. Katie led them straight to her truck. "Get in, Miles!"

She turned the key in the ignition and slammed the car into reverse, but the wheels spun. The ground had turned to sucking mud in the heavy rain.

The wheels finally gained traction when Katie ripped the truck back in reverse a second time. She barely missed the huge oak tree that was the oldest thing in her yard. Mud was flying from under the wheels, splashing the side windows, but they were free and that was all that mattered.

In that instant there was a sharp ping, like the sound of something hitting metal, and then another.

"Someone's shooting at us," Katie said low, her voice controlled. "Get the kids down, Miles."

He worked both children down into the space in front of the passenger seat. They were holding each other tightly, not making a sound. How much more of this could two little kids take?

"Keep your head down," Katie said, all matter-of-fact. "I'm getting us out of here."

She hit the gas the instant after she shifted into drive, and the truck shot forward. They heard a tremendous explosion that rocked the truck. Katie stopped the truck and jerked around, even as she dialed 911.

"Those bastards—my house is on fire!" She got her night dispatcher, Lewis, and snapped out instructions to him. "Get every deputy out to my house along with the fire department. And Lewis, Danny and Jeffrey never showed up at two o'clock to take over guard duty."

"Sheriff, they told me they were just going to be a few minutes late. Some kids busted out both their back tires."

"Yeah, right, some kids," Katie said. "Well, at least they're okay."

When she'd hung up, she said, her voice flat and calm, "Miles, you take the kids to the sheriff's office. Lock yourselves in a cell. Keely, Sam, it will be all right. Do what Miles tells you. I'll be with you as soon as I can."

"Mama!"

Katie didn't hesitate, she was out of the truck, sliding in the mud and rain, running back toward her burning house, her gun drawn.

Where were the idiots who'd fired at them? Surely there was no reason for them to stay now with Sam gone. But whoever had done this had gone over the edge. Nothing could surprise her now.

She was crouched down, until she was under tree cover again as she made her way to the side of her burning house. She felt the heat billowing off her house, felt a spark strike her hand, and shook her fingers, cursing. She looked down to see her burned flesh. It hurt like the devil, but she had nothing to wrap it up with. She shook her hand to cool it, then knew she had to forget it.

They'd thrown the bomb into the kitchen. Why? To flush them out? The kitchen was the farthest room from the guest room where Sam was sleeping. They'd probably known that. The last thing they seemed to want was to hurt Sam.

It seemed like years passed before she heard the deputies, the firemen. The bombers were gone, no reason for them to hang around since their target had escaped.

Suddenly, she heard another gunshot. At the same time, her cell phone rang. She yelled into the phone even as she rolled behind a garbage can, "Wade, stay put, that's an order! The moron who bombed the house just shot at me!"

Another shot, this one a good twenty feet away. She saw Wade coming around the corner, and yelled, "Don't come any closer, Wade! Get more deputies and get down!"

But Wade just kept running toward her, his gun fanning as he ran. Soon, four deputies were there, yelling, running into each other, trying to avoid flying sparks from Katie's burning house.

"All of you be careful," Katie yelled.

Wade was panting when he reached her. He saw the blood on her hand and turned white. "My God, your hand."

"No, I'm all right, it was a flying spark. Wade, take the guys and check in the woods. See what you can find."

Not many minutes later, she slowly rose to see Wade come running toward her through the thick rain. He was shaking his head.

"Nothing?"

"Not a single damned thing. Hell, Katie, this whole thing's so off-the-wall. What do we do now?"

"We search every inch around here and see what we can find." She pointed him to the shards of glass sticking out of the mud. "They dropped that one and broke it, but its brother went through my kitchen window." She looked down at her hand. Wade pulled a handkerchief out of his pocket and tied it around her hand. "There, that's better than nothing."

She looked up at Wade. "Thanks. At least the bastards didn't follow Miles into Jessborough. They've got to be okay."

THIRTY-ONE

Miles had got himself under control because, simply, there was no choice. "Your mama will be just fine," he said as he eased himself behind the wheel. "Now, Sam, Keely, I want you both to sit in the passenger seat and snuggle under those blankets."

They were wet and scared, their teeth chattering, and Miles turned the heat on high. "You guys know what? I'd really appreciate it if you'd sing me a song."

The children, bless their hearts, sang themselves hoarse. "Puff the Magic Dragon" had never sounded so good. He knew they were scared, knew they were dealing with it, just as he was, and he was very proud of both of them. Within minutes, he heard sirens, saw sheriff cars, red lights flashing; he pulled the truck off onto a side street while they streamed past, headed to Katie's burning house. Thank God it was raining so hard, the house just might survive.

He was praying Katie was all right as he scooped both children into his arms, charged through the door of City Hall, veered to the right, where the sheriff's department was housed.

Lewis, the night dispatcher, waved them in. Then the outer door whooshed open again and there was Linnie, running through the doors right behind them, wearing jeans, boots, a huge sweatshirt with an extra-large bomber jacket over it, and rollers in her hair.

"This way," she said and smiled down at the children, just as calm and cool as Katie had been. His own heart was pounding and he wanted to hit something.

The phone rang and Lewis was on it.

"Everything is fine," Linnie said, leaning down to hug both children. "Listen to me now, I don't want you two worrying. Your mama's really tough, Keely, you know that. And Sam, your papa's right here, big and mean, and no one would mess with him. Now, come this way and we'll get you dry."

Sam stared up at his father, his small mouth working.

Miles came down on his knees next to Sam and Keely, drew them both into the circle of his arms. "Linnie's here to take care of you guys. She's going to get you dry and warm."

The kids, pale and wet, stared up at him, saying nothing. They weren't buying it, and he was trying his very best, dammit.

"Okay, Linnie is going to watch you and keep you company, okay? She's also going to lock this place up tighter than your bank, Sam."

"Papa, you're going to leave us?"

He said simply, "I have to help Katie. Okay?"

"Don't let those bad men hurt my mama," Keely said, and burst into tears.

"I won't let anyone hurt your mama, Keely. I promise," Miles said as he stood up. "You guys, stay with Linnie."

He mouthed a thank you to Linnie, who was gathering both children against her.

"Wait, Mr. Kettering!" She tossed him a cell phone. "Use it. Call us whenever you can, right, Sam?"

"Call me, Papa."

"You got it, kid."

"I'll hug Keely," Sam said. "She's scared." Miles watched his son pull Keely close and pat her back.

As Miles drove back through the heavy cold rain, the driver's window cracked down, he could still hear sirens. He saw the glow of the flames from a mile away. With the heavy rainfall, at least the trees were protected. He pulled the truck up behind one of the deputy's cars and jumped out.

The firemen were hosing down the roof of the house, but even with the heavy rain there was no hope. Katie's house was gutted, and everything in it gone.

Miles threw back his head and yelled, "Katie!"

One of the deputies came running up, panting as he said, "Are the kids okay, Mr. Kettering?"

"They're with Linnie in jail, I mean that literally. Where's Katie?"

"I think she's still in the back."

Miles said, "They shot at the sheriff's truck. You'll probably be able to dig out the bullets, identify them. Are you sure Katie's okay?"

"I heard her yelling," the deputy said. "When she yells like that, she's okay, just real mad."

Miles nodded and ran to the back of the burning house, rain blurring his vision. He swiped his hand over his eyes, and shouted, "Katie!"

"I'm here."

He nearly ran right into her. She was leaning against a sugar maple, tying something around her hand.

"Dammit, you hurt yourself," he said, then pulled her tight against him, unable to help himself, he was so afraid.

"Nothing bad, I promise," she said, and pulled back to give him the ghost of a smile. "A flying spark burned my hand. It's not bad. The guys who bombed my house are long gone. Wade and the other deputies haven't found anything yet."

"Both of us know where they went," he said. "First, let's get your hand bandaged a bit better. I saw the paramedics out front."

Ten minutes later they were in Katie's truck, Miles driving, headed for the McCamy house.

Katie turned back to look at the devastation of her house. "Gone," she said. "Everything's gone, including all my pictures of Keely and even her chess set."

"We're alive and that's all that matters. And you've got your hat."

She was wet and dirty, her hair straggling down beneath her beautiful cream-colored straw hat, her hand hurt, but she managed a smile. "Yes, and now I want to face down the monsters who have tried to wreck our lives." She drew her ankle gun and handed it to him. Driving with one hand, he shoved it into the waistband of his jeans.

As he leaned forward to wipe his hand across the fog building up on the windshield, Miles said, "The rain is finally letting up a bit."

Katie said, "It's nearly four o'clock in the morning. Do you think the McCamys will pretend they were sleeping?"

He just shook his head, concentrating on not sliding off the road. "Unless we get lucky, and these guys have gone back to the McCamy house, I don't know what we're going to accomplish tonight."

Katie said slowly, "I've got an idea on how to get us through the front door."

Miles raised an eyebrow, but when she shook her head, he said, "Who have you called for backup?"

Again, she didn't answer. Her hand was throbbing bad now, she was sick to her stomach about her house and so mad she wanted to spit nails. Did she want backup? Sure, you always had backup, always. She just couldn't believe that she hadn't been the one to think of it.

She blew out her breath and dialed 911. "Linnie, how are the kids?"

"They're locked in a cell with Mort, the cleaning guy." There was a pause, and Linnie said, "He's teaching them how to play poker. They're distracted and that's for the best. And yes, they're in dry clothes and they're warm. Everything's okay here, Katie. We got this place lit up like Christmas, and there are four of us here, ready to bust heads if those creeps show up."

"Thank you so much for coming in, Linnie. Okay, here's the deal. I want four deputies, Wade in the lead, out at Reverend McCamy's house." Linnie, of course, already knew they were on the way. Katie imagined that she'd spoken to every one of the deputies. "Listen, Linnie, this is very important: Tell Wade not to use sirens. I want a silent approach and I want them to stay outside and search for the guys who bombed my house. Tell them to be very careful." She paused, smiled a bit. "Give the kids a kiss." She flipped her cell off. "Turn here, Miles."

Miles was hunched over the steering wheel, trying to see through the rain and the fogged windshield. "He wants Sam beyond reason or else he would have given it up. This has nothing to do with money, this has to do with a madman, and what a madman believes."

That sounded simple, and exactly right, Katie thought. She said, "He must be well over the edge now, surely what happened tonight proves it. I wonder who he found to do this on such short notice. It's got to be someone local, maybe someone from his congregation."

"I wonder if there were two guys or just one. The ability to talk just one member into doing something this crazy, much less two guys, boggles the mind. You said he was charismatic. I guess this proves it."

"When you put it like that, I guess one guy makes more sense. Still, we've got to be really careful."

Katie rolled down the window and stuck her hand out. "It's not raining as hard."

"Your hand okay?"

She didn't answer, just pointed to the big Victorian house that had just come into view. "We're not leaving without answers this time, Miles."

THIRTY-TWO

The only sound they heard when they got out of the truck was the rain and the rustling of wet leaves. It was cold and there was no moon, not a single star, just fat bloated clouds, probably gathering energy for another deluge. There were no lights on in the big Victorian house.

They were wet. Katie's hat was still clamped down on her head, her hair coming out of its French braid, the white bandage on her hand soaked with rain. She could feel her boots squish as she walked.

Katie rang the doorbell, such a mundane thing. There was no answer. She rang it again, then once more. She was smiling, as grim as Jesse Helms if he'd been a judge. Finally, she slammed her fist against the large wooden door.

She kept pounding until, at last, Reverend McCamy's angry voice shouted, "Who is this? What is going on here? Go away!"

The door jerked open. Reverend McCamy, dressed in pajamas, dressing gown, and bedroom slippers, stood there, his face a study of anger and something else, something that was beyond what they could begin to understand.

"Who is it, Reverend McCamy?"

They heard the light sound of footfalls coming down the stairs. Elsbeth McCamy came to stand beside her husband, staring at them.

She was wearing a pink silk robe that came only to her knees; it was obvious she was wearing absolutely nothing underneath. Her feet were bare. Her hair was tousled around her face and tangled down her back, and for once, she wasn't wearing her earrings.

Reverend McCamy, his dark eyes fathomless and sharp, raised his hands to his hips, and stared at them. They stared back. Finally, he said slowly, "What is the meaning of this, Sheriff? Do you have any idea at all what time it is?"

Katie actually smiled at Reverend McCamy, showing him lots of teeth, and waved her bandaged hand in a shooing motion. "Do invite us in, Reverend McCamy. And I think a cup of coffee would be nice, too. It's been a hard night."

"No, I'm not letting either of you in my house until you tell me what's going on. You both look filthy."

"Well, that's true," Katie said. "Naturally, since I've had my house burned down and we've been running around in the rain, I guess you'd have to expect that."

Still, he didn't move. "Your house caught on fire? I'm sorry about that, Sheriff, but it doesn't have anything to do with us. I don't want to give you any coffee. I want you both to leave."

Katie paused a moment. "Well, there's something else, Reverend, something you should know." She waited, letting this soak in, then said, looking straight into those mad prophet's eyes, "As a result of your hiring incompetent help, Sam is in the hospital with severe injuries."

Miles didn't blink.

Reverend McCamy's mouth worked, but nothing came out.

Elsbeth cried out, "What do you mean Sam is in the hospital? What's wrong with him?"

Reverend McCamy whispered, "No, this can't happen. Tell me he will be all right."

"We don't know yet."

"I'm a minister, I will go to him," said Reverend McCamy and turned on his heel. "I'll be ready in just a moment."

Katie called out after him, "You're not going to the hospital, Reverend McCamy. Sam's in surgery. There's nothing you can do. Best to stay here and tell us why you want Sam so much."

Elsbeth said, "You're being ridiculous, Sheriff. We had nothing to do with this. What hospital is Sam in?"

Miles said, "Do you honestly believe we'd tell you where he is? My God, you'd probably set the hospital on fire to get to him."

"I don't know what you're talking about," Reverend McCamy said, but he was backing up, one step at a time. He was pale, markedly so, and it wasn't that he was afraid of getting caught. It was because he was afraid Sam would die. His eyes, Katie thought, his eyes were quite fixed, no light in them at all.

And Elsbeth? Did she realize her husband was mad? Maybe she

didn't want to admit it, but she had to know, just as she had to be involved in all the efforts to get hold of Sam.

"My boy isn't expected to live," Miles said, his voice filled with rage. "Because of you, you fanatic bastard, my boy is probably going to die. Do you understand that, you moron? A six-year-old boy is going to die because of you! No one else, just you."

He walked toward Reverend McCamy, one step at a time, staring into those mad eyes of his until he had him backed up against the wall. He put his face right into his, grabbed his robe lapels, and shook him. He screamed in his face, "And you call yourself a man of God?" Miles yanked him close again, shaking him so hard his head lolled on his neck.

Reverend McCamy tried to pull Miles's hands away, but he couldn't. He yelled, "You fool, you conceited buffoon! *Sam doesn't belong to you!*"

Miles felt the man's spittle on his cheek. He pressed closer and yelled back, "He sure in hell doesn't belong to you!"

Reverend McCamy was shaking his head wildly, back and forth. "No! He belongs to God! And God won't let him die, he won't! I must go to the hospital, don't you understand? I must go. I'm the only one who can save him!"

Katie said, "Why won't God let him die, Reverend McCamy?"

Elsbeth said, "No, Reverend McCamy, don't let them fluster you."

Reverend McCamy slipped out of Miles's grasp and dashed past him. Miles let him go. He watched him stumble over a Victorian umbrella stand, sending it crashing onto its side and splitting it open. Two umbrellas rolled out. Reverend McCamy took off running down the long hallway.

Elsbeth stood there in her sexy pink robe, staring after her husband. Katie and Miles ignored her, and turned to run after Reverend McCamy. He tried to slam the library door in their faces, but Miles shoved it back against him. He retreated back across the room where he did his couples counseling. There were three sofa pillows on the carpet. Why, for heaven's sake?

As they closed in, he fetched up against the bookshelved wall, his hands out to ward them off.

Miles stopped in front of the desk, leaned forward and splayed his fingers on the desktop. "We want you to talk to us, Reverend McCamy. We want you to tell us why my son belongs to God."

"No!" Elsbeth shouted. "Leave him alone, do you hear me? Go away!" She turned on Katie, and smashed her fist into her jaw. Katie, focused on Miles and Reverend McCamy, lurched to the side, nearly falling. She saw stars, but felt more surprise than pain. Katie grabbed Elsbeth's arm, jerked her close, and pulled both her arms behind her. She pulled her against her, leaned over, and whispered in her ear through all that beautiful tangled blond hair, "Just hold still, Elsbeth. Assaulting a police officer isn't going to help the Reverend. We're not going to hurt him."

"No, you can't make me—" She moaned as Katie tightened her hold. Her pink silk robe came open.

"Woman, do not show your body to these sinners!"

"We're not looking at her body," Miles said, his attention never wavering from Reverend McCamy. "I'm waiting, Reverend McCamy. Why does Sam belong to God?"

Reverend McCamy's mouth was a thin pale line. Suddenly, he shouted at them, "You're not worthy, you godless cretin! Why God gave such a son to you is beyond me. But His ways are not always clear to those who worship Him. It is not our right to question Him, for we are nothing compared to Him. The Lord showed me that I must take Samuel, to teach him to understand that he is one of God's favored ones. You don't understand, do you? Sam is an ecstatic! He must learn to accept the sublime suffering he once showed as a small child. He will learn to accept it again. He will throw himself into the well of God's mercy and greet this suffering with great happiness because he was chosen by God."

Reverend McCamy walked around the desk until he came right up into Miles's face. "Don't you understand, you fool? Sam is a victim of love—God's love. He has shown the stigmata! He will experience sublime suffering for all mankind, and his suffering will be radiant in its ecstasy. His very soul will know the beauty and sacrifice of our Lord!"

Miles felt as though he'd fallen down Alice's rabbit hole. He plowed his way through all the mad words. He stood back from Reverend McCamy, studying him. "What are you talking about? What nonsense is this? So you think Sam has shown the stigmata? Is that what this is all about? There is no such thing, you fool!"

Suddenly, Elsbeth stiffened and jerked free of Katie. She ran right at Miles, her fists swinging, screaming, "Leave him alone! Reverend

McCamy, they don't understand. They never will. Say no more. Make them leave. They don't belong here. Make them leave!"

"She's right, you'll never understand," Reverend McCamy said, coming around the desk to his wife, reaching out his hands, for what reason, neither Miles nor Katie knew. Then he slammed both fists onto the desktop. "Sam—it is not his name! His name is Samuel, his biblical name. He can't die! Save the boy, oh Lord, he is part of You, he is Your beloved victim. You must save him!"

Reverend McCamy was shaking so hard that he appeared to be having a seizure. Tears streamed down his face. "Elsbeth is right. Get out, both of you!"

A man's voice came from the doorway. "I can't let you do this to him, Sheriff, I just can't. Back away from Reverend McCamy."

Reverend McCamy screamed, "Are you crazy? What are you doing here, Thomas? Get out!"

Katie turned slowly around to see Tom Boone, a local postman for twenty years, standing just inside the library door holding a rifle on her. She smiled. "Well, I think there walks my proof on the hoof. Is there anyone else getting ready to come through that door? Or was it just you, Mr. Boone?"

"It was just me, Sheriff, and I'm enough to deal with you. I'm sorry, Reverend McCamy, but she's got a gun, you know. It's right there in her belt holster. I didn't want her to hurt you. You, Mr. Kettering, you get away from Reverend McCamy!"

Miles stepped away.

Katie remembered seeing Mr. Boone on Sunday, at the Sinful Children of God. She said, "Do you believe in this madman enough to try to kill me and Keely and Mr. Kettering to get to Sam?"

"I didn't try to kill nobody."

"Just be quiet, Thomas. Go away from here."

"No, Reverend, not just yet. I've got to tell her how it really was, that I wasn't there to hurt anyone, then she'll leave you alone. I did what I had to do, Sheriff, what the Reverend and God commanded me to do."

"What are you talking about, Mr. Boone? God doesn't have anything to do with this. It was this madman who gave you your marching orders. It was this madman who ordered you to take Sam. Didn't you hear what happened to the other two men he sent to get Sam?"

"I heard, Sheriff. You killed both of them. You, a woman, killed two men. You're an abomination."

Katie could only stare at him and shake her head. "And just look at what you did. You threw gas bombs into my kitchen and fired at me in my truck. Then you stayed around and tried to kill me again. What were you thinking?"

Mr. Boone, asthmatic all his life, panted hard now because he was scared. The drizzling rain and cold air had gone into his chest, he could feel it, choking off his air. He looked at the man who had helped him before, the saintly man who'd laid his hands on his chest and prayed and had eased his breathing. Thomas had known it was a miracle. He looked over at Reverend McCamy.

"It was God's orders as well," Reverend McCamy shouted. "I promised that you would be rewarded, Thomas. I promised that I would heal your asthma forever, but only if you finished what you started."

Katie asked, "What else did the Reverend here offer you as a reward, Mr. Boone?"

"He promised me that I would be his deacon. I've always wanted that and now I'll have it, and I'll be able to breathe free and easy for the rest of my life."

Katie had dealt with teenage gang members, drug dealers, homicides, and rapes in Knoxville, but never had she heard thinking as bizarre as this.

She drew in a deep breath, and held out her hand to Mr. Boone. "Did you think even once about your mother and your grandmother, what this would do to them? Listen to me. This man isn't holy, he's insane. Do you have any idea what deep trouble you're in? Now, put down that damned rifle."

But Mr. Boone held on to the rifle like it was his lifeline, and perhaps, in his mind, it was. He kept it steady on her chest.

Katie said to Reverend McCamy, "I believe that in Hollywood they would say the jig's up, sir. Is there anything else you'd like to tell me before I take you to my cozy jail?"

"Damn you, Sheriff, why don't you believe me?"

"Of course I don't believe you," she said, warning signs going off in her head because he was losing it fast. "I'm not mad."

"You stupid woman!" He lurched away and ran to the bookshelf behind his desk. He jerked books off the shelf, hurling them to the floor, reached in and pulled out what appeared to be a videotape.

"I'll prove it to you! Look at this tape! This proves what I'm saying! I'm not insane—it's on this tape!"

"What's on the tape, Reverend?" Katie asked.

"You'll see," Reverend McCamy said, tears still running down his face, his voice feverish, trembling, quite mad. "You'll see. God, through His infinite grace, through His desire to use me to teach others, has brought me this miracle. I saw the miracle and I clasped it to my soul and swore to God that I would bring Samuel to understand and accept God's mission for him in this life."

He shoved the video into the machine slot, turned on the TV and there it was, without his doing anything else. He obviously kept the TV set to video, ready for this tape.

There was a hissing sound from the tape, and then the grainy sound and squiggly lines faded away. The focus wasn't very good, and there was motion because the camera wasn't being held steady. Miles realized that it was a home movie, of sorts. Of what? The camera came to a stop on Sam, a younger Sam, maybe three years old, lying on his old bed in his child's bedroom in their first house in Alexandria, wearing only his pajama bottoms. He was thrashing around, moaning, or delirious. He was heaving, arching his back, his arms and legs flailing. The jerking camera moved in closer. Miles thought he heard a person crying, probably the person videotaping his son. Was it Alicia?

Miles knew nothing of this, nothing. He watched Sam's arms fly over his head, watched the camera zoom in on his fisted hands. Then his small hands opened, slowly.

There was blood on Sam's palms. And it was running down his wrists.

Miles stopped breathing. Blood? Sam had been bleeding? When? Why hadn't Alicia told him?

The woman was crying loudly now, and the camera was shaking so badly everything went blurry, then suddenly, it went to black.

Reverend McCamy hit the stop button, but he didn't look away from the blank TV screen. His breath was coming fast and hard, and his dark eyes were glazed. It was almost as if he was in some sort of ecstasy. Miles watched as his hands slowly unfurled, the palms open, just like

Sam's had, and now he was panting, shivering, as if he were in that film with Sam, as if his body wanted desperately to simulate what had happened to Sam.

Reverend McCamy whispered as he continued to stare at the blank TV screen, "Did you see? The child, like Christ, is God's victim and God's sacrifice, here to make the world know His power, and through Samuel's ecstasy, understand God's love and His limitless compassion.

"Samuel, in those moments, those precious moments, was as close to God as any of us will ever be in this life."

THIRTY-THREE

Reverend McCamy stared at the screen, his wild eyes seeing what was no longer there, but was only there in his mind, so deep that he'd made himself mad with it. Or maybe the madness had come first.

There was a moment of stark silence.

Miles didn't move, just said to Reverend McCamy, his voice calm and steady, "You're telling me that you had Sam kidnapped because you saw a video of an obviously sick, delirious little boy, who, for whatever reason, had blood on his hands?"

Katie felt as if someone had smacked her upside the head and she'd never seen it coming. When Reverend McCamy had spoken of the stigmata, she'd thought of it as another of the ravings of a fanatic, certainly nothing to do with Sam.

What was all this about stigmata? From what she'd read, which wasn't much at all, the people who'd supposedly displayed the marks of the Cross seemed very ill, both physically and mentally. But why was there blood on Sam's hands in the video? Was that his mother taping this? It was obvious Miles didn't know a thing about it. Why in heaven's name hadn't Miles's wife told him about this?

"This must have happened about three years ago, Reverend McCamy," Miles said. "Why did you wait three years to take Sam?"

Reverend McCamy looked suddenly at his wife, and his eyes went even wilder. "Elsbeth, stay back! Close your robe, woman, you're showing your body to these people, to this man!"

"I'm looking at you, Reverend, not your damned wife."

"I'm sorry, Reverend McCamy, I'm so sorry." Elsbeth turned away, frantically tying the sash on her silk robe again.

Reverend McCamy looked back at Miles. "Taking the boy, it should have been so simple, but I hadn't yet seen the boy, and so how could he understand? He managed to escape. Don't you see? God wants the boy to be with me."

Miles said slowly, "I have never seen that tape. I never even knew about it, don't even know who shot it. I don't remember Sam ever being that ill. He was obviously delirious, very sick. Where did you get that tape, Reverend?"

"I won't tell you. You'll hurt the people who gave me the tape, and they were only doing God's work."

Miles rolled his eyes. "Don't be ridiculous—"

"Very well, at least tell us what you were going to do with Sam?" Katie said. "He's six years old, not a toddler."

"I was willing to leave my ministry here, to take Samuel to Phoenix with us. I've already bought property there. It wouldn't take me long to teach Samuel what he is and what he must do with his life."

"Sam is to be your successor," Katie said.

"Of course, I must go see Samuel. *Now.*" He was suddenly the leader of his flock, decisive, full of resolve. He stepped back from Miles and shook himself. "I am going to see Samuel. I will pray for him. I will intercede with God to save him. I will lay my hands upon him."

And he turned to walk out of the room.

"Reverend McCamy," Katie said quite pleasantly. "You, sir, aren't going anywhere."

In spite of Mr. Boone with his rifle pointed at her, Katie pulled her SIG out of her waistband. He said, "Please, Sheriff Benedict, put that gun down."

Katie turned as she slowly lowered her SIG to her side. "Surely, Mr. Boone, you can't think God is ordering you now to kill both me and Mr. Kettering, to go with Reverend McCamy to the hospital and try to steal Sam away again? Don't you realize that you would be sending that innocent little boy into a life of slavery and madness? Listen, Mr. Boone, I can still help you if you don't hurt anyone."

"No! That's not what the Reverend said!"

Reverend McCamy said, "Thomas, they said the boy was injured. How did that happen?"

"I was going to throw the bombs in the kitchen to get them out of the house. It's just that the sheriff was there, and I really didn't want to kill her like that. And then Mr. Kettering came into the kitchen and I believed they were going to fornicate right there, on the kitchen table!

I watched them, but you know what? Before anything happened, she sensed something, I swear it, she knew something was wrong. Maybe she saw me, but I don't think so. I was real careful. She yelled at Mr. Kettering to get the kids, that they were getting out of there. They got to the truck before I could grab Samuel. He drove off with Mr. Kettering, and he was fine."

Reverend McCamy's face turned red with rage, the pulse pounding at his temple. He shook so hard he had to hold on to the edge of the desk to keep his balance. He yelled, "God will strike you dead, Sheriff! You twisted, perverted woman. You lied!"

Katie even grinned as she said to Reverend McCamy, an eyebrow arched, "I'm a perverted woman? That language isn't particularly nice, Reverend."

"Samuel isn't in the hospital! He wasn't hurt. Where have you hidden him? Where is the boy?"

Miles knew he had to keep calm with that idiot still holding the rifle on Katie. He leaned back against a bookshelf, crossed his arms over his chest and said, "My son is safe in jail, Reverend McCamy. I believe four deputies are guarding him and he's playing poker with Mort, the cleaning guy. I'm sure the sheriff will let him out when you show up in handcuffs."

"This is the man you obeyed, Mr. Boone," Katie said. "Take a good look."

"Kill them, Thomas!"

It was obvious to Katie that Mr. Boone finally realized he was in way over his head. He was holding a rifle on a law enforcement officer, obviously so scared sweat was pouring off his forehead, and he looked ready to faint.

"Kill them!"

Mr. Boone started wheezing, bad. He gasped through the precious breaths he was able to draw, "No, Reverend McCamy, I can't, sir. I can't, sir, I know her mother!"

Everything froze for one long moment.

Then, Elsbeth McCamy grabbed the rifle from Mr. Boone's lax hands. She whirled around and aimed it at Miles, who dropped to the floor behind the desk just as she fired. Katie was on her instantly. Elsbeth screamed, trying to wrest the rifle free, but she couldn't. Katie slammed her fist into Elsbeth's stomach and took a huge handful of her gorgeous hair, pulling it until Elsbeth's head was nearly bent back over her arm. She said very quietly against her ear, "Drop the rifle, Elsbeth, or I'll pull out all that wonderful hair of yours."

Elsbeth moaned but kept struggling, trying to bring the rifle up. Katie turned her and kneed her hard in the chest, knocking the wind out of her.

"Leave my wife alone!"

Reverend McCamy lurched forward, grabbed the rifle from where his wife had dropped it on the floor, and ran, knocking Mr. Boone over a chair in his escape from the library.

They heard him running upstairs.

Miles said, "I want him, Katie. I'll get him."

She started to go with him, but then she looked at him, really looked, and knew he wouldn't do anything stupid. He had a cop's training and a cop's instincts. He'd pulled out her ankle gun. The derringer looked absurd in his big hand, but up close it could stop a man, even a madman.

"Take care, Miles. I'll get help."

She'd picked up her SIG Sauer and motioned Mr. Boone and Elsbeth to the sofa. She pulled out her cell phone and called Wade, who had to be outside by now.

But there wasn't time for Wade to even make it through the front door. Overhead, there was a huge explosion. The whole house shook with the shock and force of it.

Elsbeth screamed. Mr. Boone said, wheezing so hard Katie wondered how he could still breathe, "The Reverend's thrown one of the gasoline bombs. Why would he do that?"

Elsbeth ran out of the library. Katie wasn't about to shoot her, so there was no choice but to go after her. As for Mr. Boone, where could he go? She shouted over her shoulder, "Mr. Boone, go outside where it's safe!"

She ran out into the hallway to see Elsbeth taking the stairs two at a time. Katie stayed right on her heels. She rounded the corner at the top of the stairs and saw Elsbeth running toward the master bedroom.

Katie heard the crackling and popping of the flames before she saw them billowing out of the master bedroom, the hallway carpet already smoking. She had to get everyone out, fast.

Katie headed after Elsbeth. She saw her run into the master bedroom and yelled, "Elsbeth, don't go in there!"

But the woman disappeared into the room.

"Miles, where are you?"

Katie ran into the huge bedroom, saw the door open to the closet, and watched Elsbeth disappear inside.

"Miles!"

She heard a gunshot, not loud, just a popping noise, and she knew it was from her derringer. She started coughing from the incredible heat and the smoke. She grabbed a pillow from a chair and clamped it against her nose.

She saw Miles, breathing hard, standing in the doorway to the sex room, her derringer dangling in his right hand. "Katie, get out of here!"

"Where are Elsbeth and Reverend McCamy? My God, what happened to your face?"

"We need to get out of here. I don't know where Elsbeth is. I had to shoot Reverend McCamy. He's dead, I checked. Come on, I don't want Sam or Keely to be orphans."

But Katie had to try. "Elsbeth! Where are you? Come out or you'll die!"

There was no answer. Katie started to run toward the sex room, but Miles grabbed her hand and dragged her from the bedroom. He was right, she thought, there was no choice. She pressed the pillow she was holding against her face and ran with him down the long hallway. She stumbled on the stairs, and Miles picked her up and pulled her against him to keep her on her feet.

They ran into the entryway where Mr. Boone and several deputies were crowded together, right inside the front door. Katie said, "I see you can breathe again, Mr. Boone. Just maybe you don't need Reverend McCamy's laying on of hands."

"This is one too many burning houses, Sheriff," Charlie Fritz, one of her deputies said. "The fire department wants us out of here right away. Let's go."

Elsbeth's face flashed in Katie's mind. Had she just given up and chosen to die with her husband? No matter what she'd been a party to, Katie didn't want her to be dead. Too many were dead already.

When they were near the road, they looked back to see the beautiful old Victorian lit up from its bowels, turning the black sky orange, spewing flames upward. Its old wood exploded in shards everywhere. It was an incredible sight, as long as you were away from the devastation.

Katie stood next to Miles, aware that his arm was holding her close, for warmth, for comfort, to make the world real again, to right the madness. He said, "Reverend McCamy went into that sex room and pulled a bottle full of gasoline out of one of the drawers beneath that marble altar. He lit the wick and threw it at me. It hit the bed, and the flames shot up in an instant."

"What happened to your face?"

Miles touched his fingers to the slash along the side of his face, from his temple to his jaw. "He pulled a whip off the wall and slashed me with it."

"And you shot him?"

"I tried to grab the whip away from him, but he fought me. I could hear the fire, knew time was growing short, and then he tried to grab the gun.

"I swear to you, Katie, there was madness pouring out of him, and a frenzy that seemed to unleash all the strength inside of him. He was grinning and moaning at the same time. I felt my blood freeze.

"And then there you were with a pillow over your face."

"You never saw Elsbeth."

He shook his head. "I heard her voice, but no, I didn't see her."

"She preferred to die with that man rather than survive," Katie said, shaking her head. She looked up at Miles and shook her head again. "I think we're going to need a paramedic." She began to examine the cut and changed her mind. "It doesn't look at all deep, but no paramedics this time. I want to take you to the hospital."

Wade was standing next to them now. "The firemen are already bitching at all this work, Sheriff. Now you want to piss off the paramedics?"

Miles laughed, he threw back his head and really laughed. He looked up at the burning house. "It's over," he said, "it's finally over. It seems like it's been going on forever—and it's been only days. Amazing."

Katie nodded and smiled at him. She grabbed Miles Kettering and hugged him to her.

THIRTY-FOUR

At ten o'clock Thursday morning the rain had lightened to a thick gray mist, mixing into the low-lying fog that crept up the sides of the mountains, blanketing the land.

"Do you really think it's over?"

Keely pursed her lips, looked doubtful. "I don't know, but I sure hope so. Last night was real scary, Sam."

Sam sighed, thought that every night since early last Friday morning had been scary, and leaned in more closely. "Yeah, I know, but your mom and my dad, they took care of us." He sighed again, deeply. "But since everything is over now, you know what that means, Keely."

"Yeah, I know. You're gonna have to leave and never come back."

"I'll tell Papa that I don't want to leave, okay?"

"Do you think he'll let you stay here and live with Mama and me?"

"I want him to stay, too," Sam said, and pulled Minna's soft wool blanket more closely around both him and Keely because it was getting colder.

"If your papa doesn't want to stay, what are you going to do, Sam?"

"I don't know," Sam said finally and he fisted his eyes. "I'm only six. Nobody listens to me."

"They listen to you even less when you're five. I heard my grandma talking to Linnie just a while ago. She told Linnie that your papa and my mama should get married and that would be that."

"What would be that?"

"Well, I guess it means that if you leave, I get to leave with you."

"Oh. Well, that's good."

"Your father would be my steppapa."

"Yeah, and Katie would be my stepmama. That's weird."

"We could fight and stuff and no one could say anything about it."

Keely punched his arm, gave him a huge grin, then settled her head on his shoulder.

They were sitting in Minna's porch swing. Since Sam's legs weren't long enough to reach the porch, he'd taken a walking stick out of the umbrella stand that had belonged to Keely's grandfather. Every few minutes, he shoved the stick against the wooden floor to make the swing go back and forth.

"I don't want you to go away, Sam."

"I know and I've been thinking, Keely. Papa isn't stupid. He'll marry your mom."

Keely said, "You're six years old. You don't know if your dad's stupid or not. My mama says this is the most beautiful place in the world. Even if your dad was stupid, he could be happy here. I know, tell him we'll take him rafting on the Big Pigeon River. That's in the Smokies."

"Papa's been rafting before. I'll tell him, but you know, Keely, he's got that big helicopter business in Virginia. Since those bad men took me he hasn't gotten much work done."

Keely pondered this for a while. "I know, tell him that Mama is the best rafter in Tennessee and she'll teach him. Oh, and tell him that Sam Houston taught in a log schoolhouse when he was eighteen. I'll bet your dad will be impressed. Tell him we'll take him there. Tell him he can e-mail to his business."

"Keely, if my papa and your mama got married, what would your name be?"

Keely didn't have an answer to that. Sam shoved the walking stick against the porch floor and the swing swung out widely. They laughed and hung on.

Children's laughter, Katie thought, there was nothing like it. She and Miles were standing just inside the screened door. Neither said a word and they didn't look at each other. So this was why her mom suggested they take a look at the beautiful hazy fog that was climbing the sides of the mountains.

Miles said quietly as he stepped back, "They look like a Norman Rockwell painting."

It was true, with their heads pressed together, the swing gently going back and forth, but any words Katie would have said stuck in her throat. She nodded and looked toward the mountains, blurred and softened by the fog, like fine smoke. Her mom had told her that looking at the mountains on a morning like this was like reading without reading glasses.

"Even in the winter, when it's so cold your toes are curling under and the mountains look weighted down with snow, they're still so beautiful it makes you want to cry just looking at them. And down at Gatlinburg—"

"Katie, what the kids were talking about . . ."

She turned to face him then. The emergency room doctor hadn't stitched Miles's face, just pressed the skin together using Steri-strips. She'd told him to rub on vitamin E and there wouldn't be a scar on his handsome face, unless he wanted to look dangerous, and she'd waggled her eyebrows at him. Katie said, "I guess this means you don't want me to tell you about the Great Smoky Mountains National Park."

"Not right this minute, no."

"Okay. You mean us getting married?"

"Yes," he said. "Maybe we should give it some thought."

Katie had firmly believed, up until, say, just four minutes ago, that she'd rather be incontinent than get married again. But now?

"Katie? Miles? I brought some cinnamon nut bread for the kids."

Her mother had excellent timing, Katie thought. She always had, particularly when there'd been horny boys around during high school. She'd given them enough time to overhear the kids talking, enough time to think about it, even say it out loud. They were both smiling when they turned to see Minna coming with a platter that smelled delicious from twenty feet away.

"I'm starving," Miles said, surprised. "I hadn't realized."

"Glad I had some clothes for you, Miles. Katie's dad was tall like you, so at least your ankles aren't showing. Sweetie, those jeans are nearly white they've been washed so many times, but you look just fine. Now, I'm going to take these goodies to the kids. They're having a hard time, you know."

"Can we have some first, Mom?"

"Sure. Take as many slices as you want. You two just go into the living room and I'll take care of the kids."

Minna waltzed back into the living room a few minutes later, and announced, "Sam and Keely aren't happy campers. I don't envy you having to separate them."

And now, Katie thought, just a touch of the spurs. Katie grinned at her mother, knowing exactly what she was doing. Miles, however, didn't.

"We're not looking forward to it," he said and sighed. He leaned his head back against the sofa and closed his eyes.

Minna said, "Linnie called while you were in the shower, sweetie. She said the TBI is going nuts and they're coming in force today about noon—that was so you could nap a little bit after that long night. Evidently one of the inspectors couldn't wait to see exactly what had happened here in Jessborough, a town, he said, that's never had anything more than some dippy DUIs and underage smokers in its extremely long life, until now. Linnie said not to worry, that the inspector really sounded excited. She also said the mayor and all the aldermen couldn't wait to see you, to hear every gory detail, I expect."

Katie said, "Oh yeah, Mayor Tommy will probably want a dozen meetings to thrash everything out."

Minna nodded. "Well, it is the most excitement Tommy's had since he caught his best friend making out with his girlfriend behind the bleachers back in high school. You really can't blame him. Nor the aldermen. I'm an alderwoman, Miles, and so I've already gotten a dozen or more calls."

"No," Katie said. "You're right, it's been a long dry spell for Tommy."

Miles called his sister-in-law, Cracker, told her it was finally over. He'd considered asking Cracker if she'd ever known Sam to be ill while Miles had been away, but decided against it. He knew to his soul that if Alicia hadn't told him about taping Sam with blood on his palms, she wouldn't have told anyone else. But she had given it to someone. Who? Perhaps her ancient priest, an old man who'd been kind and was failing physically and mentally. If she gave it to him then he must have passed it on to someone else, someone who'd given it to Reverend McCamy. They would never know now, and, truth be told, it didn't matter. The video was now ashes buried beneath more ashes and shards of burned wood.

When he'd hung up the phone, Katie had nodded. The last thing Sam needed was to have the media proclaiming him the newest candidate for sainthood, or a freak, or a helpless pawn. She could just see a TV guy asking Sam to please try to make his hands bleed again for the cameras. And here was Dr. X, psychologist, to give a historical perspective on the visible stigmata. Or those proclaiming he was a fraud or a victim of abuse, and exploited for it. Thomas Boone could say whatever he wanted, but everyone knew what he'd done, so she doubted anyone would believe him if he talked crazy.

And he'd said more to himself than to Katie, "What else did she keep from me?"

Katie hadn't said anything, merely taken his hand.

They would come up with exactly what to tell everyone, including the mayor and the aldermen, including her mother, but just not now, not when they were both so tired, like they'd been hung out to dry.

She looked over at Miles, a paper plate on his lap, a half-eaten slice of cinnamon nut bread sitting in the middle. He was sound asleep.

She smiled and nodded off herself.

THIRTY-FIVE

Although two days had passed, Katie still felt unanchored, her brain adrift. She'd dealt with the TBI, attended a special town meeting called by Mayor Tommy Bledsoe, of the long-lived Sherman Bledsoes, to explain exactly what had happened. She'd swear that nearly every citizen in Jessborough was present, along with her mother, of course, and all the mill employees who'd been given the day off to hear the details. There was some media—not national media, thank God. She had told all concerned that Reverend McCamy had been mentally ill, that he had evidently seen Sam when he'd visited Washington, D.C., that something about the boy had attracted him and so he'd arranged to take him. She assumed he wanted to raise him, mold him into what he saw himself as being, make him his successor, and that was surely the truth. He had just gone over the edge. It sounded idiotic to Katie, but not as idiotic as the just plain crazy truth. She and Miles had repeated their story so often that Katie imagined she'd be believing it herself soon.

Neither she nor Miles could explain what they'd seen on the video. She wondered if they ever would. She wondered how and why it had happened to a three-year-old boy. Some sort of bloody rash? Had his fingernails pierced his palms? Or was it a reaction to a medicine? More than likely, because Sam had sure looked sick. And Alicia hadn't said anything of it to Miles. Miles was fretting over that, but Alicia was long dead, and Katie knew he'd have to let it go.

She'd even called together the congregation of the Sinful Children of God and told them how very sorry she was that Reverend and Mrs. McCamy had died in the fire at their home. She wove the same tale, telling them that Reverend McCamy had been consumed with getting Sam, no one really knew why, and then told them the scene of his final disintegration, his complete mental breakdown, and his suicide. There was a lot of grief, a lot of questions, but most of them seemed willing to let life move on, fast.

She sighed, thinking about her home. Gone, nothing left at all. She had no idea what she was going to do yet and was still just too tired to think about it coherently.

"I think it's a good idea, Katie, what we talked about."

She jerked up. Miles was talking about marriage, she knew that even though neither of them had said another thing about it since early Thursday morning. She said, "It's a huge thing, Miles, a really huge thing."

"You lost your house."

"Yeah, I was just thinking about that."

"I've got a house, a really big house, and there's lots of room, for all of us. It's colonial. Do you like colonial?"

"Yes," she said, nothing more, and continued not to look at him.

Miles looked over at Sam and Keely, who were sitting on the living room floor, their jeaned legs spread wide, rolling three red balls back and forth between them. They were evidently trying to keep the balls inside their legs.

"You hit it too hard, Sam!"

Sam said, as he batted a ball back to her, "Pay attention, Keely."

"My God, he said that just like I do," Miles said. "This parent thing, it's scary when your kid mimics you. Say yes, Katie."

"Say yes to what, Mama?"

Suddenly both small faces were concentrated on them. Miles shrugged at Katie who sighed and nodded. "Okay, what do you guys think of Katie and me getting married? Not that she's said yes yet. That way you'd be brother and sister and you could stay together." And that, Katie thought, was the primary reason for getting married, and not a bad reason, really. At least both of them would be motivated to make a happy home for their children. Sam would be hers. And that kiss, she'd felt it all the way to her size nines. The man was potent. That made her smile, but it fell off her face pretty fast. Married, after knowing a man a week.

No, not married. *Remarried.*

Katie had sworn she'd never get married again as long as there was enough breath in her lungs to say no. It was simple, really, she couldn't trust herself to choose wisely. Just look at what she'd brought home the first time—Carlo Silvestri, a weak, spoiled jerk whose father had paid her a million and a half bucks to get out of his life. Hmm. At least that was a pretty good trade-off. Carlo's father had saved the pulp mill and a lot of people's jobs. And of course, Carlo had given her Keely—she'd put up with a dozen jerks for Keely.

The fact was, bottom line, she didn't know Miles well. Not even a complete week, and those days had been filled with nonstop fear and violence and adrenaline rushes so extreme that Katie was ready to swear that her blood sugar had plummeted to her toes because there hadn't been a life-and-death crisis since the McCamy house burned down, its two occupants with it.

What was a woman with no house to do? Marry a man who did have a house? A colonial?

It was funny if you looked at it a certain way. She'd saved a little boy, his dad had come to town, lots of bad things had happened, and now he wanted her to marry him. Truth be told, it was the children who'd started it. She'd wished now that they hadn't heard Sam and Keely talking on the porch, but of course that was what her mother had intended.

Then again, she couldn't forget those minutes in her kitchen. Fact was, she'd wanted to jump him; he'd felt just that good.

Both children were staring from Miles to her and back again. Sam said slowly, "You guys going to get married?"

"As I said, Sam, she hasn't said yes yet. So, what do you think? Keely?"

"Mama, I've given this a lot of thought and I think it's a really good idea."

"Keely, Miles only told you two minutes ago, not all that much time to think about it."

Keely slid a glance at Sam, who grinned like a kid who'd just copped an early look at his Christmas presents.

"Keely and I talked about it," Sam announced. "And we think it would be okay."

"This is the way to go, Mama. We're right about this."

It was Miles and Katie's turn to stare, both at each other and at their children. Miles said slowly, "How can you be so sure? You kids didn't even know each other existed until last Saturday afternoon."

Both children gave them a look like, So what's your point?

Miles felt pumped, ready to take on the world. He knew to his soul that he wanted to do this. "Katie, what do you say? Let's do it. No reason not to." Knew even deeper that making love with Katie, watching her laugh and love his son, was the right thing.

Katie jumped to her feet, startling everyone. "Okay, guys, listen up. This is a huge decision for all of us. I'm going to think what this would mean before I commit to anything, you hear me? Sam, your father is going to be doing some heavy-duty thinking, too. You and Keely will have to be patient, and not pressure either your father or me into this."

Yeah, right, Miles thought, looking at his son.

Sunday Night
Georgetown, Washington, D.C.

After the most delicious spinach lasagna Miles could remember, sautéed winter squash, and a Caesar salad, hot dogs and chips and a token salad for Sam and Sean, Savich handed Miles a cup of coffee, black, no sugar. "Sit down, Miles. You still look pretty wrung out."

"Nah, not really. Promise me you made the coffee, Savich."

Savich grinned. "Oh yeah. I've taught Sherlock just about everything I know, but coffee still defeats her."

Sherlock called out from the kitchen, "Did I hear my name being maligned?"

"Not at all," Miles called back. "You make a mean salad, all that feta cheese you add makes it really good, but, and I have to be honest here, you just don't have the same knack with coffee that your husband has, which is amazing since he rarely drinks it."

"No one said you had to be honest," Sherlock said, coming into the living room. She handed Savich a cup of tea, fresh-brewed.

"Thanks." He took a sip, closed his eyes in bliss.

"I like your pirate face, Miles," Sherlock said, "with all those little tape pieces. It's sexy."

"You never said my back was sexy," Savich said.

She actually shuddered. "No, but I will once I stop shaking." She added to Miles, "He's much better, but it's going to take another week before he can stretch without worrying his back is going to break open."

Savich and Sherlock sat across from Miles, listening with half an ear to Sean talking a blue streak to Sam, not much of it comprehensible, but Sam seemed to understand enough. He was rolling blocks to Sean, then helping Sean roll them back to him. They were in the designated kid part of the living room, where toys and chaos could reign without adults tripping over a stray ball and breaking a neck.

Sherlock looked sleek in black slacks and a black lace top, her curly red hair flying about, her eyes blue as a summer sky. Miles saw Savich grinning at her like a fool, sighed, and thought yet again of Katie.

It had been nearly a day and a half since he'd seen her. Those thirty hours felt like a decade.

"They're still getting lots of rain in eastern Tennessee," Miles said. "I'll tell you, it kept me real alert flying out of Ackerman's Air Field, what with the rain coming down so hard. They've got several storms lined up with little respite in between. Katie and her crew were up to their noses in mud and downed wires, not to mention all the accidents, the odd cow bawling in the middle of the road, mail soaked because some kids poked holes in some mailboxes."

"Sounds like she has her hands full, all right," Savich said and leaned forward so Sherlock could lightly scratch around the wound in his back.

Miles sat back and closed his eyes. Things were really bad and he didn't see how anything could get better. His guts hurt. Sam's guts hurt. Cracker kept asking what was wrong with him. He'd stomped around his office at the plant like a wounded rhino even though there were very few employees there to see it on a Sunday afternoon. Then he'd gone back home and stomped some more.

Even though Sam was safe, he sure wasn't sound, but it was really early yet. As for himself, he felt like he'd left unfinished business he wasn't in a position to finish, and that sucked, big time.

Miles muttered something under his breath, his eyes still closed, and Sherlock figured they were better off not knowing what he'd said.

Savich raised an eyebrow at him.

Miles said, "It's been a day and a half, well, maybe a bit more than thirty hours now. Isn't that amazing?"

"Yes," Sherlock said, "absolutely amazing. Now, you're moping, Miles." She lowered her voice just a bit and moved her chair closer. "Sam and Sean are distracted. Tell us what's going on here."

He cocked open an eye and said, "Yesterday morning I asked Katie to marry me and she turned me down."

Both of them stared at him.

Sherlock said slowly, "You're saying you asked a woman to marry you after—what was it?—not even a complete and full week after meeting her?"

"That's about the size of it," Miles said. "Damned woman. What could I do? I even asked her about architecture and she said she liked colonials."

Sherlock lightly laid her hand on Savich's leg. "I've never had much to do with colonials—they're not what you'd call thick on the ground on the West Coast. Fact is, I would have married Dillon after three days, if he'd only known I was alive, colonial or not."

Savich said, "Oh, I knew, I knew." He clasped her hand and said, "You're not remembering things exactly right, sweetheart. You were so cut off from everyone at the time, including me, until finally, you happened to spend that night here, with me, and then . . . Miles has heard all of that story he's ever going to hear."

Miles looked over to see Sean stuffing a graham cracker into his mouth. "I can pretend I haven't heard any of it and you could give me some pointers, Savich." He paused a moment, then said, shaking his head, "Isn't it strange how Sam looks like me and Sean looks just like you?"

Sherlock said, "So much for the indomitable X chromosome." Then she added, "So, Katie turned you down?"

"Yeah, I suppose because it's been only a week. Too soon, really, just too soon. She wanted to think about it. I guess maybe I agreed with that. I don't think she ever had a gun out of her hand. Strange time. She's really pretty. Did you notice that?"

Savich nodded, smiling, and said, "How long does she want to think about it? Did she give you any hope at all?"

Miles shrugged. "I don't know. We didn't set a time, but I'll tell you, Sam and I aren't doing so well."

"You miss her?"

"Well, yes, and Keely, but it's Sam I'm really worried about."

"What, nightmares? Surely you've got him seeing a child shrink. What does the doctor say?"

"No, no nightmares," Miles said. "It's Keely. He's miserable without Keely. I'm telling you, those two kids bonded instantly. I've never seen anything like it. It was a nightmare separating them. Katie and I both felt like monsters, and there's Katie's mom, looking at us like she wanted to carry the pitchfork as she led the villagers. Sam is speaking to me now, but he's miserable, too quiet—not sulking, just unhappy. I'm beginning to think it's not going to go away."

"It's only been a little over a day, Miles," Sherlock said.

Savich said, "So what does the shrink say?"

"Evidently Dr. Jones called Dr. Raines in Jessborough and that's why she agreed to see Sam this morning."

"So what did she say?"

"She said I should do anything to get Katie to marry me."

They all laughed. Sam looked up, frowned at them, and went back to helping Sean build a block fort, which wasn't going too well since Sean would yell and give it a karate chop when it got three blocks high.

"So what are you going to do?" Sherlock asked.

Miles sat forward. "You know," he said slowly, "maybe it's time I was a buccaneer."

"What's a buccaneer, Papa?"

"So you heard that, did you?" Sam, holding Sean's hand, was standing next to his father. "He's learned he has to be real quiet if he wants to eavesdrop."

"Tell us, Papa."

That serious, so serious voice. "All right, Sam." Miles lifted both Sam and Sean up onto his lap. "A buccaneer was a pirate who was given permission by his country to plunder enemy ships. They were take-charge kind of guys, Sam, who did things their own way. I'm thinking that it's time for me to take charge. What do you think?"

"You're always in charge, Papa."

Sean burped against Sam's arm, raised his head and said, "Mama, apple pie."

Sherlock laughed, got up, and went to the kitchen. "Apple pie coming up. What would the buccaneer like to have?"

"Just bring me an eye patch."

Sam laughed, the first laugh that had sprung out of that little mouth since they'd left Tennessee.

THIRTY-SIX

At eleven o'clock that night, Miles landed his plane at Ackerman's Air Field. Thirty minutes later, he was driving the rental car into Minna Benedict's driveway.

It wasn't raining so hard now, but he could tell that it had really been coming down. A low-lying fog had come up, turning everything gray. The mountains brooded, blurred in a soft mist.

It felt like coming home.

He let Sam, so excited he could barely speak, knock on the door.

Minna beamed at them, clearly startled. "Good grief, Miles, Sam! Come give me a big hug, sweetie. You, Sam, not your daddy. Oh my goodness, it's wonderful to see both of you. Miles, your face looks all sort of romantic."

While Sam was enfolded in Minna's arms, Miles looked over her head for Katie. "I called, but there wasn't any answer, Minna. Where are Katie and Keely? Asleep? It's nearly midnight. I'm sorry we're so late. They are asleep, aren't they?"

Before Minna could say anything, Sam said, "We're here because Papa decided at dinner that he had to be a buccaneer. My aunt Sherlock couldn't find him an eye patch, that's why you can't tell."

"What Sam means, Minna, is that I'm here to sling my bride over my shoulder and cart her away."

"I see," Minna said. She straightened, keeping Sam pressed against her side. She gave Miles a big grin. "Well, now, isn't this the funniest thing? Katie and Keely took off in her truck this evening, headed for Virginia."

"*What?*"

"Oh wow!"

Minna smiled at the boy and the man, who, she suspected, would be related to her in no time at all. "Come in, come in. You can phone Katie on her cell. I'm surprised you didn't get her number before you left."

"She wouldn't give it to me," Miles said. "She wanted time to think without my bugging her and without Sam guilting her."

"Doesn't matter. Don't worry, Sam, Keely's been working on her around the clock."

"I told her I'd work on my dad," Sam said and gave her a huge grin.

"That's my boy," Minna said. "How long will it take Katie to drive to Colfax?"

Miles felt ready to explode. His heart was pounding, his guts were in a knot. "Minna, please tell me exactly why Katie is driving to Colfax. Spell it out for me."

"She was coming to marry you, of course. She told me if you agreed, she'd call me and we'd work things out from this end."

"You're not joking? She's really coming to marry me? She and Keely just hopped in her truck and off they went?"

"That's it, Miles. She's been stomping around here, driving everyone nuts, she's growled at all her deputies, snapped at Mayor Tommy because he wanted every gory detail about everything, three times. What with all the rain and all the problems that's brought, it hasn't helped. She even snapped Linnie's head off, blew a fit at Keely for her less-than-subtle hints, cried at her and Keely's misery, and then she gave it up. Oh goodness, look at you, Miles. I love to see a man who's trying to think."

Miles stood there with his mouth open, just shaking his head. She'd been acting just like he had, which had to mean that she was miserable without him, without Sam.

"Katie's a buccaneer," Sam shouted. "Just like Papa!" Sam whooped, grabbed his father's hand, and started dancing around.

"Why don't I get her an eye patch for her wedding present?" Minna said. "You flew your plane, Miles?"

He nodded, blinking, still getting his wits back together.

"Then I guess you'd best be on your way back home. You don't want her to get there before you do, do you? And be careful, the weather's terrible."

He thought of Cracker and hoped to God she'd let Katie and Keely in the house if Katie beat him back to Colfax.

Monday Night
Colfax, Virginia

"We're married," Sam said with a great deal of satisfaction to the group gathered with coffee, champagne, and Cracker's special triple chocolate cake in the living room.

Savich leaned over and ruffled Sam's hair. He said, "Yep, it's all official now, Sam."

Sherlock, holding a sleeping Sean in her arms, nodded. "You and Keely are brother and sister."

"Cool," said Keely, and punched Sam in the arm.

"Well, you can see where my kid stands on this," Miles said as he handed a slice of cake to Cracker, who was still looking a bit shell-shocked.

Sam leaned over and patted her hand. "It's okay, Aunt Cracker, Katie's really nice and she can shoot people dead if they bother you."

Cracker swallowed the bite the wrong way and began coughing. Sam was slapping her on the back, she was tearing up, and Keely handed her a glass of champagne.

"Just what I needed," Cracker gasped and downed the champagne.

"Oh dear," Katie said. "Would you believe, Cracker, that I'm actually known more for keeping our teenagers on the straight and narrow? No kid under eighteen smokes in my town when I'm around."

Cracker took another bite of cake and said, as she closed her eyes in bliss, "That's not gory enough, Katie. Sounds like Sam thinks you're the Terminator."

But Sam and Keely weren't listening to the adults. They were whispering to each other in the corner of the living room, every once in a while sneaking looks at their parents.

Savich stood, picked up his boy and gently laid him over his shoulder. "It's nearly ten o'clock. We accomplished the impossible—got you guys licensed and married, all in one day."

"Thanks to the no-waiting laws in old Virginia," Miles said. "Lucky the circuit court clerk is real good friends with one of the judge's wives." Miles grinned from ear to ear. "One-stop shopping."

"Married," Katie said, and her eyes crossed. "I've known Miles for a week, and I'm married."

Sam evidently heard that clearly. He and Keely both hooted with laughter.

"Not only can she kill bad guys dead, she can even cross her eyes, Sam," Sherlock said. "What more could a guy ask for?"

"Oh yes, Mama," Keely said and crossed her own eyes. "I can do that, too, Aunt Sherlock."

Katie said to Sam, "Are you still going to be happy about this when you do something bratty and I have to nail your hide to the floor? I'm tough, remember, Sam."

Keely laughed. "I told him that if he acted stupid, you would put him up in a tree, like a cat."

"Hmm," Miles said. "Sam's pretty good with climbing trees, Keely, maybe I should give Katie some pointers."

"I'm never bad," Sam said. He smiled beatifically and sat back in his chair, crossing his arms over his chest.

On that cue, Sherlock and Savich took their leave, Sean giving little snorting snores as his father carried him out.

It was nearly midnight before the kids were in bed, Keely in a lovely bedroom of pale rose and cream connected to Sam's room through a bathroom. Keely just couldn't get over that. Katie heard her tell Sam not to step a single foot into her side of the bathroom or she'd bust him. It didn't matter that her side had the toilet. Sam made sure to stick his toe over to her side before he went to bed.

Cracker had a suite in the large former attic with its curious sloping corners and polished wooden floors. As Katie brushed her teeth, she hoped that Cracker would soon get over the intense suspicion Katie had felt coming off her in waves when she'd opened the door to Katie's knock. "You're here for what?" she'd said when she'd answered the door.

"Keely and I are here to see Miles. I'm Katie Benedict. Sheriff Katie Benedict." She'd stuck out her hand and had it hesitantly shaken, then dropped.

"You're the one who saved Sam? Oh dear, Miles isn't here. He said something weird about being a buccaneer, gave me a big hug, told me to wish him luck, and off he went with Sam, I don't know where. I guess you must come in." And she'd stepped back and been perfectly pleasant until Keely said, "Mama's here to marry Miles so Sam can be my brother and Miles can be my papa."

The woman looked like she'd been slapped in the face. Speaking through a rictus of a smile, she said, "Little girls say the cutest things, don't they?"

It seemed an eternity ago, yet it had only been the previous evening. Katie brushed out her hair. She started to braid it, then dropped her hands back to her sides. This was her wedding night. How very peculiar that was. Miles was right about the one-stop shopping. They'd plunked down thirty dollars and were in business. During the brief ceremony Sam stood straight and important beside his father, Keely beside her, and everyone else just a couple of steps back. It was a pity that her mother had been fogged in, no flights out at all for the entire day. Minna promised to come in the next couple of weeks. She wanted to give them some time to themselves.

Conrad Evans, Miles's right hand at the plant, had looked as shell-shocked as Cracker. He'd been quite nice, no choice, really. The man looked like a linebacker for the Titans, and had hair as red as Sherlock's.

Katie looked down at the plain gold band. Married. She was married again. She'd killed two kidnappers, an idiot former postal employee had burned her house down, and here she was, in Virginia, married. For the second time. She felt very strange, as if her life had taken a one-eighty, which indeed it had.

Her name was now Katie Benedict Kettering. It was weird.

When she came back to the big bedroom after tucking Keely in yet again for the night, making certain the bathroom door was open on both sides, she faced Miles across the length of his bedroom. It was a big airy room with large windows, antique furniture, and a bed the size of the *Queen Mary*. Katie crossed her arms over her chest, her position defensive, her fight-flight response in high gear.

She couldn't imagine taking off her clothes in front of this man who was nearly a stranger, and also her husband. She already had in a way, not really thinking about it.

"How tall are you?" she asked.

Miles wasn't a fool. He didn't move even a single step toward her. "Six-two, something around there. I'm not planning on jumping you, by the way," he said and grinned like a schoolboy who'd just shot a three-pointer from twenty feet.

Katie shook her head, both at him and at herself. "This is all just so weird."

"But just look at what you've accomplished in the space of a very short time." He tapped off his fingers. "You've known me for this entire week, enough to know I'll make a terrific mate, and you've made our kids so happy they just might not act bratty for another week. Your new last name isn't that bad at all. The best thing is that I really like you, Katie. Really. You looked great in your wedding dress."

"Don't forget the three-inch heels that brought me eyeball to eyeball with you."

"Never." He hadn't seen her in a dress until their wedding seven hours ago.

"I'm thirty-one years old."

"Yeah, I heard you tell the county clerk. I'm thirty-five, which means I've got more experience than you, a really finely honed judgment, and you should trust me completely." He held out his hands to her, palms up, fingers spread. "These are perfectly good hands you're in, Katie."

"Yeah, yeah, you've had more years to learn how to joke around and be an all-around smart guy." She paused a moment. "I haven't really trusted anyone—a man, that is—since Carlo."

"That makes sense, since the guy was such a gold-plated jerk. But I'm me and there's no gold plating about me. I'm not a shit, Katie, believe me. Now, it's nearly midnight on a fine Monday night. I'm exhausted, you're exhausted, and even Keely and Sam didn't complain about going to bed."

"That's a first and likely a last."

"Come here and let me kiss you. Then we'll go to bed and get our first good night's sleep in a week."

Katie looked at the bed, then back at Miles. "I haven't had sex in so long I think I've forgotten what comes after a kiss."

He started ticking off on his fingers.

"What are you doing?"

"Trying to figure out when I had sex last. I've used up all my fingers. This is truly pathetic. Maybe we can figure it out together, sooner or later. What do you think?"

She wasn't thinking anything, her brain was on hold. She tugged on her sleep shirt that showed a buzzard wearing a cowboy hat singing "Howdy, Howdy, Howdy, I'm a cowboy." He'd have liked that sleep shirt to disappear. He really liked those long long legs of hers; he'd really like them wrapped around him.

"Which side of the bed do you prefer?"

She pointed to the left. After he climbed in beside her, Katie said, "Those pajamas look brand new."

"They're my official wedding pajamas."

Miles flipped off the lights. Silence fell. After about five minutes, Katie said, "What are you humming?"

"Just an old buccaneer song."

"Miles?"

"Yeah?"

"How about we try a kiss, and maybe then those wedding pajamas can go back in the drawer."

A younger man, he thought, rolling over to a beautiful woman who was also his new wife, might feel a little nervous, but all his parts that counted were working just fine.

"We'll always have fun in bed," he said against her mouth, "maybe moan and thrash about a bit, and you'll see, our problems won't follow us here. You know something else?"

"What?"

"I swear I'll respect you in the morning."

When he had her under him, those long legs of hers wrapped around his flanks, and she was panting, biting his earlobe, kissing any part of him she could reach, he said, "We're going to be just fine, Katie," and he laid his hands on her then and she would have flown out the window if he hadn't been on top of her.

THIRTY-SEVEN

Two Weeks Later
Washington, D.C.

Sherlock heard a shout and turned to wave at Sean, who was running after Keely and Sam. Then Sam turned, held out his hand, and Sean latched on to it, shrieking. She smiled as she said to Katie, "They're really good with him."

"Yes, Sam told me he had to take care of Sean because he was little and ignorant."

Sherlock laughed.

"Keely said Sean would grow up fast enough. Then she said since boys had so much to learn, she'd better start teaching him stuff now. She didn't want to have to wait and cram everything into his head when he was grown up."

Another shout. Katie looked over her shoulder to see Miles throw a Frisbee to Keely. So much laughter. It warmed her all the way to her bones.

Katie said, "It's been two weeks and no more math teacher murders. Maybe the madman has simply left the area."

"Thank God for no more murders, but I really hope he hasn't left, it would make it that much harder to get the creep. Dillon hasn't said much, just told me he's doing good old-fashioned police work, and then he smiles. We'll see. I'm busy on other cases, so it's really pretty much in his bailiwick. Calls on the hot line have dropped over the past two weeks to only about fifty a day. You wouldn't believe how many man-hours it takes to check just fifty calls, and all for nothing."

"I can't begin to imagine. I never had to do anything like that." Katie shaded her eyes and looked over the park, always coming back to

Keely, who was chasing Sam, Sean running as fast as he could behind them. She didn't realize she'd stopped walking and was staring at nothing in particular when Sherlock said, "What's up, Katie?"

Katie gave a start. She looked down at the small woman who could probably knock her on her butt. "Do you fight dirty, Sherlock?"

"Dirty? Hmm. As in would I do anything at all, no matter how rotten, to disarm a bad guy? Oh yeah. Why?"

Katie shrugged. "I was just wondering, that's all. Would you look at this gorgeous day. Can you believe this Indian summer? In early December?"

Sherlock raised her face to the sun that was bright and warm. A crisp breeze rustled through the nearly naked tree branches, ruffled her hair. Winter was lurking just around the corner, but not today. "Thank God, all that interminable rain has stopped. I swear I was starting to grow mold. At least we've got a couple of beautiful days before that snowstorm hits on Monday."

"Mom says it's finally stopped raining in Jessborough. Everything is still soggy, but things are getting back to normal. Do you know what she sent me for a wedding present?"

"A whip?"

To Sherlock's surprise, Katie looked like she would burst into tears. "What is it, Katie? What did she send you?"

Katie wiped her hand across her eyes, and shook her head. "I didn't mean to lose it like that. What you said about the whip—that's funny, but it's just that every time I think about it, how much it means to me and how she knew how much it means. She sent me copies of all her family photos, put them in three big albums. You know I lost everything when the house burned down. But now I have Keely's first five years again."

"Oh my, that was nice of her. Your mom is the greatest, Katie. Sam's a lucky little boy to have such a wonderful grandmother. You said you guys are going back to Jessborough for Christmas? And there'll be a religious ceremony this time for your mom and all your friends?"

Katie nodded. "She didn't want to come here right away. She wanted to give the four of us time to get settled in with each other." Katie sucked in a deep breath. "You know, Sherlock, it just doesn't smell like eastern Tennessee here."

"No," Sherlock said. "Here, there's always the underlying scent of car exhaust."

"No, it's more than that."

"Okay, there's also the scent of politicians, and that's worse than car exhaust. But you know, springtime in Washington is really beautiful, if you just forget politics."

Katie laughed, but to Sherlock's keen ears, it was forced. She said, "Miles mentioned yesterday that as soon as Savich was up for it, they were going to work out together."

Sherlock said, "That'll end up in lots of insults and bruises. I hope you're good with the Ben-Gay tube."

"Oh yeah, I am. I told Miles you'd take on the winner."

Sherlock looked very pleased at that. "You've been married thirteen days, Katie, which means that you and Miles have known each other for, wow, a grand total of three weeks. Now, how are things going between you?"

Katie arched an eyebrow. "I don't sleep in the guest room, if that's what you mean."

"Well, no, I would certainly hope that you don't. As I told Dillon, Miles is not only a really good guy, he has this marvelous flat stomach."

"So he does."

"And who could turn that down?"

"Not I. And I'll tell you something else, Sherlock, Miles is also the sexiest guy on earth."

Sherlock was too kind to point out the obvious, that Katie was wrong, dead wrong—Dillon was the sexiest guy, period. Anywhere. Maybe she would tell Katie when she knew her better. Sherlock said, her brow furrowed, "I would think that intimacy between two people who really like each other, who are committed to each other and to a family, well, it would help move things more quickly, take away the artificialness of the situation. Hey, you see a guy in his boxers, whiskers on his face, and the embarrassment factor goes down fast."

"It's still tough, both of us dancing around, afraid to hurt the other's feelings or piss the other off or do something that might upset one of the kids."

"And Sam and Keely are settling in together? Or is there a problem?"

"There are kid squabbles, but yeah, they're incredible together. Just this morning, both of them came bouncing in on our bed at six a.m. It felt . . . good. Sometimes I wonder how Keely could not have known Sam all her life. They're very close. As for Cracker, I haven't a clue what's going on in her head. She leaves us alone for the most part, spends lots of time in her attic suite, or is out with friends for the evenings, movies, I think. She's pleasant enough when we cross paths. I really hope she'll start dating, if she's not already."

Sherlock picked a twig off a maple tree and chewed on it. "She wanted to marry Miles, you know."

"I figured that. Still, she's trying to be nice to me. Talk about a shock for her."

"The thing is that after her sister died, she moved in to take care of Sam, which was a great thing for her to do. Both Sam and Miles were devastated and she provided stability. But it's been over two years now and you're here. It's time for her to get her own life."

"And find a good guy that isn't Miles."

"All right, Katie. What's really wrong?"

"If you want the truth, well then, I'm itchy, restless. The first week, I walked every inch of that very lovely house, raked leaves until I had blisters on my palms, spoke to my mom twice a day, played with the kids until I was too tired to stand. Then this last week . . . okay, I whined, not to Miles, to Dr. Raines—my good friend Sheila—in Jessborough. She can take it. She told me lots of things that just depressed me more. She just ended up telling me to be patient, that it'll take time to settle in, and metaphorically patted me on the head.

"As you know, I'm on a leave of absence from the Jessborough Sheriff's Department. And that puts Wade temporarily in charge, and that's okay, don't get me wrong, but—" Katie shrugged, sighed, and continued after clearing her throat once, then again. "Sorry. Of course, both kids started back to school a week and a half ago. Sam was a hero to his classmates. Unfortunately, Keely's a year behind Sam, but she appears to be doing okay. She misses her friends in Jessborough, but she has Sam and that makes up for it. Sam's included her with all his friends, and since he's the big dog among the first-graders, she's in. It's still early, we'll see. That leaves lots of hours in-between to fill up, hours I never before even dreamed existed."

"Katie—"

"Okay, okay, don't hit me. Here's the bottom line for me, Sherlock: I've got to do something real, something worthwhile—"

Yeah, like be sheriff again. Sherlock said, "I understand, truly I do. Give it just a little more time, just like Dr. Raines said. Talk to Miles about it—he's your husband now, Katie, and that means you're not alone anymore. You've got this big additional brain to add to the mix, and that's good, at least part of the time."

"Now you're going to preach to me about compromise."

"Fact is, you've got to compromise to have a good marriage, and sometimes that's so sucky I want to yell."

"Yeah, yeah. All right, I'll talk to him about it, but not yet. He's working really hard right now."

Sherlock nodded. "Tell me what else Dr. Raines said."

"Wade is doing fine as acting sheriff. She says everyone misses me and asks when I'm coming back. All I can say is 'We'll see.'"

Katie started shaking her head. "I was even studying a cookbook yesterday." She sighed. "It's so stupid really, but I never thought about what would happen two weeks after we got married, or a month, or a year, or anything. It was just the right thing to do and I didn't consider, you know, what exactly would come after the wedding. I never once wondered how it would be not to have the sheriff's job, to be living in a place I didn't know, not the streets, not the shops, not the people.

"Sorry, I'm whining again. Damn, sometimes it's really hard to be an adult."

"That's the truth," Sherlock said. "No honeymoon in sight?"

"Miles has been working his butt off at the plant. He says there's lots to be done, what with contract issues still unresolved, design problems with the helicopter guidance system, stuff like that. He's missed dinner three times this past week."

"Hmm," Sherlock said again. "Katie, you guys are going to have to talk about this, you know. Oh, quick, look at that Frisbee throw Miles just made to Sam."

Katie twisted about to see the Frisbee floating toward Sam, watched Sam leap a good foot into the air and snag it. She heard Miles and Dillon laugh. She wondered what they were talking about. Was Miles talking about her to Dillon? Saying the same things about his life that she'd been saying to Sherlock?

Savich was saying to Miles as they both watched Sam leap into the air and curl his fingers around the edge of the Frisbee to bring it in, "I've just about given up on the Redskins this year."

Miles said, "Yeah, it's hard to even turn the games on anymore, it's so depressing. I have this gut feeling about the Raiders, though, we'll see. Wasn't that catch something? Sam's nearly Olympic with the Frisbee. I've been playing with him since he was three."

"I thought I'd start Sean in six months or so. I'm also thinking the Patriots might make it to the big game. Does Katie like football?"

"You know, I don't have the foggiest idea what my wife thinks about football. That first Sunday we just relaxed, what with no Beau or Clancy to worry about, took the kids for pizza and ice cream and fell into bed at nine o'clock. We'll see if she perks up at kick-off time tomorrow."

"Hey, Sean, come back here!"

Savich was off, scooping up his son, swinging him over his head, letting his shrieks of laughter flow over him.

Miles said to Savich once he'd trotted back, Sean under one arm, "I sure like the sound of your Porsche engine. You get it tuned up recently?"

"Oh yeah. God's creation gets checked if it hiccups once. Sounds really good, huh?"

"You know it does. Sherlock was telling me that Sean loves that car, that you've promised to give it to him when he's eighteen."

"Yep, I did."

"By that time the Porsche will be in a museum."

Savich grinned. "How about that? Hey, all you've got left from McCamy is just a faint line down your cheek. It looks like it just might stay with you."

Miles touched his face. "A good thing. It'll fit my image."

Savich smiled. "How's Cracker dealing with your marriage?"

"Oh, she's fine with it. She's always a brick. No problem at all."

Savich wondered if Miles really didn't have a clue as to his sister-in-law's feelings for him, or if he was just in denial. He sincerely doubted that Cracker was a happy camper with another woman in the house and this one Miles's wife.

Suddenly, they heard a shot, sharp and clear in the still air, not at all close. It was up ahead, near Katie and Sherlock.

For a brief instant they both froze, then Miles whirled about. "Oh, damn! What's happening?"

Savich yelled, "Sherlock, Katie, gunfire! Hurry, get down!"

"Savich, get Sean behind that tree! I'll get the kids!"

There were two more shots in rapid succession, closer to them.

Savich would swear that he felt the heat of that second bullet as it tunneled past his head before he dropped to his knees behind a huge oak tree, Sean clutched against his chest. Sean was crying and his father was shaking so badly he couldn't do anything except rock his boy, holding him close, trying to cover every bit of him with his body.

He saw Sherlock crouched down behind a square garbage receptacle some thirty feet beyond them, looking all around, waiting. Katie was on her hands and knees, her cell phone out.

He heard a car door slam, but couldn't see where. He whispered nonsense to Sean, heard his boy sob, felt his small body heave, pressed very tightly against his father's body.

God, that bastard could have shot his son. He called out, "Miles?"

Miles's voice was out of breath. "I've got Keely and Sam. We're down, about twelve feet behind you. Is Sean all right?"

"Yes, just scared to his bones, like I am."

Savich heard voices, lots of them, some screams. Not all that many people in the park, thank God, but enough.

Savich was sitting on the ground, his back against the oak tree, rocking Sean back and forth in his arms, holding him as close as he could.

Not thirty seconds later, Sherlock was in his arms, Sean sandwiched between them, and she was whispering against his chin, "Thank God you're all right."

"I'm fine, sweetheart." He sounded all calm again, but he didn't let her go.

Savich heard Katie say, even as she clutched Keely tightly against her, "Hey, Sam, that was the sort of excitement I'd hoped we'd seen the last of in Jessborough, wasn't it? Did you dive behind a garbage can?"

"There sure are lots of bad guys, Katie," said Sam, who was plastered against his father's side, and blinked at her. He shook his head, "There wasn't a garbage can close. Papa grabbed up me and Keely. We were over behind that big tree." He paused a moment, his forehead wrinkled. "Who's after me this time?"

"Someone who heard you were bad," Keely said, and, bless her heart, she reached out and punched him.

"Sam, I don't think anyone was after you this time," Miles said. "You guys okay? Really?"

"You promise, Papa?" said Sam.

Smiling, Miles picked both of them up, then reached out his hand to Katie. Like Sherlock and Savich, they stood close for a very long time, at least until their hearts slowed.

Katie said, "I called nine-one-one. They'll be here any minute now."

Sherlock said, "I spotted a late-model white Camry screech out of here. I got four numbers off the license plate: WT twenty-seven—that's it."

Miles and Savich looked at each other. Savich said, "Looks like the women took care of things."

As for Katie, she needed to get to a bathroom, fast.

THIRTY-EIGHT

Nearly three hours later Katie and Miles tucked the kids into their beds. It was only seven o'clock at night, but both Sam and Keely had just folded down, an adrenaline crash.

As they walked back down the long corridor to their bedroom, Miles said, "They're out like lights, thank God. Amazing."

"Yeah. Keely was gone before I read the first page of her story. She only talked a little bit about the shooting in the park."

"Same with Sam, thank God. Did you see Sean fall asleep in his father's arms? A good thing, since Savich wasn't about to let him go. And the worry in Sherlock's face, damn, this isn't good. Why did this happen? For God's sake, we were in the park with the children."

"Miles—"

"Dear God, I know the kids seem okay right now, but what about tomorrow, the next day? I think it's smart to use a real light touch, making it all seem like an adventure, getting the spotlight off Sam. I sure hope it works. Sam didn't act like he was freaked out again, not like he was in Jessborough. And Keely seemed all right, too." He shuddered. "Somebody after Savich or Sherlock, I guess." He began emptying his pants pockets on the dresser top. "Since they weren't after Sam, it's just got to shove away at least some of the fear, don't you think?"

"Yes, I think you're right. Miles—"

"You know, Katie, I've never seen Savich freak like this before. He was white as a sheet and didn't even want to give Sean over to Sherlock. This asshole trying to shoot him right there in the middle of a park, Jesus, he could have killed Sean. He could have killed any of us, even Sam and Keely."

"Miles—"

He set his wallet on the dresser, looked over at Katie who was standing by the bathroom door. "Yes?"

"Maybe the asshole wasn't necessarily just after Savich or Sherlock."

"What do you mean?"

Katie slowly slid her arms out of her leather jacket, pulled it down, and let it slide to the floor. She lifted up her long gray sweatshirt and he saw the blood covering her upper thigh. "It could be that the asshole was after me."

He couldn't take it in, just couldn't. He stood there like a block of wood, staring at all that blood. Then his breath whooshed out. "Oh Jesus, oh God, you're hurt." He was at her side in a moment, his face flushed red, his hands shaking. "Why didn't you say anything? You didn't say a single word! I'm getting you to the emergency room. I can't believe you didn't tell me, that you sat through all the questioning with the cops, and didn't say a thing. No, just keep quiet and don't faint on me."

"I won't faint. It's not bad, the bullet just grazed me, on the side of my hip. If you could just help me off with my jeans we could take a look."

"Shut up. So that's why you excused yourself to that public bathroom in the park, that's why you left Keely with me, oh damn." He came down on his hands and knees in front of her and unzipped her jeans. He eased them down real slow and easy. She'd ripped off the bottom of her sweatshirt and wrapped it around her upper thigh. It was bloody, but not fresh blood, he didn't think. "I'm not going to undo it, it might start bleeding again." He got to his feet, helped her pull up her jeans again. "I'll tell Cracker that we're leaving the house for a bit. Stay put, Katie."

While he was gone, Katie took a couple more Tylenol. When Miles got back to her, looked at her white face in the bathroom mirror and saw the Tylenol bottle, he didn't say a word, just picked her up in his arms and carried her out to the car. "It's funny how it hurts more now that I've told you about it. Isn't that strange?"

She was breathing light shallow breaths, obviously hurting even though it was just a graze. Jesus, a bullet had gone through her. He just couldn't take it in. And she hadn't said a word.

Katie appreciated that Miles was really careful when he fastened the seat belt.

"Hang in there, Katie, the hospital's only about ten minutes away." It was hard not to floor the accelerator, but he didn't want her flying forward.

At a red light, he smacked his hands on the steering wheel. She saw the pulse pounding in his neck. He was angry, very understandable. "Okay, I can't stand it any longer. Give me one good reason, Katie, just one good reason why you didn't tell me." His voice was low and perfectly cold, not a bit of inflection. She wondered if he ever yelled.

She felt a sharp stab of pain that held her quiet until it eased.

"Well, are you going to say anything?" Now, she thought, that was close to a yell. She nearly smiled, but couldn't.

She got hold of herself and said, "The children. I just couldn't let Sam and Keely see that I'd been shot. They've been through so much, particularly Sam, I just couldn't do that to them. If I'd been shot bad, Miles, I would have hollered, but it's just not that bad. I figured it could wait until we took care of the kids. I know it was unfair of me to spring this on you."

"Yeah, right, real unfair."

Sarcasm was good, she supposed. She said, "I went to the women's room in the park, tore off some of my sweatshirt, pulled down my jeans and wrapped it tight around my hip. Really, it looked to me like a flesh wound, the bullet went right through me. I'm not going to die, Miles."

"You'd better not or I'll really be pissed. So would Sam. So would Keely."

"I don't want them to know about this."

He gunned the Mercedes into the hospital parking lot, and swerved into the circular turnabout in front of the emergency room, figuring they'd get instant attention, and so they did.

He held her hand when the nurse pulled down her jeans and untied the strips of sweatshirt she'd wrapped around herself. The piece of sweatshirt that was directly over the wound was soaked with blood. She didn't touch it. Miles was ready to yell when Dr. Pierce came barreling into the cubicle in the next instant, out of breath. "Hey, I hear we got a gunshot wound," he said, and looked down at Katie's hip. "Would you look at that. I heard about the shooting, Mr. Kettering, but they said it had to do with the FBI. They didn't say anyone was injured. I don't understand why she didn't see a doctor right away."

"We'll talk about it later, Dr. Pierce," Katie said. "Please, just clean me up."

"This is going to hurt a bit, Mrs. Kettering." He managed to get the rest of the sweatshirt off the wound, but of course it had stuck and Katie almost yelled at the pain.

But she hung in there, squeezing Miles's hand really hard when the nurse used alcohol to clean off all the dried blood.

"The bullet appears to have gone through the fleshy part of the side of your hip, Mrs. Kettering. You two know, of course, that I'll have to report this."

"Yes, of course," Miles said. "You wondered why we didn't come to the ER immediately. Well, my wife didn't want our children to know she'd been shot and that's why we're here now."

"Not very bright of you, Mrs. Kettering."

"Yeah, yeah, I just bet you'd choose to let your kids see you dripping blood if you had a choice."

Dr. Pierce paused a moment, then slowly nodded. "You're a cop, aren't you?"

"A sheriff. I know when a wound is bad and when it can wait awhile. Nothing to hit here in my hip except fat, and that always grows back without a problem."

Miles said, "Call Detective Raven at DC Metro. He'll tell you all about it. I'll bet he'll also want to smack my wife around a bit."

"Okay. Mrs. Kettering, I can see this hurts. We're going to start an IV, give you some morphine. You'll want to go to sleep on the examination table in just a minute or two. Then I can clean up this wound and stitch you together. I don't think you'll be needing any X rays. Hold on to your husband's hand real tight. That's it."

She sucked in her breath, and it was done. He left her for a moment; undoubtedly he was going to call Detective Raven.

An hour later, Katie was walking slowly out of the hospital, supported by Miles.

"You're going to be okay," he said, more for himself than for her, Katie thought, as he very carefully fastened her seat belt. "The doctor said you were lucky. Now, don't move."

"I won't."

When he was driving out of the parking lot, Katie said, "Thank you, Miles. I know this was a pain in your butt as well as mine, but, well, thank you."

"You're my damned wife. You think I'd dab some iodine on your hip and go to sleep?"

He was angry again. If she hadn't felt so dopey, her brain cotton, she would have laughed. "Where are we going?"

He turned to face her for a moment. "To the all-night pharmacy to get the Vicodin prescription filled. You're to take a couple every four hours for a day or so."

"I really feel fine."

"That's the morphine talking."

"I understand how you would get really upset what with all that dried blood on my hip."

"Don't even start with me, Katie. I am so pissed at you—"

"That's all right, just so long as we keep this from the children."

Miles sucked in a deep breath. "Tomorrow, after I'm sure you're up to it, we're going to discuss who might have shot at us. I'll bet that's what Detective Raven is wondering. Count on him coming by tomorrow, along with half the FBI."

"Bring them on, Miles." She closed her eyes and drifted off. She wasn't aware that he'd stopped at the all-night pharmacy. She hadn't awakened when he'd undressed her and tucked her into bed.

She wasn't aware that he held her hand until he woke her up at two o'clock and fed her two Vicodin. He held her hand the rest of that long night.

The next morning, the lovely morphine was a hazy memory, the pain in her hip all too present. When Miles held out two big pills to her, she took them without a fuss.

"Oh, no," she said, "where are the kids?"

"I'll take care of the kids. It's still early. When they're up, I'll tell them that you've got a bit of a stomach bug and to leave you alone until you decide to appear. Okay?"

"I can tell you're a parent. You're good. Thank you, Miles."

He paced the room in front of her, then turned back to face her. "Katie, I've been thinking quite a bit about this. I think you did the right thing. We don't know how Sam and Keely are going to be this morning, how yesterday's trauma will affect them, but I do know that if they knew you'd been shot, it would be much worse. So thank you. Now see that you heal while I think about how I'm going to keep the police away from you as long as possible."

"I'll be just fine. Say early afternoon?"

She fell asleep ten minutes later with just a pinch of pain in her hip.

Miles stood a moment in the doorway, then looked down at his watch. It was only six-thirty in the morning. The kids would be up any time now. He hated lying to them, but not this time. He hoped they could carry it off. He didn't want to see any more blank pain in Sam's eyes for as long as he lived.

THIRTY-NINE

At eight o'clock that evening, only three hours after leaving Detective Raven down at Metro Headquarters in the Daley building, Savich came to stand in the kitchen doorway, watching Sherlock wipe spaghetti sauce off Sean's mouth. Sean quickly replaced it with the next spoonful. What with all the excitement, they'd gotten home very late, and Sean was hungry, tired, and really hyped up. As for Sean's parents, they both hoped some of Savich's spaghetti would put him out. Savich said to Sherlock, not taking his eyes off his boy, "Are you ready for something you're not going to believe?"

Sherlock straightened midswipe. "I heard you talking on the phone to Miles. What's going on?"

"The shooter today. It seems he wasn't after me. He was after Katie."

"After Katie? What do you mean?"

Savich didn't say anything for a moment as Sean clattered his spoon to his plate, climbed down from his chair, and made a beeline for his orange plastic ball in the corner. They both, for a moment, listened to him tell the ball that he was going to bounce it, good.

When she looked up at him, Savich said, "He shot Katie."

"*What?* How? But that isn't possible! She never said a word, she never acted wounded, she—"

Savich leaned his head back against one of the cabinets, closed his eyes. "He shot her in the hip and she managed to hide it from all of us. The bullet went in and through. She'll be okay. Miles called from the emergency room while the nurse was getting Katie into a robe. Turns out she didn't say a word about it until after they'd gotten home and put the kids to bed. Then she tells him. He's still so shaken up he could barely speak straight."

"She's really okay?"

"Yes, soon to be out with a smile on her face from the morphine. Just a couple days rest, and she'll be fine."

Sherlock picked up a hot pad and hurled it across the kitchen. It calmed her and didn't make any noise to frighten Sean. "I don't believe this, Dillon. It's ridiculous, just plain dumb. She's wounded and doesn't even let on? No, that can't be right, it can't."

"She didn't say anything because she didn't want the kids any more frightened than they were. If you think about it, you can see Katie's point. It was an adult decision, hers to make, I guess."

Sherlock's heart was still pumping wildly. She threw another hot pad at the wall, calmed herself down. "It was brave of her." She drew in a deep breath. "I hope I would have the presence of mind to do that. But wait, Dillon, if the shooter hit her—"

"That means I wasn't the target. Or, I really was the target, and he could have shot at her first, for the fun of it."

Savich straightened, shrugged. "Maybe he, whoever *he* is, just wanted to scare us. At this point, any guess is as good as any other. Who knows, it might have been a random shooting." Neither of them believed that for an instant.

Savich picked up Sean, who was tightly clutching his orange ball, and walked to the front window in the living room. He stared out into the calm dark night. A storm was expected to hit Monday, winter coming with a grand announcement. And the temperature would plummet. Sean dropped his ball, watched it roll under an end table. He then spoke in his father's ear and patted his face, telling him things he understood, like *good spaghetti*—"I think Sean just said he wanted a puppy."

It was so ridiculous that for a moment Sherlock actually laughed and kissed her son's sleepy face.

She saw the strain on Dillon's face, saw the restless movement of his hands, saw the scars on his hands and fingers from his whittling. She knew he'd been caught off guard by the same devastating feelings she had felt when that bullet had come so close to him and to Sean. It made her want to scream and cry at the same time. He said finally, as if he'd been holding the words inside but they now had to come out, "This was too close, Sherlock, far too close. Sean could have been killed."

Of course she agreed. The corrosive fear, the sense of absolute impotence—she nodded but didn't say anything, just moved closer.

Sean's head now lay on his father's shoulder. Savich lightly smoothed his back, cupped his head. She saw a spasm of fear cross his face. He said quietly, "I've been giving a lot of thought today to what I've been doing nearly all my adult life—being a cop. What if . . . what if, because of me, some crazy kills my son? It would be my fault, Sherlock, no one else's, just mine, and it would all be because of what I choose to do for a living. I couldn't live with that, I just couldn't."

"No," she said slowly, her eyes still on his face, "neither of us could."

He plowed forward, the words forcing themselves out of his mouth. "Maybe, just maybe, I should think about another line of work." There, he'd said the unimaginable, and the earth hadn't opened up and swallowed him. It was out in the open now, those words between them, and he didn't say anything else, just let the unthinkable settle around him, and he waited. Sean suddenly lurched up against his palm, and smiled at his father. He patted his father's face again with wet fingers.

Sherlock closed in and put her arms around him, just as they had after the shooting, with Sean between them. Then she began to lightly scratch around the healing wound in his back. They stood there silently together for several minutes. Finally, she raised her face, patted his cheek with her fingers, hers thankfully not wet, and said, "Do you know, Dillon, I agree with you entirely."

He nearly fell back against the window with surprise. "You do?"

"Yes, I do. But the only thing is, you're the best cop I've ever met in my life."

"Maybe, but Sean—"

She nodded. "This was so scary that both of us nearly went round the bend. But, you know, if you just stop to think about it, the solution to this isn't difficult."

His head came up. "What solution?" He sounded irritated, and she was pleased. She could just imagine how deep he would dig in his heels if she argued with him, what with the worry and the guilt, worry and guilt that had nearly felled her as well.

She went on her tiptoes and kissed him, and again hugged her boy and her husband tight.

"Dillon, you're a smart man."

"Yeah, well, what's your point? What's this easy solution?"

She smiled up at him, kissed both him and Sean again, and said, "As I said, you're smart. But here's your problem; you're just too much of a hero, Dillon; you feel too responsible, like you have to fix every bad thing that happens anywhere around you. It's not just your job, it's who you are."

"Yeah, sure, but—"

"No buts. No more. You're a cop, Dillon, one of the very best. It's what you are, who you are. What happened in the park—it was scary, that's for sure, but the fact is there are such things as random shootings. Would you have blamed yourself for being a cop then? I'll tell you, there have been times when I've wanted to take you away to the Poconos, hide you in a cabin, and carry around six guns to protect you."

"And you don't think I've felt the same way about you?"

She gave him a big smile, reached up her hand and cupped his cheek. "I think we're both doing exactly what we were meant to do. I plan for Sean to see us both well into old age. Get over it, Dillon. It's time to move on."

He kissed her, pulled her hard against him again. Sean burped. "But—"

"I know, there's always a but. Let's just work through this one day at a time, all right? You know as well as I do that the time to make a life-altering decision isn't right after a huge scare."

Slowly, he nodded.

"We've worked through everything else that's come along and hit us in the chops. This is different because it's the first time our jobs have come close to Sean, the first time our little tiger here could have been hurt because of what we do. It will be tough, but we'll do the right thing. Don't worry, we'll sort it all out."

"Sherlock?"

She lightly bit his neck in answer.

"You want to spend some quality time with me?"

She was laughing as she licked where she'd bitten. "Can I strip you naked and kiss you all over?"

He swallowed hard, and nodded, looking at her smiling mouth. Sean burped again.

Sunday Afternoon
The Kettering Home
Colfax, Virginia

Katie didn't hurt if she stayed still, and that was a very nice thing. On the other hand, she wasn't stupid enough to laugh or make any sudden movements. She was seated in Miles's big comfortable leather chair, wearing sweats with a nice loose fleece top that hid the bandages under the sweats, her feet up on a big ottoman, her legs covered with a ratty afghan Miles's mother had knitted many years before. She was wearing a pair of thick socks, no shoes.

Cracker had taken Sam and Keely to a children's movie matinee so they wouldn't see or hear the cops. Both of them had seemed fine, thank God, neither suspecting that she had something other than the flu. She was thankfully spared enthusiastic hugs that would surely have brought a moan out of her. She smiled over Sherlock and Savich, who'd arrived a few minutes earlier.

Miles brought in coffee and tea, and a plate of scones he'd picked up at Nathan's Bakery just down on Cartwright Avenue.

Detective Benjamin Raven said the moment he sat down on the comfortable sofa in the living room, ignoring both scones and coffee, "I am royally pissed, Mrs. Kettering. That was a really stupid thing to do."

To his surprise, she nodded. "I would agree with you, Detective, if I'd been wearing your cop's shoes and not the victim's."

It was Sunday, his buddies were waiting for him down at the sports bar with peanuts, beer, and the Redskins game. Then Mr. Kettering had called. He'd been nursing his snit for a good half hour now and he wasn't about to let go without cutting loose on the woman who'd ruined his day. "You're a cop, Sheriff, yet you pulled this stunt. You've come pretty close to obstructing justice."

"An interesting point, Detective," Miles said, his voice mild, really quite reasonable now that he'd gotten over his own snit. He turned slightly in his chair and winked at Katie before he turned back. "I think it was pretty dumb, too, but we've already discussed why she did it. Can we move on to something helpful?"

Detective Raven shouted at all of them indiscriminately, "Are all you people nuts? Your macho sheriff here could have bloody bled to death!"

"I really prefer macha, Detective Raven."

"Don't you try to jolly me out of this, Sheriff!"

Miles said, "If she'd been shot bad, she would have yelled. She's not stupid." He paused a moment. "You would have yelled, wouldn't you have, Katie?"

"Oh yes. I've always believed you've got to live to fight another day." She stared at Miles, then gave him such a brilliant smile he blinked.

"Enough already," Detective Raven said at last. He snagged a scone off the plate, poured himself a cup of coffee, and said, "If you guys are through praising this crazy woman, why doesn't somebody tell me who you think fired at you."

Katie said, "I made a phone call back home to Jessborough just before you got here, Detective. Miles told you yesterday about all the hoopla we went through there. I asked about the congregation, about what was going on with them. Nothing, evidently. Interesting fact though. The place has been a disaster area what with all the storms, but once it started drying out, crews went out to the ruins of the McCamy house to start cleaning everything up and dig out the bodies. It's still really slow going. There's no word yet."

Detective Raven said, "You think one of the McCamys survived?"

"No one could have survived in that house, Detective," Miles said.

"Then what's your point?"

Katie said, "I guess maybe I was just surprised that they hadn't cleaned everything up. It's just strange, all of it."

"Basically, we ain't got anymore diddly than we had yesterday," Detective Raven said, rising, and dusting off his jeans. "I've always hated too many possibilities. It sucks, big time."

"Yeah," Miles said, "I agree."

Savich's cell phone played the *1812 Overture*. He held up a staying hand, listened, and when he hung up, he said, "That was one of my agents. The white Toyota Camry the shooter was driving was stolen two days ago from a Mr. Alfred Morley, in Rockville, Maryland. Right out of his driveway, during the night. He told the local police and they put out an APB on it."

"I don't suppose the car's turned up?" Detective Raven said.

Savich shook his head. "Not yet."

"Well, like my daddy always says, if things come too easy in life, you have more fun than you deserve. Okay, that's it then. Thanks for the scones." He looked down at his watch. "Well, damn, I've missed a good half of the game."

"The Redskins are probably losing anyway," Savich said. "No fun watching that."

FORTY

Savich was depressed, he admitted it. Sherlock was in a meeting when he left headquarters early to stop at the gym. He wanted to sweat out some of the day's frustrations and see what his back could manage. Maybe he'd find someone he could practice some easy throws with.

What he didn't want to find at the gym was Valerie Rapper; her eyes were on him the moment he came out of the men's locker room.

He nodded to her, nothing more, and headed into the big room to stretch. She followed him, stood at the barre in front of the mirrors and did some ballet moves with her toes pointed out. She said, "I've missed you, Agent Savich."

He didn't answer her, tried to concentrate on stretching out his knotted muscles. The stress had left him feeling tight and cold. At least his back wasn't bothering him.

"Would you like me to walk on your back? I'm really very good at it and you look like you could use it."

"No, thank you, I'm about all set now," he said and left the exercise room. He worked out hard, moving between the weights and the treadmill, aware that she was always near, and it was driving him nuts. When she got on the treadmill next to him nearly an hour later, he knew he had to put a stop to this.

"Ms. Rapper."

"Yes, Agent Savich?" She cocked an eyebrow at him, actually ran her tongue over her bottom lip. He stared at that slip-sliding tongue of hers, not out of overwhelming lust, but amazement that she actually did that. The only thing he knew for sure about Ms. Valerie Rapper was that she had supreme self-confidence. Hadn't any guy ever said no to her? Evidently not.

He said with a touch of humor in his voice, "Why don't you go introduce yourself to Jake Palmer? You see the good-looking guy down there doing bench presses? He's single, been divorced for a good long time, and I've heard he's ready to start dating again. I'm not in the dating market, Ms. Rapper."

"I'm glad you're not, Agent Savich. I want you all to myself."

Her arrogance astounded him, and he was silent for a moment. "I've already told you I'm married, Ms. Rapper. I've got a wife who wants me all to herself. I'm not available. Please, enough is enough. Hey, Jake can out-bench-press me."

She stretched out her hand and pressed the stop button on his treadmill. He stared at her as she stepped over onto his treadmill, right in front of him, ignoring the dozen or so people on the machines near them, and pressed herself against him. She went up on her toes, clasped her palms around his face and kissed him, hard.

There was no punch of lust, just shock at what she was doing, and then anger.

He heard a wolf whistle, but mainly there was just stupefied silence. There was a comment, within hearing, about at least taking it to the parking lot.

"Shall we go to that sexy red Porsche of yours?" She said into his mouth. "But you're a big man, Agent Savich. My Mercedes is roomier than a Porsche, so how about we go there instead?"

Savich grabbed her arms, pulled them to her sides, and held them there.

She looked up at him, her eyes on his mouth, and said, "You're really strong. I like that."

"Dillon, why is this woman taking advantage of you on the treadmill?"

Sherlock. He grinned like a loon. He was never so happy to hear her voice in his life. He let go of Valerie's arms and pushed her back, but her lower body was still close to his groin. He heard a whistle and looked onto the main floor of the gym. There was Jake, giving him a little wave. So Jake had called Sherlock. He nodded back and said to his wife, "Hi, sweetheart, I didn't hear you come in."

"No, I can see that it would have been tough given Ms. Barracuda here all over you."

"Actually, this is Valerie Rapper."

Sherlock gave a cheerful smile to the woman who was standing frozen, still too close to Dillon. "Hi, Ms. Rapper. If you don't get your hands, your mouth, and all the rest of yourself off my husband, and step off his treadmill, I will deck you. Then I will put my foot on your neck and I will rub your nose into a sweaty mat. Is that enough of a threat?"

Valerie took a step back, couldn't help herself, not knowing what to say to that miserable little red-headed monster. She wanted Savich, wanted *him,* not anyone else. He'd been playing the faithful game—oh yes, a man could be as coy and tease as well as any woman—but it would have ended quite soon. She said to him, "Would you just look at her. I'll bet she dyes all that wild red hair. There aren't any freckles on her face, and that means a dye job. It's not even well done. I can see roots."

Savich said, "I can assure you that all that wild red hair is quite natural. I'm her husband, I've got the inside track on this."

"Dillon," Sherlock said, "that's a tad indelicate. Ms. Rapper, not all redheads have freckles. Now, please remove yourself or I will take action in the next couple of seconds."

Valerie waved this away. "You know if she weren't here, you'd be pulling me out of this wretched gym in no time at all."

"Do you really think so?" Savich inquired, and a black eyebrow shot up a good inch.

"Of course I do! This is ridiculous. Don't you know who I am?"

Sherlock said, head cocked to the side, "A pushy broad with an embarrassing last name?"

"You little bitch, back off! My father is the CEO and major stockholder of Rapper Industries. I am his daughter."

"Fancy that," Savich said, looking impressed, his mouth smiling, but his eyes hard. "Actually, when you said he was your father, I figured you just might be his daughter."

"I could buy your dumb-ass FBI with my trust fund!"

Now this was interesting, Savich thought. "How ignorant of me. I hadn't realized who you were. Just imagine, the daughter of the famed Mr. Rapper. Now that I realize you're very rich as well as very beautiful, it makes all the difference. Don't you agree, sweetheart?"

Sherlock, her smile still in place, nodded. "It sure does. It makes me realize it's time to bring out my big guns." She pushed Dillon out of the way and stepped up right into Valerie Rapper's face, making three of them on the treadmill. "I don't suppose you know who we are, do you?"

Valerie Rapper blinked. "Of course, you're a couple of unimportant little cops. So what?"

"If he's so little, then why do you want him?"

"I was referring to you. I saw him on TV. I saw those women reporters looking at him. Go away now."

Sherlock didn't touch her, even though she badly wanted to. She said, not an inch from Valerie Rapper's face, "Oh no, he's mine. Now, Ms. Rapper, you won't believe my big gun—it's a cannon really. My father is the famous federal judge Sherlock. If I tell him you've been annoying me, why, he could have your father and his entire conglomerate investigated. What do you think of that, missy?"

Before Savich could throw in his own big gun and tell her he was Sarah Elliott's grandson and he controlled millions of dollars in paintings, Valerie Rapper stepped off the treadmill, grabbed her bottle of water, waved it at them. "Both of you are crazy, totally crazy. Judge Sherlock! What a ridiculous name!"

"You should know," Sherlock said.

"Don't you dare have my father investigated, do you hear me?"

"Well, I'll think about it if you leave my husband alone."

"I'll bet you dye everything so he won't guess that your hair isn't natural!"

"Gee, I didn't know that was possible. Thanks for the tip."

"What's going on here, Agent Savich?"

It was Bobby Curling, the gym manager. He looked both amused and alarmed. "We got a problem here? These two fighting over you? Since when did you become such a sex object?"

Savich grinned at his wife. "Actually, the three of us were just comparing our antecedents. It's my considered opinion that Sherlock and I come from the better gene pool."

"You're not worth my time, either of you!" Valerie Rapper whirled around. "As for you, Bobby, you can take your cheap club and shove it."

She took the stairs two at a time going down, something Savich had never seen anyone do before. Bobby grinned up at him. Savich gave Bobby a thumbs up. "No problem now, Bobby, everything's cool."

"Yeah, but you guys just lost me a customer."

"Maybe," Savich said. "But we also put on quite a show for everyone else."

"I'd say we're easier to get along with anyway," Sherlock said.

Bobby hunched his huge muscled shoulders, took a last look at Valerie Rapper stomping into the women's locker room. "She sure is pretty," he said, and sighed. "I've been watching her go after you, so I guess in the spirit of keeping marriages together, it's okay with me she's leaving." He sighed again, and turned away. "I'll bet she's really rich, huh?"

"She says she is." Savich turned to his wife, lightly touched his fingertip to her cheek. "Thanks for showing up. Good timing, as always."

"The Special Forces couldn't have moved any faster than I did getting here. I'd hug you but you're sweaty. Oh, who cares?" She plastered herself to him and whispered against his neck, "When I saw her pushing against you, I have to admit I nearly lost it. I wanted to heave one of the bicycles at her or throw her over the railing or knock her beautiful capped teeth into her tonsils."

"You were the model of restraint," he said, hugging her.

She cupped his face between her hands, pulled him down, kissed him hard. "Thank God you're so sweaty, I can't smell her on you. We're a pretty good team."

He looked down at her. "From the time I kicked your SIG Sauer out of your hand in Hogan's Alley, I knew we would be."

She bit his neck, which tasted like salt. "I called Lily. She came dashing over to watch Sean. You want to go rescue your sister?"

"Nah. Lily's always complaining that she doesn't get him to herself enough. Let's give her another hour. Now, I've got to shower. Maybe we could stop off at Dizzy Dan's and get a pizza. We could take a couple of slices home to Sean and Lily. They've both got a big pizza tooth."

Sherlock laughed. "A little kid and he loves his pizza with artichokes on it." She grinned up at him. Yes, everything was under control. "Let's do it. We'll get you the Vegetarian Nirvana, which sounds scary to me."

"Only Sean and I truly appreciate pineapple and broccoli," he said.

"You got that right. Me, I'm pure carnivore," she said, and bit his neck again.

FORTY-ONE

Agent Dane Carver said, "Glad you guys made it in time. He just made his move, see him? He's over there by the side of the house, trying to hide in the shadows, but he's too damned big. I was just on my way after him."

Sherlock said, "Would you look at that bulky wool coat he's wearing. He looks like a huge black bat."

"Let's have a closer look," Savich said. Dane gave Savich his infrared glasses and Savich saw him clearly, skulking to the side of the small 1940s cottage using the oak trees as cover.

Sherlock said, "Did you get her name?"

"Ms. Aquine Barton, single, longtime math teacher at Dentonville High School. She's in there alone, Savich."

"Okay, Dane, hang back and call the cops when I signal you. We're going to let him heave himself over the windowsill into the cottage, then we'll get him. I don't want him getting close to the teacher. Just close enough so it's the final nail in his coffin. Keep your fingers crossed he doesn't try anything stupid, and keep your gun ready."

Savich, Sherlock on his heels, ran bent over, SIG Sauers drawn, to the front of the cottage. "We're being cowboys," she said to the back of his black leather jacket.

"Not really. This guy's not going to give us any problems once we confront him. Keep down and stay behind me."

"Sometimes I hate it that you're the boss."

He grinned into the darkness as he eased the lock pick into the front-door keyhole.

It took under three seconds. The lock released and the front door slid open with just a push of his toe.

It was utterly black inside. The air smelled like jasmine, so much jasmine your nose felt stuffed with flowers.

They paused, listening. They'd watched him jimmy the window into the dining room, not more than twenty feet away from where they were crouched over in deep shadows by the front door. It was lucky he hadn't tried to go right in through a bedroom window. That, they couldn't have allowed. They walked lightly, pressing themselves against the wall in the hallway, listening to him try to get through the window. How he could get in without awakening Ms. Barton neither of them could imagine.

They heard him land hard on the dining room floor.

"That's it," Savich said and ran lightly into the dining room.

Savich said, quietly but clearly, "You can stop now, Troy. It's all over."

Troy Ward's head jerked up. He recognized Savich's voice even though he couldn't see him clearly.

He yelled at the top of his lungs, "Get away!"

As his voice echoed off the dining room walls, they heard a woman yell loud enough to make the crystals on the chandelier over the dining room table dance. "You little creep! How dare you come in here to rape me! Just look at you, all dressed in black like some sort of gangster, sneaking into my house, landing like a brick on my dining room floor! How's this, you nasty little pervert!"

There was enough light coming through the window to see Ms. Aquine Barton bring a huge old iron skillet down on Troy Ward's head. Troy's finger jerked the trigger on his gun in reflex, and a bullet slammed into the lamp on Ms. Barton's sideboard. It exploded, sending shards of glass flying all over the room.

"Get down, kids!" Aquine Barton yelled even though there were no kids around. "Look what you did, you little creep! That was my mama's lamp." She leaned over Troy Ward's still bulk and kicked him in the ribs with her bare foot. Then she looked up, saw two more shadows, heard them breathing hard, and flipped on the light, skillet raised high. "Two more of you?" She waved that skillet toward them. "You just come here and I'll lay you flat, too."

"Ms. Barton? Please don't hurt us. I'm Agent Savich and this is Agent

Sherlock. We're with the FBI. Please don't slam us with that skillet." He pulled out his shield and flipped it open.

She looked them both up and down, then checked out his FBI shield. "A woman's got to protect herself. Had this skillet under the bed for a good fifteen years now. First time I had to use it. Who is this nasty fat little man anyway?" She waved the skillet very close to Troy Ward's head. "What is all this about? What are you doing in my house at midnight? I have school tomorrow, you know."

"The man you just flattened, Ms. Barton, is the math teacher killer," Sherlock said. "And you brought him down all by yourself. Thank you very much."

Ms. Barton stood there, staring down at Troy Ward, then back at Savich. "I know who you are now. This man was one of the widowers, standing behind you, Agent Savich, on that podium. I remember thinking he really needed to go to the gym, maybe even sleep there, no food. When was that press conference? A couple of weeks ago?"

"Yes, ma'am," Savich said. "You've got a very good memory."

"But his wife was the first one killed. Oh, I see. It was him all along, the scummy little jerk." She kicked him with her bare foot. "But why was he here?" Her dark eyes widened and she whispered, "Oh my goodness, he was here to kill me, to make me his next victim, wasn't he?"

"We wouldn't have allowed that, Ms. Barton," Sherlock said. "We were right with him all the way. We just had to wait until the moment he stepped into your house. Then we were prepared to arrest him. By catching him here, we've left no way for a lawyer to get him off. There was never any danger to you. I was looking forward to taking him in myself, but you didn't give me a chance, you just bonked him on the head and laid him right out."

Bless Sherlock, Savich thought. She was excellent at distraction.

"I see now. You boobs set me up." Ms. Barton crossed her arms over her chest, still holding the skillet.

A schoolteacher who had obviously heard better excuses than Sherlock's.

"Yes, ma'am," Sherlock said. "But you're a heroine, ma'am. You've made things safe for math teachers again."

"Well, yes, I suppose I have," said Ms. Barton as she fussed over her knee-length nightgown.

Dane appeared in the doorway, out of breath. "You got him, Savich?"

Savich grinned and waved toward Aquine. "No, Ms. Barton here brought him down with her trusty iron skillet."

"Holy shit, ma'am," Dane said. He stared from Troy Ward back to her, and gave her a fat smile. "You did a fine job."

"You watch your mouth, boy."

"Sorry, ma'am, I guess the shock made me forget my manners."

"Well, I'll tell you, I've taught nasty-mouthed little high school boys for nearly thirty years now. There isn't anything I haven't heard."

Troy Ward groaned. Aquine kicked him. He shuddered, fell still again. She said, "I see what you had in mind now. You just wanted me standing in a corner, fluttering my hands, all helpless, right?"

"Yes, ma'am," Savich said, smiling. "We're the law. We're paid to hit people, occasionally. But you know, it doesn't matter who brought him down in the big equation of life. You got him, and that's just fine."

"Agent Savich, I'll just bet you got yourself smacked when you were in high school."

"Only a couple of times, ma'am," Savich said. "I was always really good in math, though."

"How did you know he was going to come after me?"

"We didn't know, ma'am. I was never certain that it was really a serial killer, I couldn't afford to be. I had all three widowers at the press conference with me so everyone watching could get a good look at them. Maybe someone would call the hot line with something on one of them. After the conference, I had both Mr. Ward and Mr. Fowler followed. Then, only Mr. Ward here because I was almost sure he was guilty, but I needed more proof, and would you look at this—he landed right in your dining room. Ms. Barton, this is Agent Dane Carver, he's the one who's been keeping a close eye on Mr. Ward tonight. He called us here."

"Hello, Ms. Barton. Aren't you cold, ma'am?"

It was in that moment Ms. Aquine Barton realized she was standing in front of three people wearing only her nightgown. She pointed the skillet at Troy Ward. "You don't let him escape, Agent Savich, and I'll get a robe on and turn up the heat in here."

They barely had time to turn Troy Ward onto his back before she was back, belting her long purple chenille bathrobe while somehow keeping a grip on the skillet.

Troy groaned, his eyelashes fluttered and he stared up at Savich. "You bastard. How did you know I was here?"

"I think the more relevant question is what you're doing here, Troy. It's kind of late to be paying a social call, don't you think? And you didn't even use the front door. Now, coming through a dining room window makes things look a little suspect, don't you think, Troy?"

"I didn't want her to hear me."

Sherlock said, "You landed a little hard, Troy."

"I'd say so," Ms. Barton said. "I can hear a boy playing with a paper clip at the back of the classroom. You sounded like a hippo trying to squeeze into a water bottle."

"Bastard. I want my lawyer."

"I'm not a bastard, you nasty little man. I'm a teacher."

"Not you, you stupid woman, him!"

Savich said, "You know, that's why I didn't call you in for a chat. You're too smart, Troy, for me to talk you into confessing, aren't you? Yeah, I'll bet you would have kept your mouth shut and demanded a lawyer. And I did wonder if I would have ever gotten enough to send you to prison for three murders and one attempted murder. So we just watched you. Thank you for climbing right in."

"I'm at the wrong house. I didn't mean to be here. It's all a mistake. I want my lawyer."

"Yep, a big mistake, I'd say. Agent Carver here followed you to the library this afternoon, saw you perusing local yearbooks. He figured you'd spotted your next victim. Fact is, though, even if we hadn't been doing our good old-fashioned police work, you picked the wrong math teacher."

"No, that's a lie. But why did you suspect me? What was there about me that made you suspicious? I can see it on your face. There was something you latched onto, wasn't there? But what? I'm a professional sports announcer, what could have made you suspect me?"

Savich saw that Aquine Barton was holding her iron skillet a little tighter. He gave her a slight shake of his head. He said, "I was in an accident several weeks ago, Troy, and they loaded me up with morphine. I was remembering our conversation, but in a morphine haze everything's different. Maybe some hidden connections came bursting through, things that I'd picked up that you hadn't actually said to me."

"And what did you pick up on, you bastard? That I wasn't like you, because you were just like all those other moron jocks? You knew I was different, didn't you?"

"I listened to you call some of the Ravens game on Sunday. You were very good, just the right mix of play calling, commentary, and sweet silence."

"Yeah, I'm the best, but it's just not enough, is it? You're just waiting to tell everyone, aren't you?"

Savich said, "That Smith and Wesson .38 of yours, Troy. Turns out when I spoke to your wife's sister, she remembered your owning a gun a long way back. A revolver, just like this .38 you brought here to Ms. Barton's house. I know there are lots of .38s in the world, Troy, but the thing is, now we'll get to test yours. Do you think we'll find a match?"

"I want a lawyer."

"You'll get your lawyer. But you might as well know we found where you bought the gun way back in 1993 in Baltimore. A small gun shop owned by a Mr. Hanratty on Willowby Street, downtown. He keeps excellent records. I'm sure your lawyer will show you a copy of the sale."

"Sounds like you better fess up, Mr. Ward," said Aquine, who now was sitting on a dining room chair, the skillet in her lap.

"Like I said, Ms. Barton, Troy here is really smart. You know, I kept worrying about motive, Troy, just couldn't understand why you'd murder your wife, even if she found out you were gay."

"I'm not gay! That's a lie! That's not a motive either."

"No, but she wasn't just going to tell the world about your being gay, Troy. I think some people already knew that and didn't really care. What she was going to tell the world was that you trade in child pornography, and that you couldn't allow."

"You can't know about that, you can't, unless—you hacked into my computer without a warrant? I'll sue your ass off, Savich! That's against the law!"

"You're right, it is. But you know, I have an agent in my unit by the name of Ruth Warnecki, and she used to be a D.C. cop. She has lots of snitches. One of them called her, told her he'd seen you on TV and knew he'd also seen you one night buying some kiddy porn on the street over on Halloran. I went there, and guess what, Troy? We found a witness who recognized your photo, said he'd seen you pay to go into a live shop with little kids parading around naked. Now, I can't prove yet exactly what went on in those shows, and if we find out who the owners of that nasty little business are, we'll nail them right along with you. But how much of that did your wife find out about, Troy? Did she even know you were gay?"

"I want a lawyer. None of that crap means anything. Witnesses are paid off all the time. I don't know anything about child pornography. Leave me alone."

"You know, Troy, we really don't need your cooperation, not after you huffed your way over the windowsill and landed in Ms. Barton's dining room with the murder weapon in your hand. That's what I'd call catching the perp dead to rights. You're a murderer, Troy, a vicious, cold-blooded murderer, and you're going down for it. All the way down. You got anything else to say?"

"I want a lawyer," Troy Ward whispered and pulled his legs into his chest.

Dane Carver hauled Troy Ward to his feet, read him his rights, and cuffed him. They left Ms. Aquine Barton with a fine story to tell the press and her students.

FORTY-TWO

Katie was sore, but she wasn't about to lie in bed and have the kids wonder if there was something else going on other than a brief bout with the flu. She showed up at the breakfast table, trying to stand straight and not limp. "Okay, I'm making waffles this morning. Miles, do you have twenty minutes?"

He really didn't, but he leaned over and kissed her. "Sure. I've never had your waffles, Katie."

"It's the best thing Mama makes," Keely said. "You're lucky. She doesn't make them often."

Miles grabbed Keely and tossed her into the air. She was his daughter, he thought, an amazing thing. She was laughing, and Sam joined in, hoping he was next. Miles, not about to let him down, swung him up and around, too, nearly crashing into the kitchen table.

"Did I hear *waffles*?"

"Aunt Cracker! That was a neat movie yesterday. And the pizza was yummy."

"Sure was," she said, reaching out and ruffling Sam's hair, then touching Keely's hair. "See, kids, Katie is just fine today. It wasn't the full-blown flu, was it, Katie? Something not quite so bad, thank God, maybe just something you ate that didn't agree with you."

"Could be," Katie said. "Thank goodness it was nothing much, whatever it was."

Katie made the largest batch of waffles ever, Miles fried up bacon, and Cracker made the coffee. The kids laughed and argued and ate until Katie thought they'd both be sick.

Forty-five minutes later, Katie dropped Keely and Sam off at the Hendricks Elementary School, with its attached preschool, only four blocks from their home. The last thing she wanted to do was go back to the house and pace and worry and wonder and make herself nuts. So she started driving. Even though she rarely saw them, she knew her two bodyguards were following her, two FBI agents assigned to protect her after the shooting in the park on Saturday, whenever she left the house.

Funny thing, but she was certain to her toes she was the one the shooter had wanted. Not Savich, not Sherlock, certainly not Miles. But who was it? She couldn't think of a single person. For an instant, Cracker's face flashed in her mind. No, that was impossible, surely. She decided to call her mother when she got back to the house. Talking to her mother always made her feel better. She wished her mother were with her right now, but no, that could be dangerous.

It was very cold, well below freezing, the sky an iron gray, the wind stiff. Snow was predicted by evening, the weather prediction of the first winter storm only a day late. It would stick and the kids would have a blast.

She turned the heater up a bit, and kept driving. She drove past Arlington National Cemetery, a place she'd first seen when she'd been not more than five years old. All those thousands upon thousands of grave markers had touched her deeply as a child, though she hadn't completely understood what they meant. Now, as an adult, all her own worries disappeared in the moments she stared over those fields of white stones. So many men, she thought, so many.

She drove around Lady Bird Johnson Park, then headed across the Arlington Memorial Bridge that spanned the Potomac. The water below was a roiling gray, moving swiftly, and looked so cold it made her lips tingle. She turned at the Lincoln Memorial when she saw the sign to Roosevelt Memorial Park. She'd first come here as a child, long before the memorial had been built, her small hand tucked in her father's as they walked along the famous Cherry Tree Walk on the Tidal Basin near the national mall. She'd brought Keely here when she'd been a baby, just after Carlo was out of her life, with her mother and father.

She shivered. It was getting colder. She turned up the heater again. The sky looked like it would snow much earlier than this evening.

She parked her Silverado in the empty parking lot at the memorial, and looked around. There was no one here, no killers, no tourists, no workers, just her. She decided to walk through the memorial once again.

One started at the beginning, since the memorial was organized chronologically, and divided into four rooms, which really weren't rooms since it was all outside, each room representing one of Roosevelt's terms in office. There were quotes, displays, and waterfalls everywhere. The place was so huge you could wander around until you dropped, but Katie didn't browse. She found herself walking directly to the third room, depicting Roosevelt's third term, where the waterfall was much larger and much louder. There, just to the left of the waterfall, was a large sculpture of FDR, and beside him sat his dog, Fala. Katie's dad had loved Fala, loved all the stories told about the little black Scottish terrier, who'd even had his own comic strip. She stood looking at the huge sculptured cape that covered Roosevelt, listening to the hammering of the water crashing against huge loose chunks of granite. She'd heard that the waterfalls froze sometimes in the winter. With the way the temperature was plummeting, she imagined it wouldn't be long before they were silent, frozen in place.

Her mind flashed to her father lifting Keely in his arms, pointing to Fala, telling her a story about how he'd performed tricks on demand. How he'd wished he'd been old enough back then to go to Washington to see him in person. Oh Lord, she missed her father, wished he'd gone to a doctor earlier, but he hadn't, just like a damned stubborn man, her mom had told her, and burst into tears. Not that it would have made much difference.

There were memories, she thought, that touched you throughout your life. She had to keep hoping that all of Sam's terrible memories would be tempered with the laughter and joy of experiences that were sweet and good.

She looked at the statue of Roosevelt and said, "If you had lived any longer, would you have announced to the country that you were willing to be president for life? And would the people have elected you?"

She half-expected an answer, and smiled at herself when the crashing water was the only thing she heard. Then there was something else, footsteps coming up behind her. She didn't turn. She thought it was one of her bodyguards, come to check on her, and that was comforting. She stood there, wishing something made sense, wishing she was back in

Jessborough, with Miles and Sam and Keely, all of them, in her house that had been magically rebuilt, her mother smiling as she came from the kitchen, carrying a tray of cinnamon buns. She craved another evening filled with tuna casserola and laughter.

She nearly jumped straight into the air when a voice behind her said, "There you are, the little princess."

Katie froze.

"That's right, just stay right where you are. Don't move a muscle."

Katie didn't even consider a twitch.

"All right. Turn around and face me."

Katie slowly turned.

"Surprised to see me, Katie?"

"Yes. Everyone believes you're dead."

Elsbeth McCamy shook her head. "They won't for much longer. I hear they've nearly dug all the way through the ruins of my beautiful house. They'll soon find just one burned body, not two. Poor Reverend McCamy, not even buried yet, left under all that rubble, all that rain pouring down on him. No! Don't you move, Katie Benedict!"

Katie held utterly still.

"I know I shot you on Saturday, but here you are, walking around this ridiculous memorial. I just couldn't believe it when I saw you leave that big fancy house of yours this morning, looking all chipper, herding those children off to school like any good little mother."

Suddenly, she started shaking, and the gun jerked in her hand. "Dammit, I shot you! Why aren't you dead like you're supposed to be?"

Katie heard hate and despair in her voice. And a bit of madness. She said, "It appears you're not a very good shot."

"I practiced, dammit, practiced for a good week before I hunted you down in that park!"

"People watch TV, see lots of violent movies, and think that when you fire a gun you kill someone, but it's just not true. No matter how good a shot you are, it's difficult to hit what you're aiming at. Don't feel too bad, you didn't miss me. You shot me in the hip." Katie lightly rested her hand against her upper thigh. "It aches a bit, but I'll live."

"I'm only two feet away from you now, Katie. When I shoot you this time, you'll die."

That was surely the truth. Where were her bodyguards?

"I had to stay back in the park since you were with those other federal agents, and that new husband of yours. You really landed on your feet, didn't you, Sheriff? Nice big house, husband kissing your feet, so much money you must think you've died and gone to heaven."

"Actually, I really didn't think of it quite like that," Katie said. Where were her bodyguards? Probably close, they surely couldn't have lost her coming through the memorial. There wasn't another soul around. Maybe they didn't want to intrude on her when there was no one here to threaten her?

"I wanted servants, but Reverend McCamy only wanted God, and me. Always God first, me second. He didn't want servants to come into our home and intrude on his privacy. So I did everything myself, even made brownies. How he loved my brownies. I made them from scratch, stirred together all that chocolate and chocolate chips and pecans, but I didn't eat any. He didn't like any fat on me, said it would be a sacrilege.

"Do you know that he studied his palms and his feet every single day? He prayed until his knees were raw, offered God everything he had, probably including me, if He would just bring back the sacred stigmata one more time. But God didn't answer his prayers."

"The story from Homer Bean was that Reverend McCamy had experienced the stigmata when he was a child. Did you believe that?"

Elsbeth McCamy nodded. "Of course. It's all he could talk about, all he could think about. He would picture it, envision it happening again over and over in his mind, but it never did. He was furious with his parents for not recording it for posterity—to show to his congregation, to prove he wasn't like those crooked loud-mouthed televangelists, that he was blessed by God himself."

"I've given it a lot of thought, Elsbeth, and do you know what I think?"

"If I don't shoot you dead right this minute, I guess you'll tell me."

Katie stayed as still and small as she could. "I don't think Sam suffered any holy stigmata. I think it was some sort of rash or exanthem, something brought on by his illness. I don't think it was blood on his palms."

"His mother believed it was blood. For God's sake, she videotaped it! She could probably smell the blood. You can, you know. Smell blood, that is." She shook her head, bringing herself back from some memory.

"She gave the tape to a senile old priest whose sister recognized its value and knew a member of the Reverend's congregation. That's how it came to Reverend McCamy. Who are you to question any of this? You're just some hick sheriff."

"Let me ask you this, Elsbeth. Was Sam the only child like that Reverend McCamy had ever heard about, had ever tracked down?"

Slowly, Elsbeth nodded her head. "Yes, but that doesn't mean anything."

"I suppose it doesn't. I'm surprised and pleased that you managed to escape the fire, Elsbeth."

"I doubt you'll be pleased much longer. If I'd burned to a crisp with Reverend McCamy, you wouldn't be looking death in the eye."

"How did you get out?"

Elsbeth McCamy shrugged. "We had a little . . . playroom at the back of the closet. There's a door that leads down from there and out of the mud room. Reverend McCamy was dead, I knew it, and I didn't want to die with him, and so I got out of there really fast."

"That little playroom, I saw it once."

"That's impossible. No one ever saw it."

"Well, yes, I did. Agent Sherlock and I looked around your house once because we thought Clancy was there. I can understand why Reverend McCamy wouldn't want servants hanging around to find it by accident. I'll admit I was really surprised that Reverend McCamy was the sort of man who tied his wife down and whipped her."

Elsbeth McCamy looked blank a moment, then she threw back her head and let out a high wild laugh, and that laugh blended in with the crashing water and sent puffs of cold breath into the air. Katie was ready, only an instant from jumping at her, when Elsbeth's head came back down, her laughter cut off like water from a spigot, and she whispered, "I want to kill you anyway, Sheriff, so please, come at me, please."

"Why did you laugh?"

"Because you're so wrong about us," she said. "Just like his damned aunt Elizabeth. I know that she snuck in there when we were building the room, looking, poking about. She believed Reverend McCamy was crazy, that he abused me and that I loved it, that I was a pathetic victim. But you're all wrong. Before I shoved that old busybody down the stairs, I told her what we were going to use that room for. I told her why Reverend McCamy was having it built, and how much he needed it. He gave himself over to me when we were in that room, and he forgave himself for his faults for a few moments at least, when he was strapped down on his belly over that fur-covered block of wood and I whipped him, whipped him until sometimes the whip cut through and brought blood. And I could smell it. He dedicated that blood to God, and prayed that God would reward him with the return of the sacred stigmata."

"Those vials in that cabinet. What did you use those for?"

"Reverend McCamy used them to help him mortify his flesh, help him transcend the pain of giving himself over to God, pain that was both corporeal and spiritual. He cried in that room, not from the pain, but from how exalted he felt in those moments when the whip split his flesh and his blood flowed off his body onto that beautiful marble altar.

"But you ruined our life, Sheriff, destroyed everything. I've thought of nothing else but killing you since my husband died."

Now! Katie dived and rolled, hoping that Roosevelt's sculpted cloak covered her, and jerked her derringer out of its ankle holster the instant she stopped rolling. It was nearly worthless at any distance at all, that little gun, but if you got close enough, it could kill.

Elsbeth fired, one shot, then another and another, all three of them striking the sculpture, ricocheting off, sending stone shards flying. Katie stayed down, protecting her face.

Elsbeth yelled, "Come out of there, Katie Benedict! You deserve to die for what you did! That statue won't help you!"

Katie stuffed herself tighter against the sculpture. "Don't come any closer, Elsbeth, I have a gun. Do you hear me? I don't want to shoot you, but I will if you force me to. Give it up. Toss the gun over here. There are bodyguards here, two of them, FBI agents. They heard the shots. You don't have a prayer, just give it up!"

Elsbeth suddenly appeared around FDR's huge cloak. She stopped not three feet from Katie, smiled down at her. She didn't see the small derringer. "You're lying to me again, Katie. You don't have a gun. You're expecting your precious bodyguards to ride up like the cavalry and save you. But there won't be time for that." And she laughed again. It made Katie's skin crawl, that laugh.

"You know something?" Elsbeth said, nearly choking. "I wish Reverend McCamy could see me now."

"I could tell he was proud of you, Elsbeth."

Those beautiful blue eyes lightened a moment with pleasure. Thank

God, Katie thought. Maybe she'd bought herself some time. That big Beretta was pointed right at her head.

Elsbeth McCamy blinked, looked momentarily confused, then shook her head so hard her ski cap fell off. "He was my dearest mentor, a great man who had God's ear and made me scream with pleasure when he made love to me. And you sent him to his death."

As she flexed her finger around the trigger of the Beretta, Katie brought up her derringer and fired its two shots point-blank into Elsbeth's chest.

Elsbeth stumbled backward, but she didn't go down. "My God, you shot me! You miserable bitch, I won't let you kill me like you did my husband!"

Katie threw herself at Elsbeth's knees. She heard a gunshot close to her head. She could smell her singed hair burning as she used all her strength to shove Elsbeth down.

The front of Elsbeth's coat was drenched with blood now. She raised the gun and fired toward Katie again, wildly now. Katie rolled into Elsbeth, pushing hard against her legs, throwing her arms up to dislodge the Beretta. She knew that at any moment a bullet would smash through her flesh.

There was a single shot, only one. Katie, her arms still pressing against Elsbeth's knees, looked up and saw a frown of faint surprise on Elsbeth's face. The frown was frozen in death. Slowly, she fell backward, landing hard. Katie jerked back and leaped to her feet. Her hip burned, and her heart was pounding.

She looked down at Elsbeth McCamy, surely dead this time, her eyes open, staring at nothing at all. Her beautiful hair spilled around her face. She looked very young, innocent even, without any evil or madness about her, just lying there on the ground, the front of her coat soaked with blood and the back of her head ruined.

She heard the sound of the cascading water and the wind whipping between the monuments. She heard the water running fast in the tidal basin, not fifty feet away. And her own harsh breathing, so deadened with relief that she couldn't move.

She heard running feet. Katie turned to see the two FBI agents, panting, their guns still drawn. "You okay, Katie?"

"Yes, I am, Ollie. I'm very glad you came when you did. That was an excellent shot. I'm also very glad that you're both all right. I didn't know if she'd killed you."

Agent Ollie Hamish shook his head, looking embarrassed and angry at himself.

Agent Ruth Warnecki patted his arm. She said to Katie even as she nodded over at Elsbeth, "She did something much smarter than try to kill us. She came right up to us, knocked on the window, and when Ollie here rolled it down, his hand on his gun, mind you, she told us she was your sister-in-law, that she had to speak to you about Sam, and she promised to keep a sharp eye out for anyone suspicious. We didn't think anything of it. You'd think after all our years of being suspicious of anything that walked on two feet—but she was so believable, so young and nice-looking. We bolted out of the car when we heard the shots."

Ollie Hamish pulled out his cell phone and dialed. "Hello, Savich? We're here at the FDR Memorial. You'll want to get down here real fast. You'll want to call Detective Raven, too."

"And Miles Kettering, please," Katie said. She looked again at Elsbeth, then slowly sank down to the ground, clasped her hands around her knees, and bowed her head.

FORTY-THREE

Detective Raven rose. "You guys like to live on the wild side, don't you?"

Katie couldn't move because Miles was holding her so tightly against his side she could barely breathe. "Oh yeah," Katie said. "I live for excitement. This time though, I think I'd like to just lie in the sun for a good long while and not think about anything but my husband's beautiful body."

"Hmm," Detective Raven said, startled. "Not just yet, okay? There'll be more questions, more discussions, particularly with the D.A., so check with me before you go off to find a nice white beach."

When he was out the door, whistling, Katie realized that Miles was holding her even more tightly and he was shaking. She was surprised, somehow, despite everything that had happened. She lightly touched her fingers to his face. "I made a small joke, Miles, just for you. It's over now, really, it's all over."

He pulled her so close she could hear his heart pounding against hers. She raised her face and kissed him, and was kissing him a second time when he said into her mouth, "When I got that call from Savich I was so afraid I nearly passed out. Here we've been worried about the kids, and I guess—"

"I know. We've been so worried about them that we didn't stop to think about how all this was affecting us." He was still shaking. She kept holding him tight, kissing him until she felt him relax a bit. She smiled. "Do you want to know something, Miles?"

"No, not unless it'll make me want to sing and dance. I can't take any more bad stuff for a while." He pressed his face against her neck. "Don't tell me, Keely wants Sam's room."

"Oh no, we've made hers even more girlie girl now and I don't think we could get her out if we tried. Just maybe, I hope, it is something that will make you want to dance and maybe hum a tune."

She could feel his mouth grinning against her. "Okay, Cracker's found a boyfriend and is moving out this afternoon?"

"Could be, but she hasn't said anything to me about finding a guy and moving. Nope, it's something else entirely."

"All right, tell me."

She said slowly, her voice dead serious now, "When I was facing Elsbeth and I knew she could raise that Beretta and shoot me just like that"—Katie snapped her fingers—"I knew for sure the last thing I wanted was to never see you or Sam or Keely again. I guess the bottom line here is that I love the kids and I love you, Miles."

He was silent as a tomb, didn't so much as flinch. He didn't do anything at all. She couldn't even feel his heart against her chest any longer.

She fidgeted, tapping her fingertips on his shoulder. "Miles?"

"Yeah?"

"Does that make you want to dance and sing?"

More silence, heavy winter silence.

"Miles? If you don't say something, I'm going to have to toss you to the floor and sit on you."

"That might be a good start," he said and bit her earlobe.

She pushed away from him to see him grinning like a thief who'd just lifted Bill Gates's wallet.

"Sit on me, Katie, do whatever you like. I don't want to sing or dance right this minute, what I do want to do is strip you naked and do everything I can think of to your injured body."

"My very serious declaration makes you horny?"

"Let me tell you what it makes me. I'm going to very gently help you upstairs to the bedroom, and then I'm going to feast. I'll set the alarm for about the time Sam and Keely come home from school."

As he carried her up the stairs, just like Rhett Butler, he whispered in her ear, "I love you, too, Katie."

Since Miles forgot to set the alarm, when Sam and Keely came running into their bedroom, they stopped in their tracks and looked at each other. They looked at their parents, sound asleep, Katie on top of Miles, the blankets, thankfully, drawn up to their ears.

"Hey, Papa, why are you home this early?" When Miles mumbled something, and waved a hand at them, Sam and Keely jumped onto the bed, laughing.

EPILOGUE

January
Jessborough, Tennessee

"Hey, Sheriff, where you been? You'll freeze your butt out there."

Sheriff Katie Kettering pulled off her gloves and tossed her cream-colored straw hat onto the small table next to Linnie's station, given to her by Sam for Christmas after her old one was destroyed in November. "It's cold but the butt isn't frozen yet," she said, rubbing her hands.

"Perfect shot. You sail that new hat as good as the old one, Sheriff," Linnie said. "You're really late. What's up?"

Katie shrugged. "Mr. Turner's rottweiler, Sugar Plum, chased Benny Phelps all the way to Molly's Diner, where he barricaded himself in, much to everyone's enjoyment."

Pete Margolis, one of the firefighters from next door, there to steal some of Linnie's coffee, said, "Oh well, Benny's the new postman and Sugar Plum just doesn't know him well enough yet. What are you going to do about it?"

"When I took Sugar Plum home and explained the problem, Mr. Turner gave me some of Sugar Plum's treats. Benny can try tossing them to her when he delivers the mail."

"After a week of the treats," Wade said, "she'll probably want to deliver mail with him."

Linnie said, "Mayor Tommy called, now he's begging. He wants you to talk to some reporters from Knoxville, help put Jessborough on the map."

"He just doesn't give up, you have to give him that. Tell him no way, again, Linnie."

"He also wants to know Miles's timetable for moving the plant here.

He's all ready to shove it through the county planning commission, and he needs the plans for the plant. He said it should sail through, given Kettering Helicopters Inc. won't be sitting any farther than fifty yards from the Benedict Pulp Mill."

"I gave Miles a real good deal on the price," Katie said.

"Mayor Tommy's rubbing his hands together about all the new jobs he'll get credit for."

Katie said, "Tell Tommy that Miles will be here tomorrow. He can talk to him then."

Deputy Neil Crooke stuck his head around the corner. "The toilet in the men's room needs work, Sheriff."

"Call Joyce at City Hall. She'll take care of it."

Wade said, "Oh yeah, Billy Bob Davis was hitting on his wife again, but when I went over there, she just snuffled and said she'd run into the door. There was nothing I could do."

Katie rolled her eyes. "You know what, Wade, why don't you and I go out to their farm and have a little chat with Billy Bob. Maybe if we rub his nose in some of the manure out there, it'll help him listen better."

Wade grinned and grabbed his leather jacket. "Sounds like a plan. I'll follow you out there."

Katie bundled up again, planted her straw hat on her head, and headed out, sucking in the sweet cold air. She walked to her newly re-painted Silverado, all the bullet holes and dents finally repaired. She smiled toward the thick fog-covered mountains. She could reach out her hand and touch them, nearly. She hummed as she revved the powerful engine. She drove slowly down Main Street, making sure none of the snowdrifts would cause any problems. She waved to Dr. Sheila Raines, running across a well-plowed Main Street after her cat, Turpentine, black as sin and easy to see against all the snow. She saw Dr. Jonah Flint wave to Sheila, then eagerly join her to go after Turpentine. Hmm, something just might be going on there.

She was still humming forty minutes later when she had her knee on the small of Billy Bob's back, pressing his face in the dirty snow in his backyard while she told him what was what.

She heard one of the Gibsons' dairy cows moo loudly into the bright blue sky. She heard the Benedict Pulp Mill's noon whistle.

It was a perfect day in the most beautiful place on God's earth.